Annotations to the Front Cover

---

1. This novel centers around Mansfield Park, a grand country house similar to the one in this painting. Such houses were a prominent feature of the English countryside, and their denizens were in the highest echelons of society and politics. The face of this house, Wentworth Woodhouse in Yorkshire, displays the classical style of architecture, most notably in its prominent columns and strict symmetry, that dominated country-house construction in the century preceding this novel. Mansfield Park, described at one point as a "spacious modern-built house," would look similar.

This picture comes from the book *Picturesque Views of Seats of Nobleman and Gentlemen of Great Britain and Ireland*, published later in the nineteenth century. Books that displayed hundreds of engraved pictures of houses in their many volumes were popular in Jane Austen's time, and a character in the novel reflects that Mansfield Park deserves to be in such a collection.

2. The same character describes Mansfield Park as being "well screened," referring to a line of trees on one side of the house akin to the one seen here. Such screens of trees were often planted to provide an attractive frame for the house when seen at a distance and to block unsightly views from the house.

3. An important episode in the novel involves a visit to another grand house, Sotherton Court. It is described as having "spacious stone steps before the principal entrance" as well as numerous windows for its many rooms, both common features of grand houses displayed prominently in this picture.

4. A large park around the house, such as is suggested here, was a basic element of country houses and the reason why many had "Park" in their name. These parks provided privacy and recreation for the inhabitants while also enhancing the house's appearance and demonstrating the wealth and taste of the owner. The deer depicted here were a frequent feature of these parks. The conversion of most of England to farmland had made deer relatively rare, and being able to set aside a large enough tract of land to support a deer population, valued both for aesthetic appeal and for food, was a sign of great wealth. Venison, treasured for this reason as a special delicacy, is mentioned as a regular part of dinner fare at Mansfield Park.

The Annotated

MANSFIELD PARK

ALSO BY DAVID M. SHAPARD

The Annotated Northanger Abbey

The Annotated Pride and Prejudice

The Annotated Persuasion

The Annotated Sense and Sensibility

The Annotated Emma

The Annotated

MANSFIELD PARK

Annotated and Edited by

DAVID M. SHAPARD

David M. Shapard is the author of *The Annotated Northanger Abbey*, *The Annotated Pride and Prejudice*, *The Annotated Persuasion*, *The Annotated Sense and Sensibility*, and *The Annotated Emma*. He graduated with a Ph.D. in European history from the University of California, Berkeley; his specialty was the eighteenth century. Since then he has taught at several colleges. He lives in upstate New York.

A young woman reading.

[From *The Repository of arts, literature, fashions, manufactures, &c*, Vol. VI (1811), p. 177]

The Annotated

MANSFIELD PARK

JANE AUSTEN

Annotated and Edited, with an Introduction, by

DAVID M. SHAPARD

ANCHOR BOOKS

A Division of Penguin Random House LLC

New York

AN ANCHOR BOOKS ORIGINAL, APRIL 2017

Library of Congress Cataloging-in-Publication Data
Names: Austen, Jane, 1775–1817, author. |
Shapard, David M., editor.
Title: The annotated Mansfield Park / by Jane Austen ;
annotated and edited, with an introduction,
by David M. Shapard.
Other titles: Mansfield Park
Description: New York : Anchor Books, 2017. |
Includes bibliographical references.
Identifiers: LCCN 2016030298 (print) |
LCCN 2016032272 (ebook)
Subjects: LCSH: Austen, Jane, 1775–1817. Mansfield Park.
| Young women—England—Fiction. | Country homes—
England—Fiction. | Children of the rich—Fiction. | Social
classes—Fiction. | Cousins—Fiction. | England—Social life
and customs—19th century—Fiction. | Domestic fiction. |
BISAC: FICTION / Literary. | GSAFD: Love stories.
Classification: LCC PR4034.M3 2017b (print) |
LCC PR4034 (ebook) | DDC 823/.7—dc23
LC record available at https://lccn.loc.gov/2016030298

Book design by Rebecca Aidlin
Maps by Robert Bull

Anchor Books Trade Paperback ISBN: 978–0-307–39079–0
eBook ISBN: 978–0-307–95025–3

www.anchorbooks.com

Printed in the United States of America
10   9   8   7   6   5   4   3

Contents

MANSFIELD PARK

VOLUME I

(Note: The following chapter headings are not found in the novel. They are added here by the editor to assist the reader.)

VOLUME II

VOLUME III

Illustrations

Notes to the Reader

Literary interpretations: Comments on the techniques and themes of the novel, more than other types of entries, represent the personal views and interpretations of the editor. Such views have been carefully considered, but inevitably they will provoke disagreement among some readers. I can only hope that even in those cases the opinions expressed provide useful food for thought.

Differences of meaning: Many words in Jane Austen's era, like many words now, had multiple meanings. The meaning of a word that is given at any particular place is intended only to apply to the way the word is used there; it does not represent a complete definition of the word in the language of the time. Thus some words are defined differently at different points, while many words are defined only in certain places, since in other places they are used in ways that remain familiar today.

Repetitions: This book has been designed so it can be used as a reference. For this reason many entries refer the reader to other pages where more complete information about a topic exists. This, however, is not practical for definitions of words, so in some cases definitions are repeated at appropriate points.

Note on the Text of the Novel

Two editions of *Mansfield Park* appeared during Jane Austen's lifetime: the first in 1814 and the second in 1816. A letter of hers to her publisher (dated December 11, 1815) indicates that she herself made corrections to the second edition. The most significant correction concerns a speech of Mr. Price's containing naval matters (see pp. 680–682 and p. 681, note 42). Other changes mostly involve punctuation, as well as in a few cases the alteration, omission, or addition of specific words. It cannot be known how many of these smaller changes were initiated by Austen herself, for printers often revised spelling and punctuation on their own (for more, see p. 337, note 32). Printers also made mistakes in typesetting, something seen in all contemporary editions of Austen's novels. For these reasons, and due to the lack of any original manuscripts of the novels, there can never be certainty as to what Austen herself intended to write.

This edition of *Mansfield Park* adopts the usual practice of relying on the 1816 edition, since it is clear that at least some of the differences between it and the earlier edition are due to Austen's own choices. It follows the 1816 text as closely as possible, altering it only in a small number of cases, mostly involving punctuation, where it seems clearly wrong.

EDITIONS AND ARTICLES CONSULTED

Chapman, R. W., ed. *The Novels of Jane Austen*, vol. III, *Mansfield Park*. Oxford: Oxford University Press, 1933.

Johnson, Claudia, ed. *Mansfield Park: A Norton Critical Edition*. New York: W. W. Norton, 1998.

Sabor, Peter. "Textual Controversies: Editing *Mansfield Park*." *Persuasions: The Jane Austen Journal* 36 (2014): 34–43.

Southam, Brian. "*Mansfield Park*—What Did Jane Austen Really Write? The Texts of 1814 and 1816," in *British Women's Writing in the Long Eighteenth Century: Authorship, Politics and History*, edited by Jennie Batchelor and Cora Kaplan. New York: Palgrave Macmillan, 2005.

Sutherland, Kathryn, ed. *Mansfield Park*. London: Penguin Books, 1996.

Wiltshire, John, ed. *The Cambridge Edition of the Works of Jane Austen: Mansfield Park*. Cambridge: Cambridge University Press, 2005.

Acknowledgments

As in all the preceding volumes of this series, my foremost debt goes to my editor, Diana Secker Tesdell. She patiently coped with some delays in the composition of the book and then provided a continual series of valuable criticisms and revisions along with numerous valuable insights and suggestions. She made it a much better book than it would have been otherwise.

I also wish to express my gratitude to Kathleen Cook for excellent work in the very difficult and important task of laying out such a complicated book, as well as the efforts of others at Anchor Books who worked on this project at its various stages.

Additional thanks are owed to the staff of the Bethlehem Public Library, the New York State Library, the New York Public Library, and the Thomas J. Watson Library at the Metropolitan Museum of Art for helping me procure the materials essential for my research.

Finally, I must extend my appreciation to the fellow members of the local Jane Austen Society of North America for their support and encouragement in my continual immersion in the rich world of Jane Austen, and to the members of my family who have provided various types of essential support over the course of my long project of annotating her novels.

Introduction

Mansfield Park, the fourth of Jane Austen's six complete novels, draws extensively—perhaps more than any of her other novels—on knowledge she acquired from her family members and on her personal experience of a variety of social levels.

Jane Austen was born on December 16, 1775, in the rural county of Hampshire in southern England. Her father, George Austen, was a clergyman, like the hero of *Mansfield Park*, and her mother, Cassandra Austen Leigh, while the daughter of a clergyman, also came from a family of landed gentry like the Bertrams. Jane Austen spent her entire youth in the same rural setting, and while her family lived modestly, they socialized with more prosperous members of the local gentry. Her parents had six boys and two girls, and they encouraged learning and a love of books among their children. Several of her brothers tried their hands at literary composition, and Jane, with family approval and support, began her own literary efforts at thirteen. These ranged from short, highly comical sketches, often parodying literature of the day, to more serious pieces that reveal the interest in delineation of character that marks all her novels. The family's interest in literature extended to plays: Jane Austen made a few brief efforts in that genre, and she and other family members participated in a number of amateur theatrical performances like the one that figures prominently in *Mansfield Park*.

As she matured, Austen began to write entire novels. The first known example was *Elinor and Marianne*, probably written in 1795, when she was nineteen. In the following year she began *First Impressions*, which upon completion impressed her family sufficiently that her father sent the manuscript to a publisher; it was, however, rejected. Her third novel, probably completed in 1799, was *Susan*, the original form of *Northanger Abbey*. Surviving letters of hers from this period show her regularly attending balls and other social events and expressing an interest in men, though no evidence exists in this period of a sustained romance or an offer of marriage. She experienced a major change in 1801 when her father retired and moved the family to the popular spa and resort town of Bath. She lived there for five years and set substantial portions of two novels there. During this period her literary production slowed; her only new effort was an unfinished novel called *The Watsons*. At some point she also returned to *Susan*, and in 1803 a revised version was submitted to a publisher, who purchased the rights but never published it. Around the same time, she rejected, after briefly accepting, her one known offer of marriage. In 1805 her father died, and in 1806 reduced financial circumstances forced Jane, her mother, and her sister to leave Bath.

Austen continued to have frequent contact, including both letters and regular visits, with her brothers, and through them she expanded her knowledge of various matters central to *Mansfield Park*. Her eldest brother, James, succeeded their father in his clerical position; at one point while writing the novel she directed an inquiry to him regarding church practices. Another brother, Edward, had the good fortune to inherit a large estate and a grand home very like Mansfield Park. During several extended visits Austen commented on her often novel experiences there; she also had occasional exposure to relatives of her mother living in similar homes, including one that served as a model for the other grand estate in the novel, Sotherton Court. Her brother Henry, with whom she was especially close, moved to London and thereby gave her regular opportunities to enjoy its pleasures and become acquainted with life there. Finally, her two youngest brothers, Francis and Charles, became naval officers and were able to furnish her with invaluable information about the navy for this novel. Moreover, when she, her mother, and her sister left Bath, they moved in with Francis and his wife in the town of Southampton. Their three years there acquainted Jane Austen with the nearby town of Portsmouth as well as the much less comfortable conditions of life depicted in the Portsmouth sections of *Mansfield Park*, for in Southampton she lived in a crowded urban home and under greater financial constraint than at any other time in her life.

Eventually, in 1809, the three women were able to move into a comfortable cottage, owned by Jane's brother Edward, in the Hampshire village of Chawton. Its quiet setting allowed Jane to dedicate herself more fully to writing. She began by revising *Elinor and Marianne* and successfully getting it published, in October 1811, as *Sense and Sensibility*; its title page said simply "By a Lady," and she maintained this anonymity in subsequent books. This book's modest success led her to revise *First Impressions*: the resulting *Pride and Prejudice*, appearing in January 1813, enjoyed even greater success. She next turned to entirely new compositions. *Mansfield Park*, which she began in 1812, was completed in 1813 and published in May 1814. While not enjoying the success of *Pride and Prejudice*, it did well enough to justify a second edition in 1816. Meanwhile, *Emma* appeared in December 1815, and a sixth novel, *Persuasion*, was already under way in that year. Unfortunately, even as knowledge and appreciation of her work was steadily growing, she began to suffer increasing illness during 1816, which probably forced her to make *Persuasion* a much shorter work than originally intended. Her health worsened in early 1817, and while still able to start another novel, *Sanditon*, she soon had to cease work. On July 18, 1817, she died. At the beginning of 1818 *Persuasion* and *Northanger Abbey* (the new title of her earlier novel *Susan*) came out together, along with a brief biographical notice by her brother Henry that finally revealed her identity to the world.

Mansfield Park occupies a curious position among Austen's novels. It is the first of her mature novels, those composed completely when she was older and already an accomplished writer. These share several features that distinguish them from her earlier novels. Their stories rely less on dramatic, or melodramatic, events and on improbable coincidences. Their characters are more muted and subtle and less like the exaggerated "types" that populated the plays and novels of the period. They also explore more fully and intricately the inner psychology of the characters, especially the heroines. Finally, they focus more on depicting and evoking the atmosphere and social milieu within which the characters operate. All this means that even if they tend to lack the general high spirits of the early novels, and the sparkling cleverness and wit of the last and best of those, *Pride and Prejudice*, they offer greater depths and are accordingly seen by most commentators—and I certainly concur—as the summit of her art. This is especially true of the two longest of the three, *Mansfield Park* and *Emma*. Their greater length compared with all the others is itself a testimony to the author's effort to extend herself artistically, and to her increased confidence.

In evaluating these two novels, recent opinion has most often rated *Emma* highest. But this was not always so. Commentators in the nineteenth and early twentieth centuries frequently preferred *Mansfield Park*. In 1862 the novelist and literary biographer Julia Kavanagh wrote that it is, "in the opinion of many, [her] most perfect novel," while the journalist and essayist H. L. Mencken stated that in 1945, deciding to try Austen, "My choice, naturally, was 'Mansfield Park,' for all the authorities seemed to agree that it was the best."* Also in 1945, the noted literary critic Edmund Wilson declared in a *New Yorker* article "that *Mansfield Park* is artistically the most nearly perfect of her novels."† A few years later Wilson recommended the novel when asked by Vladimir Nabokov for advice on English works to include in an upcoming course on European fiction. Nabokov replied, "I dislike Jane, and am prejudiced, in fact, against all women writers. They are in another class. Could never see anything in *Pride and Prejudice*." Wilson, however, persisted, declaring that Austen "is, in my opinion, one of the half-dozen greatest English writers (the others being Shakespeare, Milton, Swift, Keats, and Dickens)." This persuaded Nabokov to try *Mansfield Park*, and he was sufficiently impressed to include it in his course; his lecture notes, published in *Lectures on Literature*, contain many valuable insights.‡

* Julia Kavanagh, from *English Women of Letters*, quoted in B. C. Southam, ed., *Jane Austen: The Critical Heritage* (London: Routledge, 1968), p. 187; and H. L. Mencken, "Jane Austen," in *A Second Mencken Chrestomathy*, ed. Terry Teachout (Baltimore: Johns Hopkins University Press, 1994), p. 231.
† "A Long Talk About Jane Austen," quoted in Ian Watt, ed., *Jane Austen: A Collection of Critical Essays* (Englewood Cliffs, NJ: Prentice Hall, 1963), p. 37.
‡ Vladimir Nabokov, *Lectures on Literature*, ed. Fredson Bowers (New York: Harcourt Brace Jovanovich, 1980); above quotes are in the introduction by John Updike, p. xxi.

Yet more recently not only has *Mansfield Park* fallen somewhat in critical favor, but it has also become, along with *Northanger Abbey*, by far the least popular of Austen's novels among readers, which was not true earlier.

One probable reason for this is the serious moral and religious message of the book. The novel was influenced by the then-popular genre of evangelical fiction, which principally began with the appearance in 1808 of *Coelebs in Search of a Wife*, by Hannah More, a leader of the powerful evangelical movement and a writer of religious tracts. Her novel, the story of a morally upright man seeking a like-minded wife, inspired a spate of similar stories. Jane Austen was familiar with these books and commented on them in letters in a tone of limited respect combined with criticism. Another leading example was *Self-Control* (1811), by Mary Brunton, and Austen speaks in one letter of having tried unsuccessfully to get hold of a copy (April 30, 1811). She eventually succeeded, for she later declares, "I am looking over Self Control again, & my opinion is confirmed of its being an excellently meant, elegantly-written Work, without anything of Nature or Probability in it. I declare I do not know whether Laura's passage down the American River, is not the most natural, possible, every-day thing she ever does" (Oct. 11, 1813). She makes a similar critique of *Rosanne* (1814), by Laetitia-Matilda Hawkins: "Mrs Hawkins' great excellence is on serious subjects. There are some very delightful conversations and reflections on religion: but on lighter topics I think she falls into many absurdities; and, as to love, her heroine has very comical feelings. There are a thousand improbabilities in the story" (early 1815—exact date uncertain).

In *Mansfield Park* Jane Austen attempts a work that includes some of these novels' serious concerns and themes, but departs from them on the critical issues of probability and realism.* As always, Austen presents a variety of human types who are complex and contain mixtures of good and bad qualities. Most important, while her hero is a man who intends to be a clergyman and has a deep sense of his vocation, he also spends most of the novel infatuated with, and often

---

* The rest of this introduction will include plot spoilers, for those not familiar with the novel.

blind to the faults of, a woman who rejects most of the principles that he expounds so eloquently. Meanwhile, the similarly religious and earnest Fanny, while never making that serious an error, still succumbs at various points to feelings of jealousy or resentment. In all this Edmund and Fanny are unlike the paragons of perfection who typically served as the heroes and heroines of evangelical novels.

Yet even with this complexity of character, the story's strict moral-ity and religious themes, often an attraction to nineteenth-century readers, have proven less congenial, and even sometimes repellent, to many readers of the twentieth and twenty-first centuries, largely because of the changed mores of our times. Fanny and Edmund have been censured as sententious and priggish. The harsh punishment of the fallen Maria has provoked condemnation. Finally, the nefari-ous part played in the story by the young people's amateur theatrical production has been seen variously as incomprehensible, ridiculous, or close-minded and philistine.

Another commonly expressed reason for dislike of the novel is dis-like of Fanny Price herself. In forums and discussions on the Internet, the vehement disagreements relating to her have been sometimes labeled the "Fanny Wars." She has aroused far greater animosity than any other Austen heroine, with the possible exception of the title character of *Emma*. Yet Emma is a heroine the reader is supposed to dislike initially, at least in part, because her flaws and her gradual correction of them are the center of the story. Fanny, in contrast, is meant to be a figure of sympathy throughout, and an exemplar of wise judgment and moral correctness, so dislike of her and rejection of her wisdom and virtue are inevitably a rejection of much of the underlying moral stance of the story. This animosity stems in part from reactions against her stringent moral code; the pettiness, envy, and bitterness she does display at times; and her negative judgment of her home and parents while staying in Portsmouth, which strikes some as excessively sensitive and finicky, if not snobbish and callous.

Moreover, even many of those who do not dislike or disapprove of Fanny find it hard to feel much enthusiasm or affection toward her. She, unlike the principal heroine in every other Austen novel, is almost completely humorless (a quality she shares with Edmund). Because of her quietness and reserve she often says little of note and rarely engages in the repartee that is a frequent highlight of Austen's work. Her passivity and timidity also mean that she simply does less; the one significant action she takes in the novel is to refuse an offer of marriage. These qualities, along with her physical frailty, low social position, and frequent hardships, while they can make her an object of sympathy or even pity, form a barrier to her being an object of admiration or emulation.

Yet Fanny's particular combination of traits does offer some appealing compensations. She draws on one of the most powerful literary archetypes, the Cinderella story, thanks to her relative poverty, her mistreatment (including by two selfish stepsister-like cousins), her almost-angelic gentleness and kindness, and her eventual vindication and reward. The wish to see justice done for her drives much of the suspense and interest of the plot for many readers.

Another advantage is simply the exploration of a character type that does not often figure at the center of novels. In all her previous novels, Jane Austen offered heroines who were outgoing and energetic, and generally confident as well; her last heroine before Fanny, Elizabeth Bennet of *Pride and Prejudice*, was distinctive particularly for her confidence and outspokenness as well as her wit. Austen shows throughout her works a fascination with the varieties of human character, and creates a vast array of distinctive characters, so it is not surprising to see her attempt a heroine as different as Fanny. Moreover, in doing so she can demonstrate how such a person, the very sort who is often ignored or neglected, if not scorned, can in fact possess many interesting or valuable qualities, an underlying strength that more than once inspires her to resist external pressures that most would not, and an extremely rich inner life.

In fact, Fanny arguably has the richest inner life of any character in Jane Austen: she is in many respects both the most intellectual and the most emotional of all the heroines. She is very bookish, in part because her shyness and her lowly social position have caused her to turn to books for diversion and education and consolation. Her reliance on books, though it can lead to naivete, encourages her to relate the particulars of her experience to general principles, and this stimulates her many sustained reflections and allows important themes to emerge in her thoughts and words. At the same time, she reacts with extreme sensitivity to almost everything that occurs, which frequently causes her anguish and distress and leads at times to foolish overreactions or unattractive feelings. Her acute reactions and emotions, coupled with her strenuous efforts to guide and control her feelings through moral principles, create conflicts that can make even the most ordinary occurrence an occasion for inner drama.

These features of Fanny also result in a distinctive amount of action and drama that is not directly related to the heroine. Austen's novels always contain the dual elements of a story involving a wide array of people and a single person through whose consciousness the story unfolds. This single consciousness focuses the novel, but it also means almost everything must transpire within her observation. This limitation proves less restrictive than usual in *Mansfield Park*, in great part due to Fanny's special characteristics. Because she is so quiet and inconspicuous she is able to witness many important events, and because she is so sensitive and thoughtful she is able to understand more than others do; hence she can be peripheral to the action for much of the novel while still being present to the reader. Moreover, the continuing lively saga of her interior life means that she never ceases to be an object of interest. Finally, as a thoughtful and sympathetic listener, whose own sentiments are frequently not perceived by others, she becomes a sounding board, most notably for Edmund and Mary Crawford. They make her their confidante about their feelings for each other, while never suspecting Fanny's love for Edmund, allowing their romance to play out substantially before her. All this permits *Mansfield Park* to go further than any other Austen novel in three important ways: the depiction of a variety of social milieus, the development of a number of complex characters, and the unfolding of a plot that is both eventful and realistic.

In the matter of social milieu, while *Emma* is distinctive for its comprehensive description of a single rural community, *Mansfield Park* shines for its portrait of three very different social worlds. Its principal world is Mansfield Park itself. Grand houses were at the pinnacle of English society and play a critical role in all Austen's novels, and their particular characteristics are explored in their greatest depth here. The second world is fashionable London society, another leading element of contemporary England. It receives here its sole sustained evocation by Jane Austen, through the characters of Mary and Henry Crawford. The third world is Fanny's home in Portsmouth, the author's only foray into such a humble milieu. In these scenes she vividly describes both the personal and the material aspects that contrast the Prices' life with the wealthier and more genteel society she otherwise depicts.

The novel also uses these worlds, and the contrasts among them, to develop fundamental moral themes. Mansfield Park is ostensibly the site of an ideal blend of sound moral principles and polished manners, contrasted with fashionable London society, whose exterior elegance and politeness are accompanied by moral laxness. Yet through the Crawfords—with their wit, charm, good humor, and clever and erudite conversation, along with their fine manners—Austen acknowledges the attractiveness of their sphere and why it could exercise such influence. Furthermore, the powerful effect of the Crawfords upon the Bertrams underlines the critical weakness of the Mansfield Park family: their focus on elegant manners, and on the wealth and social position that help support them, has caused them to neglect moral principles, which leads ultimately to the tragic denouement of the story. As for the Prices, they adhere, even if imperfectly, to a basic moral code, but their lack of manners causes continual conflict and frequent unhappiness, demonstrating that while manners may be of lesser importance, they still have value. Finally, Fanny herself, who is not a full member of any of these worlds, serves as an additional locus of contrast. Her memories of Mansfield Park make her more keenly aware of the social defects in Portsmouth. Her consistently firm moral stance in her exchanges with both Crawfords highlights their moral deficiencies. Most important, she reveals more than anyone the defects at Mansfield Park. Her bookishness and her social apartness mean that the high-minded principles in books have substantially guided her; in contrast, most of the Bertrams, like so many wealthy families, have paid only lip service to those principles and instead let fashionable and worldly mores guide their behavior. Fanny's resulting independent standards allow her to perceive the failings around her in the early part of the book, to stand on principle with unexpected firmness later, and, finally, to serve as a moral corrective and source of inspiration at the end.

This complex interplay of theme and milieu is matched by similar complexity of character. In all other Austen novels, at most two characters are multifaceted ones who struggle with contradictory feelings and who evolve over the course of the story: the main heroine and either a second heroine (in *Sense and Sensibility*) or the hero (to varying degrees in the other four novels). *Mansfield Park*, however, has at least four such characters: Edmund, Mary, Henry, and Fanny. All four receive extensive treatment, with the first three revealed at times by the author's direct presentation of their thoughts or private conversations, and even more by Fanny's careful observation of them. Edmund and Mary are portrayed as being strongly attracted to each other while strongly objecting to each other's principles and priorities, which creates parallel internal conflicts. Each in turn becomes angry or frustrated with the other and vows to abandon aspirations of romance, before regretting this decision and relenting, leading to a period of positive hopes and plans, eventually dashed by reminders of the gulf between them. At the same time, their respective stories do exhibit an overall arc, as each gradually becomes more inclined to choose the other—with Mary in particular seeming to accept more and more the previously unthinkable notion of marrying a clergyman—before their siblings' scandal leads to a definitive break and a revelation of their profound differences. Even after this, both display some regret and hope for reconciliation.

Henry presents initially a less multifaceted character, seeming to be simply an intelligent man in perpetual pursuit of amusement, most notably through the temporary conquest of female hearts. But as his pursuit of Fanny gradually leads to genuine interest and then affection, he reveals additional dimensions. He comes to understand and appreciate her unusual moral qualities. He also displays, in his reaction to William Price and in conversations with Sir Thomas and Edmund, glimpses of more general moral seriousness. By the time he visits Fanny in Portsmouth, he exhibits clear evidence both of efforts toward personal reform and of his continued mercurial nature. The complexities and ambiguities of his character are such that the author takes the unusual step at the end of declaring that a trivial decision of his, one he almost made differently, could have led to a completely different outcome for him (and in consequence for the other principals). In fact, more than any other Austen character, Henry has inspired numerous readers over the centuries to wish he had made an alternative decision and met a happier fate, or to believe this should have happened, that his acting differently at the end would be more plausible. Such a sentiment seems to have been shared by Jane Austen's sister, Cassandra, the person she was far closer to than any other: a fan of Austen's novels, relating a conversation she had in the 1850s with an Austen niece, reports that the niece recalled hearing Cassandra argue with Jane that she should allow Henry to marry Fanny. In a letter the author, speaking of her brother, writes, "Henry is going on with Mansfield Park; he admires H. Crawford—I mean properly—as a clever, pleasant Man" (March 2, 1814), a sign that she was far from condemning her creation, even as her story ultimately condemns him to unhappiness.

This novel also presents a uniquely complex parental figure in Sir Thomas Bertram. All Austen heroines (and some heroes) have parents who play important roles in the story. Yet in all other cases they are primarily marked by a few characteristics and remain essentially unchanged throughout the novel. Sir Thomas, however, shows a variety of dimensions, being at the outset a man of high intelligence and responsibility and good moral principles who also, through aloofness and coldness of manner and excessive concern for social position, neglects the education and moral development of his children and remains blind to the true nature of his daughters, of Fanny, and of Mrs. Norris. Moreover, he undergoes a significant evolution that forms another important story arc, first showing, after he returns from Antigua, an increased appreciation of Fanny and doubt about Mrs. Norris, then revealing his continued limits in his reaction to Fanny's refusal of Henry, and finally realizing his profound errors. Furthermore, unlike another father forced to confront a family disaster due in part to his own negligence, Mr. Bennet of *Pride and Prejudice*, Sir Thomas experiences more than temporary regret and alters his outlook and conduct, a development made plausible by the moral seriousness and reflectiveness he has always displayed.

Finally, the variety of significant and interesting characters in *Mansfield Park* contributes to the strongest plot in all of Austen's novels. *Sense and Sensibility* and *Pride and Prejudice* are similar in having dramatic and eventful plots, but these two, especially the former, rely for their drama on melodramatic developments, including some told in a long and woeful backstory, a common device in other novels of the time that Austen ridicules in some of her writings. Moreover, both, especially *Pride and Prejudice*, contain highly improbable coincidences that are crucial for the plot, another device common in the novels Austen satirizes and that conflicts with her general preference for strict realism and ordinariness. The other three, *Northanger Abbey*, *Emma*, and *Persuasion*, are more subdued in their plots, employing less melodrama and coincidence (though all three still have some of both). But their plots are also much simpler and less eventful. The hero and heroine like and appreciate each other from the beginning, and the story mostly involves waiting for them to become fully cognizant of their affection and suitability. In *Northanger Abbey* and *Persuasion* this means a short and generally straightforward march toward the denouement, while in *Emma* progress is lengthened and complicated by subplots involving supporting characters.

In contrast, *Mansfield Park* contains no coincidences as well as no significant melodrama other than the final elopement of Henry and Maria, while its plot is full of developments and twists and remains in a state of acute uncertainty and tension until the end. It alone does not follow the pattern of having a heroine encounter early on a man who both is right for her and is, or has been, interested in her, a more typical scenario that leaves the author the option of either letting the course of true love run fairly smoothly or impeding and resolving it with often melodramatic developments. *Mansfield Park* follows a different pattern, linking the four main characters in a chain of affection, where A (Henry) loves B (Fanny), who in turn loves C (Edmund), who in turn loves D (Mary); in each case the beloved object is hostile or unconscious or ambivalent. The chain is further extended by the two lesser characters of Mr. Rushworth, who loves Maria, and Maria, who loves Henry. This situation allows new developments to arise naturally and realistically, with no recourse to extraneous causation, while leaving the final outcome in doubt until the end.

The crucial handicap of this structure, and the almost certain reason why Jane Austen does not resort to it elsewhere, is that it shifts the action away from the main heroine, the figure who is always central to her novels and through whose eyes the story always occurs. This is not a fatal problem in this case, because Fanny's passivity, along with her sensitivity and reflectiveness, allows her to serve as an excellent observer of others' actions and recipient of their confidential disclosures. Yet not everything can be witnessed or heard by Fanny; nor can the author have too many scenes occurring away from her, or too many descriptions of the thoughts of other characters, without abandoning the heroine's centrality. This problem is especially acute in the case of Henry and Maria, for their final action, if fully narrated as its importance would seem to demand, would require a substantial portion of the novel to occur outside Fanny's view.

The author attempts to resolve that problem with two devices. The first is the priority given in the first third of the novel to the visit to Sotherton and to the theatrical performances. These episodes are notable because, despite their prominence and their superb artistry, they lead in the immediate term to no significant plot developments. Edmund and Mary's relationship progresses during both episodes, but it also progresses through other incidents, rendering these scenes in no way necessary for this purpose. They are more important for Maria and Henry's relationship, but they conclude with the two characters back essentially where they started; he has resumed his usual nomadic pursuit of pleasure, and she proceeds with her marriage to Mr. Rushworth. Yet the episodes' long-term function is crucial. In both, Maria and Henry elope together in a metaphorical sense. Moreover, they reveal the characteristics that will eventually lead to their fateful final action, namely, her powerful feelings for him and his willingness, from vanity and a love of variety and amusement, to encourage her beyond what both decency and prudence would allow. Hence these episodes allow the author, through vivid early scenes that occur directly in Fanny's presence or awareness, to foreshadow and adumbrate the final scenes that can be summarized only from a distance and in retrospect.

The second device, a far less happy one, is to present many of the later plot developments in the form of letters. Nabokov, in his comments, says that in this section the novel "shows signs of disintegrating," and "this letter-writing business is a shortcut of no great artistic merit."* This underrates the usual artistry with which Austen reveals character through the content and style of letters, as well as the letters' function in giving a sustained insight into the vacillating attitudes of two important characters, Mary and Edmund. Nonetheless, the letters are a poor substitute for the vividly dramatized scenes in the rest of the novel. Mostly they are simply a necessary mechanism to keep Fanny and the reader abreast of other important characters and incidents during the Portsmouth section, which is crucial to the novel, since it highlights certain moral and social themes, teaches Fanny about her true place in the world, and provides the fatal test of Henry's reform and fidelity by separating him from Fanny.

The concluding chapters that come just after the letters have a similarly summary quality, as a long series of critical events and changes is narrated in quick succession. This makes the last part the weakest section of the novel; yet this is also a symptom of the novel's greatest strength, its embarrassment of riches when it comes to complex and fully developed story lines, characters, and themes. With so many superb elements in play, far more than in any other Austen novel, the author is forced at the end to be somewhat cursory in wrapping up all these loose strands without extending the novel to far greater length. But the riches that came before are so great, and the overall structure so harmonious and carefully integrated, that the deficiencies at the end fade in importance, and the reader is left with what is, in this writer's opinion, the finest sustained example of Jane Austen's artistic brilliance.

* Nabokov, *Lectures on Literature*, pp. 49, 52.

The Annotated

MANSFIELD PARK

VOLUME ONE

Chapter One

*A*bout thirty years ago,[1] Miss Maria Ward of Huntingdon,[2] with only seven thousand pounds,[3] had the good luck to captivate Sir Thomas Bertram, of Mansfield Park,[4] in the county of Northampton,[5] and to be thereby raised to the rank of a baronet's lady,[6] with all the comforts and consequences of an handsome[7] house and large income. All Huntingdon exclaimed on the greatness[8] of the match, and her uncle, the lawyer,[9] himself, allowed her to be at least three thousand pounds short of any equitable claim to it.[10] She had two sisters to be benefited by her elevation; and such of

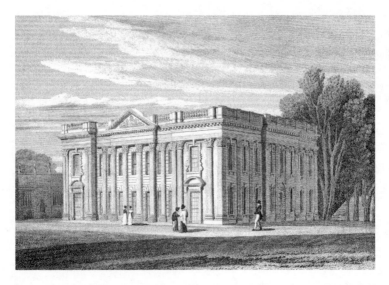

Sutton Hall, Derbyshire, a grand house fitting much of the description of Mansfield Park.

[From John Preston Neale, *Views of the Seats of Noblemen and Gentlemen*, Vol. V (London, 1822)]

1.   This is the only time that Jane Austen states at the outset of a novel how many years earlier her story began. One reason is that this novel provides by far the longest narrative (lasting several chapters) of the events leading up to the main action, including the heroine's childhood. As usual, Austen is careful and accurate in her dating. The main action begins approximately twenty-seven years after this opening event and transpires over one year. The concluding events sketched in the last few pages would logically span about two years and possibly a little more. For more detail, see the chronology, p. 853.

2.   Huntingdon is a town in eastern England and the county seat of Hunting-donshire. Since the time of this novel Huntingdonshire has been absorbed into the county of Cambridgeshire.

3.   In most wealthy families, women were allotted a fixed sum as their inheritance. It would serve as a dowry and go to her husband upon her marriage.

4.   Grand homes were always given formal names. Many names included the word "Park," for estates normally had ample grounds, and the name designated the grounds as well as the house.

5.   The county of Northampton, or Northamptonshire, is in the Midlands of England; it is to the immediate west of Huntingdonshire. Jane Austen, who was never in Northamptonshire, probably set her story there because its distance from Portsmouth, the home of the heroine, serves the plot by making travel between the two places difficult. Similar considerations determine her choice of settings for other novels. For these locations, see map, p. 882.

6.   A baronet was the highest rank in Britain below the aristocracy or peerage. It was a hereditary knighthood, which gave the holder the right to be known as "Sir" and his wife the right to be known as "Lady" but, unlike the peerage, conferred no legal or political privileges. Baronets and peers, as well as the untitled gentry who ranked just below them, derived most of their wealth from large landed estates, usually with grand residences like Mansfield Park at the center. This landed elite dominated British government and society.

7.   *handsome*: large. The word could also refer to the house's attractiveness, but in this context it probably refers mostly to its size.

8.   *greatness*: social eminence. This and its attendant privileges are what is primarily meant by the "consequences" of the match.

9.   "Lawyer" at this time could mean either a barrister, who could try cases in court, or an attorney, who could not. The uncle is likely a barrister, for barristers were considered gentlemen (for what this means, see p. 17, note 67) while attorneys were looked down upon socially; having an uncle who was an attorney would have been a formidable barrier to marrying a baronet.

10. Marriage choices among the wealthy were so heavily determined by considerations of fortune and social rank that people had a clear sense of how

their acquaintance as thought Miss Ward and Miss Frances quite as handsome[11] as Miss Maria,[12] did not scruple[13] to predict their marrying with almost equal advantage. But there certainly are not so many men of large fortune in the world, as there are pretty women to deserve them.[14] Miss Ward, at the end of half a dozen years, found herself obliged to be attached to the Rev. Mr. Norris,[15] a friend of her brother-in-law, with scarcely any private fortune, and Miss Frances fared yet worse. Miss Ward's match, indeed, when it came to the point, was not contemptible, Sir Thomas being happily able to give his friend an income in the living of Mansfield,[16] and Mr. and

A barrister of the period (Sir George Trafford Heald, K.C.).

[From Sir Walter Armstrong, *Lawrence* (London, 1913), p. 56]

much wealth on the wife's side would normally be required to attract a husband of a specific social and economic level. Lawyers would be particularly aware of this, for much of their business involved negotiating and drawing up the complicated financial settlements that elite marriages involved.

11. *handsome*: attractive. The word is frequently used in Austen's novels to describe women, with no masculine connotation intended.

12. "Miss Ward" is the eldest. The oldest unmarried daughter in a family was referred to as "Miss + last name"; her younger sisters were referred to as "Miss + first name," with the last name sometimes added. Later we learn that Maria was the next oldest, and Frances (or Fanny) the youngest (p. 734—the latter is called "some years her [Lady Betram's] junior").

13. *scruple*: hesitate.

14. This basic truth manifests itself throughout Austen's novels, and—along with women's urgent need to marry due to the absence of alternative careers—provides much of the novels' dramatic tension. The reference to a woman's prettiness underlines the importance of looks as an asset. It is almost certain that her looks were what allowed Maria to make such an advantageous marriage, for, as is soon revealed, she has almost no other attractive qualities.

15. "Rev.," short for "Reverend," indicates he is a clergyman. Clergymen were central to English rural society at this time. Jane Austen's father was a clergyman, as were two of her brothers. Clergy tended to be closely connected to the landed elite, and usually ranked next in status in the rural hierarchy. The phrase "obliged to be attached" indicates that Miss Ward married for the sake of her husband's social and economic position rather than for love, which was not unusual.

16. This living is the position as clergyman for Mansfield parish, which comes with a regular income. England was divided into parishes, which were units both of the church and of local government; each parish had a church and a clergyman belonging to the Church of England. The official state church enjoyed legal privileges and was where most people in England worshipped, including virtually everyone in rural areas like this one. In towns and cities, more people belonged to other denominations, though, while generally able to worship freely, they were still obligated to contribute to the official Anglican Church. The power to appoint someone to a church living was frequently in the hands of wealthy landowners, and it was standard for them to appoint friends and family members. Jane Austen's father was appointed to his living by a cousin, which allowed him to marry and start a family. For more on the system of church appointments, see p. 47, notes 3 and 6.

Mrs. Norris began their career of conjugal felicity with very little less than a thousand a year.[17] But Miss Frances married, in the common phrase, to disoblige her family,[18] and by fixing on[19] a Lieutenant of Marines,[20] without education, fortune, or connections,[21] did it very thoroughly. She could hardly have made a more untoward choice. Sir Thomas Bertram had interest,[22] which, from principle as well as pride, from a general wish of doing right, and a desire of seeing all that were connected with him in situations of respectability, he would have been glad to exert for the advantage of Lady Bertram's sister: but her husband's profession was such as no interest could reach;[23] and before he had time to devise any other method of assist-

A general in standard army officer uniform, similar to that of the marines.

[From William Alexander, *Picturesque Representations of the Dress and Manners of the English* (London, 1813), Plate 29]

17. This is a very comfortable income, though not nearly as grand as Sir Thomas's (which is never specified) undoubtedly is. "Conjugal felicity" was a common expression of the time, in this case used ironically, given the real motives behind the marriage.

18. This society emphasized people's obligations to their family, which included taking into account the family's wishes and interests in one's marital decisions.

19. *fixing on*: choosing, selecting.

20. The Royal Marines was a corps of soldiers who were trained like army soldiers and had similar uniforms and weaponry, but were attached to the navy. Virtually every naval ship had a contingent of marines, who existed to participate in landing parties that were sent ashore, to assist in hand-to-hand combat when a ship directly grappled with an enemy ship, and to maintain order and discipline. Commissioned military officers were considered gentlemen, but those in the marines were lower in status than army or navy officers. One reason was that, whereas commissions in the other services either had to be purchased or required years of experience, neither was the case in the marines, so those seeking marine commissions frequently had humble backgrounds and poor qualifications. This, plus the fact that lieutenant was the lowest officer rank and promotion was difficult, would make such a figure an undesirable husband for a woman from a family that could give its daughters a decent dowry and whose other daughters had married a baronet and a clergyman with a good living.

21. *connections*: relations, family ties. Such ties were highly important, both for social prestige and for the practical benefits they could confer. This man's lack of them, along with his lack of education and private fortune (he would receive only a modest salary as a marine lieutenant), would add to his undesirability from the perspective of the bride's family.

22. *interest*: influence, especially as arising from personal connections.

23. Patronage was important in the navy and marines, as in almost every other area of life in this society, but they were relatively closed societies in which the principal form of patronage was that exercised by high-ranking officers within the services. Moreover, in the case of the marines, promotion tended to operate by strict seniority, making outside interference even less possible.

ing them, an absolute breach between the sisters had taken place. It was the natural result of the conduct of each party, and such as a very imprudent marriage almost always produces.[24] To save herself from useless remonstrance, Mrs. Price never wrote to her family on the subject till actually married.[25] Lady Bertram, who was a woman of very tranquil feelings, and a temper[26] remarkably easy and indolent, would have contented herself with merely giving up her sister,[27] and thinking no more of the matter:[28] but Mrs. Norris had a spirit of activity,[29] which could not be satisfied till she had written a long and angry letter to Fanny, to point out the folly of her conduct, and threaten her with all its possible ill consequences. Mrs. Price in her turn was injured and angry; and an answer which comprehended each sister in its bitterness, and bestowed such very disrespectful reflections[30] on the pride of Sir Thomas,[31] as Mrs. Norris could not possibly keep to herself, put an end to all intercourse between them for a considerable period.[32]

Their homes were so distant, and the circles in which they moved so distinct, as almost to preclude the means of ever hearing of each other's existence during the eleven following years, or at least to make it very wonderful[33] to Sir Thomas, that Mrs. Norris should ever have it in her power to tell them, as she now and then did in an angry

Steventon Rectory, where Jane Austen grew up.

[From Mary Augusta Austen-Leigh, *Personal Aspects of Jane Austen* (New York, 1920), p. 12]

24. Austen's novels contain other examples of such breaches (as in a similar match at the outset of *Emma*), but she also shows, as in this case, that the "inevitability" results as much from pride and anger and hasty temper as from absolute necessity.

25. Once people had reached the age of twenty-one they were legally free to marry in England without parental consent, but social mores dictated that even then the couple should marry only if both could obtain consent. Mrs. Price, knowing she would not have received consent, found it more convenient not to try for it.

26. *temper*: disposition, inclinations. The term had a broader meaning then.

27. This most likely means ceasing any communication or contact with her, and no longer speaking of her to others. Such actions would minimize the possibility of others learning about the embarrassing affair, indicate one's firm disapproval to anyone who did know about it, and prevent any encounters between the offending relative and the members of one's immediate family or social circle.

28. This use of a colon where a semicolon would normally be used appears at numerous points in *Mansfield Park*. It was likely the preference of the printers, for other Austen novels use colons far less often. Variation in punctuation or other points of style, due to different standards prevailing at different printers, was common.

29. *activity*: energy, busyness.

30. *reflections*: critical reflections or comments.

31. She probably assumed that Sir Thomas's high rank made him especially proud and inclined to disapprove the match, and that this pride accounted for much of her sisters' disapproval.

32. This passage provides the first picture we have of Mrs. Norris, one of the most distinctive and memorable characters in the novel. Many people in Mrs. Norris's situation, even if angered by the words in her sister's letter, would have refrained from sharing them with her brother-in-law, for the importance of family made people anxious to minimize family quarrels.

33. *wonderful*: amazing.

voice, that Fanny had got another child.[34] By the end of eleven years, however, Mrs. Price could no longer afford to cherish pride or resentment, or to lose one connection that might possibly assist her. A large and still increasing family, an husband disabled for active service,[35] but not the less equal to company and good liquor,[36] and a very small income to supply their wants, made her eager to regain the friends[37] she had so carelessly sacrificed; and she addressed Lady Bertram in a letter which spoke so much contrition and despondence, such a superfluity of children, and such a want of almost every thing else, as could not but dispose them all to a reconciliation. She was preparing for her ninth lying-in,[38] and after bewailing the circumstance, and imploring their countenance[39] as sponsors to the expected child, she could not conceal how important she felt they might be to the future maintenance of the eight already in being. Her eldest was a boy of ten years old, a fine spirited[40] fellow who longed to be out in the world; but what could she do? Was there any chance of his being hereafter useful to Sir Thomas in the concerns of his West Indian property?[41] No situation[42] would be beneath him—or what did Sir

The West India Docks, London, with ships and warehouses related to trade there.

[From Fiona St. Aubyn, *Ackermann's Illustrated London*, illustrations by Augustus Pugin and Thomas Rowlandson (Ware, 1985), p. 7]

34. Many couples had numerous children, for methods of birth control were limited and most people believed they had an obligation to be fruitful and multiply. Jane Austen's parents had eight children, as did one of her brothers, while two other brothers each had eleven. It is not certain where Mrs. Norris obtains her information about her sister's fecundity. Most likely, she made an effort to find and befriend someone living near the Prices as a source of regular updates. She will show similar inquisitiveness on other occasions.

35. A disabled military officer would go indefinitely on half pay. Since the regular pay of a marine lieutenant was not much, half would provide little to support a family. Moreover, he would lose any chance of sharing in the most potentially lucrative part of serving on ship, the distribution of the often ample prize money allotted after the capture of an enemy vessel.

36. As will be shortly indicated, the Prices live in Portsmouth, a town on the southern coast. As it contained the main British naval base, Portsmouth would offer plenty of drinking companions for Mr. Price and plenty of establishments where they could indulge their habit.

37. *friends*: relations. The term was often used for family then.

38. Lying-in, also known as confinement, was the standard procedure surrounding the birth of a child. It started with the birth—thus "preparing for" it means primarily anticipating that she will soon give birth—and, when followed fully, continued for about a month afterward. During this period the mother remained in bed and was kept isolated from light and visitors (other than a nurse who usually attended her); this was believed to minimize the possibility of ill consequences to her. Those in less favorable circumstances like Mrs. Price would have a harder time following this regimen strictly, but the term could still be applied.

39. *countenance*: support, favor.

40. *spirited*: energetic, vigorous, enterprising.

41. Sir Thomas has property in the West Indies, or Caribbean, ample enough that a little later in the novel he will spend two years there endeavoring to put it back on a profitable footing. A variety of possible jobs would be connected with it, especially since he does not live there himself, and the slowness of communication across the Atlantic required delegating substantial responsibilities to those managing the property. For more on the West Indies and Sir Thomas's property, see p. 49, note 14.

42. *situation*: employment, position.

Thomas think of Woolwich?[43] or how could a boy be sent out to the East?[44]

The letter was not unproductive. It re-established peace and kindness. Sir Thomas sent friendly advice and professions, Lady Bertram dispatched money and baby-linen, and Mrs. Norris wrote the letters.[45]

Such were its immediate effects, and within a twelvemonth a more important advantage to Mrs. Price resulted from it. Mrs. Norris was often observing to the others, that she could not get her poor sister and her family out of her head, and that much as they had all done for her, she seemed to be wanting to do more: and at length she could not but own[46] it to be her wish, that poor Mrs. Price should be relieved from the charge and expense of one child entirely out of her great number. "What if they were among them to undertake the care of her eldest daughter, a girl now nine years old, of an age to require more attention than her poor mother could possibly give? The trouble and expense of it to them, would be nothing compared with the benevolence of the action." Lady Bertram agreed with her instantly. "I think we cannot do better," said she, "let us send for the child."

Sir Thomas could not give so instantaneous and unqualified a consent. He debated and hesitated;—it was a serious charge;—a girl so brought up must be adequately provided for, or there would be cruelty instead of kindness in taking her from her family.[47] He thought of his own four children—of his two sons—of cousins in love, &c.;[48]—but no sooner had he deliberately begun to state his objections, than Mrs. Norris interrupted him with a reply to them all whether stated or not.

"My dear Sir Thomas, I perfectly comprehend you, and do justice to the generosity and delicacy[49] of your notions, which indeed are quite of a piece with your general conduct; and I entirely agree with you in the main as to the propriety[50] of doing every thing one could by way of providing for a child one had in a manner taken into one's own hands; and I am sure I should be the last person in the world to withhold my mite[51] upon such an occasion. Having no children of my own,[52] who should I look to in any little matter I may ever have to bestow, but the children of my sisters?—and I am sure Mr. Norris is too just—but you know I am a woman of few words and profes-

43. Woolwich was the location of the Royal Military Academy for the training of army officers in the artillery and the engineers. The boy, William, who ends up entering the navy, may have already exhibited an inclination for a military career. Mrs. Price may also mention it in the hope that Sir Thomas has some influence and connections in the army.

44. The East means India, most of which was controlled either directly or indirectly by the British East India Company. India offered many opportunities to make money, though going there also meant an extremely long and difficult voyage, a long stay, very slow communication with Britain, and the continual threat of tropical diseases. Jane Austen's aunt, due to her lack of fortune, went to India as a young woman to find a wealthy husband. She succeeded, though after the couple returned and found that their wealth did not allow them to live in London with the lavishness that they had enjoyed in India, her husband returned to India to augment their fortunes and suffered commercial reverses and a decline in health that caused his death.

45. As the woman of the house, and Mrs. Price's sister, Lady Bertram would properly be the official correspondent. This is why Mrs. Price wrote to her and why she is the one who sends money and baby linen. Sir Thomas's friendly words would be conveyed indirectly via this correspondence, while Mrs. Norris writes the letters on behalf of Lady Bertram.

46. *own*: acknowledge.

47. Adequate provision for a girl would mean maintenance and education and some kind of dowry, usually essential for making a good marriage.

48. Among the landed elite, marriage between cousins, including first cousins, was completely acceptable (those at lower social levels were more likely to regard it as incestuous). One reason was the emphasis on marrying at the same rank, combined with the limited pool of possible mates at the top of the hierarchy. But Sir Thomas would not wish a son of his to marry a poor cousin.

49. *delicacy*: refined sense of what is proper and appropriate.

50. *propriety*: rightness, decency, appropriateness. The term, frequently used in Austen's novels, refers to general moral principles, not just etiquette.

51. *mite*: small amount of money. The word has biblical connotations, which Mrs. Norris exploits later; see p. 555, note 32.

52. Mr. and Mrs. Norris's lack of children, which will play an important role in the novel, was a common condition, even as many couples had extremely large families. The reason was the absence of effective treatments for infertility.

sions. Do not let us be frightened from a good deed by a trifle. Give a girl an education, and introduce her properly into the world,[53] and ten to one but she has the means of settling[54] well, without farther expense to any body.[55] A niece of our's, Sir Thomas, I may say, or, at least of *your's*, would not grow up in this neighbourhood without many advantages. I don't say she would be so handsome as her cousins. I dare say she would not; but she would be introduced into the society of this country[56] under such very favourable circumstances as, in all human probability, would get her a creditable establishment.[57] You are thinking of your sons—but do not you know that of all things upon earth *that* is the least likely to happen; brought up, as they would be, always together like brothers and sisters? It is morally impossible. I never knew an instance of it.[58] It is, in fact, the only sure way of providing against the connection.[59] Suppose her a pretty girl, and seen by Tom or Edmund for the first time seven years hence,[60] and I dare say there would be mischief.[61] The very idea of her having been suffered to grow up at a distance from us all in poverty and neglect, would be enough to make either of the dear sweet-tempered boys in love with her.[62] But breed her up with them from this time, and suppose her even to have the beauty of an angel, and she will never be more to either than a sister."[63]

"There is a great deal of truth in what you say," replied Sir Thomas,

East India House, the London headquarters of the East India Company, which governed and controlled trade with British India.

[From *The Repository of arts, literature, fashions, manufactures, &c*, Vol. III (1810), p. 184]

53. Social life among the wealthy was carefully regulated at this time, and a girl, once old enough to marry, would be presented or introduced by the family to adults of other families. This would, among other things, allow her to talk to eligible young men. For more on this system, see p. 95, note 36.

54. *settling*: marrying.

55. That is, without giving her a dowry.

56. *country*: county.

57. *establishment*: marriage, or position created by marriage. Mrs. Norris's hope has some basis, for being brought up in Sir Thomas's home would raise the status of his niece and give her more polished speech and manners. In one case in *Emma* (see note 63 below), the elegant manners and first-rate education a young woman acquires from growing up in a wealthy home allow her to attract a rich husband despite her lack of fortune. But such cases were the exception rather than the rule, and it would be irresponsible to expect a girl given no dowry to make a decent marriage.

58. It is possible that Mrs. Norris has never heard of a marriage between cousins who were raised in the same household, but she certainly would have heard of cousin marriages, for they occurred regularly.

59. *connection*: marriage.

60. Tom and Edmund are the two Bertram sons. Tom is the eldest, shown here by his being listed first—an almost invariable practice in this status-conscious society—and by his having been named after his father, a usual though not universal practice. (The custom was similar with girls: as will soon be revealed, the eldest daughter they adopt, Fanny, was named after her mother.)

61. *mischief*: trouble. The term had a stronger connotation then, referring to serious harm or injury.

62. Fiction of the time, partly reflecting the early stages of a growing democratic sentiment, often sympathetically depicted characters in circumstances of poverty and distress. In many cases these were young women whom wealthy young men, aroused by pity for their plight as well as their beauty and charm, would fall in love with and marry.

63. Taking another's child into one's home and raising it was not unusual. In Austen's *Emma*, Frank Churchill is raised by his aunt and uncle, who are far wealthier than his father and who ultimately make him their heir, while another character, Jane Fairfax, who has lost her parents and been left with no money, is taken in by a wealthy friend of her father's, who raises her with his daughter and gives her an excellent education. Still, since it was a serious and costly undertaking, most people would not give such instant assent as Lady

"and far be it from me to throw any fanciful impediment in the way of a plan which would be so consistent with the relative situations of each.[64] I only meant to observe, that it ought not to be lightly engaged in, and that to make it really serviceable to Mrs. Price, and creditable to ourselves,[65] we must secure to the child, or consider ourselves engaged to secure to her hereafter,[66] as circumstances may arise, the provision of a gentlewoman,[67] if no such establishment should offer as you are so sanguine in expecting."[68]

"I thoroughly understand you," cried Mrs. Norris; "you are every thing that is generous and considerate, and I am sure we shall never disagree on this point. Whatever I can do, as you well know, I am always ready enough to do for the good of those I love; and, though I could never feel for this little girl the hundredth part of the regard I bear your own dear children, nor consider her, in any respect, so

A panorama of London showing part of the city.

[From *The Repository of arts, literature, fashions, manufactures, &c*, Vol. III (1810), p. 184]

Bertram does; her alacrity results less from generosity than from knowing that it will cause her no trouble, since she never takes trouble over anything.

64. With Sir Thomas's reply all three of those present in this dialogue have spoken. Jane Austen uses their manner of speaking to indicate what kind of people they are, a technique she employs brilliantly throughout her works. In this case, Lady Bertram's brief, simple statement suggests the simplicity of mind and indolence that will mark her throughout, while Mrs. Norris's volubility and emphatic declarations indicate her frenetic busyness, wish to manage everything, extreme confidence in her own judgment, and lack of self-knowledge (as when she says, in the midst of her long speech, "I am a woman of few words and professions"). As for Sir Thomas, his long, complex, and often roundabout sentences reveal him as a man who is intelligent and thoughtful but also formal and ponderous in his manner and way of proceeding.

65. He is thinking partly of how it will make the family look in the eyes of others, a very important consideration in the world of Austen's novels.

66. Securing it now would mean drawing up a legal document specifying what support the child will receive, a common procedure for children of wealthy families, whether natural or adopted. It is never clear whether Sir Thomas does this, or simply, as he also suggests, resolves to provide the child with sufficient support when she reaches the age when she will need it.

67. A gentlewoman, or lady, was the counterpart of a gentleman. The terms had a precise meaning then, namely membership in the upper, or genteel, ranks of society. For men the standard criterion for gentility was either possession of a sufficient fortune, especially in landed property, enabling one not to have to work, or a career in one of the professions deemed genteel: principally army or navy officer, clergyman, or barrister. For women, membership was secured by being the wife or daughter of a man of genteel status. The division between those with this status and those without it is the most important social distinction within Austen's novels. The child being discussed, as the daughter of a marine officer, would technically already be considered a gentlewoman, but his very low rank and the family's poverty would make her status precarious, and it would sink further if she married a man who was not genteel, as she easily might do if she remains in her current circumstances.

"Genteel" and its attendant terms also had a moral significance. The possession of certain virtues, including courtesy, refinement, and generosity, was supposed to correspond to social gentility, though in practice this was not always the case. People in this society would regularly judge how genteel others were in their behavior and character; Jane Austen often does this in her letters.

68. Sir Thomas indicates his awareness that Mrs. Norris's hopes for a good marriage for the girl without a dowry are overly optimistic. If she did not marry, she would need to be able to live comfortably to maintain her status as a gentlewoman, because the only jobs a genteel woman might secure, govern-

much my own,[69] I should hate myself if I were capable of neglecting her. Is not she a sister's child? and could I bear to see her want, while I had a bit of bread to give her? My dear Sir Thomas, with all my faults I have a warm heart: and, poor as I am, would rather deny myself the necessaries of life, than do an ungenerous thing. So, if you are not against it, I will write to my poor sister to-morrow, and make the proposal; and, as soon as matters are settled, *I* will engage to get the child to Mansfield; *you* shall have no trouble about it. My own trouble, you know, I never regard. I will send Nanny to London on purpose,[70] and she may have a bed at her cousin, the sadler's,[71] and the child be appointed to meet her there. They may easily get her from Portsmouth to town[72] by the coach,[73] under the care of any creditable person that may chance to be going. I dare say there is always some reputable tradesman's wife or other going up."[74]

Except to the attack on Nanny's cousin, Sir Thomas no longer made any objection, and a more respectable, though less economical rendezvous being accordingly substituted,[75] every thing was con-

A public coach of the time.
[From Ralph Nevill, *Old Sporting Prints* (London, 1908)]

ess or schoolteacher, would probably cause her to lose that status. Arrangements for her to continue living with a member of the Bertram family would probably be necessary.

69. Mrs. Norris will prove herself true to her words about strongly preferring Sir Thomas's children to the adopted child, even though the latter has just as close a familial relationship to her. One reason is her high regard for rank, and another is the benefit, both social and economic, that she derives from close association with the Bertram family.

70. "Nanny" does not refer to the position she holds: the word as a designation for someone hired to take care of children would not arise until many decades later (at the time of this novel, such a person was called a "nurse" or "nursery maid"), and in any case the Norrises have no children. Instead, it is a diminutive form of Anne, a very common name then. When Jane Austen was young her family had two servants named Anne who were called Nanny. This woman's position is confirmed by the use of her first name: this would only be done with servants or certain close family members (and Mrs. Norris has no family living with her). The little inconvenience involved in sending this servant to London, which would mean at least two days away, is the basis of Mrs. Norris's boast about never regarding her own trouble.

71. A sadler, or saddler, is someone who makes saddles. The ubiquity of horses for transportation made it a common occupation. As a workingman, a saddler would be a likely cousin to a servant.

72. *town*: London. The term is frequently used this way in Austen's novels.

73. This means the public coach, which ran regularly between towns in England. Since Portsmouth is south of London and Northampton directly north, going via London, while not the most direct route, would not be greatly out of the way (see map, p. 882).

74. Being only ten, she would naturally need an escort, and preferably a female one. Tradesmen and their wives were not considered genteel, but they, like Mrs. Norris's servant, would be completely acceptable for a task like this, and there were many of them in Britain due to the country's commercial and industrial growth. Moreover, because Portsmouth was a good-sized town and London contained a million people, there would be plenty of travelers regularly making the trip between the two places.

75. By the "attack on Nanny's cousin," Sir Thomas means this man's being forced, without any prior consultation, to host his cousin and a stranger. Sir

sidered as settled, and the pleasures of so benevolent a scheme were already enjoyed. The division of gratifying sensations ought not, in strict justice, to have been equal; for Sir Thomas was fully resolved to be the real and consistent patron of the selected child, and Mrs. Norris had not the least intention of being at any expense whatever in her maintenance. As far as walking, talking, and contriving reached, she was thoroughly benevolent, and nobody knew better how to dictate liberality[76] to others: but her love of money was equal to her love of directing, and she knew quite as well how to save her own as to spend that of her friends. Having married on a narrower income than she had been used to look forward to,[77] she had, from the first, fancied a very strict line of economy necessary; and what was begun as a matter of prudence, soon grew into a matter of choice, as an object of that needful solicitude, which there were no children to supply.[78] Had there been a family to provide for, Mrs. Norris might never have saved her money; but having no care of that kind, there was nothing to impede her frugality, or lessen the comfort of making a yearly addition to an income which they had never lived up to. Under this infatuating[79] principle, counteracted by no real affection for her sister, it was impossible for her to aim at more than the credit of projecting and arranging so expensive a charity; though perhaps she might so little know herself, as to walk home to the Parsonage[80] after this conversation, in the happy belief of being the most liberal-minded sister and aunt in the world.

When the subject was brought forward again, her views were more fully explained; and, in reply to Lady Bertram's calm inquiry of "Where shall the child come to first, sister, to you or to us?" Sir Thomas heard, with some surprise, that it would be totally out of Mrs. Norris's power to take any share in the personal charge of her. He had been considering her as a particularly welcome addition at the Parsonage, as a desirable companion to an aunt who had no children of her own; but he found himself wholly mistaken. Mrs. Norris was sorry to say, that the little girl's staying with them, at least as things then were, was quite out of the question. Poor Mr. Norris's indifferent state of health made it an impossibility: he could no more bear the noise of a child than he could fly; if indeed he should ever get well of his gouty complaints,[81] it would be a different matter:

Thomas seems to be worrying less about the inconvenience to the cousin than about the lowliness of his position when he substitutes a more "respectable" rendezvous. This probably means having Nanny rent a room at an inn in London, and lodging the girl there for the next day's journey to Mansfield Park (both journeys are around seventy miles, a full day's travel then).

76. *liberality*: generosity, particularly in a financial sense.

77. Any hopes she had previously harbored for a wealthy match would have been inflated by her sister's marriage to Sir Thomas, which might have encouraged wealthy suitors who could see the advantage of marrying the sister-in-law of a baronet.

78. Her frugality was initially a matter of prudence because if she had children—as virtually all couples expected to—it would be best to save money in advance. Once she realized they were destined to remain childless, continued thrift became a choice, one she apparently enjoys. These matters would fall primarily under Mrs. Norris's control, for a wife's job normally involved managing household expenditures, including those for food, other necessities, and servants.

79. *infatuating*: folly-inducing.

80. The parsonage, the residence of the local clergyman, is near the village of Mansfield, which is within fairly easy walking distance of Mansfield Park. This proximity will play an important role in the novel.

81. Gout is an affliction of the joints, often centered in those of the big toe, that involves inflammation and pain, sometimes excruciating. It is not life-threatening but can immobilize the sufferer. It is caused by an excess of uric acid in the blood due to excessive consumption of alcohol and foods rich in purine (mainly various types of meat and fish). It was a common ailment, for alcohol was part of most people's daily routine, and the diet of those who could afford it consisted mostly of meat—thus it was particularly prevalent among the wealthy; Jane Austen's rich brother Edward suffered from it. It also was most likely to afflict men, due to differences in male and female physiology, and the middle-aged or elderly, since it resulted from long-term consumption of the offending items.

she should then be glad to take her turn, and think nothing of the inconvenience; but just now, poor Mr. Norris took up every moment of her time, and the very mention of such a thing she was sure would distract him.

"Then she had better come to us?" said Lady Bertram with the utmost composure. After a short pause, Sir Thomas added with dignity, "Yes, let her home be in this house. We will endeavour to do our duty by her, and she will at least have the advantage of companions of her own age, and of a regular instructress."

"Very true," cried Mrs. Norris, "which are both very important considerations: and it will be just the same to Miss Lee, whether she has three girls to teach, or only two[82]—there can be no difference. I only wish I could be more useful; but you see I do all in my power. I am not one of those that spare their own trouble; and Nanny shall fetch her, however it may put me to inconvenience to have my chief counsellor away for three days.[83] I suppose, sister, you will put the child in the little white attic, near the old nurseries. It will be much the best place for her, so near Miss Lee, and not far from the girls, and close by the housemaids,[84] who could either of them help to dress her you know, and take care of her clothes, for I suppose you would not think it fair to expect Ellis to wait on her as well as the others.[85] Indeed, I do not see that you could possibly place her any where else."

Lady Bertram made no opposition.

"I hope she will prove a well-disposed girl," continued Mrs. Norris, "and be sensible of her uncommon good fortune in having such friends."

"Should her disposition be really bad," said Sir Thomas, "we must not, for our own children's sake, continue her in the family; but there is no reason to expect so great an evil.[86] We shall probably see much to wish altered in her, and must prepare ourselves for gross ignorance, some meanness of opinions, and very distressing vulgarity of manner;[87] but these are not incurable faults—nor, I trust, can they be dangerous for her associates. Had my daughters been *younger* than herself, I should have considered the introduction of such a companion, as a matter of very serious moment; but as it is, I hope

82. Miss Lee is the family governess, the "regular instructress" mentioned by Sir Thomas, while the other two girls are his daughters, who are roughly Fanny's age. A governess was a servant, but a high-ranking one, which is why she is called "Miss." They were usually women with no money but from fairly good backgrounds, which ensured they were well educated enough to teach, and that their speech and manners were sufficiently refined for them to serve as models for their charges.

83. The mistress of a house would often have a servant who was her chief advisor and assistant in deciding on and carrying out household tasks. It is not clear why Nanny will be away three days, since it takes only two to travel to London and back. It is possible she is spending two nights in London to ensure she is present when the child arrives there the day after her first night; it is also possible that they have arranged a rendezvous south of London in order to make the child's journey from Portsmouth easier. Finally, Mrs. Norris may be exaggerating in order to magnify the trouble she will suffer by her servant's absence.

84. The top floor of a grand house like this was often the location of the nurseries, as well as the rooms for the servants, including the governess. Housemaids were the most basic type of female servant; their principal job was cleaning the house.

85. Ladies often had lady's maids, who would help them dress, fix their hair, and take care of their clothes. They were upper servants, which gave them the privilege of being called by their last name (hence "Ellis"). In this case the two daughters of Sir Thomas share a lady's maid (Lady Bertram, as revealed later, has her own). When a lady's maid was not available, a housemaid could perform her tasks instead. For a contemporary picture, see p. 493.

86. *evil*: misfortune. The word then tended to have a less strong connotation than at present.

87. Sir Thomas's low expectations reflect partly his own snobbery, but partly the reality of dramatic differences in the experience and upbringing of children depending on their social class. This was particularly marked in education: there were no government schools or standard curriculum, so while those at the top would have private governesses and instructors or go to exclusive schools, those at the bottom would receive little or no schooling. The Prices would have given their children some education, but the girls, whose education was considered less important, would likely have been taught by their mother when she was not occupied with household chores; girls also would be required to spend much of their time assisting their mother when they were old enough. The resulting lack of knowledge could produce a "meanness," i.e., baseness or littleness, in their ideas about the world. Finally, the manners

there can be nothing to fear for *them*, and every thing to hope for *her*, from the association."

"That is exactly what I think," cried Mrs. Norris, "and what I was saying to my husband this morning. It will be an education for the child said I, only being with her cousins; if Miss Lee taught her nothing, she would learn to be good and clever from *them*."

"I hope she will not tease my poor pug," said Lady Bertram; "I have but just got Julia to leave it alone."[88]

"There will be some difficulty in our way, Mrs. Norris," observed Sir Thomas, "as to the distinction proper to be made between the girls as they grow up; how to preserve in the minds of my *daughters* the consciousness of what they are, without making them think too lowly of their cousin; and how, without depressing her spirits too far, to make her remember that she is not a *Miss Bertram*. I should wish to see them very good friends, and would, on no account, authorize in my girls the smallest degree of arrogance towards their relation; but still they cannot be equals. Their rank, fortune, rights, and expectations, will always be different. It is a point of great delicacy, and you must assist us in our endeavours to choose exactly the right line of conduct."[89]

Mrs. Norris was quite at his service; and though she perfectly agreed with him as to its being a most difficult thing, encouraged him to hope that between them it would be easily managed.

It will be readily believed that Mrs. Norris did not write to her sister in vain. Mrs. Price seemed rather surprised that a girl should be fixed on, when she had so many fine boys,[90] but accepted the offer most thankfully, assuring them of her daughter's being a very well-disposed, good-humoured girl, and trusting they would never have cause to throw her off.[91] She spoke of her farther as somewhat delicate and puny, but was sanguine in the hope of her being materially better for change of air.[92] Poor woman! she probably thought change of air might agree with many of her children.[93]

taught and practiced at various social levels differed significantly, giving those lower down many characteristics that seemed vulgar to those above them.

88. Pugs, like other lapdogs, were very popular among wealthy ladies. They had been introduced into Europe during the seventeenth century by Dutch traders who encountered them in Asia. They came to England by the end of that century and became a favorite pet during the next, reaching the peak of their popularity late in the eighteenth century, when the queen was a great devotee of pugs: a dictionary written in 1780 gives as one of the two definitions of "pug" "anything tenderly loved." A number of writers of the time discuss pugs, sometimes affectionately and sometimes mockingly, for ladies' affection for small dogs was a frequent object of ridicule.

89. Sir Thomas's careful weighing of these conflicting principles reflects partly his preference for his own children—among other things, they will have greater rights within the family and a larger fortune, and therefore superior expectations of a good marriage—and his wish to behave well toward a niece he is bringing into his family. It also reflects a conflict within the society of the time, between a belief in the rightness of social hierarchy and of treating people differently according to their rank (a belief that underlay the entire social and political order), and a belief, strongly grounded in the established Christian faith, in extending compassion and concern to all people regardless of their rank. The tension between the two can be seen in many aspects of this society, and in contemporary writings.

90. Mrs. Price is later described as favoring her sons. She also might think that a boy, because he needs to pursue a career, would benefit more from an improvement in his education and in the social level of those he associates with.

91. *throw her off*: rid themselves of her.

92. Medical opinion of the time attributed many illnesses to the effects of bad air, and the air in towns like Portsmouth was often foul, due to poor sanitation and crowded living quarters.

93. This is a rare authorial exclamation in Austen's novels. Usually, she confines herself to impersonal description, though her descriptions often contain strong doses of irony and moral judgment. One reason for it here is that Fanny comes from a more deprived background than the heroines of any of the other novels, and while Jane Austen gets around to depicting this background in detail only toward the end, she wishes to give the reader some sense of its harsh reality by a brief evocation of the pity it naturally arouses.

Chapter Two

*T*he little girl performed her long journey in safety, and at Northampton was met by Mrs. Norris,[1] who thus regaled[2] in the credit of being foremost to welcome her, and in the importance of leading her in to the others, and recommending her to their kindness.

Fanny Price was at this time just ten years old, and though there might not be much in her first appearance to captivate, there was, at least, nothing to disgust her relations. She was small of[3] her age, with no glow of complexion, nor any other striking beauty; exceedingly timid and shy, and shrinking from notice; but her air,[4] though awkward, was not vulgar, her voice was sweet, and when she spoke, her countenance was pretty. Sir Thomas and Lady Bertram received her very kindly, and Sir Thomas seeing how much she needed encouragement, tried to be all that was conciliating; but he had to work against a most untoward gravity of deportment—and Lady Bertram, without taking half so much trouble, or speaking one word where he spoke ten, by the mere aid of a good-humoured smile, became immediately the less awful[5] character of the two.

The young people were all at home,[6] and sustained their share in the introduction very well, with much good humour, and no embarrassment, at least on the part of the sons, who at seventeen and sixteen, and tall of their age, had all the grandeur of men in the eyes of their little cousin. The two girls were more at a loss from being younger and in greater awe of their father, who addressed them on the occasion with rather an injudicious particularity.[7] But they were too much used to company and praise, to have any thing like natural shyness, and their confidence increasing from their cousin's total want[8] of it, they were soon able to take a full survey of her face and her frock[9] in easy indifference.

They were a remarkably fine family, the sons very well-looking,[10] the daughters decidedly handsome, and all of them well-grown

1.   The girl's two-day journey would have been either by public coach or by a smaller hired carriage (for the latter, which is the way characters in Austen's novels usually travel, see p. 483, note 22). Mrs. Norris had stipulated for the former, but it is possible Sir Thomas, who already chose a "more respectable though less economical rendezvous," would have also paid more for a means of conveyance that was far more respectable as well as more private and comfortable. In either case Northampton, meaning the principal town in Northamptonshire, would have been her last stop. Mansfield Park is described as being "seventy miles from London" (p. 114), and Northampton was around sixty-five miles by roads of that time. The short remaining distance would allow Sir Thomas to send his own carriage and horses, accompanied by Mrs. Norris, to meet his niece.

2.   *regaled*: delighted.

3.   *of*: for. This usage often occurs in Austen's novels. Immediately below, the children at Mansfield Park are described as "well-grown and forward of their age." There are also other cases where prepositions are used differently than they are today.

4.   *air*: outward character, demeanor.

5.   *awful*: imposing; tending to inspire awe or fear.

6.   This means that the boys are home from school—a little later the younger boy is said to be at boarding school (p. 44), and the older boy is almost certainly at school as well—and that means this scene takes place in August. As explained there (note 83), the younger boy's school had holidays in August and around Christmas and Easter, and since Fanny is now "just ten years old" and we later learn that her birthday is in July (she is described on page 80 as having "just reached her eighteenth year" in July), it must be August now.

7.   This means he singled them out, probably by telling them that they, as fellow girls, had a particular obligation to make their cousin feel at home, and that this backfired by making them more awkward and hesitant. Sir Thomas's inability to communicate well with his daughters or establish any rapport, due to his formality and the awe he inspires, will play an important role in the story.

8.   *want*: lack.

9.   A frock was a soft, loose gown. It was the standard wear for infants of both sexes, and continued to be worn by girls when older.

10.   *well-looking*: good-looking.

and forward[11] of their age, which produced as striking a difference between the cousins in person,[12] as education had given to their address;[13] and no one would have supposed the girls so nearly of an age as they really were. There was in fact but two years between the youngest and Fanny. Julia Bertram was only twelve, and Maria but a year older.[14] The little visitor meanwhile was as unhappy as possible. Afraid of every body, ashamed of herself, and longing for the home she had left, she knew not how to look up, and could scarcely speak to be heard, or without crying. Mrs. Norris had been talking to her the whole way from Northampton of her wonderful good fortune, and the extraordinary degree of gratitude and good behaviour which it ought to produce, and her consciousness of misery was therefore increased by the idea of its being a wicked thing for her not to be happy. The fatigue too, of so long a journey, became soon no trifling evil. In vain were the well-meant condescensions[15] of Sir Thomas, and all the officious prognostications of Mrs. Norris that she would be a good girl; in vain did Lady Bertram smile and make her sit on the sofa[16] with herself and pug,[17] and vain was even the sight of a gooseberry tart towards giving her comfort;[18] she could scarcely swallow two mouthfuls before tears interrupted her, and sleep seeming to be her likeliest friend, she was taken to finish her sorrows in bed.

"This is not a very promising beginning," said Mrs. Norris when Fanny had left the room. — "After all that I said to her as we came along, I thought she would have behaved better; I told her how much might depend upon her acquitting herself well at first. I wish there may[19] not be a little sulkiness of temper—her poor mother had a good deal; but we must make allowances for such a child—and I do not know that her being sorry to leave her home is really against her, for, with all its faults, it *was* her home, and she cannot as yet understand how much she has changed for the better; but then there is moderation in all things."

It required a longer time, however, than Mrs. Norris was inclined to allow, to reconcile Fanny to the novelty of Mansfield Park, and the separation from every body she had been used to. Her feelings were very acute, and too little understood to be properly attended to.[20]

11. *forward*: precocious.

12. *person*: personal appearance.

13. *address*: outward demeanor or manner.

14. Thus the elder Bertram girl, like Fanny, has been named after her mother.

15. *condescensions*: acts of graciousness or friendliness, especially toward an inferior.

16. Sofas, where Lady Bertram regularly stations herself, had become popular pieces of furniture in England only in the decade or two prior to this novel. For a picture, see the following page.

17. This is one of several instances where "pug" is used, by either the narrator or Lady Bertram, without an article before it. Since at a couple of points the "p" is capitalized, it seems that, rather than bothering to give her dog a specific name, she has simply chosen to call it "Pug." This would be consistent with her general indolence.

18. Tarts, especially for fruit, had long been popular in England. Since tart pastry requires less cooking than the pastry for pies (also long popular in England), tarts are better for foods that cook quickly. Gooseberries, which grow wild in England and have been cultivated there since the Middle Ages, were often used in tarts as well as other recipes. Jane Austen makes a few references in her letters to gooseberries growing in the kitchen garden adjacent to her home.

19. *wish there may*: hope there will be.

20. Fanny's very acute feelings, and the inability or unwillingness of others to understand them, whether because of their lack of concern or Fanny's quiet and withdrawn manner, will characterize her situation throughout the novel, often with significant consequences.

Nobody meant to be unkind, but nobody put themselves out of their way to secure her comfort.

The holiday allowed to the Miss Bertrams the next day on purpose to afford leisure for getting acquainted with, and entertaining their young cousin, produced little union. They could not but hold her cheap[21] on finding that she had but two sashes,[22] and had never learnt French;[23] and when they perceived her to be little struck with the duet they were so good as to play,[24] they could do no more than make her a generous present of some of their least valued toys, and leave her to herself, while they adjourned to whatever might be the favourite holiday sport[25] of the moment, making artificial flowers or wasting gold paper.[26]

Fanny, whether near or from her cousins, whether in the school-room,[27] the drawing-room,[28] or the shrubbery,[29] was equally forlorn, finding something to fear in every person and place. She was disheartened by Lady Bertram's silence, awed by Sir Thomas's grave looks, and quite overcome by Mrs. Norris's admonitions. Her elder cousins mortified her by reflections on her size, and abashed her by noticing her shyness; Miss Lee wondered at her ignorance, and the maid-servants sneered at her clothes;[30] and when to these sorrows

A sofa of the period.

[From A. E. Reveirs-Hopkins, *The Sheraton Period* (New York, 1922), Figure 7]

21. *hold her cheap*: look down on her.

22. Girls normally wore sashes at the waist around their frocks. Frocks were usually made of plain white muslin (a lightweight cotton that was very popular in this period for female fashions). Sashes, which were also worn by women, provided color and helped the frocks fit more snugly; for an example, see p. 60.

23. Modern languages, particularly French and to a lesser degree Italian, were subjects for girls, especially in the upper ranks of society; Jane Austen herself learned to read French, though she never could speak it well. Girls rarely learned Latin or Greek, which were central to boys' education at this time.

24. Music was a highly valued accomplishment for girls. Their duet is most likely played on the pianoforte (the ancestor of today's piano), which had developed in the eighteenth century and soon became the most popular instrument and a common fixture in homes. Jane Austen played the pianoforte well and practiced regularly for most of her life.

25. *sport*: amusement.

26. Girls of their class often engaged in decorative arts and crafts. This was considered an important genteel female skill, and there were books that explained how to do a variety of projects. The reference to wasting gold paper indicates the author's view of the uselessness of many of these projects, at least at this age. The artificial flowers were probably made from colored papers, which were often used in these decorative craft projects.

27. The schoolroom was a room in the house dedicated to teaching the girls (it may also have been for the boys before they went to boarding school).

28. The drawing room was the main sitting or living room in wealthier houses. A later description of the Prices' home indicates that they have only a parlor, a more modest living room found at a lower social level; hence Fanny is probably surprised and intimidated by the grandeur and elegance of the drawing room here.

29. A shrubbery was a standard feature of the area adjacent to grand houses. It was an area of formal plantings, which could include trees, that were laid out in a decorative pattern.

30. The maidservants probably help her to dress and take care of her clothes. They would perform similar duties for the other ladies of the house, giving them a good basis for seeing how inferior Fanny's clothes are. Clothes were a very important marker of status. Moreover, servants often identified with the family that employed them, and could be very snobbish toward those inferior in status to the family, even if these people were far above the servants themselves.

was added the idea of the brothers and sisters among whom she had always been important as play-fellow, instructress, and nurse,[31] the despondence that sunk her little heart was severe.

The grandeur of the house astonished, but could not console her. The rooms were too large for her to move in with ease; whatever she touched she expected to injure,[32] and she crept about in constant terror of something or other; often retreating towards her own chamber to cry; and the little girl who was spoken of in the drawing-room when she left it at night, as seeming so desirably sensible of her peculiar good fortune, ended every day's sorrows by sobbing herself to sleep. A week had passed in this way, and no suspicion of it conveyed by her quiet passive manner, when she was found one morning by her cousin Edmund, the youngest of the sons, sitting crying on the attic stairs.

"My dear little cousin," said he with all the gentleness of an excellent nature, "what can be the matter?" And sitting down by her, was at great pains to overcome her shame in being so surprised,[33] and persuade her to speak openly. "Was she ill? or was any body angry with her? or had she quarrelled with Maria and Julia? or was she puzzled about any thing in her lesson that he could explain? Did she, in short, want any thing he could possibly get her, or do for her?" For a long while no answer could be obtained beyond a "no, no—not at all—no, thank you;" but he still persevered, and no sooner had he begun to revert to her own home, than her increased sobs explained to him where the grievance lay. He tried to console her.

"You are sorry to leave Mamma, my dear little Fanny," said he, "which shows you to be a very good girl; but you must remember that you are with relations and friends, who all love you, and wish to make you happy. Let us walk out in the park,[34] and you shall tell me all about your brothers and sisters."

On pursuing the subject, he found that dear as all these brothers and sisters generally were, there was one among them who ran more in her thoughts than the rest. It was William whom she talked of most and wanted most to see. William, the eldest, a year older than herself, her constant companion and friend; her advocate with her mother (of whom he was the darling) in every distress. "William did

31. Fanny, as the oldest girl, helped her mother with the younger children. With a large family and limited help from servants, her mother would be very busy. "Nurse" then meant someone who took care of small children as well as someone who tended the sick.

32. A grand house like this would be full of expensive objects, including fine paintings, sculpture, and ceramic pieces. In addition to providing aesthetic pleasure, these were meant to proclaim the wealth and artistic taste of the owner.

33. Since the attic stairs lead only to her room and the servants' quarters, she likely did not expect a family member to see her there.

34. *park*: grounds around a house. Grand houses like this had very extensive parks, sometimes stretching for miles, and including paths for walking.

A contemporary portrait of three children.
[From *The Masterpieces of Hoppner* (London, 1912), p. 45]

not like she should come away—he had told her he should miss her very much indeed." "But William will write to you, I dare say." "Yes, he had promised he would, but he had told *her* to write first." "And when shall you do it?" She hung her head and answered, hesitatingly, "she did not know; she had not any paper."

"If that be all your difficulty, I will furnish you with paper and every other material,[35] and you may write your letter whenever you choose. Would it make you happy to write to William?"

"Yes, very."

"Then let it be done now. Come with me into the breakfast-room,[36] we shall find every thing there, and be sure of having the room to ourselves."

"But cousin—will it go to the post?"[37]

"Yes, depend upon me it shall; it shall go with the other letters; and as your uncle will frank it, it will cost William nothing."

"My uncle!" repeated Fanny with a frightened look.

"Yes, when you have written the letter, I will take it to my father to frank."[38]

Fanny thought it a bold measure, but offered no farther resistance; and they went together into the breakfast-room, where Edmund prepared her paper, and ruled her lines[39] with all the good will that her brother could himself have felt, and probably with somewhat more exactness. He continued with her the whole time of her writing, to assist her with his penknife or his orthography,[40] as either were wanted; and added to these attentions, which she felt very much, a kindness to her brother, which delighted her beyond all the rest. He wrote with his own hand his love to his cousin William, and sent him half a guinea under the seal.[41] Fanny's feelings on the occasion were such as she believed herself incapable of expressing; but her countenance and a few artless words fully conveyed all their gratitude and delight, and her cousin began to find her an interesting object. He talked to her more, and from all that she said, was convinced of her having an affectionate heart, and a strong desire of doing right; and he could perceive her to be farther entitled to attention, by great sensibility of[42] her situation, and great timidity. He had never knowingly given her pain, but he now felt that she required more positive kindness, and with that view endeavoured, in the first place, to lessen her

35. Among the materials needed for writing were a pen, an inkwell for dipping a pen into, and a pounce pot, or sander, for sprinkling a substance onto the fresh ink to help it dry.

36. Having a separate breakfast room indicates the wealth of the family. It would be less grand than the dining room, used for dinner.

37. *post*: mail.

38. Members of Parliament, as Sir Thomas is (see p. 43, note 72), as well as some other public officials, had the privilege of franking letters, or designating letters as theirs, which allowed them to be conveyed free of postage. The system had developed in the late seventeenth century and by the eighteenth had become widely used, and abused; several laws were passed in the late eighteenth century to curb the abuses, but they had limited effect and those with the privilege continued to frank letters for those they knew. In several of her letters Jane Austen mentions her intention, or another woman's, to take advantage of the presence of someone who can provide a frank for her next letter (November 1, 1800; November 8, 1800; October 11, 1813). The privilege was especially valuable at this point, for the government, which used the post office to raise revenue for general expenditures, increased rates significantly at several points during the expensive wars against France from 1793 to 1814. In 1812, the very time when this novel was being written, rates reached the highest point they ever had.

39. *ruled her lines*: drew lines on her paper using a pencil and ruler. Neat handwriting, in straight lines, was highly prized; the high cost of paper, and even more of postage (determined by number of sheets), would also make people wish to fit as much as possible on a page, which would be easier with straight and symmetrical lines. Lined paper did exist but was expensive.

40. Quill or feather pens became dull fairly quickly; a penknife was used to cut the end of the pen in order to sharpen the point. As for spelling, Fanny's young age and limited education probably led to many mistakes, and dictionaries were not as common then as they later became.

41. Because envelopes did not yet exist, letters were sealed by folding up the paper and then either placing a sticky wafer between the folds of the outer sheet or melting wax over the outer edge and stamping it. Edmund, using the latter method, has placed a coin on the paper and melted the wax over the coin before stamping it. The half-guinea, a gold coin worth a little more than half a pound (for guineas, see p. 103, note 11) and thus not insignificant in monetary value, was small and thin enough to go under a seal. Sending half-guineas in this way was a popular way to transmit money by mail.

42. *great sensibility of*: acute feelings and sensitivity regarding.

fears of them all, and gave her especially a great deal of good advice as to playing with Maria and Julia, and being as merry as possible.

From this day Fanny grew more comfortable. She felt that she had a friend, and the kindness of her cousin Edmund gave her better spirits with every body else. The place became less strange, and the people less formidable; and if there were some amongst them whom she could not cease to fear, she began at least to know their ways, and to catch the best manner of conforming to them. The little rusticities[43] and awkwardnesses which had at first made grievous inroads on the tranquillity of all, and not least of herself, necessarily wore away, and she was no longer materially afraid to appear before her uncle, nor did her aunt Norris's voice make her start very much. To her cousins she became occasionally an acceptable companion. Though unworthy, from inferiority of age and strength, to be their constant associate, their pleasures and schemes[44] were sometimes of a nature to make a third very useful, especially when that third was of an obliging, yielding temper; and they could not but own, when their aunt inquired into her faults, or their brother Edmund urged her claims to their kindness, that "Fanny was good-natured enough."

Edmund was uniformly kind himself, and she had nothing worse to endure on the part of Tom, than that sort of merriment which a young man of seventeen will always think fair with a child of ten. He was just entering into life, full of spirits,[45] and with all the liberal[46] dispositions of an eldest son, who feels born only for expense and enjoyment. His kindness to his little cousin was consistent with his situation and rights;[47] he made her some very pretty presents, and laughed at her.

As her appearance and spirits improved, Sir Thomas and Mrs. Norris thought with greater satisfaction of their benevolent plan; and it was pretty soon decided between them, that though far from clever, she showed a tractable disposition, and seemed likely to give them little trouble. A mean[48] opinion of her abilities was not confined to *them*. Fanny could read, work,[49] and write, but she had been taught nothing more; and as her cousins found her ignorant of many things with which they had been long familiar, they thought her prodigiously stupid,[50] and for the first two or three weeks were continually bringing some fresh report of it into the drawing-room. "Dear Mamma,

43. *rusticities*: qualities that are unrefined or uncouth.

44. *schemes*: plans, projects. The word is frequently used in Austen's novels, and usually with no pejorative connotation.

45. *spirits*: eagerness, animation.

46. *liberal*: unrestrained.

47. As an elder son he will inherit the family estate, so he can look forward to being very wealthy. He does not need to prepare for a profession, as his younger brother does, and so as long as his father is alive to manage the estate he can live a life of almost complete leisure.

48. *mean*: low, disdainful.

49. *work*: do needlework. Almost all girls were taught this skill, for it was a regular, if not daily, activity of women, including the wealthy (though the latter engaged more in decorative embroidery than practical sewing). The frequent use of "work" to mean needlework in Austen's novels testifies to this. Austen herself was a skilled needlewoman, and some fine samples of her delicate embroidery survive. For contemporary pictures of women doing needlework, see pp. 128 and 315; for a needlework pattern, see p. 48.

50. *stupid*: slow-witted. The word usually had a less harsh connotation than it does now.

only think, my cousin cannot put the map of Europe together[51]—or my cousin cannot tell the principal rivers in Russia—or she never heard of Asia Minor[52]—or she does not know the difference between water-colours and crayons![53]—How strange!—Did you ever hear any thing so stupid?"

"My dear," their considerate aunt would reply;[54] "it is very bad, but you must not expect every body to be as forward and quick at learning as yourself."

"But, aunt, she is really so very ignorant!—Do you know, we asked her last night, which way she would go to get to Ireland; and she said, she should cross to the Isle of Wight. She thinks of nothing but the Isle of Wight, and she calls it *the Island*, as if there were no other island in the world.[55] I am sure I should have been ashamed of myself, if I had not known better long before I was so old as she is. I cannot remember the time when I did not know a great deal that she has not the least notion of yet. How long ago it is, aunt, since we used to repeat the chronological order of the kings of England, with the dates of their accession, and most of the principal events of their reigns!"[56]

"Yes," added the other; "and of the Roman emperors as low as

A grand modern house (Langley Park, Norfolk), similar to Mansfield Park.

[From John Preston Neale, *Views of the Seats of Noblemen and Gentlemen*, Vol. III (London, 1820)]

51. Geography was a popular academic subject. Putting the map together means fitting a jigsaw puzzle whose pieces were the countries of Europe. Such puzzles were a popular, and from contemporary accounts highly effective, way to teach children geography. The jigsaw puzzle seems to have been invented in England in the 1760s for this exact purpose.

52. During the eighteenth century Russia had emerged as one of the leading powers of Europe; its vast territory contained many rivers, most notably the Dnieper, Don, and Volga. What was then called Asia Minor is currently Turkey. At that time it was the center of the Ottoman Empire, which controlled the southern Balkans and much of the Middle East and thus was a significant factor in international affairs.

53. Drawing and painting were frequently taught to girls, and watercolors and crayons were the two leading media, as they could be employed using paper and relatively inexpensive materials and were not difficult to learn. Oil painting was cultivated far less often: it was more expensive and difficult, and since there was no thought of girls becoming professional artists, there was no need for them to produce works of the highest possible quality.

54. They addressed their mother, but Mrs. Norris responds. This will happen frequently, a testament to her regular presence at Mansfield and her far greater volubility.

55. The Isle of Wight is a large island close to Portsmouth (see map, p. 882). Its prominence, and its role in forming the harbor that was the city's lifeblood, would make it natural for people there to call it simply "the Island." Jane Austen observed this usage when she lived in the neighboring town of Southampton.

56. Memorization was a central part of education. This was lamented by a number of writers on education, including Maria Edgeworth, whose novels were favorites of Jane Austen's.

Severus;[57] besides a great deal of the Heathen Mythology,[58] and all the Metals, Semi-Metals,[59] Planets, and distinguished philosophers."

"Very true, indeed, my dears, but you are blessed with wonderful memories, and your poor cousin has probably none at all. There is a vast deal of difference in memories, as well as in every thing else, and therefore you must make allowance for your cousin, and pity her deficiency. And remember that, if you are ever so forward and clever yourselves, you should always be modest; for, much as you know already, there is a great deal more for you to learn."

"Yes, I know there is, till I am seventeen.[60] But I must tell you another thing of Fanny, so odd and so stupid. Do you know, she says she does not want to learn either music or drawing."

"To be sure, my dear, that is very stupid indeed, and shows a great want of genius[61] and emulation.[62] But, all things considered, I do not know whether it is not as well that it should be so, for, though you know (owing to me) your papa and mamma are so good as to bring her up with you, it is not at all necessary that she should be as accomplished as you are;—on the contrary, it is much more desirable that there should be a difference."

Such were the counsels by which Mrs. Norris assisted to form her nieces' minds;[63] and it is not very wonderful that with all their promising talents and early information,[64] they should be entirely deficient in the less common acquirements[65] of self-knowledge, generosity, and humility. In every thing but disposition,[66] they were admirably taught.[67] Sir Thomas did not know what was wanting, because, though a truly anxious father, he was not outwardly affectionate, and the reserve of his manner repressed all the flow of their spirits before him.

To the education of her daughters, Lady Bertram paid not the smallest attention. She had not time for such cares. She was a woman who spent her days in sitting nicely dressed on a sofa, doing some long piece of needle-work, of little use and no beauty, thinking more of her pug than her children, but very indulgent to the latter, when it did not put herself to inconvenience, guided in every thing important by Sir Thomas, and in smaller concerns by her sister. Had she possessed greater leisure for the service of her girls, she would probably have supposed it unnecessary, for they were under the care

57. Severus is Septimius Severus, who was Roman emperor from 193 to 211. "As low as" means as late as. In other words, they memorized the emperors from the beginning until that point, a span of approximately 250 years and twenty emperors. The choice of Severus as an endpoint is logical, since he was the last emperor with a long and distinguished reign in the first two and a half centuries of the Roman Empire, when it was at its height. He was followed by a long succession of short-lived and unremarkable emperors, under whom the empire experienced decades of civil war and invasion that permanently weakened it.

58. The mythology of ancient Greece and Rome was central to the classical literature that formed much of men's education at this time. It also was a frequent subject of contemporary art and literature, and was a basic point of cultural reference in many contexts.

59. "Semi-metals" was the term for substances that are not malleable, including arsenic, cobalt, manganese, nickel, and zinc. Regular metals included copper, gold, iron, lead, mercury, silver, and tin. The total number in both categories was smaller than today—the periodic table of the elements did not exist, and many elements on it had yet to be identified—so memorizing all of them would not be as prodigious a feat as now.

60. Seventeen was a standard age for girls' education to end. But the statement also indicates a foolish complacency and arrogance on the part of the speaker. One important theme in Austen's work is the ignorance and folly shown by even intelligent and well-educated people, no matter what their age, and thus the need for all to be open to learning more.

61. *genius*: natural aptitude, along with inclination. At this time the word was only occasionally used to mean extraordinary ability.

62. *emulation*: ambition to equal others.

63. *minds*: characters. The term, often used in Austen's novels, usually refers to general inner state and qualities, rather than purely intellectual ones.

64. *information*: education, knowledge.

65. *acquirements*: accomplishments, attainments.

66. *disposition*: general mental character, especially regarding moral qualities.

67. Jane Austen is here commenting on matters that were the subject of great debate at the time. The eighteenth century witnessed a growing vogue for encouraging accomplishments in girls from families able to afford a good education for their daughters; in contrast, in earlier times good household management was often considered to be all that women needed to be taught. The popularity of this new standard is indicated in *Pride and Prejudice* when a character declares, "I am sure I never heard a young lady being spoken of for the first time, without being informed that she was very accomplished."

of a governess, with proper masters,[68] and could want nothing more. As for Fanny's being stupid at learning, "she could only say it was very unlucky, but some people *were* stupid, and Fanny must take more pains; she did not know what else was to be done; and except her being so dull,[69] she must add, she saw no harm in the poor little thing—and always found her very handy and quick in carrying messages, and fetching what she wanted."

Fanny, with all her faults of ignorance and timidity, was fixed[70] at Mansfield Park, and learning to transfer in its favour much of her attachment to her former home, grew up there not unhappily among her cousins. There was no positive ill-nature in Maria or Julia; and though Fanny was often mortified by their treatment of her, she thought too lowly of her own claims to feel injured by it.

From about the time of her entering the family, Lady Bertram, in consequence of a little ill-health, and a great deal of indolence, gave up the house in town,[71] which she had been used to occupy every spring, and remained wholly in the country, leaving Sir Thomas to attend his duty in Parliament,[72] with whatever increase or diminution of comfort might arise from her absence. In the country, therefore, the Miss Bertrams continued to exercise their memories, practise their duets, and grow tall and womanly; and their father saw them becoming in person, manner, and accomplishments, every thing that could satisfy his anxiety.[73] His eldest son was careless and extravagant, and had already given him much uneasiness; but his other children promised him nothing but good. His daughters he felt, while they retained the name of Bertram, must be giving it new grace, and in quitting it he trusted would extend its respectable alliances;[74] and the character of Edmund, his strong good sense and uprightness of mind, bid most fairly for utility, honour, and happiness to himself and all his connections. He was to be a clergyman.[75]

Amid the cares and the complacency[76] which his own children suggested, Sir Thomas did not forget to do what he could for the children of Mrs. Price; he assisted her liberally in the education and disposal of her sons as they became old enough for a determinate pursuit:[77] and Fanny, though almost totally separated from her family, was sensible of the truest satisfaction in hearing of any kindness

The accomplishments most cultivated, and praised, were usually some limited academic skills (especially languages), music and drawing, and skill in dancing, dress, and physical deportment. This emphasis provoked a reaction by the end of the century, as many writers, without necessarily condemning these accomplishments, argued that they were far less important than the cultivation of more substantial moral and intellectual qualities. In their view, girls and their families were focusing on decorative attributes at the expense of wisdom, deeper learning (far more than memorization), and the development of moral character. Jane Austen indicates sympathy for this view in her novels, and much of this story demonstrates its validity.

68. Masters were specialists hired to teach children particular subjects such as music, drawing, or dancing. Wealthy families often hired them; here they would supplement the work of the governess, who inevitably did not have expertise in all subjects.

69. *dull*: stupid, foolish.

70. *fixed*: settled.

71. A house in London was a mark of high status (for those with estates in the country) as well as wealth, due to its expense.

72. Spring was when the annual sessions of Parliament were held. Sir Thomas is a member, which was common for those at the top of the social hierarchy, membership being a source of prestige and influence (as well as financial benefit at times). It was also regarded as a duty for those whose wealth and leisure and education made them, in the contemporary view, particularly suited for directing the affairs of the nation. One of the main arguments for having a privileged elite was that it provided the country with a class of people who could govern it well.

73. Sir Thomas is evaluating his daughters according to the prevailing standards that emphasized surface qualities in women.

74. They would quit the name of Bertram upon marriage. The landed elite conceived of marriage as, at least in part, an alliance between families, one that could enhance the influence and social position of each.

75. The system of inheritance that prevailed among the landed elite in England at this time gave the family estate to the eldest son. Younger sons as well as daughters would inherit a sum of money, coming from the family assets but worth far less than the main estate; this would provide the daughters with a dowry and help the sons in their necessary pursuit of a profession.

76. *complacency*: pleasure, satisfaction.

77. *determinate pursuit*: definite or clearly defined career path.

towards them, or of any thing at all promising in their situation or conduct. Once, and once only in the course of many years, had she the happiness of being with William. Of the rest she saw nothing; nobody seemed to think of her ever going amongst them again, even for a visit, nobody at home seemed to want her; but William determining, soon after her removal, to be a sailor, was invited to spend a week with his sister in Northamptonshire, before he went to sea.[78] Their eager affection in meeting, their exquisite[79] delight in being together, their hours of happy mirth, and moments of serious conference, may be imagined; as well as the sanguine views[80] and spirits of the boy even to the last, and the misery of the girl when he left her. Luckily the visit happened in the Christmas holidays,[81] when she could directly look for comfort to her cousin Edmund; and he told her such charming things of what William was to do, and be hereafter, in consequence of his profession,[82] as made her gradually admit that the separation might have some use. Edmund's friendship never failed her: his leaving Eton for Oxford made no change in his kind dispositions, and only afforded more frequent opportunities of proving them.[83] Without any display of doing more than the rest, or any fear of doing too much, he was always true to her interests, and considerate of her feelings, trying to make her good qualities understood, and to conquer the diffidence which prevented their being more apparent; giving her advice, consolation, and encouragement.

Kept back as she was by every body else, his single support could not bring her forward, but his attentions were otherwise of the highest importance in assisting the improvement of her mind, and extending its pleasures. He knew her to be clever, to have a quick apprehension as well as good sense, and a fondness for reading, which, properly directed, must be an education in itself. Miss Lee taught her French, and heard her read the daily portion of History;[84] but he recommended the books which charmed her leisure hours, he encouraged her taste, and corrected her judgment; he made reading useful by talking to her of what she read, and heightened its attraction by judicious praise. In return for such services she loved him better than any body in the world except William; her heart was divided between the two.

78. This choice of a naval career would be natural for someone growing up in Portsmouth, which was completely dominated by the navy. At this point William is only eleven or twelve, but boys aspiring to be a naval officer usually began their service at that age. It took many years to master the intricacies of sailing ships, which were enormously complex mechanisms that often operated under extremely difficult conditions of weather or war. This mastery was considered more important than any academic learning that might result from remaining in school. Later another brother of Fanny's is described as starting his career in the navy at eleven.

79. *exquisite*: intense, exalted.

80. *views*: expectations, i.e., of success, and perhaps also adventure and heroism in the navy.

81. Since Fanny arrived in August (see p. 27, note 6), this is four months later, and thus a time when Fanny's and William's memories of each other are still vivid.

82. The navy did offer many opportunities for someone like William to rise in rank, especially because the war with Napoleonic France created a great demand for naval personnel and many positions were vacated due to injury or death. The navy also offered the chance of becoming wealthy, through the distribution of prize money after the capture of an enemy ship (for more, see p. 121, note 69). Finally, the crucial role the navy played in the war would make people regard serving in it as an admirable patriotic service.

83. Eton was probably the most famous and distinguished of the small number of boarding schools that were the principal venue for education of upper-class boys in England. Most graduates of such schools would go on to Oxford or Cambridge, the only two universities in England at this time. Both existed primarily to train members of the Anglican clergy, Edmund's chosen profession, though other men would also attend.

At this time Eton had three holidays during the year, a month around Christmas, two weeks around Easter, and the month of August. Oxford had four weeks around Christmas, almost three weeks around Easter, and a little more than three months from early July to early October. Hence Edmund would have substantially more time away from school after he entered Oxford. This transition would have happened not long after Fanny arrived, for he was sixteen then and students usually entered a university at eighteen.

84. History was probably the subject that contemporary writers on education were most likely to recommend as an essential part of study for girls (it was also valued for boys, though it was subordinated to the supreme emphasis on ancient languages and literature).

Chapter Three

*T*he first event of any importance in the family was the death of Mr. Norris, which happened when Fanny was about fifteen, and necessarily introduced alterations and novelties. Mrs. Norris, on quitting the parsonage, removed first to the park, and afterwards to a small house of Sir Thomas's in the village,[1] and consoled herself for the loss of her husband by considering that she could do very well without him, and for her reduction of income by the evident necessity of stricter economy.[2]

The living was hereafter for Edmund, and had his uncle died a few years sooner, it would have been duly given to some friend to hold till he were old enough for orders.[3] But Tom's extravagance[4] had, previous to that event, been so great,[5] as to render a different disposal of the next presentation necessary,[6] and the younger brother must help to pay for the pleasures of the elder. There was another family-living actually held for Edmund;[7] but though this circumstance had made the arrangement somewhat easier to Sir Thomas's conscience, he could not but feel it to be an act of injustice, and he earnestly tried to impress his eldest son with the same conviction, in the hope of its producing a better effect than any thing he had yet been able to say or do.

"I blush for you, Tom," said he, in his most dignified manner; "I blush for the expedient which I am driven on, and I trust I may pity your feelings as a brother on the occasion. You have robbed Edmund for ten, twenty, thirty years, perhaps for life, of more than half the income which ought to be his.[8] It may hereafter be in my power, or in your's (I hope it will), to procure him better preferment;[9] but it must not be forgotten, that no benefit of that sort would have been beyond his natural claims on us, and that nothing can, in fact, be an equivalent for the certain advantage which he is now obliged to forego through the urgency of your debts."

Tom listened with some shame and some sorrow; but escaping as

1. It would be normal for Sir Thomas, who probably owns much of the land in and around the village, to own some of the houses there. Jane Austen, during the latter part of her life when she wrote this and other novels, lived in a house owned by her brother, who owned a grander house and other land in the same village.

2. Her principal source of income has been her husband's annual clerical salary. For what she now lives on instead, see p. 59, note 37.

3. The right to appoint the holder of the clerical living, called an advowson, was in the hands of Sir Thomas; such advowsons were forms of property that could be bought and sold, or inherited. Sir Thomas had intended to appoint Edmund to the position, just as he earlier appointed Mr. Norris. If the latter died before Edmund was old enough to be in orders (age twenty-three), the normal expedient would be to appoint a friend on the condition that the friend would resign the living once Edmund was in a position to take it.

4. *extravagance*: unrestrained or excessive living, which in this case has also involved financial extravagance.

5. Tom has run up debts, which his father must pay. A later passage describes Tom as having engaged in gambling (p. 92), and he also may have borrowed money (his father would give him an allowance, but he might easily wish to spend more). Moneylenders would lend, though at high interest rates, to heirs of wealthy estates, who eventually would be in a position to repay.

6. The "different disposal" of the presentation means Sir Thomas is selling the right to appoint the next holder. He would be legally barred from a formal sale, permanently alienating the right of appointment, since such a sale could not occur while the living was vacant, nor would he wish to sell it permanently. But he can arrange informally to let someone else choose the next holder in return for a substantial payment. The man who appointed Jane Austen's father to his living sold the right of presentation to another living he controlled, and there were advertisements in newspapers offering to sell the next presentation to a living.

7. Sir Thomas intended for Edmund to hold both livings; many clergy did this.

8. The new holder must die or resign for Edmund to be appointed. "More than half" suggests that the salary for this living is higher than that for the family living still reserved for Edmund.

9. *preferment*: advancement to a church living. Sir Thomas may be able to procure a different living at some point, as might Tom after he inherits the estate and the church livings belonging to it.

quickly as possible, could soon with cheerful selfishness reflect, 1st, that he had not been half so much in debt as some of his friends; 2dly, that his father had made a most tiresome piece of work of it; and 3dly, that the future incumbent, whoever he might be, would, in all probability, die very soon.

On Mr. Norris's death, the presentation became the right of a Dr. Grant,[10] who came consequently to reside at Mansfield, and on proving to be a hearty man of forty-five, seemed likely to disappoint Mr. Bertram's calculations.[11] But "no, he was a short-neck'd, apoplectic sort of fellow, and, plied well with good things, would soon pop off."[12]

He had a wife about fifteen years his junior,[13] but no children, and they entered the neighbourhood with the usual fair report of being very respectable, agreeable people.

The time was now come when Sir Thomas expected his sister-in-law to claim her share in their niece, the change in Mrs. Norris's situation, and the improvement in Fanny's age, seeming not merely to do away any former objection to their living together, but even to give it the most decided eligibility; and as his own circumstances were rendered less fair than heretofore, by some recent losses on his West India Estate,[14] in addition to his eldest son's extravagance, it

A needlework pattern.

[From *The Repository of arts, literature, fashions, manufactures, &c*, Vol. XIII (1815), p. 122]

10. "Dr." means he is a doctor of divinity. Most clergy received only a bachelor's degree, and they would simply be called "Mr." A doctorate did not necessarily enhance one's chances of securing a better position, but it did confer greater prestige. The title "Dr." was not used to refer to medical men, who generally received no formal education.

11. "Mr. Bertram" is Tom. The eldest male of a family is called "Mr. + last name." Normally that is the father, but in this case he is "Sir Thomas" instead. Edmund, as a younger son, is called "Mr. Edmund Bertram."

12. "Apoplectic" means inclined toward apoplexy, the term used then for a sudden seizure, especially a stroke. (Not understanding the role of blood clots, people attributed strokes to other causes, such as overheating of the blood.) A short neck was considered one of the leading signs of being apoplectic; diagnosing susceptibility to disease through external appearance was very common, due to the lack of almost any internal diagnostic tools. A medical book of the time says of apoplexy, "The short-necked, the indolent, and such as are apt to indulge in full meals of animal food, and the free use of spirituous and vinous liquors, are generally its victims" (Richard Reece, *The Medical Guide*, 1820 ed., p. 190). This view provides the basis for Tom's hope that if "plied with good things" (as in fact Dr. Grant will be), he will soon "pop off." Tom's use of this slang expression signals his flip attitude toward serious matters.

13. This age difference was not unusual. The pressure for women to marry (for more, see p. 77, note 35) meant that women with poor marital prospects—and Mrs. Grant is shortly described as being neither good-looking nor rich—had a strong incentive to accept a man greatly their senior, especially if he could offer them a good home.

14. Many people in England had West Indian estates. During the seventeenth century England had acquired and settled a number of islands in the Caribbean, including Jamaica, Barbados, Antigua, Grenada, and St. Vincent. These colonies, which contained rich agricultural lands, attracted numerous English settlers, some of whom attained great wealth and gradually established a planter aristocracy that dominated the islands. The heyday of these colonies was the eighteenth century, when tremendous profits were made by many planters, most notably in sugar, which came to dominate production. The plantations were worked by massive numbers of imported African slaves, who became the majority population of the islands while also suffering extremely high death rates, due to brutality of treatment and the debilitating rigors involved in harvesting sugar. For this same reason, the one area of the antebellum United States that specialized in sugar cultivation, southern Louisiana, suffered far worse slave mortality than other slaveholding areas. For more on the issue of slavery, see p. 61, note 41.

During the second half of the eighteenth century many members of the planter class used their riches to move to England and live comfortably there. They and their descendants reassimilated into English life and intermarried

became not undesirable to himself to be relieved from the expense of her support, and the obligation of her future provision.[15] In the fulness of his belief that such a thing must be, he mentioned its probability to his wife; and the first time of the subject's occurring to her again, happening to be when Fanny was present, she calmly observed to her, "So, Fanny, you are going to leave us, and live with my sister. How shall you like it?"

Fanny was too much surprised to do more than repeat her aunt's words, "Going to leave you?"

"Yes, my dear, why should you be astonished? You have been five years with us, and my sister always meant to take you when Mr. Norris died. But you must come up and tack on my patterns all the same."[16]

The news was as disagreeable to Fanny as it had been unexpected. She had never received kindness from her aunt Norris, and could not love her.

"I shall be very sorry to go away," said she, with a faltering voice.

"Yes, I dare say you will; *that's* natural enough. I suppose you have had as little to vex you, since you came into this house, as any creature in the world."

"I hope I am not ungrateful, aunt," said Fanny, modestly.

"No, my dear; I hope not. I have always found you a very good girl."

"And am I never to live here again?"

"Never, my dear; but you are sure of a comfortable home. It can make very little difference to you, whether you are in one house or the other."

Fanny left the room with a very sorrowful heart; she could not feel the difference to be so small, she could not think of living with her aunt with any thing like satisfaction. As soon as she met with Edmund, she told him her distress.[17]

"Cousin," said she, "something is going to happen which I do not like at all; and though you have often persuaded me into being reconciled to things that I disliked at first, you will not be able to do it now. I am going to live entirely with my aunt Norris."

"Indeed!"

"Yes, my aunt Bertram[18] has just told me so. It is quite settled. I am

with wealthy English families. As a consequence, as a leading contemporary writer states, "Many persons there are, in Great Britain itself, who, amidst the continual fluctuation of human affairs, and the changes incident to property, find themselves possessed of estates in the West Indies which they have never seen" (Bryan Edwards, *The History, Civil and Commercial, of the British West Indies*, vol. 2, 1819 ed.). Sir Thomas Bertram's being a baronet suggests his family has been of prominent status in England for a while, which, along with the strong attachment he shows to Mansfield Park, makes it likely that the Mansfield estate is his principal source of income. Planters from the West Indies who settled in England instead tended to live in London or coastal towns with better prospects for social life and enjoyment. Yet his West Indies estate must be substantial, for he soon shows himself willing to go there for almost a year to deal with losses.

Such losses were not unusual. Many estates in the hands of absentee owners suffered difficulties, since they were managed by people, often local merchants or attorneys, who had other demands on their time or whose interests conflicted with those of the owner. Moreover, the reliance of much of the West Indies on a single export crop, and the islands' vulnerability to disruptions in international trade, produced great economic volatility. Around 1800 the islands suffered an acute downturn when Napoleon's blockade of Britain cut them off from trade with Europe and created a glut of sugar in Britain that drove the price down. This situation lasted until 1813, when this novel was being finished.

15. His assumption is that once Fanny goes to live with Mrs. Norris, the latter will naturally assume these responsibilities.

16. This is part of Lady Bertram's needlework, her principal daily activity. She would embroider a design from a pattern (many patterns for such use were printed in books and journals of the time—see the preceding page), and she has Fanny attach the pattern to the material using a "tack" or short stitch that can easily be removed.

17. Edmund is probably home on holiday from Oxford. He was sixteen when Fanny arrived, the normal age of entry was eighteen, and it is now five years later (making him twenty-one). Students studying to be clergy usually stayed four years. Since the timing of the next major event (the departure of his father and brother) suggests it is now November or December (see chronology, p. 855), this scene likely occurs during the Christmas holidays.

18. She has just spoken of "my aunt Norris," and now she says "my aunt Bertram." This usage is standard in Austen's novels. Speaking this way to Edmund about his own mother is also a mark of the prevailing formality of manners.

to leave Mansfield Park, and go to the White house,[19] I suppose, as soon as she is removed there."

"Well, Fanny, and if the plan were not unpleasant to you, I should call it an excellent one."

"Oh! Cousin!"

"It has every thing else in its favour. My aunt is acting like a sensible woman in wishing for you. She is choosing a friend and companion exactly where she ought, and I am glad her love of money does not interfere. You will be what you ought to be to her. I hope it does not distress you very much, Fanny."

"Indeed it does. I cannot like it. I love this house and every thing in it. I shall love nothing there. You know how uncomfortable I feel with her."

"I can say nothing for her manner to you as a child; but it was the same with us all, or nearly so. She never knew how to be pleasant to children. But you are now of an age to be treated better; I think she *is* behaving better already; and when you are her only companion, you *must* be important to her."

"I can never be important to any one."

"What is to prevent you?"

"Every thing—my situation[20]—my foolishness and awkwardness."

"As to your foolishness and awkwardness, my dear Fanny, believe me, you never have a shadow of either, but in using the words so improperly. There is no reason in the world why you should not be important where you are known. You have good sense, and a sweet temper, and I am sure you have a grateful heart, that could never receive kindness without wishing to return it. I do not know any better qualifications for a friend and companion."

"You are too kind," said Fanny, colouring[21] at such praise; "how shall I ever thank you as I ought, for thinking so well of me? Oh! cousin, if I am to go away, I shall remember your goodness, to the last moment of my life."

"Why, indeed, Fanny, I should hope to be remembered at such a distance as the White house. You speak as if you were going two hundred miles off, instead of only across the park.[22] But you will belong to us almost as much as ever. The two families will be meeting every day in the year. The only difference will be, that living with your

19. The capital "W" may result from its having been previously owned by a family called White. Important houses often had proper names, as in Mansfield Park, and sometimes this name included the word "House," but in that case it would be spelled with a capital "H," as it is not here.

20. Her situation is her position as an adopted child, and the more humble social and economic level of her parents in comparison to the Bertram family and to Mrs. Norris.

21. *colouring*: blushing.

22. At a later point Mrs. Norris's new house, which is in the village, is described as a quarter-mile away. Edmund's wording signals that the park that surrounds Mansfield Park extends all the way to the edge of the village.

A private library from the late eighteenth century.

[From John Swarbrick, *Robert Adam and his Brothers* (New York, 1915), p. 267]

aunt, you will necessarily be brought forward, as you ought to be. *Here*, there are too many, whom you can hide behind; but with *her* you will be forced to speak for yourself."

"Oh! do not say so."

"I must say it, and say it with pleasure. Mrs. Norris is much better fitted than my mother for having the charge of you now. She is of a temper to do a great deal for any body she really interests herself about, and she will force you to do justice to your natural powers."[23]

Fanny sighed, and said, "I cannot see things as you do; but I ought to believe you to be right rather than myself, and I am very much obliged to you for trying to reconcile me to what must be. If I could suppose my aunt really to care for me, it would be delightful to feel myself of consequence to any body!—*Here*, I know I am of none, and yet I love the place so well."

"The place, Fanny, is what you will not quit, though you quit the house. You will have as free a command of the park and gardens as ever.[24] Even *your* constant little heart need not take fright at such a nominal change. You will have the same walks to frequent,[25] the same library to choose from,[26] the same people to look at, the same horse to ride."

"Very true. Yes, dear old grey poney.[27] Ah! cousin, when I remember how much I used to dread riding, what terrors it gave me to hear it talked of as likely to do me good;—(Oh! how I have trembled at my uncle's opening his lips if horses were talked of) and then think of the kind pains you took to reason and persuade me out of my fears, and convince me that I should like it after a little while, and feel how right you proved to be, I am inclined to hope you may always prophesy as well."

"And I am quite convinced that your being with Mrs. Norris, will be as good for your mind, as riding has been for your health—and as much for your ultimate happiness, too."[28]

So ended their discourse, which, for any very appropriate service it could render Fanny, might as well have been spared, for Mrs. Norris had not the smallest intention of taking her. It had never occurred to her, on the present occasion, but as a thing to be carefully avoided. To prevent its being expected, she had fixed on the smallest habita-

23. *powers*: abilities, especially mental ones.

24. Grand houses usually had gardens near the house, both for flowers and for fruits and vegetables.

25. A typical park around a house featured walking paths, some of them extending a great distance if the park was large enough. For examples, see the picture on the next page and the pictures on pp. 189 and 197.

26. A library was a standard feature of a grand house. It often contained books collected over many generations. They would be an invaluable resource for someone devoted to reading, as Fanny is shown to be, for books were expensive and only a limited number would be easily available, even for purchase, in a rural village like Mansfield.

27. Exercise was recognized as important for health, and riding horses was almost the only form possible for women, aside from walking, since almost all outdoor sports were considered inappropriate for them. Fanny's youth, small stature for her age, and lack of physical vigor would make a pony the logical choice for her; it would also be less expensive.

28. This conversation, which turns out to concern a situation that never occurs, does have one crucial significance: it marks an incipient willingness by Fanny to judge differently from Edmund and to express that difference, despite her almost worshipful respect for him and her timidity and diffidence. That willingness will grow, and play an important role in the story.

tion which could rank as genteel among the buildings of Mansfield parish;[29] the White house being only just large enough to receive herself and her servants, and allow a spare room for a friend, of which she made a very particular point;[30]—the spare-rooms at the parsonage had never been wanted, but the absolute necessity of a spare-room for a friend was now never forgotten. Not all her precautions, however, could save her from being suspected of something better; or, perhaps, her very display of the importance of a spare-room, might have misled Sir Thomas to suppose it really intended for Fanny. Lady Bertram soon brought the matter to a certainty, by carelessly observing to Mrs. Norris,—

"I think, sister, we need not keep Miss Lee any longer, when Fanny goes to live with you?"[31]

Mrs. Norris almost started. "Live with me, dear Lady Bertram,[32] what do you mean?"

"Is not she to live with you?—I thought you had settled it with Sir Thomas?"

"Me! never. I never spoke a syllable about it to Sir Thomas, nor he to me. Fanny live with me! the last thing in the world for me to think of, or for any body to wish that really knows us both. Good heaven! what could I do with Fanny?—Me! a poor helpless, forlorn widow, unfit for any thing, my spirits quite broke down, what could I do with a girl at her time of life, a girl of fifteen! the very age of all others to need most attention and care, and put the cheerfullest spirits to the test.[33] Sure Sir Thomas could not seriously expect such a thing! Sir Thomas is too much my friend. Nobody that wishes me well, I am sure, would propose it. How came Sir Thomas to speak to you about it?"

"Indeed, I do not know. I suppose he thought it best."

"But what did he say?—He could not say he *wished* me to take Fanny. I am sure in his heart he could not wish me to do it."

"No, he only said he thought it very likely—and I thought so too. We both thought it would be a comfort to you. But if you do not like it, there is no more to be said. She is no incumbrance here."

"Dear sister! If you consider my unhappy state, how can she be any comfort to me? Here am I a poor desolate widow, deprived of the best of husbands, my health gone in attending and nursing him,[34] my

29. Mansfield parish means the local neighborhood. A rural parish usually comprised a village and the immediate surrounding countryside.

30. A house would need to be of a certain size and quality to qualify as genteel, which means having at least two bedrooms suitable for residents or guests of genteel status (rather than for servants, who would inhabit inferior rooms). Thus, Mrs. Norris, in wishing to maintain the outward signs of gentility while also avoiding having to take Fanny, must pretend that her second good bedroom is reserved for a potential guest.

31. Since Fanny is now fifteen, the two Bertram daughters are seventeen and eighteen. This means they are at the end of their education and no longer need a governess; the Bertrams are retaining Miss Lee only to continue teaching Fanny.

32. Calling her "Lady Bertram," as Mrs. Norris will continue to do, indicates her deference; in contrast, Lady Bertram has simply called her "sister." Social differences have superseded the difference in age (which favors Mrs. Norris).

33. "Cheerfullest," rather than "most cheerful," reflects a greater willingness at this time to add "-er" or "-est" to long adjectives. In other novels Austen also uses "cheerfullest" or "cheerfuller," and later in this novel she uses "forwarder."

34. Nursing had not yet emerged as a profession and was mainly done by the women of the family or by female servants.

A park next to a grand house.

[From Ercole Silva, *Dell'arte de' giardini inglesi*, Vol. I (Milano, 1813), Plate I]

spirits still worse, all my peace in this world destroyed,[35] with barely enough to support me in the rank of a gentlewoman, and enable me to live so as not to disgrace the memory of the dear departed[36] — what possible comfort could I have in taking such a charge upon me as Fanny! If I could wish it for my own sake, I would not do so unjust a thing by the poor girl. She is in good hands, and sure of doing well. I must struggle through my sorrows and difficulties as I can."

"Then you will not mind living by yourself quite alone?"

"Dear Lady Bertram! what am I fit for but solitude? Now and then I shall hope to have a friend in my little cottage (I shall always have a bed for a friend); but the most part of my future days will be spent in utter seclusion. If I can but make both ends meet, that's all I ask for."

"I hope, sister, things are not so very bad with you neither — considering Sir Thomas says you will have six hundred a year."[37]

"Lady Bertram, I do not complain. I know I cannot live as I have done, but I must retrench where I can, and learn to be a better manager. I *have been* a liberal housekeeper enough, but I shall not be ashamed to practise economy now. My situation is as much altered as my income. A great many things were due from poor Mr. Norris as clergyman of the parish, that cannot be expected from me. It is unknown how much was consumed in our kitchen by odd comers and goers.[38] At the White house, matters[39] must be better looked after. I *must* live within my income, or I shall be miserable; and I own it would give me great satisfaction to be able to do rather more — to lay by a little at the end of the year."

"I dare say you will. You always do, don't you?"[40]

"My object, Lady Bertram, is to be of use to those that come after me. It is for your children's good that I wish to be richer. I have nobody else to care for, but I should be very glad to think I could leave a little trifle among them, worth their having."

"You are very good, but do not trouble yourself about them. They are sure of being well provided for. Sir Thomas will take care of that."

"Why, you know Sir Thomas's means will be rather straitened, if the Antigua estate is to make such poor returns."

35. The use of "this world" to refer to earthly life, in contrast to the next world or heaven, was common. Mrs. Norris, as a clergyman's wife, would be very accustomed to this pious rhetoric (as also in her use of "peace," another word frequently evoked in religious contexts), even though she never gives any sense of having genuine religious feeling herself.

36. Were she to live shabbily, it could harm Mr. Norris's reputation by making it look as if he failed to provide sufficiently for his widow. She is again pretending to care about others to justify her selfishness.

37. Widows of clergymen received no pensions or other payments. Mrs. Norris's principal source of income is the 7,000 pounds that she, like her sister Lady Bertram, received from her family as her dowry. This sum, which was controlled by her husband while they were married, reverted to her after his death. It provides her with 350 pounds a year, at the standard rate of 5 percent per annum on government bonds (the main way people invested their money, aside from land). She also might have inherited her husband's own money, though because he was described at the outset as having "scarcely any private fortune," this would be unlikely to provide much. Thus she must be drawing annual returns from money she saved over the course of her married life. The Norrises were married for seventeen years (see chronology, pp. 853–855) and enjoyed an income of "very little less than a thousand a year," so she must have adopted a formidable program of frugality. To generate the entire 250 pounds a year required to bring her to 600, she would have needed to save 5,000 pounds, almost a third of the total income she and her husband received.

It is hard to convert these amounts into current equivalents. Judging by changes in retail prices, a pound from the time of the novel is equal to 65 to 70 pounds today, or around 100 U.S. dollars by current exchange rates. This would make Mrs. Norris's 600-pound annual income the equivalent of $60,000. But present societies, in the U.S. and the U.K., are far wealthier on average than the society of that time: Mrs. Norris's income would put her in the top 2 or 3 percent of the population then. Moreover, relative prices have altered significantly: in particular, goods tended to be relatively much more expensive then and labor much cheaper. Thus, according to a contemporary guide, a household with Mrs. Norris's income would normally hire four to five servants.

38. Clergy, as well as other genteel people, were expected to extend charity to the poor, which would often include feeding people who came to the house in need. Mrs. Norris's words indicate she did this grudgingly.

39. *matters*: household or financial affairs.

40. Lady Bertram's words indicate not only Mrs. Norris's habitual thriftiness but also her inclination to boast of it. Given Lady Bertram's inattentiveness and vagueness, she probably remembers this only because her sister has repeatedly spoken of her achievement.

"Oh! *that* will soon be settled. Sir Thomas has been writing about it, I know."[41]

"Well, Lady Bertram," said Mrs. Norris, moving to go, "I can only say that my sole desire is to be of use to your family—and so

A woman with a sash (see p. 31, note 22).

[From *The Repository of arts, literature, fashions, manufactures, &c*, Vol. VIII (1812), p. 174]

41. Antigua was one of the most important islands in the British West Indies, and, like most of the others, it was dominated by sugar plantations worked by slaves. Jane Austen's decision to have the principal family in her novel possess such a plantation has naturally aroused comment. It is also interesting in light of clear indications of her personal opposition to slavery. The strongest of these is in a letter written during the time she was writing this novel (January 24, 1813). In it she expresses admiration for Thomas Clarkson, author of *The History of the Rise, Progress, & Accomplishment of the Abolition of the African Slave-Trade by the British Parliament* (1808). Clarkson was a leader in the campaign to abolish the slave trade in British territories, which was achieved in 1807, and in the book he chronicles and celebrates that struggle, while also expressing his horror at the continuing institution of slavery. (The abolitionists focused on the slave trade first because they thought it would be easier to end that than to abolish slavery entirely; they turned to the latter goal afterward and finally accomplished it in 1833.)

The most obvious reason she chose to make Sir Thomas the owner of an estate in the West Indies is that it is essential for the plot. Sir Thomas leaves for an extended trip to Antigua in order to salvage the struggling estate, and this absence will permit several developments that are central to the story. A significant property overseas is necessary for this, since heads of families with large estates in England would otherwise never go away for so long. The West Indies was the one place at the time where they might have such a property. Moreover, its location is far enough away to make an absence of a year or two normal, but not so far to make a much longer absence more likely.

Some commentators have suggested that Austen also wished to raise the issues of slavery and abolition in the novel. One piece of evidence cited is its title, for it was the judge Lord Mansfield who in 1772 laid down the decision that effectively abolished slavery within England; this decision helped inspire the movement to abolish it throughout the British Empire. It is possible that Austen had this in mind when choosing the title, but far from certain, for Mansfield is a common English name, typical of those she used for the characters and places in her novels. Moreover, the paucity of references to slavery and abolition, with only one overt mention of the slave trade (see p. 366, as well as the accompanying note), makes any theory of an underlying message on the matter inherently speculative.

Another possibility is that her choice of Antigua was influenced by a perception among many that slavery there was less oppressive than elsewhere in the West Indies. In the late eighteenth century those ruling the islands had made some moves, including the passage of new laws, to improve conditions for slaves, partly because they hoped to blunt the criticisms of abolitionists. Antigua went further than others in instituting capital punishment for anyone who killed a slave. It is uncertain how much difference this and other laws really made in the lives of slaves, but people in England interested in the matter would have known of their existence. Jane Austen could have been

if Sir Thomas should ever speak again about my taking Fanny, you will be able to say, that my health and spirits put it quite out of the question—besides that, I really should not have a bed to give her, for I must keep a spare-room for a friend."

Lady Bertram repeated enough of this conversation to her husband, to convince him how much he had mistaken his sister-in-law's views; and she was from that moment perfectly safe from all expectation, or the slightest allusion to it from him. He could not but wonder at her refusing to do any thing for a niece, whom she had been so forward[42] to adopt; but as she took early care to make him, as well as Lady Bertram, understand that whatever she possessed was designed for their family, he soon grew reconciled to a distinction, which at the same time that it was advantageous and complimentary to them, would enable him better to provide for Fanny himself.[43]

Fanny soon learnt how unnecessary had been her fears of a removal; and her spontaneous, untaught felicity on the discovery, conveyed some consolation to Edmund for his disappointment in what he had expected to be so essentially serviceable to her. Mrs. Norris took possession of the White house, the Grants arrived at the parsonage, and these events over, every thing at Mansfield went on for some time as usual.

The Grants showing a disposition to be friendly and sociable, gave great satisfaction in the main among their new acquaintance. They had their faults, and Mrs. Norris soon found them out.[44] The Dr. was very fond of eating, and would have a good dinner every day; and Mrs. Grant, instead of contriving to gratify him at little expense, gave her cook as high wages as they did at Mansfield Park,[45] and was scarcely ever seen in her offices.[46] Mrs. Norris could not speak with any temper of such grievances, nor of the quantity of butter and eggs that were regularly consumed in the house.[47] "Nobody loved plenty and hospitality more than herself—nobody more hated pitiful[48] doings—the parsonage she believed had never been wanting in comforts of any sort, had never borne a bad character[49] in *her time*, but this was a way of going on that she could not understand. A fine lady in a country parsonage was quite out of place.[50] *Her* store-room she thought might have been good enough for Mrs. Grant to

exposed to information regarding Antigua because her father knew well a man who had inherited an estate on the island. She also could have read comments in Clarkson's history that cited Antigua as a place where recent missionary activity had especially improved the conditions of the slaves and as the one island in the British West Indies that had not needed to import slaves to make up for a high death rate. The choice of Antigua could allow her to give Sir Thomas a West Indian estate for the sake of the plot, while doing less violence than otherwise to her own disapproval of slavery.

42. *forward*: ardent, eager.

43. Meaning her distinction of the Bertrams for her favor, and her destining all her fortune for them.

44. Her main source of information would be village gossip, which is consistently depicted in Austen's novels as a pervasive and powerful force. Both those working in local shops and other women who shopped there would notice what Mrs. Grant spent and share that information, especially since the parson and his wife are such prominent people. Moreover, Mrs. Grant's servants, who would know everything about her household affairs, would talk to other working people, including the servants in other households, allowing someone as nosy as Mrs. Norris to pump her own servants for information.

45. Grand houses like Mansfield Park usually had highly professional cooks, in many cases male, and often from France due to the prestige of French cooking. Such male cooks would earn more than any other servant—a contemporary guide to servants specifies eighty pounds a year—and even female cooks could earn a lot. Hence matching the wages of the Mansfield cook would represent a considerable expenditure for the Grants.

46. *offices*: rooms in a house where practical tasks are performed, such as the kitchen, scullery (where dishes are cleaned), pantry, storage cellars, and laundry room. In a household with the income of the parsonage the mistress would not do such work herself but would supervise what the servants did there.

47. Butter and eggs were prominent parts of the English diet. Both were added to a wide array of recipes, and butter was also the basic fat used for cooking.

48. *pitiful*: paltry, stingy.

49. *character*: reputation—in this case, its reputation for generosity, rated a highly important virtue both for genteel people in general and for clergy.

50. "Fine lady" could refer to a woman of particularly elevated rank; it also could be used, sometimes pejoratively, to mean a woman of very refined and fastidious tastes. Mrs. Norris is probably using it in both senses, suggesting that Mrs. Grant is inappropriately acting like a fine lady.

go into.[51] Enquire where she would,[52] she could not find out that Mrs. Grant had ever had more than five thousand pounds."[53]

Lady Bertram listened without much interest to this sort of invective. She could not enter into the wrongs of an economist,[54] but she felt all the injuries of beauty in Mrs. Grant's being so well settled in life without being handsome, and expressed her astonishment on that point almost as often, though not so diffusely, as Mrs. Norris discussed the other.[55]

These opinions had been hardly canvassed[56] a year, before another event arose of such importance in the family, as might fairly claim some place in the thoughts and conversation of the ladies. Sir Thomas found it expedient to go to Antigua himself,[57] for the better arrangement of his affairs, and he took his eldest son with him in the hope of detaching him from some bad connections at home.[58] They left England with the probability of being nearly a twelvemonth absent.[59]

The necessity of the measure in a pecuniary light, and the hope of its utility to his son, reconciled Sir Thomas to the effort of quitting the rest of his family, and of leaving his daughters to the direction of others at their present most interesting[60] time of life. He could

A naval squadron in battle (see the next page).

[From J. R. Green, *A Short History of the English People*, Vol. IV (New York, 1903), p. 1797]

51. The storeroom was for long-term storage of foodstuffs like sugar, flour, and tea as well as household products like soap and candles. It was less dirty and unpleasant than other offices in a house; Mrs. Grant's alleged unwillingness even to go there would make her especially culpable in Mrs. Norris's eyes. Part of Jane Austen's household duties during the time she was writing her novels was to take care of the stores of tea, sugar, and wine.

52. Though this passage is in quotation marks, the use of "she" indicates it is reported speech rather than direct quotation. Austen uses this technique elsewhere. It allows her to summarize what the character said at greater length, or combine remarks made on numerous occasions (both are likely the case here, given Mrs. Norris's garrulousness and obsessive harping on the same points).

53. Since Mrs. Norris had seven thousand, this would mark Mrs. Grant's inferiority and undermine further her supposed pretensions to be a "fine lady."

54. *economist*: someone who advocates and practices thrift, or someone who manages a household. Both meanings would apply to Mrs. Norris.

55. The idea of women's beauty being an asset with a discernible value, and thus one that deserves an appropriate level of compensation, is found elsewhere in Austen's novels. One character in *Sense and Sensibility*, lamenting his sister's loss of beauty, says that now she is not likely to "marry a man worth more than five or six hundred a-year."

56. *canvassed*: discussed, examined.

57. As mentioned earlier (p. 49, note 14), long-term absenteeism of owners was frequently a reason for estates in the West Indies to suffer losses; hence an extended visit by the proprietor could improve things.

58. The bad connections are probably friends who have encouraged Tom in his extravagant behavior and indebtedness. Sir Thomas has a good additional justification: it would be standard for the elder son to be gradually initiated into the affairs of a family estate that he will eventually inherit. Tom is not in a position to refuse because, until he comes into his inheritance, he depends completely on an allowance from his father.

59. Since their expected return is shortly identified as September, it is likely October or early November now. From this point on, events begin to happen close enough together to make it both possible and important to place them in a particular time of year.

60. *interesting*: important.

not think Lady Bertram quite equal to supply his place with them, or rather to perform what should have been her own;[61] but in Mrs. Norris's watchful attention, and in Edmund's judgment, he had sufficient confidence to make him go without fears for their conduct.

Lady Bertram did not at all like to have her husband leave her; but she was not disturbed by any alarm for his safety, or solicitude for his comfort, being one of those persons who think nothing can be dangerous or difficult, or fatiguing to any body but themselves.

The Miss Bertrams were much to be pitied on the occasion; not for their sorrow, but for their want of it. Their father was no object of love to them, he had never seemed the friend of their pleasures, and his absence was unhappily most welcome. They were relieved by it from all restraint; and without aiming at one gratification that would probably have been forbidden by Sir Thomas, they felt themselves immediately at their own disposal, and to have every indulgence within their reach. Fanny's relief, and her consciousness of it, were quite equal to her cousins', but a more tender nature suggested that her feelings were ungrateful, and she really grieved because she could not grieve.[62] "Sir Thomas, who had done so much for her and her brothers, and who was gone perhaps never to return![63] that she should see him go without a tear!—it was a shameful insensibility."[64] He had said to her moreover, on the very last morning, that he hoped she might see William again in the course of the ensuing winter, and had charged her to write and invite him to Mansfield as soon as the squadron to which he belonged should be known to be in England.[65] "This was so thoughtful and kind!"—and would he only have smiled upon her and called her "my dear Fanny," while he said it, every former frown or cold address might have been forgotten. But he had ended his speech in a way to sink her in sad mortification, by adding, "If William does come to Mansfield, I hope you may be able to convince him that the many years which have passed since you parted, have not been spent on your side entirely without improvement—though I fear he must find his sister at sixteen in some respects too much like his sister at ten." She cried bitterly over this reflection when her uncle was gone; and her cousins, on seeing her with red eyes, set her down as a hypocrite.

61. It is normally the wife's place to supervise and guide her daughters, but since Lady Bertram has long neglected it, it has fallen by default to Sir Thomas.

62. Fanny thus contrasts to her cousins, who should have more reason to grieve their father's absence (and the dangers he is facing—see next note) but are not grieving at all. Fanny's tendency to hold herself to the strictest moral standard will continue throughout the novel, and have significant effects.

63. Voyages across the Atlantic involved serious dangers, especially because Britain was still at war. Moreover, residence in the West Indies posed a considerable risk of one contracting a fatal disease (see p. 209, note 6).

64. *insensibility*: indifference, lack of feeling.

65. The Royal Navy contained a number of permanent fleets, as well as squadrons of ships organized to perform specific tasks. The latter might return home when a task was done, either to be disbanded or reassigned to different duties.

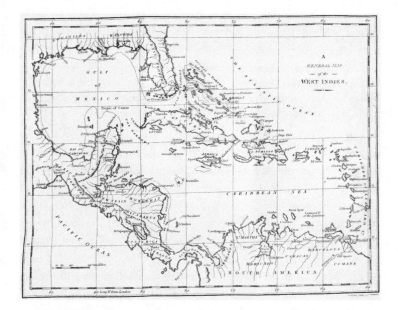

A map of the West Indies; Antigua is near the top of the chain of small islands on the far right.

[From Daniel MacKinnon, A *Tour through the British West Indies in the Years 1802 and 1803* (London, 1812)]

Chapter Four

*T*om Bertram had of late spent so little of his time at home, that
he could be only nominally missed; and Lady Bertram was soon
astonished to find how very well they did even without his father,
how well Edmund could supply his place in carving, talking to
the steward, writing to the attorney, settling with the servants,[1] and
equally saving her from all possible fatigue or exertion in every particular, but that of directing her letters.[2]

The earliest intelligence of the travellers' safe arrival in Antigua
after a favourable voyage, was received; though not before Mrs. Norris had been indulging in very dreadful fears, and trying to make
Edmund participate[3] them whenever she could get him alone; and
as she depended on being the first person made acquainted with any
fatal catastrophe, she had already arranged the manner of breaking
it to all the others, when Sir Thomas's assurances of their both being
alive and well, made it necessary to lay by her agitation and affectionate preparatory speeches for a while.

The winter came and passed without their being called for; the
accounts continued perfectly good;—and Mrs. Norris in promoting gaieties for her nieces, assisting their toilettes,[4] displaying their
accomplishments, and looking about for their future husbands,[5] had
so much to do as, in addition to all her own household cares, some
interference in those of her sister, and Mrs. Grant's wasteful doings
to overlook, left her very little occasion to be occupied even in fears
for the absent.

The Miss Bertrams were now fully established among the belles
of the neighbourhood; and as they joined to beauty and brilliant[6]
acquirements, a manner naturally easy,[7] and carefully formed to general civility and obligingness, they possessed its favour as well as its
admiration. Their vanity was in such good order, that they seemed to
be quite free from it, and gave themselves no airs; while the praises

1. These are all basic tasks of the male head of the household. Carving meant cutting the meat at the table (meat being the main food in the diet of the wealthy at the time). The steward managed the estate, while the attorney would handle its financial as well as legal affairs; he may need to be written to because he lived in a town, rather than in Mansfield village. Settling with the servants meant paying their wages; it is possible Sir Thomas, and now Edmund, also engage in more general management of the servants, a task usually done by the mistress of a household but that Lady Bertram most likely neglects.

2. Edmund can assume these duties because by this time—his father and brother left in the autumn (see p. 64 and p. 65, note 59)—he has finished his studies at Oxford. He is now twenty-two and probably finished earlier in the year. He will be at Mansfield for most of the remainder of the novel, allowing him to play a important role in the story and in the development of Fanny's feelings.

3. *participate*: share.

4. *toilettes*: getting dressed.

5. By now Maria is twenty, and Julia is either eighteen or nineteen. At these ages, young ladies would be looking to marry (poorer young women would often wait until later because they needed to earn enough for a dowry). A fundamental part of husband-hunting was the display of female accomplishments, many of which, including music and dancing, were intended to enhance the girls' charms in the eyes of potential mates.

6. *brilliant*: sparkling, splendid. This does not mean that their acquirements (accomplishments) are particularly intellectual.

7. *easy*: free from awkwardness or embarrassment.

attending such behaviour, secured, and brought round by their aunt,[8] served to strengthen them in believing they had no faults.[9]

Lady Bertram did not go into public with her daughters. She was too indolent even to accept a mother's gratification in witnessing their success and enjoyment at the expense of any personal trouble, and the charge was made over[10] to her sister, who desired nothing better than a post of such honourable representation, and very thoroughly relished the means it afforded her of mixing in society without having horses to hire.[11]

Fanny had no share in the festivities of the season; but she enjoyed being avowedly useful as her aunt's companion, when they called away the rest of the family; and as Miss Lee had left Mansfield, she naturally became every thing to Lady Bertram during the night of a ball or a party.[12] She talked to her, listened to her, read to her;[13] and the tranquillity of such evenings, her perfect security in such a *tête-à-tête* from any sound of unkindness, was unspeakably welcome to a mind which had seldom known a pause in its alarms or embarrassments. As to her cousins' gaieties, she loved to hear an account of them, especially of the balls, and whom Edmund had danced with; but thought too lowly of her own situation[14] to imagine she should ever be admitted to the same,[15] and listened therefore without an idea of any nearer concern in them. Upon the whole, it was a comfortable[16] winter to her; for though it brought no William to England, the never failing hope of his arrival was worth much.

The ensuing spring deprived her of her valued friend the old grey poney, and for some time she was in danger of feeling the loss in her health as well as in her affections, for in spite of the acknowledged importance of her riding on horseback, no measures were taken for mounting her again, "because," as it was observed by her aunts, "she might ride one of her cousin's horses at any time when they did not want them;" and as the Miss Bertrams regularly wanted their horses every fine day, and had no idea of carrying their obliging manners to the sacrifice of any real pleasure, that time of course never came. They took their cheerful rides in the fine mornings of April and May;[17] and Fanny either sat at home the whole day with one aunt, or walked beyond her strength at the instigation of the other; Lady

8. Meaning that their aunt Norris obtained the praises, apparently by prompting them from others, and then relayed them to her nieces.

9. This belief is always a sign of danger in Austen's novels, which consistently show the susceptibility of everyone toward faulty behavior, and the need to be aware of and attempt to correct one's potential faults. Jane Austen demonstrates this awareness in a letter, written when she was only a little older than Maria and Julia; in it she writes, after reporting someone's complaint about negligent treatment, "This was an oblique reproach at me, which I am sorry to have merited, and from which I will profit" (Nov. 18, 1798).

10. *made over*: handed over.

11. To attend social engagements on her own, unless they were at Mansfield Park, she would need to hire horses and probably a carriage (there is never any indication that she owns one). But if she accompanies Maria and Julia, filling the essential post of chaperone, she would be conveyed by the Bertrams' carriage and horses.

12. By now Fanny is seventeen, so a governess is no longer needed. A governess like Miss Lee sometimes stayed on as a companion to her mistress, for while technically a servant, she likely came from a fairly high social background and her speech and manners would be closer to those of her employers than to other servants. An important character in *Emma*, Miss Weston, stayed on in this way before eventually marrying.

13. Reading aloud was a common activity, especially in the evening. The high cost of artificial lighting made it more economical to have only enough light burning for one person to read to the others. This would be less of an issue for a wealthy family like the Bertrams, but even they would not disregard the expense, and Lady Bertram's indolence would undoubtedly make her prefer to have someone else do the reading in any case.

14. *situation*: social position.

15. Fanny's nonattendance at balls may result in part from her lower social status, but it also would be natural because of her younger age, combined with Mrs. Norris's determination to keep her down and the wish of Lady Bertram, who does not attend balls, to retain Fanny as a companion.

16. *comfortable*: pleasant, enjoyable.

17. At this time "morning" meant almost the entire day, which is why their morning riding confines Fanny so thoroughly.

Bertram holding exercise to be as unnecessary for every body as it was unpleasant to herself; and Mrs. Norris, who was walking all day, thinking every body ought to walk as much. Edmund was absent at this time, or the evil would have been earlier remedied. When he returned to understand how Fanny was situated, and perceived its ill effects, there seemed with him but one thing to be done, and that "Fanny must have a horse," was the resolute declaration with which he opposed whatever could be urged by the supineness of his mother, or the economy[18] of his aunt, to make it appear unimportant. Mrs. Norris could not help thinking that some steady old thing might be found among the numbers belonging to the Park, that would do vastly well,[19] or that one might be borrowed of the steward,[20] or that perhaps Dr. Grant might now and then lend them the poney he sent to the post.[21] She could not but consider it as absolutely unnecessary, and even improper, that Fanny should have a regular lady's horse of her own in the style of her cousins.[22] She was sure Sir Thomas had never intended it; and she must say, that to be making such a purchase in his absence, and adding to the great expenses of his stable at a time when a large part of his income was unsettled,[23] seemed to her very unjustifiable. "Fanny must have a horse," was Edmund's only reply. Mrs. Norris could not see it in the same light. Lady Bertram did; she entirely agreed with her son as to the necessity of it, and as to its being considered necessary by his father;—she only pleaded against there being any hurry, she only wanted him to wait till Sir Thomas's return, and then Sir Thomas might settle it all himself. He would be at home in September, and where would be the harm of only waiting till September?

Though Edmund was much more displeased with his aunt than with his mother, as evincing least regard for her niece, he could not help paying more attention to what she said, and at length determined on a method of proceeding which would obviate the risk of his father's thinking he had done too much, and at the same time procure for Fanny the immediate means of exercise, which he could not bear she should be without. He had three horses of his own, but not one that would carry a woman. Two of them were hunters; the third, a useful road-horse:[24] this third he resolved to exchange for

18. *economy*: thriftiness, frugality.

19. Mansfield Park would have horses for pulling carriages and possibly for working land on the Bertram family farm directly. Farm and carriage horses, needing great strength, tended to be heavier than horses for riding, making them unsuitable for someone like Fanny, who is small and not very strong.

20. The steward would certainly have a horse, perhaps more than one, since his job requires him to ride around frequently. Mansfield Park has a very large estate surrounding it. The bulk of it would be rented to tenant farmers, whom the steward would visit regularly to make sure everything was in order, to convey instructions from the estate, to maintain good relations, and to deal with problems or conflicts.

21. *post*: post office. The pony would be ridden by a servant, most likely a boy (boys were often employed to perform such tasks). If the pony's sole job was to ride to the village to fetch the post, it would likely be an old and feeble horse that the Grants purchased cheaply and that is suitable for little else.

22. Only some horses were considered suitable for women; in a letter Jane Austen, discussing her brother James's plan to add two new horses to the one he has, writes, "Mary [his wife] wishes the other two to be fit to carry women" (Dec. 27, 1808). Size was one determinant, which is why mares or ponies are preferred. In addition, some horses were trained to accommodate sidesaddle riding, the almost exclusive method for ladies.

23. A stable did involve considerable expense, including the costs of building and maintaining it (many were very elaborate structures) and of servants to tend to the horses. But since Sir Thomas already has a stable, the additional cost of one more horse would not be great, assuming there is room (and the absence of both Sir Thomas and Tom probably means they are not using the stable to full capacity).

24. Horses were ubiquitous in English society, used for an array of essential tasks, and were a particular interest of wealthy men, who kept them for pleasure as well as utility. Foreign travelers often remarked on the extreme interest in horses as well as the high quality of English horses. The latter resulted from the care taken with them and the extensive breeding of superior strains in England during the centuries preceding this novel, including the development of the hunter, which combined the speed of racehorses with the strength of road horses (two varieties, especially the racehorse, that had also been improved significantly through breeding). Hunters were used for fox hunting and thus needed to be able to ride fast and to leap over fences and streams.

one that his cousin might ride;[25] he knew where such a one was to be met with,[26] and having once made up his mind, the whole business was soon completed. The new mare proved a treasure; with a very little trouble,[27] she became exactly calculated[28] for the purpose, and Fanny was then put in almost full possession of her. She had not supposed before, that any thing could ever suit her like the old grey poney; but her delight in Edmund's mare was far beyond any former pleasure of the sort; and the addition it was ever receiving in the consideration of that kindness from which her pleasure sprung, was beyond all her words to express. She regarded her cousin as an example of every thing good and great, as possessing worth, which no one but herself could ever appreciate, and as entitled to such gratitude from her, as no feelings could be strong enough to pay. Her sentiments towards him were compounded of all that was respectful, grateful, confiding, and tender.

As the horse continued in name as well as fact, the property of Edmund, Mrs. Norris could tolerate its being for Fanny's use; and had Lady Bertram ever thought about her own objection again, he might have been excused in her eyes, for not waiting till Sir Thomas's return in September, for when September came, Sir Thomas was still abroad, and without any near prospect of finishing his business. Unfavourable circumstances had suddenly arisen at a moment when he was beginning to turn all his thoughts towards England, and the very great uncertainty in which every thing was then involved, determined him on sending home his son, and waiting the final arrangement by himself. Tom arrived safely, bringing an excellent account of his father's health; but to very little purpose, as far as Mrs. Norris was concerned. Sir Thomas's sending away his son, seemed to her so like a parent's care, under the influence of a foreboding of evil to himself, that she could not help feeling dreadful presentiments; and as the long evenings of autumn came on, was so terribly haunted by these ideas, in the sad solitariness of her cottage, as to be obliged to take daily refuge in the dining room of the park.[29] The return of winter engagements, however, was not without its effect;[30] and in the course of their progress, her mind became so pleasantly occupied in superintending the fortunes of her eldest niece, as tolerably to quiet her nerves. "If poor Sir Thomas were fated never to return, it

They were highly prized and also expensive. Edmund's having two indicates the wealth of the Bertram family, as well as his dedication to hunting, which is not threatened by his plan to become a clergyman: some writers of the time argued that killing for sport was incompatible with a religious vocation, but their view was a minority one. For pictures of hunters in action, see pp. 421 and 449; for a picture of racehorses, see the following page.

25. The road horse is less expensive than the hunters and thus would make a more even exchange for the smaller horse he is procuring for Fanny. He would have his own road horse—as opposed to those the family possesses for use in other carriages, such as the one that fetched Fanny from Northampton—to enable him to travel alone by carriage; for this he could use a gig, a small open carriage pulled by a single horse. Since he could also travel alone by horseback, he might consider the road horse a less essential possession.

26. Buying and selling horses was a regular pursuit of men who could afford them, so it is likely Edmund has heard acquaintances tell him of horses they, or people they know, wish to sell or exchange.

27. The "very little trouble" is probably the training needed to teach the horse to handle someone on a sidesaddle.

28. *calculated*: fitted, suited.

29. The dining room of a place like Mansfield Park was a grand room used only for dinner (as well as the after-dinner drinking of the men of the house). Hence, unlike the drawing room, it would be of limited use as a refuge from loneliness for Mrs. Norris; it would, however, since dinner was by far the largest meal of the day, be an excellent escape from having to pay for her own meals. The words "her cottage" reflect Mrs. Norris's own terminology in explaining why she must come; she also used "cottage" when explaining why she could not accommodate Fanny. Elsewhere her dwelling is called "the White house," but "cottage" sounds more pathetic.

30. Winter was prime season for parties and balls, since outdoor activities were more limited (and winter weather would usually not keep people from leaving home, since heavy snow is rare in England).

would be peculiarly[31] consoling to see their dear Maria well married," she very often thought; always when they were in the company of men of fortune, and particularly on the introduction of a young man who had recently succeeded to[32] one of the largest estates and finest places in the country.[33]

Mr. Rushworth was from the first struck with the beauty of Miss Bertram, and being inclined to marry, soon fancied himself in love. He was a heavy young man, with not more than common sense; but as there was nothing disagreeable in his figure[34] or address, the young lady was well pleased with her conquest. Being now in her twenty-first year, Maria Bertram was beginning to think matrimony a duty;[35] and as a marriage with Mr. Rushworth would give her the enjoyment of a larger income than her father's, as well as ensure her the house in town, which was now a prime object, it became, by the same rule of moral obligation, her evident duty to marry Mr. Rushworth if she could.[36] Mrs. Norris was most zealous in promoting the match, by every suggestion and contrivance, likely to enhance its desirableness to either party; and, among other means, by seeking an intimacy with the gentleman's mother, who at present lived with him, and to whom she even forced Lady Bertram to go through ten miles of indifferent road,[37] to pay a morning visit.[38] It was not long before a good under-

Racehorses.

[From William Henry Scott, *British Field Sports* (London, 1818), p. 461]

31. *peculiarly*: particularly.

32. *succeeded to*: inherited.

33. *country*: county.

34. *figure*: general appearance.

35. Many women, especially from wealthy families, would be married by the age of twenty-one. By her late twenties a woman was considered to be past prime marital age; thus, while Maria has some years to go before reaching that stage, it is natural she should be thinking now that the time has come. The pressure on young women to marry is a constant and powerful factor in Austen's novels, a reflection of social realities. Marriage was considered a duty, especially for a woman, since raising children was seen as her supreme vocation. But this ideal of duty was reinforced by powerful social and material incentives. Being married automatically conferred much greater status and prestige on a woman; in contrast, women who remained single were called old maids and could be subject to scorn and ridicule. By marrying, most woman also gained a much higher income, as well as material security for the future; Jane Austen, in a letter to a niece discussing the latter's decision whether to marry, declared, "Single Women have a dreadful propensity for being poor" (March 13, 1817). Finally, a married woman went from being a powerless dependent in another's home to having a home of her own in which she could exercise substantial influence through her role as mistress of the household, which included making most of the purchases, managing the budget, planning meals, accommodating guests, supervising the children, and, at this social level, directing the servants.

36. Having a house in London, in addition to one's country mansion, was very desirable, though also rare because of the high cost. The wording of the passage indicates that in Maria's case the ideal of a duty to marry is simply a good cover for her to pursue material advantage.

37. Rural roads were often in rough shape, for they were made of dirt and their upkeep depended on the vigilance of local authorities, which varied greatly. Such roads tended to be especially bad during this season, the winter, because of mud. Ten miles would take two hours or more each way, and passengers in the carriages of the time would be considerably jolted by uneven surfaces.

38. A visit of introduction would occur in the morning (meaning early afternoon in current parlance, since people usually stayed home early in the day). It would be important for Lady Bertram, as Maria's mother, to become formally acquainted through such a visit. Maria and Mr. Rushworth have already met at parties or balls, but this visit will help clear the way to an actual engagement.

standing took place between this lady and herself. Mrs. Rushworth acknowledged herself very desirous that her son should marry, and declared that of all the young ladies she had ever seen, Miss Bertram seemed, by her amiable[39] qualities and accomplishments, the best adapted to make him happy. Mrs. Norris accepted the compliment, and admired the nice discernment of character which could so well distinguish merit. Maria was indeed the pride and delight of them all—perfectly faultless—an angel; and of course, so surrounded by admirers, must be difficult[40] in her choice; but yet as far as Mrs. Norris could allow herself to decide on so short an acquaintance, Mr. Rushworth appeared precisely the young man to deserve and attach her.

After dancing with each other at a proper number of balls, the young people justified these opinions,[41] and an engagement, with a due reference to the absent Sir Thomas, was entered into, much to the satisfaction of their respective families, and of the general lookers-on of the neighbourhood, who had, for many weeks past, felt the expediency of Mr. Rushworth's marrying Miss Bertram.[42]

It was some months before Sir Thomas's consent could be received;[43] but in the mean while, as no one felt a doubt of his most cordial[44] pleasure in the connection, the intercourse of the two families was carried on without restraint, and no other attempt made at secrecy, than Mrs. Norris's talking of it every where as a matter not to be talked of at present.

Edmund was the only one of the family who could see a fault in the business; but no representation of his aunt's could induce him to find Mr. Rushworth a desirable companion. He could allow his sister to be the best judge of her own happiness, but he was not pleased that her happiness should centre in a large income; nor could he refrain from often saying to himself, in Mr. Rushworth's company, "If this man had not twelve thousand a year, he would be a very stupid fellow."[45]

Sir Thomas, however, was truly happy in the prospect of an alliance[46] so unquestionably advantageous, and of which he heard nothing but the perfectly good and agreeable. It was a connection exactly of the right sort; in the same county, and the same interest;[47] and his most hearty concurrence was conveyed as soon as possible. He

39. *amiable*: benevolent, pleasing, worthy of being loved. The word had a broader and stronger meaning then than now.

40. *difficult*: exacting, fastidious.

41. "A proper number" would confirm, to the couple and to the rest of the world, that they had become sufficiently acquainted for an engagement.

42. Nosiness and gossip about neighbors' affairs, especially those of elite families, is a pervasive feature of this society. Respect for rank and wealth would lead to a general approval of marriage between two people from such families.

43. There was regular mail service between Britain and its colonies in the West Indies, but it took a considerable amount of time. For more, see p. 207, note 2.

44. *cordial*: sincere, heartfelt.

45. He means that Mr. Rushworth would be regarded as very stupid without that fortune. Social and economic snobbery has distorted judgment of his true character and abilities. This revelation of his income, and the earlier statement that it is larger than Sir Thomas's, gives some sense of the latter (which is never specified). It is probably not a lot below twelve thousand, considering how comfortably the Bertrams live, even with recent losses in the West Indies and the need to provide for four children and a niece. Some commentators have guessed ten thousand a year.

46. *alliance*: marriage.

47. *interest*: party, faction, interest group. This could refer broadly to what was called "the landed interest," which both families belong to; to a political party (though these were fairly loose associations then); or to a narrower local alliance.

only conditioned[48] that the marriage should not take place before his return, which he was again looking eagerly forward to. He wrote in April, and had strong hopes of settling every thing to his entire satisfaction, and leaving Antigua before the end of the summer.

Such was the state of affairs in the month of July, and Fanny had just reached her eighteenth year,[49] when the society of the village received an addition in the brother and sister of Mrs. Grant, a Mr. and Miss Crawford, the children of her mother by a second marriage. They were young people of fortune. The son had a good estate in Norfolk,[50] the daughter twenty thousand pounds.[51] As children, their sister had been always very fond of them; but, as her own marriage had been soon followed by the death of their common parent, which left them to the care of a brother of their father, of whom Mrs. Grant knew nothing, she had scarcely seen them since. In their uncle's house they had found a kind home. Admiral and Mrs. Crawford, though agreeing in nothing else, were united in affection for these children, or at least were no farther adverse in their feelings than that each had their favourite, to whom they showed the greatest fondness of the two. The Admiral delighted in the boy, Mrs. Crawford doated on the girl;[52] and it was the lady's death which now obliged her *protegée*, after some months further trial at her uncle's house, to find another home. Admiral Crawford was a man of vicious conduct, who chose, instead of retaining his niece, to bring his mistress under his own roof;[53] and to this Mrs. Grant was indebted for her sister's proposal of coming to her, a measure quite as welcome on one side, as it could be expedient on the other; for Mrs. Grant having by this time run through the usual resources[54] of ladies residing in the country without a family of children; having more than filled her favourite sitting room with pretty furniture, and made a choice collection of plants and poultry,[55] was very much in want of some variety at home. The arrival, therefore, of a sister whom she had always loved, and now hoped to retain with her as long as she remained single, was highly agreeable; and her chief anxiety was lest Mansfield should not satisfy the habits of a young woman who had been mostly used to London.

Miss Crawford was not entirely free from similar apprehensions, though they arose principally from doubts of her sister's style of living

48. *conditioned*: stipulated.

49. This marks the beginning of the main action of the novel. From this point forward events will be narrated in far greater detail. This action will transpire over approximately one year, the same length as in all of Austen's longer novels.

50. Norfolk is a coastal county in eastern England; see map, p. 882. It is not far from Northampton.

51. This is a great deal more than Mrs. Grant's five thousand, or the seven thousand of Lady Bertram and her sisters. Among the landowning class, women's fortunes came in the form of lump sums; men's, in contrast, in the form of annual incomes, as in Mr. Rushworth's twelve thousand a year. The latter were generally much greater. Thus, while Miss Crawford's twenty thousand, as normally invested, would yield a thousand a year, we later learn that her brother's estate gives him four thousand a year. This gender disparity is also why Miss Crawford and her brother, with the same mother as Mrs. Grant but different fathers, can be so much richer than Mrs. Grant. High death rates made such second marriages fairly common in this society.

52. As with the Bertram children and with Fanny, their upbringing will manifest itself in their characters over the course of the book. They are like the Bertrams in having been indulged, but unlike them in having been brought up within a fashionable London world with somewhat different customs and standards.

53. He could have retained Mary as the new mistress to manage the household. Most single men had a female relative, if one was available, live with them for this purpose. Many wealthy men in London, where there was a wide availability of women, had mistresses, but most conducted these affairs discreetly. Admiral Crawford's open arrangement would be regarded as even worse than a clandestine affair because of its overt defiance of conventional morality. Jane Austen comments at two points in her letters on aristocratic men who have a mistress.

54. *resources*: sources or means of relaxation and amusement.

55. Poultry was the particular province of the woman of the family, including in genteel households (see the picture on p. 383 for an example). Jane Austen's mother raised poultry, and in a letter, written when the family was preparing to move, Austen mentions that a "party of fine Ladies" visited them with a view to possibly purchasing the family's hens (Jan. 14, 1801). Many women in Austen's works, including Fanny Price later, are shown liking plants. In a couple of letters Austen refers to her sister Cassandra's plants.

and tone of society;[56] and it was not till after she had tried in vain to persuade her brother to settle with her at his own country-house, that she could resolve to hazard herself among her other relations. To any thing like a permanence of abode, or limitation of society, Henry Crawford had, unluckily, a great dislike; he could not accommodate his sister in an article[57] of such importance,[58] but he escorted her, with the utmost kindness, into Northamptonshire,[59] and as readily engaged to fetch her away again at half an hour's notice, whenever she were weary of the place.

The meeting was very satisfactory on each side. Miss Crawford found a sister without preciseness[60] or rusticity—a sister's husband who looked the gentleman, and a house commodious and well fitted up;[61] and Mrs. Grant received in those whom she hoped to love better than ever, a young man and woman of very prepossessing appearance. Mary Crawford was remarkably pretty; Henry, though not handsome, had air[62] and countenance;[63] the manners[64] of both were lively and pleasant, and Mrs. Grant immediately gave them credit for every thing else. She was delighted with each, but Mary was her dearest object;[65] and having never been able to glory in beauty of her own, she thoroughly enjoyed the power of being proud of her sister's. She had not waited[66] her arrival to look out for a suitable match for her; she had fixed on Tom Bertram; the eldest son of a Baronet was not too good for a girl of twenty thousand pounds, with all the elegance and accomplishments which Mrs. Grant foresaw in her; and being a warm-hearted, unreserved woman, Mary had not been three hours in the house before she told her what she had planned.

Miss Crawford was glad to find a family of such consequence[67] so very near them, and not at all displeased either at her sister's early care, or the choice it had fallen on. Matrimony was her object, provided she could marry well,[68] and having seen Mr. Bertram in town,[69] she knew that objection could no more be made to his person than to his situation in life. While she treated it as a joke, therefore, she did not forget to think of it seriously. The scheme was soon repeated to Henry.

"And now," added Mrs. Grant, "I have thought of something to make it quite complete. I should dearly love to settle you both in this

56. She worries that her sister is living in a less grand fashion, since she has a lower income and is removed from the fancy shops of London, and that she is socializing with less genteel people, since there are fewer in a rural area and Mrs. Grant lacks the resources to travel far afield to visit other genteel families. (Mrs. Grant's anxieties seem to stem from the lack of the vast array of amusements available in London.) In an early work of Austen's, *Lady Susan*, which also contrasts the mores of London and those of the country, the fashionable title character expresses bitter regret at having to live in the country rather than in London.

57. *article*: matter.

58. Social mores dictated that an unmarried young woman must live with someone. Were Henry Crawford to establish a permanent household at his country house, his sister could live there and function as its mistress.

59. He needs to escort her because it was considered improper for women to travel alone. Jane Austen often needed to arrange with one of her brothers to accompany her when she traveled.

60. *preciseness*: rigid propriety, prudishness.

61. *fitted up*: furnished.

62. *air*: a stylish or impressive manner and appearance.

63. *countenance*: composure, confidence.

64. *manners*: outer behavior, especially in relation to others. "Manners," a term used frequently in Austen's novels, had a wider connotation than today. Here it refers to the overall conduct of the Crawfords, a complement to the description of their looks and demeanor in the first part of the sentence.

65. Austen switches to "Mary" because she is relating the thoughts and reactions of Mrs. Grant, who would call her sister by her first name.

66. *waited*: waited for. Austen frequently omits a preposition that would be used in current English.

67. *consequence*: social rank or importance.

68. To "marry well" is to marry someone of wealth and high status.

69. Tom, living a life of pleasure and associating with a great variety of friends, probably spends a lot of time in London.

country, and therefore, Henry, you shall marry the youngest Miss Bertram, a nice, handsome, good-humoured, accomplished girl, who will make you very happy."

Henry bowed and thanked her.[70]

"My dear sister," said Mary, "if you can persuade him into any thing of the sort, it will be a fresh matter of delight to me, to find myself allied to[71] any body so clever, and I shall only regret that you have not half-a-dozen daughters to dispose of.[72] If you can persuade Henry to marry, you must have the address[73] of a Frenchwoman.[74] All that English abilities[75] can do, has been tried already. I have three very particular friends who have been all dying for him in their turn; and the pains which they, their mothers, (very clever women), as well as my dear aunt and myself, have taken to reason, coax, or trick him into marrying, is inconceivable! He is the most horrible flirt that can be imagined.[76] If your Miss Bertrams do not like to have their hearts broke, let them avoid Henry."

"My dear brother, I will not believe this of you."

"No, I am sure you are too good. You will be kinder than Mary. You will allow for the doubts of youth and inexperience. I am of a cautious temper, and unwilling to risk my happiness in a hurry.[77] Nobody can think more highly of the matrimonial state than myself. I consider the blessing of a wife as most justly described in those discreet lines of the poet, 'Heaven's *last* best gift.'"[78]

"There, Mrs. Grant, you see how he dwells on one word, and only look at his smile. I assure you he is very detestable—the admiral's lessons have quite spoiled him."[79]

"I pay very little regard," said Mrs. Grant, "to what any young person says on the subject of marriage. If they profess a disinclination for it, I only set it down that they have not yet seen the right person."

Dr. Grant laughingly congratulated Miss Crawford on feeling no disinclination to the state herself.

"Oh! yes, I am not at all ashamed of it. I would have every body marry if they can do it properly; I do not like to have people throw themselves away;[80] but every body should marry as soon as they can do it to advantage."

70. Henry is the one character in the novel who bows on a number of occasions. This indicates his background in polite London society, where manners were more formal. Bowing had been more common in earlier times, but had gradually declined due to an overall relaxation of formality. This bow may be an ironic response to his sister's proposal, or a way to deflect it without rudeness.

71. "Allied to" could express close relationships of various kinds, including sisterly ones.

72. Marrying their daughters off was a prime vocation for mothers; the mother of the heroine in *Pride and Prejudice* goes to great lengths in this pursuit.

73. *address*: skill, dexterity.

74. The prevailing English view of the French at the time was of a people devoted to, and skillful at, the arts of clever conversation, refined etiquette, and the pleasing of others, all of which could make a French person adept at persuading or managing someone. This view was often accompanied by an idea of France as a country of surface charms that was inferior to England in the more solid moral virtues, a negative verdict bolstered in this period by the long war against France. Mary's more positive perspective reflects her background in fashionable London society, which was more cosmopolitan and often looked to France as a source of style, elegance, and culture.

75. *abilities*: mental powers, cleverness.

76. A male "flirt" would be someone who wooed and tried to attract women, without ever intending marriage. This behavior would be generally disapproved, given the importance of marriage for women.

77. In fact, Henry will display great confidence and boldness in many areas, but he will be careful when it comes to a definite marital commitment.

78. He is quoting John Milton's *Paradise Lost* (book V, line 19). The words are used by Adam in the Garden of Eden to describe Eve (the earlier, inferior gifts are the other living things in the garden). "Last" is not emphasized in the original, but is the point of Henry's joke here.

79. The admiral's example, considering his conduct and the lack of harmony in his marriage, would tend to convince his nephew of the greater desirability of having a mistress than a wife.

80. By "throw themselves away" she means marry someone who is not desirable from a social and economic point of view.

Chapter Five

*T*he young people were pleased with each other from the first. On each side there was much to attract, and their acquaintance soon promised as early an intimacy as good manners would warrant.[1] Miss Crawford's beauty did her no disservice with the Miss Bertrams. They were too handsome themselves to dislike any woman for being so too, and were almost as much charmed as their brothers, with her lively dark eye, clear brown complexion,[2] and general prettiness. Had she been tall, full formed,[3] and fair, it might have been more of a trial; but as it was, there could be no comparison, and she was most allowably a sweet pretty girl, while they were the finest young women in the country.

Her brother was not handsome; no, when they first saw him, he was absolutely plain, black and plain; but still he was the gentleman, with a pleasing address. The second meeting proved him not so very plain; he was plain, to be sure, but then he had so much countenance, and his teeth were so good,[4] and he was so well made, that one soon forgot he was plain; and after a third interview, after dining in company with him at the parsonage,[5] he was no longer allowed to be called so by any body. He was, in fact, the most agreeable young man the sisters had ever known, and they were equally delighted with him. Miss Bertram's engagement made him in equity the property of Julia, of which Julia was fully aware,[6] and before he had been at Mansfield a week, she was quite ready to be fallen in love with.[7]

Maria's notions on the subject were more confused and indistinct. She did not want to see or understand. "There could be no harm in her liking an agreeable man—every body knew her situation—Mr. Crawford must take care of himself."[8] Mr. Crawford did not mean to be in any danger; the Miss Bertrams were worth pleasing, and were ready to be pleased; and he began with no object but of making them like him. He did not want them to die of love; but with sense

1. Good manners dictated that people should not become intimate until they had come to know each other well. Overly rapid intimacy could lead to giving an untrustworthy person access to one's secrets and social circle. Young, unmarried women especially needed to be on guard against men who might attempt to charm them without serious intentions of matrimony.

2. This means she had a darker, but not actually brown, complexion. One reason for this terminology—similar to the later description of her brother as "black"—is that at this time there were few people in England who were not white, so even slightly darker skin tones would be noticeable.

3. *full formed*: endowed with a larger figure (and probably more buxom). A contemporary guide to beauty contrasts the "full-formed woman" with the slender one, and not with a view of disparaging the former, since the prevailing ideal of beauty was a median between fat and thin.

4. People were often judged by their teeth, for the poor quality of dentistry meant that many had very bad teeth.

5. Etiquette dictated that the first interview, or meeting, between people of different households should be a brief daytime introductory visit, followed by a similar return visit. For the third meeting one party could invite the other for dinner.

6. Ideally sisters should marry in order of seniority. Now that Maria is engaged, Julia can properly expect that she should be the intended target of any eligible man.

7. A woman was supposed to wait for the man to indicate that he had fallen in love with her, protecting her from flirtatious men who had no matrimonial intentions. In practice, of course, this did not always happen, and the reaction of Julia, as well as her sister, to this new arrival suggests an inclination to fall in love without waiting. But Julia, whatever her feelings, knows how matters should go and allows herself to imagine them occurring only in the proper sequence.

8. He must take care not to fall for her, since her engagement ensures that she would refuse him. She, like her sister, will always call him "Mr. Crawford," as will the narrator in the next sentence (in contrast to other places where his own sister, and the narrator, echoing his sister, calls him "Henry"). Women were always supposed to use the title "Mr." for a man outside the family (just as men were supposed to use "Miss" or "Mrs."). A character in *Emma* signals her vulgarity and offends the heroine by calling an unrelated man by his last name only.

and temper which ought to have made him judge and feel better, he allowed himself great latitude on such points.[9]

"I like your Miss Bertrams exceedingly, sister,"[10] said he, as he returned from attending them to their carriage after the said dinner visit; "they are very elegant, agreeable girls."[11]

"So they are, indeed, and I am delighted to hear you say it. But you like Julia best."

"Oh! yes, I like Julia best."

"But do you really? for Miss Bertram is in general thought the handsomest."

"So I should suppose. She has the advantage in every feature, and I prefer her countenance—but I like Julia best. Miss Bertram is certainly the handsomest, and I have found her the most agreeable, but I shall always like Julia best, because you order me."

"I shall not talk to you, Henry, but I know you *will* like her best at last."

"Do not I tell you, that I like her best *at first?*"

"And besides, Miss Bertram is engaged. Remember that, my dear brother. Her choice is made."

"Yes, and I like her the better for it. An engaged woman is always more agreeable than a disengaged. She is satisfied with herself. Her cares are over, and she feels that she may exert all her powers of pleasing without suspicion.[12] All is safe with a lady engaged; no harm can be done."

"Why as to that—Mr. Rushworth is a very good sort of young man, and it is a great match for her."

"But Miss Bertram does not care three straws for him; *that* is your opinion of your intimate friend. *I* do not subscribe to it. I am sure Miss Bertram is very much attached to Mr. Rushworth. I could see it in her eyes, when he was mentioned. I think too well of Miss Bertram to suppose she would ever give her hand without her heart."

"Mary, how shall we manage him?"

"We must leave him to himself I believe. Talking does no good. He will be taken in[13] at last."

"But I would not have him *taken in*, I would not have him duped; I would have it all fair and honourable."

9.   A man of sense and temper (or composure) would appreciate that if he had no intention of falling in love with and becoming engaged to a woman—what is meant by his not meaning "to be in any danger"—he should avoid any conduct that might stir her feelings toward him. Henry is not being sufficiently careful on that point.

10.   He is speaking to Mrs. Grant, not Mary (whom he calls by her first name). "Sister" is more formal, a sign of lesser intimacy and probably greater respect, since Mrs. Grant is married and is older than he is.

11.   The introduction of Henry Crawford to the Miss Bertrams, along with the mutual attraction now developing, marks a critical development in the plot. This is a standard pattern in Austen novels. In all but one, the story is prompted by the arrival into a rural neighborhood of one or more unmarried young men who proceed to attract, and be attracted to, one or more unmarried young ladies residing there (in the one exception, *Northanger Abbey*, the heroine initially visits the resort town of Bath, where numerous eligible young people of both sexes are to be found). This pattern reflects a basic reality of the society in which the novels are set. Those who are genteel can socialize only with others of the same level, but only a small number of families of this status exist within a given rural neighborhood, and slowness of travel meant that those farther afield could be visited only occasionally. This meant that unmarried young people had few opportunities for regular contact with potential mates, an especially severe limitation for young women because they could not travel on their own. Hence, for them the arrival of an eligible young man into a rural locale was a significant occasion, which in Austen's novels quickly leads to romantic interests on one or both sides.

12.   Were she to exercise these powers while unengaged, the suspicion would arise that she is aiming for an engagement.

13.   *taken in*: deceived, tricked.

"Oh! dear—Let him stand his chance and be taken in. It will do just as well. Every body is taken in at some period or other."

"Not always in marriage, dear Mary."

"In marriage especially. With all due respect to such of the present company as chance to be married, my dear Mrs. Grant,[14] there is not one in a hundred of either sex, who is not taken in when they marry. Look where I will, I see that it *is* so; and I feel that it *must* be so, when I consider that it is, of all transactions, the one in which people expect most from others, and are least honest themselves."

"Ah! You have been in a bad school for matrimony, in Hill Street."[15]

"My poor aunt had certainly little cause to love the state; but, however, speaking from my own observation, it is a manœuvring business.[16] I know so many who have married in the full expectation and confidence of some one particular advantage in the connection, or accomplishment or good quality in the person, who have found themselves entirely deceived, and been obliged to put up with exactly the reverse![17] What is this, but a take in?"

"My dear child, there must be a little imagination here. I beg your pardon, but I cannot quite believe you. Depend upon it, you see but half. You see the evil, but you do not see the consolation. There will be little rubs and disappointments every where, and we are all apt to expect too much; but then, if one scheme of happiness fails, human nature turns to another; if the first calculation is wrong, we make a second better; we find comfort somewhere—and those evil-minded observers, dearest Mary, who make much of a little, are more taken in and deceived than the parties themselves."

"Well done, sister! I honour your *esprit du corps*. When I am a wife, I mean to be just as staunch myself; and I wish my friends in general would be so too. It would save me many a heart-ache."[18]

"You are as bad as your brother, Mary; but we will cure you both. Mansfield shall cure you both—and without any taking in. Stay with us and we will cure you."

The Crawfords, without wanting to be cured, were very willing to stay. Mary was satisfied with the parsonage as a present home, and Henry equally ready to lengthen his visit. He had come, intending to spend only a few days with them, but Mansfield promised well, and there was nothing to call him elsewhere.[19] It delighted Mrs. Grant to

14. This use of "my dear" or "dear" (or "dearest," as below) occurs regularly in Austen's novels and has no special meaning.

15. Hill Street is where Admiral Crawford lives. It is an appropriate address for a wealthy man, in the Mayfair district of London, which was developed at what was then the western edge of town during the first half of the eighteenth century and soon became the most fashionable area of the city. Most characters in Austen's novels who are in London, whether as residents or visitors, live in Mayfair or in the similar, adjoining Marylebone district. For pictures from the time, of two of Mayfair's leading landmarks, see pp. 547 and 747.

16. At this time "maneuver" often referred particularly to stratagems involving trickery or deception.

17. Later Mary will provide some details on the marital difficulties of these friends—see pp. 646–648.

18. That is, if they were more committed to seeing the positive side of marriage, she would not have the frequent pain of listening to their complaints.

19. As a wealthy young man with no profession, Henry has complete freedom to go where he likes. This freedom will play a major role in the plot, and, as will be demonstrated, it has played an important role in shaping his character.

Burley House, Rutlandshire, a modern house in an elevated position (see the next page).

[From John Preston Neale, *Views of the Seats of Noblemen and Gentlemen*, Vol. V (London, 1822)]

keep them both with her, and Dr. Grant was exceedingly well contented to have it so; a talking pretty young woman like Miss Crawford, is always pleasant society to an indolent, stay-at-home man;
and Mr. Crawford's being his guest was an excuse for drinking claret
every day.[20]

The Miss Bertrams' admiration of Mr. Crawford was more raptur-
ous than any thing which Miss Crawford's habits made her likely
to feel. She acknowledged, however, that the Mr. Bertrams were
very fine young men, that two such young men were not often seen
together even in London, and that their manners, particularly those
of the eldest, were very good. *He* had been much in London,[21] and
had more liveliness and gallantry[22] than Edmund, and must, therefore, be preferred; and, indeed, his being the eldest was another
strong claim. She had felt an early presentiment that she *should* like
the eldest best. She knew it was her way.[23]

Tom Bertram must have been thought pleasant, indeed, at any
rate; he was the sort of young man to be generally liked, his agreeableness was of the kind to be oftener found agreeable than some
endowments of a higher stamp,[24] for he had easy manners, excellent
spirits, a large acquaintance, and a great deal to say; and the reversion
of Mansfield Park,[25] and a baronetcy, did no harm to all this. Miss
Crawford soon felt, that he and his situation might do. She looked
about her with due consideration, and found almost every thing in
his favour, a park, a real park five miles round, a spacious modern-
built house,[26] so well placed and well screened[27] as to deserve to be
in any collection of engravings of gentlemen's seats in the kingdom,[28]
and wanting only to be completely new furnished[29]—pleasant sisters,
a quiet mother, and an agreeable man himself—with the advantage
of being tied up from much gaming at present, by a promise to his
father,[30] and of being Sir Thomas hereafter.[31] It might do very well;
she believed she should accept him; and she began accordingly to
interest herself a little about the horse which he had to run at the
B—— races.

These races were to call him away not long after their acquaintance began; and as it appeared that the family did not, from his
usual goings on, expect him back again for many weeks, it would
bring his passion to an early proof. Much was said on his side to

20. Claret was the English name for red wine from the Bordeaux region of France. It had long been popular in England and was considered an especially fine wine (in contrast to the cheaper and more widely consumed port). Dr. Grant's preference for it indicates his love of fine food and drink, and the presence of a guest furnishes a good excuse for serving it. Moreover, as the custom was for women to withdraw at the end of dinner and men to remain to drink, a second man means Dr. Grant has an excuse to consume additional wine, with the agreeable presence of a companion.

21. London would have the men of the highest social rank, and of the most polished and fashionable manners.

22. *gallantry*: courtesy and attention to women.

23. It is her way because the eldest son inherits the family property.

24. The "endowments of a higher stamp" would be serious moral and intellectual qualities, which are not found in the list of Tom's merits.

25. The "reversion" is the right of succeeding as heir to the property.

26. A "modern-built house" was one built within the last fifty to a hundred years. During the eighteenth century a new, more spacious and comfortable style of architecture for grand houses in England emerged, inspired by the Italian Renaissance architect Andrea Palladio. Many landowning families would still have much older houses, due to the considerable expense of building anew, so a modern house would be a notable asset.

27. Newer houses were placed in higher positions than older homes traditionally were, which made them look more striking and provided better views of the surrounding park and countryside. Parts of their exterior were screened by trees, which could attractively frame the house for onlookers and block less attractive views, such as those of nearby functional buildings.

28. Books containing high-quality engravings of grand houses, along with brief descriptions, were popular. Many illustrations in this book come from a leading example of the genre, John Preston Neale's *Views of the Seats of Noblemen and Gentlemen*; it extended to many volumes.

29. She probably feels the house's furnishings, especially the furniture, are too old. Families often retained pieces for generations, whether due to respect for ancestors and their possessions or due to the high cost of buying newer pieces.

30. Presumably, in the wake of Tom's earlier losses and debts, Sir Thomas has extracted a promise from his son to refrain from substantial gaming (gambling). He may have done this while they were both in the West Indies and made Tom's agreeing a condition of being allowed to return earlier.

31. Tom will become "Sir Thomas" when his father dies. His wife will then be "Lady Bertram," a fact that is undoubtedly a consideration for Mary.

induce her to attend the races,[32] and schemes were made for a large party to them, with all the eagerness of inclination, but it would only do to be talked of.[33]

And Fanny, what was *she* doing and thinking all this while? and what was *her* opinion of the new-comers?[34] Few young ladies of eighteen could be less called on to speak their opinion than Fanny. In a quiet way, very little attended to, she paid her tribute of admiration to Miss Crawford's beauty; but as she still continued to think Mr. Crawford very plain, in spite of her two cousins having repeatedly proved the contrary, she never mentioned *him*.[35] The notice which she excited herself, was to this effect. "I begin now to understand you all, except Miss Price," said Miss Crawford, as she was walking with the Mr. Bertrams. "Pray, is she out, or is she not?—I am puzzled.— She dined at the parsonage, with the rest of you, which seemed like being *out*; and yet she says so little, that I can hardly suppose she *is*."[36]

Edmund, to whom this was chiefly addressed, replied, "I believe I know what you mean—but I will not undertake to answer the question. My cousin is grown up. She has the age and sense of a woman, but the outs and not outs are beyond me."

"And yet in general, nothing can be more easily ascertained. The distinction is so broad. Manners as well as appearance are, generally speaking, so totally different. Till now, I could not have supposed it possible to be mistaken as to a girl's being out or not. A girl not out, has always the same sort of dress; a close bonnet for instance, looks very demure, and never says a word.[37] You may smile—but it is so I assure you—and except that it is sometimes carried a little too far, it is all very proper. Girls should be quiet and modest. The most objectionable part is, that the alteration of manners on being introduced into company is frequently too sudden. They sometimes pass in such very little time from reserve to quite the opposite—to confidence![38] *That* is the faulty part of the present system. One does not like to see a girl of eighteen or nineteen so immediately up to every thing—and perhaps when one has seen her hardly able to speak the year before. Mr. Bertram, I dare say *you* have sometimes met with such changes."

"I believe I have; but this is hardly fair; I see what you are at. You are quizzing[39] me and Miss Anderson."[40]

32. Horse racing had grown steadily in popularity during the eighteenth century and would continue to grow in the nineteenth. Races large and small existed all over England, so there would be no need to specify a particular one (Jane Austen uses this technique of a blank name on other occasions). Many men, especially wealthy ones, raced their own horses, which were frequently the objects of great care and selective breeding.

33. Women often attended races, which were major social events. Jane Austen occasionally discusses them in her letters; she could have attended while visiting her brother Edward, who took his family to local races. In this case, however, Mary Crawford, in addition to possibly preferring to remain with her sister at Mansfield, would face the barrier of needing someone suitable to accompany her there, and someone to reside with once she arrived. Tom, an unrelated young man who was also a potential suitor, would definitely not qualify for either function.

34. The narrator returns to Fanny with these questions because, though the heroine of the novel, she operates almost purely as an observer in the early part of the story.

35. Fanny's conduct here is the same she will exhibit later: forming firm, independent judgments while not expressing them and remaining outwardly diffident and quiescent.

36. Formally coming out into society, a standard practice among the wealthier strata of society, was a critical event for a young woman, occurring when she reached maturity (though the exact age could vary). She moved from a life confined to her own family or to other young girls to being able to socialize with a broad range of strangers at events like balls and, most important, to meet and talk to eligible young men. Men, observing this freer behavior, would know that she was now available to be courted.

37. Both women and men almost always wore headgear when outside, and bonnets, which lacked the brims of hats, had recently become popular with women (for a picture, see p. 801). Because they encompassed the whole head, rather than sitting atop it, they tended to be "close" (close-fitting). By hiding the face from anyone not directly in front of the wearer, they would be appropriate for girls who were supposed to remain modest and unnoticed.

38. *confidence*: presumption, extreme assurance. The word could have a negative connotation then.

39. *quizzing*: making fun of, ridiculing.

40. Tom's response, moving from Miss Crawford's question and concerns to his own situation, and the two long stories about himself he proceeds to tell,

"No indeed. Miss Anderson! I do not know who or what you mean. I am quite in the dark. But I *will* quiz you with a great deal of pleasure, if you will tell me what about."

"Ah! you carry it off very well, but I cannot be quite so far imposed on.[41] You must have had Miss Anderson in your eye, in describing an altered young lady. You paint too accurately[42] for mistake. It was exactly so. The Andersons of Baker Street.[43] We were speaking of them the other day, you know. Edmund, you have heard me mention Charles Anderson. The circumstance was precisely as this lady has represented it. When Anderson first introduced me to his family, about two years ago, his sister was not *out*, and I could not get her to speak to me. I sat there an hour one morning waiting for Anderson, with only her and a little girl or two in the room—the governess being sick or run away, and the mother in and out every moment with letters of business;[44] and I could hardly get a word or a look from the young lady—nothing like a civil answer—she screwed up her mouth, and turned from me with such an air! I did not see her again for a twelvemonth. She was then *out*. I met her at Mrs. Holford's—and did not recollect her. She came up to me, claimed me as an acquaintance, stared me out of countenance,[45] and talked and laughed till I did not know which way to look. I felt that I must be the jest of the room at the time—and Miss Crawford, it is plain, has heard the story."

"And a very pretty story it is, and with more truth in it, I dare say, than does credit to Miss Anderson. It is too common a fault. Mothers certainly have not yet got quite the right way of managing their daughters. I do not know where the error lies. I do not pretend to set people right, but I do see that they are often wrong."

"Those who are showing the world what female manners *should be*," said Mr. Bertram, gallantly, "are doing a great deal to set them right."

"The error is plain enough," said the less courteous Edmund; "such girls are ill brought up. They are given wrong notions from the beginning. They are always acting upon motives of vanity—and there is no more real modesty in their behaviour *before* they appear in public than afterwards."

signal what will soon become fully apparent: that he has no particular interest in her. Thus Jane Austen uses this dialogue both to provide more information about Fanny and to develop the character and relationships of the three speakers.

41. *imposed on*: deceived.

42. *accurately*: precisely.

43. Baker Street is in the Marylebone section of London. Marylebone developed in the second half of the eighteenth century, immediately north of the Mayfair section (see p. 91, note 15). It became part of the wealthy and fashionable West End.

44. The letters of business could be to local merchants. The mother was normally in charge of purchases, and since buying on credit was standard practice, there would be letters going back and forth to handle bills.

45. *out of countenance*: into a disconcerted state.

Ramsgate (see the next page).

[From William Daniell, *A Voyage Round Great Britain*, Vol. II (London, 1815), p. 111]

"I do not know," replied Miss Crawford hesitatingly. "Yes, I cannot agree with you there. It is certainly the modestest part of the business. It is much worse to have girls *not out*, give themselves the same airs and take the same liberties as if they were, which I *have* seen done. *That* is worse than any thing—quite disgusting!"[46]

"Yes, *that* is very inconvenient indeed," said Mr. Bertram. "It leads one astray; one does not know what to do. The close bonnet and demure air you describe so well, (and nothing was ever juster), tell one what is expected; but I got into a dreadful scrape last year from the want of them. I went down to Ramsgate[47] for a week with a friend last September—just after my return from the West Indies—my friend Sneyd—you have heard me speak of Sneyd, Edmund; his father and mother and sisters were there, all new to me. When we reached Albion place they were out; we went after them, and found them on the pier.[48] Mrs. and the two Miss Sneyds, with others of their acquaintance. I made my bow in form,[49] and as Mrs. Sneyd was surrounded by men,[50] attached myself to one of her daughters, walked by her side all the way home, and made myself as agreeable as I could; the young lady perfectly easy in her manners, and as ready to talk as to listen. I had not a suspicion that I could be doing any thing wrong. They looked just the same; both well dressed, with veils and parasols like other girls;[51] but I afterwards found that I had been giving all my attention to the youngest, who was not *out*, and had most excessively offended the eldest.[52] Miss Augusta ought not to have been noticed for the next six months, and Miss Sneyd, I believe, has never forgiven me."[53]

"That was bad indeed. Poor Miss Sneyd! Though I have no younger sister, I feel for her. To be neglected before one's time, must be very vexatious. But it was entirely the mother's fault. Miss Augusta should have been with her governess.[54] Such half and half[55] doings never prosper. But now I must be satisfied about Miss Price. Does she go to balls? Does she dine out every where, as well as at my sister's?"

"No," replied Edmund, "I do not think she has ever been to a ball. My mother seldom goes into company herself, and dines no where but with Mrs. Grant, and Fanny stays at home with *her*."

"Oh! then the point is clear. Miss Price is *not* out."[56]

46. *disgusting*: distasteful. The word had a less strong connotation then. The disagreement between Miss Crawford and Edmund suggests differences in outlook that will be articulated more fully in later exchanges (see p. 180 particularly). She is focusing on modesty as an external behavior, thinking silent girls are sufficiently modest and condemning girls who act freely too soon, because of the distasteful appearance that results. He, in contrast, conceives of modesty as an inner virtue, criticizing the girls in question for lack of sincerity in their modest behavior. Here and later, she sees manners as external rules designed to facilitate social life, he as expressions of underlying moral principles.

47. Ramsgate was a seaside resort in Kent, on the southeastern coast; its proximity to London made it one of the most visited in England. Going to the seaside had developed as a popular activity during the eighteenth century, and numerous resorts had sprung up along the coasts. Jane Austen visited some of them, including Ramsgate. She liked others, but in a letter she derides someone's interest in Ramsgate as "Bad Taste!" (Oct. 14, 1813).

48. Albion Place is a street in Ramsgate next to the water. A travel book from 1805 describes dining at an inn on Albion Place, "from which there is a most admirable view," and then walking "along the two piers, which are the finest in England, running out nearly half a mile into the sea" (John Henry Manners, *Journal of a Tour Round the Southern Coasts of England*).

49. *in form*: formally, according to the prescribed rules.

50. Mrs. Sneyd's being surrounded by men suggests the possible moral looseness of Tom's friends. His casual mention of such a potentially embarrassing detail indicates his own lack of discretion.

51. Veils and parasols protect the face from the sun, a particular issue at the seaside. Tanned skin was considered unattractive, so genteel people, especially women, tried to shield themselves (see p. 149 for a picture).

52. Usually an older daughter would be out for a certain period before the younger one came out, in part to give the older a chance to secure a husband without competition from within the family.

53. Miss Sneyd is the elder, which is why only her last name is used.

54. A governess would often serve as a chaperone as well as a teacher for girls.

55. *half and half*: half one thing, half another.

56. A girl who was out would normally go to balls and dinners, so Miss Crawford's conclusion is understandable, though Edmund's remarks suggest that Fanny's limited social life may result more from Lady Bertram's selfish insistence on her company at home than from her not being out.

Chapter Six

*M*r. Bertram set off for ——, and Miss Crawford was prepared to find a great chasm in their society, and to miss him decidedly in the meetings which were now becoming almost daily between the families; and on their all dining together at the park soon after his going, she retook her chosen place near the bottom of the table,[1] fully expecting to feel a most melancholy difference in the change of masters. It would be a very flat business,[2] she was sure. In comparison with his brother, Edmund would have nothing to say. The soup would be sent round in a most spiritless manner,[3] wine drank without any smiles, or agreeable trifling,[4] and the venison cut up without supplying one pleasant anecdote of any former haunch,[5] or a single entertaining story about "my friend such a one." She must try to find amusement in what was passing at the upper end of the table, and in observing Mr. Rushworth, who was now making his appearance at Mansfield, for the first time since the Crawfords' arrival. He had been visiting a friend in a neighbouring county, and that friend having recently had his grounds laid out by an improver,[6] Mr. Rushworth was returned with his head full of the subject, and very eager to be improving his own place in the same way; and though not saying much to the purpose, could talk of nothing else. The subject had been already handled in the drawing-room; it was revived in the dining-parlour.[7] Miss Bertram's attention and opinion was evidently his chief aim; and though her deportment showed rather conscious superiority than any solicitude to oblige him, the mention of Sotherton Court,[8] and the ideas attached to it, gave her a feeling of complacency, which prevented her from being very ungracious.

"I wish you could see Compton," said he, "it is the most complete thing! I never saw a place so altered in my life. I told Smith I did not know where I was. The approach *now* is one of the finest things in the country. You see the house in the most surprising manner.

1. The hostess sits at the top of the table and the host at the bottom. With Sir Thomas gone, Tom, as the elder son, is the host (and would also carve); when he is absent, Edmund fills his place. Mary's interest in Tom led her to choose a seat near the bottom, which has become her customary one.

2. *flat business*: dull occupation or activity.

3. At this time food was served by placing dishes throughout the table; this allowed diners to see all the choices and the hosts to display their wealth and taste through the wide array on offer. Usually the meal began with soup being passed around. After that people took items from the dishes in their vicinity, with gentlemen expected to serve the ladies next to them.

4. Wine would also be passed around. The host initiated the process (as Edmund does—p. 106), in part because it was considered improper for ladies to drink wine unless solicited to do so by a man.

5. Venison seems to be served regularly here, an indication of the Bertrams' wealth, for the conversion of most land in England to farmland had made deer rare. Only those with very large estates could afford to have deer parks, which provided an exclusive form of sport and food. Tom's former haunches may include ones he enjoyed at friends' homes.

6. Improving one's grounds had become very popular, especially among those with extensive estates, who frequently hired a professional improver. In letters from a visit to her brother Edward, who inherited a wealthy estate, Jane Austen describes active discussions of such plans (Oct. 25, 1800; Nov. 8, 1800; Nov. 20, 1800). A principal impetus was a dramatic change in garden design. Traditionally gardens had been formal, characterized by straight paths, geometric shapes, and strict symmetry. But in the mid-eighteenth century in England a new style arose; it rejected symmetry in favor of grounds that looked more natural, with serpentine paths, changes in elevation, scattered groups of trees or other plants, and irregular bodies of water. This style soon predominated and inspired all who could afford it to alter their grounds according to its tenets. This could be a considerable undertaking, for the new style called ideally for shaping the entire park surrounding the house, even if it stretched for miles, and while the result was supposed to look natural, it involved a careful design of each section and substantial work, including clearing away older features, cutting down or planting large numbers of trees, raising or lowering entire hills, and shifting rivers or forming new ponds and lakes.

7. People would gather in the drawing room before dinner, and sit for a brief period, before proceeding into the dining room.

8. This is the house's formal name. Many grand houses were called "Court," since older dwellings had often been built around a central court.

I declare when I got back to Sotherton yesterday, it looked like a prison—quite a dismal old prison."[9]

"Oh! for shame!" cried Mrs. Norris. "A prison, indeed! Sotherton Court is the noblest old place in the world."[10]

"It wants improvement, ma'am, beyond any thing. I never saw a place that wanted so much improvement in my life; and it is so forlorn, that I do not know what can be done with it."

"No wonder that Mr. Rushworth should think so at present," said Mrs. Grant to Mrs. Norris, with a smile; "but depend upon it, Sotherton will have *every* improvement in time which his heart can desire."

"I must try to do something with it," said Mr. Rushworth, "but I do not know what. I hope I shall have some good friend to help me."

"Your best friend upon such an occasion," said Miss Bertram, calmly, "would be Mr. Repton, I imagine."

"That is what I was thinking of. As he has done so well by Smith, I think I had better have him at once. His terms are five guineas a day."[11]

"Well, and if they were *ten*," cried Mrs. Norris, "I am sure *you* need not regard it. The expense need not be any impediment. If I were you, I should not think of the expense. I would have every thing done in the best style, and made as nice as possible. Such a place as Sotherton Court deserves every thing that taste and money can do. You have space to work upon there, and grounds that will well reward you. For my own part, if I had any thing within the fiftieth part of the size of Sotherton, I should be always planting and improving, for naturally I am excessively fond of it. It would be too ridiculous for me to attempt any thing where I am now, with my little half acre. It would be quite a burlesque.[12] But if I had more room, I should take a prodigious delight in improving and planting. We did a vast deal in that way at the parsonage; we made it quite a different place from what it was when we first had it.[13] You young ones do not remember much about it, perhaps. But if dear Sir Thomas were here, he could tell you what improvements we made; and a great deal more would have been done, but for poor Mr. Norris's sad state of health. He could hardly ever get out, poor man, to enjoy any thing, and *that* disheartened me from doing several things that Sir Thomas and I used to talk of.[14] If it had not been for *that*, we should have carried on the

9. The man identified below as responsible for these alterations, Humphry Repton, was a real person. Repton, the leading landscape gardener of the time, placed a great importance on the approach, or road to a house. In one of his books on the subject, *Sketches and Hints on Landscape Gardening* (1795), he devotes a chapter to approaches, and a list of his main principles includes: "The house, unless very large and magnificent, should not be seen at so great a distance as to make it appear much less than it really is," and "The house should be at first presented in a pleasing point of view" (*The Art of Landscape Gardening*, p. 51). The goal was for the visitor's first sight of the house to be close and impressive, so it comes into view "in a surprising manner."

10. As explained shortly, Sotherton is an older building, which might be regarded by someone enamored of newer styles as being prison-like. Older houses tended to be less comfortable, to have thicker walls, and to enjoy less light, due to fewer or smaller windows or a more shaded location. For examples, see the pictures on pp. 108 and 110.

11. This was Humphry Repton's actual fee (a guinea was worth a pound and a shilling, and thus just over a pound; for shillings, see p. 105, note 19). Many landowners hired professionals like Repton to assist with or direct their improvements. Jane Austen's knowledge of his work stemmed from personal experience, for cousins of the Austens who owned the estate of Adlestrop, in Gloucestershire, hired Repton to redesign their grounds. Jane Austen, who had first visited in 1794, before the redesign, came again in 1806, allowing her to see the effect of his completed handiwork and to hear about the process from her cousins. Among the changes was a new approach road that improved the view of the house. On this latter visit she also stayed at another grand estate, Stoneleigh Abbey (for more, see p. 163, note 5), whose owners hired Repton a few years later. She never returned to see those alterations, but she would have heard of them, especially from her brother James, who visited in 1809, just after Repton had given the family one of his "Red Books"—books with illustrations that showed how the improved landscape would look (in this case, the family ended up following some, but not all, of his recommendations).

12. *burlesque*: grotesque or ridiculous imitation; caricature.

13. The grounds of a parsonage, though smaller than those at a grand house, could still be an object of improvement. The hero of *Northanger Abbey*, a clergyman, devotes substantial attention to alterations to his grounds, and Jane Austen's parents, at the rectory where she grew up, made a number of changes, including the creation of a decorative shrubbery.

14. As the person controlling the appointment to the clerical position, it was officially Sir Thomas's responsibility to make necessary improvements to Mansfield parsonage. He probably paid for most or all of the changes made there, and thus discussed them with Mr. and Mrs. Norris. At the same time, he may have set a limit to how much he was willing to spend, constraining any further activity by Mrs. Norris, whatever the state of her husband's health.

garden wall,[15] and made the plantation to shut out the churchyard,[16] just as Dr. Grant has done. We were always doing something, as it was. It was only the spring twelvemonth before Mr. Norris's death,[17] that we put in the apricot against the stable wall, which is now grown such a noble tree, and getting to such perfection, sir," addressing herself then to Dr. Grant.

"The tree thrives well beyond a doubt, madam," replied Dr. Grant. "The soil is good; and I never pass it without regretting, that the fruit should be so little worth the trouble of gathering."

"Sir, it is a moor park, we bought it as a moor park,[18] and it cost us—that is, it was a present from Sir Thomas, but I saw the bill, and I know it cost seven shillings,[19] and was charged as a moor park."

"You were imposed on, ma'am," replied Dr. Grant; "these potatoes have as much the flavour of a moor park apricot, as the fruit from that tree. It is an insipid fruit at the best; but a good apricot is eatable, which none from my garden are."

"The truth is, ma'am," said Mrs. Grant, pretending to whisper across the table to Mrs. Norris, "that Dr. Grant hardly knows what the natural[20] taste of our apricot is; he is scarcely ever indulged with one, for it is so valuable a fruit, with a little assistance, and ours is such a remarkably large, fair sort, that what with early tarts and preserves, my cook contrives to get them all."[21]

Mrs. Norris, who had begun to redden, was appeased, and, for a little while, other subjects took place of the improvements of Sotherton. Dr. Grant and Mrs. Norris were seldom good friends; their acquaintance had begun in dilapidations,[22] and their habits were totally dissimilar.

After a short interruption, Mr. Rushworth began again. "Smith's place is the admiration of all the country;[23] and it was a mere nothing before Repton took it in hand. I think I shall have Repton."

"Mr. Rushworth," said Lady Bertram, "if I were you, I would have a very pretty shrubbery. One likes to get out into a shrubbery in fine weather."

Mr. Rushworth was eager to assure her ladyship of his acquiescence, and tried to make out something complimentary; but between his submission to *her* taste, and his having always intended the same himself, with the super-added objects of professing attention to the comfort of ladies in general, and of insinuating, that there

15. It was standard for gardens to have walls around them, both to shield plants from the cold, thereby extending the growing season, and, in the case of gardens designed for relaxation or enjoyment, to provide privacy.

16. A "plantation" means a grouping of planted items. It often referred to trees and probably does here, since trees could shut out an adjacent yard from view. Parsonages were usually next to the church, and because a churchyard was a public space, often containing the parish graves, blocking it from sight would add to the privacy of the parsonage.

17. Meaning the spring that was at least a year before the death. Since the death probably occurred in the autumn (see chronology, p. 855), it would be about a year and a half.

18. Apricots, which were widely cultivated in ancient times, were introduced to England in the sixteenth century. The "moor park," a specific variety, was developed later and named after the estate where it was first cultivated. A book from 1818 calls it the variety of apricot that "is held in esteem over any other at present cultivated" (*Pomona Londinensis*, entry IX). For a picture of an apricot tree from a contemporary book on cultivating fruit trees, see p. 113.

19. A shilling was, along with pounds and pence, one of the basic units of monetary value; account records were normally kept with one column for each of the three. Twelve pence made a shilling, and twenty shillings made a pound. Hence seven shillings would not be a large sum.

20. *natural*: normal.

21. Fruit was often used for tarts and preserves rather than eaten raw, in part from a belief that raw fruit could harm people's digestion.

22. "Dilapidations" in this context means actions causing the parsonage to fall into a state of decay or damage; it could also mean sums charged to pay for repairs. In the English church then it was the responsibility of the holder of a clerical living to maintain the parsonage, and sometimes, whether from negligence or lack of means, the incumbent failed in this task. The new holder could then charge him or his heirs the appropriate sum. Considering Mr. Norris's poor health and Mrs. Norris's stinginess, it makes sense that the parsonage fell into disrepair during their residence, while Mr. Grant's taste for comfortable living makes it logical for him to have sought redress.

23. An important reason for landscaping improvements was to allow the owner to show off his fine estate, and thus his wealth and good taste, to his friends or to other prominent families in the country (i.e., county).

was one only whom he was anxious to please, he grew puzzled,[24] and Edmund was glad to put an end to his speech by a proposal of wine. Mr. Rushworth, however, though not usually a great talker, had still more to say on the subject next his heart. "Smith has not much above a hundred acres altogether in his grounds, which is little enough, and makes it more surprising that the place can have been so improved. Now, at Sotherton, we have a good seven hundred, without reckoning the water meadows;[25] so that I think, if so much could be done at Compton, we need not despair. There have been two or three fine old trees cut down that grew too near the house, and it opens the prospect[26] amazingly,[27] which makes me think that Repton, or any body of that sort, would certainly have the avenue at Sotherton down; the avenue that leads from the west front to the top of the hill you know,"[28] turning to Miss Bertram particularly as he spoke. But Miss Bertram thought it most becoming to reply:

"The avenue! Oh! I do not recollect it. I really know very little of Sotherton."[29]

Fanny, who was sitting on the other side of Edmund, exactly opposite Miss Crawford, and who had been attentively listening, now looked at him, and said in a low voice,

"Cut down an avenue! What a pity! Does not it make you think of Cowper? 'Ye fallen avenues, once more I mourn your fate unmerited.'"[30]

He smiled as he answered, "I am afraid the avenue stands a bad chance, Fanny."

A depiction by Repton of a garden and its view after his improvements.

[From Humphry Repton, *Fragments on the Theory and Practice of Landscape Gardening* (London, 1816), p. 214]

24. Elsewhere in Austen's novels people speak of the need to pay particular attention to ladies' comfort. Maria is the lady whom Mr. Rushworth is keen to please; he can only insinuate that because it was not proper to express very strong affection, especially in public, for someone to whom one is only engaged.

25. Water meadows are deliberately flooded by a stream or river during part of the year, a common practice that had developed during the preceding two centuries. The water stimulated the growth of grass, thereby providing better pasturage for livestock, and shielded the grass from cold during the winter, thereby promoting early growth. The meadows were drained in the spring, once sufficient grass had grown, and then, after the animals had exhausted them and moved to later-blossoming dry meadows, reflooded until the next year.

26. *prospect*: view.

27. *amazingly*: exceedingly.

28. Since having a beautiful and expansive view from the house was a prime goal of Repton and other landscape gardeners of the time, trees that blocked the view were often removed, including from avenues — roads lined with trees, usually in a straight line and at regular intervals. Such avenues were popular in earlier periods, when landscaping ideals emphasized order and symmetry, and were a prominent feature of the grounds around older homes. Repton himself did not call for all avenues to be removed, for he believed in adjusting his recommendations to the particular characteristics of each setting, but he did consider them generally to be a drawback, especially because of their interference with the view. For an older house with trees, see p. 110.

29. Maria may think it becoming to profess ignorance of her betrothed's estate due to prevailing standards of feminine modesty, which emphasized the need for women not to show romantic eagerness; but she also may wish to signal to Henry Crawford her relative lack of attachment to Mr. Rushworth.

30. William Cowper (1731–1800) was one of the most popular poets of the period; he is a particular favorite of Marianne Dashwood, the romantic heroine of *Sense and Sensibility*. Jane Austen also liked him, and refers to him in her letters. His poems center around the depiction and celebration of nature, frequently mixed with a religious message. Fanny is quoting from his most renowned work, "The Task," a long philosophical poem that includes, in its many evocations of the beauties of the country and rural life, the famous line "God made the country, and man made the town." His lamentations regarding disappearing avenues commence with praise of "Our fathers" for knowing

"I should like to see Sotherton before it is cut down, to see the place as it is now, in its old state; but I do not suppose I shall."

"Have you never been there? No, you never can; and unluckily it is out of distance for a ride.[31] I wish we could contrive it."

"Oh! it does not signify. Whenever I do see it, you will tell me how it has been altered."

"I collect,"[32] said Miss Crawford, "that Sotherton is an old place, and a place of some grandeur. In any particular style of building?"

"The house was built in Elizabeth's time, and is a large, regular, brick building—heavy, but respectable looking, and has many good rooms.[33] It is ill placed. It stands in one of the lowest spots of the park;[34] in that respect, unfavourable for improvement. But the woods are fine, and there is a stream, which, I dare say, might be made a good deal of.[35] Mr. Rushworth is quite right, I think, in meaning to give it a modern dress,[36] and I have no doubt that it will be all done extremely well."

Heslington Hall, Yorkshire: like Sotherton Court, an Elizabethan house that is large, regular, and brick. The courtyard in front is another common feature of older houses, a sign of limited interest in the view. Its stone steps leading to the front entrance are another feature shared with Sotherton Court.

[From John Preston Neale, *Views of the Seats of Noblemen and Gentlemen*, Vol. V (London, 1822)]

the value of "shaded walks / And long protracted bow'rs" to protect us from the sun. He soon returns to the theme with the passage cited by Fanny:

> Ye fallen avenues! once more I mourn
> Your fate unmerited, once more rejoice
> That yet a remnant of your race survives.
> How airy and how light the graceful arch,
> Yet awful as the consecrated roof
> Re-echoing pious anthems!

This is followed by a celebration of the delightful play of light and shadow beneath the leaves of the avenue. Later he offers a further criticism of the new landscaping fashion, declaring, "Improvement too, the idol of the age / Is fed with many a victim" and describing how the elaborate changes involve tearing down the venerable "abode of our forefathers" and frequently impoverish the owner of the estate.

31. As explained earlier, Sotherton is ten miles away, and a trip would take around two hours in each direction, far beyond what Fanny, who is soon described as of limited strength in her horse-riding abilities, could do in a day.

32. *collect*: gather.

33. Queen Elizabeth reigned from 1558 to 1603. Many of the grand houses in England dated from previous centuries, so people would be well acquainted with earlier architectural styles. Houses in Elizabethan, or Tudor, style tended to be both regular and heavy.

34. Older houses were usually in a low-lying and sheltered position. In the century preceding this novel, that had changed, as the fashion grew for having houses that could command a sweeping view of the surrounding landscape.

35. Water played a critical role in landscaping improvements of the time, with rivers or streams regularly being altered, through changing their direction or damming them to create or enlarge a lake. Repton discusses the subject frequently in his writings, and in a brief passage regarding Adlestrop, the estate where Jane Austen was able to witness his changes, he explains how he eliminated "a small pool" near the house to keep it from "attracting the eye and preventing its range over the lawn and falling ground beyond." Instead "a lively stream of water has been led through a flower garden, where its progress down the hill is occasionally obstructed by ledges of rocks, and after a variety of interesting circumstances it falls into a lake at a considerable distance" (*The Art of Landscape Gardening*, p. 96). He says the result is a delightful view from the dwellings on the estate. For similar plans of his, see the next page.

36. *dress*: appearance, adornment.

Miss Crawford listened with submission, and said to herself, "He is a well bred[37] man; he makes the best of it."

"I do not wish to influence Mr. Rushworth," he continued, "but had I a place to new fashion, I should not put myself into the hands of an improver. I would rather have an inferior degree of beauty, of my own choice, and acquired progressively. I would rather abide by my own blunders than by his."

"*You* would know what you were about of course—but that would not suit *me*. I have no eye or ingenuity for such matters, but as they are before me; and had I a place of my own in the country, I should be most thankful to any Mr. Repton who would undertake it, and give me as much beauty as he could for my money; and I should never look at it, till it was complete."

"It would be delightful to *me* to see the progress of it all," said Fanny.

"Ay—you have been brought up to it.[38] It was no part of my education; and the only dose I ever had, being administered by not the

Abington Abbey, Northamptonshire: an older house with trees.

[From John Preston Neale, *Views of the Seats of Noblemen and Gentlemen*, Second Series, Vol. II (1825)]

37. *well bred*: polite, courteous.

38. Those residing at Mansfield Park not only were used to elaborate land-scaped grounds but also would have seen work done on them, for they required considerable maintenance and needed at times minor alterations.

Two plans by Humphry Repton for improving landscaped grounds through the cre-ation of a river or of a waterfall and lake.

[From Humphry Repton, *The Art of Landscape Gardening* (Boston, 1907; reprint edition), p. 100, and *Fragments on the Theory and Practice of Landscape Gardening* (London, 1816), p. 48]

first favourite in the world, has made me consider improvements *in hand*[39] as the greatest of nuisances. Three years ago, the admiral, my honoured uncle, bought a cottage at Twickenham for us all to spend our summers in;[40] and my aunt and I went down to it quite in raptures; but it being excessively pretty, it was soon found necessary to be improved; and for three months we were all dirt and confusion, without a gravel walk to step on, or a bench fit for use. I would have every thing as complete as possible in the country, shrubberies and flower gardens, and rustic seats innumerable;[41] but it must be all done without my care. Henry is different, he loves to be doing."

Edmund was sorry to hear Miss Crawford, whom he was much disposed to admire, speak so freely of her uncle. It did not suit his sense of propriety,[42] and he was silenced, till induced by further smiles and liveliness,[43] to put the matter by[44] for the present.

An elegant cottage. The original illustration included a floor plan of the cottage showing various rooms as well as an extensive veranda, partly revealed in this picture.

[From *The Repository of arts, literature, fashions, manufactures, &c*, Series Two, Vol. I (1816), p. 542]

39. *in hand*: in process.

40. During the eighteenth century the town of Twickenham became a popular place of residence for the wealthy, since it offered country living in close proximity to the capital, with the added attraction of being along the river Thames. For its location, see map, p. 882.

By "a cottage" she does not mean a small, humble dwelling but what was then known as a "Cottage Ornée" (from the French for "adorned" or "decorated"). The first couple of decades of the nineteenth century witnessed a brief vogue for such cottages among the wealthy, who, in line with the prevailing Romanticism of the period, were attracted by the simple and rustic associations they evoked. These cottages were built in a deliberately primitive style, with thatched roofs and crude stone walls and many intentional irregularities. But while smaller than grand houses like Mansfield Park, they were still fairly substantial buildings, with many rooms and all the latest luxuries and conveniences.

41. Gravel walks, benches along paths, shrubberies, and flower gardens were standard features of landscaped grounds. Rustic seats, which meant chairs or benches done in a rough-hewn style, were also popular, a product of the same taste that made "cottages" for the wealthy popular.

42. Edmund disapproves of her sarcastic reference to him as "my honoured uncle" and her statement that he wished to improve the cottage because it was "excessively pretty." She also called him "not the first favourite in the world."

43. *liveliness*: playfulness, jocular talk, inclination to be merry.

44. *put the matter by*: set it aside, let it alone.

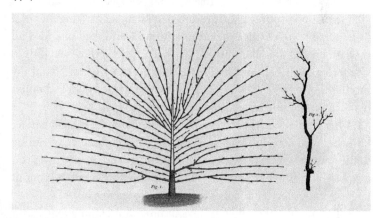

An apricot tree; the image on the right is a branch of the tree.

[From William Forsyth, *A Treatise on the Culture and Management of Fruittrees* (London, 1802)]

"Mr. Bertram,"[45] said she, "I have tidings of my harp at last.[46] I am assured that it is safe at Northampton; and there it has probably been these ten days, in spite of the solemn assurances we have so often received to the contrary." Edmund expressed his pleasure and surprise. "The truth is, that our inquiries were too direct; we sent a servant, we went ourselves: this will not do seventy miles from London—but this morning we heard of it in the right way. It was seen by some farmer, and he told the miller, and the miller told the butcher, and the butcher's son-in-law left word at the shop."[47]

"I am very glad that you have heard of it, by whatever means; and hope there will be no farther delay."

"I am to have it to-morrow; but how do you think it is to be conveyed? Not by a waggon or cart;—Oh! no, nothing of that kind could be hired in the village. I might as well have asked for porters and a hand-barrow."[48]

"You would find it difficult, I dare say, just now, in the middle of a very late hay harvest, to hire a horse and cart?"[49]

"I was astonished to find what a piece of work was made of it! To want a horse and cart in the country seemed impossible, so I told my maid to speak for one directly;[50] and as I cannot look out of my dressing-closet[51] without seeing one farm yard, nor walk in the shrubbery without passing another, I thought it would be only ask and have, and was rather grieved that I could not give the advantage to all. Guess my surprise, when I found that I had been asking the most unreasonable, most impossible thing in the world, had offended all the farmers, all the labourers, all the hay in the parish.[52] As for Dr. Grant's bailiff, I believe I had better keep out of *his* way;[53] and my brother-in-law himself, who is all kindness in general, looked rather black upon me, when he found what I had been at."[54]

"You could not be expected to have thought on the subject before, but when you *do* think of it, you must see the importance of getting in the grass. The hire of a cart at any time, might not be so easy as you suppose; our farmers are not in the habit of letting them out; but in harvest, it must be quite out of their power to spare a horse."

"I shall understand all your ways in time; but coming down with the true London maxim, that every thing is to be got with money,

45. She calls Edmund "Mr. Bertram" here because, with Tom gone, there is no need to distinguish between the two brothers.

46. The harp was, after the piano, the most popular instrument for young ladies to learn to play. For more, see p. 127, note 7.

47. The shop can be referred to that simply because it is most likely a general village store. Since almost everyone would frequent it, news shared there would quickly spread. The network of local gossip she describes was a basic feature of rural life, as often seen in Austen's novels.

48. *hand-barrow*: a rectangular frame for carrying items; it has bars going across the frame to place the items upon, and is lifted and conveyed by means of poles sticking out at each end, as with a stretcher.

49. The hay harvest was a central event in the rural calendar, starting in June and usually continuing into July. The hay would be mown and then gathered first into piles and then into a haystack before being carted away into storage, furnishing the food necessary to enable livestock to survive the winter. Since the labor involved was substantial, and speed was important to reduce the chance of cut hay being rained on (it needed to be dry for gathering), all available labor and resources, including horses and carts, would be mobilized. A very late harvest (it is currently after the middle of July—see chronology, p. 855), probably caused by bad weather earlier, would add to the sense of urgency.

50. *speak for one directly*: order one immediately. Her maid is her lady's maid, who, unlike other servants, would travel with her mistress. Mary's having her own indicates her wealth; Maria and Julia Bertram share a maid.

51. *dressing-closet*: small room for dressing, attached to the bedroom.

52. Farmers, distinct from laborers, were basically the rural middle class: they rented large tracts of land from estate owners like Sir Thomas, and hired laborers, the rural lower class, to work the land under their supervision. In *Emma* a character who is a farmer has a nice house and employs servants. Hence Mary's list involves three categories of descending importance, allowing her cleverly to suggest the steadily increasing absurdity of the offense she has aroused.

53. A bailiff in this context is someone who superintends the operation of a farm. The farm here is Dr. Grant's glebe land, which is given to a resident clergyman as part of the living to help furnish his income.

54. Dr. Grant's own income is derived from agriculture, whether the products of his glebe land or what he receives in tithes (payments from his parishioners based on a percentage of their produce). Hence he would have a keen sense of the need not to interfere with something as essential as the hay harvest.

I was a little embarrassed at first by the sturdy independence of your country customs. However, I am to have my harp fetched tomorrow. Henry, who is good-nature itself, has offered to fetch it in his barouche. Will it not be honourably conveyed?"[55]

Edmund spoke of the harp as his favourite instrument, and hoped to be soon allowed to hear her. Fanny had never heard the harp at all, and wished for it very much.

"I shall be most happy to play to you both," said Miss Crawford; "at least, as long as you can like to listen; probably much longer, for I dearly love music myself, and where the natural taste is equal, the player must always be best off, for she is gratified in more ways than one.[56] Now, Mr. Bertram, if you write to your brother, I entreat you to tell him that my harp *is* come, he heard so much of my misery about it. And you may say, if you please, that I shall prepare my most plaintive airs against his return, in compassion to his feelings, as I know his horse will lose."[57]

"If I write, I will say whatever you wish me; but I do not at present foresee any occasion for writing."

"No, I dare say, nor if he were to be gone a twelvemonth, would you ever write to him, nor he to you, if it could be helped. The occasion would never be foreseen. What strange creatures brothers are! You would not write to each other but upon the most urgent necessity in the world; and when obliged to take up the pen to say that such a horse is ill, or such a relation dead, it is done in the fewest possible words. You have but one style among you. I know it perfectly. Henry, who is in every other respect exactly what a brother should be, who loves me, consults me, confides in me, and will talk to me by the hour together, has never yet turned the page in a letter; and very often it is nothing more than, 'Dear Mary, I am just arrived. Bath seems full,[58] and every thing as usual. Your's sincerely.' That is the true manly style; that is a complete brother's letter."[59]

"When they are at a distance from all their family," said Fanny, colouring for William's sake, "they can write long letters."

"Miss Price has a brother at sea," said Edmund, "whose excellence as a correspondent, makes her think you too severe upon us."[60]

"At sea, has she? — In the King's service of course."[61]

55. A barouche is a type of carriage (see the picture on the next page). Its principal feature is a folding roof that renders it suitable for both warm and cold weather. This made it desirable, though also expensive due to the cost of a mechanism that was regularly opened and closed. Henry Crawford's possessing one testifies to both his wealth and his wish to own a highly fashionable carriage. Jane Austen speaks in a letter of riding in a barouche: "I liked my solitary elegance, & was ready to laugh all the time, at my being where I was—I could not but feel that I had naturally small right to be parading about London in a Barouche" (May 24, 1813). This is why Mary says the harp will be "honourably conveyed."

56. Where the musical taste of the listener equals that of the performer, the latter has the advantage, for both her love of her music and her vanity are gratified. Her use of "she" for the player, at a time when "he" was regularly used to refer to people in general, indicates how much playing an instrument was an almost exclusively female activity in this social world.

57. Tom has been attending the horse races. Mary's mention indicates that she is still thinking of him as a potential mate, though this scene also marks the beginning of a greater interest in Edmund. Her writing to Tom herself would be improper, so she must send messages through Edmund.

58. During the eighteenth century Bath became the leading spa and resort town in England, and while by this time it was facing increased competition from seaside resorts, it was still very popular. Its many entertainments and busy social life made it a natural venue for a wealthy man of leisure like Henry. Bath was most frequently full, or crowded, during the winter months.

59. The two main characters in *Emma* both describe women as writing longer and more detailed letters. Henry's willingness to send such a short letter indicates selfishness: letters were very expensive and the charge, by the page, was laid upon the recipient. Therefore most letter writers would at least turn the page (write on the reverse side), and many, including Jane Austen, took special pains to cram every available space with writing.

60. Men serving in the navy were often assiduous correspondents. Long overseas postings made them anxious to communicate news of themselves to their families and to receive news from home. Ships carried mail regularly between Britain and naval stations abroad, and those serving in the navy (or army) were legally entitled to send and receive letters at extremely low postal rates. Jane Austen maintained a regular correspondence with her two brothers who were serving in the navy.

61. "The King's service" is the navy. The alternative, serving in the merchant marine, was much less prestigious. Mary thus assumes the navy, though her comment may be intended as a question, since the lower status of Fanny's

Fanny would rather have had Edmund tell the story, but his determined silence obliged her to relate her brother's situation; her voice was animated in speaking of his profession, and the foreign stations he had been on, but she could not mention the number of years that he had been absent without tears in her eyes.[62] Miss Crawford civilly wished him an early promotion.

"Do you know any thing of my cousin's captain?" said Edmund; "Captain Marshall? You have a large acquaintance in the navy, I conclude?"[63]

"Among Admirals, large enough; but," with an air of grandeur; "we know very little of the inferior ranks. Post captains may be very good sort of men, but they do not belong to *us*.[64] Of various admirals I could tell you a great deal; of them and their flags, and the gradation of their pay,[65] and their bickerings and jealousies. But in general, I can assure you that they are all passed over, and all very ill used.[66] Certainly, my home at my uncle's brought me acquainted with a circle of admirals. Of *Rears*, and *Vices*, I saw enough. Now, do not be suspecting me of a pun, I entreat."[67]

A barouche.

[From Ralph Straus, *Carriages and Coaches* (London, 1912), p. 232]

family could naturally raise doubt; in fact, a younger brother of hers is later described as serving on a merchant vessel (p. 684).

62. Britain had naval bases in various parts of the world, and many in the navy would be stationed abroad for years.

63. Edmund is maybe hoping that if Mary does know the captain she could help persuade him to promote Fanny's brother.

64. A post captain was an officer who could command large ships; it was the highest rank below admiral.

65. Admirals were divided among three different flags—the red, white, and blue—and traditionally ships sailed under the flag of the admiral commanding them. This practice had long ceased, but the flags remained as a distinction of rank, with red the highest, then white, then blue. There were also three types of admirals: full (the highest), vice (the next highest), and rear. A man would start as a rear admiral of the blue, then become in turn rear admiral of the white, rear admiral of the red, vice admiral of the blue, and so forth, until reaching full admiral of the red; a tenth supreme rank, full admiral of the fleet, was added in 1805. As an admiral rose in rank, his pay also increased.

66. Admirals were promoted automatically to the next rank after serving enough years in their existing rank. But promotion did not confer any particular post, so many high-ranking admirals, if judged less worthy, would be given insignificant posts or no post at all, while lower-ranking admirals could be given prominent ones. Posts also differed in the opportunities they offered for prize money (see p. 121, note 69). All this could foster jealousy among admirals, and a sense of being passed over unfairly.

67. She refers to types of admirals (see above). The possible pun would involve a vice relating to rears, a very risqué comment by the strict standards of genteel society, which is why the straitlaced Edmund looks grave. Some commentators have suggested she is referring to male homosexuality, which in later times was sometimes associated with the navy (one source being an apocryphal quote by Winston Churchill that naval tradition is "nothing but rum, sodomy, and the lash"). This, however, is extremely unlikely. Male homosexual acts were extremely taboo, subject to serious punishment, and almost never discussed in public. A genteel lady, even a daring one, would never introduce the topic in a dinner conversation, nor would Jane Austen, or her publisher, have sanctioned its mention in print. Moreover, sexual relations between men seem to have been very rare in the navy then, in part because crowded conditions and strict discipline limited opportunities for it.

Instead, one writer has suggested, "Mary's naughty innuendo clearly concerns flagellation: utterly unfit for a lady's conversation, but legal . . . and familiar enough to any citizen who ever glanced in a print-shop window at the satirical cartoons of Gillray or Rowlandson, in which birches and but-

Edmund again felt grave, and only replied, "It is a noble profession."[68]

"Yes, the profession is well enough under two circumstances; if it make the fortune, and there be discretion in spending it.[69] But, in short, it is not a favourite profession of mine. It has never worn an amiable form to *me*."

Edmund reverted to the harp, and was again very happy in the prospect of hearing her play.

The subject of improving grounds meanwhile was still under consideration among the others; and Mrs. Grant could not help addressing her brother, though it was calling his attention from Miss Julia Bertram. "My dear Henry, have *you* nothing to say? You have been an improver yourself, and from what I hear of Everingham, it may vie with any place in England. Its natural beauties, I am sure, are great. Everingham as it *used* to be was perfect in my estimation;[70] such a happy fall of ground,[71] and such timber![72] What would not I give to see it again!"

"Nothing could be so gratifying to me as to hear your opinion of it," was his answer. "But I fear there would be some disappointment. You would not find it equal to your present ideas.[73] In extent it is a mere nothing—you would be surprised at its insignificance; and as for improvement, there was very little for me to do; too little—I should like to have been busy much longer."

"You are fond of the sort of thing?" said Julia.

"Excessively: but what with the natural advantages of the ground, which pointed out even to a very young eye what little remained to be done, and my own consequent resolutions, I had not been of age three months before Everingham was all that it is now.[74] My plan was laid at Westminster—a little altered perhaps at Cambridge,[75] and at one and twenty executed. I am inclined to envy Mr. Rushworth for having so much happiness yet before him. I have been a devourer of my own."

"Those who see quickly, will resolve quickly and act quickly," said Julia. "*You* can never want employment. Instead of envying Mr. Rushworth, you should assist him with your opinion."

Mrs. Grant hearing the latter part of this speech, enforced[76] it warmly, persuaded that no judgment could be equal to her brother's; and as Miss Bertram caught at the idea likewise, and gave it

tocks made frequent appearances" (Josephine Ross, *Jane Austen: A Companion*, p. 148). During the eighteenth and nineteenth century, books appeared discussing the practice and sexual appeal of flagellation, and special "parlors" existed catering to those with a taste for it. It was often associated with upper-class men—a standard explanation was that they acquired the predilection in public schools, where caning was common—and its popularity in England was such that during the nineteenth century it became known in Europe as the "English Vice." The topic would also fit naturally with a pun involving the navy, in which flogging was prevalent as a means of discipline.

68. The navy was held in especially high regard during this period because Britain was in the midst of a long war with Napoleonic France, and the navy had been its principal weapon, saving Britain from French invasion. Mary's speaking of it in the next sentence in purely mercenary terms would be a patriotic failing on her part, as well as disrespectful of her uncle.

69. Naval pay was not particularly high, but it offered the opportunity to make a substantial fortune through capture of enemy vessels. The navy, after determining the value of the ship, would distribute this sum among the crew as prize money, with those of highest rank receiving the most. Some officers became very wealthy in this fashion. The suddenness of the acquisition could be a temptation to spend it recklessly.

70. Mrs. Grant would have lived there before she married, when their father was alive and owned the estate.

71. *fall of ground*: slope or declivity of the ground. Current landscaping ideals celebrated hills and steep slopes.

72. Timber was often an important product of estates. Mrs. Grant shows that she appreciates the economic value as well as the beauties of an estate.

73. He means now that Mrs. Grant has lived next to Mansfield Park. Seeing it may have increased Henry's own sense of the smallness of his estate.

74. People came of age when they turned twenty-one. Before this, Henry, while the designated heir, would not yet have legal control of the estate, which, after the death of his father, would have been vested in one or more other family members until he came of age.

75. Westminster was one of the leading boarding schools for upper-class boys. Heirs to wealthy estates had no need to attend Oxford or Cambridge, unlike those (such as Edmund) training to be clergymen. But it was normal for them to attend for at least a year or two to acquire additional education and polish. They did not pursue rigorous courses of study, were segregated from other students, and could receive honorary degrees when they left.

76. *enforced*: urged, reaffirmed.

her full support, declaring that in her opinion it was infinitely better to consult with friends and disinterested advisers, than immediately to throw the business into the hands of a professional man,[77] Mr. Rushworth was very ready to request the favour of Mr. Crawford's assistance; and Mr. Crawford after properly depreciating his own abilities, was quite at his service in any way that could be useful. Mr. Rushworth then began to propose Mr. Crawford's doing him the honour of coming over to Sotherton, and taking a bed there; when Mrs. Norris, as if reading in her two nieces' minds their little approbation of a plan which was to take Mr. Crawford away, interposed with an amendment. "There can be no doubt of Mr. Crawford's willingness; but why should not more of us go?—Why should not we make a little party?[78] Here are many that would be interested in your improvements, my dear Mr. Rushworth, and that would like to hear Mr. Crawford's opinion on the spot, and that might be of some small use to you with *their* opinions; and for my own part I have been long wishing to wait upon your good mother again; nothing but having no horses of my own, could have made me so remiss; but now I could go and sit a few hours with Mrs. Rushworth while the rest of you walked about and settled things,[79] and then we could all return to a late dinner here, or dine at Sotherton just as might be most agreeable to your mother,[80] and have a pleasant drive home by moonlight.[81] I dare say Mr. Crawford would take my two nieces and me in his barouche, and Edmund can go on horseback,[82] you know, sister, and Fanny will stay at home with you."

Lady Bertram made no objection, and every one concerned in the going, was forward in expressing their ready concurrence, excepting Edmund, who heard it all and said nothing.

77. Earlier Maria was recommending the employment of Repton. Now, however, she sees an opportunity to please Henry by enthusiastic support of his participation; she also may be spurred by competition with Julia, who suggested the idea. It gives both of them an excuse to have more of his company.

78. *party*: social gathering. The word could refer to modest as well as grand occasions.

79. Mrs. Norris, who loves activity, sees an opportunity for an outing at no expense to herself. When she actually goes, she spends little time with Mrs. Rushworth, instead focusing on inquiring into others' affairs and trying to procure valuable gifts from them.

80. Dinner was usually at four or five o'clock, so it could occur during or after an excursion for the day.

81. The moon was the only source of nighttime illumination on country roads, other than the limited light provided by carriages. People often arranged evening activities to coincide with a full or nearly full moon.

82. Men frequently went on horseback rather than going in a carriage.

An approach to Harleston Park, Northamptonshire; see p. 103, note 9.

[From Humphry Repton, *Fragments on the Theory and Practice of Landscape Gardening* (London, 1816), p. 23]

Chapter Seven

"Well Fanny, and how do you like Miss Crawford *now*?" said Edmund the next day, after thinking some time on the subject himself. "How did you like her yesterday?"

"Very well—very much. I like to hear her talk. She entertains me; and she is so extremely pretty, that I have great pleasure in looking at her."

"It is her countenance that is so attractive. She has a wonderful play of feature! But was there nothing in her conversation that struck you Fanny, as not quite right?"

"Oh! yes, she ought not to have spoken of her uncle as she did. I was quite astonished. An uncle with whom she has been living so many years, and who, whatever his faults may be, is so very fond of her brother, treating him, they say, quite like a son. I could not have believed it!"[1]

"I thought you would be struck. It was very wrong—very indecorous."[2]

"And very ungrateful I think."

"Ungrateful is a strong word. I do not know that her uncle has any claim to her *gratitude*; his wife certainly had; and it is the warmth of her respect for her aunt's memory which misleads her here. She is awkwardly circumstanced. With such warm feelings and lively spirits it must be difficult to do justice to her affection for Mrs. Crawford, without throwing a shade[3] on the admiral. I do not pretend to know which was most to blame in their disagreements, though the admiral's present conduct might incline one to the side of his wife: but it is natural and amiable that Miss Crawford should acquit her aunt entirely. I do not censure her *opinions*; but there certainly *is* impropriety in making them public."

"Do not you think," said Fanny, after a little consideration, "that this impropriety is a reflection itself upon Mrs. Crawford, as her

1. Fanny disapproves strongly of what Mary said, but her first reply to Edmund only praised Mary. After Edmund has made a critical comment himself, Fanny feels emboldened to express her true feelings.

2. *indecorous*: improper.

3. *throwing a shade*: casting a negative light.

"*Harmony Before Marriage*": *a contemporary illustration showing the romantic effects of a harp (see the next page).*

[From *Works of James Gillray* (London, 1849), Figure 538]

niece has been entirely brought up by her? She cannot have given her right notions of what was due to the admiral."

"That is a fair remark. Yes, we must suppose the faults of the niece to have been those of the aunt; and it makes one more sensible of the disadvantages she has been under. But I think her present home must do her good. Mrs. Grant's manners are just what they ought to be. She speaks of her brother with a very pleasing affection."

"Yes, except as to his writing her such short letters. She made me almost laugh; but I cannot rate so very highly the love or good nature of a brother, who will not give himself the trouble of writing any thing worth reading, to his sisters, when they are separated. I am sure William would never have used *me* so, under any circumstances. And what right had she to suppose, that *you* would not write long letters when you were absent?"

"The right of a lively mind, Fanny, seizing whatever may contribute to its own amusement or that of others; perfectly allowable, when untinctured by ill humour or roughness; and there is not a shadow of either in the countenance or manner of Miss Crawford, nothing sharp, or loud, or coarse. She is perfectly feminine,[4] except in the instances we have been speaking of. *There* she cannot be justified. I am glad you saw it all as I did."[5]

Having formed her mind and gained her affections, he had a good chance of her thinking like him; though at this period, and on this subject, there began now to be some danger of dissimilarity, for he was in a line of admiration of Miss Crawford, which might lead him where Fanny could not follow. Miss Crawford's attractions did not lessen. The harp arrived, and rather added to her beauty, wit,[6] and good humour, for she played with the greatest obligingness,[7] with an expression and taste which were peculiarly becoming,[8] and there was something clever to be said at the close of every air. Edmund was at the parsonage every day to be indulged with his favourite instrument; one morning secured an invitation for the next, for the lady could not be unwilling to have a listener, and every thing was soon in a fair train.[9]

A young woman, pretty, lively, with a harp as elegant as herself; and both placed near a window, cut down to the ground, and opening on

4.   Prevailing ideals of femininity put particular emphasis on being delicate and restrained and gentle in speech and behavior.

5.   It is actually clear from Fanny's own words that her overall verdict is less positive than his, but he, wanting her to agree fully with him, fails to perceive it, and Fanny is too deferential to correct his error. This misperception on his part will continue for most of the novel and play an important role in the plot.

6.   *wit*: the quality of being cleverly amusing.

7.   Many young ladies played the harp. It had long existed but became more widely used after the development at the beginning of the eighteenth century of pedals, an innovation that significantly increased its musical range. Late in the century, the French queen Marie Antoinette's love of harp playing enhanced its status and popularity, especially among women, throughout Europe because of the cultural prominence of the French court. Many portrait paintings from the late eighteenth and early nineteenth centuries show elegant, aristocratic young women playing the harp. A critical attraction was the gracefulness the harp imparted to the person playing it; it also put the lady's arms on full display and often caused her feet and ankles to be exposed as she pressed the pedals. These were important considerations, since a principal reason for young women to learn a musical instrument, or learn to sing well, was that musical performance was believed to enhance considerably her attractiveness and value in the marriage market. Jane Austen presents several cases of women who gave up, or planned to give up, their music making after marriage (when it would no longer be needed for this purpose).

8.   A musical dictionary of the time defines "expression" as "that quality in a composition or performance from which we receive a kind of sentimental appeal to our feelings, and which constitutes one of the first of musical requisites" (Thomas Busby, *A Dictionary of Music*, 1813 ed.). Taste is described at various points in Austen's novels as one of the critical ingredients of successful musicianship.

9.   *fair train*: good course or direction (for greater intimacy between the two).

a little lawn,[10] surrounded by shrubs in the rich foliage of summer, was enough to catch any man's heart. The season, the scene, the air, were all favourable to tenderness and sentiment. Mrs. Grant and her tambour frame were not without their use;[11] it was all in harmony; and as every thing will turn to account when love is once set going, even the sandwich tray,[12] and Dr. Grant doing the honours of it,[13] were worth looking at. Without studying the business, however, or knowing what he was about, Edmund was beginning, at the end of a week of such intercourse, to be a good deal in love; and to the credit of the lady it may be added, that without his being a man of the world[14] or an elder brother, without any of the arts of flattery or the gaieties of small talk, he began to be agreeable to her. She felt it to be so, though she had not foreseen and could hardly understand it; for

A woman at an embroidery frame.

[From Max von Boehn, *Modes & Manners of the Nineteenth Century*, Vol. I (London, 1909), p. 70]

10. Windows stretching to the floor, called French windows, had recently become popular. They appealed to the growing taste for natural beauty and the outdoors, for they offered a fuller view of the outside and often access as well, since many such windows functioned as doors.

11. A tambour frame is a round frame over which a piece of cloth is tightly stretched, allowing someone to embroider it easily by passing the thread back and forth through the cloth. "Tambouring" had become very popular in the late eighteenth century; in *Northanger Abbey* the heroine owns a gown that is decorated with tamboured embroidery.

12. Sandwiches were a recent English invention, created around 1760 by the Earl of Sandwich. They were normally served as a snack or part of a light meal, normal during the day due to the absence of a regular meal between breakfast and a late-afternoon dinner. They were also suitable for serving in a sitting room, as here; nobody would think of serving a regular meal in such a setting.

13. *doing the honours of it*: performing the courtesies of a host with it.

14. *world*: fashionable world, high society.

French windows opening onto a picturesque scene.

[From *The Repository of arts, literature, fashions, manufactures, &c*, Vol. VI (1811), p. 291]

he was not pleasant by any common rule, he talked no nonsense, he paid no compliments, his opinions were unbending, his attentions tranquil and simple. There was a charm, perhaps, in his sincerity, his steadiness, his integrity, which Miss Crawford might be equal to feel, though not equal to discuss with herself.[15] She did not think very much about it, however; he pleased her for the present; she liked to have him near her; it was enough.

Fanny could not wonder that Edmund was at the parsonage every morning; she would gladly have been there too, might she have gone in uninvited and unnoticed to hear the harp; neither could she wonder, that when the evening stroll was over, and the two families parted again, he should think it right to attend Mrs. Grant and her sister to their home, while Mr. Crawford was devoted to the ladies of the park; but she thought it a very bad exchange, and if Edmund were not there to mix the wine and water for her, would rather go without it than not.[16] She was a little surprised that he could spend so many hours with Miss Crawford, and not see more of the sort of fault which he had already observed, and of which *she* was almost always reminded by a something of the same nature whenever she was in her company; but so it was. Edmund was fond of speaking to her of Miss Crawford, but he seemed to think it enough that the admiral had since been spared; and she scrupled to point out her own remarks to him, lest it should appear like ill-nature. The first actual pain which Miss Crawford occasioned her, was the consequence of an inclination to learn to ride, which the former caught soon after her being settled at Mansfield from the example of the young ladies at the park,[17] and which, when Edmund's acquaintance with her increased, led to his encouraging the wish, and the offer of his own quiet mare for the purpose of her first attempts, as the best fitted for a beginner that either stable could furnish.[18] No pain, no injury, however, was designed by him to his cousin in this offer: *she* was not to lose a day's exercise by it. The mare was only to be taken down to the parsonage half an hour before her ride were to begin; and Fanny, on its being first proposed, so far from feeling slighted, was almost overpowered with gratitude that he should be asking her leave for it.

Miss Crawford made her first essay with great credit to herself, and no inconvenience to Fanny. Edmund, who had taken down the mare

15. The suggestion, confirmed at other points, is that neither Mary's education nor her background, centering on the admiral's home and fashionable London society, has given her much knowledge or experience of these virtues. Thus, while she has sufficient intelligence and natural decency to perceive and appreciate them, she cannot really understand them. This sort of analysis is found elsewhere in Jane Austen, who consistently treats virtue, especially in its highest forms, as the product of education and rational understanding as well as benevolent inclinations. In some cases she shows people, through a conscious intellectual effort, teaching themselves to correct their faults and become better people. Mary's incapacity or disinclination even to "discuss with herself" these new sensations might not bode well for this process of improvement.

16. Women often mixed wine with water (men did so also but not as much). Jane Austen describes doing it herself in a letter (Sept. 16, 1813), and mentions women drinking it or being offered it at two other points in her novels, always in the evening. One reason was the strong social taboo against female alcohol consumption except in strict moderation; in contrast, men frequently drank heavily. A book commended by Jane Austen in a letter, Thomas Gisborne's *An Enquiry into the Duties of the Female Sex*, says that "among women, in whom feminine delicacy and feeling have not been almost obliterated, . . . intemperance in wine, and the use of profane language, are unknown; and she who should be guilty of either crime, would be generally regarded as having debased herself to the level of a brute" (p. 33). A wish not to seem eager for drink also caused women to often wait for men to offer them alcohol or, in this case, to mix it for them.

17. Horseback riding was not very common for ladies (it became more so later in the nineteenth century); only a few female characters in Austen's novels engage in it. Mary would be especially unlikely to have pursued it previously, since she has mostly lived in London until now.

18. Meaning either the stable at Mansfield Park or the one at the parsonage.

and presided at the whole, returned with it in excellent time, before either Fanny or the steady old coachman, who always attended her when she rode without her cousins,[19] were ready to set forward. The second day's trial was not so guiltless. Miss Crawford's enjoyment of riding was such, that she did not know how to leave off. Active and fearless, and, though rather small, strongly made, she seemed formed for a horsewoman; and to the pure genuine pleasure of the exercise, something was probably added in Edmund's attendance and instructions, and something more in the conviction of very much surpassing her sex in general by her early progress, to make her unwilling to dismount. Fanny was ready and waiting, and Mrs. Norris was beginning to scold her for not being gone, and still no horse was announced, no Edmund appeared. To avoid her aunt, and look for him, she went out.

The houses, though scarcely half a mile apart, were not within sight of each other; but by walking fifty yards from the hall door,[20] she could look down the park, and command a view of the parsonage and all its demesnes,[21] gently rising beyond the village road;[22] and in Dr. Grant's meadow she immediately saw the group—Edmund and Miss Crawford both on horseback, riding side by side, Dr. and Mrs. Grant, and Mr. Crawford, with two or three grooms, standing about and looking on.[23] A happy party it appeared to her—all interested in one object—cheerful beyond a doubt, for the sound of merriment ascended even to her. It was a sound which did not make *her* cheerful; she wondered that Edmund should forget her, and felt a pang. She could not turn her eyes from the meadow, she could not help watching all that passed. At first Miss Crawford and her companion made the circuit of the field, which was not small, at a foot's pace; then, at *her* apparent suggestion, they rose into a canter; and to Fanny's timid nature it was most astonishing to see how well she sat. After a few minutes, they stopt entirely, Edmund was close to her, he was speaking to her, he was evidently directing her management of the bridle, he had hold of her hand; she saw it, or the imagination supplied what the eye could not reach. She must not wonder at all this; what could be more natural than that Edmund should be making himself useful, and proving his good-nature by any one? She could not but think indeed that Mr. Crawford might as well have saved him

19. A coachman was the servant who drove the family's carriage(s), which could mean carriages other than a coach. He also frequently took care of the horses, those used for carriages and those used for riding.

20. This is the main entrance to the house. While "hall" could refer to a large room within the house, it most frequently meant (especially when preceded by "the") the one where people entered.

21. *demesnes*: lands. In this case the lands, including the meadow referred to immediately below, are the glebe lands that, like the parsonage, come with the clerical position that Dr. Grant holds.

22. The village road leads from the village. The description indicates that the parsonage is a little removed from the village; in the previous chapter Mary said she saw and encountered farm yards all around her residence. Many, though by no means all, parsonages were situated thus, including the one where Jane Austen lived when young.

23. Grooms are servants who take care of horses. They have taken the horses out of the stable, have perhaps helped some people to mount, and are ready to assist further if needed and to take the horses back once the ride is finished.

Marston House, Somersetshire, which is screened on one side by trees—see p. 93, note 27.

[From John Preston Neale, *Views of the Seats of Noblemen and Gentlemen*, Vol. V (London, 1822)]

the trouble; that it would have been particularly proper and becoming in a brother to have done it himself; but Mr. Crawford, with all
his boasted good-nature, and all his coachmanship,[24] probably knew
nothing of the matter, and had no active kindness in comparison
of[25] Edmund. She began to think it rather hard upon the mare to
have such double duty; if she were forgotten the poor mare should
be remembered.[26]

Her feelings for one and the other were soon a little tranquillized,
by seeing the party in the meadow disperse, and Miss Crawford still
on horseback, but attended by Edmund on foot, pass through a gate
into the lane, and so into the park, and make towards the spot where
she stood. She began then to be afraid of appearing rude and impatient; and walked to meet them with a great anxiety to avoid the suspicion.

"My dear Miss Price," said Miss Crawford, as soon as she was at all
within hearing, "I am come to make my own apologies for keeping
you waiting—but I have nothing in the world to say for myself—I
knew it was very late, and that I was behaving extremely ill; and,
therefore, if you please, you must forgive me. Selfishness must always
be forgiven you know, because there is no hope of a cure."[27]

Fanny's answer was extremely civil, and Edmund added his conviction that she could be in no hurry. "For there is more than time
enough for my cousin to ride twice as far as she ever goes," said he,
"and you have been promoting her comfort by preventing her from
setting off half an hour sooner; clouds are now coming up, and she
will not suffer from the heat as she would have done then. I wish
you may not be fatigued by so much exercise. I wish you had saved
yourself this walk home."[28]

"No part of it fatigues me but getting off this horse, I assure you,"
said she, as she sprang down with his help; "I am very strong. Nothing ever fatigues me, but doing what I do not like. Miss Price, I give
way to you with a very bad grace; but I sincerely hope you will have
a pleasant ride, and that I may have nothing but good to hear of this
dear, delightful, beautiful animal."

The old coachman, who had been waiting about with his own
horse, now joining them, Fanny was lifted on her's, and they set off

24. His coachmanship is his skill in driving a carriage. It is soon apparent that Henry drives his own carriage; other young men in Austen's novels do this, though their carriages are smaller than Henry's barouche.

25. *in comparison of*: compared with.

26. This passage marks the first signs of Fanny's jealousy of Mary Crawford, which will continue for most of the novel. It also shows the author taking a more critical stance toward Fanny by showing how she, in order to avoid admitting her jealousy, first criticizes Henry Crawford for not helping his sister, and then pretends that her objection to the scene results only from concern for the mare.

27. Mary's final comment shows her cleverness and wit, but it also shows her using humor to rationalize a bad action and to disarm criticism.

28. She could have dismounted near the parsonage and let Edmund walk the horse back alone.

across another part of the park; her feelings of discomfort not lightened by seeing, as she looked back, that the others were walking
down the hill together to the village; nor did her attendant do her
much good by his comments on Miss Crawford's great cleverness as
a horsewoman, which he had been watching with an interest almost
equal to her own.

"It is a pleasure to see a lady with such a good heart for riding!"
said he. "I never see one sit a horse better. She did not seem to have
a thought of fear. Very different from you, miss, when you first began,
six years ago come next Easter. Lord bless me! how you did tremble
when Sir Thomas first had you put on!"[29]

In the drawing-room Miss Crawford was also celebrated. Her
merit in being gifted by nature with strength and courage was fully
appreciated by the Miss Bertrams; her delight in riding was like their
own; her early excellence in it was like their own, and they had great
pleasure in praising it.

"I was sure she would ride well," said Julia; "she has the make for
it. Her figure is as neat[30] as her brother's."

"Yes," added Maria, "and her spirits are as good, and she has the
same energy of character. I cannot but think that good horsemanship
has a great deal to do with the mind."

When they parted at night, Edmund asked Fanny whether she
meant to ride the next day.

"No, I do not know, not if you want the mare," was her answer.

"I do not want her at all for myself," said he; "but whenever you
are next inclined to stay at home, I think Miss Crawford would be
glad to have her for a longer time—for a whole morning in short. She
has a great desire to get as far as Mansfield common, Mrs. Grant has
been telling her of its fine views,[31] and I have no doubt of her being
perfectly equal to it. But any morning will do for this. She would be
extremely sorry to interfere with you. It would be very wrong if she
did.—She rides only for pleasure, you for health."

"I shall not ride to-morrow, certainly," said Fanny; "I have been
out very often lately, and would rather stay at home. You know I am
strong enough now to walk very well."

Edmund looked pleased, which must be Fanny's comfort, and
the ride to Mansfield common took place the next morning;—the

29. This passage gives a good sense of servants' language. As with lower-class language in general, it involves simpler sentences and grammatical errors. It also contains the use of the Lord's name, which was considered improper, and frequent use of exclamation points, whereas genteel speech was supposed to be restrained and, ideally, understated. Jane Austen does not give many examples of lower-class speech, but those she gives display similar features, ones she would have noticed from her own experience. At the same time, she does not caricature it or make it sound ridiculous, unlike many writers of the time who introduced lower-class characters for the purpose of comic relief and had them speak in an exaggerated or grotesque style.

30. *neat*: of an elegant form; well made and proportioned.

31. A common was a piece of land owned by the lord of the manor, who was usually the leading landowner in the area (Sir Thomas in this case), but which others in the community have the right to use for various purposes, such as grazing animals. Traditionally most places had commons, though the enclosure movement of the late eighteenth and early nineteenth centuries was causing many commons to be converted into purely private land that could be cultivated more productively by the landowner; this often caused hardships for poor people who had gathered material for fuel or used the commons in other ways. The commons tended to be mostly open land, which is why in this case it offers fine views.

A sofa.

[From K. Warren Clouston, *The Chippendale Period in English Furniture* (New York, 1897), p. 187]

party included all the young people but herself,[32] and was much enjoyed at the time, and doubly enjoyed again in the evening discussion. A successful scheme of this sort generally brings on another; and the having been to Mansfield common, disposed them all for going somewhere else the day after. There were many other views to be shewn, and though the weather was hot, there were shady lanes wherever they wanted to go. A young party is always provided with a shady lane. Four fine mornings successively were spent in this manner, in shewing the Crawfords the country, and doing the honours of its finest spots. Every thing answered;[33] it was all gaiety and good-humour, the heat only supplying inconvenience enough to be talked of with pleasure — till the fourth day, when the happiness of one of the party was exceedingly clouded. Miss Bertram was the one. Edmund and Julia were invited to dine at the parsonage, and *she* was excluded. It was meant and done by Mrs. Grant, with perfect good humour, on Mr. Rushworth's account, who was partly expected at the park that day; but it was felt as a very grievous injury, and her good manners were severely taxed to conceal her vexation and anger, till she reached home.[34] As Mr. Rushworth did *not* come, the injury was increased, and she had not even the relief of shewing her power over him; she could only be sullen to her mother, aunt, and cousin, and throw as great a gloom as possible over their dinner and dessert.

Between ten and eleven, Edmund and Julia walked into the drawing-room,[35] fresh with the evening air, glowing and cheerful, the very reverse of what they found in the three ladies sitting there, for Maria would scarcely raise her eyes from her book, and Lady Bertram was half asleep; and even Mrs. Norris, discomposed by her niece's ill-humour, and having asked one or two questions about the dinner, which were not immediately attended to, seemed almost determined to say no more. For a few minutes, the brother and sister were too eager in their praise of the night and their remarks on the stars, to think beyond themselves; but when the first pause came, Edmund, looking around, said, "But where is Fanny? — Is she gone to bed?"

"No, not that I know of," replied Mrs. Norris; "she was here a moment ago."

32. From this point on in the novel, Fanny will frequently be alone and therefore forced to rely on her own resources. Edmund will still help her at times, but his absorption in Mary distracts him much of the time. This new situation will lead to a number of tests of Fanny's character.

33. *answered*: was satisfactory.

34. That not being invited to dinner would so severely tax, or try, Maria's good manners indicates a flaw in her character; it also shows her preference for dining with Henry Crawford over Mr. Rushworth.

35. Wealthy people tended to keep late hours, while those who could not easily afford artificial light and who had to work long hours rose early to take full advantage of daylight and rarely stayed up late. Edmund and Julia would be especially likely to stay out late in the summer, when England's northerly latitudes cause the day to be very long.

A flower garden of the time.

[From Humphry Repton, *The Art of Landscape Gardening* (Boston, 1907; reprint edition), p. 144]

Her own gentle voice speaking from the other end of the room, which was a very long one,[36] told them that she was on the sofa. Mrs. Norris began scolding.

"That is a very foolish trick, Fanny, to be idling away all the evening upon a sofa.[37] Why cannot you come and sit here, and employ yourself as *we* do?—If you have no work of your own, I can supply you from the poor-basket.[38] There is all the new calico that was bought last week,[39] not touched yet. I am sure I almost broke my back by cutting it out.[40] You should learn to think of other people; and take my word for it, it is a shocking trick[41] for a young person to be always lolling upon a sofa."[42]

Before half this was said, Fanny was returned to her seat at the table, and had taken up her work again; and Julia, who was in high good-humour, from the pleasures of the day, did her the justice of exclaiming, "I must say, ma'am, that Fanny is as little upon the sofa as any body in the house."

"Fanny," said Edmund, after looking at her attentively; "I am sure you have the headach?"

She could not deny it, but said it was not very bad.

"I can hardly believe you," he replied; "I know your looks too well. How long have you had it?"

"Since a little before dinner. It is nothing but the heat."

"Did you go out in the heat?"

"Go out! to be sure she did," said Mrs. Norris; "would you have her stay within such a fine day as this? Were not we *all* out? Even your mother was out to-day for above an hour."

"Yes, indeed, Edmund," added her ladyship, who had been thoroughly awakened by Mrs. Norris's sharp reprimand to Fanny; "I was out above an hour. I sat three quarters of an hour in the flower garden, while Fanny cut the roses,[43] and very pleasant it was I assure you, but very hot. It was shady enough in the alcove,[44] but I declare I quite dreaded the coming home again."[45]

"Fanny has been cutting roses, has she?"

"Yes, and I am afraid they will be the last this year. Poor thing! *She* found it hot enough, but they were so full blown,[46] that one could not wait."

36. Drawing rooms in wealthy homes were very large, since they were often the principal gathering room in the house; for examples of large drawing rooms of the time, see pp. 271 and 325.

37. Reclining on a sofa, especially for a long time, was believed to be a sign of laxness and self-indulgence. Traditionally it was considered improper for any-one not sick or physically incapable to do other than sit up straight when not standing. This attitude had relaxed somewhat in the decades leading to this novel, part of a general relaxation of social formality that led to sofas emerging as a popular piece of furniture in England. But the traditional attitude still held much force.

38. The poor-basket contains materials that could be used to make clothing for the poor; Fanny could help with it if she has no needlework of her own. Charity to the local poor was a basic duty and activity of the wealthy then, especially women.

39. Calico is a type of cotton cloth originally from India that in the last part of the eighteenth century began to be commonly manufactured and worn in England. It is a relatively sturdy cotton, in contrast to the lightweight muslin that was even more popular then, so it would be a useful material to make items for the poor (though it also could be used to make fine clothes).

40. Cloth was purchased in large pieces, which would then need to be cut and sewn into clothes. Wealthy people hired others to do this, but Mrs. Norris's cheapness and love of activity make her inclined to do it herself.

41. *trick*: capricious or thoughtless act.

42. Mrs. Norris will continue meting out such abuse on Fanny, who is the only non-servant who is clearly below Mrs. Norris in status, especially now the Bertram children are adults.

43. Roses, which have been widely cultivated since ancient times, have long been popular in England.

44. Many gardens had alcoves, which meant any covered retreat, whether constructed or formed by trees.

45. This is the only time Lady Bertram is ever described going out of doors, except on a couple of occasions to travel to another house. Here all she seems to do is sit in the shade while Fanny cuts roses; the three-quarters of an hour for that activity was probably stretched into her being out "above an hour" by the time spent in walking to the flower garden and back—and such gardens were normally close to the house.

46. *full blown*: fully in bloom or blossom.

"There was no help for it certainly," rejoined Mrs. Norris, in a rather softened voice; "but I question whether her headach might not be[47] caught *then*, sister. There is nothing so likely to give it as standing and stooping in a hot sun. But I dare say it will be well to-morrow. Suppose you let her have your aromatic vinegar;[48] I always forget to have mine filled."

"She has got it," said Lady Bertram; "she has had it ever since she came back from your house the second time."

"What!" cried Edmund; "has she been walking as well as cutting roses; walking across the hot park to your house,[49] and doing it twice, ma'am? — No wonder her head aches."

Mrs. Norris was talking to Julia, and did not hear.

"I was afraid it would be too much for her," said Lady Bertram; "but when the roses were gathered, your aunt wished to have them, and then you know they must be taken home."[50]

"But were there roses enough to oblige her to go twice?"

"No; but they were to be put into the spare room to dry; and, unluckily, Fanny forgot to lock the door of the room and bring away the key, so she was obliged to go again."[51]

Edmund got up and walked about the room, saying, "And could nobody be employed on such an errand but Fanny? — Upon my word, ma'am, it has been a very ill-managed business."

"I am sure I do not know how it was to have been done better," cried Mrs. Norris, unable to be longer deaf; "unless I had gone myself indeed; but I cannot be in two places at once; and I was talking to Mr. Green at that very time about your mother's dairymaid,[52] by *her* desire, and had promised John Groom to write to Mrs. Jefferies about his son,[53] and the poor fellow was waiting for me half an hour. I think nobody can justly accuse me of sparing myself upon any occasion, but really I cannot do every thing at once. And as for Fanny's just stepping down to my house for me, it is not much above a quarter of a mile,[54] I cannot think I was unreasonable to ask it. How often do I pace it three times a-day, early and late, ay and in all weathers too, and say nothing about it."

"I wish Fanny had half your strength, ma'am."

"If Fanny would be more regular in her exercise, she would not be knocked up[55] so soon. She has not been out on horseback now

47. *might not be*: may not have been.

48. Books of the time use the term "aromatic vinegar" to refer to various substances made from vinegar, used to purify rooms rife with foul odors or disease. The *Encyclopaedia Britannica* provides one recipe (also given in a leading medical guide) that involves soaking rosemary, sage, lavender flowers, and cloves in vinegar for a week and then straining the liquid, which is "sometimes given as a stimulus."

49. Parks usually consisted of substantial tracts of open grass, so they would become hot on a sunny day in summer.

50. Mrs. Norris is avid for the cut roses because they were used for a variety of practical purposes. The petals or the rose hips formed a key ingredient in some medicinal remedies as well as perfumes or cosmetics; they also were used to flavor sweet dishes or to make syrups, conserves, and jellies.

51. This is presumably the same spare room that Mrs. Norris insisted she needed to keep empty for the sake of a friend who might visit (p. 56). If so, it is an indoor room, which would not necessarily need to be locked. Mrs. Norris may keep it always locked due to suspicion of her servants, or she may wish to lock it now because she considers the roses too valuable to leave unsecured.

52. The dairymaid is called his mother's maid because the dairy was often the province of the lady of the house (see p. 205, note 43, and the picture on p. 203). Given Lady Bertram's indolence and Mrs. Norris's busyness, the latter probably manages it, which is why she concerns herself with the dairymaid. Mr. Green, who is never mentioned elsewhere, may be the steward who supervises the estate; Mrs. Norris would not call someone of low status "Mr."

53. John Groom may not be his actual name; he may simply be a groom named John. Lower-class people were sometimes referred to in this manner; in *Emma* a character speaks of John ostler, though in that case "ostler," which is someone attending horses at an inn, is not capitalized. This usage, even more common in earlier times when poor people often did not have last names, makes clear how a large class of English surnames, such as Smith or Taylor or Cooper, developed. In this case John Groom likely works on the estate and is seeking employment for his son with Mrs. Jefferies, whose title indicates she is of high enough status to hire someone to work for her. Helping relatives of one's servants get jobs was standard practice and is something other characters in Austen's novels are shown doing.

54. This reveals that the village is closer to Mansfield Park than the parsonage, which was recently described as half a mile away (p. 132).

55. *knocked up*: exhausted, overcome with fatigue.

this long while, and I am persuaded, that when she does not ride, she ought to walk. If she had been riding before, I should not have asked it of her. But I thought it would rather do her good after being stooping[56] among the roses; for there is nothing so refreshing as a walk after a fatigue of that kind; and though the sun was strong, it was not so very hot. Between ourselves, Edmund," nodding significantly at his mother, "it was cutting the roses, and dawdling about in the flower-garden, that did the mischief."

"I am afraid it was, indeed," said the more candid[57] Lady Bertram, who had overheard her, "I am very much afraid she caught the head-ach there, for the heat was enough to kill any body. It was as much as I could bear myself. Sitting and calling to Pug, and trying to keep him from the flower-beds, was almost too much for me."

Edmund said no more to either lady; but going quietly to another table, on which the supper tray yet remained,[58] brought a glass of Madeira to Fanny, and obliged her to drink the greater part.[59] She wished to be able to decline it; but the tears which a variety of feelings created, made it easier to swallow than to speak.

Vexed as Edmund was with his mother and aunt, he was still more angry with himself. His own forgetfulness of her was worse than any thing which they had done. Nothing of this would have happened had she been properly considered; but she had been left four days together without any choice of companions or exercise, and without any excuse for avoiding whatever her unreasonable aunts might require. He was ashamed to think that for four days together she had not had the power of riding, and very seriously resolved, however unwilling he must be to check a pleasure of Miss Crawford's, that it should never happen again.

Fanny went to bed with her heart as full as on the first evening of her arrival at the Park. The state of her spirits had probably had its share in her indisposition; for she had been feeling neglected, and been struggling against discontent and envy for some days past. As she leant on the sofa, to which she had retreated that she might not be seen, the pain of her mind had been much beyond that in her head; and the sudden change which Edmund's kindness had then occasioned, made her hardly know how to support herself.

56. *being stooping*: stooping. This construction, an older grammatical form, is used elsewhere in Austen's novels.

57. *candid*: impartial, just.

58. Among the wealthy supper was a light meal, since it came after a dinner, the big meal of the day, which was served at four or five or even later for the very wealthy and fashionable. Hence supper has been brought into the drawing room on a tray.

59. Madeira is wine from the archipelago of that name in the Atlantic. It was popular in England then; one reason was Britain's close commercial ties with the owner of the archipelago, Portugal. Wine was often used as a restorative.

A riding habit, such as Fanny or Mary might wear.

[From *The Repository of arts, literature, fashions, manufactures, &c*, Vol. VI (1811), p. 358]

Chapter Eight

*F*anny's rides recommenced the very next day, and as it was a pleasant fresh-feeling morning, less hot than the weather had lately been, Edmund trusted that her losses both of health and pleasure would be soon made good. While she was gone, Mr. Rushworth arrived, escorting his mother, who came to be civil, and to shew her civility especially, in urging the execution of the plan for visiting Sotherton, which had been started[1] a fortnight before, and which, in consequence of her subsequent absence from home, had since lain dormant.[2] Mrs. Norris and her nieces were all well pleased with its revival, and an early day was named, and agreed to, provided Mr. Crawford should be disengaged; the young ladies did not forget that stipulation, and though Mrs. Norris would willingly have answered for his being so, they would neither authorize the liberty, nor run the risk; and at last on a hint from Miss Bertram, Mr. Rushworth discovered that the properest thing to be done, was for him to walk down to the parsonage directly, and call on Mr. Crawford, and inquire whether Wednesday would suit him or not.[3]

Before his return Mrs. Grant and Miss Crawford came in. Having been out some time, and taken a different route to the house, they had not met him. Comfortable[4] hopes, however, were given that he would find Mr. Crawford at home. The Sotherton scheme was mentioned of course. It was hardly possible indeed that any thing else should be talked of, for Mrs. Norris was in high spirits about it, and Mrs. Rushworth, a well-meaning, civil, prosing,[5] pompous woman, who thought nothing of consequence, but as it related to her own and her son's concerns, had not yet given over pressing Lady Bertram to be of the party. Lady Bertram constantly declined it; but her placid manner of refusal made Mrs. Rushworth still think she wished to come, till Mrs. Norris's more numerous words and louder tone convinced her of the truth.[6]

"The fatigue would be too much for my sister, a great deal too

1. *started*: proposed, introduced.

2. It is now early August; see chronology, p. 856.

3. Mrs. Rushworth has already asked the ladies at Mansfield Park, but it would be proper for the invitation to Mr. Crawford to come from another man.

4. *Comfortable*: encouraging, reassuring.

5. *prosing*: tedious.

6. Good manners, especially for ladies, would dictate resisting an invitation at first in order not to appear too eager. On the next page Mary Crawford, who does wish to come, waits to accept until she has been pressed a little.

A parsonage; not all at the time were this nice.

[From *The Repository of arts, literature, fashions, manufactures, &c*, Series Two, Vol. II (1816), p. 191]

much I assure you, my dear Mrs. Rushworth. Ten miles there, and then back, you know. You must excuse my sister on this occasion, and accept of our two dear girls and myself without her. Sotherton is the only place that could give her a *wish* to go so far, but it cannot be indeed. She will have a companion in Fanny Price you know, so it will all do very well; and as for Edmund, as he is not here to speak for himself, I will answer for his being most happy to join the party. He can go on horseback, you know."

Mrs. Rushworth being obliged to yield to Lady Bertram's staying at home, could only be sorry. "The loss of her Ladyship's company would be a great drawback,[7] and she should have been extremely happy to have seen the young lady too, Miss Price, who had never been at Sotherton yet, and it was a pity she should not see the place."

"You are very kind, you are all kindness, my dear madam," cried Mrs. Norris; "but as to Fanny, she will have opportunities in plenty of seeing Sotherton. She has time enough before her; and her going now is quite out of the question. Lady Bertram could not possibly spare her."

"Oh! no—I cannot do without Fanny."

Mrs. Rushworth proceeded next, under the conviction that every body must be wanting to see Sotherton, to include Miss Crawford in the invitation; and though Mrs. Grant, who had not been at the trouble of visiting[8] Mrs. Rushworth on her coming into the neighbourhood,[9] civilly declined it on her own account, she was glad to secure any pleasure for her sister; and Mary, properly pressed and persuaded, was not long in accepting her share of the civility. Mr. Rushworth came back from the parsonage successful; and Edmund made his appearance just in time to learn what had been settled for Wednesday, to attend Mrs. Rushworth to her carriage, and walk half way down the park with the two other ladies.

On his return to the breakfast-room, he found Mrs. Norris trying to make up her mind as to whether Miss Crawford's being of the party were desirable or not, or whether her brother's barouche would not be full without her. The Miss Bertrams laughed at the idea, assuring her that the barouche would hold four perfectly well, independent of the box, on which *one* might go with him.[10]

"But why is it necessary," said Edmund, "that Crawford's carriage,

7. *drawback*: diminution.

8. *been at the trouble of visiting*: taken the trouble to visit.

9. This means Mrs. Grant's coming into the neighborhood. She may have decided that Mrs. Rushworth lived too far away. Whatever the reason, she has not visited Sotherton and thus is a prime candidate for an invitation.

10. The box is the seat in the front of the carriage on which the driver sits; it is large enough for a second person. For a picture, see p. 118.

A woman outdoors with a parasol and a veil.

[From *The Repository of arts, literature, fashions, manufactures, &c*, Vol. VI (1811), p. 52]

or his *only* should be employed? Why is no use to be made of my mother's chaise?[11] I could not, when the scheme was first mentioned the other day, understand why a visit from the family were not to be made in the carriage of the family."

"What!" cried Julia: "go box'd up three in a post-chaise in this weather,[12] when we may have seats in a barouche![13] No, my dear Edmund, that will not quite do."

"Besides," said Maria, "I know that Mr. Crawford depends upon taking us. After what passed at first, he would claim it as a promise."

"And my dear Edmund," added Mrs. Norris, "taking out *two* carriages when *one* will do, would be trouble for nothing;[14] and between ourselves, coachman is not very fond of the roads between this and Sotherton; he always complains bitterly of the narrow lanes scratching his carriage,[15] and you know one should not like to have dear Sir Thomas when he comes home find all the varnish scratched off."[16]

"That would not be a very handsome reason for using Mr. Crawford's," said Maria; "but the truth is, that Wilcox is a stupid old fellow, and does not know how to drive.[17] I will answer for it that we shall find no inconvenience from narrow roads on Wednesday."

"There is no hardship, I suppose, nothing unpleasant," said Edmund, "in going on the barouche box."

"Unpleasant!" cried Maria; "Oh! dear, I believe it would be generally thought the favourite seat. There can be no comparison as to one's view of the country. Probably, Miss Crawford will choose the barouche box herself."

"There can be no objection then to Fanny's going with you; there can be no doubt of your having room for her."[18]

"Fanny!" repeated Mrs. Norris; "my dear Edmund, there is no idea of her going with us. She stays with her aunt. I told Mrs. Rushworth so. She is not expected."

"You can have no reason I imagine madam," said he, addressing his mother, "for wishing Fanny *not* to be of the party, but as it relates to yourself, to your own comfort. If you could do without her, you would not wish to keep her at home?"

"To be sure not, but I *cannot* do without her."

"You can, if I stay at home with you, as I mean to do."

There was a general cry out at this. "Yes," he continued, "there is

11. A chaise is an enclosed carriage that seats three people, all facing forward (for a picture, see the following page); the largest of all carriages then, the coach, is also enclosed but seats six, with three facing forward and three facing backward. Though Edmund calls the chaise his mother's, it is probably a family carriage (Lady Bertram travels little, even around the neighborhood), but because Sir Thomas is currently absent, its ownership is attributed to his wife.

12. A post-chaise, strictly speaking, means a chaise used for traveling post, the main method for long distances (for an explanation, see p. 483, note 22). The chaise was the normal carriage used, since its being enclosed meant protection from the elements and its small size meant it required fewer horses than a coach. Because chaises were used so often for travel, the term "post-chaise" was sometimes used to refer to any of them.

13. Since a barouche's top opens, it would be more suitable for warm weather.

14. Carriages suffered serious wear and tear on the mostly dirt roads of the time, and could need extensive repairs; moreover, horses would eventually exhaust themselves from work and have to be replaced. Hence any trip would impose some cost.

15. An earlier passage described the roads to Sotherton as "indifferent" (p. 76). The coachman would not wish the carriage to be scratched, since he is in charge of maintaining and repairing it and since, in part because of this responsibility, he takes pride in the vehicle.

16. Carriages, which could be highly decorated in various ways, were normally painted and then varnished to preserve the paint.

17. Wilcox, the coachman, is called by his last name because he is an upper servant. His employment despite his age and, if Maria's charge is accurate, his incompetence would be typical. The ethos of the time dictated that long-time servants, in return for their service and their deferential devotion to their employers, be cared for and, if possible, employed as they aged.

18. The plan is for four passengers in the barouche: Maria, Julia, Mary Crawford, and Mrs. Norris. If one can sit next to Henry as he drives, then Fanny could join the other three in the main part of the carriage.

no necessity for my going, and I mean to stay at home. Fanny has a great desire to see Sotherton. I know she wishes it very much. She has not often a gratification of the kind, and I am sure ma'am you would be glad to give her the pleasure now?"

"Oh! yes, very glad, if your aunt sees no objection."

Mrs. Norris was very ready with the only objection which could remain, their having positively assured Mrs. Rushworth, that Fanny could not go, and the very strange appearance there would consequently be in taking her, which seemed to her a difficulty quite impossible to be got over. It must have the strangest appearance! It would be something so very unceremonious, so bordering on disrespect for Mrs. Rushworth, whose own manners were such a pattern of good-breeding and attention,[19] that she really did not feel equal to it. Mrs. Norris had no affection for Fanny, and no wish of procuring her pleasure at any time, but her opposition to Edmund *now* arose more from partiality for her own scheme because it *was* her own, than from any thing else. She felt that she had arranged every thing extremely well, and that any alteration must be for the worse. When Edmund, therefore, told her in reply, as he did when she would give him the hearing,[20] that she need not distress herself on Mrs. Rushworth's account, because he had taken the opportunity as he walked with her through the hall,[21] of mentioning Miss Price as one who would probably be of the party, and had directly received a very sufficient invitation for his cousin, Mrs. Norris was too much vexed to submit with a very good grace, and would only say, "Very well, very well, just as you choose, settle it your own way, I am sure I do not care about it."

"It seems very odd," said Maria, "that you should be staying at home instead of Fanny."

"I am sure she ought to be very much obliged to you," added Julia, hastily leaving the room as she spoke, from a consciousness that she ought to offer to stay at home herself.[22]

"Fanny will feel quite as grateful as the occasion requires," was Edmund's only reply, and the subject dropt.

Fanny's gratitude when she heard the plan, was in fact much greater than her pleasure. She felt Edmund's kindness with all, and more than all, the sensibility which he, unsuspicious of her fond attachment, could be aware of; but that he should forego any enjoy-

19. *attention*: formal courtesy.

20. *give him the hearing*: listen to him.

21. It was earlier stated that he attended her out, which would have meant going through the hall.

22. Julia could be expected to offer, since, unlike Fanny, she presumably saw Sotherton on an earlier family visit, and since she, as a woman, would be a more logical companion for Lady Bertram than Edmund.

PLATE 38. AN ENGLISH POST CHAISE OF 1790.

A chaise.

[From G. A. Thrupp, *History of Coaches* (London, 1877), p. 77]

ment on her account gave her pain, and her own satisfaction in seeing Sotherton would be nothing without him.

The next meeting of the two Mansfield families produced another
alteration in the plan, and one that was admitted with general approbation. Mrs. Grant offered herself as companion for the day to Lady
Bertram in lieu of her son, and Dr. Grant was to join them at dinner. Lady Bertram was very well pleased to have it so, and the young
ladies were in spirits again. Even Edmund was very thankful for an
arrangement which restored him to his share of the party; and Mrs.
Norris thought it an excellent plan, and had it at her tongue's end,
and was on the point of proposing it when Mrs. Grant spoke.

Wednesday was fine, and soon after breakfast the barouche arrived,
Mr. Crawford driving his sisters; and as every body was ready, there
was nothing to be done but for Mrs. Grant to alight and the others to
take their places. The place of all places, the envied seat, the post of
honour, was unappropriated. To whose happy lot was it to fall? While
each of the Miss Bertrams were meditating how best, and with most
appearance of obliging the others, to secure it, the matter was settled
by Mrs. Grant's saying, as she stepped from the carriage, "As there are
five of you, it will be better that one should sit with Henry, and as you
were saying lately, that you wished you could drive, Julia, I think this
will be a good opportunity for you to take a lesson."[23]

Happy Julia! Unhappy Maria! The former was on the barouche-
box in a moment, the latter took her seat within, in gloom and mortification; and the carriage drove off amid the good wishes of the two
remaining ladies, and the barking of Pug in his mistress's arms.

Their road was through a pleasant country; and Fanny, whose
rides had never been extensive, was soon beyond her knowledge, and
was very happy in observing all that was new, and admiring all that
was pretty. She was not often invited to join in the conversation of the
others, nor did she desire it. Her own thoughts and reflections were
habitually her best companions; and in observing the appearance of
the country, the bearings of the roads, the difference of soil, the state
of the harvest, the cottages, the cattle, the children, she found entertainment that could only have been heightened by having Edmund
to speak to of what she felt. That was the only point of resemblance
between her and the lady who sat by her; in every thing but a value[24]

23. Mrs. Grant was earlier described as wanting Henry to prefer Julia, so she naturally promotes their riding together. Women did not drive carriages often, and when they did, would use ones smaller than a barouche.

24. *value*: liking, regard.

Salisbury Cathedral, considered at the time to be the greatest of all Gothic cathedrals in England. For the interest in Gothic architecture then, see p. 159, note 35.

[From *Winkle's Architectural and Picturesque Illustrations of the Cathedral Churches of England and Wales*, Vol. I (London, 1836), Plate 6]

for Edmund, Miss Crawford was very unlike her. She had none of
Fanny's delicacy of taste, of mind, of feeling; she saw nature, inanimate nature, with little observation; her attention was all for men
and women, her talents for the light and lively. In looking back after
Edmund, however, when there was any stretch of road behind them,
or when he gained on them in ascending a considerable hill, they
were united, and a "there he is" broke at the same moment from
them both, more than once.[25]

For the first seven miles Miss Bertram had very little real comfort;
her prospect always ended in Mr. Crawford and her sister sitting side
by side full of conversation and merriment;[26] and to see only his
expressive profile as he turned with a smile to Julia, or to catch the
laugh of the other was a perpetual source of irritation, which her own
sense of propriety could but just smooth over.[27] When Julia looked
back, it was with a countenance of delight, and whenever she spoke
to them, it was in the highest spirits; "her view of the country was
charming, she wished they could all see it, &c." but her only offer of
exchange was addressed to Miss Crawford, as they gained the summit of a long hill, and was not more inviting than this, "Here is a
fine burst[28] of country. I wish you had my seat, but I dare say you
will not take it, let me press you ever so much," and Miss Crawford could hardly answer, before they were moving again at a good
pace.

When they came within the influence of Sotherton associations,
it was better for Miss Bertram, who might be said to have two strings
to her bow. She had Rushworth-feelings, and Crawford-feelings,
and in the vicinity of Sotherton, the former had considerable effect.
Mr. Rushworth's consequence was hers. She could not tell Miss
Crawford that "those woods belonged to Sotherton," she could not
carelessly observe that "she believed it was now all Mr. Rushworth's
property on each side of the road," without elation of heart;[29] and it
was a pleasure to increase with their approach to the capital freehold
mansion,[30] and ancient manorial residence of the family,[31] with all
its rights of Court-Leet and Court-Baron.[32]

"Now we shall have no more rough road, Miss Crawford, our difficulties are over. The rest of the way is such as it ought to be. Mr.
Rushworth has made it since he succeeded to the estate. Here begins

25. The carriage would go at least as fast on level ground as Edmund does on horseback, since, while much heavier, it would be pulled by multiple horses. But a carriage would slow much more while going up a hill, allowing him to reduce the gap. A similar phenomenon can be seen on modern highways when heavy vehicles like trucks slow down ascending an incline.

26. The carriage's being open means an unencumbered "prospect," or view, of those driving in front, and Maria and Mrs. Norris are the two facing forward; Fanny and Mary have just been described as looking back toward Edmund. The former two probably claimed their position, which was regarded as superior due to the possibility of motion sickness in carriages, because of their greater age and social position; by now Maria may have come to regret the choice.

27. That is, her sense of propriety barely enables her to control or suppress her irritation.

28. *burst*: view that suddenly opens up.

29. It is notable that her "Rushworth-feelings," in contrast to her "Crawford-feelings," seem to be inspired almost completely by the man's possessions and social positions, rather than his character.

30. A capital mansion is the principal residence of the owner: many wealthy landowners had multiple properties and homes but would primarily reside in one; this was the case with Jane Austen's brother Edward, who inherited a wealthy estate from distant cousins. Freehold property is owned outright, in contrast to copyhold property, which is held under lease. Both capital and freehold status would add to the value of a mansion.

31. A manor meant land that has tenants on it, which almost all large land-holdings did; it also could refer to an older feudal status, in which land was held in trust from the king and the owner had certain legal rights over its tenants. "Ancient manorial residence" would suggest this earlier status of the estate as well as the antiquity of the house.

32. These were two rights held by the lord of the manor under the old feudal arrangements. He was empowered to hold a court leet, usually annually or semiannually, presided over by him or his steward; it judged petty offenses and could also exercise supervision over local matters like rules for the use of land or selling goods. A court-baron (derived from an early meaning of "baron" as one who held something, such as a manor, from the king) decided civil disputes between tenants; the lord also had jurisdiction over it. Both courts were gradually superseded by more regular law courts and by the time of this novel were mostly historical memories. Nonetheless, the earlier possession of these rights would add significantly to the prestige of a family and its estate.

the village.[33] Those cottages are really a disgrace.[34] The church spire is reckoned remarkably handsome.[35] I am glad the church is not so close to the Great House as often happens in old places. The annoyance of the bells must be terrible.[36] There is the parsonage; a tidy looking house, and I understand the clergyman and his wife are very decent people. Those are alms-houses, built by some of the family.[37] To the right is the steward's house; he is a very respectable man.[38] Now we are coming to the lodge gates;[39] but we have nearly a mile through the park still. It is not ugly, you see, at this end; there is some fine timber, but the situation of the house is dreadful. We go down hill to it for half-a-mile, and it is a pity, for it would not be an ill-looking place if it had a better approach."[40]

Miss Crawford was not slow to admire; she pretty well guessed Miss Bertram's feelings, and made it a point of honour to promote her enjoyment to the utmost. Mrs. Norris was all delight and volubility; and even Fanny had something to say in admiration, and might be

A poor family's cottage.

[From Sir Walter Gilbey and E. D. Cuming, *George Morland: His Life and Works* (London, 1907), p. 234]

33. That they have already been traveling through Mr. Rushworth's property before reaching the village, which is still some distance from the mansion, suggests the extent of his holdings.

34. The cottages are the residences of laborers and other poor people, likely to present a dilapidated or unattractive sight. During the late eighteenth century, and continuing into the nineteenth, many landowners rebuilt local cottages, or in some cases even entire villages. This was done from concern for the welfare of the residents but also from a wish to make the buildings near or around the estate look more attractive and picturesque. Maria may already envision such a rebuilding effort once she becomes mistress of the estate.

35. This period witnessed a growing interest in church architecture, both exemplified and spurred by a number of books about architecture, especially that of churches, that appeared after 1800. Two series by the same publisher, *Architectural Antiquities of Great Britain* and *Cathedral Antiquities,* enjoyed wide success. They were accompanied by elaborate engravings of their subject matter, as were many books in this period; for an example, see the illustatrion on p. 155. This interest was connected to a growing interest in Gothic architecture of earlier centuries, the style in which most of Britain's grandest cathedrals and many of her ordinary churches had been built.

36. In earlier times the local church was often near the "Great House," whose owner would frequently be its main patron. Grand houses constructed more recently were often farther away because of the desire to surround the house with a large landscaped park. The change also indicated a decline in strict piety. Maria's dislike of the church bells, which would be rung as part of daily routine as well as for special occasions, marks her lack of piety. At this time, when religion and morality were considered to be inextricably intertwined, this lack could also portend moral weakness.

37. Almshouses are residences for poor people, especially the elderly. Wealthy landowners often built them for the poor in their area. Limited public assistance made such types of private charity critical, and helping the poor was considered an essential duty of those in the higher ranks.

38. Here "respectable" means worthy and decent, but not genteel.

39. The lodge gates mark the entrance to the park surrounding the house. The lodge, sometimes known as the gatehouse, would be staffed and inhabited by a porter, who controlled entry. A lodge could also impress visitors and thus had become more common as visiting grand houses increased in popularity (see p. 165, note 8); many lodges were fairly grand in appearance. For an example, see the following page.

40. Maria, like Mr. Rushworth earlier, expresses prevailing taste in wishing for an elevated situation, i.e., position, and an impressive approach.

heard with complacency. Her eye was eagerly taking in every thing within her reach; and after being at some pains to get a view of the house, and observing that "it was a sort of building which she could not look at but with respect," she added, "Now, where is the avenue? The house fronts[41] the east, I perceive. The avenue, therefore, must be at the back of it. Mr. Rushworth talked of the west front."

"Yes, it is exactly behind the house; begins at a little distance, and ascends for half-a-mile to the extremity of the grounds. You may see something of it here—something of the more distant trees. It is oak entirely."[42]

Miss Bertram could now speak with decided information of what she had known nothing about, when Mr. Rushworth had asked her opinion, and her spirits were in as happy a flutter as vanity and pride could furnish, when they drove up to the spacious stone steps before the principal entrance.[43]

An entrance gate to an estate.

[From John Buonaratti Papworth, *Rural Residences* (London, 1832), p. 81]

41. *fronts*: faces.

42. Oak trees were, and are, the most common trees in England. Maria may mention them because they had a particular prestige in this period, since oak's hardness made it the material for building the warships of the all-important British navy. "Heart of Oak," composed in the eighteenth century, was one of the navy's most popular songs.

43. Grand houses often had an impressive set of stone steps leading to the main entrance. For examples, see pp. 108 and 236.

A park lodge.

[From John Buonaratti Papworth, *Rural Residences* (London, 1832), p. 77]

Chapter Nine

*M*r. Rushworth was at the door to receive his fair lady, and the whole party were welcomed by him with due attention. In the drawing-room they were met with equal cordiality by the mother, and Miss Bertram had all the distinction with each that she could wish. After the business of arriving was over, it was first necessary to eat, and the doors were thrown open to admit them through one or two intermediate rooms into the appointed dining-parlour, where a collation[1] was prepared with abundance and elegance. Much was said, and much was ate, and all went well. The particular object of the day was then considered. How would Mr. Crawford like, in what manner would he choose, to take a survey of the grounds?— Mrs. Rushworth mentioned his curricle.[2] Mr. Crawford suggested the greater desirableness of some carriage which might convey more than two. "To be depriving themselves of the advantage of other eyes and other judgments, might be an evil even beyond the loss of present pleasure."[3]

Mrs. Rushworth proposed that the chaise should be taken also; but this was scarcely received as an amendment;[4] the young ladies neither smiled nor spoke. Her next proposition, of shewing the house to such of them as had not been there before, was more acceptable, for Miss Bertram was pleased to have its size displayed, and all were glad to be doing something.

The whole party rose accordingly, and under Mrs. Rushworth's guidance were shewn through a number of rooms, all lofty, and many large, and amply furnished in the taste of fifty years back, with shining floors, solid mahogany, rich damask, marble, gilding and carving, each handsome in its way.[5] Of pictures there were abundance, and some few good, but the larger part were family portraits,[6] no longer any thing to any body but Mrs. Rushworth, who had been at great pains to learn all that the housekeeper could teach, and was

1. *collation*: light meal.

2. A curricle is a small open carriage drawn by two horses (unlike the similar gig, which used one horse). This made it fast; moreover, it was a very fashionable carriage, usually owned by the wealthy. For a picture, see the next page.

3. He may not wish to spend all his time with Rushworth alone; he also may be thinking of spending more time with Maria or Julia.

4. He presumably owns a chaise also. It would convey three more people, but its enclosed nature means they could not see much.

5. These are all prominent features of interior decor of fifty years earlier, around 1765. By Austen's time there was much greater use of wallpaper and of carpets, including wall-to-wall carpets in some cases, due to manufacturing advances that lowered their cost. This meant less emphasis on beautiful flooring and on ornamenting the walls with gilding and carving or with marble. (Marble had become popular during the eighteenth century, but its expense and weight led many to substitute scagliola, a plaster made to resemble marble, on the surfaces of walls, doorways, and columns; it is possible the author is thinking as much of that as of real marble.) Manufacturing advances also led to a preference for less expensive and more easily washable cotton fabrics over damask—a fabric of silk, linen, or wool woven in a manner that allowed elaborate decorative patterns, which was widely used in the seventeenth and eighteenth centuries for furniture coverings, table linens, and wall and bed hangings. Mahogany, the most prized wood for furniture in the eighteenth century, continued to be popular but in the years preceding this novel had begun to be superseded by lighter woods, such as satinwood.

This description, along with other features of Sotherton Court, suggest that Jane Austen used as her model an actual house, Stoneleigh Abbey in Warwickshire (a Midlands county adjacent to the Northamptonshire of the novel). In 1806, while she, her sister, and her mother were visiting their first cousin Thomas Leigh in nearby Gloucestershire, a very distant cousin who owned Stoneleigh Abbey died. Because of the lack of direct descendants and uncertainty regarding the inheritance of the property, Thomas Leigh, a possible heir, was advised by his lawyer to take immediate possession to strengthen his claim. The three Austen women accompanied him and stayed for a brief visit, giving Jane an intimate look at a house of this grandeur. The house still stands, is open for tours (including a special Jane Austen tour at certain times), and looks very much as it did during her day.

6. The long-standing practice in wealthy families was for the reigning master and mistress, as well as sometimes other family members, to have their

now almost equally well qualified to shew the house.[7] On the present occasion, she addressed herself chiefly to Miss Crawford and Fanny, but there was no comparison in the willingness of their attention, for Miss Crawford, who had seen scores of great houses, and cared for none of them,[8] had only the appearance of civilly listening, while Fanny, to whom every thing was almost as interesting as it was new, attended with unaffected earnestness to all that Mrs. Rushworth could relate of the family in former times, its rise and grandeur, regal visits and loyal efforts,[9] delighted to connect any thing with history already known, or warm her imagination with scenes of the past.

The situation of the house excluded the possibility of much prospect from any of the rooms, and while Fanny and some of the others were attending Mrs. Rushworth, Henry Crawford was looking grave and shaking his head at the windows.[10] Every room on the west front looked across a lawn to the beginning of the avenue immediately beyond tall iron palisades and gates.[11]

Having visited many more rooms than could be supposed to be of any other use than to contribute to the window tax, and find employ-

A curricle (Astead Park, a country house, is in the background).

[From John Preston Neale, *Views of the Seats of Noblemen and Gentlemen*, Vol. V (London, 1822)]

portraits painted. These would be preserved in the house, so that families like the Rushworths that had been prominent for many generations would have a large collection. Such families would usually also collect other works of art, both to beautify the home and to display their wealth and taste. The pictures could vary greatly in quality.

7.   The housekeeper was the principal female servant and normally showed the house to visitors; hence, she would know best its history and its objects. Mrs. Rushworth is taking over her functions now because of the special nature of the guests.

8.   She could have seen such houses on previous visits to acquaintances or relatives, or while touring England with others; the heroine of *Pride and Prejudice* visits several houses while touring with her aunt and uncle. During the eighteenth century tourism became a common activity among the minority who could afford it, and grand houses were a popular destination, often featured in the many travel guidebooks that appeared to cater to this new taste. Houses did not charge admission; traditions of upper-class hospitality along with an interest in displaying their magnificence led families to allow such visitors. But visitors were expected to tip the housekeeper (as well as the gardener, if they toured the grounds), giving the housekeeper a strong incentive to develop extensive knowledge of the house.

9.   Monarchs, when visiting an area where no royal residence existed, would stay in the home of a prominent person; this had been especially common in earlier centuries when monarchs and their courts spent a good part of the year traveling around the kingdom. Such visits were great sources of pride and prestige, and to encourage them, great houses frequently had a special set of rooms, grander than any other, set aside solely to be used by visiting royalty. "Loyal efforts" most likely refers to support given by the family to the monarchy when it was challenged by rebellion. A number of such rebellions had occurred over the centuries, most notably during the 1640s, when the monarchy was temporarily overthrown. The Leighs of Stoneleigh Abbey had been ardent supporters of the deposed king, Charles I, and at one point in 1642 he took refuge at the house, an event remembered and retold with pride by the family.

10.   He is probably disappointed both because of the intrinsic disadvantage of a poor view and because it prevents him from surveying the grounds in order to suggest improvements.

11.   An iron palisade is a fence made of iron.

ment for housemaids,[12] "Now," said Mrs. Rushworth, "we are coming to the chapel,[13] which properly we ought to enter from above, and look down upon; but as we are quite among friends, I will take you in this way, if you will excuse me."

They entered. Fanny's imagination had prepared her for something grander than a mere, spacious, oblong room, fitted up for the purpose of devotion—with nothing more striking or more solemn than the profusion of mahogany,[14] and the crimson velvet cushions appearing over the ledge of the family gallery above.[15] "I am disappointed," said she, in a low voice, to Edmund. "This is not my idea of a chapel. There is nothing awful[16] here, nothing melancholy, nothing grand. Here are no aisles, no arches, no inscriptions, no banners.[17] No banners, cousin, to be 'blown by the night wind of Heaven.' No signs that a 'Scottish monarch sleeps below.'"[18]

"You forget, Fanny, how lately all this has been built, and for how confined a purpose, compared with the old chapels of castles and

A room, in Lansdowne House, with some of the features characteristic of an earlier period, especially the prominence of marble (see p. 163, note 5).

[From E. Beresford Chancellor, *The XVIIIth Century in London* (New York, 1921), p. 164]

12. The British government imposed a tax on homes according to the number of windows they contained. During their visit to Stoneleigh Abbey, Jane Austen's mother was sufficiently impressed by the windows that she counted the number in front and related it in a letter—her total, forty-five, is still accurate today. She also declares that "there are 26 Bed Chambers in the new part of the house, & a great many . . . in the Old" (quoted in Wilson, *At Home with Jane Austen*, p. 72). Housemaids would be responsible for keeping the rooms clean and well aired.

13. Traditionally grand houses had a chapel that the inhabitants could use for daily prayers. They would still attend a regular church for Sunday services.

14. Mahogany is what the pews and other fixtures are made of.

15. The "family gallery above" is a special room overlooking the chapel, entered separately from the floor above, for the family to worship in; the servants would use the main part of the chapel where the visitors are now standing. Wealthy families would normally worship separately from others, including in regular churches, and such places would naturally tend to have more luxurious furnishings (the main part of the chapel presumably lacks velvet cushions). All the features mentioned here, including the mahogany and the cushions, are found in the chapel at Stoneleigh Abbey.

16. *awful*: impressive, solemn, worthy of awe.

17. These would all be features of older and larger chapels. Arches, in particular pointed ones, were a central feature of medieval churches; Austen's period witnessed a strong revival of interest in the Gothic architecture characterizing such churches, linked to the prevailing cultural Romanticism of the time. Inscriptions on tombs and monuments for the dead would be found throughout churches (Winchester Cathedral, where Jane Austen is buried, contains lengthy inscriptions for her both on the stone under which she lies and on a commemorative monument on the adjacent wall). Banners, which were widely used in the Middle Ages, including on the battlefield, in ceremonies, and in religious processions, were common features of older churches. All these, particularly the inscriptions, were also likely to be found in the aisles, a term used then almost exclusively for areas of a church, especially those on its sides. The chapel at Stoneleigh Abbey has only a simple aisle in the middle, and none of these other elements.

18. These lines are both quotations, a little garbled, from Sir Walter Scott's *The Lay of the Last Minstrel* (1805). It was the first of his long narrative poems that, along with his later novels, made him by far the best-selling author of the age. Two other highly popular poems, *Marmion* and *The Lady of the Lake*, are the subject of enthusiastic discussion between the heroine and a young man

monasteries. It was only for the private use of the family. They have been buried, I suppose, in the parish church. *There* you must look for the banners and the achievements."[19]

"It was foolish of me not to think of all that, but I am disappointed."

Mrs. Rushworth began her relation.[20] "This chapel was fitted up as you see it, in James the Second's time.[21] Before that period, as I understand, the pews were only wainscot;[22] and there is some reason to think that the linings and cushions of the pulpit and family-seat were only purple cloth; but this is not quite certain. It is a handsome chapel, and was formerly in constant use both morning and evening. Prayers were always read in it by the domestic chaplain, within the memory of many. But the late Mr. Rushworth left it off."[23]

"Every generation has its improvements," said Miss Crawford, with a smile, to Edmund.

Mrs. Rushworth was gone to repeat her lesson to Mr. Crawford; and Edmund, Fanny, and Miss Crawford remained in a cluster together.

"It is a pity," cried Fanny, "that the custom should have been discontinued. It was a valuable part of former times. There is something in a chapel and chaplain so much in character with a great house, with one's ideas of what such a household should be! A whole family[24] assembling regularly for the purpose of prayer, is fine!"

"Very fine indeed!" said Miss Crawford, laughing. "It must do the heads of the family a great deal of good to force all the poor housemaids and footmen to leave business and pleasure,[25] and say their prayers here twice a day, while they are inventing excuses themselves for staying away."

"*That* is hardly Fanny's idea of a family assembling," said Edmund. "If the master and mistress do *not* attend themselves, there must be more harm than good in the custom."

"At any rate, it is safer to leave people to their own devices on such subjects. Every body likes to go their own way—to choose their own time and manner of devotion. The obligation of attendance, the formality, the restraint, the length of time—altogether it is a formidable thing, and what nobody likes: and if the good people who used to kneel and gape[26] in that gallery could have foreseen that the time would ever come when men and women might lie another ten minutes in bed,[27] when they woke with a headach, without danger

in Jane Austen's *Persuasion*. Stories of love and war in sixteenth-century Scotland, all three poems express an interest in earlier times and in melancholy or awe-inspiring events, which were also basic features of Romanticism and have inspired Fanny's regrets regarding the chapel.

The two lines appear in a passage in which a monk and another man explore Melrose Abbey (which Scott, in a footnote, calls "the finest specimen of Gothic architecture and Gothic sculpture which Scotland can boast"), and the features of the abbey are evocatively described. The first line appears as they enter the area around the altar: "Full many a scutcheon and banner riven, / Shook to the cold night-wind of heaven." The second line comes soon after: "They sate them down on a marble stone, / (A Scottish monarch slept below)."

19. Monasteries as well as medieval castles, which were built to withstand sieges and could contain an entire community, often included a regular church.

20. *relation*: account, narrative.

21. James II reigned from 1685 to 1688. Such a dating poses a serious challenge for a chapel full of mahogany, which did not come into general use in England until the early 1700s. In the late 1600s it was extremely rare. Jane Austen may intend to signal how wealthy the Rushworths are, but it is also possible that she simply erred in assuming mahogany was used regularly before the eighteenth century. The Stoneleigh Abbey chapel, with all its mahogany, was built in the early 1700s.

22. *wainscot*: a high-quality imported oak.

23. It had long been customary for wealthy families to employ domestic chaplains to perform religious duties in their homes. In her letter from Stoneleigh Abbey Mrs. Austen mentions everyone gathering each morning in the chapel to say prayers, though she says nothing about a chaplain. She also uses "handsome" to describe the chapel. The century preceding this novel witnessed a steady decrease in the percentage of grand houses employing a domestic chaplain, and many newly built houses no longer contained a chapel. One reason was a general decline in piety; another was the growing emphasis on private rather than communal religious devotion.

24. *family*: household.

25. Footmen were lower-ranking servants who would deliver messages, wait on table, or answer doors. In a large house they were the most numerous male servants, just as housemaids were the most numerous female servants.

26. *gape*: yawn.

27. It is only ten minutes because daily prayers were short.

of reprobation, because chapel was missed, they would have jumped with joy and envy. Cannot you imagine with what unwilling feelings the former belles of the house of Rushworth did many a time repair[28] to this chapel? The young Mrs. Eleanors and Mrs. Bridgets[29]— starched up[30] into seeming piety, but with heads full of something very different—especially if the poor chaplain were not worth looking at—and, in those days, I fancy parsons were very inferior even to what they are now."[31]

For a few moments she was unanswered. Fanny coloured and looked at Edmund, but felt too angry for speech; and *he* needed a little recollection[32] before he could say, "Your lively[33] mind can hardly be serious even on serious subjects.[34] You have given us an amusing sketch, and human nature cannot say it was not so. We must all feel *at times* the difficulty of fixing our thoughts as we could wish; but if you are supposing it a frequent thing, that is to say, a weakness grown into a habit from neglect, what could be expected from the *private* devotions of such persons? Do you think the minds which are suffered, which are indulged in wanderings in a chapel, would be more collected in a closet?"[35]

"Yes, very likely. They would have two chances at least in their favour. There would be less to distract the attention from without, and it would not be tried so long."

"The mind which does not struggle against itself under *one* circumstance, would find objects to distract it in the *other*, I believe; and the influence of the place and of example may often rouse better feelings than are begun with. The greater length of the service, however, I admit to be sometimes too hard a stretch[36] upon the mind. One wishes it were not so—but I have not yet left Oxford long enough to forget what chapel prayers are."[37]

While this was passing, the rest of the party being scattered about the chapel, Julia called Mr. Crawford's attention to her sister, by saying, "Do look at Mr. Rushworth and Maria, standing side by side, exactly as if the ceremony were going to be[38] performed. Have not they completely the air of it?"

Mr. Crawford smiled his acquiescence, and stepping forward to Maria, said, in a voice which she only could hear, "I do not like to see Miss Bertram so near the altar."[39]

28. *repair*: proceed, make their way.

29. Mary is consciously evoking an earlier age by using archaic language—in the phrase "did many a time"; in the names Bridget and Eleanor, both of which were regarded as somewhat old-fashioned, though they were still used; and, most of all, in the use of "Mrs." for the "belles," i.e., young ladies. "Mistress," or "Mrs." (its abbreviation), had long been used to refer to all women, but during the eighteenth century both were replaced for young, unmarried women by "Miss" (also derived from "Mistress" and first appearing in the late seventeenth century).

30. *starched up*: made rigid or formal.

31. Mary's ridicule of religious piety and the clergy, found almost nowhere else in Austen's novels (even among characters who do not seem at all pious), indicates her background in fashionable London society, many of whose members had adopted such an attitude. This disrespect is also seen in her calling clergymen "parsons," a term often used by those who wished to disparage the clergy. Mary's uses of the word, here and once later, represent two of its only three appearances in Austen's novels; Austen never employs it in her other writings or her letters. As we soon discover, Mary is unaware that Edmund intends to become a clergyman.

32. *recollection*: recovery of composure.

33. *lively*: merry, lighthearted.

34. "Serious" sometimes referred particularly to religious subjects, and that is undoubtedly at least part of Edmund's meaning here.

35. *closet*: a secluded, private room.

36. *stretch*: strain.

37. The primary function of Oxford, and Cambridge, at this time was to train clergy for the Church of England, and only members of the Church were admitted to the university. One of its features was daily morning chapel, at which attendance was mandatory.

38. *going to be*: about to be.

39. Just as Julia's mention of the upcoming marriage is intended to direct Henry's attention away from Maria and toward herself, his expression of distaste for the possibility signals to Maria his interest in her, regardless of her engagement. But he must do it covertly, since open flirtation with a woman engaged to another man would be a gross breach of propriety.

Starting, the lady instinctively moved a step or two, but recovering herself in a moment, affected to laugh, and asked him, in a tone not much louder, "if he would give her away?"[40]

"I am afraid I should do it very awkwardly," was his reply, with a look of meaning.

Julia joining them at the moment, carried on the joke.

"Upon my word, it is really a pity that it should not take place directly, if we had but a proper license,[41] for here we are altogether, and nothing in the world could be more snug[42] and pleasant." And she talked and laughed about it with so little caution, as to catch the comprehension of Mr. Rushworth and his mother, and expose her sister to the whispered gallantries of her lover, while Mrs. Rushworth spoke with proper smiles and dignity of its being a most happy event to her whenever it took place.

"If Edmund were but in orders!" cried Julia, and running to where he stood with Miss Crawford and Fanny; "My dear Edmund, if you were but in orders now, you might perform the ceremony directly. How unlucky that you are not ordained, Mr. Rushworth and Maria are quite ready."[43]

Miss Crawford's countenance, as Julia spoke, might have amused a disinterested observer. She looked almost aghast under the new idea she was receiving. Fanny pitied her. "How distressed she will be at what she said just now," passed across her mind.

"Ordained!" said Miss Crawford; "what, are you to be a clergyman?"

"Yes, I shall take orders soon after my father's return—probably at Christmas."

Miss Crawford rallying her spirits, and recovering her complexion, replied only, "If I had known this before, I would have spoken of the cloth with more respect,"[44] and turned[45] the subject.

The chapel was soon afterwards left to the silence and stillness which reigned in it with few interruptions throughout the year. Miss Bertram, displeased with her sister, led the way, and all seemed to feel that they had been there long enough.

The lower part of the house had been now entirely shown, and Mrs. Rushworth, never weary in the cause, would have proceeded towards the principal stair-case,[46] and taken them through all the

40. Maria's initial discomposure indicates she is stirred by Henry's declaration, the most explicit he has yet made of his affection. Her reply once she recovers is meant to make her appear indifferent to him, because propriety demands it and because, not knowing if Henry is serious in his intentions, she does not wish to break her engagement to Rushworth. At the same time, her remark gives Henry a chance, through his negative reply, to confirm her hopes.

41. A proper license means one that is legally valid. By law a marriage required either the prior public reading of banns, a procedure mainly used by the poor, or the procuring of an ecclesiastical license. The standard license allowed the couple to marry only in a parish church, not in a private home. But very wealthy and prominent families could obtain a special license from the Archbishop of Canterbury, the head of the Church of England, that allowed a marriage to be performed anywhere.

42. *snug*: comfortable.

43. All valid marriages had to be conducted by an ordained clergyman of the Church of England (except in the case of Quakers and Jews, who were allowed to conduct separate ceremonies).

44. Mary's reply gives a sense of her values, which would be shared by many of her social set. She is irreverent toward religion, so she makes no apologies for the substance of her remarks. But she believes strongly in good manners, which would dictate not expressing such irreverence before a clergyman, and she does express regret for that.

45. *turned*: changed.

46. Grand houses normally had a large and impressive staircase, often with ornate carvings, near the entrance.

rooms above, if her son had not interposed with a doubt of there being time enough. "For if," said he, with the sort of self-evident proposition which many a clearer head does not always avoid— "we are *too* long going over the house, we shall not have time for what is to be done out of doors. It is past two, and we are to dine at five."

Mrs. Rushworth submitted, and the question of surveying the grounds, with the who and the how, was likely to be more fully agitated, and Mrs. Norris was beginning to arrange by what junction of carriages and horses most could be done, when the young people, meeting with an outward door, temptingly open on a flight of steps which led immediately to turf and shrubs, and all the sweets of pleasure-grounds,[47] as by one impulse, one wish for air and liberty, all walked out.

"Suppose we turn down here for the present," said Mrs. Rushworth, civilly taking the hint and following them. "Here are the greatest number of our plants, and here are the curious pheasants."[48]

"Query," said Mr. Crawford, looking round him, "whether we may not find something to employ us here, before we go farther? I see walls of great promise.[49] Mr. Rushworth, shall we summon a council on this lawn?"

"James," said Mrs. Rushworth to her son, "I believe the wilderness will be new to all the party. The Miss Bertrams have never seen the wilderness yet."[50]

No objection was made, but for some time there seemed no inclination to move in any plan, or to any distance. All were attracted at first by the plants or the pheasants, and all dispersed about in happy independence. Mr. Crawford was the first to move forward, to examine the capabilities of that end of the house. The lawn, bounded on each side by a high wall, contained beyond the first planted ærea, a bowling-green,[51] and beyond the bowling-green a long terrace walk, backed by iron palissades, and commanding a view over them into the tops of the trees of the wilderness immediately adjoining. It was a good spot for fault-finding. Mr. Crawford was soon followed by Miss Bertram and Mr. Rushworth, and when after a little time the others

47. *pleasure-grounds*: areas of ornamental plantings near a house, such as shrubberies and flower gardens. They contrast with the park, which was dominated by extensive lawns and woods.

48. Wealthy landowners often cultivated a great variety of plants in their gardens and greenhouses; many would then be transplanted onto the estate grounds. That variety had increased greatly in recent times due to the importation of plant species from around the world, especially from North America. A similar spirit of inquiry and experimentation inspired the procurement or breeding of new strains of animals.

49. Walls near the house, often around gardens, were a common feature of older houses, and they formed a popular target of demolition for those improving grounds in the latest fashion, which usually centered around providing more open and spectacular views. Hence for Henry the walls are "of great promise" as an object to be removed.

50. A wilderness is an area of trees or shrubs that has pathways arranged in an elaborate pattern. Wildernesses had been very popular in the seventeenth and early eighteenth centuries but had been superseded by shrubberies. The latter, in keeping with newer tastes in landscaping, tended to have winding and irregular paths, while the former were more geometric. Hence the author, reflecting the newer taste, will shortly describe this wilderness as "laid out with too much regularity," another feature that reflects the old-fashioned nature of Sotherton Court.

51. Stoneleigh Abbey had a bowling green. It was a feature more common in the grounds of older houses, for lawn bowling, while still played, had declined in popularity among the wealthy.

A garden with walls.

[From Humphry Repton, *Fragments on the Theory and Practice of Landscape Gardening* (London, 1816), p. 138]

began to form into parties, these three were found in busy consultation on the terrace by Edmund, Miss Crawford and Fanny, who seemed as naturally to unite, and who after a short participation of their regrets and difficulties, left them and walked on. The remaining three, Mrs. Rushworth, Mrs. Norris, and Julia, were still far behind; for Julia, whose happy star no longer prevailed, was obliged to keep by the side of Mrs. Rushworth, and restrain her impatient feet to that lady's slow pace, while her aunt, having fallen in with[52] the housekeeper, who was come out to feed the pheasants, was lingering behind in gossip with her. Poor Julia, the only one out of the nine not tolerably satisfied with their lot, was now in a state of complete penance, and as different from the Julia of the barouche-box as could well be imagined. The politeness which she had been brought up to practise as a duty, made it impossible for her to escape; while the want of that higher species of self-command, that just consideration of others, that knowledge of her own heart, that principle of right which had not formed any essential part of her education, made her miserable under it.

"This is insufferably hot," said Miss Crawford when they had taken one turn on the terrace, and were drawing a second time to the door in the middle which opened to the wilderness. "Shall any of us object to being comfortable? Here is a nice little wood, if one can but get into it. What happiness if the door should not be locked!—but of course it is, for in these great places, the gardeners are the only people who can go where they like."[53]

The door, however, proved not to be locked, and they were all agreed in turning joyfully through it, and leaving the unmitigated glare of day behind. A considerable flight of steps landed them in the wilderness, which was a planted wood of about two acres, and though chiefly of larch and laurel, and beech cut down, and though laid out with too much regularity, was darkness and shade, and natural beauty, compared with the bowling-green and the terrace.[54] They all felt the refreshment of it, and for some time could only walk and admire. At length, after a short pause, Miss Crawford began with, "So you are to be a clergyman, Mr. Bertram. This is rather a surprise to me."

52. *fallen in with*: encountered.

53. The gardener is the principal servant taking care of the grounds, and thus the one most likely to possess the key to locked sections.

54. These trees provide more shade than an open space, though not a lot. Larches at this time were small trees, described by a leading writer on nature

Carvings on the wall, a popular feature of earlier decoration (see p. 162), at God-mersham Park, Kent, the home of Edward Austen and a place Jane regularly visited.

[From J. Alfred Gotch, *The English Home from Charles I to George IV* (New York, 1918), p. 357]

"Why should it surprise you? You must suppose me designed for some profession, and might perceive that I am neither a lawyer, nor a soldier, nor a sailor."[55]

"Very true; but, in short, it had not occurred to me. And you know there is generally an uncle or a grandfather to leave a fortune to the second son."[56]

"A very praiseworthy practice," said Edmund, "but not quite universal. I am one of the exceptions, and *being* one, must do something for myself."

"But why are you to be a clergyman? I thought *that* was always the lot of the youngest, where there were many to choose before him."

"Do you think the church itself never chosen then?"

"*Never* is a black word. But yes, in the *never* of conversation which means *not very often*, I do think it. For what is to be done in the church? Men love to distinguish themselves, and in either[57] of the other lines, distinction may be gained, but not in the church. A clergyman is nothing."[58]

"The *nothing* of conversation has its gradations, I hope, as well as the *never*. A clergyman cannot be high in state[59] or fashion.[60] He must not head mobs, or set the ton[61] in dress. But I cannot call that situation nothing, which has the charge of all that is of the first importance to mankind, individually or collectively considered, temporally and eternally—which has the guardianship of religion and morals, and consequently of the manners which result from their influence.[62] No one here can call the *office* nothing. If the man who holds it is so, it is by the neglect of his duty, by foregoing its just importance, and stepping out of his place to appear what he ought not to appear."

"*You* assign greater consequence to the clergyman than one has been used to hear given, or than I can quite comprehend. One does not see much of this influence and importance in society, and how can it be acquired where they are so seldom seen themselves? How can two sermons a week, even supposing them worth hearing, supposing the preacher to have the sense to prefer Blair's to his own,[63] do all that you speak of? govern the conduct and fashion the manners of a large congregation for the rest of the week? One scarcely sees a clergyman out of his pulpit."

as "the puny inhabitant of a garden" (William Gilpin, *Remarks on Forest Scenery*, vol. I, p. 76). Laurels were mostly used for shrubberies; their being evergreens made them popular, but their limbs did not stretch wide. In contrast, beeches are tall deciduous trees, but these have been cut down, perhaps to harmonize with the other species.

55. These three professions were, along with clergyman, the ones considered genteel at the time, and thus acceptable for younger sons from elite families. "Soldier" or "sailor" would mean an army or navy officer. "Lawyer" would mean a barrister, the type of lawyer allowed to handle cases in court; attorneys, who did other legal work, especially ordinary property transactions, and who formed the majority of lawyers, were not considered genteel.

56. It was not unusual, thanks to high death rates, for owners of large estates to have no direct heir, and in such cases they might bequeath the estate to a young male relative who was a younger son and would not be a landowner otherwise.

57. *either*: any. "Either" (like "neither") could refer then to more than two.

58. Clergy tended to be lower in prestige than members of the other genteel professions. In *Sense and Sensibility* the main male character faces resistance to his wish to become a clergyman from his wealthy and status-conscious family.

59. *state*: power, splendor, grandeur.

60. *fashion*: social standing or importance. The term was most commonly used at this time to denote high society and its ways.

61. *ton*: fashion, vogue.

62. Edmund succinctly summarizes the prevailing view of religion, as a matter essential both to the individual's own soul and eternal salvation and to society as the source of morality and good behavior.

63. People normally went to both a morning and an evening service on Sunday, and hence would hear two sermons. As Mary's statement suggests, social norms dictated that everyone attend these services, even those (like her) who had little religious feeling. Hugh Blair, a Scottish minister and professor, was a leading author in eighteenth-century Britain, and among his books were five volumes of sermons. Many clergy used his, or other published sermons, when preaching; there was no general expectation that they must compose their own.

"*You* are speaking of London, *I* am speaking of the nation at large."

"The metropolis, I imagine, is a pretty fair sample of the rest."

"Not, I should hope, of the proportion of virtue to vice throughout the kingdom. We do not look in great cities for our best morality.[64] It is not there, that respectable people of any denomination can do most good; and it certainly is not there, that the influence of the clergy can be most felt. A fine preacher is followed and admired; but it is not in fine preaching only that a good clergyman will be useful in his parish and his neighbourhood, where the parish and neighbourhood are of a size capable of knowing his private character, and observing his general conduct, which in London can rarely be the case. The clergy are lost there in the crowds of their parishioners. They are known to the largest part only as preachers.[65] And with regard to their influencing public manners, Miss Crawford must not misunderstand me, or suppose I mean to call them the arbiters of good breeding, the regulators of refinement and courtesy, the masters of the ceremonies of life. The *manners* I speak of, might rather be called *conduct*,[66] perhaps, the result of good principles; the effect, in short, of those doctrines which it is their duty to teach and recommend; and it will, I believe, be every where found, that as the clergy are, or are not what they ought to be, so are the rest of the nation."[67]

Preaching a sermon (the church is laid out very differently than was typical then).

[From William Combe, *The Tour of Doctor Syntax in Search of the Picturesque* (London, 1817; 1903 reprint), p. 178]

64. The question of the respective value of city and country life was a frequent subject of debate in Austen's time and earlier. Advocates for the city lauded it as the source of greater sophistication and opportunities to socialize and gain knowledge of the world, while others condemned it as an encouragement to a host of vices, including greed, concern for status, and sexual misconduct. Jane Austen, in a letter when young, indicates a knowledge of this debate, which was conducted among ordinary people as well as writers, when she jokes, after arriving in London, "Here I am once more in this Scene of Dissipation & vice, and I begin already to find my Morals corrupted" (Aug. 23, 1796). In later writings she approaches the issue more seriously, and generally favors the country side of the debate, though not without complexity and nuance.

65. The recent rapid growth of London—it had reached a population of more than a million in the recent 1811 census—caused many London parishes to be very populous, which made it impossible for the parish priest to have personal contact with most of his parishioners.

66. Books of the time about history or current affairs often refer to the "manners" of a people or society, using that as a comprehensive term for customs and habits. The contrast Edmund draws, between external refinement and courtesy and a more profound commitment to good behavior and principles, plays an important role in the novel. At various points the author describes the way that Maria and Julia have been educated well in the former virtues but poorly in the latter, including in the passage above about Julia's inability to be more than outwardly polite when she ends up unhappily stuck with Mrs. Rushworth. Mary Crawford, though sometimes behaving more sympathetically than Maria or Julia, displays a similar discrepancy in her character, and this feature of all three young ladies will play a critical role in the plot.

67. Edmund's emphatic speech could be seen as a reflection of the growing evangelical movement in England, which during the early nineteenth century strove to inspire greater piety within the Church of England, improve religious and moral conduct throughout society, and eliminate certain social evils, such as the slave trade. Its efforts, which had a wide effect, were an important factor in the more earnest and morally strict culture that characterized Victorian England in the mid to late nineteenth century. Jane Austen refers to the movement in two letters, one from 1809 stating, "I do not like the Evangelicals," and one from 1814 declaring, "I am by no means convinced that we ought not all to be Evangelicals" (Jan. 24, 1809; Nov. 18, 1814). The contrast between the two comments may reflect a change in her attitude in the intervening years, one that occurred within many in England at the time, though it may also result merely from different contexts—the first comment occurs when she is expressing her dislike of a moralistic novel by a leading evangelical writer, Hannah More, and the second when she is counseling her niece about the proposal of a man whom her niece worries is too evangelical.

"Certainly," said Fanny with gentle earnestness.

"There," cried Miss Crawford, "you have quite convinced Miss Price already."

"I wish I could convince Miss Crawford too."

"I do not think you ever will," said she with an arch smile; "I am just as much surprised now as I was at first that you should intend to take orders. You really are fit for something better. Come, do change your mind. It is not too late.[68] Go into the law."[69]

"Go into the law! with as much ease as I was told to go into this wilderness."

"Now you are going to say something about law being the worst wilderness of the two, but I forestall you; remember I have forestalled you."[70]

"You need not hurry when the object is only to prevent my saying a bon-mot, for there is not the least wit in my nature. I am a very matter of fact, plain spoken being, and may blunder on the borders of a repartee for half an hour together without striking it out."[71]

A general silence succeeded. Each was thoughtful. Fanny made the first interruption by saying, "I wonder that I should be tired with only walking in this sweet wood; but the next time we come to a seat, if it is not disagreeable to you, I should be glad to sit down for a little while."

"My dear Fanny," cried Edmund, immediately drawing her arm within his, "how thoughtless I have been! I hope you are not very tired. Perhaps," turning to Miss Crawford, "my other companion may do me the honour of taking an arm."

"Thank you, but I am not at all tired." She took it, however, as she spoke, and the gratification of having her do so, of feeling such a connection for the first time, made him a little forgetful of Fanny. "You scarcely touch me," said he. "You do not make me of any use. What a difference in the weight of a woman's arm from that of a man! At Oxford I have been a good deal used to have a man lean on me for the length of a street,[72] and you are only a fly in the comparison."[73]

"I am really not tired, which I almost wonder at for we must have walked at least a mile in this wood. Do not you think we have?"

"Not half a mile," was his sturdy answer; for he was not yet so

68. One possible model for Mary Crawford, and her relationship with Edmund, is a cousin of Jane Austen's, Eliza de Feuillide. Eliza, who had married a Frenchman who was executed during the Reign of Terror, was a woman of great charm, intelligence, and vivacity; she also was flirtatious, hedonistic, and frequently self-centered. Jane's brother Henry, who had long been enamored of Eliza, married her after her first husband died, and this probably caused him to abandon his plans to become a clergyman and to move later to London, whose fashionable social life Eliza loved.

69. The law and the navy offered the best opportunities for someone to earn a large fortune and thereby rise socially, but the navy required an officer to begin his career when he was in his teens. In contrast, a man like Edmund with a university degree required only three years of legal education at one of the Inns of Court. Mary may also judge that Edmund would be more suited to a legal career than a military one. Finally, because barristers were always based in London, the wife of one could enjoy the social life of the capital.

70. The English legal system, which was based on centuries of precedent rather than a comprehensive legislated code and which contained a variety of court systems with often overlapping jurisdiction, was extremely complex and often confusing.

71. *striking it out*: producing it, coming up with it. Edmund will demonstrate this character throughout the novel; in fact, he is the least witty hero in all Austen's novels (just as Fanny is her most serious heroine). In contrast, Mary Crawford is one of the wittiest characters in all the novels. Jane Austen herself, in addition to displaying tremendous wit in her novels, shows a great love of wit in her letters, and she calls the heroine of *Pride and Prejudice*, the wittiest of all her characters, "as delightful a creature as ever appeared in print" (Jan. 29, 1813). But Austen also reveals another side. In a letter, the same one mentioned in note 67 above about the man with evangelical tendencies, she cautions her niece against rejecting him for lack of wit, for "Wisdom is certainly better than Wit, & in the long run will certainly have the laugh on her side" (Nov. 18, 1814); and in *Pride and Prejudice* the heroine learns to temper her love of wit after it causes unhappiness to herself and to others. In this novel a central question will be whether Mary Crawford can learn the same lesson.

72. He may have done this for men who were drunk. Oxford was notorious at this time for the frequent drunkenness of the students; the lax educational standards allowed those attending to neglect studying in favor of other pursuits. In *Northanger Abbey* a boorish Oxford student expresses contempt for his fellow students because most do not exceed four pints of wine a day (and a pint in England is twenty ounces).

73. Though it seems Edmund offered his arm purely from concern for her, it becomes an opportunity for him to also make this offer to Mary. Propri-

much in love as to measure distance, or reckon time, with feminine lawlessness.[74]

"Oh! you do not consider how much we have wound about. We have taken such a very serpentine course; and the wood itself must be half a mile long in a straight line, for we have never seen the end of it yet, since we left the first great path."[75]

"But if you remember, before we left that first great path, we saw directly to the end of it. We looked down the whole vista, and saw it closed by iron gates, and it could not have been more than a furlong in length."[76]

"Oh! I know nothing of your furlongs, but I am sure it is a very long wood; and that we have been winding in and out ever since we came into it; and therefore when I say that we have walked a mile in it, I must speak within compass."[77]

"We have been exactly a quarter of an hour here," said Edmund, taking out his watch.[78] "Do you think we are walking four miles an hour?"

"Oh! do not attack me with your watch. A watch is always too fast or too slow. I cannot be dictated to by a watch."[79]

A few steps farther brought them out at the bottom of the very walk they had been talking of; and standing back, well shaded and sheltered, and looking over a ha-ha into the park,[80] was a comfortable-sized bench, on which they all sat down.

"I am afraid you are very tired, Fanny," said Edmund, observing her; "why would not you speak sooner? This will be a bad day's amusement for you, if you are to be knocked up.[81] Every sort of exercise fatigues her so soon, Miss Crawford, except riding."

"How abominable in you, then, to let me engross her horse as I did all last week! I am ashamed of you and of myself, but it shall never happen again."

"*Your* attentiveness and consideration make me more sensible of my own neglect. Fanny's interest seems in safer hands with you than with me."

"That she should be tired now, however, gives me no surprise; for there is nothing in the course of one's duties so fatiguing as what we have been doing this morning—seeing a great house, dawdling from one room to another—straining one's eyes and one's attention—

ety would normally prohibit him from doing so, for physical contact between unmarried and unrelated young people was discouraged, but in this case it can be justified as politeness, since it avoids the possible rudeness of singling out Fanny for courtesy.

74. *lawlessness*: licentiousness. The idea is that women are capricious or careless in reckoning time and distance.

75. *great path*: large or main path.

76. A furlong is 660 feet, or one-eighth of a mile.

77. *within compass*: within the bounds of moderation.

78. He is taking the watch out of his pocket. Watches had become common accessories by this time, but wristwatches were rare.

79. Watches often were inaccurate then, due to the difficulty of constructing a timekeeping mechanism on a very small scale, but Mary's objection to them here is probably founded on her own willfulness.

80. A ha-ha is a sunken fence, or more precisely a narrow trench in which at least one side is held in place by a barrier to prevent the dirt from collapsing into the empty space (the other side can take the form of a slope). Ha-has had been developed in the eighteenth century for the landscaped grounds of grand houses. Livestock grazed these grounds, for they were part of working agricultural estates, and the livestock also kept the grass low. Pictures of such grounds often show cattle or sheep on the grass as well as people strolling—for an example, see p. 110. These animals needed to be penned in, but the new taste for extensive views over the grounds made the visual interference of fences undesirable. The ha-ha, an effective barrier that was invisible from a distance, solved this problem. It is not certain how the name arose; one theory is that because people could see the trench only when they were almost on top of it, this led to surprised exclamations of "ha-ha!" For a picture, see the following page.

81. *knocked up*: worn out, exhausted.

hearing what one does not understand—admiring what one does not care for.—It is generally allowed to be the greatest bore in the world, and Miss Price has found it so, though she did not know it."

"I shall soon be rested," said Fanny; "to sit in the shade on a fine day, and look upon verdure, is the most perfect refreshment."

After sitting a little while, Miss Crawford was up again. "I must move," said she, "resting fatigues me.—I have looked across the ha-ha till I am weary. I must go and look through that iron gate at the same view, without being able to see it so well."

Edmund left the seat likewise. "Now, Miss Crawford, if you will look up the walk, you will convince yourself that it cannot be half a mile long, or half half a mile."

"It is an immense distance," said she; "I see *that* with a glance."

He still reasoned with her, but in vain. She would not calculate, she would not compare. She would only smile and assert. The greatest degree of rational consistency could not have been more engaging, and they talked with mutual satisfaction. At last it was agreed, that they should endeavour to determine the dimensions of the wood by walking a little more about it. They would go to one end of it, in the line they were then in (for there was a straight green walk along the bottom by the side of the ha-ha), and perhaps turn a little way in some other direction, if it seemed likely to assist them, and be back in a few minutes. Fanny said she was rested, and would have moved too, but this was not suffered.[82] Edmund urged her remaining where she was with an earnestness which she could not resist,[83] and she was left on the bench to think with pleasure of her cousin's care, but with great regret that she was not stronger. She watched them till they had turned the corner, and listened till all sound of them had ceased.

82. *suffered*: allowed.

83. Edmund is concerned that Fanny rest, but his earnestness probably also results from his wish to be alone with Mary Crawford. It would be improper for two unmarried young people of the opposite sex to go off deliberately on their own, for there was always the fear that this could lead to something untoward, or lead to gossip. But this situation, in which Edmund and Mary were walking with a third person who then needed to rest, presents them with an ideal opportunity for a blameless tête-à-tête.

A side view of a ha-ha; the trench would have a wooden structure to hold the dirt in place.

[From John Plaw, *Ferme Ornée* (London, 1795), Plate II]

Chapter Ten

A quarter of an hour, twenty minutes, passed away, and Fanny was still thinking of Edmund, Miss Crawford, and herself, without interruption from any one. She began to be surprised at being left so long, and to listen with an anxious desire of hearing their steps and their voices again. She listened, and at length she heard; she heard voices and feet approaching; but she had just satisfied herself that it was not those she wanted, when Miss Bertram, Mr. Rushworth, and Mr. Crawford, issued from the same path which she had trod herself, and were before her.

"Miss Price all alone!" and "My dear Fanny, how comes this?" were the first salutations. She told her story. "Poor dear Fanny," cried her cousin, "how ill you have been used by them! You had better have staid with us."

Then seating herself with a gentleman on each side, she resumed the conversation which had engaged them before, and discussed the possibility of improvements with much animation. Nothing was fixed on—but Henry Crawford was full of ideas and projects, and, generally speaking, whatever he proposed was immediately approved, first by her, and then by Mr. Rushworth, whose principal business seemed to be to hear the others, and who scarcely risked an original thought of his own beyond a wish that they had seen his friend Smith's place.

After some minutes spent in this way, Miss Bertram observing the iron gate, expressed a wish of passing through it into the park,[1] that their views and their plans might be more comprehensive. It was the very thing of all others to be wished, it was the best, it was the only way of proceeding with any advantage, in Henry Crawford's opinion; and he directly saw a knoll not half a mile off, which would give them exactly the requisite command of the house. Go therefore they must to that knoll, and through that gate; but the gate was locked. Mr. Rushworth wished he had brought the key; he had been very near thinking whether he should not bring the key; he was deter-

1. The gate and the ha-ha both border the park. Mary Crawford just expressed a wish of looking through the gate into the park, and she and Edmund subsequently walked alongside the ha-ha (rather than passing directly into the park, as the others now intend).

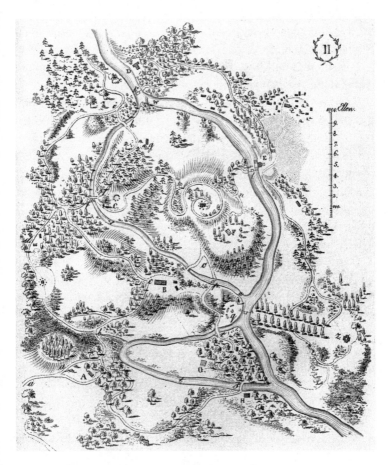

The layout of a park with a stream and meandering paths.

[From C. L. Stieglitz and K. A. Siegel, *Descriptions pittoresques de jardins du goût le plus modernes* (Leipzig, 1802), Plate II]

mined he would never come without the key again; but still this did not remove the present evil. They could not get through; and as Miss Bertram's inclination for so doing did by no means lessen,[2] it ended in Mr. Rushworth's declaring outright that he would go and fetch the key. He set off accordingly.

"It is undoubtedly the best thing we can do now, as we are so far from the house already," said Mr. Crawford, when he was gone.

"Yes, there is nothing else to be done. But now, sincerely, do not you find the place altogether worse than you expected?"

"No, indeed, far otherwise. I find it better, grander, more complete in its style, though that style may not be the best.[3] And to tell you the truth," speaking rather lower, "I do not think that *I* shall ever see Sotherton again with so much pleasure as I do now. Another summer will hardly improve it to me."[4]

After a moment's embarrassment the lady replied, "You are too much a man of the world not to see with the eyes of the world. If other people think Sotherton improved, I have no doubt that you will."[5]

"I am afraid I am not quite so much the man of the world as might be good for me in some points. My feelings are not quite so evanescent, nor my memory of the past under such easy dominion as one finds to be the case with men of the world."[6]

This was followed by a short silence. Miss Bertram began again. "You seemed to enjoy your drive here very much this morning. I was glad to see you so well entertained. You and Julia were laughing the whole way."

"Were we? Yes, I believe we were; but I have not the least recollection at what. Oh! I believe I was relating to her some ridiculous stories of an old Irish groom of my uncle's.[7] Your sister loves to laugh."

"You think her more light-hearted than I am."

"More easily amused," he replied, "consequently you know," smiling, "better company. I could not have hoped to entertain *you* with Irish anecdotes during a ten miles' drive."[8]

"Naturally, I believe, I am as lively as Julia, but I have more to think of now."

"You have undoubtedly—and there are situations in which very

2.   The implication is that her inclination for going through has increased from learning that Mr. Rushworth must leave to fetch the key. This gives her and Henry Crawford an opportunity to be alone (as Edmund and Mary have just seized a similar opportunity).

3.   He means the older style of landscaping, which Mr. Rushworth wishes to replace on his property.

4.   Maria and Mr. Rushworth are planning to be married by next summer, and Henry flirtatiously expresses his displeasure at the prospect.

5.   "A man of the world" usually means a denizen of high or fashionable society. Her meaning is that such a man would have the sense to adopt the views of society in general on the suitability of her marriage, whatever his true feelings about that event might be.

6.   The man of the world, according to the usual stereotype, has complete command of his feelings. Henry's avowal of his lack of command, like his previous words about regretting another summer, seems to represent an admission of amorous feelings toward Maria; each statement reduces her to embarrassment or silence. At the same time, by making his admission obliquely he is protecting himself. Current social norms dictated that a man's direct avowal of his love for a woman was tantamount to a proposal of marriage, from which he could not retreat without suffering social censure and a stain on his honor.

7.   Irish servants were not uncommon in England. In some cases people from Ireland, due to the widespread poverty there, emigrated to England in search of work. In other cases, those with property in Ireland brought their servants with them to England, for there were close ties between the Irish and English upper classes. In *Emma* the daughter of a wealthy family has recently married an Irishman and gone to live there; in *Persuasion* the principal family has aristocratic relations living in Ireland.

8.   Irish anecdotes, meaning funny or ridiculous stories about Irish people, were very popular in England. At this time, the Irish were regarded by the English as a humorous and amusing people (later in the century, as Ireland was the scene of increasing rebellion, sometimes violent, against British rule, a nastier, more brutish stereotype developed). The Irishman was a stock character in English drama, usually introduced for comic relief. Some of the comedy derived from stereotypical Irish customs that were regarded as strange, some from verbal malapropisms committed by the Irish characters, who were regarded as particularly prone to such mishaps, commonly described as Irish "bulls" (or blunders). In 1802 Maria Edgeworth, a leading novelist of the time (admired by Jane Austen) who was from Ireland, wrote, along with her father, *Essay on Irish Bulls* in order to refute this notion; one of her main points was that since English was a foreign language to most Irish people, those who came to England would naturally struggle to speak it correctly.

high spirits would denote insensibility. Your prospects, however, are too fair to justify want of spirits. You have a very smiling scene before you."[9]

"Do you mean literally or figuratively? Literally, I conclude. Yes, certainly, the sun shines and the park looks very cheerful. But unluckily that iron gate, that ha-ha, give me a feeling of restraint and hardship.[10] I cannot get out, as the starling said."[11] As she spoke, and it was with expression, she walked to the gate; he followed her. "Mr. Rushworth is so long fetching this key!"[12]

"And for the world you would not get out without the key and without Mr. Rushworth's authority and protection, or I think you might with little difficulty pass round the edge of the gate, here, with my assistance; I think it might be done, if you really wished to be more at large, and could allow yourself to think it not prohibited."

"Prohibited! nonsense! I certainly can get out that way, and I will. Mr. Rushworth will be here in a moment you know—we shall not be out of sight."[13]

"Or if we are, Miss Price will be so good as to tell him, that he will find us near that knoll, the grove of oak on the knoll."

Fanny, feeling all this to be wrong,[14] could not help making an effort to prevent it. "You will hurt yourself, Miss Bertram," she cried, "you will certainly hurt yourself against those spikes—you will tear

A sloping landscape with deer, such as was popular at the time.

[From Humphry Repton, *The Art of Landscape Gardening* (Boston, 1907; reprint edition), p. 138]

9. He is playing on two meanings of "prospect": prospect regarding a future event (as in today's English) and view of the surrounding landscape. Henry has now advanced to testing Maria's views, by in effect asking if she truly regards favorably the prospect of marriage.

10. Maria, grasping his two meanings, responds to both: one prospect (the view) is good, while the other (her engagement) makes her feel trapped. But she, like he, is careful to avoid explicitness, so she cleverly suggests that it is the gate and ha-ha that create the trapped feeling. Direct avowals of affection would be considered improperly forward of a woman, and since he has not declared himself openly, prudence would dictate care in revealing too much herself. She is being imprudent, however, in even implying that she wishes to escape her engagement.

11. She here alludes to a famous passage from Laurence Sterne's *Sentimental Journey Through France and Italy* (1768). This novel, which helped popularize the word "sentimental," played an important role in the rise of the sentimental novel, the dominant type of novel in the late eighteenth century and the object of Jane Austen's satire in many of her youthful works. It recounts the narrator's desultory wanderings and adventures, as well as his strong emotional reactions. Maria refers to an episode in which, alarmed by the possibility of being sent to the Bastille for lacking a passport, he perceives a starling in a cage and seems to hear it saying repeatedly, "I can't get out." This magnifies his anguish and dread regarding his situation, a reaction similar to Maria's before the gate. Sterne's narrator also compares his situation to "the millions of my fellow-creatures born to no inheritance but slavery," which could be seen as an allusion to the issue of slavery raised elsewhere in this novel.

12. Her words continue to suggest her strong feelings. In contrast, Henry, while claiming he is overcome by feeling, continues to speak calmly.

13. Henry has presented her with the temptation of escaping the constraints placed on her by her fiancé, and thus figuratively by the engagement itself, and she has accepted his offer. This passage is a rare example in Austen's novels of clear use of symbolism.

14. It is a surprising feature that this dialogue, filled with such pointed allusions, occurs in the presence of Fanny. Both Henry and Maria know they are bordering on impropriety and would be unlikely to do so in the presence of a third person. This possible solecism may suggest a clue to one of the mysteries surrounding this novel. In a letter to her sister written during the period of composition, Jane Austen states, "If you c^d discover whether Northamptonshire is a Country of Hedgerows, I sh^d be glad again" (Jan. 29, 1813). The answer she received was presumably negative, for there are only two passing and insignificant references to hedgerows or hedges in *Mansfield Park* (pp. 384 and 440). But in fact Northamptonshire was full of hedgerows then: it, along with many other counties in the Midlands, had recently experienced a wave of enclosures that had converted most of the land into pasture for live-

your gown—you will be in danger of slipping into the ha-ha.[15] You had better not go."

Her cousin was safe on the other side, while these words were spoken, and smiling with all the good-humour of success, she said, "Thank you, my dear Fanny, but I and my gown are alive and well, and so good bye."

Fanny was again left to her solitude, and with no increase of pleasant feelings, for she was sorry for almost all that she had seen and heard, astonished at Miss Bertram, and angry with Mr. Crawford. By taking a circuitous, and as it appeared to her, very unreasonable direction to the knoll, they were soon beyond her eye;[16] and for some minutes longer she remained without sight or sound of any companion. She seemed to have the little wood all to herself. She could almost have thought, that Edmund and Miss Crawford had left it, but that it was impossible for Edmund to forget her so entirely.

She was again roused from disagreeable musings by sudden footsteps, somebody was coming at a quick pace down the principal walk. She expected Mr. Rushworth, but it was Julia, who hot and out of breath, and with a look of disappointment, cried out on seeing her, "Hey-day! Where are the others? I thought Maria and Mr. Crawford were with you."

Fanny explained.

"A pretty trick,[17] upon my word! I cannot see them any where," looking eagerly into the park. "But they cannot be very far off, and I think I am equal to as much as Maria, even without help."

"But, Julia, Mr. Rushworth will be here in a moment with the key. Do wait for Mr. Rushworth."

"Not I, indeed. I have had enough of the family for one morning. Why, child, I have but this moment escaped from his horrible mother. Such a penance as I have been enduring, while you were sitting here so composed and so happy! It might have been as well, perhaps, if you had been in my place, but you always contrive to keep out of these scrapes."

This was a most unjust reflection, but Fanny could allow[18] for it, and let it pass; Julia was vexed, and her temper was hasty, but she felt that it would not last, and therefore taking no notice, only asked her if she had not seen Mr. Rushworth.[19]

stock, and creating vast numbers of hedgerows was fundamental to this process. Moreover, Austen's query itself seems odd, for hedgerows were a basic feature of the landscape through most of England, and it is not clear how they would figure importantly enough into the story to make them worth a special inquiry.

The oddity disappears, however, if one supposes that she actually meant a specific, less common type of hedgerow, namely the one that her nephew James Edward Austen-Leigh, in his A *Memoir of Jane Austen*, identifies as a common feature of the countryside around her childhood home, "an irregular border of copse-wood and timber, often wide enough to contain within it a winding footpath, or a rough cart track." In *Persuasion*, written a few years later, the hero and a woman he is wooing walk down the middle path of a hedgerow; they cannot see that the heroine is sitting just outside it, and thus, they exchange crucial information and opinions regarding her within her hearing. Austen may have envisioned a similar scene for *Mansfield Park*. If so, this is probably that scene, and she intended Fanny to overhear Henry and Maria unobserved (giving Fanny an even stronger reason not to reveal later the contents of Maria and Henry's conversation). If Austen then learned that Northamptonshire's continuous expanses of pasture did not typically contain this type of hedgerow, she may have changed her plans, being always a stickler for strict accuracy. Since this dialogue and Fanny's hearing it are critical to the plot, she has Henry and Maria talk in front of her, figuring perhaps that their perception of Fanny's insignificance renders it at least somewhat plausible.

15. This passage suggests that the gate exists at a break in the ha-ha. Henry and Maria have carefully stepped around the gate, which is why he just spoke of passing "with little difficulty . . . round the edge" and why Fanny warns of falling into the ha-ha. The spikes she mentions presumably stick out of the side of the gate to prevent livestock from executing a similar maneuver.

16. A lengthy and indirect path would delay their reaching the knoll, where Mr. Rushworth is supposed to meet them, and would also make less likely their encountering him on the way there.

17. *trick*: contrivance, scheme (often with a connotation of deceit).

18. *allow*: make allowance.

19. Julia's arrival means that all seven of the young people around whom the story is centered appear at this one place. The resulting action develops and reveals several of the principal plotlines: the romance of Edmund and Mary, the illicit flirtation of Maria and Henry, and the jealousy of Julia and Rushworth. Fanny, meanwhile, carefully observes all these developments while participating little in them, which is her role throughout the early part of the novel.

"Yes, yes, we saw him. He was posting[20] away, as if upon life and death, and could but just spare time to tell us his errand, and where you all were."

"It is a pity that he should have so much trouble for nothing."

"*That* is Miss Maria's concern. I am not obliged to punish myself for *her* sins. The mother I could not avoid, as long as my tiresome aunt was dancing about with the housekeeper,[21] but the son I *can* get away from."

And she immediately scrambled across the fence, and walked away,[22] not attending to Fanny's last question of whether she had seen any thing of Miss Crawford and Edmund. The sort of dread in which Fanny now sat of seeing Mr. Rushworth prevented her thinking so much of their continued absence, however, as she might have done. She felt that he had been very ill-used, and was quite unhappy in having to communicate what had passed. He joined her within five minutes after Julia's exit; and though she made the best of the story, he was evidently mortified and displeased in no common degree. At first he scarcely said any thing; his looks only expressed his extreme surprise and vexation, and he walked to the gate and stood there, without seeming to know what to do.

"They desired me to stay—my cousin Maria charged me to say that you would find them at that knoll, or thereabouts."[23]

"I do not believe I shall go any further," said he sullenly; "I see nothing of them. By the time I get to the knoll, they may be gone some where else. I have had walking enough."

And he sat down with a most gloomy countenance by Fanny.

"I am very sorry," said she; "it is very unlucky." And she longed to be able to say something more to the purpose.

After an interval of silence, "I think they might as well have staid for me," said he.

"Miss Bertram thought you would follow her."

"I should not have had to follow her if she had staid."

This could not be denied, and Fanny was silenced. After another pause, he went on. "Pray, Miss Price, are you such a great admirer of this Mr. Crawford as some people are? For my part, I can see nothing in him."

"I do not think him at all handsome."

20. *posting*: hurrying. The usage derives from traveling by post (see p. 483, note 22), the fastest means of transportation at the time.

21. Mrs. Norris will soon reveal how she talked at length to the housekeeper and procured favors from her.

22. This probably means she passed the gate and ha-ha in the same manner as Maria and Henry; "fence" could be used for various types of barriers.

23. Actually, it was Henry who delivered this charge. Fanny may attribute it to Maria because of Rushworth's dislike and jealousy of Henry, which would have naturally been aroused by seeing the latter's friendliness with Maria, even though he did not witness the worst of it.

Landscaped grounds with a stream and bridge.

[From Ercole Silva, *Dell'arte de' giardini inglesi*, Vol. II (Milano, 1813), p. 121]

"Handsome! Nobody can call such an under-sized man hand-some. He is not five foot nine. I should not wonder if he was not more than five foot eight.[24] I think he is an ill-looking fellow. In my opinion, these Crawfords are no addition at all. We did very well without them."

A small sigh escaped Fanny here, and she did not know how to contradict him.[25]

"If I had made any difficulty about fetching the key, there might have been some excuse, but I went the very moment she said she wanted it."

"Nothing could be more obliging than your manner, I am sure, and I dare say you walked as fast as you could; but still it is some distance, you know, from this spot to the house, quite into the house; and when people are waiting, they are bad judges of time, and every half minute seems like five."

He got up and walked to the gate again, and "wished he had had the key about him at the time." Fanny thought she discerned in his standing there, an indication of relenting, which encouraged her to another attempt, and she said, therefore, "It is a pity you should not join them. They expected to have a better view of the house from that part of the park, and will be thinking how it may be improved; and nothing of that sort, you know, can be settled without you."

She found herself more successful in sending away, than in retaining a companion. Mr. Rushworth was worked on. "Well," said he, "if you really think I had better go; it would be foolish to bring the key for nothing." And letting himself out, he walked off without further ceremony.

Fanny's thoughts were now all engrossed by the two who had left her so long ago, and getting quite impatient, she resolved to go in search of them. She followed their steps along the bottom walk, and had just turned up into another, when the voice and the laugh of Miss Crawford once more caught her ear; the sound approached, and a few more windings brought them before her. They were just returned into the wilderness from the park, to which a side gate, not fastened, had tempted them very soon after their leaving her, and they had been across a portion of the park into the very avenue which Fanny had been hoping the whole morning to reach at last;[26] and

24. Rushworth, who was earlier described as "heavy" and thus is probably large, may naturally turn to Henry Crawford's smaller size—the only way, aside from his income, that he is clearly superior to Henry. His statement also provides a clue about a frequent matter of historical debate, the relative size of people in the past. Records of army recruits, in general the best source for past heights, show average heights for men of just under five feet, six inches, in Britain (and in the United States), which would be four inches below the current average of just under five feet, ten inches. At the same time, various sources suggest that those from upper-class backgrounds were several inches taller than the general population, and thus similar to people today. This would fit with Mr. Rushworth's statement, for the heights he denigrates, less than five feet eight or nine, are only a little shorter than the current norm. The better diet of the wealthy, in both quantity and quality, accounted for the class difference (which still exists now but is far smaller), one more factor sharply distinguishing the elite from most people in this society.

25. Fanny and Rushworth have both seen the person they love lured away by one of the Crawfords.

26. Fanny had asked about the avenue when they were approaching Sotherton in the carriage, the same avenue that, in the initial dinner conversation about altering Sotherton, Rushworth had spoken of cutting down, to Fanny's regret.

A winding path; landscaped grounds usually had buildings of various kinds to enchance the views.

[From C. L. Stieglitz and K. A. Siegel, *Descriptions pittoresques de jardins du goût le plus moderns* (Leipzig, 1802), Plate IE]

had been sitting down under one of the trees. This was their history. It was evident that they had been spending their time pleasantly, and were not aware of the length of their absence. Fanny's best consolation was in being assured that Edmund had wished for her very much, and that he should certainly have come back for her, had she not been tired already; but this was not quite sufficient to do away the pain of having been left a whole hour, when he had talked of only a few minutes, nor to banish the sort of curiosity she felt, to know what they had been conversing about all that time; and the result of the whole was to her disappointment and depression, as they prepared, by general agreement, to return to the house.

On reaching the bottom of the steps to the terrace, Mrs. Rushworth and Mrs. Norris presented themselves at the top, just ready for the wilderness, at the end of an hour and half from their leaving the house. Mrs. Norris had been too well employed to move faster. Whatever cross accidents had occurred to intercept the pleasures of her nieces, she had found a morning of complete enjoyment—for the housekeeper, after a great many courtesies on the subject of pheasants, had taken her to the dairy, told her all about their cows, and given her the receipt[27] for a famous cream cheese;[28] and since Julia's leaving them, they had been met by the gardener, with whom she had made a most satisfactory acquaintance, for she had set him right as to his grandson's illness, convinced him it was an ague,[29] and promised him a charm for it;[30] and he, in return, had shewn her all his choicest nursery of plants, and actually presented her with a very curious specimen of heath.[31]

On this rencontre[32] they all returned to the house together, there to lounge[33] away the time as they could with sofas, and chit-chat, and Quarterly Reviews,[34] till the return of the others, and the arrival of dinner. It was late before the Miss Bertrams and the two gentlemen came in, and their ramble did not appear to have been more than partially agreeable, or at all productive of any thing useful with regard to the object of the day. By their own accounts they had been all walking after each other, and the junction which had taken place at last seemed, to Fanny's observation, to have been as much too late for re-establishing harmony, as it confessedly had been for determining on any alteration. She felt, as she looked at Julia and Mr. Rush-

27. *receipt*: recipe.

28. Grand houses normally had dairies nearby to supply milk and milk products for the family. Similarly, they would procure vegetables and fruits from nearby gardens, and meat from the livestock grazing on the grounds.

29. Ague was the current term for malaria, a disease that existed in much of Europe at this time. Contemporary medical opinion did not understand its true nature as a parasite spread by mosquitoes, but they did know that it was particularly prevalent in swampy areas and that use of bark from the Peruvian cinchona tree, which contains quinine, can assist in treating it. It would make sense that someone would suffer from ague now, in summer, when mosquitoes are most active.

30. Wealthy, educated people at this time no longer believed in using charms or other supernatural remedies for illnesses, but many poorer people still did seek assistance from a local person renowned for special healing powers. Mrs. Norris's indulgence of the gardener's superstition signals her willingness to stoop to any means to obtain profitable favors.

31. Large estates kept nurseries growing a variety of plants. Plants would start off there, when it was too cold for them elsewhere, and then be moved and transplanted later, allowing them to bloom earlier in the season than would be possible otherwise.

32. *rencontre*: encounter.

33. *lounge*: idle, occupy oneself indolently.

34. The *Quarterly Review* was one of the two leading literary journals of the time (the other was the *Edinburgh Review*). As its name implied, it appeared four times a year and consisted of many lengthy reviews of books, covering a wide range of subject matters. Both reviews had a wide circulation. The main difference was that the *Quarterly Review* was conservative in its politics, while the other was liberal. Its appearance here would be appropriate, for the country gentry, the class consistently depicted in Austen's novels, tended to be conservative; the peerage (meaning titled aristocrats) and the urban middle class tended to be liberal. In 1816, two years after the publication of this novel, the *Quarterly Review* published a review of Jane Austen's novels by Walter Scott, the most important article about her work to appear during her lifetime.

worth, that her's was not the only dissatisfied bosom amongst them; there was gloom on the face of each. Mr. Crawford and Miss Bertram were much more gay, and she thought that he was taking particular pains, during dinner, to do away any little resentment of the other two, and restore general good humour.

Dinner was soon followed by tea and coffee, a ten miles' drive home allowed no waste of hours,[35] and from the time of their sitting down to table, it was a quick succession of busy nothings till the carriage came to the door, and Mrs. Norris, having fidgetted about, and obtained a few pheasant's eggs and a cream cheese from the housekeeper, and made abundance of civil speeches to Mrs. Rushworth, was ready to lead the way. At the same moment Mr. Crawford approaching Julia, said, "I hope I am not to lose my companion, unless she is afraid of the evening air in so exposed a seat."[36] The request had not been foreseen, but was very graciously received, and Julia's day was likely to end almost as well as it began. Miss Bertram had made up her mind to something different, and was a little disappointed—but her conviction of being really the one preferred, comforted her under it,[37] and enabled her to receive Mr. Rushworth's parting attentions as she ought. He was certainly better pleased to hand her into the barouche than to assist her in ascending the box—and his complacency seemed confirmed by the arrangement.

"Well, Fanny, this has been a fine day for you, upon my word!" said Mrs. Norris, as they drove through the park. "Nothing but pleasure from beginning to end! I am sure you ought to be very much obliged to your aunt Bertram and me, for contriving to let you go. A pretty good day's amusement you have had!"

Maria was just discontented enough to say directly, "I think *you* have done pretty well yourself, ma'am. Your lap seems full of good things, and here is a basket of something between us, which has been knocking my elbow unmercifully."

"My dear, it is only a beautiful little heath, which that nice old gardener would make me take; but if it is in your way, I will have it in my lap directly. There Fanny, you shall carry that parcel for me—take great care of it—do not let it fall; it is a cream cheese, just like the excellent one we had at dinner.[38] Nothing would satisfy that

35. Tea and coffee, accompanied by breads and cakes, would normally be served an hour or two after dinner. The interval has been reduced in this case to allow the party to leave for home.

36. People feared the effect on their health of the damp, cool air of the evening. In an early work by Jane Austen, "Catharine, or the Bower," a elderly hypochondriac panics upon realizing she has been out in the evening air, and worries that she may not recover her health until almost a year later.

37. This shows Henry Crawford's inclination, and ability, to keep both women satisfied, at least for the time being.

38. At this time, the middle of summer, the cows' milk would be at its richest, and thus a fresh cheese like cream cheese would be especially good.

A dairymaid churning butter (see the next page).

[From William Alexander, *Picturesque Representations of the Dress and Manners of the English* (London, 1813), Plate 30]

good old Mrs. Whitaker,[39] but my taking one of the cheeses. I stood out[40] as long as I could, till the tears almost came into her eyes, and I knew it was just the sort that my sister would be delighted with. That Mrs. Whitaker is a treasure! She was quite shocked when I asked her whether wine was allowed at the second table,[41] and she has turned away two housemaids for wearing white gowns.[42] Take care of the cheese, Fanny. Now I can manage the other parcel and the basket very well."

"What else have you been spunging?" said Maria, half pleased that Sotherton should be so complimented.

"Spunging, my dear! It is nothing but four of those beautiful pheasant's eggs, which Mrs. Whitaker would quite force upon me; she would not take a denial. She said it must be such an amusement to me, as she understood I lived quite alone, to have a few living creatures of that sort; and so to be sure it will. I shall get the dairy maid to set them under the first spare hen,[43] and if they come to good I can have them moved to my own house and borrow a coop;[44] and it will be a great delight to me in my lonely hours to attend to them. And if I have good luck, your mother shall have some."

It was a beautiful evening, mild and still,[45] and the drive was as pleasant as the serenity of nature could make it; but when Mrs. Norris ceased speaking it was altogether[46] a silent drive to those within. Their spirits were in general exhausted—and to determine whether the day had afforded[47] most pleasure or pain, might occupy the meditations of almost all.

39. Mrs. Whitaker is the housekeeper, with whom Mrs. Norris was talking earlier. Upper servants were usually called by their last name alone. However, particularly high-ranking servants, like housekeepers, could be given the title "Mr./Mrs./Miss" as well, and "Mrs." was frequently used as a courtesy for older women in this position even if they had never married (as servants usually had not).

40. *stood out*: resisted, held out.

41. The second table is where upper servants ate (the first table was for the family owning the house). Grand houses like this had enough servants that the upper ones would have a separate place for eating, and usually better fare, than lower servants. This might include wine instead of only beer or ale, the staple drink of ordinary people in England, but not everywhere, as Mrs. Norris's question and Mrs. Whitaker's response indicate.

42. White gowns were associated with fine dressing, whereas servants were expected to be simple in their dress (for more, see p. 735, note 3). Mrs. Norris reveals that she does not favor being indulgent to servants, as her later actions will also reveal. This fits with her denigration and bullying of Fanny, who is also socially lower than Mrs. Norris. In contrast, she flatters and courts assiduously those who are above her.

43. The dairymaid is a servant who takes care of the dairy cows or of the egg-producing poultry, as well as of the various activities involved in the production of milk, milk products such as butter, or eggs. A spare hen is one not at the moment nurturing an egg of its own.

44. In other words, the dairymaid and hen are part of the Bertrams' estate. Hence Mrs. Norris is seeking to make use of them, as well as one of the Bertrams' coops, to cultivate pheasants for herself.

45. This line echoes the opening line of a famous sonnet by William Wordsworth, "It is a beauteous evening, calm and free." The sonnet was published in 1807, and Jane Austen mentions Wordsworth in her last, unfinished novel, *Sanditon*. The evocation of the natural beauty of the evening forms a contrast with the picture of human egoism, conflict, and discontent that the visit to Sotherton has revealed.

46. *altogether*: on the whole.

47. *afforded*: provided.

Chapter Eleven

*T*he day at Sotherton, with all its imperfections, afforded the Miss Bertrams much more agreeable feelings than were derived from the letters from Antigua, which soon afterwards reached Mansfield. It was much pleasanter to think of Henry Crawford than of their father; and to think of their father in England again within a certain period, which these letters obliged them to do, was a most unwelcome exercise.

November was the black month fixed for his return. Sir Thomas wrote of it with as much decision[1] as experience and anxiety could authorize. His business was so nearly concluded as to justify him in proposing to take his passage in the September packet,[2] and he consequently looked forward with the hope of being with his beloved family again early in November.[3]

Maria was more to be pitied than Julia, for to her the father brought a husband, and the return of the friend most solicitous for her happiness, would unite her to the lover, on whom she had chosen that happiness should depend. It was a gloomy prospect,[4] and all that she could do was to throw a mist over it, and hope when the mist cleared away, she should see something else. It would hardly be *early* in November, there were generally delays, a bad passage or *something*; that favouring *something* which every body who shuts their eyes while they look, or their understandings while they reason, feels the comfort of. It would probably be the middle of November at least; the middle of November was three months off. Three months comprised thirteen weeks. Much might happen in thirteen weeks.

Sir Thomas would have been deeply mortified by a suspicion of half that his daughters felt on the subject of his return, and would hardly have found consolation in a knowledge of the interest it excited in the breast of another young lady. Miss Crawford, on walking up with her brother to spend the evening at Mansfield Park, heard the good news; and though seeming to have no concern in the

1. *decision*: determination, firmness.

2. The "packet" is the ship carrying mail between Britain and overseas destinations (the name derives from their packet of mail). Packet service was established during the seventeenth century, first for Ireland, then the European continent, and then the North American colonies. Finally, in the early eighteenth century a similar service began for the British colonies in the West Indies; it would have conveyed the letter they just received from Sir Thomas. These ships sailed at regular intervals, with ones to nearby locations going several times a week and the one for the Leeward Islands, which includes Antigua, going twice a month. These ships also took paying passengers, and at least for a distant destination like the West Indies were the only public means of transport; regular passenger ships across the Atlantic developed only later in the nineteenth century.

3. The passage would normally take at least several weeks, with the amount varying greatly according to weather in the Atlantic.

4. The irony of the passage, in which arrival of the friend (i.e., her father) most concerned with her happiness is an unhappy occasion, suggests the problematic nature of Maria's situation.

A family of the period gathered around a pianoforte (picture by Jean-Auguste-Dominique Ingres).

[From Max von Boehn, *Modes & Manners of the Nineteenth Century*, Vol. I (London, 1909), p. 59]

affair beyond politeness, and to have vented all her feelings in a quiet congratulation, heard it with an attention not so easily satisfied. Mrs. Norris gave the particulars of the letters, and the subject was dropt; but after tea, as Miss Crawford was standing at an open window with Edmund and Fanny looking out on a twilight scene, while the Miss Bertrams, Mr. Rushworth, and Henry Crawford, were all busy with candles at the pianoforte,[5] she suddenly revived it by turning round towards the group, and saying, "How happy Mr. Rushworth looks! He is thinking of November."

Edmund looked round at Mr. Rushworth too, but had nothing to say.

"Your father's return will be a very interesting event."

"It will, indeed, after such an absence; an absence not only long, but including so many dangers."[6]

"It will be the fore-runner also of other interesting events; your sister's marriage, and your taking orders."

"Yes."

"Don't be affronted," said she laughing; "but it does put me in mind of some of the old heathen heroes, who after performing great exploits in a foreign land, offered sacrifices to the gods on their safe return."[7]

"There is no sacrifice in the case," replied Edmund with a serious smile, and glancing at the pianoforte again, "it is entirely her own doing."

"Oh! yes, I know it is. I was merely joking. She has done no more than what every young woman would do; and I have no doubt of her being extremely happy.[8] My other sacrifice of course you do not understand."

"My taking orders I assure you is quite as voluntary as Maria's marrying."

"It is fortunate that your inclination and your father's convenience should accord so well. There is a very good living kept for you, I understand, hereabouts."[9]

"Which you suppose has biassed me."

"But *that* I am sure it has not," cried Fanny.

"Thank you for your good word, Fanny, but it is more than I would affirm myself. On the contrary, the knowing that there was such a

5. "Pianoforte" is the original name for piano; it derives from Italian, where it means "soft-strong," because the great advance of the piano over previous instruments was that it permitted playing the same note either delicately or forcefully, resulting in variation of volume. Pianos were invented in the early eighteenth century and by Jane Austen's time were by far the most popular instrument for the home. In other novels of hers, the piano is often referred to simply as "the instrument." They are busy with candles because, now that it is twilight, they need artificial lighting for whoever plays it.

6. The dangers are the passage across the ocean and, even more, residence in the West Indies. The death rate for English people there was very high, due to the ubiquity of tropical diseases and the lack of inherited immunity to them among those from a northerly climate. The fiancé of Jane Austen's sister, Cassandra, died of yellow fever before they could marry, while serving on a ship in the West Indies.

7. The heathen heroes are those from the literature and history of ancient Greece and Rome. Classical antiquity was central to education and culture at the time, and while women, unlike men, would not learn Latin or Greek, they would still encounter it through translated works or frequent allusions to antiquity in contemporary ones. It also could be part of schooling: earlier the Bertram girls boasted of learning "Heathen Mythology."

8. Mary's comments suggest that she has sensed Maria Bertram's interest in Henry Crawford, and thus her mixed feelings about her engagement to Rushworth.

9. This means someone else, probably a friend of the family, has been appointed to the living, or clerical position, on condition that he resign it when Edmund has been ordained and can be appointed.

provision for me, probably did bias me. Nor can I think it wrong that it should. There was no natural disinclination to be overcome, and I see no reason why a man should make a worse clergyman for knowing that he will have a competence[10] early in life. I was in safe hands. I hope I should not have been influenced myself in a wrong way, and I am sure my father was too conscientious to have allowed it.[11] I have no doubt that I was biassed, but I think it was blamelessly."

"It is the same sort of thing," said Fanny, after a short pause, "as for the son of an admiral to go into the navy, or the son of a general to be in the army, and nobody sees any thing wrong in that. Nobody wonders that they should prefer the line where their friends can serve them best,[12] or suspects them to be less in earnest in it than they appear."

"No, my dear Miss Price, and for reasons good. The profession, either navy or army, is its own justification. It has every thing in its favour; heroism, danger, bustle, fashion. Soldiers and sailors are always acceptable in society. Nobody can wonder that men are soldiers and sailors."[13]

"But the motives of a man who takes orders with the certainty of preferment, may be fairly suspected, you think?" said Edmund. "To be justified in your eyes, he must do it in the most complete uncertainty of any provision."

"What! take orders without a living! No, that is madness indeed, absolute madness!"

"Shall I ask you how the church is to be filled, if a man is neither to take orders with a living, nor without? No, for you certainly would not know what to say. But I must beg some advantage to the clergyman from your own argument. As he cannot be influenced by those feelings which you rank highly as temptation and reward to the soldier and sailor in their choice of a profession, as heroism, and noise, and fashion are all against him, he ought to be less liable to the suspicion of wanting sincerity or good intentions in the choice of his."

"Oh! no doubt he is very sincere in preferring an income ready made, to the trouble of working for one; and has the best intentions of doing nothing all the rest of his days but eat, drink, and grow fat. It is indolence Mr. Bertram, indeed. Indolence and love of ease[14]—a want of all laudable ambition, of taste for good company, or of inclination to take the trouble of being agreeable, which make men

10. *competence*: sufficiency of means.

11. That is, his father is too conscientious to appoint someone to the living who was not suitable to fill the position properly. In principle, all those who controlled church appointments should follow this tenet, and many did, but by no means everyone.

12. "Friends" included family members. Patronage was a fundamental part of this society, and as Fanny's words indicate, it was accepted almost universally.

13. Army and navy officers did usually have higher status than clergymen, and this would matter to wealthy and fashionable people (what she means by "society") because of the value they placed on status, as well as their relative lack of religious piety.

14. The essential duties of a clergyman, preaching in church and presiding over ceremonies like weddings and funerals, did not require heavy labor. He

An army officer.

[From William Alexander, *Picturesque Representations of the Dress and Manners of the English* (London, 1813), Plate 50]

clergymen.[15] A clergyman has nothing to do but to be slovenly and selfish—read the newspaper, watch the weather,[16] and quarrel with his wife. His curate does all the work,[17] and the business of his own life is to dine."

"There are such clergymen, no doubt, but I think they are not so common as to justify Miss Crawford in esteeming[18] it their general character. I suspect that in this comprehensive and (may I say) common-place censure, you are not judging from yourself, but from prejudiced persons, whose opinions you have been in the habit of hearing. It is impossible that your own observation can have given you much knowledge of the clergy. You can have been personally acquainted with very few of a set of men you condemn so conclusively. You are speaking what you have been told at your uncle's table."[19]

"I speak what appears to me the general opinion; and where an opinion is general, it is usually correct. Though *I* have not seen much of the domestic lives of clergymen, it is seen by too many to leave any deficiency of information."[20]

"Where any one body of educated men, of whatever denomination, are condemned indiscriminately, there must be a deficiency of information, or (smiling) of something else. Your uncle, and his brother admirals, perhaps, knew little of clergymen beyond the chaplains whom, good or bad, they were always wishing away."[21]

"Poor William! He has met with great kindness from the chaplain of the Antwerp,"[22] was a tender apostrophe of Fanny's, very much to the purpose of her own feelings, if not of the conversation.

"I have been so little addicted to take my opinions from my uncle," said Miss Crawford, "that I can hardly suppose;—and since you push me so hard, I must observe, that I am not entirely without the means of seeing what clergymen are, being at this present time the guest of my own brother, Dr. Grant. And though Dr. Grant is most kind and obliging to me, and though he is really a gentleman, and I dare say a good scholar and clever,[23] and often preaches good sermons, and is very respectable, *I* see him to be an indolent selfish bon vivant, who must have his palate consulted in every thing, who will not stir a finger for the convenience of any one, and who, moreover, if the cook makes a blunder, is out of humour with his excellent wife. To own the truth, Henry and I were partly driven out this very evening,

was also expected to perform other duties, such as visiting the poor and sick and counseling his parishioners, but he still would usually have ample leisure time.

15. In her terms, "laudable ambition" is for distinction and accomplishment, while "good company" means people of elite society. As for being agreeable, that would be useful for those like military officers who were under others' authority and needed to work with others. In contrast, a clergyman, once appointed, could mostly direct his own affairs.

16. At this time the principal way people predicted the weather was by watching the skies. Barometers did exist, but not other instruments, and there were no official weather forecasts.

17. A curate is a clergyman hired by the holder of a living to perform its duties. Curates were clergy who lacked regular positions, and because there were many of them, they could not command high salaries. Regular clergy would most often hire a curate if they were in charge of more than one parish and could not attend to both, but sometimes they hired one in their own parish simply to relieve themselves of work.

18. *esteeming*: considering.

19. Her uncle, Admiral Crawford, was already described as "a man of vicious conduct" who lived with his mistress, so he would not be likely to associate much with clergymen. Edmund repeats the point in his next statement, a sign that he considers it an important one.

20. *leave any deficiency of information*: allow for the possibility that there is a lack of knowledge (on the part of those who condemn clergymen).

21. Naval ships were supposed to have chaplains to attend to the spiritual needs of the crew, though in practice only the largest ships had them. Chaplains received low pay, were often held in contempt, and experienced, like everyone else, the harsh and dangerous conditions on board a naval vessel. For these reasons there were never nearly enough eligible candidates who applied for the post, and those who did were often disreputable. Many ship captains disliked chaplains, believing they got in the way of normal operations.

22. *Antwerp* is the name of the ship. It is likely it was originally a French ship, for Antwerp, which as part of Belgium had been controlled by France since 1795, has a superb harbor. Britain captured many foreign warships, converting each ship to its own use while retaining its original name.

23. Being a scholar was considered a valuable qualification for a clergyman. Many men of scholarly bent became clergy, and took advantage of the leisure

by a disappointment about a green goose, which he could not get the better of.[24] My poor sister was forced to stay and bear it."

"I do not wonder at your disapprobation, upon my word. It is a great defect of temper, made worse by a very faulty habit of self-indulgence; and to see your sister suffering from it, must be exceedingly painful to such feelings as your's. Fanny, it goes against us. We cannot attempt to defend Dr. Grant."

"No," replied Fanny, "but we need not give up his profession for all that; because, whatever profession Dr. Grant had chosen, he would have taken a —— not a good temper into it; and as he must either in the navy or army have had a great many more people under his command than he has now, I think more would have been made unhappy by him as a sailor or soldier than as a clergyman. Besides, I cannot but suppose that whatever there may be to wish otherwise in Dr. Grant, would have been in a greater danger of becoming worse in a more active and worldly profession, where he would have had less time and obligation—where he might have escaped that knowledge of himself, the *frequency*, at least, of that knowledge which it is impossible he should escape as he is now. A man—a sensible man like Dr. Grant, cannot be in the habit of teaching others their duty every week, cannot go to church twice every Sunday and preach such very good sermons in so good a manner as he does, without being the better for it himself. It must make him think, and I have no doubt that he oftener endeavours to restrain himself than he would if he had been any thing but a clergyman."

"We cannot prove the contrary, to be sure—but I wish you a better fate Miss Price, than to be the wife of a man whose amiableness depends upon his own sermons; for though he may preach himself into a good humour every Sunday, it will be bad enough to have him quarrelling about green geese from Monday morning till Saturday night."

"I think the man who could often quarrel with Fanny," said Edmund, affectionately, "must be beyond the reach of any sermons."

Fanny turned farther into the window; and Miss Crawford had only time to say in a pleasant manner, "I fancy Miss Price has been more used to deserve praise than to hear it;" when being earnestly invited by the Miss Bertrams to join in a glee,[25] she tripped off to

offered to pursue this interest. A large number of important books were written by clergy, not just about religion but in other areas like history and science.

24. A green goose could mean either an undercooked goose, in which case that is the cook's blunder Mary refers to, or a young one. If the latter, the cook's error is uncertain but could be a particular disappointment to Dr. Grant, since young geese were delicacies.

25. A glee is a part song, or song for multiple vocal parts, designed for three or more voices: the need for a third is probably why the Miss Bertrams seek Miss Crawford so earnestly. Glees had emerged as a distinct musical genre in the middle of the eighteenth century in England, and quickly grew in popularity, reaching their height in the years around 1800 before declining in the following century. They were initially songs for unaccompanied male voices performed in gentlemen's clubs, but they gradually spread to public performances and then to performances in the home, and as they did, many glees were written for female voices and for accompaniment by an instrument, especially the piano. They were influenced by madrigals, a type of song that flourished in the sixteenth and seventeenth centuries, but glees had more unified harmonies instead of the counterpoint of separate harmonies in madrigals (in this respect they reflected a general trend in music in this period). Glees also put particularly strong emphasis on the words of the song, reflecting the great love of poetry and language in eighteenth-century England. Many practitioners and advocates celebrated this aspect and, appealing to English nationalism, contrasted it with the more purely instrumental music from the European continent. Glees were also characterized—unlike the bawdy catch songs popular in taverns—by lyrics that were, in the words of a contemporary publisher, "consistent with female delicacy." This made them suitable for domestic performers, who could make use, as those here are undoubtedly doing, of the many books of glees published then.

the instrument, leaving Edmund looking after her in an ecstacy of admiration of all her many virtues, from her obliging manners down to her light and graceful tread.[26]

"There goes good humour I am sure," said he presently. "There goes a temper which would never give pain! How well she walks! and how readily she falls in with the inclination of others! joining them the moment she is asked. What a pity," he added, after an instant's reflection, "that she should have been in such hands!"[27]

Fanny agreed to it, and had the pleasure of seeing him continue at the window with her, in spite of the expected glee; and of having his eyes soon turned like her's towards the scene without, where all that was solemn and soothing, and lovely, appeared in the brilliancy of an unclouded night, and the contrast of the deep shade of the woods. Fanny spoke her feelings. "Here's harmony!" said she, "Here's repose! Here's what may leave all painting and all music behind, and what poetry only can attempt to describe. Here's what may tranquillize every care, and lift the heart to rapture! When I look out on such a night as this, I feel as if there could be neither wickedness nor sorrow in the world; and there certainly would be less of both if the sublimity of Nature were more attended to, and people were carried more out of themselves by contemplating such a scene."[28]

"I like to hear your enthusiasm, Fanny. It is a lovely night, and they are much to be pitied who have not been taught to feel in some degree as you do—who have not at least been given a taste for nature in early life. They lose a great deal."

"*You* taught me to think and feel on the subject, cousin."[29]

"I had a very apt scholar.[30] There's Arcturus looking very bright."

"Yes, and the bear. I wish I could see Cassiopeia."[31]

"We must go out on the lawn for that. Should you be afraid?"[32]

"Not in the least. It is a great while since we have had any stargazing."

"Yes, I do not know how it has happened." The glee began. "We will stay till this is finished, Fanny," said he, turning his back on the window; and as it advanced, she had the mortification of seeing him advance too, moving forward by gentle degrees towards the instrument, and when it ceased, he was close by the singers, among the most urgent in requesting to hear the glee again.

26. Women were often praised for walking gracefully.

27. Meaning the hands of those who raised her.

28. Fanny's rhapsody to nature, and to the beneficent effects its beauties can have on the heart and soul, echoes many strains of thought from this period. Eighteenth-century writers often identified the wonders and harmony of nature as proof of God's wisdom and benevolence, as well as a critical source of moral inspiration. A significant example was the poem by William Cowper, *The Task*, that Fanny earlier cited in her lament over fallen avenues. The Romantic movement that blossomed in the early nineteenth century went even further in celebrating nature, while shifting the focus somewhat away from God and toward personal experience. Fanny's speech seems close to this, though she also reveals during the novel a strong religious faith. Her attitude may also represent a partial shift in Jane Austen's view of Romanticism. In two early novels, *Northanger Abbey* and *Sense and Sensibility*, she satirizes aspects of it, but in this novel she presents a sympathetic heroine with many Romantic elements; she will do that again more mildly with the heroine of her last novel, *Persuasion*. At the same time, in that last novel Austen criticizes excess of Romantic sentiment, and here it is possible she is treating Fanny with a degree of irony: her speech sounds a little stilted and didactic, and suggests how much the youthful and inexperienced Fanny has derived her ideas directly from books (as is also true of the youthful Romantic heroines satirized in *Northanger Abbey* and *Sense and Sensibility*).

29. While Edmund calls Fanny by her name, she, here and elsewhere, calls him by the more deferential term "cousin." This suggests the unequal nature of their relationship, which will play a critical role in the plot.

30. *scholar*: pupil.

31. Arcturus is, after Sirius, the brightest star visible in the northern hemisphere, and is part of the constellation called "the Bear." Cassiopeia is a constellation. Astronomy was often recommended for girls to learn, as was seen earlier in a limited way with Maria and Julia (p. 40). There were also celestial atlases published that had maps of all the constellations.

32. He refers to the fear of damp night air, mentioned in the last chapter in relation to the carriage ride home from Sotherton.

Fanny sighed alone at the window till scolded away by Mrs. Norris's threats of catching cold.

A woman looking at sheet music.

[From *The Repository of arts, literature, fashions, manufactures, &c*, Vol. X (1813), p. 242]

Shooting a pheasant.

[From William Henry Scott, *British Field Sports* (London, 1818), p. 232]

A gamekeeper (see the next page).

[From W. B. Daniel, *Rural Sports* (London, 1807), p. 135]

Chapter Twelve

Sir Thomas was to return in November, and his eldest son had duties to call him earlier home. The approach of September brought tidings of Mr. Bertram first in a letter to the gamekeeper,[1] and then in a letter to Edmund;[2] and by the end of August, he arrived himself, to be gay, agreeable, and gallant again as occasion served, or Miss Crawford demanded, to tell of races and Weymouth,[3] and parties and friends, to which she might have listened six weeks before with some interest, and altogether to give her the fullest conviction, by the power of actual comparison, of her preferring his younger brother.

It was very vexatious, and she was heartily sorry for it; but so it was; and so far from now meaning to marry the elder, she did not even want to attract him beyond what the simplest claims of conscious beauty required;[4] his lengthened absence from Mansfield, without any thing but pleasure in view, and his own will to consult, made it perfectly clear that he did not care about her; and his indifference was so much more than equalled by her own, that were he now to step forth the owner of Mansfield Park, the Sir Thomas complete, which he was to be in time, she did not believe she could accept him.[5]

The season and duties which brought Mr. Bertram back to Mansfield, took Mr. Crawford into Norfolk.[6] Everingham could not do without him in the beginning of September. He went for a fortnight; a fortnight of such dulness to the Miss Bertrams, as ought to have put them both on their guard, and made even Julia admit in her jealousy of her sister, the absolute necessity of distrusting his attentions, and wishing him not to return; and a fortnight of sufficient leisure in the intervals of shooting and sleeping, to have convinced the gentleman that he ought to keep longer away, had he been more in the habit of examining his own motives, and of reflecting to what the indulgence of his idle vanity was tending; but, thoughtless and

1.   September brought the commencement of outdoor sports, which were matters of vital importance to most country gentlemen and thus are referred to here humorously as "duties," for on September 1 it became legal to shoot partridges, one of the two principal game birds (the season for the other bird, pheasants, along with that for hunting foxes and hares, began later in the autumn). The gamekeeper was the servant in charge of the game on an estate; his duties included breeding game, protecting it from predators, assisting sportsmen in the pursuit of game, and stopping poachers, for which last the owner of the estate could confer on him the power of arrest.

2.   He would write to Edmund because he is currently managing the affairs of the house and because, as later revealed, he will also participate in the sport. It is notable that Tom writes to him only after writing to the gamekeeper. Sport is his priority.

3.   He had earlier left Mansfield to attend horse races. He went subsequently to Weymouth, a town in southwestern England that was one of the most fashionable seaside resorts of the time. Its popularity and prestige were enhanced by its being a favorite destination of the current king, George III. A leading tourist book, John Feltham's *A Guide to All the Watering and Sea-Bathing Places* (1804), says of it, "As a bathing place it is perhaps unparalleled." Bathing, or swimming in the sea, emerged as a recreation during the eighteenth century, recommended by medical opinion for health and also simply enjoyed by many people, and seaside resorts gradually sprang up all over the coast of England. Many other characters in Austen's novels take vacations at the seaside, as did Jane Austen herself and her family.

4.   Meaning she wishes to have her beauty and attractiveness confirmed by some attention on his part, but does not wish for a stronger interest.

5.   In other words, even if Sir Thomas were now to die and Tom to inherit the property and the title, she would not marry Tom. Thus Mary, as concerned as she is with wealth and position, also cares about less mercenary factors; in this she contrasts with Maria Bertram and her willingness to become engaged to Mr. Rushworth despite a lack of any feeling for him on her part.

6.   Henry Crawford's estate is in Norfolk, and he would wish to go there for the shooting, for like any large estate it would have its own game.

selfish from prosperity and bad example, he would not look beyond the present moment.[7] The sisters, handsome, clever, and encouraging, were an amusement to his sated mind; and finding nothing in Norfolk to equal the social pleasures of Mansfield, he gladly returned to it at the time appointed, and was welcomed thither quite as gladly by those whom he came to trifle with farther.

Maria, with only Mr. Rushworth to attend to her, and doomed to the repeated details of his day's sport,[8] good or bad, his boast of his dogs,[9] his jealousy of his neighbours,[10] his doubts of their qualification,[11] and his zeal after poachers,[12]—subjects which will not find their way to female feelings without some talent on one side, or some attachment[13] on the other, had missed Mr. Crawford grievously; and Julia, unengaged and unemployed, felt all the right of missing him much more. Each sister believed herself the favourite. Julia might be justified in so doing by the hints of Mrs. Grant, inclined to credit what she wished, and Maria by the hints of Mr. Crawford himself. Every thing returned into the same channel as before his absence; his manners being to each so animated and agreeable, as to lose no ground with either, and just stopping short of the consistence, the steadiness, the solicitude, and the warmth which might excite general notice.[14]

Fanny was the only one of the party who found any thing to dislike; but since the day at Sotherton, she could never see Mr. Crawford with either sister without observation, and seldom without wonder or censure; and had her confidence in her own judgment been equal to her exercise of it in every other respect, had she been sure that she was seeing clearly, and judging candidly,[15] she would probably have made some important communications to her usual confidant. As it was, however, she only hazarded a hint, and the hint was lost. "I am rather surprised," said she, "that Mr. Crawford should come back again so soon, after being here so long before, full seven weeks; for I had understood he was so very fond of change and moving about, that I thought something would certainly occur when he was once gone, to take him elsewhere. He is used to much gayer places than Mansfield."

"It is to his credit," was Edmund's answer, "and I dare say it gives his sister pleasure. She does not like his unsettled habits."

7. This is an important theme in Jane Austen, who frequently shows the adverse effects of enjoying too much wealth and importance or of poor education. She begins her longest book, *Emma*, by declaring that the heroine's two main disadvantages are "the power of having rather too much her own way, and a disposition to think a little too well of herself."

8. Meaning detailed accounts of his shooting ("sport" then referred only to the pursuit of game).

9. Dogs played a central role in shooting by locating the birds through their scent and fetching those that had been shot. Sportsmen devoted great effort to breeding and raising their dogs, and took great pride in the result.

10. His jealousy could be simple competitiveness about who killed the most birds. But it also could be a worry that others are killing game on his land. Landowners tried by various means to maximize their supply of game; at the same time, improved killing methods during this period, most notably better guns, often caused the supply to become exhausted. This made landowners zealous to prevent any loss of their own game to others; in *Persuasion* three neighboring proprietors are said to be "each more careful and jealous than the other" regarding their game.

11. By law the right to kill game was restricted to those owning a fairly large estate, but others sometimes also pursued game, in many cases with the permission of landowners, who used this as a way to confer favors and enhance their social and political position in the community.

12. Poaching was a serious issue in rural England at this time: landowners tried hard to stop it and got Parliament, which they dominated, to pass draconian laws against it, but it persisted. Ordinary people believed that wild game should be free to all, and thus that poaching, unlike stealing domestic livestock, was not wrong. In addition, game meat was highly desired and commanded very high prices; landowners got Parliament to outlaw the sale of game, but this only created a lucrative black market for it and thus even better money for those willing to poach.

13. *attachment*: affection.

14. If he attracted general notice, it might lead to an open conflict with Mr. Rushworth regarding Maria or, in the case of Julia, to an expectation that he was courting her, and from that an opinion that he was honor-bound to marry her. Henry's avoidance of this shows him to be skilled and practiced in flirting with and pursuing women.

15. *candidly*: generously, justly. "Candour" and "candid," frequently used in Austen's novels, refer principally not to frankness, as now, but to a tendency or willingness to think well of others.

"What a favourite he is with my cousins!"

"Yes, his manners to women are such as must please. Mrs. Grant, I believe, suspects him of a preference for Julia; I have never seen much symptom of it, but I wish it may be so. He has no faults but what a serious attachment would remove."

"If Miss Bertram were not engaged," said Fanny, cautiously, "I could sometimes almost think that he admired her more than Julia."

"Which is, perhaps, more in favour of his liking Julia best, than you, Fanny, may be aware; for I believe it often happens, that a man, before he has quite made up his own mind, will distinguish[16] the sister or intimate friend of the woman he is really thinking of, more than the woman herself. Crawford has too much sense to stay here if he found himself in any danger from Maria; and I am not at all afraid for her, after such a proof as she has given, that her feelings are not strong."[17]

Fanny supposed she must have been mistaken, and meant to think differently in future; but with all that submission to Edmund could do, and all the help of the coinciding looks and hints which she occasionally noticed in some of the others, and which seemed to say that Julia was Mr. Crawford's choice, she knew not always what to think.[18] She was privy, one evening, to the hopes of her aunt Norris on this subject, as well as to her feelings, and the feelings of Mrs. Rushworth, on a point of some similarity, and could not help wondering as she listened; and glad would she have been not to be obliged to listen, for it was while all the other young people were dancing, and she sitting, most unwillingly, among the chaperons at the fire,[19] longing for the re-entrance of her elder cousin, on whom all her own hopes of a partner then depended.[20] It was Fanny's first ball, though without the preparation or splendour of many a young lady's first ball, being the thought only of the afternoon,[21] built on[22] the late[23] acquisition of a violin player in the servants' hall,[24] and the possibility of raising five couple with the help of Mrs. Grant and a new intimate friend of Mr. Bertram's just arrived on a visit.[25] It had, however, been a very happy one to Fanny through four dances, and she was quite grieved to be losing even a quarter of an hour.[26] —While waiting and wishing, looking now at the dancers and now at the door, this dialogue between the two above-mentioned ladies was forced on her.

16. *distinguish*: single out, pay particular notice to.

17. He means that Maria's willingness to become engaged to a man like Rush-worth whom she does not love deeply—it is not clear if Edmund has con-cluded this from observation or from assuming that no sensible woman could be deeply in love with Rushworth—indicates that she lacks strong romantic feelings.

18. Fanny's deference to Edmund's judgment and unwillingness to contra-dict him, even though she has had more opportunity of observing the matter under discussion and has not been distracted by wooing someone else, as he has, will continue for much of the novel and have momentous consequences.

19. The chaperons are the older women who watch the dancing to ensure nothing improper occurs; the older men at balls, who also would not dance, usually go off by themselves to play cards. In a letter Jane Austen describes how she, being older, now serves as a chaperon at a ball, and says that it has its compensations, since "I am put on the Sofa near the Fire & can drink as much wine as I like" (Nov. 6, 1813).

20. In other words, Tom has left; his reason for leaving will soon be revealed.

21. Since "morning" comprised most of the day at this time, "afternoon" refers only to the period of an hour or two between dinner and the onset of evening.

22. *built on*: founded upon.

23. *late*: recent.

24. This would not be a professional musician but simply a servant capable of playing the violin.

25. Their party otherwise consists of eight young people: the four Bertram children, the two Crawfords, Mr. Rushworth, and Fanny. An additional man and woman allow for five dancing couples. With Tom temporarily gone, one woman is left without a partner, and it is natural that it is Fanny, the lowest in social status of the women.

26. A dance normally lasted a quarter of an hour.

"I think, ma'am," said Mrs. Norris—her eyes directed towards Mr. Rushworth and Maria, who were partners for the second time[27]— "we shall see some happy faces again now."

"Yes, ma'am, indeed"—replied the other, with a stately[28] simper— "there will be some satisfaction in looking on *now*, and I think it was rather a pity they should have been obliged to part. Young folks in their situation should be excused complying with the common forms.[29]—I wonder my son did not propose it."

"I dare say he did, ma'am.—Mr. Rushworth is never remiss. But dear Maria has such a strict sense of propriety, so much of that true delicacy which one seldom meets with now-a-days, Mrs. Rushworth, that wish of avoiding particularity![30]—Dear ma'am, only look at her face at this moment;—how different from what it was the two last dances!"[31]

Miss Bertram did indeed look happy, her eyes were sparkling with pleasure, and she was speaking with great animation, for Julia and her partner, Mr. Crawford, were close to her; they were all in a cluster together. How she had looked before, Fanny could not recollect, for she had been dancing with Edmund herself, and had not thought about her.

Mrs. Norris continued, "It is quite delightful, ma'am, to see young people so properly happy, so well suited, and so much the thing! I cannot but think of dear Sir Thomas's delight. And what do you say, ma'am, to the chance of another match? Mr. Rushworth has set a good example, and such things are very catching."

Mrs. Rushworth, who saw nothing but her son, was quite at a loss. "The couple above, ma'am.[32] Do you see no symptoms there?"

"Oh! dear—Miss Julia and Mr. Crawford. Yes, indeed, a very pretty match. What is his property?"

"Four thousand a year."[33]

"Very well.—Those who have not more, must be satisfied with what they have.—Four thousand a year is a pretty estate, and he seems a very genteel, steady young man, so I hope Miss Julia will be very happy."

"It is not a settled thing, ma'am, yet.—We only speak of it among friends. But I have very little doubt it *will be*.—He is growing extremely particular in his attentions."

27. Dancing couples stayed together for a pair of dances, thus for half an hour, and then each person selected a new partner for the next pair. This change of partners was standard etiquette: in *Sense and Sensibility* a couple too wrapped up in each other to be willing to dance with anyone else must sit down for every other pair in order to avoid breaching etiquette; even so, their exclusiveness attracts ridicule. In this case, Maria and Mr. Rushworth were together for the first pair, were then separated, and are now reunited for the third pairing (four dances have been completed).

28. *stately*: haughty, excessively dignified.

29. She means that those engaged should be free from standard dancing etiquette, i.e., "the common forms," and be allowed to dance continuously with each other.

30. Mrs. Norris reveals her naivete and blindness regarding Maria and her feelings for Rushworth, a blindness she will continue to show throughout the novel. A more discerning observer could easily guess that Maria's insistence on changing partners might have other motives than strict propriety.

31. Meaning the previous pair of dances.

32. The couple above are the ones preceding them in the line of dancers. Dances involved a number of couples together: two facing lines, one of each sex, were formed, and couples would take turns performing dance steps; the most common procedure was for the couple at the top of the lines to take their turn and move at the end to the bottom of the lines, after which everyone else would advance one position. For an example of a dance like this from the time, see the diagram on p. 231. The substantial periods of standing and watching others allowed the participants to perform so many dances without needing to rest.

33. Austen's novels consistently portray a society in which knowledge of other people's incomes is almost universal. One source would be marriage settlements, which were agreements between families that involved explicit calculations of their respective worth as well as stipulations as to what the bride and the groom were to have; another would be wills. Once, via whatever source, the information was known, it would be widely shared without hesitation.

Fanny could listen no farther. Listening and wondering were all suspended for a time, for Mr. Bertram was in the room again, and though feeling it would be a great honour to be asked by him,[34] she thought it must happen. He came towards their little circle; but instead of asking her to dance, drew a chair near her, and gave her an account of the present state of a sick horse, and the opinion of the groom, from whom he had just parted.[35] Fanny found that it was not to be, and in the modesty of her nature immediately felt that she had been unreasonable in expecting it. When he had told of his horse, he took a newspaper from the table,[36] and looking over it said in a languid way, "If you want to dance, Fanny, I will stand up[37] with you."—With more than equal civility the offer was declined;—she did not wish to dance.—"I am glad of it," said he in a much brisker tone, and throwing down the newspaper again—"for I am tired to death. I only wonder how the good people can keep it up so long.—They had need be *all* in love, to find any amusement in such folly—and so they are, I fancy.—If you look at them, you may see they are so many couple of lovers—all but Yates and Mrs. Grant—and, between ourselves, she, poor woman! must want a lover as much as any one of them. A desperate dull life her's must be with the doctor," making a sly face as he spoke towards the chair of the latter, who proving, however, to be close at his elbow, made so instantaneous a change of expression and subject necessary, as Fanny, in spite of every thing, could hardly help laughing at.—"A strange business this in America, Dr. Grant![38]—What is your opinion?—I always come to you to know what I am to think of public matters."

"My dear Tom," cried his aunt soon afterwards, "as you are not dancing, I dare say you will have no objection to join us in a rubber;[39] shall you?"—then, leaving her seat, and coming to him to enforce the proposal, added in a whisper—"We want to make a table for Mrs. Rushworth, you know.[40]—Your mother is quite anxious about it, but cannot very well spare time to sit down herself, because of her fringe.[41] Now, you and I and Dr. Grant will just do; and though *we* play but half-crowns, you know you may bet half-guineas with *him*."[42]

"I should be most happy," replied he aloud, and jumping up with alacrity, "it would give me the greatest pleasure—but that I am this

34. As the elder son of the host family, he is the leading man at the ball (and thus opposite in position to Fanny).

35. Thus he left the ball to check on his horse; this gives a sense of his priorities. The groom would be tending to the horse.

36. Newspapers had become a standard feature of life in England, at least among the affluent (they were expensive). They are shown in Austen's novels as particularly the favorite reading matter of men, who were the only ones who could participate in politics.

37. *stand up*: dance.

38. The "strange business" is probably the War of 1812, which Tom would have been reading about in the newspaper. The war arose principally from disputes between Britain and the United States over restrictions on maritime trade imposed by Britain and the impressment of sailors by the British navy, both of which grew out of Britain's long and difficult war with Napoleonic France. War was declared by the United States in June 1812 and lasted until February 1815. The first two years centered around attempts by the United States to invade Canada, all of which ultimately failed. The last part, coming after Napoleon had been defeated in the spring of 1814 and Britain could devote more resources to the fight, involved British attacks on the United States, which also were ultimately repulsed. At the end both sides agreed to restore the status quo ante. Jane Austen started writing this novel sometime in 1812 and finished it in 1813, so this war would have been a regular subject of newspaper articles (there is every indication that this novel, like all her novels, is set in the time when it is written).

39. A rubber is a set of card games, usually three.

40. As revealed shortly, they are playing whist, which requires four players, and Mrs. Norris needs a fourth person.

41. Her fringe is part of Lady Bertram's needlework, her main occupation. As the mistress of the house and thus the nominal hostess of the event, she should be principally responsible for entertaining guests, especially female ones, but she still cannot be bothered to leave her normal activity. It is unclear if she is really anxious about Mrs. Rushworth, or if Mrs. Norris is simply attributing her own anxiety to her sister.

42. Betting was standard for card playing. Half-crowns and half-guineas were both coins; the first was worth two and a half shillings, the second ten and a half. Thus changing from one to the other will slightly more than quadru-

moment going to dance. Come, Fanny,"—taking her hand—"do not be dawdling any longer, or the dance will be over."

Fanny was led off very willingly, though it was impossible for her to feel much gratitude towards her cousin, or distinguish, as he certainly did, between the selfishness of another person and his own.

"A pretty modest request upon my word!" he indignantly exclaimed as they walked away. "To want to nail me to a card table for the next two hours with herself and Dr. Grant, who are always quarrelling, and that poking[43] old woman, who knows no more of whist than of algebra.[44] I wish my good aunt would be a little less busy! And to ask me in such a way too! without ceremony,[45] before them all, so as to leave me no possibility of refusing! *That* is what I dislike most particularly. It raises my spleen more than any thing, to have the pretence of being asked, of being given a choice, and at the same time addressed in such a way as to oblige one to do the very thing— whatever it be! If I had not luckily thought of standing up with you, I could not have got out of it. It is a great deal too bad. But when my aunt has got a fancy in her head, nothing can stop her."

A whist game.
[From *Works of James Gillray* (London, 1849), Figure 413]

ple the stakes. Mrs. Norris assumes that Tom, whose love of horse racing has already been revealed, would prefer to gamble for higher stakes.

43. *poking*: inclined to putter around in a desultory manner.

44. Whist, which emerged in the eighteenth century, had become the most popular game in England by this time. It is essentially bridge without bidding or the complicated point system.

45. *without ceremony*: in an offhand way, without formal courtesy.

ALL THE LADIES AND GENTLEMEN LEAD THROUGH.
Fig. 1.

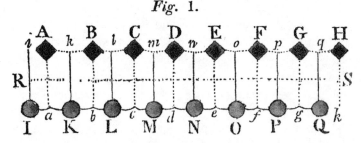

The Ladies at A B C D E F G H, and the Gentlemen at I K L M N O P Q, join hands and lead over to the line R S, where they pass between each other, the Ladies to *a b c d e f g h*, and the Gentlemen to *i k l m n o p q*.

The outline of a dance, performed with two facing lines of dancers.

[From Thomas Wilson, *Analysis of Country Dancing* (London, 1808), p. 110]

Chapter Thirteen

The Honourable John Yates,[1] this new friend, had not much to recommend him beyond habits of fashion and expense, and being the younger son of a lord with a tolerable independence;[2] and Sir Thomas would probably have thought his introduction at Mansfield by no means desirable. Mr. Bertram's acquaintance with him had begun at Weymouth, where they had spent ten days together in the same society,[3] and the friendship, if friendship it might be called, had been proved and perfected by Mr. Yates's being invited to take Mansfield in his way, whenever he could, and by his promising to come; and he did come rather earlier than had been expected, in consequence of the sudden breaking-up of a large party assembled for gaiety at the house of another friend, which he had left Weymouth to join. He came on the wings of disappointment, and with his head full of acting, for it had been a theatrical party;[4] and the play, in which he had borne a part, was within two days of representation, when the sudden death of one of the nearest connections[5] of the family had destroyed the scheme and dispersed the performers.[6] To be so near happiness, so near fame, so near the long paragraph in praise of the private theatricals at Ecclesford,[7] the seat of the Right Hon. Lord Ravenshaw,[8] in Cornwall,[9] which would of course have immortalized the whole party for at least a twelvemonth! and being so near, to lose it all, was an injury to be keenly felt, and Mr. Yates could talk of nothing else. Ecclesford and its theatre, with its arrangements and dresses,[10] rehearsals and jokes, was his never-failing subject, and to boast of the past his only consolation.

Happily for him, a love of the theatre is so general, an itch for acting so strong among young people, that he could hardly out-talk the interest of his hearers. From the first casting of the parts, to the epilogue,[11] it was all bewitching, and there were few who did not wish to have been a party concerned, or would have hesitated to try

1.   "The Honourable" is a courtesy title given to sons of the three lowest ranks of the peerage or nobility, which are, in descending order, earl, viscount, and baron; we later learn that Mr. Yates is the son of a baron. Sons of the two highest peerage ranks, duke and marquess, are given the title "Lord" before their name. Courtesy titles, unlike the titles of actual peers, do not confer any legal privileges on the bearer.

2.   *independence*: income or fortune providing financial independence. Usually younger sons, who would not inherit the family title or estate, would receive a monetary inheritance. In his case, we later learn, he has his own estate, separate from the main family one.

3.   One of the attractions of fashionable resorts like Weymouth was that they contained many people of high social rank.

4.   Private theatricals at home were a long-standing amusement that became extremely popular from the 1770s through the time of this novel. Families often organized special parties and sent invitations to carefully selected guests, who would help fill the casts of the plays.

5.   *connections*: relations.

6.   There were strict customs relating to funerals and mourning for family members that would have dictated dropping frivolous entertainments.

7.   Ecclesford, a fictional name, is the house where Yates was visiting. The long paragraph would have appeared in a local newspaper, which had become increasingly common in England: by 1821, fewer than ten years after the composition of this novel, one-third of all stamps sold by the Post Office were for local newspapers, and by 1830 more than 150 such papers were being published.

8.   "Right Hon.," or "Right Honourable," is a title used for an earl, viscount, or baron in formal contexts; in this case it is what would have been printed in the newspaper. It would not be employed in normal conversation. Its specific use here indicates that Lord Ravenshaw is a baron: for the other two ranks the formal designation would be "Right Honourable the Earl . . ." or "Right Honourable Lord Viscount . . ."

9.   Cornwall is a county in the farthest southwestern corner of England. It is not far from Weymouth. For both locations, see map, p. 882.

10. *dresses*: costumes.

11. Epilogues, usually spoken by one of the characters, had long been a common feature of plays. Jane Austen's brother James wrote special epilogues for some of the dramas performed in their home.

their skill. The play had been Lovers' Vows,[12] and Mr. Yates was to have been Count Cassel. "A trifling part," said he, "and not at all to my taste, and such a one as I certainly would not accept again; but I was determined to make no difficulties. Lord Ravenshaw and the duke had appropriated the only two characters worth playing before I reached Ecclesford; and though Lord Ravenshaw offered to resign his to me, it was impossible to take it, you know. I was sorry for *him* that he should have so mistaken his powers, for he was no more equal to the Baron! A little man, with a weak voice, always hoarse after the first ten minutes! It must have[13] injured the piece materially; but *I* was resolved to make no difficulties. Sir Henry thought the duke not equal to Frederick,[14] but that was because Sir Henry wanted the part himself; whereas it was certainly in the best hands of the two. I was surprised to see Sir Henry such a stick.[15] Luckily the strength of the piece did not depend upon him. Our Agatha was inimitable, and the duke was thought very great by many. And upon the whole it would certainly have gone off wonderfully."

"It was a hard case, upon my word;" and, "I do think you were very much to be pitied;" were the kind responses of listening sympathy.

"It is not worth complaining about, but to be sure the poor old dowager[16] could not have died at a worse time; and it is impossible to help wishing, that the news could have been suppressed for just the three days we wanted. It was but three days; and being only a grandmother, and all happening two hundred miles off, I think there would have been no great harm, and it *was* suggested, I know; but Lord Ravenshaw, who I suppose is one of the most correct men in England, would not hear of it."

"An after-piece instead of a comedy,"[17] said Mr. Bertram. "Lovers' Vows were at an end, and Lord and Lady Ravenshaw left to act My Grandmother by themselves.[18] Well, the jointure may comfort *him*;[19] and perhaps, between friends, he began to tremble for his credit[20] and his lungs in the Baron, and was not sorry to withdraw; and to make *you* amends, Yates, I think we must raise a little theatre at Mansfield, and ask you to be our manager."[21]

This, though the thought of the moment, did not end with the moment; for the inclination to act was awakened, and in no one more strongly than in him who was now master of the house; and

12. *Lovers' Vows* was a popular play of the time; Count Cassel is a character in it, as are other names mentioned in this paragraph: the Baron, Frederick, and Agatha. For much more on the play, see the next chapter.

13. *must have*: certainly would have.

14. Sir Henry is either a baronet or a knight. The presence of a duke, a "Lord," and a "Sir" indicates the elite nature of the party.

15. *stick*: wooden actor. Mr. Yates's speech, with its inappropriate denigration of his companions, including the man who was his host, to listeners who have never met them, introduces his character. It also reveals the sort of petty rivalries and jealousies that were attendant to the play's production and that will soon appear as well among the Mansfield party.

16. *dowager*: a wealthy, often titled widow. For more, see p. 375, note 38.

17. Professional theatrical shows of the time normally included an after-piece, which was a short play, usually lighthearted, that succeeded the main drama.

18. *My Grandmother*, by Prince Hoare, was a popular play that was usually acted as an after-piece because it had two acts instead of the standard five. Tom contrasts it to *Lovers' Vow*, a full-length comedy. Tom's clever allusion also has a cruel edge, for since *My Grandmother* was a farce, it suggests the empty or ludicrous nature of Lord Ravenshaw's mourning.

19. A jointure is a provision in a marriage settlement giving a lifetime annual sum to the wife after the husband dies; it was usually set at 10 percent of the dowry brought by the wife, based on the calculation that on average the wife outlived her husband by ten years (there typically was an age disparity at marriage) and thus she would receive back the same amount from the family that she had contributed when she married into it. The jointure in this case was going to the grandmother of Lord Ravenshaw while she was alive. She was probably fairly old, and, given generally low life expectancy at the time, there is a good chance she had been a widow for many years. Thus Lord Ravenshaw, at least in Tom's opinion, may derive significant comfort from being relieved of this annual financial burden; in *Sense and Sensibility* a mercenary woman complains of how hard it is to have to pay annuities to those who live a long time.

20. *credit*: reputation, good name.

21. "Manager" was the term for the person in charge of a theatrical production; the term and concept of a theatrical director did not exist then.

who having so much leisure as to make almost any novelty a certain good, had likewise such a degree of lively talents and comic taste, as were exactly adapted to the novelty of acting. The thought returned again and again. "Oh! for the Ecclesford theatre and scenery to try something with." Each sister could echo the wish; and Henry Crawford, to whom, in all the riot[22] of his gratifications it was yet an untasted pleasure, was quite alive at[23] the idea. "I really believe," said he, "I could be fool enough at this moment to undertake any character that ever was written, from Shylock or Richard III.[24] down to the singing hero of a farce in his scarlet coat and cocked hat.[25] I feel as if I could be any thing or every thing, as if I could rant and storm, or sigh, or cut capers[26] in any tragedy or comedy in the English language. Let us be doing something. Be it only half a play—an act—a scene; what should prevent us? Not these countenances I am sure," looking towards the Miss Bertrams, "and for a theatre, what signifies a theatre? We shall be only amusing ourselves. Any room in this house might suffice."

"We must have a curtain," said Tom Bertram, "a few yards of green baize for a curtain,[27] and perhaps that may be enough."

"Oh! quite enough," cried Mr. Yates, "with only just a side wing or two run up, doors in flat, and three or four scenes to be let down;[28] nothing more would be necessary on such a plan as this. For mere amusement among ourselves, we should want nothing more."

"I believe we must be satisfied with *less*," said Maria. "There would not be time, and other difficulties would arise.[29] We must

Ditchley Park, Oxfordshire: a grand house similar to where Mr. Yates has just been.

[From John Preston Neale, *Views of the Seats of Noblemen and Gentlemen*, Vol. V (London, 1822)]

22. *riot*: extravagance, dissipation.

23. *alive at*: aroused by.

24. Shylock and Richard III were two of the most popular dramatic roles of the time. Records for the main London theaters show *Richard III* and *The Merchant of Venice* as, respectively, the third and fifth most produced Shakespeare plays during the second half of the eighteenth century (the first, second, and fourth most produced were, respectively, *Romeo and Juliet*, *Hamlet*, and *Macbeth*). *The Merchant of Venice* also underwent a transformation during this period, in which Shylock, previously portrayed as a comical supporting character, became a diabolical figure who was the main focus of the drama. Since *Richard III* was also valued at this time for the monstrous iniquity of its title character, Henry mentions roles that would give him the greatest opportunity for melodramatic acting; they also provide the sharpest contrast to the farcical figure he next mentions.

25. Farces frequently involved music. Scarlet coats and cocked hats were outmoded fashions and hence appropriate to a farce. During this time dark, sober colors had become standard for men's principal attire, while cocked hats, which had been popular throughout the eighteenth century, had declined in favor of the top hat. A cocked hat had opposing brims turned up together to make either two points (bicorn) or three (tricorn).

26. *cut capers*: act fantastically.

27. Baize is a coarse woolen fabric, commonly used in this period for curtains and furniture; in a letter Jane Austen mentions two new tables being covered with green baize (Nov. 8, 1800). Green was the traditional color for stage curtains.

28. These are elements of contemporary stagecraft. Side wings are pieces of movable scenery for the side of the stage. "Doors in flat" mean doors that are part of the flat, a standing backdrop that was also movable; stage directions in plays of the time call for actors to enter or exit by a "door in flat." "Scenes" here mean large painted hangings that can be let down to form an even larger backdrop. A trend during this period was for scenery and props to become more elaborate and to play a larger role in the drama. Most home theatricals could not afford scenery like this, though some aristocratic families put on comparable productions, and the one Mr. Yates just left is probably an example. That would account for his suggestions, as well as his familiarity with technical stage terminology.

29. The principal other difficulty would be the return of Sir Thomas. She herself has particular reason to wish to accelerate the performance of the play, since it would be likely to retain Henry Crawford at Mansfield.

rather adopt Mr. Crawford's views, and make the *performance*, not the *theatre*, our object. Many parts of our best plays are independent of scenery."

"Nay," said Edmund, who began to listen with alarm. "Let us do nothing by halves. If we are to act, let it be in a theatre completely fitted up with pit, box, and gallery, and let us have a play entire from beginning to end;[30] so as it be[31] a German play,[32] no matter what, with a good tricking, shifting after-piece,[33] and a figure-dance, and a hornpipe, and a song between the acts.[34] If we do not out do Ecclesford, we do nothing."

"Now, Edmund, do not be disagreeable," said Julia. "Nobody loves a play better than you do, or can have gone much farther to see one."

"True, to see real acting, good hardened real acting; but I would hardly walk from this room to the next to look at the raw efforts of those who have not been bred to the trade,[35]—a set of gentlemen and ladies, who have all the disadvantages of education and decorum to struggle through."[36]

After a short pause, however, the subject still continued, and was discussed with unabated eagerness, every one's inclination increasing by the discussion, and a knowledge of the inclination of the rest; and though nothing was settled but that Tom Bertram would prefer a comedy, and his sisters and Henry Crawford a tragedy, and that nothing in the world could be easier than to find a piece which would please them all, the resolution to act something or other, seemed so decided, as to make Edmund quite uncomfortable. He was determined to prevent it, if possible, though his mother, who equally heard the conversation which passed at table, did not evince the least disapprobation.

The same evening afforded him an opportunity of trying his strength. Maria, Julia, Henry Crawford, and Mr. Yates, were in the billiard-room.[37] Tom returning from them into the drawing-room, where Edmund was standing thoughtfully by the fire, while Lady Bertram was on the sofa at a little distance, and Fanny close beside her arranging her work, thus began as he entered. "Such a horribly vile billiard-table as ours, is not to be met with, I believe, above ground! I can stand it no longer, and I think, I may say, that nothing shall ever tempt me to it again. But one good thing I have just ascertained. It is

30. The boxes, the pit, and the galleries were the three seating sections of a theater then. They also expressed a social division. The boxes, which covered the sides of the theater as well as usually the lower part of the back, were where the wealthiest patrons sat; the pit, in the middle, was for those of more moderate means; and the galleries, in the upper sections of the back, had the cheapest seats and the poorest customers. Edmund is conjuring up an image of enormous size—the leading London theaters then, which had recently been rebuilt, contained seating for several thousand people—that he reinforces by talk of an entire play. For pictures of the two principal London theaters, including the boxes and pit of one, see pp. 243 and 245.

31. *so as it be*: so long as it is.

32. *Lovers' Vow* was a translation of a play by a German playwright, August F. F. von Kotzebue. His plays had become popular recently, as to a lesser degree had those of other Germans. This popularity was denounced by some writers due to the alleged immorality of German plays as well as the radical political views of many, including Kotzebue's.

33. "Tricking" could refer to the use of artifice or deceptive stagecraft that fooled and surprised the audience; "trick" also could mean a prank or frolic or act of roguery. "Shift" could also denote acts of trickery and deceit, or could refer to changes of scenery or costume. All of these meanings would be suitable for the farcical productions that were typical of after-pieces.

34. A figure-dance is a dance with several figures or parts, while a hornpipe can refer either to a musical instrument of the time or to a lively dance often accompanied by it. Theatrical productions frequently added songs and dances to the program, including during the intervals between acts.

35. Acting was a trade then, which people were frequently apprenticed to when young, as in other trades. It was not very respectable socially and was considered especially improper for ladies.

36. Gentlemen and ladies of the time were educated in strict conventions of decorum, which emphasized the importance of restraint and propriety and would therefore preclude much of the behavior found on the stage.

37. Billiards was a popular amusement, especially for gentlemen, and many grand houses had a billiard room. The house of Jane Austen's wealthy brother Edward contained one, and in *Sense and Sensibility* a man complains of the lack of such a room in a house where he is staying. For a contemporary illustration of men playing billiards, see p. 247.

the very room for a theatre, precisely the shape and length for it, and the doors at the farther end, communicating with each other as they may be made to do in five minutes, by merely moving the bookcase in my father's room, is the very thing we could have desired, if we had set down to wish for it. And my father's room will be an excellent green-room.[38] It seems to join the billiard-room on purpose."

"You are not serious, Tom, in meaning to act?" said Edmund in a low voice, as his brother approached the fire.

"Not serious! never more so, I assure you. What is there to surprise you in it?"

"I think it would be very wrong. In a *general* light, private theatricals are open to some objections,[39] but as *we* are circumstanced, I must think it would be highly injudicious, and more than injudicious, to attempt any thing of the kind. It would show great want of feeling[40] on my father's account, absent as he is, and in some degree of constant danger;[41] and it would be imprudent, I think, with regard to Maria, whose situation is a very delicate one, considering every thing, extremely delicate."[42]

"You take up a thing so seriously! as if we were going to act three times a week till my father's return, and invite all the country. But it is not to be a display of that sort. We mean nothing but a little amusement among ourselves, just to vary the scene, and exercise our powers in something new. We want no audience, no publicity. We may be trusted, I think, in choosing some play most perfectly unexceptionable, and I can conceive no greater harm or danger to any of us in conversing in the elegant written language of some respectable author than in chattering in words of our own. I have no fears, and no scruples.[43] And as to my father's being absent, it is so far from an objection, that I consider it rather as a motive; for the expectation of his return must be a very anxious period to my mother,[44] and if we can be the means of amusing[45] that anxiety, and keeping up her spirits for the next few weeks, I shall think our time very well spent, and so I am sure will he.—It is a *very* anxious period for her."

As he said this, each looked towards their mother. Lady Bertram, sunk back in one corner of the sofa, the picture of health, wealth, ease, and tranquillity, was just falling into a gentle doze, while Fanny was getting through the few difficulties of her work for her.

38. The greenroom, a term still in use, is a room next to the side of the stage where the actors wait until it is time for them to appear onstage. Theater plans of the time consistently include a greenroom.

39. Some people objected to private theatricals, especially under the influence of the growing evangelical movement of the time. An example is Thomas Gisborne in *An Enquiry into the Duties of the Female Sex* (1797), which Jane Austen read in 1805 and praised in a letter. Gisborne condemns private theatricals on the grounds that many plays are improper and morally dangerous, that acting in plays encourages vanity, and that they "destroy diffidence, by the unrestrained familiarity with persons of the other sex, which inevitably results from being joined with them in the drama" (p. 175). It is not clear that Austen agrees with this verdict. When young she participated in her family's frequent play-acting, and around the time that she read this book she joined in a theatrical production among people she was visiting. But past experience may have alerted her to potential dangers. In 1787–88, when Jane was twelve, her charming, hedonistic, and flirtatious cousin Eliza de Feuillide (see p. 183, note 68) played a leading role in the dramas the family was putting on, and seems to have fascinated and attracted two of Jane's brothers, James and Henry, especially the latter (soon after, she expressed a strong interest in Henry, even though she was married to another man at the time). Jane's perception of their flirtation was registered in a youthful story she wrote in this period entitled "Henry and Eliza," in which the title characters elope.

40. *want of feeling*: lack of sensitivity, tenderness.

41. The principal objection here is probably that acting would mean taking advantage of his absence to engage in an activity, and to make alterations to his house, of which Sir Thomas might not approve.

42. He means her engagement, which might be imperiled by any appearance of impropriety on her part. In general, social conventions did not permit a man to withdraw from an engagement, but in this case Mr. Rushworth could plausibly argue that he was not breaking a formal pact since the engagement has not been officially sanctioned by Sir Thomas.

43. *scruples*: doubts, uncertainties.

44. Tom's use of "my father" and "my mother," even though he is speaking to his own brother, was standard at the time for genteel people. Along with the similar use of "my sister" and "my brother," it is regularly found in Austen's novels and in her letters. In a letter to her sister she comments, with evident bemusement, on a servant's consistently saying "Mother" rather than "my mother" (Jan. 24, 1809).

45. *amusing*: diverting, distracting.

Edmund smiled and shook his head.

"By Jove! this won't do" — cried Tom, throwing himself into a chair with a hearty laugh. "To be sure, my dear mother, your anxiety — I was unlucky there."

"What is the matter?" asked her ladyship in the heavy tone of one half roused, — "I was not asleep."

"Oh! dear, no ma'am — nobody suspected you — Well, Edmund," he continued, returning to the former subject, posture, and voice, as soon as Lady Bertram began to nod again — "But *this* I *will* maintain — that we shall be doing no harm."

"I cannot agree with you — I am convinced that my father would totally disapprove it."

"And I am convinced to the contrary. — Nobody is fonder of the exercise of talent in young people, or promotes it more, than my father; and for any thing of the acting, spouting, reciting kind, I think he has always a decided taste. I am sure he encouraged it in us as boys. How many a time have we mourned over the dead body of Julius Cæsar, and *to be'd* and *not to be'd*,[46] in this very room, for his amusement! And I am sure, *my name was Norval*,[47] every evening of my life through one Christmas holidays."[48]

"It was a very different thing. — You must see the difference yourself. My father wished us, as school-boys, to speak well,[49] but he would never wish his grown up daughters to be acting plays. His sense of decorum is strict."[50]

"I know all that," said Tom, displeased. "I know my father as well as you do, and I'll take care that his daughters do nothing to distress him. Manage your own concerns, Edmund, and I'll take care of the rest of the family."

"If you are resolved on acting," replied the persevering Edmund, "I must hope it will be in a very small and quiet way; and I think a theatre ought not to be attempted. — It would be taking liberties with my father's house in his absence which could not be justified."

"For every thing of that nature, I will be answerable," — said Tom, in a decided tone. — "His house shall not be hurt. I have quite as great an interest in being careful of his house as you can have;[51] and as to such alterations as I was suggesting just now, such as moving a bookcase, or unlocking a door, or even as using the billiard-room for

46. Tom refers to two of the most famous speeches in Shakespeare, Marc Antony's funeral oration for the title character in *Julius Caesar* and Hamlet's soliloquy.

47. "My name is Norval" is the beginning of a speech in the tragedy *Douglas* by John Home; the play, appearing in the 1750s, became one of the most popular tragedies of the age and was acclaimed by some as superior to Shakespeare.

48. The Christmas holidays were when Tom and Edmund were home from school.

49. Learning to speak well was considered an important part of education. It could also be especially important for Tom and Edmund, the former because, as the heir to the title and estate, he would be expected to succeed his father as a member of Parliament, where oratory was an essential skill, and the latter because, as a prospective clergyman, he will eventually have to deliver regular sermons.

50. Sir Thomas presumably shares the objection to female acting alluded to above, which would apply particularly to grown-up—i.e., sexually mature—women.

51. This is a deliberate understatement, for Tom will inherit the house.

Drury Lane Theatre, one of the two regular theaters operating in London.

[From *The Repository of arts, literature, fashions, manufactures, &c*, Vol. VIII (1812), p. 287]

the space of a week without playing at billiards in it, you might just as well suppose he would object to our sitting more in this room, and less in the breakfast-room, than we did before he went away, or to my sister's[52] pianoforte being moved from one side of the room to the other.—Absolute nonsense!"

"The innovation, if not wrong as an innovation, will be wrong as an expense."

"Yes, the expense of such an undertaking would be prodigious! Perhaps it might cost a whole twenty pounds.[53]—Something of a theatre we must have undoubtedly, but it will be on the simplest plan;—a green curtain and a little carpenter's work—and that's all; and as the carpenter's work may be all done at home by Christopher Jackson himself,[54] it will be too absurd to talk of expense;—and as long as Jackson is employed, every thing will be right with Sir Thomas.—Don't imagine that nobody in this house can see or judge but yourself.—Don't act yourself, if you do not like it, but don't expect to govern every body else."

"No, as to acting myself," said Edmund, "*that* I absolutely protest against."

Tom walked out of the room as he said it, and Edmund was left to sit down and stir the fire in thoughtful vexation.

Fanny, who had heard it all, and borne Edmund company in every feeling throughout the whole, now ventured to say, in her anxiety to suggest some comfort, "Perhaps they may not be able to find any play to suit them. Your brother's taste, and your sisters', seem very different."

"I have no hope there, Fanny. If they persist in the scheme they will find something—I shall speak to my sisters, and try to dissuade *them*, and that is all I can do."

"I should think my aunt Norris would be on your side."

"I dare say she would; but she has no influence with either Tom or my sisters that could be of any use; and if I cannot convince them myself, I shall let things take their course, without attempting it through her. Family squabling is the greatest evil of all, and we had better do any thing than be altogether by the ears."[55]

His sisters, to whom he had an opportunity of speaking the next morning, were quite as impatient of his advice, quite as unyielding

52. Most editions of the novel amend this to "sisters'," and it is possible that Jane Austen meant to refer to both sisters and it was accidentally altered by those printing the book. But it is also possible that the pianoforte was given to only one sister, most likely to Maria as the elder, and considered hers, even if both play on it.

53. This is a small sum for Tom, whose family's income is certainly in the thousands per annum. At the same time, it exceeds the annual income of many laborers of the time.

54. Christopher Jackson is the carpenter for the estate; large estates often had various types of workers on staff.

55. *by the ears*: at variance, in a state of conflict.

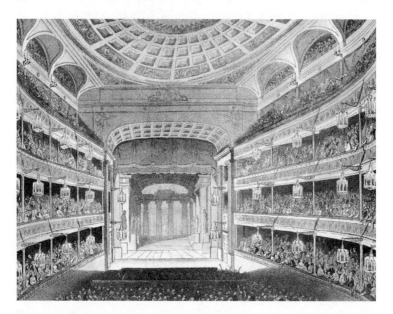

Theatre Royal, Covent Garden, the other main theater. The picture shows the pit and the boxes on the side; it also indicates the elaborate scenery standard onstage.

[From Fiona St. Aubyn, *Ackermann's Illustrated London*, illustrations by Augustus Pugin and Thomas Rowlandson (Ware, 1985), p. 133]

to his representation,[56] quite as determined in the cause of plea-sure, as Tom.—Their mother had no objection to the plan, and they were not in the least afraid of their father's disapprobation.—There could be no harm in what had been done in so many respectable families, and by so many women of the first consideration; and it must be scrupulousness run mad, that could see any thing to cen-sure in a plan like their's, comprehending only brothers and sisters, and intimate friends, and which would never be heard of beyond themselves. Julia *did* seem inclined to admit that Maria's situation might require particular caution and delicacy—but that could not extend to *her*—*she* was at liberty; and Maria evidently considered her engagement as only raising her so much more above restraint, and leaving her less occasion than Julia, to consult either father or mother.[57] Edmund had little to hope, but he was still urging the sub-ject, when Henry Crawford entered the room, fresh from the Parson-age, calling out, "No want of hands in our Theatre, Miss Bertram. No want of under strappers[58]—My sister desires her love, and hopes to be admitted into the company, and will be happy to take the part of any old Duenna or tame Confidante, that you may not like to do yourselves."[59]

Maria gave Edmund a glance, which meant, "What say you now? Can we be wrong if Mary Crawford feels the same?" And Edmund silenced, was obliged to acknowledge that the charm of acting might well carry fascination to the mind of genius;[60] and with the ingenuity of love, to dwell more on the obliging, accommodating purport of the message than on any thing else.[61]

The scheme advanced. Opposition was vain; and as to Mrs. Nor-ris, he was mistaken in supposing she would wish to make any. She started no difficulties that were not talked down in five minutes by her eldest nephew and niece, who were all-powerful with her; and, as the whole arrangement was to bring very little expense to any body, and none at all to herself, as she foresaw in it all the comforts of hurry, bustle and importance, and derived the immediate advantage of fancying herself obliged to leave her own house, where she had been living a month at her own cost,[62] and take up her abode in their's, that every hour might be spent in their service; she was, in fact, exceedingly delighted with the project.

56. *representation*: argument, remonstrance.

57. Maria's probable reasoning is that because she is committed to a future husband she is less likely to engage in improper flirtation, and that others would be less likely to misinterpret her friendly behavior toward unrelated men as a sign of romantic interest.

58. *under strappers*: assistants.

59. A duenna is an elderly female chaperone; many plays of the time contained duennas, and the leading playwright of late eighteenth-century England, Richard Brinsley Sheridan, wrote a comic opera entitled *The Duenna*. A confidante is an intimate companion to a woman. Confidantes had long been common characters in dramas, since they provided a mechanism for the playwright to have important female characters express their inner thoughts aloud. Both duennas and confidantes are usually supporting roles, which is why Mary mentions them to indicate her willingness and flexibility.

60. *mind of genius*: character of talent or natural ability.

61. Meaning that he focuses on how kind Mary is to offer to help, rather than on her eagerness to engage in a plan he considers inappropriate.

62. In the period leading up to the expedition to Sotherton, she had been frequently at Mansfield Park. Since then, nothing important has occurred to furnish her an excuse for coming there for extended periods.

Billiards.

[From William Combe, *The Dance of Life* (London, 1817; 1903 reprint), p. 234]

Chapter Fourteen

*F*anny seemed nearer being right than Edmund had supposed. The business[1] of finding a play that would suit every body, proved to be no trifle; and the carpenter had received his orders and taken his measurements, had suggested and removed at least two sets of difficulties, and having made the necessity of an enlargement of plan and expense fully evident, was already at work, while a play was still to seek. Other preparations were also in hand. An enormous roll of green baize had arrived from Northampton, and been cut out by Mrs. Norris (with a saving, by her good management, of full three quarters of a yard), and was actually forming[2] into a curtain by the housemaids, and still the play was wanting;[3] and as two or three days passed away in this manner, Edmund began almost to hope that none might ever be found.

There were, in fact, so many things to be attended to, so many people to be pleased, so many best characters required, and above all, such a need that the play should be at once both tragedy and comedy, that there did seem as little chance of a decision, as any thing pursued by youth and zeal could hold out.

On the tragic side were the Miss Bertrams, Henry Crawford, and Mr. Yates; on the comic, Tom Bertram, not *quite* alone, because it was evident that Mary Crawford's wishes, though politely kept back, inclined the same way; but his determinateness[4] and his power, seemed to make allies unnecessary; and independent of this great irreconcileable difference, they wanted a piece containing very few characters in the whole, but every character first-rate, and three principal women. All the best plays were run over in vain.[5] Neither Hamlet, nor Macbeth, nor Othello, nor Douglas, nor the Gamester,[6] presented any thing that could satisfy even the tragedians; and the Rivals, the School for Scandal, Wheel of Fortune, Heir at Law,[7] and a long etcetera, were successively dismissed with yet warmer objections. No piece could be proposed that did not supply somebody with

1. *business*: task.

2. *forming*: being formed. This usage is found elsewhere in Austen's novels and letters as well as in other writings of the time.

3. *wanting*: lacking.

4. *determinateness*: determination, decidedness of choice.

5. They are going through published copies of plays, of which there were many available.

6. *Hamlet*, *Macbeth*, and *Othello* were, after *Romeo and Juliet*, Shakespeare's most popular tragedies at the time. For *Douglas*, see p. 243, note 47. *The Gamester* (1753), by Edward Moore, was another popular tragedy; it concerns a man destroyed by excessive gambling.

7. These are all comedies. *The Rivals* (1775) and *The School for Scandal* (1777) are the two most renowned pieces by the leading playwright of the age, Richard Brinsley Sheridan; the first centers around the romantic complications of two couples, while the second is a satire of fashionable London society. *The Wheel of Fortune* (1795), by Richard Cumberland, is a sentimental comedy about a man who ultimately renounces revenge on a man who wronged him in the past. *The Heir at Law* (1797) is by the popular comic dramatist George Colman the Younger; for more, see note 11 below.

A contemporary picture of gambling, a popular pastime, especially among the wealthy, and a subject of various literary works, including The Gamester.
[From Joseph Grego, *Rowlandson the Caricaturist*, Vol. I (London, 1880), p. 46]

a difficulty, and on one side or the other it was a continual repetition of, "Oh! no, *that* will never do. Let us have no ranting tragedies. Too many characters—Not a tolerable woman's part in the play—Any thing but *that*, my dear Tom. It would be impossible to fill it up—One could not expect any body to take such a part—Nothing but buffoonery from beginning to end. *That* might do, perhaps, but for the low parts[8]—If I *must* give my opinion, I have always thought it the most insipid play in the English language—*I* do not wish to make objections, I shall be happy to be of any use, but I think we could not choose worse."

Fanny looked on and listened, not unamused to observe the self-ishness which, more or less disguised, seemed to govern them all, and wondering how it would end. For her own gratification she could have wished that something might be acted, for she had never seen even half a play, but every thing of higher consequence was against it.

"This will never do," said Tom Bertram at last. "We are wasting time most abominably. Something must be fixed on. No matter what, so that something is chosen. We must not be so nice.[9] A few characters too many must not frighten us. We must *double* them. We must descend a little. If a part is insignificant, the greater our credit in making any thing of it. From this moment *I* make no difficulties. I take any part you choose to give me, so as it be comic. Let it but be comic, I condition for nothing more."

For about the fifth time he then proposed the Heir at Law, doubt-ing[10] only whether to prefer Lord Duberley or Dr. Pangloss for him-self, and very earnestly, but very unsuccessfully, trying to persuade the others that there were some fine tragic parts in the rest of the Dramatis Personæ.[11]

The pause which followed this fruitless effort was ended by the same speaker, who taking up one of the many volumes of plays that lay on the table, and turning it over, suddenly exclaimed, "Lovers' Vows! And why should not Lovers' Vows do for *us* as well as for the Ravenshaws?[12] How came it never to be thought of before? It strikes me as if it would do exactly. What say you all?—Here are two capital tragic parts for Yates and Crawford, and here is the rhyming butler for

8. These would be the characters of low social rank. Such characters almost always played supporting roles in plays of the time, and were usually comical, if not buffoonish.

9. *nice*: fastidious, choosy.

10. *doubting*: wondering.

11. *The Heir at Law* is a broad comedy that does not have "fine tragic parts." Lord Duberly and Dr. Pangloss are leading roles, both highly comical. The first is a crude merchant seeking education; the second, the most celebrated character in the play, is a pedantic and greedy scholar who is hired for the task. Tom wishes for this play particularly because it would allow him to play one of these two figures.

12. *Lovers' Vows* is based on *Das Kind der Liebe* by August F. F. von Kotzebue, which appeared in 1790. An English version by the popular playwright and novelist Elizabeth Inchbald was first performed in London in 1798, and quickly attained great success; it became a popular part of the theatrical repertoire and also appeared in various printed versions. Inchbald, who did not know German and based her version on someone else's literal translation, made substantial changes to the play. This included changing the title, which translates to "love child," for the play centers around a child born out of wedlock. Inchbald, knowing this to be a controversial if not taboo subject in England, substituted a more innocuous title, while also altering other important elements to create a drama more suitable to English taste, as she avows in a preface to the first printed edition. Even so, the drama, while praised by many, provoked condemnation for treating sympathetically a female character who had borne an illegitimate child.

The story begins with this character, Agatha, returning to the town where she had earlier had the child in order to look for him, now a full-grown man who has become a soldier; she is also on the verge of starvation. Her son, Frederick, soon appears, and he and his mother recognize each other and embrace. He determines to find food for her. Meanwhile Agatha's seducer, Baron Wildenhaim, has just returned to his nearby castle after a long absence. He is entertaining Count Cassel, a suitor to his daughter Amelia. The Count, however, is vain and foolish, and Amelia prefers instead Anhalt, her teacher and the family chaplain. She declares her love to him, and Anhalt, after admitting the same passion, fears the Baron will never approve because he is not a nobleman. Meanwhile Frederick accosts the Count and the Baron, ignorant of the latter's identity, and begs them for money for his mother; when the Baron does not give as much as he needs, Frederick pulls out his sword and demands more, which leads to his arrest and imprisonment at the casme[13]—if nobody else wants it—a trifling part, but the sort of thing I should not dislike, and as I said before, I am determined to take anything and do my best. And as for the rest, they may be filled up by any-body. It is only Count Cassel and Anhalt."[14]

The suggestion was generally welcome. Every body was growing weary of indecision, and the first idea with every body was, that nothing had been proposed before so likely to suit them all. Mr. Yates was particularly pleased; he had been sighing and longing to do the Baron at Ecclesford, had grudged every rant of Lord Ravenshaw's, and been forced to re-rant it all in his own room.[15] To storm through Baron Wildenhaim was the height of his theatrical ambition, and with the advantage of knowing half the scenes by heart already, he did now with the greatest alacrity offer his services for the part. To do him justice, however, he did not resolve to appropriate it—for remembering that there was some very good ranting ground in Frederick, he professed an equal willingness for that. Henry Crawford was ready to take either. Whichever Mr. Yates did not choose, would perfectly satisfy him, and a short parley[16] of compliment ensued. Miss Bertram feeling all the interest of an Agatha in the question,[17] took on her to decide it, by observing to Mr. Yates, that this was a point in which height and figure ought to be considered, and that *his* being the tallest, seemed to fit him peculiarly for the Baron.[18] She was acknowledged to be quite right, and the two parts being accepted accordingly, she was certain of the proper Frederick. Three of the characters were now cast, besides Mr. Rushworth, who was always answered for by Maria as willing to do any thing; when Julia, meaning like her sister to be Agatha, began to be scrupulous on Miss Crawford's account.

"This is not behaving well by the absent," said she. "Here are not women enough. Amelia and Agatha may do for Maria and me, but here is nothing for your sister, Mr. Crawford."

Mr. Crawford desired *that* might not be thought of; he was very sure his sister had no wish of acting, but as she might be useful, and that she would not allow herself to be considered in the present case. But this was immediately opposed by Tom Bertram, who asserted the part of Amelia to be in every respect the property of Miss Crawford if she would accept it. "It falls as naturally, as necessarily to her," said

tle. While there he learns the Baron is his father and reveals this to him; the Baron, who has long been stricken with remorse, decides to make amends, finds Agatha in the village, reconciles with her and Frederick, and agrees to marry her. Inspired by the same pure and generous spirit, he also gives his previously withheld permission for his daughter to marry Anhalt.

13. The butler, a comical supporting character, delivers information in the form of his own verses, even after being requested to speak in prose.

14. Tom is thinking only of the male parts in saying that is all. This may indicate his general disinterest in women as well as a self-centered focus on how each drama they are considering suits him personally.

15. Ranting, which could also mean simply speaking in a boisterous or declamatory manner, was considered an essential part of acting then. The vast size of theaters made loud tones and exaggerated gestures more necessary to communicate with the audience, and prevailing theories also stressed the importance of expressing each emotion through emphatic outward behavior. At the same time, some writers criticized actors who went too far in this direction, and praised more naturalistic performances. Henry Fielding's *Tom Jones*, the most popular and renowned of all eighteenth-century novels, contains an episode in which Tom's servant is held up for ridicule because, after disparaging the actor playing Hamlet (identified as David Garrick, the greatest actor of his age and one renowned for his naturalism) on the grounds that he acted just as a man would act in those situations, he praises instead the actor playing the king, since "he speaks all his Words distinctly, half as loud again as the other.—Any Body may see he is an Actor." Hence Yates's ambition to rant would be criticized by many, including Jane Austen, who frequently ridicules the tendency toward melodramatic exaggeration in contemporary fiction.

16. *parley*: dialogue, exchange.

17. Agatha and Frederick have a long and tender scene of reconciliation and explanation, including several embraces, so Maria would naturally hope to play the role opposite Henry Crawford.

18. Since the Baron is Frederick's father, and a figure of authority, his being taller could be seen as appropriate.

he, "as Agatha does to one or other of my sisters. It can be no sacrifice on their side, for it is highly comic."[19]

A short silence followed. Each sister looked anxious; for each felt the best claim to Agatha, and was hoping to have it pressed on her by the rest. Henry Crawford, who meanwhile had taken up the play, and with seeming carelessness was turning over the first act,[20] soon settled the business. "I must entreat Miss *Julia* Bertram," said he, "not to engage in the part of Agatha, or it will be the ruin of all my solemnity. You must not, indeed you must not—(turning to her). I could not stand your countenance dressed up in woe and paleness. The many laughs we have had together would infallibly come across me,[21] and Frederick and his knapsack would be obliged to run away."[22]

Pleasantly, courteously it was spoken; but the manner was lost in the matter to Julia's feelings. She saw a glance at Maria, which confirmed the injury to herself; it was a scheme—a trick; she was slighted, Maria was preferred; the smile of triumph which Maria was trying to suppress shewed how well it was understood, and before Julia could command herself enough to speak, her brother gave his weight against her too, by saying, "Oh! yes, Maria must be Agatha. Maria will be the best Agatha. Though Julia fancies she prefers tragedy, I would not trust her in it. There is nothing of tragedy about her. She has not the look of it. Her features are not tragic features, and she walks too quick, and speaks too quick, and would not keep her countenance. She had better do the old countrywoman; the Cottager's wife;[23] you had, indeed, Julia. Cottager's wife is a very pretty[24] part I assure you. The old lady relieves the high-flown benevolence of her husband with a good deal of spirit.[25] You shall be Cottager's wife."

"Cottager's wife!" cried Mr. Yates. "What are you talking of? The most trivial, paltry, insignificant part; the merest common-place—not a tolerable speech in the whole.[26] Your sister do that! It is an insult to propose it. At Ecclesford the governess was to have done it. We all agreed that it could not be offered to any body else.[27] A little more justice, Mr. Manager, if you please. You do not deserve the office,[28] if you cannot appreciate the talents of your company a little better."[29]

"Why as to *that*, my good friend, till I and my company have really acted there must be some guesswork; but I mean no disparagement

19. Tom exaggerates, probably due to his own preference for comedy, for Amelia has a number of tender and serious scenes. But she also expresses wit and humor, and her scenes are far more lighthearted than those of Agatha, who spends virtually the entire play in a pitiable state of misery and remorse.

20. The play opens with Agatha, and she dominates the first act.

21. *come across me*: cross my path, i.e., occur to me (often unintentionally or by chance).

22. In Act 1, Frederick makes his entrance wearing a soldier's uniform and carrying a knapsack, which was mostly associated with soldiers at the time.

23. After the encounter of Agatha and Frederick, they are befriended and given succor by a cottager, the inhabitant of a cottage and thus a man of humble means, along with his wife.

24. *pretty*: nice, proper.

25. *spirit*: ardor, vigor. The wife differs with her husband in her inclination to speak critically of others despite his admonitions against it.

26. Cottager's wife, while definitely a secondary role, does appear in several scenes and has numerous lines, albeit mostly short ones. Yates's contempt for the role indicates his love of declamation, which more important characters engage in through long speeches explaining their situation and feelings.

27. A governess's lower status makes her more appropriate for a lesser role as a poorer character. At the same time, unlike a servant, who would actually be closer to the rank of cottager's wife, a governess's better social background made her a suitable companion for joining in the amusements of the presiding family in the house.

28. *office*: position, function.

29. Yates begins to reveal his partiality for Julia.

to Julia. We cannot have two Agathas, and we must have one Cottager's wife; and I am sure I set her the example of moderation myself in being satisfied with the old Butler. If the part is trifling she will have more credit in making something of it; and if she is so desperately bent against every thing humorous, let her take Cottager's speeches instead of Cottager's wife's,[30] and so change the parts all through; *he* is solemn and pathetic[31] enough I am sure. It could make no difference in the play; and as for Cottager himself, when he has got his wife's speeches, *I* would undertake him with all my heart."

"With all your partiality for Cottager's wife," said Henry Crawford, "it will be impossible to make any thing of it fit for your sister, and we must not suffer her good nature to be imposed on. We must not *allow* her to accept the part. She must not be left to her own complaisance. Her talents will be wanted in Amelia. Amelia is a character more difficult to be well represented than even Agatha. I consider Amelia as the most difficult character in the whole piece. It requires great powers, great nicety,[32] to give her playfulness and simplicity without extravagance. I have seen good actresses fail in the part. Simplicity, indeed, is beyond the reach of almost every actress by profession. It requires a delicacy of feeling which they have not.[33] It requires a gentlewoman—a Julia Bertram. You *will* undertake it I hope?" turning to her with a look of anxious entreaty, which softened her a little; but while she hesitated what to say, her brother again interposed with Miss Crawford's better claim.

"No, no, Julia must not be Amelia. It is not at all the part for her. She would not like it. She would not do well. She is too tall and robust. Amelia should be a small, light, girlish, skipping figure.[34] It is fit for Miss Crawford and Miss Crawford only. She looks the part, and I am persuaded will do it admirably."

Without attending to this, Henry Crawford continued his supplication. "You must oblige us," said he, "indeed you must. When you have studied the character, I am sure you will feel it suit you. Tragedy may be your choice, but it will certainly appear that comedy chooses *you*. You will be to[35] visit me in prison with a basket of provisions; you will not refuse to visit me in prison? I think I see you coming in with your basket."[36]

30. Cottager and his wife appear together in all their scenes, and have a comparable number of lines, so the only difference is that, as Tom says, Cottager is a less humorous role.

31. *pathetic*: affecting, moving.

32. *nicety*: delicacy, subtlety.

33. "Simplicity" is a term that had assumed mostly positive connotations in the language of the time, and is consistently used that way in Austen's novels. It most commonly occurs in descriptions of a person's character, where it means sincerity and naturalness or lack of affectation and artifice; it is also used in this sense to describe Amelia at one point in the play. The word could also be employed in an aesthetic sense, meaning a suitable plainness and an absence of ornamentation or excessive elaboration. Henry is probably using the term in both senses when asserting the debility of professional actresses—though it is not clear how much he really believes this, since he is obviously searching for whatever argument he can use to mollify Julia. In this respect, as in many over the course of the novel, he is the opposite of moral simplicity, as defined at the time.

34. Nothing is said in the play about Amelia's size, or exact age, but she is described as young, and she acts girlish, especially through her enthusiastic eagerness and her naivete about the ways of the world.

35. *be to*: have to, be required to.

36. Amelia pities Frederick when he is imprisoned in the castle, and upon hearing he is being provided only with bread and water, she fills a basket with better fare, including wine, and brings it to him. They have a short dialogue there in which Frederick learns the Baron is his father.

The influence of his voice was felt. Julia wavered: but was he only trying to soothe and pacify her, and make her overlook the previous affront? She distrusted him. The slight had been most determined. He was, perhaps, but at treacherous play with her. She looked suspiciously at her sister; Maria's countenance was to decide it; if she were vexed and alarmed—but Maria looked all serenity and satisfaction, and Julia well knew that on this ground Maria could not be happy but at her expense. With hasty indignation therefore, and a tremulous voice, she said to him, "You do not seem afraid of not keeping your countenance when I come in with a basket of provisions—though one might have supposed[37]—but it is only as Agatha that I was to be so overpowering!"—She stopped—Henry Crawford looked rather foolish, and as if he did not know what to say. Tom Bertram began again,

"Miss Crawford must be Amelia.—She will be an excellent Amelia."

"Do not be afraid of *my* wanting the character," cried Julia with angry quickness;—"I am *not* to be Agatha, and I am sure I will do nothing else; and as to Amelia, it is of all parts in the world the most disgusting to me. I quite detest her. An odious, little, pert, unnatural, impudent[38] girl.[39] I have always protested against comedy, and this is comedy in its worst form." And so saying, she walked hastily out of the room, leaving awkward feelings to more than one, but exciting small compassion in any except Fanny, who had been a quiet auditor of the whole, and who could not think of her as under the agitations of *jealousy*, without great pity.[40]

A short silence succeeded her leaving them; but her brother soon returned to business and Lovers' Vows, and was eagerly looking over the play, with Mr. Yates's help, to ascertain what scenery would be necessary—while Maria and Henry Crawford conversed together in an under voice,[41] and the declaration with which she began of, "I am sure I would give up the part to Julia most willingly, but that though I shall probably do it very ill, I feel persuaded *she* would do it worse," was doubtless receiving all the compliments it called for.

When this had lasted some time, the division of the party was completed by Tom Bertram and Mr. Yates walking off together to consult farther in the room now beginning to be called *the Theatre*, and Miss Bertram's resolving to go down to the Parsonage herself with the offer of Amelia to Miss Crawford; and Fanny remained alone.[42]

37. Since Frederick is in acute distress during the scene with Amelia, the danger Henry earlier alluded to of losing his solemnity while acting opposite Julia could also apply here. In fact, as Julia seems to be on the verge of stating, the danger might be greater there, for while his character is serious throughout their dialogue, she, unlike Agatha in all her scenes, speaks in a way that might arouse inappropriate laughter in the actor playing Frederick, most notably when she says, regarding Frederick's drawing his sword against the Baron, "if you had murdered any one, you had better have killed the Count; nobody would have missed him."

38. *impudent*: shameless.

39. Amelia is bold and uninhibited in her conversation, especially when it comes to matters of love (see note 43 below), and makes a number of cheeky or caustic remarks, as in the quotation in note 37 above. This was often condemned at the time, especially in the case of women, who were urged to be modest and discreet and diffident and believed to be naturally inclined toward those virtues.

40. Fanny would be especially inclined to sympathize due to her own jealousy of Mary Crawford. This may be why the author puts the word in italics.

41. *under voice*: low or suppressed voice.

42. It would be appropriate for Maria, as another woman, to visit Mary Crawford and offer the part to her. At the same time, going to the parsonage now means she can walk with Henry Crawford, who is returning there himself (since he neither walks off with Tom and Mr. Yates nor remains with Fanny). She also knows that securing Mary's services would both please Henry, who is eager for the play, and ensure that Julia will not play a role that would involve acting opposite Henry.

The first use she made of her solitude was to take up the volume which had been left on the table, and begin to acquaint herself with the play of which she had heard so much. Her curiosity was all awake, and she ran through it with an eagerness which was suspended only by intervals of astonishment, that it could be chosen in the present instance—that it could be proposed and accepted in a private Theatre! Agatha and Amelia appeared to her in their different ways so totally improper for home representation—the situation of one, and the language of the other, so unfit to be expressed by any woman of modesty,[43] that she could hardly suppose her cousins could be aware of what they were engaging in; and longed to have them roused as soon as possible by the remonstrance which Edmund would certainly make.

43. Agatha has had a child out of wedlock. Amelia's impropriety may be not only her outspokenness and frequent sauciness, but especially her behavior toward her beloved, Anhalt. Instead of waiting for him to initiate any talk of love, as was considered absolutely incumbent on women at the time, she signals her love to him first, and then coaxes and persuades him into a similar declaration. For this reason, her character was, according to the English adapter of the play, Elizabeth Inchbald, "a very particular object of my solicitude and alteration." Since "the forward and unequivocal manner, in which she announces her affection, in the original, would have been revolting to an English audience," she made Amelia proceed by "whimsical insinuations, rather than by coarse abruptness." Even so, Mary Crawford, who is far bolder and less morally strict than Fanny, will later balk at some of the lines she is supposed to utter as Amelia (p. 316).

An ordinary soldier, such as Frederick is in the play.

[From William Alexander, *Picturesque Representations of the Dress and Manners of the English* (London, 1813), Plate 45]

Chapter Fifteen

Miss Crawford accepted the part very readily, and soon after Miss Bertram's return from the Parsonage, Mr. Rushworth arrived, and another character was consequently cast. He had the offer of Count Cassel and Anhalt, and at first did not know which to choose, and wanted Miss Bertram to direct him, but upon being made to understand the different style of the characters, and which was which, and recollecting that he had once seen the play in London, and had thought Anhalt a very stupid fellow,[1] he soon decided for the Count. Miss Bertram approved the decision, for the less he had to learn the better;[2] and though she could not sympathize in his wish that the Count and Agatha might be to act together, nor wait very patiently while he was slowly turning over the leaves with the hope of still discovering such a scene, she very kindly took his part in hand,[3] and curtailed every speech that admitted being shortened;— besides pointing out the necessity of his being very much dressed,[4] and choosing his colours. Mr. Rushworth liked the idea of his finery very well, though affecting to despise it,[5] and was too much engaged with what his own appearance would be, to think of the others, or draw any of those conclusions, or feel any of that displeasure, which Maria had been half prepared for.[6]

Thus much was settled before Edmund, who had been out all the morning, knew any thing of the matter; but when he entered the drawing-room before dinner, the buz of discussion was high between Tom, Maria, and Mr. Yates; and Mr. Rushworth stepped forward with great alacrity to tell him the agreeable news.

"We have got a play," said he.—"It is to be Lovers' Vows; and I am to be Count Cassel, and am to come in first with a blue dress,[7] and a pink satin cloak, and afterwards am to have another fine fancy suit by way of a shooting dress.[8]—I do not know how I shall like it."

Fanny's eyes followed Edmund, and her heart beat for him as

1. Anhalt is certainly not unintelligent, but "stupid" frequently meant dull then, and Mr. Rushworth may have found him that, since he is thoughtful and unassuming, in contrast to the confident and flashy Count. His negative memory of Anhalt may also have been shaped by Maria's current description of the characters, for she prefers that he not choose Anhalt.

2. Count Cassel is a smaller role than Anhalt.

3. *in hand*: under her control.

4. *very much dressed*: highly adorned.

5. Maria presumably knows of Mr. Rushworth's love of fine dressing.

6. His displeasure, if he was at all perceptive, would be at Maria and Henry Crawford choosing to play roles that lead to a very affectionate scene between them.

7. *dress*: costume. The term then referred to everything one was wearing, not one specific garment, and it is frequently used in relation to men in Austen's novels. What we call a dress was then called a gown.

8. There is a scene in which Count Cassel and the Baron are out shooting, i.e., hunting, together.

Men in shooting dress.

[From *The Repository of arts, literature, fashions, manufactures, &c*, Vol. IV (1810), p. 93]

she heard this speech, and saw his look, and felt what his sensations must be.

"Lovers' Vows!"—in a tone of the greatest amazement, was his only reply to Mr. Rushworth; and he turned towards his brother and sisters as if hardly doubting a contradiction.

"Yes," cried Mr. Yates.—"After all our debatings and difficulties, we find there is nothing that will suit us altogether so well, nothing so unexceptionable, as Lovers' Vows. The wonder is that it should not have been thought of before. My stupidity was abominable, for here we have all the advantage of what I saw at Ecclesford; and it is so useful to have any thing of a model!—We have cast almost every part."

"But what do you do for women?" said Edmund gravely, and looking at Maria.

Maria blushed in spite of herself as she answered, "I take the part which Lady Ravenshaw was to have done, and (with a bolder eye) Miss Crawford is to be Amelia."[9]

"I should not have thought it the sort of play to be so easily filled up, with *us*," replied Edmund, turning away to the fire where sat his mother, aunt, and Fanny, and seating himself with a look of great vexation.

Mr. Rushworth followed him to say, "I come in three times, and have two and forty speeches.[10] That's something, is not it?—But I do not much like the idea of being so fine.[11]—I shall hardly know myself in a blue dress, and a pink satin cloak."

Edmund could not answer him.—In a few minutes Mr. Bertram was called out of the room to satisfy some doubts of the carpenter, and being accompanied by Mr. Yates, and followed soon afterwards by Mr. Rushworth, Edmund almost immediately took the opportunity of saying, "I cannot before Mr. Yates speak what I feel as to this play, without reflecting on his friends at Ecclesford—but I must now, my dear Maria, tell *you*, that I think it exceedingly unfit for private representation, and that I hope you will give it up.—I cannot but suppose you *will* when you have read it carefully over.—Read only the first Act aloud, to either your mother or aunt, and see how you can approve it.—It will not be necessary to send you to your *father's* judgment, I am convinced."

"We see things very differently," cried Maria—"I am perfectly

9.   Maria's blush indicates her sense of the possible impropriety of her choice. Mentioning Lady Ravenshaw is likely a means of making it seem more proper, while mentioning Mary Crawford would help deflect Edmund's censure due to his partiality toward Mary.

10. Count Cassel does have forty-two lines, or speeches; Mr. Rushworth has counted precisely. What he has not said is that almost all Count Cassel's lines are short—and Maria has cut those that are not.

11. *fine*: ornately dressed.

A lord, or peer, in fancy dress.

[From William Pyne, *The Costume of Great Britain* (London, 1804; 1989 reprint), Plate XXXVII]

acquainted with the play, I assure you—and with a very few omissions, and so forth, which will be made, of course, I can see nothing objectionable in it; and *I* am not the *only* young woman you find, who thinks it very fit for private representation."

"I am sorry for it," was his answer—"But in this matter it is *you* who are to lead. *You* must set the example.—If others have blundered, it is your place to put them right, and shew them what true delicacy[12] is.—In all points of decorum, *your* conduct must be law to the rest of the party."

This picture of her consequence had some effect, for no one loved better to lead than Maria;—and with far more good humour she answered, "I am much obliged to you, Edmund;—you mean very well, I am sure—but I still think you see things too strongly; and I really cannot undertake to harangue all the rest upon a subject of this kind.—*There* would be the greatest indecorum I think."

"Do you imagine that I could have such an idea in my head? No—let your conduct be the only harangue.—Say that, on examining the part, you feel yourself unequal to it, that you find it requiring more exertion and confidence than you can be supposed to have.—Say this with firmness, and it will be quite enough.—All who can distinguish, will understand your motive.—The play will be given up, and your delicacy honoured as it ought."

"Do not act any thing improper, my dear," said Lady Bertram. "Sir Thomas would not like it.—Fanny, ring the bell;[13] I must have my dinner.—To be sure Julia is dressed by this time."[14]

"I am convinced, madam," said Edmund, preventing Fanny, "that Sir Thomas would not like it."

"There, my dear, do you hear what Edmund says?"

"If I were to decline the part," said Maria with renewed zeal, "Julia would certainly take it."

"What!"—cried Edmund, "if she knew your reasons!"

"Oh! she might think the difference between us—the difference in our situations—that *she* need not be so scrupulous as *I* might feel necessary. I am sure she would argue so. No, you must excuse me, I cannot retract my consent. It is too far settled; every body would be so disappointed. Tom would be quite angry; and if we are so very nice, we shall never act any thing."

12. *delicacy*: refined sense of what is proper and appropriate.

13. The bell is to call for a servant. Wealthy houses then did not use hand bells but ropes, or bell-pulls, hanging along the wall that were linked by wires to bells in the servants' quarters; there was a different bell for each room, allowing the servants to know where they were wanted.

14. Ladies and gentlemen changed into evening clothes for dinner; Lady Bertram is calling for her lady's maid to help her change. Since Julia is not participating in the play preparations, she has been able to change already.

A woman in evening dress.

[From *The Repository of arts, literature, fashions, manufactures, &c*, Vol. VIII (1812), p. 174]

"I was just going to say the very same thing," said Mrs. Norris. "If every play is to be objected to, you will act nothing—and the preparations will be all so much money thrown away—and I am sure *that* would be a discredit to us all. I do not know the play; but, as Maria says, if there is any thing a little too warm (and it is so with most of them) it can be easily left out.[15]—We must not be over precise[16] Edmund. As Mr. Rushworth is to act too, there can be no harm.—I only wish Tom had known his own mind when the carpenters began, for there was the loss of half a day's work about those side-doors.[17]— The curtain will be a good job, however. The maids do their work very well, and I think we shall be able to send back some dozens of the rings.—There is no occasion to put them so very close together. I *am* of some use I hope in preventing waste and making the most of things. There should always be one steady head to superintend so many young ones. I forgot to tell Tom of something that happened to me this very day.—I had been looking about me in the poultry yard, and was just coming out, when who should I see but Dick Jackson making up[18] to the servants' hall door with two bits of deal board in his hand,[19] bringing them to father, you may be sure; mother had chanced to send him of a message to father, and then father had bid him bring up them two bits of board, for he could not no how do without them.[20] I knew what all this meant, for the servants' dinner bell was ringing at the very moment over our heads,[21] and as I hate such encroaching people, (the Jacksons are very encroaching, I have always said so,—just the sort of people to get all they can), I said to the boy directly—(a great lubberly fellow of ten years old you know, who ought to be ashamed of himself), *I'll* take the boards to your father, Dick; so get you home again as fast as you can.[22]—The boy looked very silly and turned away without offering a word, for I believe I might speak pretty sharp; and I dare say it will cure him of coming marauding about the house for one while,—I hate such greediness—so good as your father is to the family, employing the man all the year round!"[23]

Nobody was at the trouble of an answer; the others soon returned, and Edmund found that to have endeavoured to set them right must be his only satisfaction.

15. "Warm" means racy. Many plays were criticized for having inappropriate content.

16. *precise*: particular, punctilious.

17. Lady Bertram has just demonstrated her inadequacy as a substitute for Sir Thomas in guiding the family by, in response to Edmund, expressing concern only briefly and then changing immediately to discussing dinner. Mrs. Norris now shows her unsuitability by quickly seguing from the important moral issues raised by Edmund to trivial questions of how the work is proceeding and whether small amounts of money are being saved.

18. *making up*: advancing.

19. Deal board is board of fir or pine. The servants' hall door is the one servants use to enter the area where they work. Dick Jackson is the son of Christopher Jackson, the estate carpenter.

20. She is imitating lower-class speech, through the use of "father" and "mother" with no "my" and through several ungrammatical constructions: "chanced to send him of," "them two bits," and "could not no how." Class differences in speech were very marked then, due to the vast gulf in education—there were no state schools and children of humble background received at most a few years of limited schooling—and to the limited interaction between classes. Jane Austen records these differences when she has servants speak, and all the characters in her novels would be aware of them. But Mrs. Norris is the only one who openly ridicules lower-class speech. The norm among genteel people was to be consistently polite toward social inferiors, while remaining distant.

21. In other words, the boy, hearing dinner announced in the servants' hall, wishes to partake; he would normally eat dinner with his family.

22. The father is not at home but in the house, working on the theatrical project. In carrying the boards to him, Mrs. Norris is actually performing a task regarded as ungenteel. Moreover, most people of her social level would hardly worry about the boy's behavior: a certain amount of petty pilfering by servants was commonplace and was either ignored or accepted as unavoidable. Mrs. Norris's going to such lengths to prevent a young boy from procuring a little food, like her mockery of his speech, indicates her exceptional pettiness and meanness.

23. He presumably works solely for the Bertrams, and it is possible Sir Thomas at times needs to find work for him to keep him continually employed. But this would not be simply charity, for preventing him from ever needing to seek

Dinner passed heavily.[24] Mrs. Norris related again her triumph over Dick Jackson, but neither play nor preparation were otherwise much talked of, for Edmund's disapprobation was felt even by his brother, though he would not have owned it. Maria, wanting Henry Crawford's animating support, thought the subject better avoided.[25] Mr. Yates, who was trying to make himself agreeable to Julia, found her gloom less impenetrable on any topic than that of his regret at her secession from their company, and Mr. Rushworth having only his own part, and his own dress in his head, had soon talked away all that could be said of either.

But the concerns of the theatre were suspended only for an hour or two; there was still a great deal to be settled; and the spirits of evening giving fresh courage, Tom, Maria, and Mr. Yates, soon after their being reassembled in the drawing-room,[26] seated themselves in committee at a separate table, with the play open before them, and were just getting deep in the subject when a most welcome inter-ruption was given by the entrance of Mr. and Miss Crawford, who, late and dark and dirty[27] as it was, could not help coming, and were received with the most grateful joy.

"Well, how do you go on?" and "What have you settled?" and "Oh! we can do nothing without you," followed the first salutations; and Henry Crawford was soon seated with the other three at the table, while his sister made her way to Lady Bertram, and with pleasant attention was complimenting *her*. "I must really congratulate your ladyship," said she, "on the play being chosen; for though you have borne it with exemplary patience, I am sure you must be sick of all our noise and difficulties. The actors may be glad, but the by-standers must be infinitely more thankful for a decision; and I do sincerely give you joy, madam, as well as Mrs. Norris, and every body else who is in the same predicament," glancing half fearfully, half slily, beyond Fanny to Edmund.

She was very civilly answered by Lady Bertram, but Edmund said nothing. His being only a by-stander was not disclaimed. After con-tinuing in chat with the party round the fire a few minutes, Miss Crawford returned to the party round the table; and standing by them, seemed to interest herself in their arrangements till, as if struck by a sudden recollection, she exclaimed, "My good friends, you are

employment elsewhere means he is always available if an important task at Mansfield Park arises.

24. *heavily*: gloomily, listlessly.

25. Henry, like his sister, has gone back to the parsonage for dinner. Mr. Yates and Mr. Rushworth, however, are there because they are staying with the Bertrams.

26. At the end of dinner, the ladies left for the drawing room while the men stayed and talked among themselves, before eventually rejoining the ladies.

27. *dirty*: muddy.

A grand drawing room of the period.

[From John Swarbrick, *Robert Adam and his Brothers* (New York, 1915), p. 99]

most composedly at work upon these cottages and ale-houses, inside and out[28]—but pray let me know my fate in the meanwhile. Who is to be Anhalt? What gentleman among you am I to have the pleasure of making love to?"[29]

For a moment no one spoke; and then many spoke together to tell the same melancholy truth—that they had not yet got any Anhalt. "Mr. Rushworth was to be Count Cassel, but no one had yet undertaken Anhalt."

"I had my choice of the parts," said Mr. Rushworth; "but I thought I should like the Count best—though I do not much relish the finery I am to have."

"You chose very wisely, I am sure," replied Miss Crawford, with a brightened look. "Anhalt is a heavy part."

"*The Count* has two and forty speeches," returned Mr. Rushworth, "which is no trifle."

"I am not at all surprised," said Miss Crawford, after a short pause, "at this want of an Anhalt. Amelia deserves no better. Such a forward[30] young lady may well frighten the men."

"I should be but too happy in taking the part if it were possible," cried Tom, "but unluckily the Butler and Anhalt are in together. I will not entirely give it up, however—I will try what can be done—I will look it over again."

"Your *brother* should take the part," said Mr. Yates, in a low voice. "Do not you think he would?"

"*I* shall not ask him," replied Tom, in a cold, determined manner.

Miss Crawford talked of something else, and soon afterwards rejoined the party at the fire. "They do not want me at all," said she, seating herself. "I only puzzle[31] them, and oblige them to make civil speeches. Mr. Edmund Bertram, as you do not act yourself, you will be a disinterested adviser; and, therefore, I apply to *you*. What shall we do for an Anhalt? Is it practicable for any of the others to double it? What is your advice?"

"My advice," said he, calmly, "is that you change the play."

"*I* should have no objection," she replied; "for though I should not particularly dislike the part of Amelia if well supported—that is, if every thing went well—I shall be sorry to be an inconvenience—

28. Act 1 takes place on a road, next to an inn (i.e., alehouse) and a cottage. The second act begins inside the cottage. They are now presumably working on the scenery for those two scenes.

29. *making love*: professing love. The term, often used, did not imply sexual relations. Normally, however, it was the man who made love; Miss Crawford's asking the question may result from her finding it so unusual to be in that position herself, at least as a character in a play.

30. *forward*: bold, presumptuous.

31. *puzzle*: embarrass, bewilder, leave at a loss.

Contemporary tea tables (see the following page).

[From Esther Singleton, *The Furniture of our Forefathers* (New York, 1916), p. 232]

but as they do not choose to hear your advice at *that table*—(looking round)—it certainly will not be taken."

Edmund said no more.

"If *any* part could tempt *you* to act, I suppose it would be Anhalt," observed the lady, archly, after a short pause—"for he is a clergyman you know."

"*That* circumstance would by no means tempt me," he replied, "for I should be sorry to make the character ridiculous by bad acting. It must be very difficult to keep Anhalt from appearing a formal, solemn lecturer;[32] and the man who chooses the profession itself, is, perhaps, one of the last who would wish to represent it on the stage."

Miss Crawford was silenced; and with some feelings of resentment and mortification, moved her chair considerably nearer the tea-table,[33] and gave all her attention to Mrs. Norris, who was presiding there.

"Fanny," cried Tom Bertram, from the other table, where the conference was eagerly carrying on, and the conversation incessant, "we want your services."

Fanny was up in a moment, expecting some errand, for the habit of employing her in that way was not yet overcome, in spite of all that Edmund could do.

"Oh! we do not want to disturb you from your seat. We do not want your *present* services. We shall only want you in our play. You must be Cottager's wife."

"Me!" cried Fanny, sitting down again with a most frightened look. "Indeed you must excuse me. I could not act any thing if you were to give me the world. No, indeed, I cannot act."

"Indeed but you must, for we cannot excuse you. It need not frighten you; it is a nothing of a part, a mere nothing, not above half a dozen speeches altogether, and it will not much signify if nobody hears a word you say, so you may be as creepmouse[34] as you like, but we must have you to look at."

"If you are afraid of half a dozen speeches," cried Mr. Rushworth, "what would you do with such a part as mine? I have forty-two to learn."

"It is not that I am afraid of learning by heart," said Fanny, shocked

32. Anhalt offers moral lessons to other characters similar to those found in a sermon or educational book.

33. A "tea-table" could mean a special table, normally small and round, built for serving tea, or any table where tea (which in this case includes food and probably coffee as well) is served.

34. *creepmouse*: shy, furtive; tending to creep like a mouse.

A poor woman (a match girl).

[From William Alexander, *Picturesque Representations of the Dress and Manners of the English* (London, 1813), Plate 19]

to find herself at that moment the only speaker in the room, and to feel that almost every eye was upon her; "but I really cannot act."

"Yes, yes, you can act well enough for *us*. Learn your part, and we will teach you all the rest. You have only two scenes, and as I shall be Cottager, I'll put you in and push you about; and you will do it very well I'll answer for it."

"No, indeed, Mr. Bertram,[35] you must excuse me. You cannot have an idea. It would be absolutely impossible for me. If I were to undertake it, I should only disappoint you."

"Phoo! Phoo! Do not be so shamefaced. You'll do it very well. Every allowance will be made for you. We do not expect perfection. You must get a brown gown, and a white apron, and a mob cap,[36] and we must make you a few wrinkles, and a little of the crowsfoot at the corner of your eyes, and you will be a very proper, little old woman."

"You must excuse me, indeed you must excuse me," cried Fanny,[37] growing more and more red from excessive agitation, and looking distressfully at Edmund, who was kindly observing her, but unwilling to exasperate his brother by interference, gave her only an encouraging smile. Her entreaty had no effect on Tom; he only said again what he had said before; and it was not merely Tom, for the requisition was now backed by Maria and Mr. Crawford, and Mr. Yates, with an urgency which differed from his, but in being more gentle or more ceremonious, and which altogether was quite overpowering to Fanny; and before she could breathe after it, Mrs. Norris completed the whole, by thus addressing her in a whisper at once angry and audible: "What a piece of work here is about nothing,—I am quite ashamed of you, Fanny, to make such a difficulty of obliging your cousins in a trifle of this sort,—So kind as they are to you!—Take the part with a good grace, and let us hear no more of the matter, I entreat."

"Do not urge her, madam," said Edmund. "It is not fair to urge her in this manner.—You see she does not like to act.—Let her choose for herself as well as the rest of us.—Her judgment may be quite as safely trusted.—Do not urge her any more."

"I am not going to urge her,"—replied Mrs. Norris sharply, "but I shall think her a very obstinate, ungrateful girl, if she does not do what her aunt and cousins wish her—very ungrateful indeed, considering who and what she is."[38]

35. Fanny calls him "Mr. Bertram"; she never addresses him as Tom. Like her consistently calling Edmund "cousin" rather than using his first name, this marks her deference and sense of her lower status.

36. A mobcap is a soft cloth hat or bonnet normally worn by women when inside, or underneath a regular hat when going outside. It would often be worn by an older woman, since it was simple and practical and protected the hair (almost all women wore caps for this purpose), but did not look as fashionable and attractive as a regular hat. A brown gown and an apron would be characteristic of a poorer woman: wealthy women, whose daily routines did not involve activities that could soil their clothes, tended to wear white or brightly colored gowns, and they would not wear aprons. For a picture of a poor woman in a dark gown and an apron, see the previous page.

37. Fanny's continued refusal, despite the pressure being exerted on her, shows that beneath her timid exterior she has an inner strength of character, at least when she believes that she is morally right.

38. Mrs. Norris expresses an important truth about Fanny's dependent status, though nobody else would be cruel enough to mention it openly, especially since Fanny herself never acts in a way to make it seem as if she needs reminding.

A woman in a mobcap.

[From Elisabeth McClellan, *Historic Dress in America, 1800–1870* (Philadelphia, 1910), p. 59]

Edmund was too angry to speak; but Miss Crawford looking for a moment with astonished eyes at Mrs. Norris,[39] and then at Fanny, whose tears were beginning to show themselves, immediately said with some keenness, "I do not like my situation;[40] this *place* is too hot for me"—and moved away her chair to the opposite side of the table close to Fanny,[41] saying to her in a kind low whisper as she placed herself, "Never mind, my dear Miss Price—this is a cross evening,—every body is cross and teasing[42]—but do not let us mind them;" and with pointed attention continued to talk to her and endeavour to raise her spirits, in spite of being out of spirits herself.—By a look at her brother, she prevented any farther entreaty from the theatrical board, and the really good feelings by which she was almost purely governed, were rapidly restoring her to all the little she had lost in Edmund's favour.

Fanny did not love Miss Crawford; but she felt very much obliged to her for her present kindness; and when from taking notice of her work and wishing *she* could work as well, and begging for the pattern,[43] and supposing Fanny was now preparing for her *appearance* as of course she would come out when her cousin was married,[44] Miss Crawford proceeded to inquire if she had heard lately from her brother at sea, and said that she had quite a curiosity to see him, and imagined him a very fine young man, and advised Fanny to get his picture drawn before he went to sea again[45]—She could not help admitting it to be very agreeable flattery,[46] or help listening, and answering with more animation than she had intended.

The consultation upon the play still went on, and Miss Crawford's attention was first called from Fanny by Tom Bertram's telling her, with infinite regret, that he found it absolutely impossible for him to undertake the part of Anhalt in addition to the Butler;—he had been most anxiously trying to make it out to be feasible,—but it would not do,—he must give it up.—"But there will not be the smallest difficulty in filling it," he added.—"We have but to speak the word; we may pick and choose.—I could name at this moment at least six young men within six miles of us,[47] who are wild[48] to be admitted into our company, and there are one or two that would not disgrace us.—I should not be afraid to trust either of the Olivers or Charles Maddox.—Tom Oliver is a very clever fellow, and Charles Maddox

39. Her astonishment does not derive from any special sympathy for Fanny. Until now she has mostly ignored her except when the two of them have both been conversing with Edmund, and then, while always courteous to Fanny, she has never shown any particular interest in her. Yet that same sense of courtesy, which she displays consistently and which reflects her background in fashionable society, makes her shocked at Mrs. Norris's words. In the world she has lived in, certain types of immoral behavior were often tolerated, but open rudeness was considered reprehensible and was therefore rare.

40. *situation*: position, location.

41. Because the sole source of heat is the fireplace, and it needs to burn fiercely to heat an entire room, especially a large room such as this one, sitting near the fire can be excessively hot. Thus people sometimes move away from it to escape the heat or closer to escape the chill. This fact of daily life gives Mary an excuse to move close enough to Fanny to avoid overtly chastising Mrs. Norris, which would be against Mary's code of politeness.

42. *teasing*: bothersome, irritating.

43. The pattern is part of Fanny's needlework, which Mary is admiring.

44. Coming out will allow her to mingle freely with eligible young men (see p. 94 for an earlier discussion of Fanny's status in this regard, which is also the only time previously that Mary showed much interest in Fanny). A family normally preferred to avoid having too many girls out at once, in order to keep the younger from competing with the elder and thereby imperiling her marital chances. Once Maria is married, it would make sense for Fanny to come out. Exactly when this occurs is never made clear, but she is able later to dance with eligible young men at a ball, and Mary's supposition is a reasonable one.

45. A small drawing or painting, often a miniature painting, of a beloved person was something people often kept with them during separations.

46. A little earlier Mary showed a similar skill in flattery when she complimented Lady Bertram on the patience she supposedly showed in withstanding the bustle of the play, even though Mary must have known that Lady Bertram pays little attention to almost anything happening among others.

47. Six miles would probably take a little more than an hour in a carriage on country roads, and a little less for a young man on horseback. It is close enough for someone to travel each day for something important, but not to allow the frequent mixing that the families at Mansfield Park and the parsonage have enjoyed.

48. *wild*: passionately eager or excited.

is as gentlemanlike a man as you will see any where, so I will take my horse early to-morrow morning, and ride over to Stoke,[49] and settle with one of them."

While he spoke, Maria was looking apprehensively round at Edmund in full expectation that he must oppose such an enlargement of the plan as this—so contrary to all their first protestations; but Edmund said nothing.—After a moment's thought, Miss Crawford calmly replied, "As far as I am concerned, I can have no objection to any thing that you all think eligible. Have I ever seen either of the gentlemen?—Yes, Mr. Charles Maddox dined at my sister's one day, did not he Henry?—A quiet-looking young man. I remember him. Let *him* be applied to, if you please, for it will be less unpleasant to me than to have a perfect stranger."

Charles Maddox was to be the man.—Tom repeated his resolution of going to him early on the morrow; and though Julia, who had scarcely opened her lips before, observed in a sarcastic manner, and with a glance, first at Maria, and then at Edmund, that "the Mansfield Theatricals would enliven the whole neighbourhood exceedingly"[50]—Edmund still held his peace, and shewed his feelings only by a determined gravity.

"I am not very sanguine as to our play"—said Miss Crawford in an under voice, to Fanny, after some consideration; "and I can tell Mr. Maddox, that I shall shorten some of *his* speeches, and a great many of *my own*, before we rehearse together.—It will be very disagreeable, and by no means what I expected."[51]

49. Stoke is a common place name in England; it is unlikely Jane Austen had a specific town or village in mind. The most famous Stoke, Stoke on Trent in Staffordshire, is too far from Northampton to be meant here.

50. Julia hopes that the suggestion that the play will become a formal event involving the whole neighborhood will provoke Edmund into protesting again, and also make Maria feel less comfortable with her participation.

51. Their scene together involves mutual declarations of affection, especially on her side, and she assumes that will make them both uncomfortable.

Two miniatures of the general period (the first is from the late eighteenth century).

[From Alice Morse Earle, *Two Centuries of Costume in America* (New York, 1903), pp. 483 and 736]

Chapter Sixteen

*I*t was not in Miss Crawford's power to talk Fanny into any real forgetfulness of what had passed.—When the evening was over, she went to bed full of it, her nerves still agitated by the shock of such an attack from her cousin Tom, so public and so persevered in, and her spirits sinking under her aunt's unkind reflection and reproach. To be called into notice in such a manner, to hear that it was but the prelude to something so infinitely worse, to be told that she must do what was so impossible as to act; and then to have the charge of obstinacy and ingratitude follow it, enforced[1] with such a hint at the dependence of her situation, had been too distressing at the time, to make the remembrance when she was alone much less so,—especially with the superadded dread of what the morrow might produce in continuation of the subject. Miss Crawford had protected her only for the time; and if she were applied to again among themselves with all the authoritative urgency that Tom and Maria were capable of; and Edmund perhaps away—what should she do? She fell asleep before she could answer the question, and found it quite as puzzling when she awoke the next morning. The little white attic, which had continued her sleeping room ever since her first entering the family, proving incompetent to suggest any reply, she had recourse, as soon as she was dressed, to another apartment,[2] more spacious and more meet[3] for walking about in, and thinking, and of which she had now for some time been almost equally mistress. It had been their school-room;[4] so called till the Miss Bertrams would not allow it to be called so any longer, and inhabited as such to a later period.[5] There Miss Lee had lived, and there they had read and written, and talked and laughed, till within the last three years, when she had quitted them.[6]—The room had then become useless, and for some time was quite deserted, except by Fanny, when she visited her plants, or wanted one of the books, which she was still glad to keep there, from the deficiency of space and accommodation[7] in her

1. *enforced*: emphasized, reinforced.

2. *apartment*: room.

3. *meet*: suitable, well-adapted.

4. Wealthy families who educated their children at home often had a special schoolroom. Jane Austen could have drawn on memories of visits to her brother's house of Godmersham Park; she never mentions a schoolroom in her letters from there, but it was certainly large enough to have one and her brother had many children. She does mention frequently playing with her nieces and nephews there and helping them with their lessons.

5. On p. 284, the author states that the room's name was changed to "the East room" when Maria turned sixteen and thus finished her schooling; she may have thought there should no longer be a room in the house called a schoolroom. It is also possible that Julia, a year younger and therefore probably still using the schoolroom, did not like a term that emphasized her inferiority to her sister.

6. Since Fanny is two years younger than Julia, for a period of that approximate length she alone would have received lessons from Miss Lee and shared the room with her.

7. *accommodation*: comfort.

A mantelpiece of the period; people often put decorative items on top or above.

[From *The Repository of arts, literature, fashions, manufactures, &c*, Series Two, Vol. I (1816), p. 542]

little chamber above;—but gradually, as her value for the comforts of it increased, she had added to her possessions, and spent more of her time there; and having nothing to oppose her, had so naturally and so artlessly worked herself into it, that it was now generally admitted to be her's. The East room as it had been called, ever since Maria Bertram was sixteen, was now considered Fanny's, almost as decidedly as the white attic;—the smallness of the one making the use of the other so evidently reasonable, that the Miss Bertrams, with every superiority in their own apartments, which their own sense of superiority could demand, were entirely approving it;—and Mrs. Norris having stipulated for there never being a fire in it on Fanny's account, was tolerably resigned to her having the use of what nobody else wanted, though the terms in which she sometimes spoke of the indulgence, seemed to imply that it was the best room in the house.

The aspect[8] was so favourable, that even without a fire it was habitable in many an early spring, and late autumn morning, to such a willing mind as Fanny's, and while there was a gleam of sunshine, she hoped not to be driven from it entirely, even when winter came. The comfort of it in her hours of leisure was extreme. She could go there after any thing unpleasant below, and find immediate consolation in some pursuit, or some train of thought at hand.—Her plants, her books[9]—of which she had been a collector, from the first hour of her commanding a shilling[10]—her writing desk,[11] and her works of charity and ingenuity,[12] were all within her reach;—or if indisposed for employment, if nothing but musing would do, she could scarcely see an object in that room which had not an interesting remembrance connected with it.—Every thing was a friend, or bore her thoughts to a friend; and though there had been sometimes much of suffering to her—though her motives had been often misunderstood, her feelings disregarded, and her comprehension undervalued; though she had known the pains of tyranny, of ridicule, and neglect, yet almost every recurrence of either had led to something consolatory; her aunt Bertram had spoken for her, or Miss Lee had been encouraging, or what was yet more frequent or more dear—Edmund had been her champion and her friend;—he had supported her cause, or explained her meaning, he had told her not to cry, or had given her some proof of affection which made her tears delightful—and

8. *aspect*: position facing the outside.

9. Fanny's geraniums are mentioned on p. 286, and she evinces an interest in nature and in plants particularly (see especially p. 386). Other women in Austen's novels exhibit this interest, which was encouraged by the emergence of botany as a popular study for young ladies in the eighteenth century and the appearance of writings designed to teach the subject to them. These books could include practical advice for cultivating plants, and Fanny, by keeping her geraniums inside in the winter while also giving them air (see the next page), is following advice delivered in contemporary books on botany and gardening.

10. This suggests she received a regular allowance from Sir Thomas. Books were not cheap then: Jane Austen's first three novels, *Sense and Sensibility*, *Pride and Prejudice*, and *Mansfield Park*, each cost eighteen shillings; her next, *Emma*, cost twenty-one; and the initial edition of *Persuasion* and *Northanger Abbey*, published together, cost twenty-four. Each of these sums exceeds the weekly income of most people in England then. Thus Fanny would have needed to save carefully. Her doing so, even though she has access to Sir Thomas's undoubtedly large library (p. 54), indicates her dedication to reading.

11. A writing desk could be either a stand-alone piece of furniture, similar to a desk of today, or a small wooden item that would be placed on a desk or table. This device would contain paper and writing materials, such as pen and ink in slots, as well as a flap that, when open, provides a surface for writing. The description of the desk being within reach, as well as the limited furnishings of Fanny's room, signals that it is this smaller type. Jane Austen owned such a desk, which is currently on display at the British Library in London.

12. Works of ingenuity are those involving skill, and in Fanny's case this probably means needlework. They may be the same as her works of charity: she is sewing items to donate to the poor. Charity was a fundamental duty of those who were genteel, especially women. Fanny, though a poor relative to the Bertrams, is still genteel, and living in a grand house, and her strict moral standards and natural benevolence would make her feel especially obliged to be charitable. Thus she has chosen to employ her needle, which she has already been described as skillful with, to supply what her purse cannot. In *Persuasion* a woman who had been wealthy, and is now living under very straitened circumstance, uses her knitting skills to assist one or two poor families.

the whole was now so blended together, so harmonized by distance, that every former affliction had its charm. The room was most dear to her, and she would not have changed its furniture[13] for the handsomest in the house, though what had been originally plain, had suffered all the ill-usage of children—and its greatest elegancies and ornaments were a faded footstool of Julia's work, too ill done for the drawing-room,[14] three transparencies, made in a rage for transparencies, for the three lower panes of one window,[15] where Tintern Abbey held its station between a cave in Italy, and a moonlight lake in Cumberland;[16] a collection of family profiles thought unworthy of being anywhere else,[17] over the mantlepiece, and by their side and pinned against the wall, a small sketch of a ship sent four years ago from the Mediterranean by William, with H. M. S. Antwerp at the bottom, in letters as tall as the mainmast.[18]

To this nest of comforts Fanny now walked down to try its influence on an agitated, doubting spirit—to see if by looking at Edmund's profile she could catch any of his counsel, or by giving air to her geraniums she might inhale a breeze of mental strength herself. But she had more than fears of her own perseverance to remove; she

Rev. George Austen   Mrs. Austen

Silhouettes of Jane Austen's parents.

[From Emma Austen-Leigh, *Jane Austen and Bath* (London, 1939), pp. 30 and 36]

13. *furniture*: furnishings.

14. Julia embroidered the cloth that forms the stool's cover. Such works by the ladies of the house would often be used for decoration.

15. Transparencies were a fashionable artistic activity during this period. They involved drawing or painting a picture onto a sheet of paper, and then applying various substances, most notably turpentine, to render the paper transparent. It could then be affixed to windows to let light through. In this case Maria, Julia, and Fanny probably each made one transparency: the first two girls had been taught drawing before Fanny arrived, and she would have been taught the subject subsequently.

16. The three scenes represent popular subjects of this period, which exhibited a particular fondness for landscape painting, especially scenes that were melancholy or mysterious. Tintern Abbey is a medieval abbey in Wales, on its border with England, that fell into ruin after the dissolution of the monasteries in the early 1500s. In the later part of the eighteenth century the rise of tourism and the growing interest in natural beauty caused the mountainous and picturesque valley of the Wye river, where the abbey lies, to become a popular spot for vacationers. The abbey was a highlight of the area, often recommended in guidebooks, due to the concurrent increasing fascination with ruins; in *Sense and Sensibility* the romantic Marianne Dashwood plans to visit the nearby ruins of a monastic order. Tintern Abbey became the subject of several poems, and in 1798 William Wordsworth was inspired by a visit to the area to write one of his most famous, "Lines Composed a Few Miles Above Tintern Abbey," in which he develops his view of the spiritual solace and inspiration provided by nature. Tintern Abbey was also painted several times by the leading painter of the age, J. M. W. Turner. Similar interests made the rugged landscape of Italy a leading subject for Turner and other painters, and inspired a fascination with the Lake District of northwestern England (which includes Cumberland) among artists, poets, and tourists. Books giving instructions on making transparencies advised that they were particularly appropriate for scenes involving moonlight or ruins or dark venues, due to the striking contrasts created by the light streaming through the paper from behind. For contemporary pictures of the Wye valley and the Lake District, see pp. 289 and 291.

17. People often had profiles, or silhouettes, of themselves drawn; they were simple to make and cost little. There are surviving profiles of Jane Austen as well as other family members; see the facing page. At the same time, they were less attractive than regular drawings or paintings, something the Bertrams could afford, so it makes sense that they are relegated to this room.

18. The mainmast, in the center of the ship, would stick up higher than any other element. Those in the navy were often taught to sketch so they could make accurate pictures when undertaking reconnaissance missions.

had begun to feel undecided as to what she *ought to do*; and as she walked round the room her doubts were increasing. Was she *right* in refusing what was so warmly asked, so strongly wished for? What might be so essential to a scheme on which some of those to whom she owed the greatest complaisance,[19] had set their hearts? Was it not ill-nature—selfishness—and a fear of exposing herself?[20] And would Edmund's judgment, would his persuasion of Sir Thomas's disapprobation of the whole, be enough to justify her in a determined denial in spite of all the rest? It would be so horrible to her to act, that she was inclined to suspect the truth and purity of her own scruples,[21] and as she looked around her, the claims of her cousins to being obliged, were strengthened by the sight of present upon present that she had received from them. The table between the windows was covered with work-boxes and netting-boxes,[22] which had been given her at different times, principally by Tom; and she grew bewildered as to the amount of the debt which all these kind remembrances produced. A tap at the door roused her in the midst of this attempt to find her way to her duty, and her gentle "come in," was answered by the appearance of one, before whom all her doubts were wont to be laid. Her eyes brightened at the sight of Edmund.

"Can I speak with you, Fanny, for a few minutes?" said he.

"Yes, certainly."

"I want to consult. I want your opinion."

"My opinion!" she cried, shrinking from such a compliment, highly as it gratified her.

"Yes, your advice and opinion. I do not know what to do. This acting scheme gets worse and worse you see. They have chosen almost as bad a play as they could; and now, to complete the business, are going to ask the help of a young man very slightly known to any of us. This is the end of all the privacy and propriety which was talked about at first. I know no harm of Charles Maddox; but the excessive intimacy which must spring from his being admitted among us in this manner, is highly objectionable, the *more* than intimacy— the familiarity.[23] I cannot think of it with any patience—and it does appear to me an evil of such magnitude as must, *if possible*, be prevented. Do not you see it in the same light?"

"Yes, but what can be done? Your brother is so determined?"

19. *complaisance*: deference, compliance with others' wishes.

20. *exposing herself*: making herself look ridiculous.

21. In other words, she fears that the personal misery she would suffer in acting is biasing her judgment of whether it is morally right to do so.

22. A workbox holds needlework supplies. A netting box holds supplies for netting, which involved forming loops around a special shuttle or netting needle in order to create fabrics of varying density. Boxes like this were very popular, due to the important place these activities held in the lives of genteel women, and were often precious objects in their own right, carefully made and elaborately decorated with expensive materials. They also usually had fitted compartments inside, each one designed to hold specific implements. Sometimes women carried their boxes with them on visits, where they could be admired for their beauty while also furnishing the tools needed for doing needlework together, a popular female social activity. In *Northanger Abbey* the heroine and a young lady she is visiting take out a netting box in the morning with the intention of passing the time with it.

23. *familiarity*: undue intimacy or intercourse.

A picturesque view on the river Wye.

[From James Merigot, *The Amateur's Portfolio, or the New Drawing Magazine*, Vol. I (London, 1815–1816), No. 6, Plate 3]

"There is but *one* thing to be done, Fanny. I must take Anhalt myself. I am well aware that nothing else will quiet Tom."

Fanny could not answer him.

"It is not at all what I like," he continued. "No man can like being driven into the *appearance* of such inconsistency. After being known to oppose the scheme from the beginning, there is absurdity in the face of my joining them *now*, when they are exceeding their first plan in every respect; but I can think of no other alternative. Can you, Fanny?"

"No," said Fanny, slowly, "not immediately—but——"

"But what? I see your judgment is not with me. Think it a little over. Perhaps you are not so much aware as I am, of the mischief that *may*, of the unpleasantness that *must*, arise from a young man's being received in this manner—domesticated among us—authorized to come at all hours—and placed suddenly on a footing which must do away all restraints. To think only of the license which every rehearsal must tend to create.[24] It is all very bad! Put yourself in Miss Crawford's place, Fanny. Consider what it would be to act Amelia with a stranger. She has a right to be felt for, because she evidently feels for herself. I heard enough of what she said to you last night, to understand her unwillingness to be acting with a stranger; and as she probably engaged in the part with different expectations—perhaps, without considering the subject enough to know what was likely to be, it would be ungenerous, it would be really wrong to expose her to it. Her feelings ought to be respected. Does not it strike you so, Fanny? You hesitate."

"I am sorry for Miss Crawford; but I am more sorry to see you drawn in to do what you had resolved against, and what you are known to think will be disagreeable to my uncle. It will be such a triumph to the others!"

"They will not have much cause of triumph, when they see how infamously I act. But, however, triumph there certainly will be, and I must brave it. But if I can be the means of restraining the publicity[25] of the business, of limiting the exhibition, of concentrating our folly, I shall be well repaid. As I am now, I have no influence, I can do nothing; I have offended them, and they will not hear me; but when I have put them in good humour by this concession, I am not with-

24. The license he has particularly in mind is that involving close and continual contact between Charles Maddox, who is presumably young and unmarried, and the young women at Mansfield, especially Mary Crawford, who would be acting opposite him. At this time genteel families would hesitate to admit strangers into their home. They could meet at formal public settings like a ball, and then proceed by gradual stages to greater intimacy. Or strangers could be introduced by someone they already know well, as happened with Henry and Mary Crawford, introduced by Mrs. Grant. Through these means they could acquire, through their own acquaintance or the recommendation of someone they trusted, some assurance of a good character. This was especially crucial when it came to accepting a stranger who was a potential romantic partner, for granting such access to a bad person could lead to disastrous consequences.

25. *publicity*: notoriety, general knowledge.

Derwent Water, one of the leading sites in the Lake District.

[From John Britton, *The Beauties of England and Wales*, Vol. VIII (London, 1813), p. 38]

out hopes of persuading them to confine the representation within a much smaller circle than they are now in the high road for. This will be a material gain. My object is to confine it to Mrs. Rushworth and the Grants. Will not this be worth gaining?"

"Yes, it will be a great point."

"But still it has not your approbation. Can you mention any other measure by which I have a chance of doing equal good?"

"No, I cannot think of any thing else."

"Give me your approbation, then, Fanny. I am not comfortable without it."

"Oh! cousin."

"If you are against me, I ought to distrust myself—and yet—But it is absolutely impossible to let Tom go on in this way, riding about the country in quest of any body who can be persuaded to act—no matter whom; the look of a gentleman is to be enough. I thought *you* would have entered more into Miss Crawford's feelings."

"No doubt she will be very glad. It must be a great relief to her," said Fanny, trying for greater warmth of manner.

"She never appeared more amiable than in her behaviour to you last night. It gave her a very strong claim on my good will."

"She *was* very kind indeed, and I am glad to have her spared.". . .

She could not finish the generous effusion. Her conscience stopt her in the middle, but Edmund was satisfied.

"I shall walk down immediately after breakfast," said he, "and am sure of giving pleasure there. And now, dear Fanny, I will not interrupt you any longer. You want to be reading. But I could not be easy till I had spoken to you, and come to a decision. Sleeping or waking, my head has been full of this matter all night. It is an evil—but I am certainly making it less than it might be. If Tom is up, I shall go to him directly and get it over; and when we meet at breakfast we shall be all in high good humour at the prospect of acting the fool together with such unanimity. *You* in the meanwhile will be taking a trip into China, I suppose. How does Lord Macartney go on?[26]—(opening a volume on the table and then taking up some others). And here are Crabbe's Tales,[27] and the Idler,[28] at hand to relieve you, if you tire of your great[29] book. I admire your little establishment[30] exceedingly; and as soon as I am gone, you will empty your head of all this non-

26. George Macartney, 1st Earl Macartney, was a diplomat who during the 1790s led the first British embassy to China. It failed in opening China to greater foreign trade, but it did bring back information about China. In 1807 Sir John Barrow, who assisted Lord Macartney, published *Some Account of the Public Life and a Selection from the Unpublished Writings, of the Earl of Macartney*. A lengthy two-volume work, it contained Barrow's narrative of Macartney's career along with the latter's own writings, including the journal he kept of his embassy to China.

27. This is *Tales in Verse* by George Crabbe, which appeared in 1812, the very year in which Jane Austen started writing this novel. Crabbe, who had published several previous volumes of poetry, wrote realistic stories of ordinary life. Austen was a great lover of his work; she may even have taken the name Fanny Price from a character in his *Parish Register* of 1807. Her nephew James Edward Austen-Leigh and her niece Caroline Austen, in their memoirs of Jane Austen, both mention her love of Crabbe, which her nephew says was "perhaps on account of a certain resemblance to herself in minute and highly finished detail." He adds that she "would sometimes say, in jest, that, if she ever married at all, she could fancy being Mrs. Crabbe," while her niece writes that her admiration of the poet made her take "a keen interest in finding out *who* he was." This is confirmed in Austen's letters. In one, started upon just arriving in London, she says, "I have not yet seen Mr Crabbe," and then, a day later, she mentions going to the theater and being "particularly disappointed at seeing nothing of Mr Crabbe" (Sept. 15–16, 1813)—Crabbe was in fact at this time in London, which was not his home, and it is possible she had heard this and hoped to see him. In the following month, having learned of the recent death of Mrs. Crabbe, she writes, playing on the jest that she might marry him, "Poor woman! I will comfort *him* as well as I can, but I do not undertake to be good to her children. She had better not leave any" (Oct. 21, 1813). According to her niece, Jane Austen was eventually able "by diligent enquiry . . . to inform the rest of the family that he [Crabbe] held the Living of Trowbridge, and had recently married a second time."

28. *The Idler* (1758–60) was a series of essays, principally by the leading eighteenth-century literary figure Samuel Johnson, that were very popular and often reprinted. The essays ranged from general moral reflections to satirical pictures of current life to comments on literature and writing. Jane Austen refers to Johnson several times in her letters, and echoes of his moral reflections and his satire, especially the former, can be found in her novels; for an example in this work, see p. 384 and p. 385, note 21.

29. *great*: large. This refers only to size, not quality; "great" in the sense of "extremely good" had not appeared by this time, except within certain limited contexts.

30. *establishment*: arrangement.

sense of acting, and sit comfortably down to your table. But do not stay here to be cold."

He went; but there was no reading, no China, no composure for Fanny. He had told her the most extraordinary, the most inconceivable, the most unwelcome news; and she could think of nothing else. To be acting! After all his objections—objections so just and so public! After all that she had heard him say, and seen him look, and known him to be feeling. Could it be possible? Edmund so inconsistent. Was he not deceiving himself? Was he not wrong? Alas! it was all Miss Crawford's doing. She had seen her influence in every speech, and was miserable. The doubts and alarms as to her own conduct, which had previously distressed her, and which had all slept while she listened to him, were become of little consequence now. This deeper anxiety swallowed them up. Things should take their course; she cared not how it ended. Her cousins might attack, but could hardly tease her. She was beyond their reach; and if at last obliged to yield—no matter—it was all misery *now*.

A young woman distracted while reading.

[From *The Repository of arts, literature, fashions, manufactures, &c*, Vol. XIII (1815), p. 119]

Chapter Seventeen

*I*t was, indeed, a triumphant day to Mr. Bertram and Maria. Such a victory over Edmund's discretion had been beyond their hopes, and was most delightful. There was no longer any thing to disturb them in their darling project, and they congratulated each other in private on the jealous weakness to which they attributed the change, with all the glee of feelings gratified in every way.[1] Edmund might still look grave, and say he did not like the scheme in general, and must disapprove the play in particular; their point was gained; he was to act, and he was driven to it by the force of selfish inclinations only. Edmund had descended from that moral elevation which he had maintained before, and they were both as much the better as the happier for the descent.

They behaved very well, however, *to him* on the occasion, betraying no exultation beyond the lines about the corners of the mouth, and seemed to think it as great an escape to be quit of the intrusion of Charles Maddox, as if they had been forced into admitting him against their inclination. "To have it quite in their own family circle was what they had particularly wished. A stranger among them would have been the destruction of all their comfort," and when Edmund, pursuing that idea, gave a hint of his hope as to the limitation of the audience, they were ready, in the complaisance of the moment, to promise any thing. It was all good humour and encouragement. Mrs. Norris offered to contrive his dress, Mr. Yates assured him, that Anhalt's last scene with the Baron admitted a good deal of action and emphasis,[2] and Mr. Rushworth undertook to count his speeches.

"Perhaps," said Tom, "*Fanny* may be more disposed to oblige us now. Perhaps you may persuade *her*."

"No, she is quite determined. She certainly will not act."

"Oh! very well." And not another word was said: but Fanny felt herself again in danger, and her indifference to the danger was beginning to fail her already.

1.   They believe he is motivated by a fear of another man acting with Mary Crawford.

2.   In this scene Anhalt entreats the Baron to lay aside his class prejudice and follow the dictates of his conscience by marrying Agatha; the Baron initially refuses but is eventually persuaded.

A baron in ceremonial robes.

[From William Alexander, *Picturesque Representations of the Dress and Manners of the English* (London, 1813), Plate 35]

There were not fewer smiles at the parsonage than at the park on this change in Edmund; Miss Crawford looked very lovely in her's, and entered with such an instantaneous renewal of cheerfulness into the whole affair, as could have but one effect on him. "He was certainly right in respecting such feelings; he was glad he had determined on it." And the morning wore away in satisfactions very sweet, if not very sound. One advantage resulted from it to Fanny; at the earnest request of Miss Crawford, Mrs. Grant had with her usual good humour agreed to undertake the part for which Fanny had been wanted—and this was all that occurred to gladden *her* heart during the day; and even this, when imparted by Edmund, brought a pang with it, for it was Miss Crawford to whom she was obliged, it was Miss Crawford whose kind exertions were to excite her gratitude, and whose merit in making them was spoken of with a glow of admiration. She was safe; but peace and safety were unconnected here. Her mind had been never farther from peace. She could not feel that she had done wrong herself, but she was disquieted in every other way. Her heart and her judgment were equally against Edmund's decision; she could not acquit his unsteadiness; and his happiness under it made her wretched. She was full of jealousy and agitation. Miss Crawford came with looks of gaiety which seemed an insult, with friendly expressions towards herself which she could hardly answer calmly. Every body around her was gay and busy, prosperous[3] and important, each had their object of interest, their part, their dress, their favourite scene, their friends and confederates, all were finding employment in consultations and comparisons, or diversion in the playful conceits they suggested. She alone was sad and insignificant; she had no share in any thing; she might go or stay, she might be in the midst of their noise, or retreat from it to the solitude of the East room, without being seen or missed. She could almost think any thing would have been preferable to this.[4] Mrs. Grant was of consequence; *her* good nature had honourable mention—her taste and her time were considered—her presence was wanted—she was sought for and attended,[5] and praised; and Fanny was at first in some danger of envying her the character she had accepted. But reflection brought better feelings, and shewed her that Mrs. Grant was entitled to respect, which could never have belonged to *her*, and that had she

3. *prosperous*: fortunate, flourishing.

4. This passage presents a less attractive picture of Fanny by showing her motivated by envy and pique, though it also shows her soon struggling against those feelings. Jane Austen consistently tries to avoid idealizing her heroines. In a letter regarding the wish for ideal heroines in novels, a common phenomenon then, she declares, "pictures of perfection as you know make me sick & wicked" (March 23, 1817).

5. *attended*: awaited.

A woman in morning dress.

[From *The Repository of arts, literature, fashions, manufactures, &c*, Vol. VIII (1812), p. 230]

received even the greatest, she could never have been easy in joining a scheme which, considering only her uncle, she must condemn altogether.

Fanny's heart was not absolutely the only saddened one amongst them, as she soon began to acknowledge herself.—Julia was a sufferer too, though not quite so blamelessly.

Henry Crawford had trifled with her feelings; but she had very long allowed and even sought his attentions, with a jealousy of her sister so reasonable as ought to have been their cure; and now that the conviction of his preference for Maria had been forced on her, she submitted to it without any alarm for Maria's situation, or any endeavour at rational tranquillity for herself.—She either sat in gloomy silence, wrapt in such gravity as nothing could subdue, no curiosity touch, no wit amuse; or allowing the attentions of Mr. Yates, was talking with forced gaiety to him alone, and ridiculing the acting of the others.

For a day or two after the affront was given, Henry Crawford had endeavoured to do it away by the usual attack of gallantry and compliment, but he had not cared enough about it to persevere against a few repulses; and becoming soon too busy with his play to have time for more than one flirtation, he grew indifferent to the quarrel, or rather thought it a lucky occurrence, as quietly putting an end to what might ere long have raised expectations in more than Mrs. Grant.[6]—She was not pleased to see Julia excluded from the play, and sitting by disregarded; but as it was not a matter which really involved her happiness, as Henry must be the best judge of his own, and as he did assure her, with a most persuasive smile, that neither he nor Julia had ever had a serious thought of each other,[7] she could only renew her former caution as to the elder sister, entreat him not to risk his tranquillity by too much admiration there, and then gladly take her share in any thing that brought cheerfulness to the young people in general, and that did so particularly promote the pleasure of the two so dear to her.

"I rather wonder Julia is not in love with Henry," was her observation to Mary.

"I dare say she is," replied Mary, coldly. "I imagine both sisters are."

6. This is the expectation that Henry will marry Julia, which Mrs. Grant has already expressed. Were others to observe Henry's flirtation with Julia they might draw similar conclusions, for in this society people are very quick to detect the possibility of matrimony. In *Persuasion* the hero finds that his friendliness toward an unmarried young woman has convinced almost everyone around them, including her family, that he intends to propose to her. This makes him feel honor-bound to become engaged to her if she indicates a continued interest in him. Henry is not as scrupulous, but he would wish to avoid the social censure and complications that would result from raising such an expectation with Julia, for social rules dictated that a man should not pay prolonged attention to an unmarried woman unless he had serious intentions.

7. Henry, though correct about his own feelings, is being disingenuous, for he has flirted with Julia and is intelligent and experienced enough to have discerned her interest in him.

The House of Commons (see the next page), the most important of the two houses of the British Parliament. The House of Lords, though its members had a higher social status, exercised less political power.

[From Fiona St. Aubyn, *Ackermann's Illustrated London*, illustrations by Augustus Pugin and Thomas Rowlandson (Ware, 1985), p. 37]

"Both! no, no, that must not be. Do not give him a hint of it. Think of Mr. Rushworth."

"You had better tell Miss Bertram to think of Mr. Rushworth. It may do *her* some good. I often think of Mr. Rushworth's property and independence, and wish them in other hands—but I never think of *him*. A man might represent the county with such an estate; a man might escape a profession and represent the county."[8]

"I dare say he *will* be in parliament soon. When Sir Thomas comes, I dare say he will be in for some borough,[9] but there has been nobody to put him in the way of[10] doing any thing yet."

"Sir Thomas is to achieve mighty things when he comes home," said Mary, after a pause. "Do you remember Hawkins Browne's 'Address to Tobacco,' in imitation of Pope?—

'Blest leaf! whose aromatic gales dispense
To Templars modesty, to Parsons sense.'[11]

I will parody them:

Blest Knight![12] whose dictatorial looks dispense
To Children affluence, to Rushworth sense.

Will not that do, Mrs. Grant? Every thing seems to depend upon Sir Thomas's return."

"You will find his consequence very just and reasonable when you see him in his family, I assure you. I do not think we do so well without him. He has a fine dignified manner, which suits the head of such a house, and keeps every body in their place. Lady Bertram seems more of a cipher now than when he is at home; and nobody else can keep Mrs. Norris in order. But, Mary, do not fancy that Maria Bertram cares for Henry. I am sure *Julia* does not, or she would not have flirted as she did last night with Mr. Yates; and though he and Maria are very good friends, I think she likes Sotherton too well to be inconstant."

"I would not give much for Mr. Rushworth's chance, if Henry stept in before the articles were signed."[13]

8. She means being a member of the House of Commons representing a county (rather than a borough). Each county in Britain elected two representatives to the House, while an even larger number were elected to represent boroughs, which were much smaller than counties. Representing the county was especially prestigious, one of the highest honors a man could attain—probably why Mary repeats the phrase for emphasis. It also required greater resources, restricting it to the very wealthiest men, for a candidate needed to appeal to a larger number of electors. At the same time, he would still need to impress the electors with his personal qualities, which is why Mary laments the possession of the necessary wealth by someone like Mr. Rushworth.

9. Mrs. Grant's hope is that Sir Thomas, who is himself a member of the House of Commons, will help Mr. Rushworth attain the lesser prize of representing a borough. Many boroughs had electorates that were small, due to various restrictions on the franchise, or that consisted mostly of people dependent on a wealthy landowner. This would allow someone with sufficient funds, or personal connections and influence, to sway the electorate to support him or his favored candidate. Mrs. Grant hopes that Sir Thomas will use his influence in a nearby borough, or his connection to another person with influence, to secure a seat for Mr. Rushworth. Such use of personal influence and patronage was a standard part of political life at the time.

10. *in the way of*: in a favorable position for.

11. She is thinking of *A Pipe of Tobacco: In Imitation of Six Several Authors* (1736), by the poet Isaac Hawkins Browne. It consists of six short humorous sections, each imitating the style of a different poet and praising tobacco. The fifth, which opens with the lines quoted by Mary, imitates Alexander Pope, the leading English poet of the eighteenth century.

12. Sir Thomas is a baronet rather than a knight, but the terms were linked, as a baronet was in effect a hereditary knight; occasionally the term "knight baronet" was used to refer to baronets. Mary presumably prefers "knight" for the sake of the rhythm of the verse. She also may wish to allude to the idea of a knight as a heroic warrior who performs great deeds, a meaning that would resonate particularly because of this period's many popular narrative poems and novels, most notably by Sir Walter Scott, involving chivalric knights of earlier times.

13. She means the articles of the marriage contract. Marriages between wealthy families were the subject of elaborate negotiations, usually involving lawyers from each family, in which the exact financial terms were settled, including how much money or other assets the bride would bring, how much

"If you have such a suspicion, something must be done, and as soon as the play is all over, we will talk to him seriously, and make him know his own mind; and if he means nothing, we will send him off, though he is Henry, for a time."[14]

Julia *did* suffer, however, though Mrs. Grant discerned it not, and though it escaped the notice of many of her own family likewise. She had loved, she did love still, and she had all the suffering which a warm temper and a high spirit were likely to endure under the disappointment of a dear, though irrational hope, with a strong sense of ill-usage. Her heart was sore and angry, and she was capable only of angry consolations. The sister with whom she was used to[15] be on easy terms, was now become her greatest enemy; they were alienated from each other, and Julia was not superior to the hope of some distressing end to the attentions which were still carrying on there, some punishment to Maria for conduct so shameful towards herself, as well as towards Mr. Rushworth.[16] With no material fault of temper, or difference of opinion, to prevent their being very good friends while their interests were the same, the sisters, under such a trial as this, had not affection or principle enough to make them merciful or just, to give them honour or compassion.[17] Maria felt her triumph, and pursued her purpose careless of Julia; and Julia could never see Maria distinguished by Henry Crawford, without trusting that it would create jealousy, and bring a public disturbance at last.

Fanny saw and pitied much of this in Julia; but there was no outward fellowship between them. Julia made no communication, and Fanny took no liberties. They were two solitary sufferers, or connected only by Fanny's consciousness.

The inattention of the two brothers and the aunt to Julia's discomposure, and their blindness to its true cause, must be imputed to the fulness of their own minds. They were totally pre-occupied. Tom was engrossed by the concerns of his theatre, and saw nothing that did not immediately relate to it. Edmund, between his theatrical and his real part, between Miss Crawford's claims and his own conduct, between love and consistency,[18] was equally unobservant; and Mrs. Norris was too busy in contriving and directing the general little

money would be set aside for her either while married or after she was widowed, and what the children of the marriage would inherit.

14. Thus both Mary and Mrs. Grant have noticed the danger to Maria's and Mr. Rushworth's engagement posed by her attraction to Henry. But neither intends to take action, at least for now. Mary, who perceives the danger fully, is clearly unconcerned, while Mrs. Grant, who worries at the prospect, is reluctant to acknowledge the unpleasant reality or to confront her brother and so prefers to hope that everything will turn out well.

15. *was used to*: used to. There are other cases in Austen's novels of this usage.

16. Julia represents another person who perceives the flirtation between Maria and Henry, but she hopes it will result in misery, which means she will not deliver a warning to anyone.

17. This harkens back to an early description of the sisters' education, in which it is stated that "they were admirably taught" in most things, but were "entirely deficient in the less common acquirements of self-knowledge, generosity, and humility." Later episodes have shown them displaying polished and agreeable manners, but also acting with complete selfishness on most matters.

18. His "consistency" is his adherence to his own principles. By joining in the play he has been inconsistent, but he would still be struggling with this and trying to violate his principles as little as he can.

matters of the company, superintending their various dresses with economical expedient, for which nobody thanked her, and saving, with delighted integrity,[19] half-a-crown here and there to the absent Sir Thomas, to have leisure for watching the behaviour, or guarding the happiness of his daughters.[20]

The Speaker of the House of Commons.

[From William Pyne, *The Costume of Great Britain* (London, 1804; 1989 reprint), Plate XXXVI]

19. Meaning she delights in her own integrity in taking great pains to save someone else money.

20. Thus three other members of the party fail even to notice anything amiss in the behavior of Maria and Henry. Since Lady Bertram hardly ever notices what does not involve herself, and Fanny, who is the keenest observer of all, is unwilling to speak up after having her earlier vague warning dismissed by Edmund, there is no one remaining to intervene.

Chapter Eighteen

*E*very thing was now in a regular train;[1] theatre, actors, actresses, and dresses, were all getting forward: but though no other great impediments arose, Fanny found, before many days were past, that it was not all uninterrupted enjoyment to the party themselves, and that she had not to witness the continuance of such unanimity and delight, as had been almost too much for her at first. Every body began to have their vexation. Edmund had many. Entirely against *his* judgment, a scene painter arrived from town, and was at work,[2] much to the increase of the expenses, and what was worse, of the eclat[3] of their proceedings; and his brother, instead of being really guided by him as to the privacy of the representation, was giving an invitation to every family who came in his way. Tom himself began to fret over the scene painter's slow progress, and to feel the miseries of waiting. He had learned his part—all his parts—for he took every trifling one that could be united with the Butler, and began to be impatient to be acting; and every day thus unemployed, was tending to increase his sense of the insignificance of all his parts together, and make him more ready to regret that some other play had not been chosen.

Fanny, being always a very courteous listener, and often the only listener at hand, came in for the complaints and distresses of most of them. *She* knew that Mr. Yates was in general thought to rant dreadfully, that Mr. Yates was disappointed in Henry Crawford, that Tom Bertram spoke so quick he would be unintelligible, that Mrs. Grant spoilt every thing by laughing, that Edmund was behind-hand[4] with his part, and that it was misery to have any thing to do with Mr. Rushworth, who was wanting a prompter through every speech. She knew, also, that poor Mr. Rushworth could seldom get any body to rehearse with him; *his* complaint came before her as well as the rest; and so decided to her eye was her cousin Maria's avoidance of him, and so needlessly often the rehearsal of the first scene between her

1. *in a regular train*: proceeding in an orderly fashion.

2. The increased use of a wide array of large painted backdrops in theaters led to greater prominence of professional scene painters (see p. 313 for an example of painted scenery). Starting in the 1770s, the names of scene painters were printed in playbills and sometimes even in the published texts of plays.

3. *eclat*: public display or notice.

4. *behind-hand*: backward, tardy.

Daytime dress.

[From Andrew Tuer, *The Follies and Fashions of our Grandfathers* (London, 1887), p. 232]

and Mr. Crawford,[5] that she had soon all the terror of other complaints from *him*. — So far from being all satisfied and all enjoying, she found every body requiring something they had not, and giving occasion of discontent to the others. — Every body had a part either too long or too short; — nobody would attend as they ought, nobody would remember on which side they were to come in — nobody but the complainer would observe any directions.[6]

Fanny believed herself to derive as much innocent enjoyment from the play as any of them; — Henry Crawford acted well, and it was a pleasure to *her* to creep into the theatre, and attend the rehearsal of the first act — in spite of the feelings it excited in some speeches for Maria.[7] — Maria she also thought acted well — too well;[8] — and after the first rehearsal or two, Fanny began to be their only audience — sometimes as prompter, sometimes as spectator — and was often very useful. — As far as she could judge, Mr. Crawford was considerably the best actor of all; he had more confidence than Edmund, more judgment than Tom, more talent and taste than Mr. Yates. — She did not like him as a man, but she must admit him to be the best actor, and on this point there were not many who differed from her.[9] Mr. Yates, indeed, exclaimed against his tameness and insipidity — and the day came at last, when Mr. Rushworth turned to her with a black look, and said — "Do you think there is any thing so very fine in all this? For the life and soul of me, I cannot admire him; — and between ourselves, to see such an undersized, little, mean[10]-looking man, set up for a fine actor, is very ridiculous in my opinion."[11]

From this moment there was a return of his former jealousy, which Maria, from increasing hopes of Crawford, was at little pains to remove; and the chances of Mr. Rushworth's ever attaining to the knowledge of his two and forty speeches became much less. As to his ever making any thing *tolerable* of them, nobody had the smallest idea of that except his mother — *She*, indeed, regretted that his part was not more considerable, and deferred coming over to Mansfield till they were forward[12] enough in their rehearsal to comprehend all his scenes, but the others aspired at nothing beyond his remembering the catchword,[13] and the first line of his speech, and being able to follow the prompter through the rest. Fanny, in her pity and kindheartedness, was at great pains to teach him how to learn, giving him

5. Their first scene, a long one, is where their characters reconcile and express their love of each other.

6. In this sentence the author switches to expressing the collective complaints of the participants against one another.

7. Maria's character, Agatha, has a series of long speeches in which she relates her story, including how she became pregnant out of wedlock. This would perturb Fanny, who earlier felt shock at reading of Agatha's situation.

8. The scene calls for her to express love and tenderness toward the character played by Henry, and she would naturally act that well, if it even could be called acting. Such conduct demonstrates the dangers created by the play, for it allows Maria to behave in a manner toward Henry that prevailing social and moral rules would absolutely prohibit if she were acting in her own character.

9. Henry's ability as an actor will reappear in a later scene in which he reads from Shakespeare. It also manifests itself throughout his conduct, for he displays an almost chameleon-like ability and inclination to adapt his behavior toward whatever situation he is in and whichever people he is trying to influence.

10. *mean*: inferior, undistinguished.

11. It is notable that the only two who criticize Henry's acting are the most foolish of the participants, and both Mr. Yates and Mr. Rushworth condemn him according to their particular obsessions: the virtue of ranting when acting and the virtue of being tall.

12. *forward*: advanced.

13. *catchword*: the last word in an actor's speech, which cues the next speaker to begin. He would need to remember the catchword of those acting opposite him to know when to speak himself.

all the helps and directions in her power, trying to make an artificial memory for him, and learning every word of his part herself, but without his being much the forwarder.[14]

Many uncomfortable, anxious, apprehensive feelings she certainly had; but with all these, and other claims on her time and attention, she was as far from finding herself without employment or utility amongst them, as without a companion in uneasiness; quite as far from having no demand on her leisure as on her compassion. The gloom of her first anticipations was proved to have been unfounded. She was occasionally useful to all; she was perhaps as much at peace as any.

There was a great deal of needle-work to be done moreover, in which her help was wanted; and that Mrs. Norris thought her quite as well off as the rest, was evident by the manner in which she claimed it: "Come Fanny," she cried, "these are fine times for you, but you must not be always walking from one room to the other and doing the lookings on, at your ease, in this way,—I want you here.—I have been slaving myself till I can hardly stand, to contrive Mr. Rushworth's cloak without sending for any more satin; and now I think you may give me your help in putting it together.—There are but three seams, you may do them in a trice.—It would be lucky for me if I had nothing but the executive part[15] to do.—*You* are best off, I can tell you; but if nobody did more than *you*, we should not get on very fast."

Fanny took the work very quietly, without attempting any defence; but her kinder aunt Bertram observed on her behalf,

"One cannot wonder, sister, that Fanny *should* be delighted; it is all new to her, you know,—you and I used to be very fond of a play ourselves—and so am I still;—and as soon as I am a little more at leisure, *I* mean to look in at their rehearsals too. What is the play about, Fanny, you have never told me?"

"Oh! sister, pray do not ask her now; for Fanny is not one of those who can talk and work at the same time.[16]—It is about Lovers' Vows."

"I believe," said Fanny to her aunt Bertram, "there will be three acts rehearsed to-morrow evening, and that will give you an opportunity of seeing all the actors at once."

"You had better stay[17] till the curtain is hung," interposed Mrs.

14. In this passage Jane Austen arouses some sympathy for Mr. Rushworth, which she does not always do for her foolish and comical characters. In this case it serves the function of underlining the wrongness of Maria's and Henry's conduct.

15. *executive part*: role of executing or carrying out the task. Mrs. Norris sees herself as having the managing or directing part.

16. This is a sign of Mrs. Norris's obtuseness, for anyone who has been around Fanny over the course of many years should have realized by now that she is intelligent. In fact, since Fanny seems to be regularly doing needlework in the drawing room, Mrs. Norris has almost certainly observed her talking while working on numerous occasions. But Mrs. Norris believes what she wants to believe—that Fanny is inferior in personal qualities as well as social position. She shows a similar blindness toward Maria, in that case refusing to believe negative truths.

17. *stay*: wait. She means Lady Bertram should wait until the curtain is hung to watch a rehearsal.

The eighteenth-century Bath theater, with curtains festooned at the top and painted scenery at the back.

[From Mowbray Aston Green, *The Eighteenth Century Architecture of Bath* (Bath, 1904), p. 214]

Norris—"the curtain will be hung in a day or two,—there is very little sense in a play without a curtain—and I am much mistaken if you do not find it draw up into very handsome festoons."[18]

Lady Bertram seemed quite resigned to waiting.—Fanny did not share her aunt's composure; she thought of the morrow a great deal,—for if the three acts were rehearsed, Edmund and Miss Crawford would then be acting together for the first time;—the third act would bring a scene between them which interested her most particularly, and which she was longing and dreading to see how they would perform. The whole subject of it was love—a marriage of love was to be described by the gentleman,[19] and very little short of a declaration of love be made by the lady.

She had read, and read the scene again with many painful, many wondering emotions, and looked forward to their representation of it as a circumstance almost too interesting. She did not *believe* they had yet rehearsed it, even in private.

The morrow came, the plan for the evening continued, and Fanny's consideration of it did not become less agitated. She worked very diligently under her aunt's directions, but her diligence and her silence concealed a very absent,[20] anxious mind; and about noon she made her escape with her work to the East room, that she might have no concern in another, and, as she deemed it, most unnecessary rehearsal of the first act, which Henry Crawford was just proposing, desirous at once of having her time to herself, and of avoiding the sight of Mr. Rushworth. A glimpse, as she passed through the hall, of the two ladies walking up from the parsonage, made no change in her wish of retreat, and she worked and meditated in the East room, undisturbed, for a quarter of an hour, when a gentle tap at the door was followed by the entrance of Miss Crawford.

"Am I right?—Yes; this is the East room. My dear Miss Price, I beg your pardon, but I have made my way to you on purpose to entreat your help."

Fanny, quite surprised, endeavoured to show herself mistress of the room by her civilities, and looked at the bright bars of her empty grate with concern.[21]

"Thank you—I am quite warm, very warm. Allow me to stay here a little while, and do have the goodness to hear me my third act. I

18. Mrs. Norris has earlier spoken of her work on the curtain, and the ways she saved money on it, so she naturally wishes to emphasize that she still managed to make it attractive. Stage curtains then were normally drawn up by festoons rather than pulled to the sides. This meant spectators could see and potentially admire them throughout the performance. For an illustration, see the preceding page.

19. In this scene Anhalt, Edmund's character, delivers a lengthy speech that eloquently evokes the beauty and happiness of a marriage based on love.

20. *absent*: absentminded, inattentive.

21. These are the bars of her fire grate. As explained earlier, Mrs. Norris has stipulated that Fanny never have a fire in her room, and Fanny now feels remiss as a hostess. The bars are bright because they have long been untouched by embers or ashes.

A woman doing needlework.

[From Mary Augusta Austen-Leigh, *Personal Aspects of Jane Austen* (New York, 1920), p. 167]

have brought my book, and if you would but rehearse it with me, I should be *so* obliged! I came here to-day intending to rehearse it with Edmund—by ourselves—against[22] the evening, but he is not in the way;[23] and if he *were*, I do not think I could go through it with *him*, till I have hardened myself a little, for really there *is* a speech or two—You will be so good, won't you?"

Fanny was most civil in her assurances, though she could not give them in a very steady voice.

"Have you ever happened to look at the part I mean?" continued Miss Crawford, opening her book. "Here it is. I did not think much of it at first—but, upon my word—. There, look at *that* speech, and *that*, and *that*. How am I ever to look him in the face and say such things? Could you do it?[24] But then he is your cousin, which makes all the difference. You must rehearse it with me, that I may fancy *you* him, and get on by degrees. You *have* a look of *his* sometimes."

"Have I?—I will do my best with the greatest readiness—but I must *read* the part, for I can *say* very little of it."

"*None* of it, I suppose. You are to have the book of course. Now for it. We must have two chairs at hand for you to bring forward to the front of the stage.[25] There—very good school-room chairs, not made for a theatre, I dare say; much more fitted for little girls to sit and kick their feet against when they are learning a lesson. What would your governess and your uncle say to see them used for such a purpose? Could Sir Thomas look in upon us just now, he would bless himself, for we are rehearsing all over the house. Yates is storming away in the dining room. I heard him as I came up stairs, and the theatre is engaged of course by those indefatigable rehearsers, Agatha and Frederick. If *they* are not perfect, I *shall* be surprised. By the bye, I looked in upon them five minutes ago, and it happened to be exactly at one of the times when they were trying *not* to embrace,[26] and Mr. Rushworth was with me. I thought he began to look a little queer, so I turned it off[27] as well as I could, by whispering to him, 'We shall have an excellent Agatha, there is something so *maternal* in her manner, so completely *maternal* in her voice and countenance.'[28] Was not that well done of me? He brightened up directly. Now for my soliloquy."

She began, and Fanny joined in with all the modest feeling which

22. *against*: before.

23. *in the way*: at hand.

24. The passage likely provoking Mary's concern begins with a declaration by her character, Amelia, "I am in love." She follows this with a lament that the object of her love does not love her, which leads Anhalt to say, "Who is there that would not?" and her to reply, "Would you?" His resulting confusion causes her first to propose teaching him about her own feelings of love, and then to declare that he has actually taught her about love and that she wishes him to do so again. When he persists in trying to change the subject, she finally proclaims, quoting from his earlier speech on the glories of married love, "Ay, I see how it is—You have no inclination to experience with me 'the good part of matrimony:' I am not the female, with whom you would like to go 'hand in hand up hills, and through labyrinths.'" This finally forces him to admit that he does love her passionately. The social rules prevailing at this time would forbid even a man from speaking such words to a potential lover unless they were part of a proposal, and would forbid an unmarried woman from uttering them under any circumstances.

25. Early in this scene the stage direction reads, "*He [Anhalt] places chairs, and they sit.*" Since Fanny is playing Anhalt now, she would do that.

26. There is no point in the scene when the characters try *not* to embrace, so she means that Maria and Henry are trying to avoid embracing at the several points when their characters are supposed to do so. Some remaining sense of propriety, which would absolutely forbid even slight contact in their normal life, may inhibit them; it is also possible that they do embrace when rehearsing alone, but desist in the presence of others. Whatever the case, Mary's description suggests that avoiding an embrace requires a struggle, one clear enough to an onlooker.

27. *turned it off*: altered the effect, gave it a different sense.

28. Agatha is Frederick's mother, and her embraces thus are supposed to be maternal.

the idea of representing Edmund was so strongly calculated[29] to inspire; but with looks and voice so truly feminine, as to be no very good picture of a man. With such an Anhalt, however, Miss Crawford had courage enough, and they had got through half the scene, when a tap at the door brought a pause, and the entrance of Edmund the next moment, suspended it all.

Surprise, consciousness, and pleasure, appeared in each of the three on this unexpected meeting; and as Edmund was come on the very same business that had brought Miss Crawford, consciousness and pleasure were likely to be more than momentary in *them.* He too had his book, and was seeking Fanny, to ask her to rehearse with him, and help him to prepare for the evening, without knowing Miss Crawford to be in the house; and great was the joy and animation of being thus thrown together—of comparing schemes—and sympathizing in praise of Fanny's kind offices.

She could not equal them in their warmth. *Her* spirits sank under the glow of theirs, and she felt herself becoming too nearly nothing to both, to have any comfort in having been sought by either. They must now rehearse together. Edmund proposed, urged, entreated it—till the lady, not very unwilling at first, could refuse no longer—and Fanny was wanted only to prompt and observe them. She was invested, indeed, with the office of judge and critic, and earnestly desired to exercise it and tell them all their faults; but from doing so every feeling within her shrank, she could not, would not, dared not attempt it; had she been otherwise qualified for criticism, her conscience must have restrained her from venturing at disapprobation. She believed herself to feel too much of it in the aggregate for honesty or safety in particulars.[30] To prompt them must be enough for her; and it was sometimes *more* than enough; for she could not always pay attention to the book. In watching them she forgot herself; and agitated by the increasing spirit of Edmund's manner,[31] had once closed the page and turned away exactly as he wanted help. It was imputed to very reasonable weariness, and she was thanked and pitied; but she deserved their pity, more than she hoped they would ever surmise. At last the scene was over, and Fanny forced herself to add her praise to the compliments each was giving the other; and when again alone and able to recall the whole, she was inclined

29. *calculated:* apt, likely.

30. In other words, her feelings of distress and jealousy at seeing Edmund and Mary speaking words of love to each other, even in the guise of other characters, make Fanny doubt that any criticism she offered could possibly be honest and fair. She also worries that she might inadvertently reveal some of her own feelings, which would mortify her; avoiding this is what is meant by "safety."

31. Meaning his increasing animation under the influence of the scene.

A fire grate by a leading designer of the period.

[From John Swarbrick, *Robert Adam and his Brothers* (New York, 1915), p. 80]

to believe their performance would, indeed, have such nature and feeling in it, as must ensure their credit, and make it a very suffering exhibition to herself. Whatever might be its effect, however, she must stand the brunt of it again that very day.

The first regular[32] rehearsal of the three first acts was certainly to take place in the evening; Mrs. Grant and the Crawfords were engaged to return for that purpose as soon as they could after dinner; and every one concerned was looking forward with eagerness. There seemed a general diffusion of cheerfulness on the occasion; Tom was enjoying such an advance towards the end, Edmund was in spirits from the morning's rehearsal, and little vexations seemed every where smoothed away. All were alert and impatient; the ladies moved soon, the gentlemen soon followed them, and with the exception of Lady Bertram, Mrs. Norris, and Julia, every body was in the theatre at an early hour,[33] and having lighted it up as well as its unfinished state admitted,[34] were waiting only the arrival of Mrs. Grant and the Crawfords to begin.

They did not wait long for the Crawfords, but there was no Mrs. Grant. She could not come. Dr. Grant, professing an indisposition, for which he had little credit with his fair sister-in-law, could not spare his wife.

"Dr. Grant is ill," said she, with mock solemnity. "He has been ill ever since; he did not eat any of the pheasant to day. He fancied it tough—sent away his plate—and has been suffering ever since."

Here was disappointment! Mrs. Grant's non-attendance was sad indeed. Her pleasant manners and cheerful conformity[35] made her always valuable amongst them—but *now* she was absolutely necessary. They could not act, they could not rehearse with any satisfaction without her. The comfort of the whole evening was destroyed. What was to be done? Tom, as Cottager, was in despair.[36] After a pause of perplexity, some eyes began to be turned towards Fanny, and a voice or two, to say, "If Miss Price would be so good as to *read* the part." She was immediately surrounded by supplications, every body asked it, even Edmund said, "Do Fanny, if it is not *very* disagreeable to you."

But Fanny still hung back. She could not endure the idea of it. Why was not Miss Crawford to be applied to as well?[37] Or why had

32. *regular*: proper, formally organized.

33. They still follow the normal ritual of departure after dinner, but do so in a way that delays only a little their moving to the theater.

34. The lack of powerful spotlights at the time meant that illumination of the stage required a number of lights at different places. Theaters normally had footlights with candles, as well as candles or oil lamps on the sides of the stage. They needed to be fixed in place to minimize the danger of fire. Installation would require some effort, and the task has only been partially completed here.

35. *conformity*: compliance, acquiescence.

36. Mrs. Grant is playing Cottager's wife, and their principal scenes occur early in the play.

37. Since Miss Crawford's character never appears in the same scene with Cottager's wife, she could easily read the part on this one occasion.

not she rather gone to her own room, as she had felt to be safest, instead of attending the rehearsal at all? She had known it would irritate and distress her—she had known it her duty to keep away.[38] She was properly punished.

"You have only to *read* the part," said Henry Crawford with renewed entreaty.

"And I do believe she can say every word of it," added Maria, "for she could put Mrs. Grant right the other day in twenty places. Fanny, I am sure you know the part."

Fanny could not say she did *not*—and as they all persevered—as Edmund repeated his wish, and with a look of even fond dependence on her good nature, she must yield. She would do her best. Every body was satisfied—and she was left to the tremors of a most palpitating heart, while the others prepared to begin.

They *did* begin—and being too much engaged in their own noise, to be struck by an usual[39] noise in the other part of the house, had proceeded some way, when the door of the room was thrown open, and Julia appearing at it, with a face all aghast, exclaimed, "My father is come! He is in the hall at this moment."[40]

END OF VOL. I.

38. It would be her duty because it could arouse feelings of jealousy and resentment, which were sinful.

39. Many editions change "an usual" to "unusual," assuming it was a printer's error, which is certainly possible, because the noise turns out to be that resulting from Sir Thomas's unexpected arrival—unusual after his having been away for two years. But it is also possible that "usual" is meant, as the same sort of noise would arise from anyone entering through the main door of the house. Since both these theories are plausible, this edition stays with the spelling present in both the editions published in Jane Austen's lifetime.

40. Sir Thomas's arrival forms a dramatic end to the first of the novel's three volumes. It also occurs just as Fanny, after resisting so long, is finally about to be drawn into participating in the play. Thus it allows her to remain unsullied by it.

VOLUME TWO

Chapter One

*H*ow is the consternation of the party to be described? To the greater number it was a moment of absolute horror. Sir Thomas in the house! All felt the instantaneous conviction. Not a hope of imposition or mistake was harboured any where. Julia's looks were an evidence of the fact that made it indisputable; and after the first starts and exclamations, not a word was spoken for half a minute; each with an altered countenance was looking at some other, and almost each was feeling it a stroke the most unwelcome, most ill-timed, most appalling![1] Mr. Yates might consider it only as a vexatious interruption for the evening, and Mr. Rushworth might imagine it a blessing, but every other heart was sinking under some degree of self-condemnation or undefined alarm, every other heart was suggesting "What will become of us? what is to be done now?" It was a terrible pause; and terrible to every ear were the corroborating sounds of opening doors and passing footsteps.[2]

Julia was the first to move and speak again. Jealousy and bitterness had been suspended: selfishness was lost in the common cause; but at the moment of her appearance, Frederick was listening with looks of devotion to Agatha's narrative,[3] and pressing her hand to his heart,[4] and as soon as she could notice this, and see that, in spite of the shock of her words, he still kept his station and retained her sister's hand,[5] her wounded heart swelled again with injury, and looking as red as she had been white before, she turned out of the room, saying "*I* need not be afraid of appearing before him."

Her going roused the rest; and at the same moment, the two brothers stepped forward, feeling the necessity of doing something. A very few words between them were sufficient. The case admitted no difference of opinion; they must go to the drawing-room directly. Maria joined them with the same intent, just then the stoutest of the three;

1. *appalling*: dismaying, terrifying.

2. Their reaction suggests that, despite their earlier confidence and determination in embarking on the play, they almost all have an awareness of doing something wrong, or at least something their father would not at all approve.

3. This occurs in the first scene of the play, and before Cottager and his wife appear, so the appearance of Sir Thomas means the play is stopped before Fanny ever has to perform in it.

4. At one point in the scene the stage direction reads: "FREDERICK, *with his eyes cast down, takes her hand, and puts it to his heart.*" Agatha then narrates her history at length while Frederick, presumably with her hand still at his heart, listens. At the end of her longest speech, the stage directions read, *"He embraces her."*

5. By continuing to hold her hand, even as Julia reveals that the rehearsal must be immediately terminated, he goes beyond what is required by the part, causing Julia to react so strongly and Maria, as described below, to be profoundly affected.

A drawing room of the period.

[From John Swarbrick, *Robert Adam and his Brothers* (New York, 1915), p. 80]

for the very circumstance which had driven Julia away, was to her the sweetest support. Henry Crawford's retaining her hand at such a moment, a moment of such peculiar proof and importance, was worth ages of doubt and anxiety. She hailed it as an earnest[6] of the most serious determination, and was equal even to encounter her father. They walked off, utterly heedless of Mr. Rushworth's repeated question of, "Shall I go too?—Had not I better go too?—Will not it be right for me to go too?" but they were no sooner through the door than Henry Crawford undertook to answer the anxious inquiry, and encouraging him by all means to pay his respects to Sir Thomas without delay, sent him after the others with delighted haste.

Fanny was left with only the Crawfords and Mr. Yates. She had been quite overlooked by her cousins; and as her own opinion of her claims on Sir Thomas's affection was much too humble to give her any idea of classing herself with his children, she was glad to remain behind and gain a little breathing time. Her agitation and alarm exceeded all that was endured by the rest, by the right of a disposition which not even innocence could keep from suffering. She was nearly fainting: all her former habitual dread of her uncle was returning, and with it compassion for him and for almost every one of the party on the development before him—with solicitude on Edmund's account indescribable. She had found a seat, where in excessive trembling she was enduring all these fearful thoughts, while the other three, no longer under any restraint, were giving vent to their feelings of vexation, lamenting over such an unlooked-for premature arrival as a most untoward event, and without mercy wishing poor Sir Thomas had been twice as long on his passage, or were still in Antigua.

The Crawfords were more warm on the subject than Mr. Yates, from better understanding the family and judging more clearly of the mischief that must ensue. The ruin of the play was to them a certainty, they felt the total destruction of the scheme to be inevitably at hand; while Mr. Yates considered it only as a temporary interruption, a disaster for the evening, and could even suggest the possibility of the rehearsal being renewed after tea, when the bustle of receiving Sir Thomas were over and he might be at leisure to be amused by it. The Crawfords laughed at the idea; and having soon agreed on the propriety of their walking quietly home and leaving the family to

6. *earnest*: indication or pledge of what is to come.

A portrait of a young woman (the Duchess of Wellington) by the leading portrait painter of the age, Sir Thomas Lawrence.

[From Lord Ronald Sutherland Gower, *Sir Thomas Lawrence* (London, 1900), p. 152]

themselves, proposed Mr. Yates's accompanying them and spending the evening at the Parsonage.[7] But Mr. Yates, having never been with those who thought much of parental claims, or family confidence,[8] could not perceive that any thing of the kind was necessary, and therefore, thanking them, said, "he preferred remaining where he was that he might pay his respects to the old gentleman handsomely since he *was* come; and besides, he did not think it would be fair by the others to have every body run away."

Fanny was just beginning to collect herself, and to feel that if she staid longer behind it might seem disrespectful, when this point was settled, and being commissioned with the brother and sister's apology,[9] saw them preparing to go as she quitted the room herself to perform the dreadful duty of appearing before her uncle.

Too soon did she find herself at the drawing-room door, and after pausing a moment for what she knew would not come, for a courage which the outside of no door had ever supplied to her, she turned the lock in desperation, and the lights of the drawing-room and all the collected family were before her. As she entered, her own name caught her ear. Sir Thomas was at that moment looking round him, and saying "But where is Fanny?—Why do not I see my little Fanny?," and on perceiving her, came forward with a kindness which astonished and penetrated[10] her, calling her his dear Fanny, kissing her affectionately, and observing with decided pleasure how much she was grown! Fanny knew not how to feel, nor where to look. She was quite oppressed.[11] He had never been so kind, so *very* kind to her in his life. His manner seemed changed; his voice was quick[12] from the agitation of joy, and all that had been awful[13] in his dignity seemed lost in tenderness. He led her nearer the light and looked at her again—inquired particularly after her health, and then correcting himself, observed, that he need *not* inquire, for her appearance spoke sufficiently on that point. A fine blush having succeeded the previous paleness of her face, he was justified in his belief of her equal improvement in health and beauty. He inquired next after her family, especially William; and his kindness altogether was such as made her reproach herself for loving him so little, and thinking his return a misfortune; and when, on having courage to lift her eyes to his face, she saw that he was grown thinner and had the burnt, fagged,[14] worn look of fatigue and a hot climate,[15] every

7.   The Crawfords demonstrate a basic sense of propriety that Mr. Yates lacks. Sir Thomas will perceive the difference, for while disapproving of Mr. Yates, he will come to like and appreciate the Crawfords.

8.   *confidence*: privacy, intimacy.

9.   Apology for not being able to stay and see Sir Thomas—the polite way to excuse themselves and avoid intruding on the family reunion.

10. *penetrated her*: pierced her heart, affected her deeply.

11. *oppressed*: overwhelmed.

12. *quick*: animated, lively.

13. *awful*: imposing; tending to inspire awe or fear.

14. *fagged*: wearied, exhausted.

15. The baleful effects of a hot climate on people's health and appearance are a frequent theme in English writings of the time; one reason was the tendency of English people, due to their pale skin, to be burnt by the tropical sun.

Liverpool harbor (see the next page).

[From Richard Ayton and William Daniell, *A Voyage Round Great Britain*, Vol. II (London, 1815)]

tender feeling was increased, and she was miserable in considering how much unsuspected vexation was probably ready to burst on him.

Sir Thomas was indeed the life of the party, who at his suggestion now seated themselves round the fire. He had the best right to be the talker; and the delight of his sensations in being again in his own house, in the centre of his family, after such a separation, made him communicative and chatty in a very unusual degree; and he was ready to give every information[16] as to his voyage, and answer every question of his two sons almost before it was put. His business in Antigua had latterly been prosperously rapid, and he came directly from Liverpool,[17] having had an opportunity of making his passage thither in a private vessel, instead of waiting for the packet;[18] and all the little particulars of his proceedings and events, his arrivals and departures, were most promptly delivered, as he sat by Lady Bertram and looked with heartfelt satisfaction on the faces around him—interrupting himself more than once, however, to remark on his good fortune in finding them all at home—coming unexpectedly as he did—all collected together exactly as he could have wished, but dared not depend on. Mr. Rushworth was not forgotten; a most friendly reception and warmth of hand-shaking had already met him, and with pointed attention he was now included in the objects most intimately connected with Mansfield. There was nothing disagreeable in Mr. Rushworth's appearance, and Sir Thomas was liking him already.

By not one of the circle was he listened to with such unbroken unalloyed enjoyment as by his wife, who was really extremely happy to see him, and whose feelings were so warmed by his sudden arrival, as to place her nearer agitation than she had been for the last twenty years. She had been *almost* fluttered for a few minutes, and still remained so sensibly animated as to put away her work, move Pug from her side, and give all her attention and all the rest of her sofa to her husband. She had no anxieties for any body to cloud *her* pleasure; her own time had been irreproachably spent during his absence; she had done a great deal of carpet work and made many yards of fringe;[19] and she would have answered as freely for the good conduct and useful pursuits of all the young people as for her own. It was so agreeable to her to see him again, and hear him talk, to have

16. *information*: communication.

17. Liverpool was, after London, the leading port in England at this time, and its position on the west coast made it especially prominent in trade with the Atlantic (see map, p. 882).

18. The packet boats went on a fixed schedule (see p. 207, note 2). The private vessel was probably a merchant ship going between Antigua and England. Many ships made this voyage, for Antigua, like other colonies in the West Indies, exported most of what it produced and imported most of what it consumed. As the owner of a plantation engaged in export, Sir Thomas might also have already had commercial dealings with the merchant who owned this vessel.

19. Carpet work involved stitching threads of colored wool onto a canvas in order to make hangings, cushions, rugs, or coverings for furniture; the original meaning of "carpet," still used in the eighteenth century alongside our cur-

A mantelpiece such as the Bertrams' drawing room might contain.
[From John Swarbrick, *Robert Adam and his Brothers* (New York, 1915), p. 79]

her ear amused and her whole comprehension filled by his narra-
tives, that she began particularly to feel how dreadfully she must have
missed him, and how impossible it would have been for her to bear
a lengthened absence.

Mrs. Norris was by no means to be compared in happiness to her
sister. Not that *she* was incommoded by many fears of Sir Thomas's
disapprobation when the present state of his house should be known,
for her judgment had been so blinded, that except by the instinctive caution with which she had whisked away Mr. Rushworth's pink
satin cloak as her brother-in-law entered, she could hardly be said
to shew any sign of alarm;[20] but she was vexed by the *manner* of his
return. It had left her nothing to do. Instead of being sent for out of
the room, and seeing him first, and having to spread the happy news
through the house, Sir Thomas, with a very reasonable dependence
perhaps on the nerves of his wife and children, had sought no confidant but the butler, and had been following him almost instanta-
neously into the drawing-room.[21] Mrs. Norris felt herself defrauded
of an office[22] on which she had always depended, whether his arrival
or his death were to be the thing unfolded; and was now trying to
be in a bustle without having any thing to bustle about, and labour-
ing to be important where nothing was wanted but tranquillity and
silence. Would Sir Thomas have consented to eat, she might have
gone to the housekeeper with troublesome directions, and insulted
the footmen with injunctions of dispatch;[23] but Sir Thomas reso-
lutely declined all dinner; he would take nothing, nothing till tea
came—he would rather wait for tea. Still Mrs. Norris was at intervals
urging something different, and in the most interesting moment of
his passage to England, when the alarm of a French privateer was at
the height,[24] she burst through his recital with the proposal of soup.
"Sure, my dear Sir Thomas, a basin of soup would be a much better
thing for you than tea. Do have a basin of soup."

Sir Thomas could not be provoked. "Still the same anxiety for
every body's comfort, my dear Mrs. Norris," was his answer. "But
indeed I would rather have nothing but tea."

"Well then, Lady Bertram, suppose you speak for tea directly, suppose you hurry Baddeley a little,[25] he seems behind hand to-night."
She carried this point, and Sir Thomas's narrative proceeded.

rent meaning, was a thick fabric covering, such as a tablecloth or a bedspread. Carpet work was a common activity at the time for wealthy ladies, especially older ones; in *Emma* the heroine anticipates engaging in it when she grows old. Bedcovers as well as other items often had elaborate fringes.

20. She contrasts here with the young people, who thus show themselves wiser than she is.

21. The butler, the highest-ranking male servant, would normally answer the door, or, if a footman had answered it, would have been summoned in the event of such an important arrival. In either case, the butler would then conduct Sir Thomas toward the drawing room. The standard ritual would be for the butler to announce him, while Sir Thomas waited and then entered, but Sir Thomas's eagerness makes him hardly wait at all.

22. *office:* duty, task.

23. The housekeeper receives instructions regarding food, and the footmen bring it from the kitchen.

24. A privateer was a ship authorized by a government at war to capture enemy vessels and seize their contents; in effect, it was a legalized pirate ship. At this time Britain and France had been at war for twenty years, and the British navy had succeeded in destroying much of the French navy or blockading it in harbor. This was also true of French privateers, but a small number were still active.

25. Baddeley, as later revealed, is the butler. As an upper servant, he is called by his last name.

At length there was a pause. His immediate communications were exhausted, and it seemed enough to be looking joyfully around him, now at one, now at another of the beloved circle; but the pause was not long: in the elation of her spirits Lady Bertram became talkative, and what were the sensations of her children upon hearing her say, "How do you think the young people have been amusing themselves lately, Sir Thomas? They have been acting. We have been all alive with acting."

"Indeed! and what have you been acting?"

"Oh! They'll tell you all about it."

"The *all* will be soon told," cried Tom hastily, and with affected unconcern; "but it is not worth while to bore my father with it now. You will hear enough of it to-morrow, sir. We have just been trying, by way of[26] doing something, and amusing my mother, just within the last week, to get up a few scenes, a mere trifle. We have had such incessant rains almost since October began, that we have been nearly confined to the house for days together. I have hardly taken out a gun since the 3d. Tolerable sport the first three days, but there has been no attempting any thing since.[27] The first day I went over Mansfield Wood, and Edmund took the copses beyond Easton,[28] and we brought home six brace[29] between us, and might each have killed six times as many; but we respect your pheasants, sir, I assure you, as much as you could desire.[30] I do not think you will find your woods by any means worse stocked than they were. *I* never saw Mansfield Wood so full of pheasants in my life as this year. I hope you will take a day's sport there yourself, sir, soon."

For the present the danger was over, and Fanny's sick feelings subsided; but when tea was soon afterwards brought in, and Sir Thomas, getting up, said that he found he could not be any longer in the house without just looking into his own dear room, every agitation was returning. He was gone before any thing had been said to prepare him for the change he must find there; and a pause of alarm followed his disappearance. Edmund was the first to speak:

"Something must be done," said he.

"It is time to think of our visitors," said Maria, still feeling her hand pressed to Henry Crawford's heart, and caring little for any thing else.—"Where did you leave Miss Crawford, Fanny?"

26. *by way of*: for the purpose of.

27. October 1 is the beginning of the legal season for shooting pheasants, one of the two principal game birds (the other, partridge, was the object of the September shooting mentioned earlier in the novel). It is now early to mid-October—see chronology, p. 856.

28. Easton, which is fictional and never mentioned elsewhere, is simply meant to be a nearby locale. A large estate like Sir Thomas's would likely have more than one place where game abounded.

29. *six brace*: twelve. A brace means two birds.

30. Stocking the woods of an estate with plenty of game (through measures to encourage breeding) and preserving that stock were imperatives for those who prized shooting. Improved methods of killing during this period, including better guns, meant that stocks of birds could easily become exhausted.

Pheasant shooting.

[From *The Repository of arts, literature, fashions, manufactures, &c*, Vol. VIII (1810), p. 243]

Fanny told of their departure, and delivered their message.

"Then poor Yates is all alone," cried Tom. "I will go and fetch him. He will be no bad assistant when it all comes out."[31]

To the Theatre he went, and reached it just in time to witness the first meeting of his father and his friend. Sir Thomas had been a good deal surprized[32] to find candles burning in his room;[33] and on casting his eye round it, to see other symptoms of recent habitation, and a general air of confusion in the furniture. The removal of the bookcase from before the billiard room door struck him especially, but he had scarcely more than time to feel astonished at all this, before there were sounds from the billiard room to astonish him still further. Some one was talking there in a very loud accent[34]—he did not know the voice—*more* than talking—almost hallooing.[35] He stept to the door rejoicing at that moment in having the means of immediate communication, and opening it, found himself on the stage of a theatre, and opposed to[36] a ranting young man, who appeared likely to knock him down backwards. At the very moment of Yates perceiving Sir Thomas, and giving perhaps the very best start he had ever given in the whole course of his rehearsals,[37] Tom Bertram entered at the other end of the room; and never had he found greater difficulty in keeping his countenance. His father's looks of solemnity and amazement on this his first appearance on any stage, and the gradual metamorphosis of the impassioned Baron Wildenhaim into the well-bred and easy[38] Mr. Yates, making his bow and apology to Sir Thomas Bertram, was such an exhibition, such a piece of true acting as he would not have lost upon any account. It would be the last—in all probability the last scene on that stage; but he was sure there could not be a finer. The house[39] would close with the greatest eclat.

There was little time, however, for the indulgence of any images of merriment. It was necessary for him to step forward too and assist the introduction, and with many awkward sensations he did his best. Sir Thomas received Mr. Yates with all the appearance of cordiality which was due to his own character, but was really as far from pleased with the necessity of the acquaintance as with the manner of its commencement. Mr. Yates's family and connections were sufficiently known to him, to render his introduction as the "particu-

31. He means that Yates will be of help in explaining and justifying their acting scheme to Sir Thomas. This proves to be a miscalculation, a sign of Tom's blindness with regard to his friend.

32. This spelling of "surprise" will continue throughout volume II, before volume III resumes our current spelling using an "s" (which already appeared in volume I). The variation reflects publishing practices of the day. Books were not, as they are today, copyedited by the publisher to correct mistakes and ensure uniform stylistic conventions. Instead, publishers sent authors' manuscripts directly to the printer, which then corrected them for spelling, punctuation, and capitalization. Since each printer had its own house rules on these matters, and different printers were often employed for the same book, variation within the same text could result. The 1816 edition of *Mansfield Park* used a different printer for each volume, producing this inconsistency of spelling as well as other inconsistencies.

A number of words in the eighteenth century were spelled using "z" where "s" is now used. In the case of "surprise," the "z" form was fading. This is reflected in Austen's own letters and unpublished manuscripts: in her youth she used both spellings, but later only the current one. Both continued to appear in her published works (*Emma*, the novel published after this one, also has a division by volume, with the "z" spelling in the first two and the "s" in the last).

33. Candles were expensive, so they would never be left burning in an unused room; with the entire family gathered in the drawing room, Sir Thomas would not expect to see candles burning elsewhere.

34. *accent*: tone.

35. *hallooing*: shouting, especially to attract attention. Yates is practicing his part in the play in his usual exaggerated manner.

36. *opposed to*: opposite.

37. At four points in the play the stage directions specify that Mr. Yates's character, the Baron, should "start" due to the surprising or shocking nature of something he has heard.

38. *easy*: unembarrassed, affable.

39. *house*: playhouse.

lar friend," another of the hundred particular friends of his son,[40] exceedingly unwelcome; and it needed all the felicity of being again at home, and all the forbearance it could supply, to save Sir Thomas from anger on finding himself thus bewildered in his own house, making part of a ridiculous exhibition in the midst of theatrical non-sense, and forced in so untoward a moment to admit the acquaintance of a young man whom he felt sure of disapproving, and whose easy indifference and volubility in the course of the first five minutes seemed to mark him the most at home of the two.[41]

Tom understood his father's thoughts, and heartily wishing he might be always as well disposed to give them but partial expression, began to see more clearly than he had ever done before that there might be some ground of offence — that there might be some reason for the glance his father gave towards the ceiling and stucco of the room;[42] and that when he inquired with mild gravity after the fate of the billiard table, he was not proceeding beyond a very allowable curiosity. A few minutes were enough for such unsatisfactory sensations on each side; and Sir Thomas, having exerted himself so far as to speak a few words of calm approbation in reply to an eager appeal of Mr. Yates, as to the happiness of the arrangement, the three gentlemen returned to the drawing-room together, Sir Thomas with an increase of gravity which was not lost on all.

"I come from your theatre," said he composedly, as he sat down; "I found myself in it rather unexpectedly. Its vicinity to my own room — but in every respect indeed it took me by surprize, as I had not the smallest suspicion of your acting having assumed so serious a character. It appears a neat job, however, as far as I could judge by candle-light, and does my friend Christopher Jackson credit."[43] And then he would have changed the subject, and sipped his coffee in peace over domestic matters of a calmer hue; but Mr. Yates, without discernment to catch Sir Thomas's meaning, or diffidence,[44] or delicacy, or discretion enough to allow him to lead the discourse while he mingled among the others with the least obtrusiveness himself, would keep him on the topic of the theatre, would torment him with questions and remarks relative to it, and finally would make him hear the whole history of his disappointment at Ecclesford. Sir Thomas listened most politely, but found much to offend his ideas

40. Tom's habits have apparently led him to form quick acquaintances with many young men over the years, and to describe them as his good friends, despite barely knowing them.

41. As a guest in the presence of the owner of the house, Mr. Yates should be restrained and quiet, and let his host take the lead and set the tone.

42. Stucco in this context means plaster carved into shapes for interior decoration. Grand English houses of the time used plaster carvings extensively, especially around the tops of walls (see the picture on the next page); Sir Thomas looks at the stucco at the same time as the ceiling to ascertain if either has been damaged by the activity and alterations in the room.

43. His use of "friend" for Christopher Jackson, the estate carpenter, is typical of the time. It does not mean that Sir Thomas regards him as an equal or associates with him socially—he would certainly do neither—but that he regards him as a good acquaintance with whom he has friendly relations and toward whom he feels goodwill.

44. *diffidence*: modesty. The word was often used in a positive sense then.

Pheasants.

[From *The Repository of arts, literature, fashions, manufactures, &c*, Vol. II (1809), p. 180]

of decorum and confirm his ill opinion of Mr. Yates's habits of think-ing from the beginning to the end of the story; and when it was over, could give him no other assurance of sympathy than what a slight bow conveyed.[45]

"This was in fact the origin of *our* acting," said Tom after a moment's thought. "My friend Yates brought the infection from Ecclesford, and it spread as those things always spread you know, sir—the faster probably from *your* having so often encouraged the sort of thing in us formerly.[46] It was like treading old ground again."

Mr. Yates took the subject from his friend as soon as possible, and immediately gave Sir Thomas an account of what they had done and were doing, told him of the gradual increase of their views,[47] the happy conclusion of their first difficulties, and present promising state of affairs; relating every thing with so blind an interest as made him not only totally unconscious of the uneasy movements of many of his friends as they sat, the change of countenance, the fidget, the hem! of unquietness, but prevented him even from seeing the expres-sion of the face on which his own eyes were fixed—from seeing Sir Thomas's dark brow contract as he looked with inquiring earnestness at his daughters and Edmund, dwelling particularly on the latter, and speaking a language, a remonstrance, a reproof, which *he* felt at his heart. Not less acutely was it felt by Fanny, who had edged back her chair behind her aunt's end of the sofa, and, screened from notice herself, saw all that was passing before her. Such a look of reproach at Edmund from his father she could never have expected to witness; and to feel that it was in any degree deserved, was an aggravation indeed. Sir Thomas's look implied, "On your judgment, Edmund, I depended; what have you been about?"—She knelt in spirit to her uncle,[48] and her bosom swelled to utter, "Oh! not to *him*. Look so to all the others, but not to *him*!"

Mr. Yates was still talking. "To own the truth, Sir Thomas, we were in the middle of a rehearsal when you arrived this evening. We were going through the three first acts, and not unsuccessfully upon the whole. Our company is now so dispersed from the Crawfords being gone home, that nothing more can be done to-night; but if you will give us the honour of your company to-morrow evening, I should not

45. A silent bow allows Sir Thomas to avoid the rudeness of not responding at all, for anything he said in reply would either be a lie or an indication of his disapproval.

46. He means what he earlier mentioned to Edmund, their reciting of speeches from plays in front of Sir Thomas when they were young — see p. 242.

47. *views*: plans, designs.

48. Meaning she imagines pleading for mercy for Edmund.

An elegant house of the period with stucco on the walls.

[From J. Alfred Gotch, *The English Home from Charles I to George IV* (New York, 1918), p. 363]

be afraid of the result. We bespeak your indulgence, you understand, as young performers; we bespeak your indulgence."[49]

"My indulgence shall be given, sir," replied Sir Thomas gravely, "but without any other rehearsal."—And with a relenting smile he added, "I come home to be happy and indulgent." Then turning away towards any or all of the rest, he tranquilly said, "Mr. and Miss Crawford were mentioned in my last letters from Mansfield. Do you find them agreeable acquaintance?"

Tom was the only one at all ready with an answer, but he being entirely without particular regard for either, without jealousy either in love or acting, could speak very handsomely of both. "Mr. Crawford was a most pleasant gentleman-like man;—his sister a sweet, pretty, elegant, lively girl."

Mr. Rushworth could be silent no longer. "I do not say he is not gentleman-like, considering; but you should tell your father he is not above five feet eight, or he will be expecting a well-looking man."

Sir Thomas did not quite understand this, and looked with some surprize at the speaker.

"If I must say what I think," continued Mr. Rushworth, "in my opinion it is very disagreeable to be always rehearsing. It is having too much of a good thing. I am not so fond of acting as I was at first. I think we are a great deal better employed, sitting comfortably here among ourselves, and doing nothing."

Sir Thomas looked again, and then replied with an approving smile, "I am happy to find our sentiments on this subject so much the same. It gives me sincere satisfaction. That I should be cautious and quick-sighted,[50] and feel many scruples which my children do *not* feel, is perfectly natural; and equally so that *my* value for domestic tranquillity, for a home which shuts out noisy pleasures, should much exceed theirs. But at your time of life to feel all this, is a most favourable circumstance for yourself and for every body connected with you; and I am sensible[51] of the importance of having an ally of such weight."

Sir Thomas meant to be giving Mr. Rushworth's opinion in better words than he could find himself. He was aware that he must not expect a genius in Mr. Rushworth; but as a well-judging steady young man, with better notions than his elocution[52] would do justice to, he

49. To bespeak, i.e., request, someone's indulgence was a common phrase at the time, often in formal contexts such as an official address. Here the phrase fits with Mr. Yates's preceding "give us the honour of your company."

50. By "quick-sighted" he means quick or keen in perceiving the dangers of an activity like this, a keenness that his greater experience of life has given him.

51. *sensible*: conscious, cognizant.

52. *elocution*: manner or power of expression.

Reading by candlelight.

[From *The Repository of arts, literature, fashions, manufactures, &c*, Vol. IX (1813), p. 168]

intended to value him very highly. It was impossible for many of the others not to smile. Mr. Rushworth hardly knew what to do with so much meaning; but by looking, as he really felt, most exceedingly pleased with Sir Thomas's good opinion, and saying scarcely any thing, he did his best towards preserving that good opinion a little longer.[53]

53. This incident is one more way the theatrical project affects the story. Mr. Rushworth's denunciation of it, though motivated solely by jealousy of Henry Crawford, has helped to delay Sir Thomas's discovery of the foolish character of his prospective son-in-law, and this delay will have critical consequences (p. 372).

A man in evening dress.

[From *The Repository of arts, literature, fashions, manufactures, &c*, Vol. III (1812), p. 27]

Chapter Two

*E*dmund's first object the next morning was to see his father alone, and give him a fair statement of the whole acting scheme, defending his own share in it as far only as he could then, in a soberer moment, feel his motives to deserve, and acknowledging with perfect ingenuousness that his concession had been attended with such partial good as to make his judgment in it very doubtful. He was anxious, while vindicating himself, to say nothing unkind of the others; but there was only one amongst them whose conduct he could mention without some necessity of defence or palliation. "We have all been more or less to blame," said he, "every one of us, excepting Fanny. Fanny is the only one who has judged rightly throughout, who has been consistent. *Her* feelings have been steadily against it from first to last. She never ceased to think of what was due to you. You will find Fanny every thing you could wish."

Sir Thomas saw all the impropriety of such a scheme among such a party, and at such a time, as strongly as his son had ever supposed he must; he felt it too much indeed for many words; and having shaken hands with Edmund,[1] meant to try to lose the disagreeable impression, and forget how much he had been forgotten himself as soon as he could, after the house had been cleared of every object enforcing the remembrance, and restored to its proper state. He did not enter into any remonstrance with his other children: he was more willing to believe they felt their error, than to run the risk of investigation.[2] The reproof of an immediate conclusion of every thing, the sweep of every preparation would be sufficient.

There was one person, however, in the house whom he could not leave to learn his sentiments merely through his conduct. He could not help giving Mrs. Norris a hint of his having hoped, that her advice might have been interposed to prevent what her judgment must certainly have disapproved. The young people had been very inconsiderate[3] in forming the plan; they ought to have been capable

1.   Shaking hands was not done with any person one met; the gesture usually signified particular friendship and affection. In this case Sir Thomas probably uses it to indicate his forgiveness of Edmund and his hope that they can put the incident behind them.

2.   Meaning the risk that, upon investigating their feelings, he might learn that they do not feel their error as they ought. Hence Sir Thomas, in avoiding possible bad news, keeps from learning more of the true moral and emotional state of his three more wayward children.

3.   *inconsiderate*: rash, lacking in consideration.

of a better decision themselves; but they were young,[4] and, excepting Edmund, he believed of unsteady characters; and with greater
surprize therefore he must regard her acquiescence in their wrong
measures,[5] her countenance of their unsafe amusements, than that
such measures and such amusements should have been suggested.
Mrs. Norris was a little confounded, and as nearly being silenced as
ever she had been in her life; for she was ashamed to confess having never seen any of the impropriety which was so glaring to Sir
Thomas, and would not have admitted that her influence was insufficient, that she might have talked in vain. Her only resource was
to get out of the subject as fast as possible, and turn the current of
Sir Thomas's ideas[6] into a happier channel. She had a great deal to
insinuate in her own praise as to *general* attention to the interest and
comfort of his family, much exertion and many sacrifices to glance
at in the form of hurried walks and sudden removals from her own
fire-side, and many excellent hints of distrust and economy to Lady
Bertram and Edmund to detail, whereby a most considerable saving
had always arisen, and more than one bad servant been detected.[7]
But her chief strength lay in Sotherton. Her greatest support and
glory was in having formed the connection[8] with the Rushworths.
There she was impregnable. She took to herself all the credit of bringing Mr. Rushworth's admiration of Maria to any effect. "If I had not
been active," said she, "and made a point of being introduced to his
mother, and then prevailed on my sister to pay the first visit, I am as
certain as I sit here, that nothing would have come of it—for Mr.
Rushworth is the sort of amiable modest young man who wants a
great deal of encouragement, and there were girls enough on the
catch for him[9] if we had been idle. But I left no stone unturned. I
was ready to move heaven and earth to persuade my sister, and at
last I did persuade her. You know the distance to Sotherton; it was
in the middle of winter, and the roads almost impassable, but I did
persuade her."[10]

"I know how great, how justly great your influence is with Lady
Bertram and her children, and am the more concerned that it should
not have been"——

"My dear Sir Thomas, if you had seen the state of the roads *that*
day! I thought we should never have got through them, though we

4.   There was a tendency to make allowances for youth in judging bad actions or decisions, along with a tendency to believe young people needed supervision and should not be allowed complete autonomy.

5.   *measures*: plans, course of action.

6.   *ideas*: thoughts.

7.   Lady Bertram, as the mistress of the house, is in charge of household affairs, including decisions on purchases and spending as well as the supervision of servants. With Tom often away, Edmund is left to fulfill Sir Thomas's place, and, given his mother's complete indolence, he must take effective charge of many of her concerns. The "hints of distrust" would be regarding a bad servant. Mrs. Norris is consistently shown chastising servants or criticizing their behavior.

8.   *connection*: engagement, and the connection with the whole family that will result. The use of "connection" to refer to an engagement or marriage reflects the view of marriage as a means of linking two entire families for their mutual advantage.

9.   *on the catch for him*: waiting or looking for an opportunity to snare him as a husband.

10.   Lady Bertram's visit to Sotherton (p. 76) was important in helping to form the engagement. It was described as being over "indifferent road."

Grounds with plantations in the distance.

[From C. L. Stieglitz and K. A. Siegel, *Descriptions pittoresques de jardins du goût le plus moderns* (Leipzig, 1802), Plate IIA]

had the four horses of course;[11] and poor old coachman would attend us, out of his great love and kindness, though he was hardly able to sit the box[12] on account of the rheumatism[13] which I had been doctoring him for, ever since Michaelmas.[14] I cured him at last; but he was very bad all the winter[15]—and this was such a day, I could not help going to him up in his room before we set off to advise him not to venture: he was putting on his wig[16]—so I said, 'Coachman, you had much better not go, your Lady and I shall be very safe; you know how steady Stephen is, and Charles has been upon the leaders so often now, that I am sure there is no fear.'[17] But, however, I soon found it would not do; he was bent upon going, and as I hate to be worrying and officious, I said no more; but my heart quite ached for him at every jolt, and when we got into the rough lanes about Stoke,[18] where what with frost and snow upon beds of stones, it was worse than any thing you can imagine,[19] I was quite in an agony about him. And then the poor horses too!—To see them straining away! You know how I always feel for the horses. And when we got to the bottom of Sandcroft Hill, what do you think I did? You will laugh at me—but I got out and walked up. I did indeed. It might not be saving them much, but it was something, and I could not bear to sit at my ease, and be dragged up at the expense of those noble animals.[20]

A contemporary drawing of a chaise with the driver on the horse.

[From John Ashton, *Social England under the Regency* (London, 1899), p. 350]

11. They probably went in a chaise, described elsewhere as the family carriage. A chaise usually was driven by two horses, but four would allow it to go faster and to perform better over difficult roads. They would also help to impress the Rushworths with the Bertrams' wealth, making a match with Maria seem more desirable.

12. *sit the box*: sit on the box (the driver's seat at the front of the carriage).

13. *rheumatism*: arthritis, specifically what is now called osteoarthritis. Rheumatoid arthritis was usually called rheumatic gout then.

14. *Michaelmas*: September 29. It was one of the dates used to divide the year into quarters; the others were Christmas, Lady Day (March 25), and Midsummer (June 24). Rents and other regular payments were often due on those days, and many contracts began and ended on one of them.

15. His arthritis might naturally worsen in the winter, especially since houses then could be cold and damp. Mrs. Norris was shown earlier giving medical advice. Her boast of curing is an exaggeration, for one cannot really cure arthritis, but she may have given the coachman something to relieve his symptoms.

16. Servants' rooms were usually on the top floor of the house, unless they were in a separate wing. Wigs for men had ceased to be fashionable in the 1790s, but they still were often worn by coachmen.

17. Stephen and Charles are lower-ranking servants, who probably assist the coachman with the carriages and horses. An establishment with many horses would have a number of servants taking care of them. The "leaders" are the two horses in front; and Charles sits on one to help manage them. Horses pulling carriages, especially chaises, were often driven solely by a rider on one of the horses. In this case, they may be combining that with a driver on the carriage, which could make driving easier over rough conditions and would also look more impressive when they arrive at Sotherton.

18. Stoke was already mentioned as a nearby place.

19. The usual way to make ordinary roads then was to pile gravel or stones on top of flattened dirt; this could naturally become very uneven.

20. Horses were expensive, and they would eventually become exhausted from years of work and have to be retired. Hence lightening their labor would represent a small saving, though this, like many other of Mrs. Norris's boasts, is a minor matter compared with the issue of the play.

I caught a dreadful cold, but *that* I did not regard. My object was accomplished in the visit."

"I hope we shall always think the acquaintance worth any trouble that might be taken to establish it. There is nothing very striking in Mr. Rushworth's manners,[21] but I was pleased last night with what appeared to be his opinion on *one* subject—his decided preference of a quiet family-party to the bustle and confusion of acting. He seemed to feel exactly as one could wish."

"Yes, indeed,—and the more you know of him, the better you will like him. He is not a shining[22] character, but he has a thousand good qualities! and is so disposed to look up to you, that I am quite laughed at about it, for every body considers it as my doing. 'Upon my word, Mrs. Norris,' said Mrs. Grant, the other day, 'if Mr. Rushworth were a son of your own he could not hold Sir Thomas in greater respect.'"

Sir Thomas gave up the point, foiled by her evasions, disarmed by her flattery; and was obliged to rest satisfied with the conviction that where the present pleasure of those she loved was at stake, her kindness did sometimes overpower her judgment.

It was a busy morning with him. Conversation with any of them occupied but a small part of it. He had to reinstate himself in all the wonted concerns of his Mansfield life, to see his steward and his bailiff—to examine and compute[23]—and, in the intervals of business, to walk into his stables and his gardens, and nearest plantations;[24] but active and methodical, he had not only done all this before he resumed his seat as master of the house at dinner, he had also set the carpenter to work in pulling down what had been so lately put up in the billiard room, and given the scene painter his dismissal, long enough to justify the pleasing belief of his being then at least as far off as Northampton.[25] The scene painter was gone, having spoilt only the floor of one room, ruined all the coachman's sponges,[26] and made five of the under-servants idle and dissatisfied;[27] and Sir Thomas was in hopes that another day or two would suffice to wipe away every outward memento of what had been, even to the destruction of every unbound copy of "Lovers' Vows" in the house, for he was burning all that met his eye.[28]

Mr. Yates was beginning now to understand Sir Thomas's intentions, though as far as ever from understanding their source. He and

21. *manners*: general conduct or behavior.

22. *shining*: distinguished, brilliant.

23. The steward was in charge of the whole estate, including the part leased out to tenant farmers. The bailiff, who was often under the steward, took charge specifically of the home farm, the smaller piece of land that the owning family farmed directly to produce food for their own consumption. Both of their jobs included keeping financial accounts, with which the computing described is probably concerned.

24. His plantations probably are areas of planted trees, the principal meaning of the term then. Trees helped beautify the land while also providing timber, a valuable product.

25. Northampton, the nearest large town, is his first stop on the way back to London. He may, after having been driven to Northampton in the Bertrams' carriage, switch to a public coach.

26. The coachman uses sponges to clean the carriages, which could get very dirty under prevailing road conditions. If the painter used them to clean up paint, the sponges would no longer be useful for other cleaning.

27. The principal task of the most common of under-servants, housemaids, was cleaning the rooms, and the scene-painters' presence would impede their ability to do that. This could distress the servants, who would also know they faced a huge job returning the rooms to their normal state when he left.

28. Books were normally published unbound then; a purchaser would pay to have one bound, choosing the style and quality of the binding according to his or her taste and budget. In this case, as they bought copies of the play to use for only a short period, they elected to forgo the trouble and expense of having them bound.

his friend had been out with their guns the chief of the morning, and Tom had taken the opportunity of explaining, with proper apologies for his father's particularity,[29] what was to be expected. Mr. Yates felt it as acutely as might be supposed. To be a second time disappointed in the same way was an instance of very severe ill-luck; and his indignation was such, that had it not been for delicacy towards his friend and his friend's youngest sister, he believed he should certainly attack the Baronet on the absurdity of his proceedings, and argue him into a little more rationality. He believed this very stoutly while he was in Mansfield Wood, and all the way home; but there was a something in Sir Thomas, when they sat round the same table, which made Mr. Yates think it wiser to let him pursue his own way, and feel the folly of it without opposition. He had known many disagreeable fathers before, and often been struck with the inconveniences they occasioned, but never in the whole course of his life, had he seen one of that class, so unintelligibly moral, so infamously tyrannical as Sir Thomas.[30] He was not a man to be endured but for his children's sake, and he might be thankful to his fair daughter Julia that Mr. Yates did yet mean to stay a few days longer under his roof.[31]

The evening passed with external smoothness, though almost every mind was ruffled; and the music which Sir Thomas called for from his daughters helped to conceal the want of real harmony.[32] Maria was in a good deal of agitation. It was of the utmost consequence to her that Crawford should now lose no time in declaring himself,[33] and she was disturbed that even a day should be gone by without seeming to advance that point. She had been expecting to see him the whole morning—and all the evening too was still expecting him. Mr. Rushworth had set off early with the great news for Sotherton;[34] and she had fondly hoped for such an immediate eclaircissement as might save him the trouble of ever coming back again. But they had seen no one from the Parsonage—not a creature, and had heard no tidings beyond a friendly note of congratulation and inquiry from Mrs. Grant to Lady Bertram. It was the first day for many, many weeks, in which the families had been wholly divided. Four-and-twenty hours had never passed before,

29. *particularity*: peculiarity.

30. Fathers were usually the principal barrier to the pleasures pursued by wealthy young men like Mr. Yates. Fathers who disapproved of their sons' extravagances could cut off or reduce their allowances, generally the sons' sole or principal source of income while their fathers were alive. The *Loiterer*, a periodical written by Jane Austen's brother James while he was at Oxford, to which she may have contributed an essay, contains a satirical portrayal, in the form of an imaginary diary, of an idle and dissipated student. He relates having received, to his dissatisfaction, "a letter from my father, no money, and a great deal of advice—wants to know how my last quarter's allowance went—how the devil should I know?—he knows I keep no account—Do think fathers are the greatest *Bores* in nature."

31. This is an example of Jane Austen's technique of writing from the point of view of a character, instead of as an objective narrator, and thereby giving a vivid picture of the character's thoughts. The eighteenth-century novels that shaped her development as a writer were often written in the form of letters or diaries, a technique that allows the reader to enter completely into the inner thoughts and perspective of a character. In her youth she tried writing a few pieces in this manner, and may have even written initial drafts of *Sense and Sensibility* or *Pride and Prejudice* in the form of letters. While she eventually rejected the technique, which has serious handicaps in telling a complex story with many characters, she still exhibits its influence by including passages where characters do, in effect, speak their thoughts for themselves through the medium of the narrator. In this passage Mr. Yates reveals his vanity and folly by imagining that his host is thankful for his continued presence in his house.

32. They play the pianoforte, and possibly sing, since young ladies were often taught that as well and the most common piano pieces were songs with words. The teaching of music allowed people to play for family and friends; otherwise the only music most people heard was at church.

33. Thinking of him as "Crawford," with no "Mr.," indicates her belief in their intimacy, for women would do that with unrelated men of their own rank only if they were very close, and even then many did not.

34. The great news is Sir Thomas's return, which will allow his wedding to Maria to finally take place.

since August began, without bringing them together in some way or other.[35] It was a sad anxious day; and the morrow, though differing in the sort of evil, did by no means bring less. A few moments of feverish enjoyment were followed by hours of acute suffering. Henry Crawford was again in the house; he walked up with Dr. Grant, who was anxious to pay his respects to Sir Thomas,[36] and at rather an early hour they were ushered into the breakfast room,[37] where were most of the family. Sir Thomas soon appeared, and Maria saw with delight and agitation the introduction of the man she loved to her father. Her sensations were indefinable, and so were they a few minutes afterwards upon hearing Henry Crawford, who had a chair between herself and Tom, ask the latter in an under voice, whether there were any plan for resuming the play after the present happy interruption, (with a courteous glance at Sir Thomas), because in that case, he should make a point of returning to Mansfield, at any time required by the party; he was going away immediately, being to meet his uncle at Bath without delay,[38] but if there were any prospect of a renewal of "Lovers' Vows," he should hold himself positively engaged, he should break through[39] every other claim, he should absolutely condition[40] with his uncle for attending them whenever he might be wanted. The play should not be lost by *his* absence.

"From Bath, Norfolk, London, York—wherever I may be,"[41] said he, "I will attend you from any place in England, at an hour's notice."

It was well at that moment that Tom had to speak and not his sister. He could immediately say with easy fluency, "I am sorry you are going—but as to our play, *that* is all over—entirely at an end (looking significantly at his father). The painter was sent off yesterday, and very little will remain of the theatre to-morrow.—I knew how *that* would be from the first.—It is early for Bath.—You will find nobody there."

"It is about my uncle's usual time."[42]

"When do you think of going?"

"I may perhaps get as far as Banbury to-day."[43]

"Whose stables do you use at Bath?"[44] was the next question; and while this branch of the subject was under discussion, Maria, who

35. Henry had been completely absent during the first two weeks of September, but Maria, with the vivid memory of recent weeks when he was constantly present, may have largely forgotten that by now.

36. Just as Mrs. Grant sent a note of congratulation to Lady Bertram, so Dr. Grant, being a man, is the one to pay his respects to Sir Thomas.

37. Usually a call like this would not occur so early. The reason for coming now, in addition to the anxiousness of Dr. Grant, is soon revealed.

38. Bath, in southwest England, was a spa town that for at least a century had been the country's leading resort. Jane Austen, who lived in Bath for five years, set half of two novels there; it is also the only town aside from London mentioned in all her novels. For a picture of Bath from the time, see p. 360.

39. *break through*: violate, cast aside.

40. *condition*: insist, stipulate.

41. Norfolk is where his estate lies. York is never otherwise mentioned in the novel. Henry mentions it not because he is likely to be there but to emphasize his willingness to come from anywhere; York, in the north of England, is farther from Northampton than any of the other places.

42. Bath was at its height during the winter, and during October was much less lively. His uncle may go there now because he, like many visitors, was going for his health; Bath initially became popular because of its abundant hot springs, believed to have medicinal qualities.

43. Banbury is on the route to Bath (see map, p. 882). The total distance from Northampton, which is several miles from Mansfield, to Bath was around ninety-eight miles by current roads. This would take more than a day using normal means of travel. Banbury is before the halfway point, but Henry will have only part of this day for travel. His wish to get started as soon as possible is the likely reason for the early hour of his and Dr. Grant's visit. Such reasoning, of course, as well as his speaking first to Tom, indicates the relative unimportance of Maria to his thoughts.

44. Bath had many stables to accommodate visitors. Stables, along with related matters of horses and carriages, are a frequent topic of conversation among men in Austen's novels. Tom's question, like his earlier comment about Bath's emptiness at this season, indicates his familiarity with the town. As a young man frequently traveling in pursuit of pleasure, he has undoubtedly gone there more than once; it would be a natural place to meet other idle and pleasure-loving young men.

wanted neither pride nor resolution, was preparing to encounter her share of it with tolerable calmness.[45]

To her he soon turned, repeating much of what he had already said, with only a softened air and stronger expressions of regret. But what availed his expressions or his air?—He was going—and if not voluntarily going, voluntarily intending to stay away; for, excepting what might be due to his uncle, his engagements were all self-imposed.—He might talk of necessity, but she knew his independence.[46]—The hand which had so pressed her's to his heart!—The hand and the heart were alike motionless and passive now! Her spirit supported her, but the agony of her mind was severe.—She had not long to endure what arose from listening to language, which his actions contradicted, or to bury the tumult of her feelings under the restraint of society; for general civilities soon called his notice from her, and the farewell visit, as it then became openly acknowledged, was a very short one.—He was gone—he had touched her hand for the last time,[47] he had made his parting bow, and she might seek directly[48] all that solitude could do for her. Henry Crawford was gone—gone from the house, and within two hours afterwards from the parish; and so ended all the hopes his selfish vanity had raised in Maria and Julia Bertram.[49]

Julia could rejoice that he was gone.—His presence was beginning to be odious to her; and if Maria gained him not, she was now cool enough to dispense with any other revenge.—She did not want exposure to be added to desertion.[50]—Henry Crawford gone, she could even pity her sister.

With a purer spirit did Fanny rejoice in the intelligence.[51]—She heard it at dinner and felt it a blessing. By all the others it was mentioned with regret, and his merits honoured with due gradation of feeling, from the sincerity of Edmund's too partial regard, to the unconcern of his mother speaking entirely by rote. Mrs. Norris began to look about her and wonder that his falling in love with Julia had come to nothing; and could almost fear that she had been remiss herself in forwarding it; but with so many to care for, how was it possible for even *her* activity[52] to keep pace with her wishes?

Another day or two, and Mr. Yates was gone likewise. In *his* departure Sir Thomas felt the chief interest; wanting to be alone with his

45. Maria has surmised that Henry is about to abandon her, despite all his earlier attentions. She is anguished and mortified, but, anticipating that he will speak to her next, she determines to avoid humiliation by maintaining an air of outward calm.

46. *independence*: financial independence. Mr. Crawford's fortune not only allows him to travel freely, but also means he can stay anywhere as long as he likes, since most business involving the management of his estate can be conducted by letter.

47. He may have simply shaken her hand, perhaps very lightly, as a parting gesture.

48. *directly*: immediately.

49. Henry's decision to leave now is prompted partly by the end of the play, which may make him wish for a fresh source of amusement. But he also undoubtedly fears further flirtation with Maria now that her father has returned, for Sir Thomas would probably notice their closeness, creating complications for Henry. Sir Thomas's sudden arrival may also have spurred Henry to pause and reflect, and to realize that he needs to pull back to avoid becoming seriously entangled with Maria.

50. That is, exposure of Maria's love for Henry Crawford, despite her engagement to another man, and her attempts through flirtation and close contact to draw him toward an offer of marriage. Such conduct would be scandalous, and knowledge of it could seriously harm Maria's reputation.

51. *intelligence*: news, information.

52. *activity*: vigor, diligence.

family, the presence of a stranger superior to Mr. Yates must have been irksome; but of him, trifling and confident, idle and expensive[53] it was every way vexatious. In himself he was wearisome, but as the friend of Tom and the admirer of Julia he became offensive.[54] Sir Thomas had been quite indifferent to Mr. Crawford's going or staying—but his good wishes for Mr. Yates's having a pleasant journey, as he walked with him to the hall door, were given with genuine satisfaction. Mr. Yates had staid to see the destruction of every theatrical preparation at Mansfield, the removal of every thing appertaining to the play; he left the house in all the soberness of its general character; and Sir Thomas hoped, in seeing him out of it, to be rid of the worst object connected with the scheme, and the last that must be inevitably reminding him of its existence.

Mrs. Norris contrived to remove one article from his sight that might have distressed him. The curtain over which she had presided with such talent and such success, went off with her to her cottage, where she happened to be particularly in want[55] of green baize.

Milsom Street, one of the leading shopping and residential streets in Bath.

[From J. Alfred Gotch, *The English Home from Charles I to George IV* (New York, 1918), p. 297]

53. *expensive*: extravagant.

54. Knowing of his son's propensity to behave foolishly and irresponsibly, Sir Thomas would not want him around a friend who could draw him further in that direction. He also knows that, with her sister about to marry, Julia may be thinking of marriage too, and he would not want her associating with a young man whose wealth and social rank might make him seem a desirable husband but whose character makes him highly undesirable in Sir Thomas's eyes.

55. *want*: need.

A pianoforte of the period.

[From Esther Singleton, *The Furniture of our Forefathers* (New York, 1916), p. 585]

Chapter Three

Sir Thomas's return made a striking change in the ways of the family,[1] independent of Lovers' Vows. Under his government, Mansfield was an altered place. Some members of their society sent away and the spirits of many others saddened, it was all sameness and gloom, compared with the past; a sombre family-party rarely enlivened. There was little intercourse with the Parsonage. Sir Thomas drawing back from intimacies in general, was particularly disinclined, at this time, for any engagements but in one quarter. The Rushworths were the only addition to his own domestic circle which he could solicit.

Edmund did not wonder that such should be his father's feelings, nor could he regret any thing but the exclusion of the Grants. "But they," he observed to Fanny, "have a claim. They seem to belong to us—they seem to be part of ourselves. I could wish my father were more sensible of their very great attention to my mother and sisters while he was away. I am afraid they may feel themselves neglected. But the truth is that my father hardly knows them. They had not been here a twelvemonth when he left England. If he knew them better, he would value their society as it deserves, for they are in fact exactly the sort of people he would like. We are sometimes a little in want of animation among ourselves; my sisters seem out of spirits, and Tom is certainly not at his ease. Dr. and Mrs. Grant would enliven us, and make our evenings pass away with more enjoyment even to my father."

"Do you think so?" said Fanny. "In my opinion, my uncle would not like *any* addition. I think he values the very quietness you speak of, and that the repose of his own family-circle is all he wants. And it does not appear to me that we are more serious than we used to be; I mean before my uncle went abroad. As well as I can recollect, it was always much the same. There was never much laughing in his presence; or, if there is any difference, it is not more I think than such an

1. *family*: household. The term could include servants as well, and probably does so here.

A wedding dress of the period.

[From Elisabeth McClellan, *Historic Dress in America, 1800–1870* (Philadelphia, 1910), p. 79]

absence has a tendency to produce at first. There must be a sort of shyness. But I cannot recollect that our evenings formerly were ever merry, except when my uncle was in town.[2] No young people's are, I suppose, when those they look up to are at home."

"I believe you are right, Fanny," was his reply, after a short consideration. "I believe our evenings are rather returned to what they were, than assuming a new character. The novelty was in their being lively.—Yet, how strong the impression that only a few weeks will give! I have been feeling as if we had never lived so before."[3]

"I suppose I am graver than other people," said Fanny. "The evenings do not appear long to me. I love to hear my uncle talk of the West Indies. I could listen to him for an hour together. It entertains *me* more than many other things have done—but then I am unlike other people I dare say."

"Why should you dare say *that*? (smiling)—Do you want to be told that you are only unlike other people in being more wise and discreet? But when did you or any body ever get a compliment from me, Fanny? Go to my father if you want to be complimented. He will satisfy you. Ask your uncle what he thinks, and you will hear compliments enough; and though they may be chiefly on your person, you must put up with it, and trust to his seeing as much beauty of mind in time."

Such language was so new to Fanny that it quite embarrassed her.

"Your uncle thinks you very pretty, dear Fanny—and that is the long and the short of the matter. Any body but myself would have made something more of it, and any body but you would resent that you had not been thought very pretty before; but the truth is, that your uncle never did admire you till now—and now he does. Your complexion is so improved!—and you have gained so much countenance![4]—and your figure[5]—Nay, Fanny, do not turn away about it—it is but an uncle. If you cannot bear an uncle's admiration what is to become of you?[6] You must really begin to harden yourself to the idea of being worth looking at.—You must try not to mind growing up into a pretty woman."

"Oh! don't talk so, don't talk so," cried Fanny, distressed by more feelings than he was aware of; but seeing that she was distressed, he had done with the subject, and only added more seriously, "Your

2.   He would have been in town, i.e., London, when attending sessions of Parliament.

3.   They have been seeing the Grants and the Crawfords for several months, but it was in the last few weeks that Edmund and Mary Crawford became especially close and saw each other frequently at Mansfield.

4.   *countenance*: composure, calm demeanor.

5.   *figure*: general appearance or form.

6.   Of course, though Edmund does not realize this, it is the fact that he expresses his agreement with his father's new assessment of Fanny that affects her so strongly.

uncle is disposed to be pleased with you in every respect; and I only wish you would talk to him more.—You are one of those who are too silent in the evening circle."

"But I do talk to him more than I used. I am sure I do. Did not you hear me ask him about the slave-trade last night?"[7]

"I did—and was in hopes the question would be followed up by others. It would have pleased your uncle to be inquired of farther."

"And I longed to do it—but there was such a dead silence! And while my cousins were sitting by without speaking a word, or seeming at all interested in the subject, I did not like—I thought it would appear as if I wanted to set myself off at their expense, by shewing a curiosity and pleasure in his information which he must wish his own daughters to feel."[8]

"Miss Crawford was very right in what she said of you the other day—that you seemed almost as fearful of notice and praise as other women were of neglect. We were talking of you at the Parsonage, and those were her words. She has great discernment. I know nobody who distinguishes characters better.—For so young a woman it is remarkable! She certainly understands *you* better than you are understood by the greater part of those who have known you so long; and with regard to some others, I can perceive, from occasional lively hints, the unguarded expressions of the moment, that she could define *many* as accurately, did not delicacy forbid it. I wonder what she thinks of my father! She must admire him as a fine looking man, with most gentleman-like, dignified, consistent manners; but perhaps having seen him so seldom, his reserve may be a little repulsive.[9] Could they be much together I feel sure of their liking each other. He would enjoy her liveliness—and she has talents to value his powers.[10] I wish they met more frequently!—I hope she does not suppose there is any dislike on his side."

"She must know herself too secure of the regard of all the rest of you," said Fanny with half a sigh, "to have any such apprehension. And Sir Thomas's wishing just at first to be only with his family is so very natural, that she can argue[11] nothing from that. After a little while I dare say we shall be meeting again in the same sort of way, allowing for the difference of the time of year."

"This is the first October that she has passed in the country since

7. The slave trade had been a prominent political issue in Britain since a major campaign to abolish it began in the 1780s. The campaign organized the formation of local committees across the country, and the gathering of petitions with hundreds of thousands of signatures to submit to Parliament. It also inspired numerous writings, as well as paintings and political cartoons and even special medallions by the leading porcelain manufacturer Wedgwood, that denounced the slave trade. This eventually led Parliament to abolish the trade (though not slavery itself) in 1807, but knowledge of the issue would have lingered, further spurred by criticisms of the continuation of slavery and measures like an act that made slave-trading a felony in 1811, the year before the composition of this novel began.

All this would make it natural for Fanny, whose reading of a book on Britain's recent mission to China indicates some curiosity about public affairs, to ask about the issue when listening to Sir Thomas discuss the West Indies, long the main end point of the trade in slaves. The end of the trade brought new conditions to the economy there, and forced estate owners like Sir Thomas to make adjustments. Some, knowing they could no longer buy replacement slaves, undertook new efforts to improve conditions among their existing slaves in order to lessen the death rate, efforts also encouraged in some cases by increased humanitarian concerns. Sir Thomas's own efforts in this regard, or other changes made in response to the end of the slave trade, may have partly caused the delay in his return. He also could discuss his experience in Parliament while the trade was being debated and abolished.

Finally, Fanny's interest could have been further spurred by her regular correspondence with her brother in the navy. While the navy had long protected Britain's slave trade, it was tasked after its abolition in 1807 with trying to suppress other nations' trade; Jane Austen's naval brothers, Francis and Charles, both captained ships whose duties included stopping slave ships. Moreover, some naval officers' experience overseas had turned them against slavery. In 1807, after Francis Austen's ship visited an island with slaves, he wrote that while it was not as harsh there as in the West Indies, "slavery however much it may be modified is still slavery, and it is much to be regretted that any trace of it should be found to exist in countries dependent on England, or colonised by her subjects" (quoted in John H. Hubback, *Jane Austen's Sailor Brothers*, p. 192).

8. In other words, Sir Thomas answered Fanny's question, furnishing her with information (and demonstrating that his ownership of a slave-holding estate does not make him unwilling to discuss the subject), but everyone else maintained the "dead silence."

9. *repulsive*: repellent.

10. *powers*: qualities, abilities.

11. *argue*: infer, conclude.

her infancy.[12] I do not call Tunbridge or Cheltenham the country;[13] and November is a still more serious month, and I can see that Mrs. Grant is very anxious for her not finding Mansfield dull as winter comes on."

Fanny could have said a great deal, but it was safer to say nothing, and leave untouched all Miss Crawford's resources,[14] her accomplishments, her spirits,[15] her importance, her friends, lest it should betray her into any observations seemingly unhandsome. Miss Crawford's kind opinion of herself deserved at least a grateful forbearance, and she began to talk of something else.

"To-morrow, I think, my uncle dines at Sotherton, and you and Mr. Bertram too. We shall be quite a small party at home. I hope my uncle may continue to like Mr. Rushworth."

"That is impossible, Fanny. He must like him less after to-morrow's visit, for we shall be five hours in his company.[16] I should dread the stupidity[17] of the day, if there were not a much greater evil to follow — the impression it must leave on Sir Thomas. He cannot much longer deceive himself. I am sorry for them all, and would give something that Rushworth and Maria had never met."

In this quarter, indeed, disappointment was impending over Sir Thomas. Not all his good-will for Mr. Rushworth, not all Mr. Rushworth's deference for him, could prevent him from soon discerning some part of the truth — that Mr. Rushworth was an inferior young man, as ignorant in business as in books,[18] with opinions in general unfixed,[19] and without seeming much aware of it himself.

He had expected a very different son-in-law; and beginning to feel grave on Maria's account, tried to understand *her* feelings. Little observation there was necessary to tell him that indifference was the most favourable state they could be in.[20] Her behaviour to Mr. Rushworth was careless and cold. She could not, did not like him. Sir Thomas resolved to speak seriously to her. Advantageous as would be the alliance,[21] and long standing and public as was the engagement,[22] her happiness must not be sacrificed to it. Mr. Rushworth had perhaps been accepted on too short an acquaintance, and on knowing him better she was repenting.

With solemn kindness Sir Thomas addressed her; told her his

12. Little information is given about the childhood of the Crawfords except that at some point they lost both parents and were raised by an uncle and aunt (p. 80). When their father was alive, they could have spent much of their time on the family estate in Norfolk. After that, those they lived with, like many wealthy town-dwellers, may have gone to the country only during the summer; earlier Mary spoke of her uncle's preparing a summer place in Twickenham, which is near London but was still fairly rural then.

13. Tunbridge, or Tunbridge Wells, and Cheltenham were fashionable spa towns where many wealthy people went; the first is south of London, the second is in western England. Because they were not large like Bath, they might be described as in the countryside. But since spa visitors would normally concentrate on the pleasures of the town itself, including mingling with visitors of a similar social rank, they would have a very different experience there than in a true rural district, where opportunities for activity were limited during colder months and few other genteel people were close enough for regular socializing.

14. She means her inner resources, specifically her ability to find means of entertaining herself.

15. *spirits*: animation, cheerfulness.

16. After Sir Thomas's arrival Rushworth went home with the news, and he has presumably been there since, so Sir Thomas has yet to spend much time with him.

17. *stupidity*: dullness.

18. Business for him is primarily the management of his estate, which includes matters of finance and investments and those of farming. Sir Thomas may also discuss community affairs, for wealthy landowners normally participated in local government and other concerns of their parish, such as its church.

19. That is, he simply repeats others' opinions and has no real convictions or ideas of his own.

20. Sir Thomas's rapidity in noticing demonstrates how critical his long absence was for allowing the engagement to go forward. Had he been present when it was being formed he would have noticed Mr. Rushworth's mental inferiority, as well as possibly Maria's lack of strong affection, and would probably have discouraged the engagement.

21. *alliance*: marriage. It would be very advantageous to be linked to a family as wealthy and socially prominent as the Rushworths.

22. The breaking of an engagement by a woman would damage both her reputation—causing her to be known as a jilt—and the standing of the fam-

fears, inquired into her wishes, entreated her to be open[23] and sincere, and assured her that every inconvenience should be braved, and the connection entirely given up, if she felt herself unhappy in the prospect of it. He would act for her and release her. Maria had a moment's struggle as she listened, and only a moment's: when her father ceased, she was able to give her answer immediately, decidedly, and with no apparent agitation. She thanked him for his great attention, his paternal kindness, but he was quite mistaken in supposing she had the smallest desire of breaking through her engagement, or was sensible of any change of opinion or inclination since her forming it. She had the highest esteem for Mr. Rushworth's character and disposition,[24] and could not have a doubt of her happiness with him.

Sir Thomas was satisfied; too glad to be satisfied perhaps to urge the matter quite so far as his judgment might have dictated to others. It was an alliance which he could not have relinquished without pain; and thus he reasoned. Mr. Rushworth was young enough to improve;—Mr. Rushworth must and would improve in good society; and if Maria could now speak so securely of her happiness with him, speaking certainly without the prejudice, the blindness of love, she ought to be believed. Her feelings probably were not acute; he had never supposed them to be so; but her comforts might not be less on that account, and if she could dispense with seeing her husband a leading, shining character, there would certainly be every thing else in her favour. A well-disposed young woman, who did not marry for love, was in general but the more attached to her own family, and the nearness of Sotherton to Mansfield must naturally hold out the greatest temptation, and would, in all probability, be a continual supply of the most amiable and innocent enjoyments.[25] Such and such-like were the reasonings of Sir Thomas—happy to escape the embarrassing evils of a rupture, the wonder, the reflections,[26] the reproach that must attend it, happy to secure a marriage which would bring him such an addition of respectability and influence, and very happy to think any thing of his daughter's disposition that was most favourable for the purpose.

To her the conference closed as satisfactorily as to him. She was

ily; it could also provoke resentment and bitterness on the part of the man and his family. Jane Austen, after receiving her one known offer of marriage and accepting it, then changed her mind. Whether from fear of the anger of the groom's family or from embarrassment and the awkwardness of the situation, she insisted on immediately leaving this family's house, where they were staying, despite the inconveniences involved. In that case no lasting damage was done to the friendship between the Austens and the other family, but her engagement had lasted only a single night and had never been announced. The long-standing nature of Maria's engagement would add significantly to her censure for not knowing her mind and mistreating Mr. Rushworth, and add to his resentment, while its public nature would ensure that the faults and humiliations of the parties were widely known.

23. *open*: frank, unreserved.

24. *disposition*: general mental character or bent.

25. Meaning regular visits by Maria, which her proximity to Mansfield and lack of strong affection for her husband would encourage.

26. *reflections*: imputations.

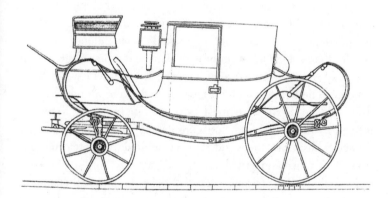

A chariot (see p. 375, note 37).

[From T. Fuller, *An Essay on Wheel Carriages* (London, 1828), Plate 1]

in a state of mind to be glad that she had secured her fate beyond recall—that she had pledged herself anew to Sotherton—that she was safe from the possibility of giving Crawford the triumph of governing her actions, and destroying her prospects; and retired in proud resolve, determined only to behave more cautiously to Mr. Rushworth in future, that her father might not be again suspecting her.

Had Sir Thomas applied to his daughter within the first three or four days after Henry Crawford's leaving Mansfield, before her feelings were at all tranquillized, before she had given up every hope of him, or absolutely resolved on enduring his rival, her answer might have been different; but after another three or four days, when there was no return, no letter, no message—no symptom of a softened heart—no hope of advantage from separation—her mind became cool enough to seek all the comfort that pride and self-revenge could give.[27]

Henry Crawford had destroyed her happiness, but he should not know that he had done it; he should not destroy her credit,[28] her prosperity too. He should not have to think of her as pining in the retirement of Mansfield for *him*, rejecting Sotherton and London, independence and splendour for *his* sake.[29] Independence was more needful than ever;[30] the want of it at Mansfield more sensibly[31] felt. She was less and less able to endure the restraint which her father imposed. The liberty which his absence had given was now become absolutely necessary. She must escape from him and Mansfield as soon as possible,[32] and find consolation in fortune and consequence,[33] bustle and the world,[34] for a wounded spirit. Her mind was quite determined and varied not.

To such feelings, delay, even the delay of much preparation, would have been an evil, and Mr. Rushworth could hardly be more impatient for the marriage than herself. In all the important preparations of the mind she was complete; being prepared for matrimony by an hatred of home, restraint, and tranquillity; by the misery of disappointed affection, and contempt of the man she was to marry. The rest might wait. The preparations of new carriages and furniture might wait for London and spring,[35] when her own taste could have fairer play.[36]

27. Her "self-revenge" may mean simply showing Henry that she does not need him. She also may think that becoming a wealthier and more prominent member of fashionable London society than Henry is a way of getting back at him.

28. She worries that her credit, i.e., reputation, will suffer if others suspect that she loved him and tried to win him, only to be jilted, and breaking off her engagement to Mr. Rushworth would feed that suspicion.

29. Thus anger against Henry plays the critical role in Maria's decision to go ahead with her marriage. Had there been no flirtation with Henry, then after Sir Thomas returned and perceived Mr. Rushworth's deficiencies, she may well have accepted his offer to cancel the engagement.

30. Once married, a woman gained more freedom to travel without a chaperone; moreover, as mistress of a household, she would be able to arrange her own affairs there.

31. *sensibly*: fervently, acutely.

32. This of course is the opposite of Sir Thomas's hope that marriage to Mr. Rushworth will allow her to be often at Mansfield.

33. *consequence*: social rank or importance.

34. *world*: fashionable world, high society.

35. As revealed on p. 374, the couple will spend the winter in Brighton and then settle into their new home in London in the spring. Buying new furniture and a new carriage were standard premarital activities for an engaged couple, at least among those who could afford it.

36. *fairer play*: better scope. She may fear that before the wedding others, such as Mrs. Rushworth, will interfere in their decisions, or she may expect that once they are married, her husband will cede control of such matters.

The principals being all agreed in this respect, it soon appeared that a very few weeks would be sufficient for such arrangements as must precede the wedding.

Mrs. Rushworth was quite ready to retire, and make way for the fortunate young woman whom her dear son had selected;—and very early in November removed herself, her maid, her footman, and her chariot,[37] with true dowager propriety,[38] to Bath[39]—there to parade[40] over the wonders of Sotherton in her evening-parties—enjoying them as thoroughly perhaps in the animation of a card-table as she had ever done on the spot[41]—and before the middle of the same month the ceremony had taken place, which gave Sotherton another mistress.

It was a very proper wedding. The bride was elegantly dressed—the two bridesmaids were duly inferior[42]—her father gave her away—her mother stood with salts in her hand, expecting to be agitated[43]—her aunt tried to cry—and the service was impressively read by Dr. Grant. Nothing could be objected to when it came under the discussion of the neighbourhood, except that the carriage which conveyed the bride and bridegroom and Julia from the church door to Sotherton, was the same chaise which Mr. Rushworth had used for a twelvemonth before.[44] In every thing else the etiquette of the day might stand the strictest investigation.

It was done, and they were gone. Sir Thomas felt as an anxious father must feel, and was indeed experiencing much of the agitation which his wife had been apprehensive of for herself, but had fortunately escaped. Mrs. Norris, most happy to assist in the duties of the day, by spending it at the Park to support her sister's spirits, and drinking the health of Mr. and Mrs. Rushworth in a supernumerary glass or two, was all joyous delight—for she had made the match—she had done every thing—and no one would have supposed, from her confident triumph,[45] that she had ever heard of conjugal infelicity in her life, or could have the smallest insight into the disposition of the niece who had been brought up under her eye.

The plan of the young couple was to proceed after a few days to Brighton, and take a house there for some weeks.[46] Every public place was new to Maria, and Brighton is almost as gay in winter as

37. Most family servants would remain at Sotherton, but a lady's maid would accompany her mistress. Mrs. Rushworth may also want a familiar footman, the servant who answers the door. A chariot is a carriage similar to a chaise; unlike the latter, it was mostly used for transport around town.

38. A dowager is a widow; the term is applied especially to one whose son has married, thereby installing his wife in the position formerly occupied by his mother (in the case of titled nobility, where the term is most commonly used, the wife becomes the new "Lady —" and the widow becomes the "Dowager Lady —"). In this case no titles are involved, but Maria has replaced Mrs. Rushworth as mistress of a grand estate. As someone who once occupied a position of great importance, a dowager would have particular reason to act with dignity and propriety and impress people with her continued importance.

39. During this period Bath, which was beginning to decline as a pleasure resort, was becoming very popular as a retirement destination, especially for widows. In the country it was often difficult for them to travel and they did not pursue the outdoor sports popular with men; in contrast, Bath was compact, easy to get around in, and full of both a wide array of entertainments and numerous other people of leisure.

40. *parade*: talk ostentatiously in order to impress others.

41. Cards were the principal activity at evening parties, which were very popular in Bath. In *Persuasion* the heroine explains that since she is "no card-player," she has no interest in the Bath evening parties.

42. At the time brides did not wear special, or even necessarily white, wedding gowns. But they would wear a very elegant dress, with various accoutrements, including in many cases a veil (for an example, see p. 363). Bridesmaids were a long-established custom. The two in this case are Julia and Fanny.

43. Smelling salts, made of ammonium carbonate, were often carried by women and used to revive people, especially those who fainted.

44. Since buying a new carriage was common practice before a wedding, those in the neighborhood would expect one here, especially given the wealth of the groom. But, as explained on p. 372, Maria chose to wait to do this in order to accelerate the wedding.

45. *triumph*: elation, exultation.

46. Brighton, on the southern coast of England, had become its most popular seaside resort during this period, in part because it was the favorite venue of

in summer.[47] When the novelty of amusement there were over, it would be time for the wider range of London.

Julia was to go with them to Brighton.[48] Since rivalry between the sisters had ceased, they had been gradually recovering much of their former good understanding; and were at least sufficiently friends to make each of them exceedingly glad to be with the other at such a time. Some other companion than Mr. Rushworth was of the first consequence to his lady, and Julia was quite as eager for novelty and pleasure as Maria, though she might not have struggled through so much to obtain them, and could better bear a subordinate situation.

Their departure made another material change at Mansfield, a chasm which required some time to fill up. The family circle became greatly contracted, and though the Miss Bertrams had latterly added little to its gaiety, they could not but be missed. Even their mother missed them—and how much more their tender-hearted cousin, who wandered about the house, and thought of them, and felt for them, with a degree of affectionate regret which they had never done much to deserve!

A distant view of Brighton.

[From William Daniell, *A Voyage Round Great Britain*, Vol. II (London, 1815), p. 139]

the Prince Regent, the current ruler of Britain (his father, George III, was still king, but the king's madness caused Parliament to appoint his son as the effective ruler, or regent; this is why the period is often called the Regency). Seaside resorts were the most popular venues for honeymoons.

47. Summer was Brighton's principal season. By "public place" the author means a place where many people congregate.

48. Julia was earlier described as leaving the wedding in the same carriage as the bride and groom. Brides often took other women as companions on their honeymoon and even after that. Marriage revolved much less then around companionship, and it was expected that husbands and wives would live somewhat separate lives. Moreover, men and women often had completely different amusements. A female companion gave the bride someone to talk to and amuse herself with, allowing the husband to devote much of his time to activities with other men.

Brighton along the sea.

[From William Daniell, A *Voyage Round Great Britain*, Vol. VII (London, 1824), p. 141]

Chapter Four

*F*anny's consequence increased on the departure of her cousins. Becoming, as she then did, the only young woman in the drawing-room, the only occupier of that interesting[1] division of a family in which she had hitherto held so humble a third, it was impossible for her not to be more looked at, more thought of and attended to, than she had ever been before; and "where is Fanny?" became no uncommon question, even without her being wanted for any one's convenience.

Not only at home did her value increase, but at the Parsonage too. In that house which she had hardly entered twice a year since Mr. Norris's death, she became a welcome, an invited guest; and in the gloom and dirt[2] of a November day, most acceptable to Mary Crawford. Her visits there, beginning by chance, were continued by solicitation. Mrs. Grant, really eager to get any change for her sister, could by the easiest self-deceit persuade herself that she was doing the kindest thing by Fanny, and giving her the most important opportunities of improvement in pressing her frequent calls.

Fanny, having been sent into the village on some errand by her aunt Norris, was overtaken by a heavy shower close to the Parsonage, and being descried from one of the windows endeavouring to find shelter under the branches and lingering leaves of an oak just beyond their premises,[3] was forced, though not without some modest reluctance on her part, to come in. A civil servant she had withstood; but when Dr. Grant himself went out with an umbrella,[4] there was nothing to be done but to be very much ashamed and to get into the house as fast as possible; and to poor Miss Crawford, who had just been contemplating the dismal rain in a very desponding[5] state of mind, sighing over the ruin of all her plan of exercise for that morning, and of every chance of seeing a single creature beyond themselves for the next twenty-four hours; the sound of a little bustle at the front door, and the sight of Miss Price dripping with wet in

1. *interesting*: significant.

2. *dirt*: mud.

3. Earlier descriptions indicated that the parsonage is a little beyond the village, from the perspective of Mansfield Park. Fanny's errand may have taken her to a place on the edge of the village that is visible from the parsonage.

4. Umbrellas had first begun to be used widely as a protection against the rain in the early eighteenth century (they had previously been used in many places for shielding people from the sun or for ceremonial functions). There was some initial resistance to them in England, but by the end of the century they had become a common accessory, especially for wealthier people.

5. *desponding*: despondent.

A woman in walking dress with a shawl, hat, and parasol.

[From *The Repository of arts, literature, fashions, manufactures, &c*, Vol. II (1809), p. 258]

the vestibule,[6] was delightful. The value of an event on a wet day in the country, was most forcibly brought before her. She was all alive[7] again directly, and among the most active in being useful to Fanny, in detecting her to be wetter than she would at first allow, and providing her with dry clothes; and Fanny, after being obliged to submit to all this attention, and to being assisted and waited on by mistresses and maids,[8] being also obliged on returning down stairs, to be fixed in their drawing-room for an hour while the rain continued, the blessing of something fresh to see and think of was thus extended to Miss Crawford, and might carry on her spirits to the period of dressing and dinner.

The two sisters were so kind to her and so pleasant, that Fanny might have enjoyed her visit could she have believed herself not in the way, and could she have foreseen that the weather would certainly clear at the end of the hour, and save her from the shame of having Dr. Grant's carriage and horses out to take her home, with which she was threatened. As to anxiety for any alarm that her absence in such weather might occasion at home, she had nothing to suffer on that score; for as her being out was known only to her two aunts, she was perfectly aware that none would be felt, and that in whatever cottage aunt Norris might chuse to establish her during the rain, her being in such cottage would be indubitable to aunt Bertram.[9]

It was beginning to look brighter, when Fanny, observing a harp in the room, asked some questions about it, which soon led to an acknowledgment of her wishing very much to hear it, and a confession, which could hardly be believed, of her having never yet heard it since its being in Mansfield.[10] To Fanny herself it appeared a very simple and natural circumstance. She had scarcely ever been at the Parsonage since the instrument's arrival, there had been no reason that she should; but Miss Crawford, calling to mind an early-expressed wish on the subject,[11] was concerned at her own neglect;—and "shall I play to you now?"—and "what will you have?" were questions immediately following with the readiest good humour.

She played accordingly; happy to have a new listener, and a listener who seemed so much obliged, so full of wonder at the performance, and who shewed herself not wanting in taste. She played till

6. A vestibule was a standard feature of a larger house, and the parsonage, though not as grand as Mansfield Park, is still a spacious and comfortable home.

7. *all alive*: fully aroused.

8. The "mistresses" are Mrs. Grant and Mary Crawford. The term could apply to any woman in an important position.

9. There would be many cottages in the village, since most who live there are of modest means.

10. Earlier Mary played the harp often for Edmund (p. 126), but Fanny was never with him.

11. This was during a dinner conversation in which Mary related the arrival of her harp to Fanny and Edmund (pp. 114–116).

A party with a woman playing a harp.

[From William Combe, *The Dance of Life* (London, 1817; 1903 reprint), p. 232]

Fanny's eyes, straying to the window on the weather's being evidently fair, spoke what she felt must be done.

"Another quarter of an hour," said Miss Crawford, "and we shall see how it will be. Do not run away the first moment of its holding up.[12] Those clouds look alarming."

"But they are passed over," said Fanny.—"I have been watching them.—This weather is all from the south."

"South or north, I know a black cloud when I see it; and you must not set forward while it is so threatening. And besides, I want to play something more to you—a very pretty piece—and your cousin Edmund's prime favourite. You must stay and hear your cousin's favourite."

Fanny felt that she must; and though she had not waited for that sentence to be thinking of Edmund, such a memento made her particularly awake to his idea,[13] and she fancied him sitting in that room again and again, perhaps in the very spot where she sat now, listening with constant delight to the favourite air, played, as it appeared to her, with superior tone and expression;[14] and though pleased with it herself, and glad to like whatever was liked by him, she was more sincerely impatient to go away at the conclusion of it than she had been before; and on this being evident, she was so kindly asked to call again, to take them in her walk whenever she could, to come and hear more of the harp, that she felt it necessary to be done, if no objection arose at home.

Such was the origin of the sort of intimacy which took place between them within the first fortnight after the Miss Bertrams' going away, an intimacy resulting principally from Miss Crawford's desire of something new, and which had little reality in Fanny's feelings. Fanny went to her every two or three days; it seemed a kind of fascination; she could not be easy without going, and yet it was without loving her, without ever thinking like her, without any sense of obligation for being sought after now when nobody else was to be had; and deriving no higher pleasure from her conversation than occasional amusement, and *that* often at the expense of her judgment, when it was raised[15] by pleasantry on people or subjects which she wished to be respected. She went however, and they sauntered about together many an half hour in Mrs. Grant's shrubbery, the

12. *holding up*: clearing up, ceasing to rain.

13. *awake to his idea*: inclined to recollect his image.

14. "Expression" denoted the ability of music to appeal to feelings (see p. 127, note 8); hence it would be a good complement to the more purely aural or technical category of "tone."

15. *raised*: aroused.

A lady feeding poultry. The clothing is from a slightly earlier period.
[From Malcolm Salaman, *Old English Colour Prints* (New York, 1909), Plate XI]

weather being unusually mild for the time of year; and venturing sometimes even to sit down on one of the benches now comparatively unsheltered,[16] remaining there perhaps till in the midst of some tender ejaculation of Fanny's, on the sweets of so protracted an autumn, they were forced by the sudden swell of a cold gust shaking down the last few yellow leaves about them, to jump up and walk for warmth.

"This is pretty—very pretty," said Fanny, looking around her as they were thus sitting together one day: "Every time I come into this shrubbery I am more struck with its growth and beauty. Three years ago, this was nothing but a rough hedgerow along the upper side of the field,[17] never thought of as any thing, or capable of becoming any thing; and now it is converted into a walk,[18] and it would be difficult to say whether most valuable as a convenience or an ornament; and perhaps in another three years we may be forgetting—almost forgetting what it was before. How wonderful, how very wonderful the operations of time, and the changes of the human mind!" And following the latter train of thought, she soon afterwards added: "If any one faculty of our nature may be called *more* wonderful than the rest, I do think it is memory. There seems something more speakingly[19] incomprehensible in the powers, the failures, the inequalities of memory, than in any other of our intelligences.[20] The memory is sometimes so retentive, so serviceable, so obedient—at others, so bewildered and so weak—and at others again, so tyrannic, so beyond controul!—We are to be sure a miracle every way—but our powers of recollecting and of forgetting, do seem peculiarly past finding out."[21]

Miss Crawford, untouched and inattentive, had nothing to say; and Fanny, perceiving it, brought back her own mind to what she thought must interest.

"It may seem impertinent[22] in *me* to praise, but I must admire the taste Mrs. Grant has shewn in all this. There is such a quiet simplicity in the plan of the walk!—not too much attempted!"[23]

"Yes," replied Miss Crawford carelessly, "it does very well for a place of this sort. One does not think of extent *here*—and between ourselves, till I came to Mansfield, I had not imagined a country parson ever aspired to a shrubbery or any thing of the kind."

16. The bench is unsheltered now because the leaves shading it have fallen. Shrubberies then often contained trees as well as bushes.

17. On the subject of hedgerows, see p. 193, note 14.

18. It was almost exactly three years ago that the Grants arrived at the parsonage, so they are responsible for the improvements.

19. *speakingly*: strikingly.

20. *intelligences*: mental faculties.

21. Fanny's ideas on memory probably derive in part from her reading of Samuel Johnson's *The Idler*, mentioned on p. 292. Of *The Idler's* 104 short essays, numbers 44, 72, and 74—"Use of memory," "Regulation of memory," and "Memory rarely deficient"—deal with the subject. None of the essays make Fanny's exact points about the mysteries and particular variability of memory compared with other mental faculties, but they do discuss memory's central importance to the mind, its frequent tendency to fail, the pain that memories of bad events can cause, and the great difficulty of either improving or controlling our memories. Fanny (or Jane Austen) could easily have been stimulated by these arguments to develop her own related reflections.

22. *impertinent*: presumptuous; inclined to meddle with matters that are not one's business.

23. The property here is small, and trying to emulate the landscaping that set the standards of fashion at large places like Sotherton could lead to creating too many features for its size.

A sheltered bench in a garden.

[From John Plaw, *Ferme Ornée* (London, 1795), Plate IV]

"I am so glad to see the evergreens thrive!" said Fanny in reply. "My uncle's gardener always says the soil here is better than his own,[24] and so it appears from the growth of the laurels and evergreens in general. — The evergreen! — How beautiful, how welcome, how wonderful the evergreen![25] — When one thinks of it, how astonishing a variety of nature! — In some countries we know the tree that sheds its leaf is the variety,[26] but that does not make it less amazing, that the same soil and the same sun should nurture plants differing in the first rule and law of their existence. You will think me rhapsodizing; but when I am out of doors, especially when I am sitting out of doors, I am very apt to get into this sort of wondering strain. One cannot fix one's eyes on the commonest natural production without finding food for a rambling fancy."[27]

"To say the truth," replied Miss Crawford, "I am something like the famous Doge at the court of Lewis XIV; and may declare that I see no wonder in this shrubbery equal to seeing myself in it.[28] If anybody had told me a year ago that this place would be my home, that I should be spending month after month here, as I have done, I certainly should not have believed them! — I have now been here nearly five months![29] and moreover the quietest five months I ever passed."

"*Too* quiet for you I believe."

"I should have thought so *theoretically* myself, but" — and her eyes brightened as she spoke — "take it all and all, I never spent so happy a summer. — But then" — with a more thoughtful air and lowered voice — "there is no saying what it may lead to."

Fanny's heart beat quick, and she felt quite unequal to surmising or soliciting any thing more. Miss Crawford however, with renewed animation, soon went on:

"I am conscious of being far better reconciled to a country residence than I had ever expected to be. I can even suppose it pleasant to spend *half* the year in the country, under certain circumstances — very pleasant. An elegant, moderate-sized house in the centre of family connections — continual engagements among them — commanding the first society in the neighbourhood — looked-up to perhaps as leading it even more than those of larger fortune,[30] and turning from the cheerful round of such amusements to nothing worse than a tête-à-tête with the person one feels most agreeable in the world. There is

24. Fanny's speaking regularly to the gardener indicates her interest in the subject; she was described earlier as having plants in her room.

25. In this period there was a great fascination and taste for evergreens, many of which had been introduced into England from abroad.

26. *variety*: deviation or departure from the norm.

27. Fanny's enthusiasm for nature, which appears throughout the novel, has sometimes been seen as in conflict with Jane Austen's emphasis on reason and her critique of romanticism in her heroines and her stories, most notably in the character of Marianne Dashwood in *Sense and Sensibility*. But Marianne errs by the excess of her romantic enthusiasm and reliance on her feelings. Jane Austen never criticizes feelings per se, as long as they are compatible with reason; thus Fanny, when she perceives herself being swayed by wrong or destructive feelings, attempts to curb them. Austen also displays a love of nature in her letters, and attributes it to many sensible characters in her novels. Fanny combines her rhapsodizing with careful, rational observation, as in her discussion of the different soils or where the wind is coming from, and, unlike Marianne Dashwood, Fanny appreciates nature that has been shaped by human hands, such as a shrubbery, as much as wild or untamed nature.

28. Doge was the title of the elected head of state of certain republics in Italy, most notably Venice and Genoa. This anecdote concerns the doge of Genoa and appeared in Voltaire's history *Le Siècle de Louis XIV*. According to Voltaire, the doge, visiting Louis XIV's court at Versailles on state business, revealed his wit when, upon being "asked what he found most remarkable at Versailles, he responded, 'Seeing myself there.'" Mary, whose conversation suggests a knowledge of French, could have read the popular work in the original, or in several English editions published in the second half of the eighteenth century under the title *The Age of Louis XIV*; she also could have encountered the tale through a version related by Samuel Johnson in a letter and published in *Letters to and from the Late Samuel Johnson* (1788), by Hester Lynch Piozzi. Those are the possible sources for Jane Austen also, who read French well.

29. This would make it toward the end of November, since the Crawfords arrived in Mansfield in early July; see chronology, p. 857.

30. She may be thinking of the influence and importance of a clergyman in local society, despite his not having great wealth, or of the ability of those of superior ability and character to lead and impress others. One example she may have in mind is her brother's ability to inspire affection and respect at Mansfield Park despite having much less wealth than Mr. Rushworth, and probably less than the Bertrams.

nothing frightful in such a picture, is there, Miss Price? One need not envy the new Mrs. Rushworth with such a home as *that*." "Envy Mrs. Rushworth!" was all that Fanny attempted to say. "Come, come, it would be very unhandsome in us to be severe on Mrs. Rushworth, for I look forward to our owing her a great many gay, brilliant, happy hours. I expect we shall be all very much at Sotherton another year. Such a match as Miss Bertram has made is a public blessing, for the first pleasures of Mr. Rushworth's wife must be to fill her house,[31] and give the best balls in the country."[32]

Fanny was silent—and Miss Crawford relapsed into thought-fulness, till suddenly looking up at the end of a few minutes, she exclaimed, "Ah! here he is." It was not Mr. Rushworth, however, but Edmund, who then appeared walking towards them with Mrs. Grant. "My sister and Mr. Bertram—I am so glad your eldest cousin is gone that he *may* be Mr. Bertram again.[33] There is something in the sound of Mr. *Edmund* Bertram so formal, so pitiful, so younger-brother-like, that I detest it."

"How differently we feel!" cried Fanny. "To me, the sound of *Mr.* Bertram is so cold and nothing-meaning—so entirely without warmth or character!—It just stands for a gentleman, and that's all.[34] But there is nobleness in the name of Edmund. It is a name of heroism and renown—of kings, princes, and knights; and seems to breathe the spirit of chivalry and warm affections."[35]

"I grant you the name is good in itself, and *Lord* Edmund or *Sir* Edmund sound delightfully; but sink it under the chill, the annihila-tion of a Mr.—and Mr. Edmund is no more than Mr. John or Mr. Thomas.[36] Well, shall we join and disappoint them of half their lec-ture upon sitting down out of doors at this time of year, by being up before they can begin?"[37]

Edmund met them with particular pleasure. It was the first time of his seeing them together since the beginning of that better acquain-tance which he had been hearing of with great satisfaction. A friend-ship between two so very dear to him was exactly what he could have wished; and to the credit of the lover's understanding[38] be it stated, that he did not by any means consider Fanny as the only, or even as the greater gainer by such a friendship.

31. She means filling the house with guests, whether for specific events or for longer stays. Inviting other prominent people for extended stays was common among the elite in England. Few if any other families of their own rank would reside in their immediate neighborhood, and the difficulty and discomfort of travel made people wish to make the most of visits by staying longer.

32. *country*: county. These would be her leading pleasures, since Mr. Rushworth's character would keep his wife from wishing to spend much time alone with him, while his wealth would give her the means to engage in such activities.

33. With Tom gone, Edmund can be called "Mr. Bertram" again.

34. Traditionally only gentlemen were called "Mr." Men below that rank, if middle class, were called "Goodman," and lower-class men were not given any title at all. By the eighteenth century "Mr." was applied more broadly, but Fanny, who here and elsewhere indicates an interest in history, would be aware of the older form.

35. Two English kings were named Edmund: Edmund the Magnificent, who reigned from 939 to 946, and Edmund Ironside, who reigned in 1016. It was also the name of a number of English princes, sons of kings who never ascended the throne, and of English aristocrats, including knights. Most of these Edmunds lived in earlier ages, which Fanny is associating with chivalry and, most likely, with the "warm affections" of courtly love. She is probably influenced here by Walter Scott, whose *Lay of the Last Minstrel* she quoted earlier, and who in this and other highly popular narrative poems celebrated the chivalry and tender passions of earlier centuries in Scotland and England. Two of those poems, *Marmion* and *Rokeby*, contain characters named Edmund.

36. John and Thomas were, along with William, the most common male names in England; approximately half the male population had one of these three names.

37. There was a great concern at the time about sickness resulting from becoming chilled. One reason for worry was that there were very limited means of fighting infections, which therefore could turn serious easily.

38. *understanding*: intellect, judgment.

"Well," said Miss Crawford, "and do not you scold us for our imprudence? What do you think we have been sitting down for but to be talked to about it, and entreated and supplicated never to do so again?"

"Perhaps I might have scolded," said Edmund, "if either of you had been sitting down alone; but while you do wrong together I can overlook a great deal."

"They cannot have been sitting long," cried Mrs. Grant, "for when I went up for my shawl[39] I saw them from the staircase window,[40] and then they were walking."

"And really," added Edmund, "the day is so mild, that your sitting down for a few minutes can be hardly thought imprudent. Our weather must not always be judged by the Calendar. We may sometimes take greater liberties in November than in May."

"Upon my word," cried Miss Crawford, "you are two of the most disappointing and unfeeling kind friends I ever met with! There is no giving you a moment's uneasiness. You do not know how much we have been suffering, nor what chills we have felt! But I have long thought Mr. Bertram one of the worst subjects to work on,[41] in any little manœuvre against common sense that a woman could be plagued with.[42] I had very little hope of *him* from the first; but you, Mrs. Grant, my sister, my own sister, I think I had a right to alarm you a little."

"Do not flatter yourself, my dearest Mary. You have not the smallest chance of moving me. I have my alarms, but they are quite in a different quarter: and if I could have altered the weather, you would have had a good sharp east wind blowing on you the whole time[43]—for here are some of my plants which Robert *will* leave out because the nights are so mild,[44] and I know the end of it will be that we shall have a sudden change of weather, a hard frost setting in all at once, taking every body (at least Robert) by surprize, and I shall lose every one; and what is worse, cook has just been telling me that the turkey, which I particularly wished not to be dressed[45] till Sunday, because I know how much more Dr. Grant would enjoy it on Sunday after the fatigues of the day,[46] will not keep beyond to-morrow.[47] These are something like grievances, and make me think the weather most unseasonably close."[48]

39. Shawls were a basic female accessory in this period, due to the prevalence of thin and lightweight materials like muslin in women's fashions. Cashmere shawls were the most popular: they were first imported into Britain from India in the early eighteenth century, in connection with increased British commercial and colonial activity in India, and by this time they were also being manufactured in Britain. For examples of women with shawls, see pp. 379 and 561.

40. Staircases often had windows to provide illumination.

41. *work on*: influence, persuade.

42. Here the maneuver is the design she just claimed of sitting down in order to be scolded and supplicated by Edmund. In fact, she and Fanny sat down before they even saw Edmund and Mrs. Grant, but Mary, as elsewhere, hopes to draw Edmund's attention and conversation by teasing and provoking him. The very imperturbability she complains of in him may make her even more determined in this pursuit.

43. East winds in England tend to be cold, for they come from the cold North Sea. In contrast, west winds come from waters that are warmed by the transatlantic Gulf Stream.

44. Robert is a lower servant.

45. *dressed*: prepared, cooked.

46. Dr. Grant conducts two services on Sunday, each of which could last a long while.

47. Lack of artificial refrigeration then meant that, in the absence of cold weather, food could spoil quickly.

48. *close*: stifling, sultry. Mrs. Grant's worries, and her knowledge of what is happening in both the garden and the kitchen, indicate she is a careful and conscientious housekeeper, contrary to Mrs. Norris's earlier aspersions.

"The sweets of housekeeping in a country village!" said Miss Crawford archly. "Commend me to the nurseryman and the poulterer."[49]

"My dear child, commend Dr. Grant to the deanery of Westminster or St. Paul's,[50] and I should be as glad of your nurseryman and poulterer as you could be. But we have no such people in Mansfield. What would you have me do?"

"Oh! you can do nothing but what you do already; be plagued very often and never lose your temper."

"Thank you — but there is no escaping these little vexations, Mary, live where we may; and when you are settled in town and I come to see you, I dare say I shall find you with yours, in spite of the nurseryman and the poulterer — or perhaps on their very account. Their remoteness and unpunctuality,[51] or their exorbitant charges and frauds will be drawing forth bitter lamentations."

"I mean to be too rich to lament or to feel any thing of the sort. A large income is the best recipe for happiness I ever heard of. It certainly may secure all the myrtle and turkey part of it."[52]

"You intend to be very rich," said Edmund, with a look which, to Fanny's eye, had a great deal of serious meaning.

"To be sure. Do not you? — Do not we all?"

"I cannot intend any thing which it must be so completely beyond my power to command. Miss Crawford may chuse her degree of wealth. She has only to fix on her number of thousands a year, and there can be no doubt of their coming. My intentions are only not to be poor."

"By moderation and economy, and bringing down your wants to your income, and all that. I understand you — and a very proper plan it is for a person at your time of life, with such limited means and indifferent connections.[53] — What can *you* want but a decent maintenance? You have not much time before you;[54] and your relations are in no situation to do any thing for you, or to mortify you by the contrast of their own wealth and consequence.[55] Be honest and poor, by all means — but I shall not envy you; I do not much think I shall even respect you. I have a much greater respect for those that are honest and rich."

"Your degree of respect for honesty, rich or poor, is precisely what I have no manner of concern with. I do not mean to be poor. Poverty

49. These are men with shops selling plants and poultry, with the latter offering a larger variety of fowl than is customary now. Neither would normally be found in the country, as Mrs. Grant points out in a moment. Instead, the lady of the house would often undertake the cultivation of both plants and poultry; for an example of the latter, see p. 383.

50. A deanery is a position as dean, the leader of a cathedral or collegiate church. In most cases in the Anglican Church it is a cathedral, a church that is the seat of a diocese and its presiding bishop. Cathedrals then had on average twenty-five to thirty resident clergy under the supervision of a dean. Hence a deanery was a position of great prestige; it also usually offered a high salary. Westminster Abbey and St. Paul's Cathedral were the two churches in London with a dean—desirable posts in themselves as well as in the opportunity they offered to live in the capital. For a contemporary picture of St. Paul's, see p. 397.

51. Tradesmen frequently delivered their products, so if they were unpunctual, customers would be forced to wait.

52. By "myrtle and turkey" she simply means the typical products of a nurseryman and a poulterer, respectively.

53. Meaning mediocre family connections, who cannot procure a highly advantageous position for Edmund.

54. Being twenty-four, Edmund needs to decide on his career soon.

55. She suggests that if Edmund had more wealthy and high-ranking relations, he might, from envy or a wish to emulate them, be motivated to choose a career that offered greater possibilities of financial and social success. This harkens back to her earlier charge regarding Edmund's lack of ambition (pp. 210–212).

is exactly what I have determined against. Honesty, in the something between, in the middle state of worldly circumstances,[56] is all that I am anxious for your not looking down on."

"But I do look down upon it, if it might have been higher. I must look down upon any thing contented with obscurity when it might rise to distinction."

"But how may it rise?—How may my honesty at least rise to any distinction?"

This was not so very easy a question to answer, and occasioned an "Oh!" of some length from the fair lady before she could add "You ought to be in parliament, or you should have gone into the army ten years ago."

"*That* is not much to the purpose now; and as to my being in parliament, I believe I must wait till there is an especial assembly for the representation of younger sons who have little to live on.[57] No, Miss Crawford," he added, in a more serious tone, "there *are* distinctions which I should be miserable if I thought myself without any chance—absolutely without chance or possibility of obtaining—but they are of a different character."[58]

A look of consciousness as he spoke, and what seemed a consciousness of manner on Miss Crawford's side as she made some laughing answer, was sorrowful food for Fanny's observation; and finding herself quite unable to attend as she ought to Mrs. Grant, by whose side she was now following the others, she had nearly resolved on going home immediately, and only waited for courage to say so, when the sound of the great clock at Mansfield Park,[59] striking three, made her feel that she had really been much longer absent than usual, and brought the previous self-inquiry of whether she should take leave or not just then, and how, to a very speedy issue.[60] With undoubting decision she directly began her adieus; and Edmund began at the same time to recollect, that his mother had been inquiring for her, and that he had walked down to the Parsonage on purpose to bring her back.

Fanny's hurry increased; and without in the least expecting Edmund's attendance, she would have hastened away alone; but the general pace was quickened, and they all accompanied her into the house, through which it was necessary to pass.[61] Dr. Grant was

56. Edmund's conception of a "middle state" is highly relative, for even the clerical position he aspires toward would place him within the top few percent of the population in income as well as social position. This attitude is frequently found in Austen's novels: her mostly genteel characters judge almost exclusively by the standards of their own class, and often label as poor those who lack what others of their class possess, even while this "poverty" places them far above the living standards of the great majority of the populace.

57. Since running for Parliament involved expense, often considerable, men in the position Edmund describes have almost no chance of being elected.

58. He means the distinction of marrying her, as opposed to the distinction in his career she has been evoking.

59. The great clock would be a very large outdoor one, most likely at the top of a tower or other high feature in the building, that can be heard from far away. Some grand houses had such clocks.

60. Fanny may be thinking, at least partly, of dinner, which may be at five o'clock—a standard time then and the time earlier stated for the Rushworths' dinner (p. 174) and soon to be suggested for the Grants' (p. 406 and p. 407, note 17). Fanny and Edmund still need to make their adieus, walk back, and change before dinner. Fanny may also feel a need to check whether Lady Bertram needs any assistance, and she would dread even the remote possibility of being late and thereby delaying others.

61. In other words, the garden does not have a direct route to the outside.

A village in the distance, surrounded by farmland.

[From Samuel Prout, *Progressive Fragments, Drawn and Etched in a Broad and Simple Manner* (London, 1818), Plate 24]

in the vestibule, and as they stopt to speak to him, she found from Edmund's manner that he *did* mean to go with her.—He too was taking leave.—She could not but be thankful.—In the moment of parting, Edmund was invited by Dr. Grant to eat his mutton with him the next day;[62] and Fanny had barely time for an unpleasant feeling on the occasion, when Mrs. Grant, with sudden recollection, turned to her and asked for the pleasure of her company too. This was so new an attention, so perfectly new a circumstance in the events of Fanny's life, that she was all surprize and embarrassment; and while stammering out her great obligation, and her—"but she did not suppose it would be in her power," was looking at Edmund for his opinion and help.—But Edmund, delighted with her having such an happiness offered, and ascertaining with half a look, and half a sentence, that she had no objection but on her aunt's account, could not imagine that his mother would make any difficulty of sparing her, and therefore gave his decided open advice that the invitation should be accepted; and though Fanny would not venture, even on his encouragement, to such a flight of audacious independence, it was soon settled that if nothing were heard to the contrary, Mrs. Grant might expect her.

"And you know what your dinner will be," said Mrs. Grant, smiling—"the turkey—and I assure you a very fine one; for, my dear"—turning to her husband—"cook insists upon the turkey's being dressed tomorrow."

"Very well, very well," cried Dr. Grant, "all the better. I am glad to hear you have any thing so good in the house. But Miss Price and Mr. Edmund Bertram,[63] I dare say, would take their chance. We none of us want to hear the bill of fare. A friendly meeting, and not a fine dinner, is all we have in view. A turkey or a goose, or a leg of mutton, or whatever you and your cook chuse to give us."[64]

The two cousins walked home together; and except in the immediate discussion of this engagement, which Edmund spoke of with the warmest satisfaction, as so particularly desirable for her in the intimacy which he saw with so much pleasure established, it was a silent walk—for having finished that subject, he grew thoughtful and indisposed for any other.

62. To "eat one's mutton" with someone was a long-standing expression for dining with someone, regardless of whether mutton was actually served. It was a natural expression in a country where sheep were ubiquitous.

63. Dr. Grant continues to use "Mr. Edmund," still the more formal and correct name.

64. His casual expressed attitude toward his meals contrasts to his behavior on many occasions. He may be genuinely unaware of how demanding he can be, or he may not wish his finicky habits to be paraded before others.

St. Paul's Cathedral.

[From Fiona St. Aubyn, *Ackermann's Illustrated London*, illustrations by Augustus Pugin and Thomas Rowlandson (Ware, 1985), p. 111]

Chapter Five

But why should Mrs. Grant ask Fanny?" said Lady Bertram. "How came she to think of asking Fanny?—Fanny never dines there, you know, in this sort of way. I cannot spare her, and I am sure she does not want to go.—Fanny, you do not want to go, do you?"

"If you put such a question to her," cried Edmund, preventing his cousin's speaking, "Fanny will immediately say, no; but I am sure, my dear mother,[1] she would like to go; and I can see no reason why she should not."

"I cannot imagine why Mrs. Grant should think of asking her.— She never did before.—She used to ask your sisters now and then, but she never asked Fanny."[2]

"If you cannot do without me, ma'am," said Fanny, in a self-denying tone—

"But my mother will have my father with her all the evening."

"To be sure, so I shall."

"Suppose you take my father's opinion, ma'am."

"That's well thought of. So I will, Edmund. I will ask Sir Thomas, as soon as he comes in, whether I can do without her."

"As you please, ma'am, on that head; but I meant my father's opinion as to the *propriety* of the invitation's being accepted or not; and I think he will consider it a right thing by Mrs. Grant, as well as by Fanny, that being the *first* invitation it should be accepted."[3]

"I do not know. We will ask him. But he will be very much surprized that Mrs. Grant should ask Fanny at all."

There was nothing more to be said, or that could be said to any purpose, till Sir Thomas were present; but the subject involving, as it did, her own evening's comfort for the morrow, was so much uppermost in Lady Bertram's mind, that half an hour afterwards, on his looking in for a minute in his way from his plantation to his dressing-

1.   Characters in Austen's novels frequently say "my dear" or "my dearest" when addressing others close to them. Jane Austen often begins her letters to her sister with "my dear Cassandra" or "my dearest Cassandra" (see below).

2.   Fanny dined at the Grants' once, just after the Crawfords arrived (p. 94), but she was accompanying the others from Mansfield Park; no particular invitation was extended to her. This is what Lady Bertram meant earlier when she said, "Fanny never dines there, you know, in this sort of way."

3.   It would be a proper and right thing by, or with regard to, Mrs. Grant, because refusing her first invitation to Fanny would be rude.

A *letter* by *Jane Austen to her sister, which begins* "My dear Cassandra."

[From Oscar Fay Adams, *The Story of Jane Austen's Life* (Boston, 1896), p. 7]

room,[4] she called him back again, when he had almost closed the door, with "Sir Thomas, stop a moment—I have something to say to you."

Her tone of calm languor, for she never took the trouble of raising her voice, was always heard and attended to; and Sir Thomas came back. Her story began; and Fanny immediately slipped out of the room; for to hear herself the subject of any discussion with her uncle, was more than her nerves could bear. She was anxious, she knew—more anxious perhaps than she ought to be—for what was it after all whether she went or staid?—but if her uncle were to be a great while considering and deciding, and with very grave looks, and those grave looks directed to her, and at last decide against her, she might not be able to appear properly submissive and indifferent. Her cause meanwhile went on well. It began, on Lady Bertram's part, with, "I have something to tell you that will surprize you. Mrs. Grant has asked Fanny to dinner!"

"Well," said Sir Thomas, as if waiting[5] more to accomplish the surprize.

"Edmund wants her to go. But how can I spare her?"

"She will be late," said Sir Thomas, taking out his watch, "but what is your difficulty?"

Edmund found himself obliged to speak and fill up the blanks in his mother's story. He told the whole, and she had only to add, "So strange! for Mrs. Grant never used to ask her."

"But is not it very natural," observed Edmund, "that Mrs. Grant should wish to procure so agreeable a visitor for her sister?"

"Nothing can be more natural," said Sir Thomas, after a short deliberation; "nor, were there no sister in the case, could any thing in my opinion be more natural. Mrs. Grant's shewing civility to Miss Price,[6] to Lady Bertram's niece, could never want explanation. The only surprize I can feel is that this should be the *first* time of its being paid. Fanny was perfectly right in giving only a conditional answer. She appears to feel as she ought. But as I conclude that she must wish to go, since all young people like to be together, I can see no reason why she should be denied the indulgence."[7]

"But can I do without her, Sir Thomas?"

"Indeed I think you may."

4.   A dressing room is a small room, usually attached to the bedroom, for getting dressed. Heads of the household were particularly likely to have a dressing room; Lady Bertram is also later described as having one. Sir Thomas is going there now to change for dinner, which men did as well as women. He will probably be assisted by a valet, who also takes care of his clothes.

5.   *waiting*: awaiting.

6.   Sir Thomas, in line with his general formality and correctness, designates Fanny by the title that Mrs. Grant would use.

7.   *indulgence*: favor.

A woman in a muslin dress of the time.
[From Malcolm Salaman, *Old English Colour Prints* (New York, 1909), Plate X]

"She always makes tea, you know, when my sister is not here."

"Your sister perhaps may be prevailed on to spend the day with us, and I shall certainly be at home."

"Very well, then, Fanny may go, Edmund."

The good news soon followed her. Edmund knocked at her door in his way to his own.

"Well, Fanny, it is all happily settled, and without the smallest hesitation on your uncle's side. He had but one opinion. You are to go."

"Thank you, I am *so* glad," was Fanny's instinctive reply; though when she had turned from him and shut the door, she could not help feeling, "And yet, why should I be glad? for am I not certain of seeing or hearing something there to pain me?"

In spite of this conviction, however, she was glad. Simple as such an engagement might appear in other eyes, it had novelty and importance in her's, for excepting the day at Sotherton, she had scarcely ever dined out before; and though now going only half a mile and only to three people, still it was dining out, and all the little interests of preparation were enjoyments in themselves. She had neither sympathy nor assistance from those who ought to have entered into her feelings and directed her taste; for Lady Bertram never thought of being useful to any body, and Mrs. Norris, when she came on the morrow, in consequence of an early call and invitation from Sir Thomas, was in a very ill humour, and seemed intent only on lessening her niece's pleasure, both present and future, as much as possible.

"Upon my word, Fanny, you are in high luck to meet with such attention and indulgence! You ought to be very much obliged to Mrs. Grant for thinking of you, and to your aunt for letting you go, and you ought to look upon it as something extraordinary: for I hope you are aware that there is no real occasion[8] for your going into company in this sort of way, or ever dining out at all; and it is what you must not depend upon ever being repeated. Nor must you be fancying, that the invitation is meant as any particular compliment to *you*; the compliment is intended to your uncle and aunt, and me. Mrs. Grant thinks it a civility due to *us* to take a little notice of you, or else it would never have come into her head, and you may be very certain, that if your cousin Julia had been at home, you would not have been asked at all."

8. *occasion*: need.

A spotted muslin dress (see p. 409, note 23).

[From *The Repository of arts, literature, fashions, manufactures, &c*, Vol. XIII (1815), p. 366]

Mrs. Norris had now so ingeniously done away all Mrs. Grant's part of the favour, that Fanny, who found herself expected to speak, could only say that she was very much obliged to her aunt Bertram for sparing her, and that she was endeavouring to put her aunt's evening work in such a state as to prevent her being missed.[9]

"Oh! depend upon it, your aunt can do very well without you, or you would not be allowed to go. *I* shall be here, so you may be quite easy about your aunt. And I hope you will have a very *agreeable* day and find it all mighty *delightful*.[10] But I must observe, that five is the very awkwardest of all possible numbers to sit down to table;[11] and I cannot but be surprized that such an *elegant* lady as Mrs. Grant should not contrive better![12] And round their enormous great wide table too, which fills up the room so dreadfully! Had the Doctor been contented to take my dining table when I came away, as any body in their senses would have done, instead of having that absurd new one of his own, which is wider, literally wider than the dinner table here—how infinitely better it would have been! and how much more he would have been respected! for people are never respected when they step out of their proper sphere. Remember *that*, Fanny. Five, only five to be sitting round that table! However, you will have dinner enough on it for ten I dare say."

Mrs. Norris fetched breath and went on again.

"The nonsense and folly of people's stepping out of their rank and trying to appear above themselves, makes me think it right to give *you* a hint, Fanny, now that you are going into company without any of us; and I do beseech and intreat you not to be putting yourself forward, and talking and giving your opinion as if you were one of your cousins—as if you were dear Mrs. Rushworth or Julia.[13] *That* will never do, believe me. Remember, wherever you are, you must be the lowest and last; and though Miss Crawford is in a manner at home, at the Parsonage, you are not to be taking place of her.[14] And as to coming away at night, you are to stay just as long as Edmund chuses. Leave him to settle *that*."

"Yes, ma'am, I should not think of any thing else."

"And if it should rain, which I think exceedingly likely, for I never saw it more threatening for a wet evening in my life—you must manage as well as you can, and not be expecting the carriage to be sent

9.   Meaning Lady Bertram's needlework.

10. Mrs. Norris adds to her disparaging sarcasm by speaking of an "agreeable day." A dinner at five, indicated below to be the Grants' time, would still be technically considered part of the day, but normally dinner guests remain well into the evening. By saying "day" Mrs. Norris suggests Fanny will not remain long.

11. The five are Fanny, Edmund, Mary Crawford, and the Grants.

12. Mrs. Norris is satirizing Mrs. Grant. Her earlier criticisms of Mrs. Grant for spending too much included the idea that a "fine lady in a country parsonage was quite out of place." She believed Mrs. Grant aspired to being more fine or elegant than was warranted by her social and economic position, and Mrs. Norris is now happy to condemn her for what might seem lack of elegance in her dinner arrangements.

13. That one should accept one's social rank and behave in the manner appropriate to it was a generally accepted principle in this society, though Mrs. Norris takes it farther than most would.

14. By "taking place of her" she means Fanny's assuming the position as the leading lady of the company ahead of Mary Crawford. Etiquette dictates that Fanny, as the sole female guest, should have this position—this is why Mrs. Norris grudgingly admits that "Miss Crawford is in a manner at home," for if she were a guest she would precede Fanny—but Mrs. Norris still insists that Fanny decline the honor.

for you. I certainly do not go home to night, and, therefore, the carriage will not be out on my account;[15] so you must make up your mind to what may happen, and take your things accordingly."

Her niece thought it perfectly reasonable. She rated her own claims to comfort as low even as Mrs. Norris could; and when Sir Thomas, soon afterwards, just opening the door, said, "Fanny, at what time would you have the carriage come round?" she felt a degree of astonishment which made it impossible for her to speak.

"My dear Sir Thomas!" cried Mrs. Norris, red with anger, "Fanny can walk."

"Walk!" repeated Sir Thomas, in a tone of most unanswerable dignity, and coming farther into the room. — "My niece walk to a dinner engagement at this time of the year![16] Will twenty minutes after four suit you?"[17]

"Yes, sir," was Fanny's humble answer, given with the feelings almost of a criminal towards Mrs. Norris; and not bearing to remain with her in what might seem a state of triumph, she followed her uncle out of the room, having staid behind him only long enough to hear these words spoken in angry agitation:

"Quite unnecessary! — a great deal too kind! But Edmund goes; — true — it is upon Edmund's account. I observed he was hoarse on Thursday night."

But this could not impose on[18] Fanny. She felt that the carriage was for herself and herself alone; and her uncle's consideration of her, coming immediately after such representations from her aunt, cost her some tears of gratitude when she was alone.

The coachman drove round to a minute;[19] another minute brought down the gentleman, and as the lady had, with a most scrupulous fear of being late, been many minutes seated in the drawing-room, Sir Thomas saw them off in as good time as his own correctly punctual habits required.

"Now I must look at you, Fanny," said Edmund, with the kind smile of an affectionate brother, "and tell you how I like you; and as well as I can judge by this light, you look very nicely indeed. What have you got on?"

"The new dress that my uncle was so good as to give me on my cousin's marriage.[20] I hope it is not too fine;[21] but I thought I ought

15. If Mrs. Norris were going home tonight, instead of staying at Mansfield Park, the family carriage would take her, and could then easily fetch Fanny back from the nearby parsonage. Taking a carriage out involved the trouble of getting horses ready and hitching them to it.

16. Taking a carriage rather than walking to any formal occasion was considered more proper for a genteel person; in *Emma* the heroine chastises the hero for being too inclined to walk in such cases. This imperative would be reinforced by its being the end of November, when, in addition to the cold, the roads may be muddy and it will get dark early.

17. This suggests that dinner will be at five. It is only a short carriage ride, but 4:20 would be too late to leave for a 4:30 dinner, especially since people normally did not proceed into dinner immediately, and too early for a 5:30 dinner.

18. *impose on*: deceive.

19. *to a minute*: at the precise time expected.

20. Fanny's new dress is probably what she wore at the wedding as Maria's bridesmaid but could have simply been a gift. It was common for the marrying couple to give presents to relatives attending the ceremony, and Sir Thomas could have given Fanny a present on behalf of his daughter.

21. *fine*: fancy or ornate. Fanny may have Mrs. Norris's strictures in mind, or may simply be expressing her usual humility.

to wear it as soon as I could, and that I might not have such another opportunity all the winter. I hope you do not think me too fine."

"A woman can never be too fine while she is all in white.[22] No, I see no finery about you; nothing but what is perfectly proper. Your gown seems very pretty. I like these glossy spots.[23] Has not Miss Crawford a gown something the same?"

In approaching the Parsonage they passed close by the stable-yard and coach-house.[24]

"Hey day!" said Edmund, "here's company, here's a carriage! who have they got to meet us?" And letting down the side-glass to distinguish,[25] "'Tis Crawford's, Crawford's barouche, I protest![26] There are his own two men pushing it back into its old quarters.[27] He is here of course. This is quite a surprize, Fanny. I shall be very glad to see him."

There was no occasion, there was no time for Fanny to say how very differently she felt; but the idea of having such another to observe her, was a great increase of the trepidation with which she performed the very aweful[28] ceremony of walking into the drawing-room.

In the drawing-room Mr. Crawford certainly was; having been just long enough arrived to be ready for dinner;[29] and the smiles and pleased looks of the three others standing round him, shewed how welcome was his sudden resolution of coming to them for a few days on leaving Bath.[30] A very cordial meeting passed between him and Edmund; and with the exception of Fanny, the pleasure was general; and even to *her*, there might be some advantage in his presence, since every addition to the party must rather forward her favourite indulgence of being suffered to sit silent and unattended to. She was soon aware of this herself; for though she must submit, as her own propriety of mind directed, in spite of her aunt Norris's opinion, to being the principal lady in company,[31] and to all the little distinctions consequent thereon, she found, while they were at table, such a happy flow of conversation prevailing in which she was not required to take any part—there was so much to be said between the brother and sister about Bath, so much between the two young men about hunting,[32] so much of politics between Mr. Crawford and Dr. Grant, and of every thing, and all together between Mr. Crawford and Mrs. Grant, as to leave her the fairest prospect of having only to listen in

22. White was the most popular color for female gowns in this period. In a letter Jane Austen says two women's gowns "look so white and so nice" (May 21, 1801). One reason was the influence, in both fashion and interior design, of classical antiquity; white was associated with ancient dress because of the absence of surviving color on ancient statues. In addition, muslin, a light cotton from India that became the leading fabric for gowns, could be rinsed to a purer whiteness than other fabrics. It could also be washed more easily, meaning white clothing now suffered less from the problem of keeping it clean than in earlier times. For examples of muslin gowns, see pp. 401 and 403.

23. The plainness of white muslin gowns encouraged the addition of decorative adornments, usually created by embroidering colored figures, often of a shinier material. "Spots" could refer to a variety of such figures.

24. The coach-house is a building where carriages are kept, near to the stable. Both buildings were probably there before the Grants moved in, for they are never described as using a carriage and horses, except for one occasion when Henry dropped off Mrs. Grant at Mansfield Park using his own carriage.

25. *distinguish*: perceive clearly or distinctly. Carriages had a window, i.e., "side-glass," on each side, which could be opened by sliding it down.

26. *protest*: declare. The barouche was previously identified as Crawford's vehicle, and it is probably the only barouche around, since they were expensive and fashionable carriages. Edmund may also recognize certain distinctive features, which carriages, being custom-made, often had.

27. These are his two servants, who would accompany him when he traveled. One may be a valet, the other his carriage driver.

28. *aweful*: awful, i.e., fearful.

29. Henry has changed into evening clothes for dinner, and has joined others in the drawing room before they proceed into the dining room.

30. As indicated shortly, Henry's ultimate destination is his home in Norfolk, and a traveler going from Bath to Norfolk would not veer much off the route by stopping in Northampton (see map, p. 882).

31. Meaning that her own strong sense of what is right and proper leads her to understand, despite Mrs. Norris, that she, as the sole female guest, must be the principal lady.

32. Hunting, which meant the pursuit of land animals, especially foxes, was the other main outdoor sport engaged in by gentlemen. While shooting began early in the autumn, hunting's main season was late autumn and winter.

quiet, and of passing a very agreeable day. She could not compliment the newly-arrived gentleman however with any appearance of interest in a scheme for extending his stay at Mansfield, and sending for his hunters from Norfolk,[33] which, suggested by Dr. Grant, advised by Edmund, and warmly urged by the two sisters, was soon in possession of his mind, and which he seemed to want to be encouraged even by her to resolve on. Her opinion was sought as to the probable continuance of the open weather,[34] but her answers were as short and indifferent as civility allowed. She could not wish him to stay, and would much rather not have him speak to her.

Her two absent cousins, especially Maria, were much in her thoughts on seeing him; but no embarrassing remembrance affected *his* spirits. Here he was again on the same ground where all had passed before, and apparently as willing to stay and be happy without the Miss Bertrams, as if he had never known Mansfield in any other state. She heard them spoken of by him only in a general way, till they were all re-assembled in the drawing-room, when Edmund, being engaged apart in some matter of business with Dr. Grant, which seemed entirely to engross them,[35] and Mrs. Grant occupied at the tea-table,[36] he began talking of them with more particularity to his other sister. With a significant smile, which made Fanny quite hate him, he said, "So! Rushworth and his fair bride are at Brighton, I understand—Happy man!"

"Yes, they have been there—about a fortnight, Miss Price, have they not?—And Julia is with them."

"And Mr. Yates, I presume, is not far off."

"Mr. Yates!—Oh! we hear nothing of Mr. Yates. I do not imagine he figures much in the letters to Mansfield Park; do you, Miss Price?[37]—I think my friend Julia knows better than to entertain her father with Mr. Yates."[38]

"Poor Rushworth and his two-and-forty speeches!" continued Crawford. "Nobody can ever forget them. Poor fellow!—I see him now;—his toil and his despair. Well, I am much mistaken if his lovely Maria will ever want him to make two-and-forty speeches to her"—adding, with a momentary seriousness, "She is too good for him—much too good." And then changing his tone again to one of gentle gallantry, and addressing Fanny, he said, "You were Mr. Rushworth's

33. This signals that he was heading to Norfolk for the hunting. Now he is leaning toward sending for his hunters, i.e., horses for hunting, and pursuing the sport here instead.

34. *open weather*: weather free of frost. Excessive cold, or heavy snow, would end the hunting season.

35. Their business is church business, which would naturally engage both; for more on its specifics, see p. 415, note 47.

36. After the men left the dinner table and rejoined the ladies in the drawing room, tea was usually served. This was a task normally performed by ladies of the house, especially the hostess.

37. Mary's twice referring to Fanny may partly result from Mary's manners, which dictate that Fanny, as the principal lady of the gathering, should not be left out of the conversation.

38. Julia probably writes to her mother, but her mother would show the letters to Sir Thomas or relate their contents.

Fox hunting.
[From William Henry Scott, *British Field Sports* (London, 1818), p. 419]

best friend. Your kindness and patience can never be forgotten, your indefatigable patience in trying to make it possible for him to learn his part—in trying to give him a brain which nature had denied—to mix up an understanding for him out of the superfluity of your own! *He* might not have sense enough himself to estimate your kindness, but I may venture to say that it had honour from all the rest of the party."[39]

Fanny coloured,[40] and said nothing.

"It is as a dream, a pleasant dream!" he exclaimed, breaking forth again after few minutes musing. "I shall always look back on our theatricals with exquisite pleasure. There was such an interest, such an animation, such a spirit diffused! Every body felt it. We were all alive. There was employment, hope, solicitude, bustle, for every hour of the day. Always some little objection, some little doubt, some little anxiety to be got over. I never was happier."[41]

With silent indignation, Fanny repeated to herself, "Never happier!—never happier than when doing what you must know was not justifiable!—never happier than when behaving so dishonourably and unfeelingly!—Oh! what a corrupted mind!"[42]

"We were unlucky, Miss Price," he continued in a lower tone, to avoid the possibility of being heard by Edmund, and not at all aware of her feelings, "we certainly were very unlucky. Another week, only one other week, would have been enough for us. I think if we had had the disposal of events—if Mansfield Park had had the government of the winds just for a week or two about the equinox,[43] there would have been a difference. Not that we would have endangered his safety by any tremendous[44] weather—but only by a steady contrary wind, or a calm. I think, Miss Price, we would have indulged ourselves with a week's calm in the Atlantic at that season."[45]

He seemed determined to be answered; and Fanny, averting her face, said with a firmer tone than usual, "As far as *I* am concerned, sir, I would not have delayed his return for a day. My uncle disapproved it all so entirely when he did arrive, that in my opinion, every thing had gone quite far enough."

She had never spoken so much at once to him in her life before, and never so angrily to any one; and when her speech was over, she trembled and blushed at her own daring. He was surprized; but after a few moments silent consideration of her,[46] replied in a calmer,

39. Actually, the others involved in the play seemed too absorbed in their own parts and other personal concerns to notice Fanny much, except when she might assist them. It was also stated that they wished to have as little to do with Mr. Rushworth as possible. That Henry did notice, and remembers it now, despite being involved with his flirtation with Maria, indicates his perceptiveness. It also indicates his interest in complimenting her, whether from general politeness or from a particular wish to please her, perhaps because she is the only woman here besides his sisters.

40. *coloured*: blushed.

41. His love of the activity, and his focus particularly on how fully it occupied his mind and absorbed all his attention, even with annoyances, suggests the character of his life. With plenty of money, and no responsibilities or need to pursue a career, he has lived a life of pure leisure and pleasure, and has clearly become somewhat bored and sated. Hence any busy activity, even one as unremarkable as rehearsing for a private theatrical production, stands out for engaging all his faculties in a way that his normal pleasures do not. This same search for variety, and a purposeful task, stimulate the significant resolution he announces in the next chapter.

42. *mind*: inner character.

43. The autumnal equinox, the day when the sun is directly over the equator and in consequence the duration of night and day is equal throughout the globe, occurs on September 22 or 23. Since Sir Thomas left Antigua in September (and not at the very end, since he was originally going to leave on a scheduled September packet boat and ended up departing earlier) and arrived home in mid-October, he would have been at sea during the equinox.

44. *tremendous*: terrible, dreadful.

45. Since all ships then traveled by sail, a contrary wind would slow one considerably. A calm would be even worse, preventing a ship from moving at all (in a contrary wind, a ship could make incremental progress by tacking back and forth). At the same time, a calm would not be dangerous, so it would only delay Sir Thomas. Henry would know about such matters due to having lived long with his uncle, the admiral, and heard the conversations between his uncle and other navy men.

46. As he indicates in the next chapter to his sister, he expected, based on past experience with other women, that his charm and gallantry would affect her favorably. His surprise at his failure then leads to consideration of his next move, followed by a change to a more serious tone.

graver tone, and as if the candid result of conviction, "I believe you are right. It was more pleasant than prudent. We were getting too noisy." And then turning the conversation, he would have engaged her on some other subject, but her answers were so shy and reluctant that he could not advance in any.

Miss Crawford, who had been repeatedly eyeing Dr. Grant and Edmund, now observed, "Those gentlemen must have some very interesting point to discuss."

"The most interesting in the world," replied her brother—"how to make money—how to turn a good income into a better. Dr. Grant is giving Bertram instructions about the living he is to step into so soon.[47] I find he takes orders in a few weeks. They were at it in the dining-parlour. I am glad to hear Bertram will be so well off.[48] He will have a very pretty income to make ducks and drakes with,[49] and earned without much trouble. I apprehend he will not have less than seven hundred a year. Seven hundred a year is a fine thing for a younger brother; and as of course he will still live at home, it will be all for his *menus plaisirs*;[50] and a sermon at Christmas and Easter, I suppose, will be the sum total of sacrifice."[51]

His sister tried to laugh off her feelings by saying, "Nothing amuses me more than the easy manner with which every body settles the abundance of those who have a great deal less than themselves. You would look rather blank, Henry, if your *menus plaisirs* were to be limited to seven hundred a year."

"Perhaps I might; but all *that* you know is entirely comparative. Birthright and habit must settle the business.[52] Bertram is certainly well off for a cadet[53] of even a Baronet's family. By the time he is four or five-and-twenty he will have seven hundred a year, and nothing to do for it."

Miss Crawford *could* have said that there would be a something to do and to suffer for it, which she could not think lightly of;[54] but she checked herself and let it pass; and tried to look calm and unconcerned when the two gentlemen shortly afterwards joined them.

"Bertram," said Henry Crawford, "I shall make a point of coming to Mansfield to hear you preach your first sermon. I shall come on purpose to encourage a young beginner. When is it to be? Miss Price, will not you join me in encouraging your cousin? Will not

47. Dr. Grant's advice centers around improving the revenue of the living (that is what Henry means by turning "a good income into a better," which he would have heard them discussing while all the men were still at the dinner table). To do so he could make his glebe land more productive, or try to raise his tithes by proving he was not receiving the correct amount, often because the tithes did not reflect recent improvements in the productivity of the land. Jane Austen's father improved his clerical income by this latter procedure, and she expresses her hope in a letter that he can attain six hundred pounds a year through this means (Jan. 3, 1801). In another letter she wonders whether someone else's meager living "may be improvable" (Jan. 21, 1799).

48. His calling him "Bertram" twice in this paragraph, and elsewhere, was standard practice among men who knew each other well. Edmund called Henry "Crawford" when he was arriving and saw the barouche. In contrast, women refer to other women by their first names, if intimate or related, or by the more formal "Miss/Mrs." This latter practice is also followed when women refer to men, or men refer to women.

49. *make ducks and drakes with*: squander, use idly or recklessly. The phrase originated from its being the name for skipping flat stones across water, a symbol of idle activity (hence also the reference to aquatic fowl).

50. menus plaisirs: little or daily pleasures. It is a French phrase, particularly likely to be used by denizens of fashionable London society like Henry and Mary.

51. Henry assumes that Edmund will hire a curate to perform the regular duties of his position. Such a curate would cost some money, but not a lot, and Edmund would save money on housekeeping by living at Mansfield Park.

52. The favoring of the oldest son was a long-standing and generally accepted custom, though Henry's own comfort with the principle is obviously assisted by his being such a son himself, and his having inherited a large estate.

53. *cadet*: younger son or brother.

54. She means his renouncing marriage with her, since, as her reflections below indicate, she is determined not to have him if he does become a clergyman.

you engage to attend with your eyes steadily fixed on him the whole time—as I shall do—not to lose a word; or only looking off just to note down any sentence pre-eminently beautiful?[55] We will provide ourselves with tablets and a pencil.[56] When will it be? You must preach at Mansfield, you know, that Sir Thomas and Lady Bertram may hear you."

"I shall keep clear of you, Crawford, as long as I can," said Edmund, "for you would be more likely to disconcert me, and I should be more sorry to see you trying at it, than almost any other man."[57]

"Will he not feel this?" thought Fanny. "No, he can feel nothing as he ought."

The party being now all united, and the chief talkers attracting each other, she remained in tranquillity; and as a whist table was formed after tea[58]—formed really for the amusement of Dr. Grant, by his attentive wife, though it was not to be supposed so—and Miss Crawford took her harp, she had nothing to do but to listen, and her tranquillity remained undisturbed the rest of the evening, except when Mr. Crawford now and then addressed to her a question or observation, which she could not avoid answering. Miss Crawford was too much vexed by what had passed to be in a humour for any thing but music. With that, she soothed herself and amused her friend.[59]

The assurance of Edmund's being so soon to take orders, coming upon her like a blow that had been suspended, and still hoped uncertain and at a distance, was felt with resentment and mortification. She was very angry with him. She had thought her influence more. She *had* begun to think of him—she felt that she had—with great regard, with almost decided intentions; but she would now meet him with his own cool feelings. It was plain that he could have no serious views, no true attachment, by fixing himself in a situation[60] which he must know she would never stoop to.[61] She would learn to match him in his indifference. She would henceforth admit his attentions without any idea beyond immediate amusement. If *he* could so command his affections, *her's* should do her no harm.

55. Henry focuses on the style of a sermon rather than the substance.

56. A tablet was a small item used for writing notes or memoranda; it usually consisted of two stiff surfaces, of varying material, that were joined by a hinge and could be folded together. This allowed it to fit into a pocket, and made it ideal for carrying places. A pencil was the common accompaniment to a tablet, for it was easy to pull out and use in any situation. In contrast, pens of the time required the accompanying presence of a bottle of liquid ink, which took up space and could spill if not on a flat, secure surface.

57. Edmund has shown that he likes Henry very much, but he has also perceived that Henry, like his sister, treats lightly moral and religious principles that Edmund regards seriously. He therefore would hate to see that side of Henry's character emerge, and spoil his opinion of his friend.

58. The table, or set of four players necessary for the game, includes Henry, Edmund, and Dr. and Mrs. Grant.

59. The friend is Fanny, who is not part of the card game and also has no taste for participating in whatever conversation occurs during intervals in the game.

60. *situation*: position in life.

61. In her recent conversation with Edmund in the Grants' shrubbery, as well as previously at Sotherton, she demonstrated clearly her disapproval of his intention to take orders and be a clergyman, and she is disappointed and angry that her words had such little effect.

Chapter Six

*H*enry Crawford had quite made up his mind by the next morning to give another fortnight to Mansfield, and having sent for his hunters and written a few lines of explanation to the Admiral,[1] he looked round at his sister as he sealed and threw the letter from him, and seeing the coast clear of the rest of the family, said, with a smile, "And how do you think I mean to amuse myself, Mary, on the days that I do not hunt? I am grown too old to go out more than three times a week;[2] but I have a plan for the intermediate days, and what do you think it is?"

"To walk and ride with me, to be sure."

"Not exactly, though I shall be happy to do both, but *that* would be exercise only to my body, and I must take care of my mind. Besides *that* would be all recreation and indulgence, without the wholesome alloy of labour, and I do not like to eat the bread of idleness.[3] No, my plan is to make Fanny Price in love with me."

"Fanny Price! Nonsense! No, no. You ought to be satisfied with her two cousins."

"But I cannot be satisfied without Fanny Price, without making a small hole in Fanny Price's heart.[4] You do not seem properly aware of her claims to notice. When we talked of her last night, you none of you seemed sensible of the wonderful improvement that has taken place in her looks within the last six weeks.[5] You see her every day, and therefore do not notice it, but I assure you, she is quite a different creature from what she was in the autumn.[6] She was then merely a quiet, modest, not plain looking girl, but she is now absolutely pretty. I used to think she had neither complexion nor countenance; but in that soft skin of her's, so frequently tinged with a blush as it was yesterday, there is decided beauty; and from what I observed of her eyes and mouth, I do not despair of their being capable of expression enough when she has any thing to express. And then—her air,[7] her

1. Henry may write to Admiral Crawford from a general habit of keeping him informed of his whereabouts. It is also possible the admiral was planning to join Henry at his estate, perhaps for the hunting.

2. Hunting could be rigorous exercise, for it meant riding a horse fast over miles of countryside and jumping obstacles, such as fences and streams (see the illustration on the following page).

3. His words derive from Proverbs 31, verse 27, part of a famous passage listing the attributes of a virtuous woman: "She looketh well to the ways of her household, and eateth not the bread of idleness." Henry, and almost certainly his listener, would know this passage from regular attendance at church.

4. In announcing his plan Henry places himself in the ranks of one of Jane Austen's most familiar male character types, the potential seducer of the heroine. All her six completed novels contain a young man, figuring prominently in the plot, who courts the heroine but who also has serious flaws or vices that she is ignorant of initially. In all but one, *Northanger Abbey*, he is also a charming and intelligent man who genuinely attracts the heroine. In one case, Willoughby of *Sense and Sensibility*, he makes the heroine (one of two in that novel) fall deeply in love with him before cruelly abandoning her; in two cases, Wickham of *Pride and Prejudice* and Mr. Elliot of *Persuasion*, he attracts her more moderately and then turns out to be unscrupulous and mercenary; in the last, Frank Churchill of *Emma*, he is more irresponsible and thoughtless than villainous and mostly flirts idly with the heroine. Of all these figures Henry Crawford plays the largest role in his story, and he is also the most complex character, so much so that his true nature and his final actions and fate remain in doubt until the very end. Moreover, he is a rare case of someone whom many readers and critics of the novel have felt could or should have acted differently and met a different fate; even the author herself, at the very end, asserts that he came close to following an alternative course that would have created an entirely different denouement to the story.

5. He left a few days after Sir Thomas's arrival, which was mid-October or a little before (see chronology, p. 856).

6. In England at that time, autumn usually meant the period from August through October.

7. *air*: outward character, demeanor.

manner, her tout ensemble[8] is so indescribably improved! She must be grown two inches, at least, since October."

"Phoo! phoo! This is only because there were no tall women to compare her with, and because she has got a new gown, and you never saw her so well dressed before. She is just what she was in October, believe me. The truth is, that she was the only girl in company for you to notice, and you must have a somebody. I have always thought her pretty—not strikingly pretty—but 'pretty enough' as people say; a sort of beauty that grows on one. Her eyes should be darker, but she has a sweet smile; but as for this wonderful degree of improvement, I am sure it may all be resolved into a better style of dress and your having nobody else to look at; and therefore, if you do set about a flirtation with her, you never will persuade me that it is in compliment to her beauty, or that it proceeds from any thing but your own idleness and folly."[9]

Her brother gave only a smile to this accusation, and soon afterwards said, "I do not quite know what to make of Miss Fanny. I do not understand her. I could not tell what she would be at yesterday. What is her character?—Is she solemn?—Is she queer?—Is she prudish? Why did she draw back and look so grave at me? I could hardly get her to speak. I never was so long in company with a girl in my life—trying to entertain her—and succeed so ill! Never met with a girl who looked so grave on me! I must try to get the better of this. Her looks say, 'I will not like you, I am determined not to like you,' and I say, she shall."[10]

"Foolish fellow! And so this is her attraction after all! This it is— her not caring about you—which gives her such a soft skin and makes her so much taller, and produces all these charms and graces! I do desire that you will not be making her really unhappy; a *little* love perhaps may animate and do her good, but I will not have you plunge her deep,[11] for she is as good a little creature as ever lived, and has a great deal of feeling."

"It can be but for a fortnight," said Henry, "and if a fortnight can kill her, she must have a constitution which nothing could save. No, I will not do her any harm, dear little soul! I only want her to look kindly on me, to give me smiles as well as blushes, to keep a chair for me by herself wherever we are, and be all animation when I take it

8. *tout ensemble*: general appearance, overall or complete effect. Once again Henry Crawford employs a French phrase; it had become somewhat common in England but was by no means a standard part of the language.

9. Thus Mary indicates her knowledge of Henry's irresponsibility, but, as with his behavior toward Maria and Julia Bertram, she makes no attempt to persuade him to act otherwise.

10. His words show how much he has made a career of conquering female hearts—though there is never any indication he has gone further in his conduct. A French commentator on Jane Austen, Léonie Villard, calls him a platonic Don Juan.

11. Mary may be alluding to the words "plung'd me deep in woe" from a song by the leading Scottish poet of the time, Robert Burns—though similar phrases are found occasionally in other contemporary writings.

Jumping over a stream during a hunt, one of the main hazards of the sport.
[From Ralph Nevill, *Old Sporting Prints* (London, 1908)]

and talk to her; to think as I think, be interested in all my possessions and pleasures, try to keep me longer at Mansfield, and feel when I go away that she shall be never happy again. I want nothing more."[12]

"Moderation itself!" said Mary. "I can have no scruples[13] now. Well, you will have opportunities enough of endeavouring to recommend yourself, for we are a great deal together."

And without attempting any further remonstrance, she left Fanny to her fate—a fate which, had not Fanny's heart been guarded in a way unsuspected by Miss Crawford, might have been a little harder than she deserved; for although there doubtless are such unconquerable young ladies of eighteen (or one should[14] not read about them) as are never to be persuaded into love against their judgment by all that talent, manner,[15] attention, and flattery can do,[16] I have no inclination to believe Fanny one of them, or to think that with so much tenderness of disposition, and so much taste as belonged to her,[17] she could have escaped heart-whole[18] from the courtship (though the courtship only of a fortnight) of such a man as Crawford, in spite of there being some previous ill-opinion of him to be overcome, had not her affection been engaged elsewhere. With all the security which love of another and disesteem of him could give to the peace of mind he was attacking, his continued attentions—continued, but not obtrusive, and adapting themselves more and more to the gentleness and delicacy of her character,—obliged her very soon to dislike him less than formerly. She had by no means forgotten the past, and she thought as ill of him as ever; but she felt his powers; he was entertaining, and his manners were so improved,[19] so polite, so seriously and blamelessly polite, that it was impossible not to be civil to him in return.[20]

A very few days were enough to effect this; and at the end of those few days, circumstances arose which had a tendency rather to forward his views of pleasing her, inasmuch as they gave her a degree of happiness which must dispose her to be pleased with every body. William, her brother, the so long absent and dearly loved brother, was in England again.[21] She had a letter from him herself, a few hurried happy lines, written as the ship came up Channel, and sent into Portsmouth, with the first boat that left the Antwerp, at anchor, in Spithead;[22] and when Crawford walked up with the newspaper in

12. He actually achieved this effect, or something close to it, with Maria, and seems now to feel no remorse about it. The previous night he lamented to Fanny that Maria was too good for Mr. Rushworth, but without ever seeming to trouble himself about his role in the whole affair.

13. *scruples*: hesitations.

14. *should*: would.

15. *manner*: polished or distinguished air or deportment.

16. Many novels of the time contained heroines (or heroes) who are extreme paragons of virtue, and this formed one of the main objects of Jane Austen's satire. She includes several ludicrous examples of excessive virtue in short humorous pieces she wrote as an adolescent, and in *Northanger Abbey*, which focuses on satirizing common fictional conventions, she makes a point at the beginning of relating her heroine's lack of extraordinary talent or virtue, adding at one point in the description, "What a strange, unaccountable character!" She returned to the theme again toward the end of her life, with a "Plan of a novel" that caricatures various fictional absurdities; it includes a heroine and hero who are faultless, with the heroine receiving "repeated offers of Marriage—which she always refers wholly to her Father, exceedingly angry that he sh^d not be first applied to."

17. By taste she means an ability to appreciate artistic beauty of various kinds, cultivated manners, and, more generally, harmony and elegance in any aspect of life. This is a quality Jane Austen often evokes in her novels as an important attribute and always gives to her heroines, with the partial exception of the untutored heroine of *Northanger Abbey*. At the same time, taste is never as important for her as moral virtue and benevolence: a kind but vulgar person is preferable to a polished but callous one, if that is the choice.

18. *heart-whole*: with an undamaged or unengaged heart.

19. *improved*: cultivated, refined.

20. Thus Henry has appealed, as predicted, to Fanny's taste, even as he has not altered her more significant condemnation of his moral character.

21. Since Fanny came to Mansfield she has only once seen William, when he visited her for a week just before he joined the navy. That was eight years ago (see chronology, pp. 854 and 857).

22. The *Antwerp*, William's ship, sailed up the English Channel from the Atlantic, and headed toward Portsmouth, Britain's largest naval base, in the center of the channel. It stopped in Spithead, the body of water just outside

his hand, which he had hoped would bring the first tidings, he found her trembling with joy over this letter, and listening with a glowing, grateful countenance to the kind invitation which her uncle was most collectedly dictating in reply.

It was but the day before, that Crawford had made himself thoroughly master of the subject, or had in fact become at all aware of her having such a brother, or his being in such a ship, but the interest then excited had been very properly lively, determining him on his return to town to apply for information as to the probable period of the Antwerp's return from the Mediterranean,[23] &c.;[24] and the good luck which attended his early examination of ship news,[25] the next morning, seemed the reward of his ingenuity in finding out such a method of pleasing her, as well as of his dutiful attention to the Admiral, in having for many years taken in the paper esteemed to have the earliest naval intelligence. He proved, however, to be too late. All those fine first feelings, of which he had hoped to be the excitor, were already given. But his intention, the kindness of his intention, was thankfully acknowledged—quite thankfully and warmly, for she was elevated beyond the common timidity of her mind by the flow of her love for William.

This dear William would soon be amongst them. There could be no doubt of his obtaining leave of absence immediately, for he was still only a midshipman;[26] and as his parents, from living on the spot, must already have seen him and be seeing him perhaps daily, his direct[27] holidays might with justice be instantly given to the sister,[28] who had been his best correspondent through a period of seven years, and the uncle who had done most for his support and advancement; and accordingly the reply to her reply, fixing a very early day for his arrival, came as soon as possible; and scarcely ten days had passed since Fanny had been in the agitation of her first dinner visit, when she found herself in an agitation of a higher nature—watching[29] in the hall, in the lobby,[30] on the stairs, for the first sound of the carriage which was to bring her a brother.

It came happily while she was thus waiting; and there being neither ceremony nor fearfulness to delay the moment of meeting, she was with him as he entered the house, and the first minutes of exquisite[31] feeling had no interruption and no witnesses, unless the ser-

Portsmouth Harbor that served as anchorage: since its harbor could not contain the numerous ships using the base, Spithead provided a place for ships to wait before docking, as is happening here, or to assemble and wait prior to sailing out to sea. Once at anchorage the *Antwerp* would send a small rowboat from the ship to inform the base of its arrival and to perform other errands, including in this case the dispatch of letters from the crew.

23. William was earlier described as having sent Fanny a picture, from the *Antwerp* in the Mediterranean, four years ago. The Mediterranean was a critical center of operation for the British navy, due to France's having major naval bases on its coast there and to Spain's and Italy's being important areas of conflict. The navy had two bases in the Mediterranean, at Malta and Gibraltar (for the latter, see also p. 429, note 40). A posting of four years or more in the same area was not unusual for a ship. William's having been with the same ship at least that long is a sign of his lack of promotion, an abiding concern of his (see later in this chapter and the next chapter).

24. Once back in London he could ask his uncle, who would know people with important positions in the navy, to find the information.

25. Newspapers often printed stories relating to the navy, with naval battles being a major news item. Most papers also had a section called "Ship News," containing information regarding ships' arrivals and departures in England or ships lost at sea; this assisted families curious about their loved ones, as well as merchants interested in the fate of their vessels.

26. Midshipmen were boys and young men preparing to be officers, so their continued presence would not be vitally important to the captain. Ordinary sailors could also have difficulty obtaining leave, due to fear of desertion, but this would not apply to midshipmen or officers.

27. *direct*: immediate.

28. The ship will probably remain in Portsmouth awhile for repairs, so he will have opportunities then to see the main part of his family.

29. *watching*: waiting, being on the alert. The term then could also mean looking out for, but here she is "watching" for a sound.

30. "Lobby" could refer to a hall or corridor, but here it probably means an open area at the top of the stairs, a common feature of grand houses. It is used in that way a little later (p. 486).

31. *exquisite*: intense, exalted.

vants chiefly intent upon opening the proper doors could be called such.[32] This was exactly what Sir Thomas and Edmund had been separately conniving at, as each proved to the other by the sympathetic alacrity with which they both advised Mrs. Norris's continuing where she was, instead of rushing out into the hall as soon as the noises of the arrival reached them.

William and Fanny soon shewed themselves; and Sir Thomas had the pleasure of receiving, in his protégé, certainly a very different person from the one he had equipped seven years ago, but a young man of an open, pleasant countenance, and frank, unstudied,[33] but feeling[34] and respectful manners, and such as confirmed him his friend.

It was long before Fanny could recover from the agitating happiness of such an hour as was formed by the last thirty minutes of expectation and the first of fruition; it was some time even before her happiness could be said to make her happy, before the disappointment inseparable from the alteration of person had vanished, and she could see in him the same William as before, and talk to him, as her heart had been yearning to do, through many a past year. That time, however, did gradually come, forwarded by an affection on his side as warm as her own, and much less incumbered by refinement or self-distrust. She was the first object of his love, but it was a love which his stronger spirits, and bolder temper, made it as natural for him to express as to feel. On the morrow they were walking about together with true enjoyment, and every succeeding morrow renewed a tête-à-tête, which Sir Thomas could not but observe with complacency,[35] even before Edmund had pointed it out to him.

Excepting the moments of peculiar[36] delight, which any marked or unlooked-for instance of Edmund's consideration of her in the last few months had excited, Fanny had never known so much felicity in her life, as in this unchecked, equal, fearless intercourse with the brother and friend, who was opening all his heart to her, telling her all his hopes and fears, plans, and solicitudes respecting that long thought of, dearly earned, and justly valued blessing of promotion[37]—who could give her direct and minute[38] information of the father and mother, brothers and sisters, of whom she very seldom heard—who was interested in all the comforts and all the little

32. The servants would open the doors to each room as they passed through them. Servants were supposed to be invisible and were often regarded as so, though in fact they would hear much that happened and relate the gossip eagerly to other servants (and from there it often passed outside the house).

33. A young man who had spent his adolescence in the navy would usually not have acquired the formal and polished manners of someone bred continually in genteel society like the denizens of Mansfield Park. On p. 428, William's "warm hearted, blunt fondness" is mentioned, and *Persuasion* contains several passages in which the friendly, sincere, and spontaneous manners of navy men are evoked, generally in a positive sense.

34. *feeling*: sensitive.

35. *complacency*: pleasure, satisfaction.

36. *peculiar*: particular.

37. Promotion from midshipman to lieutenant, the next rank in the navy. For more, see p. 454 and p. 455, notes 78 and 80.

38. *minute*: precise, detailed.

A sailor and a midshipman (on right).

[From J. R. Green, *A Short History of the English People*, Vol. IV (New York, 1903), p. 1797]

hardships of her home, at Mansfield—ready to think of every member of that home as she directed, or differing only by a less scrupulous opinion, and more noisy abuse of their aunt Norris—and with whom (perhaps the dearest indulgence of the whole) all the evil and good of their earliest years could be gone over again, and every former united pain and pleasure retraced with the fondest recollection. An advantage this, a strengthener of love, in which even the conjugal tie is beneath the fraternal. Children of the same family, the same blood, with the same first associations and habits, have some means of enjoyment in their power, which no subsequent connections can supply; and it must be by a long and unnatural estrangement, by a divorce which no subsequent connection can justify, if such precious remains of the earliest attachments are ever entirely outlived. Too often, alas! it is so.—Fraternal love, sometimes almost every thing, is at others worse than nothing. But with William and Fanny Price, it was still a sentiment in all its prime and freshness, wounded by no opposition of interest, cooled by no separate attachment, and feeling the influence of time and absence only in its increase.

An affection so amiable[39] was advancing each in the opinion of all who had hearts to value any thing good. Henry Crawford was as much struck with it as any. He honoured the warm hearted, blunt fondness of the young sailor, which led him to say, with his hand stretched towards Fanny's head, "Do you know, I begin to like that queer fashion already, though when I first heard of such things being done in England I could not believe it, and when Mrs. Brown, and the other women, at the Commissioner's, at Gibraltar,[40] appeared in the same trim,[41] I thought they were mad; but Fanny can reconcile me to any thing"—and saw, with lively admiration, the glow of Fanny's cheek, the brightness of her eye, the deep interest, the absorbed attention, while her brother was describing any of the imminent hazards, or terrific[42] scenes, which such a period, at sea, must supply.

It was a picture which Henry Crawford had moral taste enough to value.[43] Fanny's attractions increased—increased two-fold—for the sensibility[44] which beautified her complexion and illumined her countenance, was an attraction in itself. He was no longer in doubt of the capabilities of her heart. She had feeling, genuine feeling. It would be something to be loved by such a girl, to excite the

39. *amiable*: kind, benevolent, good-natured.

40. Gibraltar, at the mouth of the Mediterranean, was one of Britain's most important overseas bases, and thus a natural place for ships to stop. Jane Austen's naval brother Francis is known to have stopped there in 1805 to resupply his ship. It also contained a number of people living and working at the base, including many employed at the dockyard, which repaired ships. The commissioner, who was appointed directly by the Navy Board, was the highest authority at the dockyard. William and other officers probably attended a social function at the commissioner's residence; his wife, almost certainly "Mrs. Brown," and some other women of relatively high rank would have also attended.

This passage represents one of the only known amendments Jane Austen made to the novel. In a letter she confides, "I learn from Sir J. Carr that there is no Government House at Gibraltar.—I must alter it to the Commissioner's" (Jan. 24, 1813). A "government house" is the residence of the governor of a colony, and she may have assumed Gibraltar was a colony (it did not acquire that status until later in the century). The authority she mentions is Sir John Carr, author of *Descriptive Travels in the Southern and Eastern Portions of Spain* (1811), which contains a lengthy description of Gibraltar. While it does not discuss its precise political status, the book does mention both the residence of the governor (who would have a different authority than a colonial governor) and the "official house of the commissioner." It also states in passing, "The society is here altogether gloomy, for want of more females." Austen may have chosen to place the event at the commissioner's house because it was described as "official," or because he has a direct connection with the navy while the governor is a civil authority.

41. *trim*: style, fashion, adornment. Since he pointed to Fanny's head he could mean a new hairstyle or a new type of headdress or ornamentation on the head; both frequently changed during this period. The women at Gibraltar could learn about new styles from women on board ships stopping there, or from published journals that included information on the latest fashions. For examples of pictures showing such fashions, including headdresses, from one of the leading journals of the time, see pp. 433 and 471.

42. *terrific*: dreadful, terrifying.

43. Moral taste is the ability to appreciate good moral qualities, especially in others. It is not the same as having those qualities oneself, but it would make one more open to the salutary influence of others.

44. *sensibility*: aroused feelings; strong capacity for feeling.

first ardours of her young, unsophisticated mind! She interested him more than he had foreseen. A fortnight was not enough. His stay became indefinite.

William was often called on by his uncle to be the talker. His recitals were amusing[45] in themselves to Sir Thomas, but the chief object in seeking them, was to understand the recitor, to know the young man by his histories; and he listened to his clear, simple, spirited details[46] with full satisfaction—seeing in them, the proof of good principles, professional knowledge, energy, courage, and cheerfulness—every thing that could deserve or promise well. Young as he was, William had already seen a great deal. He had been in the Mediterranean—in the West Indies—in the Mediterranean again[47]—had been often taken on shore by the favour of his Captain,[48] and in the course of seven years had known every variety of danger, which sea and war together could offer.[49] With such means in his power he had a right to be listened to; and though Mrs. Norris could fidget about the room, and disturb every body in quest of two needlefulls of thread or a second hand shirt button in the midst of her nephew's account of a shipwreck or an engagement,[50] every body else was attentive; and even Lady Bertram could not hear of such horrors unmoved, or without sometimes lifting her eyes from her work to say, "Dear me! how disagreeable.—I wonder any body can ever go to sea."

To Henry Crawford they gave a different feeling. He longed to have been at sea, and seen and done and suffered as much. His heart was warmed, his fancy fired, and he felt the highest respect for a lad who, before he was twenty, had gone through such bodily hardships, and given such proofs of mind.[51] The glory of heroism, of usefulness, of exertion, of endurance, made his own habits of selfish indulgence appear in shameful contrast; and he wished he had been a William Price, distinguishing himself and working his way to fortune and consequence with so much self-respect and happy ardour, instead of what he was!

The wish was rather eager than lasting.[52] He was roused from the reverie of retrospection and regret produced by it, by some inquiry from Edmund as to his plans for the next day's hunting; and he found it was as well to be a man of fortune at once with horses and grooms at

45. *amusing*: interesting.

46. *details*: detailed accounts.

47. He may have gone to the West Indies, another prime area of naval activity due to its importance to British commerce, while assigned to a different ship before the *Antwerp*. Or he may have gone with the *Antwerp*. Ships were often assigned to different stations; they could also be commanded to engage in a short, single mission to another part of the world.

48. This would be when the ship docked in overseas ports. Whether members of the crew went onshore, and for how long, was at the discretion of the captain.

49. Among the many hazards were naval engagements or battles, storms at sea, and fights on land (see note 54 below). Even more deaths—80 percent of the total during this period—were from disease or accidents on board (which were frequent due to the need to perform many difficult and dangerous tasks amid heavy pieces of equipment on a crowded ship).

50. Women frequently did needlework during conversations, which could include sewing new buttons onto shirts ("second hand" means not original to the garment). But most would not interrupt a speaker with a search for supplies, especially in the midst of such dramatic stories.

51. *proofs of mind*: testaments of character.

52. This episode gives an important glimpse into Henry's character. His moral taste allows him to appreciate another person's qualities, and his honesty and intelligence allow him to perceive his own deficiency in this regard, but his lack of self-discipline or willingness to sacrifice his pleasures keeps him from turning that perception into self-reform. His reaction also shows his inclination to imagine himself in different roles, which already allowed him to be an excellent actor.

his command. In one respect it was better, as it gave him the means of conferring a kindness where he wished to oblige. With spirits, courage, and curiosity up to any thing, William expressed an inclination to hunt; and Crawford could mount him without the slightest inconvenience to himself, and with only some scruples to obviate in Sir Thomas, who knew better than his nephew the value of such a loan,[53] and some alarms to reason away in Fanny. She feared for William; by no means convinced by all that he could relate of his own horsemanship in various countries, of the scrambling parties in which he had been engaged,[54] the rough horses and mules he had ridden, or his many narrow escapes from dreadful falls,[55] that he was at all equal to the management of a high-fed[56] hunter in an English fox-chase;[57] nor till he returned safe and well, without accident or discredit, could she be reconciled to the risk, or feel any of that obligation to Mr. Crawford for lending the horse which he had fully intended it should produce. When it was proved however to have done William no harm, she could allow it to be a kindness, and even reward the owner with a smile when the animal was one minute tendered to his use again; and the next, with the greatest cordiality, and in a manner not to be resisted, made over to his use entirely so long as he remained in Northamptonshire.

53. Hunters were very expensive, and there was always the danger that one could be injured, perhaps fatally, during a hunt.

54. "Scrambling parties" probably means excursions onshore, which often involved scrambling up land formations or over rough terrain; this interpretation is strengthened by the immediate reference to rides on horses or mules. The navy often sent men onto foreign shores, whether to gather intelligence about the terrain or the enemy, to place cannons onshore so they could engage in more effective bombardment, or to attack enemy forces or fortifications—all naturally dangerous.

55. The falls could be part of the landing parties, or on ship. Sailors regularly had to scale the ship's rigging, whether to adjust the sails or to perform other tasks, and the rigging's height, the precariousness of the places for standing or walking, the frequent tossing of the ship in the waves, and windy or rainy weather created continual danger of serious falls.

56. *high-fed:* well-fed.

57. The hunt was literally a chase over a long distance, at the end of which, when the fox was cornered, dogs would be set on it to finish it. The task of the hunters on horseback was simply to follow along (dogs were also the ones who found the fox, forced it to flee, and finally trapped it).

A picture showing a current hairstyle.

[From *The Repository of arts, literature, fashions, manufactures, &c*, Vol. V (1811), p. 361]

Chapter Seven

*T*he intercourse of the two families was at this period more nearly restored to what it had been in the autumn, than any member of the old intimacy had thought ever likely to be again. The return of Henry Crawford, and the arrival of William Price, had much to do with it, but much was still owing to Sir Thomas's more than toleration of the neighbourly attempts at the Parsonage. His mind, now disengaged from the cares which had pressed on him at first, was at leisure to find the Grants and their young inmates[1] really worth visiting;[2] and though infinitely above scheming or contriving for any the most advantageous matrimonial establishment that could be among the apparent possibilities of any one most dear to him, and disdaining even as a littleness the being quick-sighted on such points,[3] he could not avoid perceiving in a grand and careless way that Mr. Crawford was somewhat distinguishing[4] his niece—nor perhaps refrain (though unconsciously) from giving a more willing assent to invitations on that account.

His readiness, however, in agreeing to dine at the Parsonage, when the general invitation was at last hazarded, after many debates and many doubts as to whether it were worth while,[5] "because Sir Thomas seemed so ill inclined! and Lady Bertram was so indolent!"— proceeded from good breeding[6] and good-will alone, and had nothing to do with Mr. Crawford, but as being one in an agreeable group; for it was in the course of that very visit, that he first began to think, that any one in the habit of such idle observations *would have thought* that Mr. Crawford was the admirer of Fanny Price.

The meeting was generally felt to be a pleasant one, being composed in a good proportion of those who would talk and those who would listen; and the dinner itself was elegant and plentiful, according to the usual style of the Grants, and too much according to the usual habits of all to raise any emotion except in Mrs. Norris, who could never behold either the wide table or the number of dishes on

1. *inmates*: mates or associates of someone who reside in the latter's home.

2. *visiting*: socializing or maintaining friendly intercourse with.

3. Meaning he considers it would be little or petty to be quick to perceive a possible advantageous marriage.

4. *distinguishing*: paying particular notice to.

5. The Grants would naturally wish to invite Sir Thomas and Lady Bertram, both as a courtesy after his return and in order to reestablish more intimate relations with the leading figure in the neighborhood.

6. *good breeding*: good manners, courtesy.

A village of the time.

[From Geoffrey Holme, ed., *Early English Water-colour Drawings* (London, 1919), Plate XLVIII]

it with patience, and who did always contrive to experience some evil[7] from the passing of the servants behind her chair,[8] and to bring away some fresh conviction of its being impossible among so many dishes but that some must be cold.[9]

In the evening it was found, according to the pre-determination of Mrs. Grant and her sister, that after making up[10] the Whist table there would remain sufficient for a round game,[11] and every body being as perfectly complying, and without a choice as on such occasions they always are, Speculation was decided on almost as soon as Whist;[12] and Lady Bertram soon found herself in the critical situation of being applied to for her own choice between the games, and being required either to draw a card for Whist or not. She hesitated. Luckily Sir Thomas was at hand.

"What shall I do, Sir Thomas?—Whist and Speculation; which will amuse me most?"

Sir Thomas, after a moment's thought, recommended Speculation. He was a Whist player himself, and perhaps might feel that it would not much amuse him to have her for a partner.[13]

"Very well," was her ladyship's contented answer—"then Speculation if you please, Mrs. Grant. I know nothing about it, but Fanny must teach me."

Here Fanny interposed however with anxious protestations of her own equal ignorance; she had never played the game nor seen it played in her life; and Lady Bertram felt a moment's indecision again—but upon every body's assuring her that nothing could be so easy, that it was the easiest game on the cards, and Henry Crawford's stepping forward with a most earnest request to be allowed to sit between her ladyship and Miss Price, and teach them both, it was so settled; and Sir Thomas, Mrs. Norris, and Dr. and Mrs. Grant, being seated at the table of prime intellectual state and dignity, the remaining six, under Miss Crawford's direction, were arranged round the other. It was a fine arrangement for Henry Crawford, who was close to Fanny, and with his hands full of business,[14] having two persons[15] cards to manage as well as his own—for though it was impossible for Fanny not to feel herself mistress of the rules of the game in three minutes,[16] he had yet to inspirit[17] her play, sharpen her avarice, and harden her heart, which, especially in any competition with Wil-

7. *evil*: misfortune, mischief.

8. The servants pass behind the guests to serve the food and drink, and a wider table in a small room could force them to step closer to the guests and thereby possibly bother them. Mrs. Norris is stretching for grounds to further condemn Mrs. Grant's rejection of her table in preference for a grander one.

9. Since dishes were all laid out on the table at once, and there could be many at a large dinner party, some might become cold before they were eaten.

10. *making up*: collecting sufficient numbers for.

11. A round game of cards is one where any number can play, and each player acts alone. There are ten people here, and only four will play whist.

12. Speculation was a popular game for multiple people. A character in Jane Austen's unfinished novel *The Watsons*, probably written around 1804, declares, "*Speculation* is the only round game at Croydon now." Austen herself seems to have been fond of the game: in a letter she states, "Our evening was equally agreeable in its way; I introduced *speculation*, and it was so much approved that we hardly knew how to leave off" (Oct. 25, 1808). A short time later, after hearing that those she had introduced to speculation had rejected it in favor of another game, she writes, "it mortifies me deeply, because Speculation was under my patronage," adding, "When one comes to reason upon it, it [the other game] cannot stand its' ground against Speculation" (Jan. 10, 1809). For the rules for speculation, see note 16 below.

13. He would be expected to partner with his own wife if she played, and since one's success at whist depended on the quality of one's partner, she would represent a substantial handicap for Sir Thomas.

14. *business*: occupation, duties.

15. "Persons" has no apostrophe in the original, but some editions have added one. Austen often omits an apostrophe in places where it would be used now.

16. Fanny can understand quickly because speculation is a fairly simple game. Each player is dealt three cards, and then a final card is turned over to determine which suit is trumps; the players also contribute to a common pool a specified number of counters or chips (often called fish because they were usually made in that shape). The players never look at their own cards—this is why Henry can manage the hands of Fanny and Lady Bertram as well as his own. Play consists in having each player in turn reveal one card from his or her hand. Whoever at the end possesses the highest card in the trump suit wins, and gains the entire pool. Moreover, after any player turns over a trump card, the other players may bid to purchase that card with their counters.

17. *inspirit*: animate.

liam, was a work of some difficulty; and as for Lady Bertram, he must continue in charge of all her fame and fortune through the whole evening; and if quick enough to keep her from looking at her cards when the deal began, must direct her in whatever was to be done with them to the end of it.

He was in high spirits, doing every thing with happy ease, and pre-eminent in all the lively turns, quick resources, and playful impu-dence that could do honour to the game; and the round table was altogether a very comfortable[18] contrast to the steady sobriety and orderly silence of the other.[19]

Twice had Sir Thomas inquired into the enjoyment and success of his lady, but in vain; no pause was long enough for the time his mea-sured manner needed; and very little of her state could be known till Mrs. Grant was able, at the end of the first rubber, to go to her and pay her compliments.

"I hope your ladyship is pleased with the game."

"Oh! dear, yes.—Very entertaining indeed. A very odd game. I do not know what it is all about. I am never to see my cards; and Mr. Crawford does all the rest."[20]

"Bertram," said Crawford some time afterwards, taking the oppor-tunity of a little languor in the game, "I have never told you what happened to me yesterday in my ride home." They had been hunt-ing together, and were in the midst of a good run, and at some dis-tance from Mansfield,[21] when his horse being found to have flung a shoe, Henry Crawford had been obliged to give up, and make the best of his way back. "I told you I lost my way after passing that old farm house, with the yew trees,[22] because I can never bear to ask; but I have not told you that, with my usual luck—for I never do wrong without gaining by it[23]—I found myself in due time in the very place which I had a curiosity to see. I was suddenly, upon turning the cor-ner of a steepish downy[24] field, in the midst of a retired little village between gently rising hills; a small stream before me to be forded, a church standing on a sort of knoll to my right—which church was strikingly large and handsome for the place, and not a gentleman or half a gentleman's house to be seen excepting one—to be presumed the Parsonage,[25] within a stone's throw of the said knoll and church. I found myself in short in Thornton Lacey."

18. *comfortable*: pleasant, enjoyable.

19. Since competitive bidding for cards is at the heart of speculation, a table where it is played would be lively and talkative.

20. This demonstrates Lady Bertram's unthinking politeness: she automatically answers that she is enjoying the game, while also revealing that she is completely puzzled by it.

21. The chase or run after the fox could extend for many miles.

22. Yew trees are one of the few coniferous trees native to Britain. As evergreens they would be noticeable and easily distinguishable from other trees during the winter.

23. This credo permeates Henry's confident attitude toward life, and is undoubtedly one factor encouraging him in his extended flirtations with women he has no interest in marrying. It will ultimately lead him into trouble.

24. *downy field*: elevated or hilly area that is treeless. Such areas were called "downs."

25. Villages were primarily inhabited by laborers, craftsmen, and shopkeepers. Aside from the clergyman, usually at most one genteel, or near-genteel (which is what is meant by "half a gentleman"), family would live there. Few genteel people would be in the vicinity at all, and they would most likely have homes outside the village.

"It sounds like it," said Edmund; "but which way did you turn after passing Sewell's farm?"

"I answer no such irrelevant and insidious questions; though were I to answer all that you could put in the course of an hour, you would never be able to prove that it was *not* Thornton Lacey—for such it certainly was."

"You inquired then?"

"No, I never inquire. But I *told* a man mending a hedge that it was Thornton Lacey, and he agreed to it."[26]

"You have a good memory. I had forgotten having ever told you half so much of the place."

Thornton Lacey was the name of his impending living, as Miss Crawford well knew; and her interest in a negociation for William Price's knave[27] increased.[28]

"Well," continued Edmund, "and how did you like what you saw?"

"Very much indeed. You are a lucky fellow. There will be work for five summers at least before the place is live-able."

"No, no, not so bad as that. The farm-yard must be moved, I grant you; but I am not aware of any thing else. The house is by no means bad, and when the yard is removed, there may be a very tolerable approach to it."[29]

"The farm-yard must be cleared away entirely, and planted up to shut out the blacksmith's shop.[30] The house must be turned to front[31] the east instead of the north—the entrance and principal rooms, I mean, must be on that side, where the view is really very pretty;[32] I am sure it may be done. And *there* must be your approach—through what is at present the garden. You must make a new garden at what is now the back of the house; which will be giving it the best aspect[33] in the world—sloping to the south-east. The ground seems precisely formed for it. I rode fifty yards up the lane between the church and the house in order to look about me; and saw how it might all be. Nothing can be easier. The meadows beyond what *will be* the garden, as well as what now *is*, sweeping round from the lane I stood in to the north-east, that is, to the principal road through the village, must be all laid together of course; very pretty meadows they are, finely sprinkled with timber. They belong to the living, I suppose.[34] If not, you must purchase them.[35] Then the stream—something

26. Henry also declared, on p. 438, that he never asks for directions, and without any apparent shame, even though he admitted that his not asking had led to his getting lost; Jane Austen probably noticed this characteristic among some men of her acquaintance. Here, however, he finds a way to procure information without stooping to inquire directly.

27. *knave*: jack.

28. She, and perhaps others, are negotiating over the price of his knave. The bargaining was tricky because nobody could know if the knave would turn out to be the highest trump, thereby securing its possessor the common pool, or if a queen, king, or ace of trumps would turn up later, rendering the knave worthless.

29. As discussed earlier in connection with Sotherton (p. 103, note 9), an attractive approach to a house was an essential part of contemporary landscaping, and a farmyard could ruin it (for a contemporary picture of a farmyard, displaying some unsightly qualities, see p. 453). Many clergy engaged in farming to help support themselves; Edmund will probably not abandon those activities, only move the farmyard to a less visible area.

30. A blacksmith was a basic feature of any village, due to the need for shoeing horses and other work involving iron. But the griminess of the work means that it would present a very unsightly appearance. In this case it cannot be moved, but adjacent plantings can block it from view.

31. *front*: face.

32. Improvers sometimes altered the house so that its entrance was on a different side, especially those focused on improving the view of the surroundings. Humphry Repton recommended repositioning a house's entrance in some of his proposals for specific places.

33. *aspect*: position facing its surroundings.

34. They would belong to the living if they are part of his glebe land.

35. He must purchase any of these meadows outside his glebe land in order to fulfill Henry's dictum of their all being "laid together," i.e., joined, and to make them all part of one grand landscaping plan.

must be done with the stream; but I could not quite determine what. I had two or three ideas."[36]

"And I have two or three ideas also," said Edmund, "and one of them is that very little of your plan for Thornton Lacey will ever be put in practice. I must be satisfied with rather less ornament and beauty. I think the house and premises may be made comfortable, and given the air of a gentleman's residence without any very heavy expense, and that must suffice me; and I hope may suffice all who care about me."[37]

Miss Crawford, a little suspicious and resentful of a certain tone of voice and a certain half-look attending the last expression of his hope, made a hasty finish of her dealings with William Price,[38] and securing his knave at an exorbitant rate, exclaimed, "There, I will stake my last like a woman of spirit.[39] No cold prudence for me. I am not born to sit still and do nothing. If I lose the game, it shall not be from not striving for it."

The game was her's, and only did not pay her for what she had given to secure it.[40] Another deal proceeded, and Crawford began again about Thornton Lacey.

"My plan may not be the best possible; I had not many minutes to form it in: but you must do a good deal. The place deserves it, and you will find yourself not satisfied with much less than it is capable of.—(Excuse me, your ladyship must not see your cards. There, let them lie just before you.) The place deserves it, Bertram. You talk of giving it the air of a gentleman's residence. *That* will be done, by the removal of the farm-yard, for, independent of that terrible nuisance, I never saw a house of the kind which had in itself so much the air of a gentleman's residence, so much the look of a something above a mere Parsonage House,[41] above the expenditure of a few hundreds a year. It is not a scrambling[42] collection of low single rooms, with as many roofs as windows[43]—it is not cramped into the vulgar compactness of a square farm-house—it is a solid, roomy, mansion-like looking house, such as one might suppose a respectable old country family had lived in from generation to generation, through two centuries at least, and were now spending from two to three thousand a year in." Miss Crawford listened, and Edmund agreed to this. "The air of a gentleman's residence, therefore, you cannot but give it, if

36. Water was important to landscaping improvements; see p. 109, note 35. Since it could be channeled and altered in various ways, Henry is torn between different ideas. He shows throughout this conversation the same zeal for improvement he displayed in connection with Sotherton.

37. He is expressing his hope that Mary, the most important of the "all who care about me," will accept him in these modest circumstances.

38. Mary's resentment of Edmund's hope now spurs her to compensate by securing victory in the card negotiation, at any price.

39. *spirit*: courage. The courage comes from paying a high price even though she cannot know if the knave will turn out to be the highest trump.

40. Thus the knave did win her the game—there were probably not many cards left to be drawn when she secured it—but she paid more counters for it than she gained when she won the pool. This is symbolic for Mary, whose bold and determined spirit sometimes leads her to judge and act imprudently.

41. Many parsonage houses were modest dwellings.

42. *scrambling*: irregular, rambling.

43. Such houses were the product of owners who wished to expand their dwelling but did not have sufficient funds to tear down and build anew, and hence were forced to join extensions to the existing core.

A view over landscaped grounds with a stream.

[From Humphry Repton, *Fragments on the Theory and Practice of Landscape Gardening* (London, 1816), p. 106]

you do any thing. But it is capable of much more. (Let me see, Mary; Lady Bertram bids a dozen for that queen; no, no, a dozen is more than it is worth. Lady Bertram does *not* bid a dozen.[44] She will have nothing to say to it. Go on, go on.) By some such improvements as I have suggested, (I do not really require you to proceed upon my plan, though by the bye I doubt any body's striking out a better) — you may give it a higher character. You may raise it into a *place*.[45] From being the mere gentleman's residence, it becomes, by judicious improvement, the residence of a man of education, taste, modern manners,[46] good connections.[47] All this may be stamped on it; and that house receive such an air as to make its owner be set down as[48] the great land-holder of the parish, by every creature travelling the road; especially as there is no real squire's house to dispute the point;[49] a circumstance between ourselves to enhance the value of such a situation[50] in point of privilege and independence beyond all calculation. *You* think with me, I hope — (turning with a softened voice to Fanny). — Have you ever seen the place?"

Fanny gave a quick negative, and tried to hide her interest in the subject by an eager attention to her brother, who was driving as hard a bargain and imposing on her as much as he could; but Crawford pursued with "No, no, you must not part with the queen. You have bought her too dearly, and your brother does not offer half her value.[51] No, no, sir, hands off — hands off. Your sister does not part with the queen. She is quite determined. The game will be yours, turning to her again — it will certainly be yours."[52]

"And Fanny had much rather it were William's," said Edmund, smiling at her. "Poor Fanny! not allowed to cheat herself as she wishes!"

"Mr. Bertram," said Miss Crawford, a few minutes afterwards, "you know Henry to be such a capital improver, that you cannot possibly engage in any thing of the sort at Thornton Lacey, without accepting his help. Only think how useful he was at Sotherton! Only think what grand things were produced there by our all going with him one hot day in August to drive about the grounds, and see his genius[53] take fire. There we went, and there we came home again; and what was done there is not to be told!"[54]

Fanny's eyes were turned on Crawford for a moment with an

44. Mary has turned over a queen of trumps, a strong potential winner, and other players are bidding on it. Henry, acting on behalf of Lady Bertram, may have first been spurred to top another's offer, before realizing it was too high. The pool probably consists of twenty-six counters, or fish, since, according to the contemporary Hoyle's guide to games, "the dealer pools six fish, and every other player four," and there are six players here. If Henry considers a dozen too high it must be early in the game, when there is still a good chance a king or an ace of trumps will appear.

45. place: a grand country house or mansion.

46. "Modern manners" could include various aspects of contemporary ways of living that are reflected in the style of architecture. For example, privacy had become more valued in recent times, and this led to changes in house design, most notably the development of corridors during the eighteenth century so that people could reach their own rooms without passing through others' rooms. It is not clear if Henry envisages such a dramatic change as that, but he does recommend making the house as suitable as possible for contemporary ideals of living.

47. *connections*: family ties and background.

48. *set down as*: considered to be.

49. "Squire" was a traditional term for a member of the gentry, especially a locally prominent landowner. In some eighteenth- and nineteenth-century novels a man in that position is called by others "Squire —." In many villages the local squire would live in the most impressive dwelling in the area. But in the absence of a squire, the parson was usually the next most prominent and wealthy figure in local rural society, and his dwelling could stand supreme.

50. *situation*: place to live.

51. This indicates that Fanny won the queen that Henry earlier declined on behalf of Lady Bertram, and paid what Henry regards as too high a price, perhaps because she is not as fierce a bargainer.

52. Presumably more cards have been turned up since the earlier bargaining for the queen, and with no king or ace of trumps appearing, the queen is now looking like a highly probable winner.

53. *genius*: mental powers or aptitude.

54. She means his flirtation with Maria and Julia, especially the former. Mary brings this up from a wish to get back at her brother, who has angered her by

expression more than grave, even reproachful; but on catching his were instantly withdrawn. With something of consciousness he shook his head at his sister, and laughingly replied, "I cannot say there was much done at Sotherton; but it was a hot day, and we were all walking after each other and bewildered." As soon as a general buz gave him shelter, he added, in a low voice directed solely at Fanny, "I should be sorry to have my powers of *planning* judged of by the day at Sotherton. I see things very differently now. Do not think of me as I appeared then."[55]

Sotherton was a word to catch Mrs. Norris, and being just then in the happy leisure which followed securing the odd trick[56] by Sir Thomas's capital play and her own, against Dr. and Mrs. Grant's great hands,[57] she called out in high good-humour, "Sotherton! Yes, that is a place indeed, and we had a charming day there. William, you are quite out of luck; but the next time you come I hope dear Mr. and Mrs. Rushworth will be at home, and I am sure I can answer for your being kindly received by both. Your cousins are not of a sort to forget their relations, and Mr. Rushworth is a most amiable man. They are at Brighton now, you know—in one of the best houses there, as Mr. Rushworth's fine fortune gives them a right to be. I do not exactly know the distance, but when you get back to Portsmouth, if it is not very far off, you ought to go over and pay your respects to them;[58] and I could send a little parcel by you that I want to get conveyed to your cousins."[59]

"I should be very happy, aunt—but Brighton is almost by Beachey Head;[60] and if I could get so far, I could not expect to be welcome in such a smart place as that—poor scrubby midshipman as I am."

Mrs. Norris was beginning an eager assurance of the affability[61] he might depend on, when she was stopped by Sir Thomas's saying with authority, "I do not advise your going to Brighton, William, as I trust you may soon have more convenient opportunities of meeting, but my daughters would be happy to see their cousins any where; and you will find Mr. Rushworth most sincerely disposed to regard all the connections of our family as his own."

"I would rather find him private secretary to the first Lord than any thing else,"[62] was William's only answer, in an under voice, not meant to reach far, and the subject dropped.

his extended discussion with Edmund regarding the parsonage at Thornton Lacey. Not only did Henry thereby force Mary to confront more fully the reality of Edmund's impending ordination, but, by speaking so positively of the possibilities offered by the parsonage Edmund will soon inhabit, Henry has provided implicit endorsement and encouragement for Edmund's decision to become a clergyman instead of seeking one of the more fashionable and remunerative careers Mary has suggested.

55. Henry noticed Fanny's disapproving glare, though he may also anticipate her disapproval from knowledge of her character. It is not clear whether Henry has any sense of the intrinsic faults of his behavior, nor whether his statement about now judging things differently refers to understanding the wrongness of his act, or to appreciating that Fanny is a more worthy object of attention than Maria and Julia.

56. *odd trick*: the thirteenth and last trick in whist when the two teams are tied at six tricks apiece; hence the deciding trick.

57. This would be Mrs. Norris's own description, for naturally she wishes to boast of her skill in overcoming the strong hands of her adversaries. She also includes Sir Thomas in her boast, due to politeness and to her consistent inclination to flatter him.

58. Brighton and Portsmouth are both on the southern coast, and are around fifty miles apart by road, which would take almost seven hours by normal carriage speeds on main roads.

59. Since postage rates were high during this period, sending a parcel could cost a fair amount, though less than the cost of traveling fifty miles and back.

60. Beachey Head is a promontory a little east of Brighton; see map, p. 882. There is no town there, but sailors would notice and remember it as a prominent feature along the English Channel.

61. *affability*: courtesy or kindness, especially of a superior to an inferior.

62. The First Lord of the Admiralty was a member of the cabinet and the highest figure in the navy. His private secretary is his assistant, rather than a mere clerical worker, and would thus exercise great authority; he would also have high social origins. William would like to have a connection with him for assistance in gaining a promotion. For a picture of the Admiralty boardroom of the time, see p. 451.

As yet Sir Thomas had seen nothing to remark in Mr. Crawford's behaviour; but when the Whist table broke up at the end of the second rubber, and leaving Dr. Grant and Mrs. Norris to dispute over their last play, he became a looker-on at the other, he found his niece the object of attentions, or rather of professions of a somewhat pointed character.

Henry Crawford was in the first glow of another scheme about Thornton Lacey, and not being able to catch Edmund's ear, was detailing it to his fair neighbour with a look of considerable earnestness. His scheme was to rent the house himself the following winter,[63] that he might have a home of his own in that neighbourhood; and it was not merely for the use of it in the hunting season (as he was then telling her), though *that* consideration had certainly some weight, feeling as he did, that in spite of all Dr. Grant's very great kindness, it was impossible for him and his horses to be accommodated where they now were without material inconvenience;[64] but his attachment to that neighbourhood did not depend upon one amusement or one season of the year: he had set his heart upon having a something there that he could come to at any time, a little home-stall[65] at his command where all the holidays of his year might be spent, and he might find himself continuing, improving, and *perfecting* that friendship and intimacy with the Mansfield Park family which was increasing in value to him every day. Sir Thomas heard and was not offended. There was no want of respect in the young man's address;[66] and Fanny's reception of it was so proper and modest, so calm and uninviting, that he had nothing to censure in her.[67] She said little, assented only here and there, and betrayed no inclination either of appropriating any part of the compliment to herself or of strengthening his views in favour of Northamptonshire. Finding by whom he was observed, Henry Crawford addressed himself on the same subject to Sir Thomas, in a more every day tone, but still with feeling.

"I want to be your neighbour, Sir Thomas, as you have perhaps heard me telling Miss Price. May I hope for your acquiescence and for your not influencing your son against such a tenant?"

Sir Thomas, politely bowing, replied—"It is the only way, sir, in which I could *not* wish you established as a permanent neighbour;

63. Henry assumes that Edmund could reside at Mansfield Park, since the other parish is close enough that he could ride over there for the day, whether on Sunday or on days when a special occasion, such as a wedding or funeral, would require his attendance.

64. Henry has horses for his carriage as well as his hunters; he is later described as using four horses to travel (p. 482), and while those might have been rented, that could be the number he habitually uses. Many who were dedicated to the hunt, and able to afford it, would have several hunters, so that they could hunt even if one horse suffered an injury, or if a horse was too tired from a previous day's hunt. Moreover, owners would often take more than two or three horses with them on a hunt: the spare ones would be ridden by lightweight servants until the owner's horse became tired, and he could switch to one of the others and continue to ride fast.

65. *home-stall*: dwelling with its land and accompanying buildings (such as a stable).

66. Since a man was not allowed to make an open declaration of his affection for a woman, unless he was making an offer of marriage, he would need to speak in this oblique way to signal his intentions. Sir Thomas comprehends immediately that Henry is signaling this interest in Fanny.

67. A woman was not supposed to indicate any strong interest in a man who was courting her.

Racing across a field during a hunt; this is why multiple horses were useful.
[From Ralph Nevill, *Old Sporting Prints* (London, 1908)]

but I hope, and believe, that Edmund will occupy his own house at Thornton Lacey. Edmund, am I saying too much?"

Edmund, on this appeal, had first to hear what was going on, but on understanding the question, was at no loss for an answer.

"Certainly, sir, I have no idea but of residence. But, Crawford, though I refuse you as a tenant, come to me as a friend. Consider the house as half your own every winter, and we will add to the stables on your own improved plan, and with all the improvements of your improved plan that may occur to you this spring."

"We shall be the losers," continued Sir Thomas. "His going, though only eight miles, will be an unwelcome contraction of our family circle; but I should have been deeply mortified, if any son of mine could reconcile himself to doing less. It is perfectly natural that you should not have thought much on the subject, Mr. Crawford. But a parish has wants and claims which can be known only by a clergyman constantly resident, and which no proxy can be capable of satisfying to the same extent. Edmund might, in the common phrase, do the duty of Thornton, that is, he might read prayers and preach, without giving up Mansfield Park; he might ride over, every Sunday, to a house nominally inhabited, and go through divine service; he might be the clergyman of Thornton Lacey every seventh day, for three or four hours,[68] if that would content him. But it will not. He knows that human nature needs more lessons than a weekly sermon can convey, and that if he does not live among his parishioners and prove himself by constant attention their well-wisher and friend, he does very little either for their good or his own."[69]

Mr. Crawford bowed his acquiescence.

"I repeat again," added Sir Thomas, "that Thornton Lacey is the only house in the neighbourhood in which I should *not* be happy to wait on[70] Mr. Crawford as occupier."

Mr. Crawford bowed his thanks.

"Sir Thomas," said Edmund, "undoubtedly understands the duty of a parish priest.—We must hope his son may prove that *he* knows it too."

Whatever effect Sir Thomas's little harangue might really produce on Mr. Crawford, it raised some awkward sensations in two of the others, two of his most attentive listeners, Miss Crawford and

68. There were two services every Sunday, and each could last awhile; hence three to four hours total.

69. Sir Thomas articulates an ideal of an active and engaged clergyman that was becoming increasingly popular at the time, partly due to the rising evangelical movement. But not all subscribed to this view, and there was an active debate over how much a clergyman needed to be resident in his parish. Edmund himself, in his earlier discussion with Mary (p. 180), declared that it was precisely that constant daily interaction with his parishioners, instead of relying simply on Sunday sermons, that allowed a clergyman to exercise a powerful moral influence on them.

70. *wait on*: visit.

The boardroom of the Admiralty.

[From Fiona St. Aubyn, *Ackermann's Illustrated London*, illustrations by Augustus Pugin and Thomas Rowlandson (Ware, 1985), p. 51]

Fanny.—One of whom, having never before understood that Thornton was so soon and so completely to be his home, was pondering with downcast eyes on what it would be, *not* to see Edmund every day; and the other, startled from the agreeable fancies she had been previously indulging on the strength of her brother's description, no longer able, in the picture she had been forming of a future Thornton, to shut out the church, sink[71] the clergyman, and see only the respectable, elegant, modernized, and occasional residence of a man of independent fortune[72]—was considering Sir Thomas, with decided ill-will, as the destroyer of all this, and suffering the more from that involuntary forbearance which his character and manner commanded, and from not daring to relieve herself by a single attempt at throwing ridicule on his cause.

All the agreeable of *her* speculation was over for that hour. It was time to have done with cards if sermons prevailed, and she was glad to find it necessary to come to a conclusion and be able to refresh her spirits by a change of place and neighbour.

The chief[73] of the party were now collected irregularly round the fire, and waiting the final break up. William and Fanny were the most detached. They remained together at the otherwise deserted card-table, talking very comfortably and not thinking of the rest, till some of the rest began to think of them. Henry Crawford's chair was the first to be given a direction towards them, and he sat silently observing them for a few minutes; himself in the meanwhile observed by Sir Thomas, who was standing in chat with Dr. Grant.

"This is the Assembly night," said William. "If I were at Portsmouth, I should be at it perhaps."[74]

"But you do not wish yourself at Portsmouth, William?"

"No, Fanny, that I do not. I shall have enough of Portsmouth, and of dancing too, when I cannot have you. And I do not know that there would be any good in going to the Assembly, for I might not get a partner. The Portsmouth girls turn up their noses at any body who has not a commission. One might as well be nothing as a midshipman.[75] One *is* nothing indeed. You remember the Gregorys; they are grown up amazing fine girls, but they will hardly speak to *me*, because Lucy is courted by a lieutenant."[76]

"Oh! shame, shame!—But never mind it, William. (Her own

71. *sink*: eliminate, deduct.

72. Mary earlier exhibited annoyance at her brother's positive description of the parsonage as Edmund's future residence, but she reacted with appreciation to Henry's second proposal, of the parsonage being Henry's residence, at least part of the year, and subject to his improvements, while Edmund remains at Mansfield. This reaction, even if it is now spoiled by Sir Thomas, shows how much she is still thinking of Edmund as a possible husband, despite her professions of never marrying him if he takes orders.

73. *chief*: greater part.

74. He means the regular night for holding an assembly, a public gathering usually centering around dancing. Assemblies had become popular during the eighteenth century and could be found occasionally in even the smallest towns. A large town like Portsmouth would have many of them. They were generally open to whoever bought tickets or a subscription.

75. Officers, unlike midshipmen, had commissions.

76. Lieutenant was the lowest commissioned rank, and thus the position that others of William's age who had been promoted would now have.

A farmyard.

[From Sir Walter Gilbey and E. D. Cuming, *George Morland: His Life and Works* (London, 1907), p. 118]

cheeks in a glow of indignation as she spoke.) It is not worth minding. It is no reflection on *you*; it is no more than what the greatest admirals have all experienced, more or less, in their time. You must think of that; you must try to make up your mind to it as one of the hardships which fall to every sailor's share—like bad weather and hard living[77]—only with this advantage, that there will be an end to it, that there will come a time when you will have nothing of that sort to endure. When you are a lieutenant!—only think, William, when you are a lieutenant, how little you will care for any nonsense of this kind."[78]

"I begin to think I shall never be a lieutenant, Fanny. Every body gets made[79] but me."[80]

"Oh! my dear William, do not talk so, do not be so desponding. My uncle says nothing, but I am sure he will do every thing in his power to get you made. He knows, as well as you do, of what consequence it is."

She was checked by the sight of her uncle much nearer to them than she had any suspicion of, and each found it necessary to talk of something else.

"Are you fond of dancing, Fanny?"

"Yes, very;—only I am soon tired."

"I should like to go to a ball with you and see you dance. Have you never any balls at Northampton?[81]—I should like to see you dance, and I'd dance with you if you *would*, for nobody would know who I was here, and I should like to be your partner once more. We used to jump about together many a time, did not we? when the hand-organ was in the street?[82] I am a pretty good dancer in my way, but I dare say you are a better."—And turning to his uncle, who was now close to them—"Is not Fanny a very good dancer, sir?"

Fanny, in dismay at such an unprecedented question, did not know which way to look, or how to be prepared for the answer. Some very grave reproof, or at least the coldest expression of indifference must be coming to distress her brother, and sink her to the ground. But, on the contrary, it was no worse than, "I am sorry to say that I am unable to answer your question. I have never seen Fanny dance since she was a little girl;[83] but I trust we shall both think she acquits herself like a gentlewoman when we do see her, which perhaps we may have an opportunity of doing ere long."

77. Life on ship involved exposure to all sorts of harsh weather, not just storms but also extremes of heat or cold, depending on where a ship sailed. The hard conditions included, in addition to many dangers, very crowded living quarters, poor diets due to the frequent absence of fresh food, and long periods of never seeing land.

78. Acquiring a commission was the crucial step in a young officer's career. It was supposed to involve passing an oral exam about seamanship before a board of three captains once he was nineteen or older, though in many cases people were promoted earlier. But even after passing the exam a candidate needed an appointment to a specific berth, and these were not available for everyone.

79. *made*: promoted.

80. Promotions came faster than usual during wartime, which is why William has probably seen many fellow midshipmen get them. Jane Austen's two naval brothers were both promoted to lieutenant when they were eighteen. At the same time, there were even larger numbers of midshipmen awaiting a promotion—almost two thousand in 1813. Receiving one often required the patronage of a more senior officer, or someone with influence in the naval administration, and since William's father is only an inactive marine, he is poorly positioned for that.

81. As a large town Northampton would hold regular assemblies, but the Bertrams are later described as only occasionally attending them. They may not frequent them because assemblies, being open to those willing to pay, attracted many middle-class as well as genteel people, and the Bertrams may mostly avoid such social mixing. Early in *Pride and Prejudice* the status-conscious and very wealthy hero speaks with disdain of those attending a public assembly.

82. A hand-organ was a portable barrel organ operated by turning a hand crank. They were played by street musicians, who provided entertainment in larger towns. William and Fanny may have prized hand-organs especially because their parents were not able to afford to buy musical instruments or to attend public concerts.

83. He probably saw Fanny while she was being taught to dance. It was considered an important skill, especially for women, and wealthy families would hire dancing masters to teach their children.

"I have had the pleasure of seeing your sister dance, Mr. Price," said Henry Crawford, leaning forward, "and will engage to answer every inquiry which you can make on the subject, to your entire satisfaction. But I believe (seeing Fanny look distressed) it must be at some other time. There is *one* person in company who does not like to have Miss Price spoken of."[84]

True enough, he had once seen Fanny dance;[85] and it was equally true that he would now have answered for her gliding about with quiet, light elegance, and in admirable time, but in fact he could not for the life of him recall what her dancing had been, and rather took it for granted that she had been present than remembered any thing about her.

He passed, however, for an admirer of her dancing; and Sir Thomas, by no means displeased, prolonged the conversation on dancing in general, and was so well engaged in describing the balls of Antigua,[86] and listening to what his nephew could relate of the different modes of dancing which had fallen within his observation,[87] that he had not heard his carriage announced, and was first called to the knowledge of it by the bustle of Mrs. Norris.

"Come, Fanny, Fanny, what are you about? We are going. Do not you see your aunt is going? Quick, quick. I cannot bear to keep good old Wilcox waiting. You should always remember the coachman and horses. My dear Sir Thomas, we have settled it that the carriage should come back for you, and Edmund, and William."[88]

Sir Thomas could not dissent, as it had been his own arrangement, previously communicated to his wife and sister; but *that* seemed forgotten by Mrs. Norris, who must fancy that she settled it all herself.

Fanny's last feeling in the visit was disappointment—for the shawl which Edmund was quietly taking from the servant to bring and put round her shoulders,[89] was seized by Mr. Crawford's quicker hand, and she was obliged to be indebted to his more prominent attention.

84. Henry's statement demonstrates both his grasp of Fanny's shy character and his assiduous attempt to adapt his conduct to it.

85. The one time was in September, approximately three months ago (see chronology, pp. 856–857). Fanny danced some, though at one point when Tom left the dance she had to sit down (p. 224). She was never mentioned then as dancing with Henry, for he was focusing on Maria and Julia and at that time would have neglected Fanny as the lowest-ranking female at the dance.

86. Antigua contained many wealthy planters like Sir Thomas who might hold balls.

87. William could have experienced a variety of types of dancing from his stops in different parts of the world with the navy. Dances on board ship were also a popular way for sailors to pass the time, and being all-male and normally done to the accompaniment of a fiddle rather than an orchestra or piano, as was usual in dances in homes and at assemblies, sailors' dances would have a distinctive character.

88. The Bertrams' carriage is a chaise, which seats only three. Hence it is first taking the three women, Lady Bertram, Fanny, and Mrs. Norris (the latter may be staying the night at Mansfield Park, or she may be about to be dropped off at her home), and then returning for the three men.

89. The servant is at the door, ready to hand shawls or coats to guests. Helping a woman with her shawl was a standard male courtesy.

Chapter Eight

William's desire of seeing Fanny dance, made more than a momentary impression on his uncle. The hope of an opportunity, which Sir Thomas had then given, was not given to be thought of no more. He remained steadily inclined to gratify so amiable a feeling—to gratify any body else who might wish to see Fanny dance, and to give pleasure to the young people in general; and having thought the matter over and taken his resolution in quiet independence, the result of it appeared the next morning at breakfast, when, after recalling and commending what his nephew had said, he added, "I do not like, William, that you should leave Northamptonshire without this indulgence. It would give me pleasure to see you both dance. You spoke of the balls at Northampton. Your cousins have occasionally attended them; but they would not altogether[1] suit us now. The fatigue would be too much for your aunt.[2] I believe, we must not think of a Northampton ball. A dance at home would be more eligible,[3] and if"—

"Ah! my dear Sir Thomas," interrupted Mrs. Norris, "I knew what was coming. I knew what you were going to say. If dear Julia were at home, or dearest Mrs. Rushworth at Sotherton, to afford[4] a reason, an occasion for such a thing, you would be tempted to give the young people a dance at Mansfield. I know you would. If *they* were at home to grace the ball, a ball you would have this very Christmas.[5] Thank your uncle, William, thank your uncle."

"My daughters," replied Sir Thomas, gravely interposing, "have their pleasures at Brighton, and I hope are very happy; but the dance which I think of giving at Mansfield, will be for their cousins. Could we be all assembled, our satisfaction would undoubtedly be more complete, but the absence of some is not to debar the others of amusement."

Mrs. Norris had not another word to say. She saw decision[6] in his looks, and her surprize and vexation required some minutes silence

1. *altogether*: on the whole.

2. It is only four miles to Northampton, which would take less than an hour by carriage, but that is still too much for Lady Bertram.

3. *eligible*: desirable, suitable.

4. *afford*: provide.

5. It is nearing Christmas now, and the ball will be held on the 22nd (see p. 460).

6. *decision*: determination, firmness.

Breakfast (from a contemporary journal).

[From Max von Boehn, *Modes & Manners of the Nineteenth Century*, Vol. I (London, 1909), p. 105]

to be settled into composure. A ball at such a time! His daughters absent and herself not consulted! There was comfort, however, soon at hand. *She* must be the doer of every thing; Lady Bertram would of course be spared all thought and exertion, and it would all fall upon *her.* She should have to do the honours[7] of the evening, and this reflection quickly restored so much of her good humour as enabled her to join in with the others, before their happiness and thanks were all expressed.

Edmund, William, and Fanny, did, in their different ways, look and speak as much grateful pleasure in the promised ball, as Sir Thomas could desire. Edmund's feelings were for the other two. His father had never conferred a favour or shewn a kindness more to his satisfaction.

Lady Bertram was perfectly quiescent and contented, and had no objections to make. Sir Thomas engaged for its giving her very little trouble, and she assured him, "that she was not at all afraid of the trouble, indeed she could not imagine there would be any."

Mrs. Norris was ready with her suggestions as to the rooms he would think fittest to be used, but found it all prearranged; and when she would have conjectured and hinted about the day, it appeared that the day was settled too. Sir Thomas had been amusing himself with shaping a very complete outline of the business; and as soon as she would listen quietly, could read his list of the families to be invited, from whom he calculated, with all necessary allowance for the shortness of the notice, to collect young people enough to form twelve or fourteen couple; and could detail the considerations which had induced him to fix on the 22d, as the most eligible day. William was required to be at Portsmouth on the 24th; the 22d would therefore be the last day of his visit;[8] but where the days were so few it would be unwise to fix on any earlier. Mrs. Norris was obliged to be satisfied with thinking just the same, and with having been on the point of proposing the 22d herself, as by far the best day for the purpose.

The ball was now a settled thing, and before the evening a proclaimed thing to all whom it concerned. Invitations were sent with dispatch, and many a young lady went to bed that night with her head full of happy cares as well as Fanny.[9]—To her, the cares were sometimes almost beyond the happiness; for young and inexperienced,

7.   *do the honours*: render the necessary courtesies or civilities (especially of a hostess).

8.   A direct trip to Portsmouth requires one full day of travel plus the better part of a second day, so he will need to leave on the 23rd (for the route and times of later journeys between Mansfield and Portsmouth, see pp. 674 and 802).

9.   This indicates that the messages arrived that day. They could have been sent via servants, traveling on horseback or by carriage. They must have gone primarily to families living in close proximity, for the description of the ball does not suggest an enormous number of people attending.

Chawton Cottage, where Jane Austen wrote her novels and the location of the current Jane Austen's House Museum.

[From Mary Augusta Austen-Leigh, *Personal Aspects of Jane Austen* (New York, 1920), p. 112]

with small means of choice and no confidence in her own taste—the "how she should be dressed" was a point of painful solicitude; and the almost solitary ornament in her possession, a very pretty amber cross which William had brought her from Sicily,[10] was the greatest distress of all, for she had nothing but a bit of ribbon to fasten it to; and though she had worn it in that manner once, would it be allowable at such a time, in the midst of all the rich ornaments which she supposed all the other young ladies would appear in? And yet not to wear it! William had wanted to buy her a gold chain too, but the purchase had been beyond his means,[11] and therefore not to wear the cross might be mortifying him. These were anxious considerations; enough to sober her spirits even under the prospect of a ball given principally for her gratification.

The preparations meanwhile went on, and Lady Bertram continued to sit on her sofa without any inconvenience from them. She had some extra visits from the housekeeper,[12] and her maid was rather hurried in making up a new dress for her;[13] Sir Thomas gave orders and Mrs. Norris ran about, but all this gave *her* no trouble, and as she had foreseen, "there was in fact no trouble in the business."

Edmund was at this time particularly full of cares; his mind being deeply occupied in the consideration of two important events now at hand, which were to fix his fate in life—ordination and matrimony—events of such a serious character as to make the ball, which would be very quickly followed by one of them, appear of less moment in his eyes than in those of any other person in the house. On the 23d he was going to a friend near Peterborough in the same situation as himself,[14] and they were to receive ordination in the course of the Christmas week. Half his destiny would then be determined[15]—but the other half might not be so very smoothly wooed. His duties would be established,[16] but the wife who was to share, and animate, and reward those duties might yet be unattainable. He knew his own mind, but he was not always perfectly assured of knowing Miss Crawford's. There were points on which they did not quite agree, there were moments in which she did not seem propitious,[17] and though trusting altogether to her affection, so far as to be resolved (almost resolved) on bringing it to a decision within a very short time, as soon as the variety of business before him were arranged,[18] and he

10. He would have stopped in Sicily while serving in the Mediterranean. Jewelry with sentimental associations, such as a link to a family member, was popular at this time.

11. Jane Austen received a cross, though not an amber one, and a chain from her brother Charles; both, along with a cross given to Jane's sister, Cassandra, were preserved by family members, and are now on display in the Jane Austen House Museum in Chawton. She speaks of them in a letter, while also discussing the sort of financial concerns that prevented William from buying a chain for Fanny: "He [Charles] has received 30£ for his share of the privateer & expects 10£ more—but of what avail is it to take prizes if he lays out the produce in presents to his Sisters. He has been buying Gold chains & Topaze Crosses for us;—he must be well scolded" (May 27, 1801). For prize money in the navy, see p. 121, note 69.

12. The housekeeper would normally consult with the mistress of the house regarding arrangements for a special event, since they were the two people who, along with in many cases the butler, managed the household and servants. Lady Bertram's housekeeper probably simply informs her of what she has decided and arranged.

13. Her lady's maid would not be creating an actual gown or other garment; that would normally be done by a professional mantua-maker (who made gowns) or milliner (who made smaller items). Instead she is combining articles of clothing and adornment to make a new outfit, the meaning of "dress" then.

14. Peterborough is a cathedral town that was then in Northamptonshire; it is now part of Cambridgeshire. A cathedral is the seat of a bishop, who would conduct the examination that allowed a candidate to be ordained as a clergyman. Northampton, the county seat, lacked a cathedral and bishop.

15. Thus he will be away over Christmas. This is not remarkable, for Christmas was a modest holiday then—for more, see p. 519, note 20.

16. *established*: fixed, settled. To be ordained the candidate had to take the oaths of allegiance and supremacy, in which one pledged allegiance to the monarch and acknowledged the supremacy of the Church of England, and subscribe to the Thirty-Nine Articles, which laid down the theological principles of the Anglican Church. These last included some sacred religious duties, and there were other basic duties understood to be part of being a clergyman.

17. *propitious*: favorably inclined.

18. These would be the various matters related to his ordination, a subject Jane Austen inquired about while writing this novel. In a letter to her sister she

knew what he had to offer her—he had many anxious feelings, many doubting hours as to the result. His conviction of her regard for him was sometimes very strong; he could look back on a long course of encouragement, and she was as perfect in disinterested attachment as in every thing else. But at other times doubt and alarm intermingled with his hopes, and when he thought of her acknowledged disinclination for privacy and retirement,[19] her decided preference of a London life—what could he expect but a determined rejection? unless it were an acceptance even more to be deprecated, demanding such sacrifices of situation and employment on his side as conscience must forbid.

The issue of all depended on one question. Did she love him well enough to forego what had used to be essential points—did she love him well enough to make them no longer essential? And this question, which he was continually repeating to himself, though oftenest answered with a "Yes," had sometimes its "No."

Miss Crawford was soon to leave Mansfield, and on this circumstance the "no" and the "yes" had been very recently in alternation. He had seen her eyes sparkle as she spoke of the dear friend's letter, which claimed a long visit from her in London, and of the kindness of Henry, in engaging to remain where he was till January, that he might convey her thither;[20] he had heard her speak of the pleasure of such a journey with an animation which had "no" in every tone. But this had occurred on the first day of its being settled, within the first hour of the burst of such enjoyment, when nothing but the friends she was to visit, was before her. He had since heard her express herself differently—with other feelings—more chequered feelings; he had heard her tell Mrs. Grant that she should leave her with regret; that she began to believe neither the friends nor the pleasures she was going to were worth those she left behind; and that though she felt she must go, and knew she should enjoy herself when once away, she was already looking forward to being at Mansfield again. Was there not a "yes" in all this?

With such matters to ponder over, and arrange, and re-arrange, Edmund could not, on his own account, think very much of the evening, which the rest of the family were looking forward to with a more equal degree of strong interest. Independent of his two cousins'

mentions the subject and adds, "I am glad to find your enquiries have ended so well" (Jan. 19, 1813). Her sister was then visiting their eldest brother, James, who had long been a clergyman and therefore would be an ideal source for information on the matter. It is not known what specific inquiries Austen had her sister make. She may have wished to know how long the process would take, for the plot requires that Edmund, even after leaving to become ordained, does not soon assume his clerical position at Thornton Lacey.

19. *retirement*: seclusion.

20. This is due to social norms dictating that a woman, especially a genteel one, travel with a male escort, usually a relative. An escort would help prevent danger as well as any sexual impropriety.

A bishop, like the one who could ordain Edmund.

[From William Pyne, *The Costume of Great Britain* (London, 1804; 1989 reprint), Plate XXII]

enjoyment in it, the evening was to him of no higher value than any other appointed[21] meeting of the two families might be. In every meeting there was a hope of receiving further confirmation of Miss Crawford's attachment; but the whirl of a ball-room perhaps was not particularly favourable to the excitement or expression of serious feelings. To engage her early for the two first dances,[22] was all the command of individual happiness which he felt in his power, and the only preparation for the ball which he could enter into, in spite of all that was passing around him on the subject, from morning till night.

Thursday was the day of the ball: and on Wednesday morning, Fanny, still unable to satisfy herself, as to what she ought to wear, determined to seek the counsel of the more enlightened, and apply to Mrs. Grant and her sister, whose acknowledged taste would certainly bear her blameless; and as Edmund and William were gone to Northampton, and she had reason to think Mr. Crawford likewise out, she walked down to the Parsonage without much fear of wanting[23] an opportunity for private discussion; and the privacy of such a discussion was a most important part of it to Fanny, being more than half ashamed of her own solicitude.

She met Miss Crawford within a few yards of the Parsonage, just setting out to call on her, and as it seemed to her, that her friend, though obliged to insist on turning back, was unwilling to lose her walk, she explained her business at once and observed that if she would be so kind as to give her opinion, it might be all talked over as well without doors as within. Miss Crawford appeared gratified by the application, and after a moment's thought, urged Fanny's returning with her in a much more cordial manner than before, and proposed their going up into her room,[24] where they might have a comfortable coze,[25] without disturbing Dr. and Mrs. Grant, who were together in the drawing-room. It was just the plan to suit Fanny; and with a great deal of gratitude on her side for such ready and kind attention, they proceeded in doors and upstairs, and were soon deep in the interesting subject. Miss Crawford, pleased with the appeal, gave her all her best judgment and taste, made every thing easy by her suggestions, and tried to make every thing agreeable by her encouragement. The dress being settled in all its grander parts,[26] — "But what

21. *appointed*: agreed upon, scheduled.

22. Dances were done in pairs; see p. 227, note 27.

23. *wanting*: lacking.

24. In other words, after they first agreed to walk to Mansfield Park together, Mary has decided they should instead enter the parsonage, which is right near them.

25. *coze*: a familiar, friendly talk or chat.

26. Meaning they have settled the larger elements of the outfit, which would be a gown as well as perhaps the shoes, gloves, and headdress. For a picture of female evening or ball dress of the time, see pp. 497 and 510.

A London clothing store; the customers would select from strips of cloth, which could be unfurled from the rolls at the top of the store, and then have a dress made to their specifications.

[From *The Repository of arts, literature, fashions, manufactures, &c*, Vol. I (1809), p. 187]

shall you have by way of[27] necklace?" said Miss Crawford. "Shall not you wear your brother's cross?" And as she spoke she was undoing a small parcel, which Fanny had observed in her hand when they met. Fanny acknowledged her wishes and doubts on this point; she did not know how either to wear the cross, or to refrain from wearing it. She was answered by having a small trinket-box placed before her,[28] and being requested to chuse from among several gold chains and necklaces.[29] Such had been the parcel with which Miss Crawford was provided, and such the object of her intended visit; and in the kindest manner she now urged Fanny's taking one for the cross and to keep for her sake, saying every thing she could think of to obviate the scruples which were making Fanny start back at first with a look of horror at the proposal.

"You see what a collection I have," said she, "more by half than I ever use or think of. I do not offer them as new. I offer nothing but an old necklace. You must forgive the liberty and oblige me."

Fanny still resisted, and from her heart. The gift was too valuable. But, Miss Crawford persevered, and argued the case with so much affectionate earnestness through all the heads[30] of William and the cross, and the ball, and herself, as to be finally successful. Fanny found herself obliged to yield, that she might not be accused of pride or indifference, or some other littleness; and having with modest reluctance given her consent, proceeded to make the selection. She looked and looked, longing to know which might be least valuable; and was determined in her choice at last, by fancying there was one necklace more frequently placed before her eyes than the rest.[31] It was of gold prettily worked;[32] and though Fanny would have preferred a longer and a plainer chain as more adapted for her purpose, she hoped in fixing on this, to be chusing what Miss Crawford least wished to keep. Miss Crawford smiled her perfect approbation; and hastened to complete the gift by putting the necklace round her and making her see how well it looked.

Fanny had not a word to say against its becomingness, and excepting what remained of her scruples, was exceedingly pleased with an acquisition so very apropos. She would rather perhaps have been obliged to some other person. But this was an unworthy feeling. Miss Crawford had anticipated her wants with a kindness which proved

27. *by way of*: to serve as a.

28. At that time "trinket" could mean any small article of jewelry or adornment, with no connotation of insignificance or low value.

29. Necklaces, as well as crosses that could be attached to a chain, had become popular in this period because they suited well the prevailing fashion for low necklines.

30. *heads*: points, topics.

31. That Mary is encouraging the choice of one necklace in particular will be revealed on the next page.

32. *prettily worked*: attractively or skillfully fashioned. "Pretty" at the time could mean generally good or admirable as well as attractive in appearance.

her a real friend. "When I wear this necklace I shall always think of you," said she, "and feel how very kind you were."

"You must think of somebody else too when you wear that necklace," replied Miss Crawford. "You must think of Henry, for it was his choice in the first place. He gave it to me, and with the necklace I make over[33] to you all the duty of remembering the original giver. It is to be a family remembrancer.[34] The sister is not to be in your mind without bringing the brother too."

Fanny, in great astonishment and confusion, would have returned the present instantly. To take what had been the gift of another person—of a brother too—impossible!—it must not be!—and with an eagerness and embarrassment quite diverting to her companion, she laid down the necklace again on its cotton, and seemed resolved either to take another or none at all. Miss Crawford thought she had never seen a prettier consciousness.[35] "My dear child," said she laughing, "what are you afraid of? Do you think Henry will claim the necklace as mine, and fancy you did not come honestly by it?—or are you imagining he would be too much flattered by seeing round your lovely throat an ornament which his money purchased three years ago, before he knew there was such a throat in the world?—or perhaps—looking archly—you suspect a confederacy between us, and that what I am now doing is with his knowledge and at his desire?"

With the deepest blushes Fanny protested against such a thought.

"Well then," replied Miss Crawford more seriously but without at all believing her,[36] "to convince me that you suspect no trick, and are as unsuspicious of compliment as I have always found you, take the necklace, and say no more about it. Its being a gift of my brother's need not make the smallest difference in your accepting it, as I assure you it makes none in my willingness to part with it. He is always giving me something or other. I have such innumerable presents from him that it is quite impossible for me to value, or for him to remember half. And as for this necklace, I do not suppose I have worn it six times; it is very pretty—but I never think of it; and though you would be most heartily welcome to any other in my trinket-box, you have happened to fix on the very one which, if I have a choice, I would rather part with and see in your possession than any other. Say no

33. *make over*: transfer.

34. *remembrancer*: memento.

35. *consciousness*: sense of guilt, uneasiness.

36. Mary attributes her own more cynical state of mind to Fanny. An additional reason for her suspicion appears later (p. 648).

Walking dress.

[From *The Repository of arts, literature, fashions, manufactures, &c*, Vol. VIII (1812), p. 111]

more against it, I entreat you. Such a trifle is not worth half so many words."

Fanny dared not make any further opposition; and with renewed but less happy thanks accepted the necklace again, for there was an expression in Miss Crawford's eyes which she could not be satisfied with.

It was impossible for her to be insensible of Mr. Crawford's change of manners. She had long seen it. He evidently tried to please her—he was gallant—he was attentive—he was something like what he had been to her cousins: he wanted, she supposed, to cheat her of her tranquillity as he had cheated them; and whether he might not have some concern in this necklace!—She could not be convinced that he had not, for Miss Crawford, complaisant as a sister, was careless as a woman and a friend.[37]

Reflecting and doubting, and feeling that the possession of what she had so much wished for, did not bring much satisfaction, she now walked home again—with a change rather than a diminution of cares since her treading that path before.

37. In *Emma* the heroine worries that, by voicing her suspicions of another woman's possible sexual impropriety, she has "transgressed the duty of woman by woman." Fanny's idea is probably that a woman should be especially protective and supportive of another woman when it comes to affairs of the heart.

Evening dress.

[From *The Repository of arts, literature, fashions, manufactures, &c,* Vol. X (1813), p. 176]

Chapter Nine

*O*n reaching home, Fanny went immediately up stairs to deposit this unexpected acquisition, this doubtful good of a necklace, in some favourite box in the east room which held all her smaller treasures; but on opening the door, what was her surprize to find her cousin Edmund there writing at the table! Such a sight having never occurred before, was almost as wonderful[1] as it was welcome.

"Fanny," said he directly, leaving his seat and his pen, and meeting her with something in his hand, "I beg your pardon for being here. I come to look for you, and after waiting a little while in hope of your coming in, was making use of your inkstand to explain my errand.[2] You will find the beginning of a note to yourself; but I can now speak my business, which is merely to beg your acceptance of this little trifle—a chain for William's cross. You ought to have had it a week ago, but there has been a delay from my brother's not being in town by several days so soon as I expected;[3] and I have only just now received it at Northampton.[4] I hope you will like the chain itself, Fanny. I endeavoured to consult the simplicity of your taste, but at any rate I know you will be kind to my intentions, and consider it, as it really is, a token of the love of one of your oldest friends."

And so saying, he was hurrying away, before Fanny, overpowered by a thousand feelings of pain and pleasure, could attempt to speak; but quickened by one sovereign wish she then called out, "Oh! cousin, stop a moment, pray stop."

He turned back.

"I cannot attempt to thank you," she continued in a very agitated manner, "thanks are out of the question. I feel much more than I can possibly express. Your goodness in thinking of me in such a way is beyond"—

"If this is all you have to say, Fanny," smiling and turning away again—

"No, no, it is not. I want to consult you."

1.   *wonderful*: amazing, astonishing.

2.   Inkstands were common accessories at the time. They included a tray for pens, an inkwell for dipping the pen into, and a pounce pot or sander, which contained a fine substance like chalk that the writer would shake over fresh ink to make it dry quickly and thereby keep it from smudging.

3.   He sent instructions to Tom in a letter to buy the item when in London, which would have far better jewelry shops than Northampton. Tom, in keeping with his general carelessness, probably came to London a few days later than he promised to Edmund.

4.   The package was sent to Northampton by Tom. At this time, packages were not conveyed by the postal service: a parcel post service developed only later in the nineteenth century. But public coaches (see p. 483, note 22) would transport parcels.

Almost unconsciously she had now undone the parcel he had just put into her hand, and seeing before her, in all the niceness[5] of jewellers' packing, a plain gold chain perfectly simple and neat,[6] she could not help bursting forth again. "Oh! this is beautiful indeed! this is the very thing, precisely what I wished for! this is the only ornament I have ever had a desire to possess. It will exactly suit my cross. They must and shall be worn together. It comes too in such an acceptable moment. Oh! cousin, you do not know how acceptable it is."

"My dear Fanny, you feel these things a great deal too much. I am most happy that you like the chain, and that it should be here in time for to-morrow: but your thanks are far beyond the occasion. Believe me, I have no pleasure in the world superior to that of contributing to yours. No, I can safely say, I have no pleasure so complete, so unalloyed. It is without a drawback."[7]

Upon such expressions of affection, Fanny could have lived an hour without saying another word; but Edmund, after waiting a moment, obliged her to bring down her mind from its heavenly flight by saying, "But what is it that you want to consult me about?"

It was about the necklace, which she was now most earnestly longing to return, and hoped to obtain his approbation of her doing. She gave the history of her recent visit, and now her raptures might well be over, for Edmund was so struck with the circumstance, so delighted with what Miss Crawford had done, so gratified by such a coincidence[8] of conduct between them, that Fanny could not but admit the superior power of *one* pleasure over his own mind, though it might have its drawback. It was some time before she could get his attention to her plan, or any answer to her demand of his opinion; he was in a reverie of fond reflection, uttering only now and then a few half sentences of praise; but when he did awake and understand, he was very decided in opposing what she wished.

"Return the necklace! No, my dear Fanny, upon no account. It would be mortifying her severely. There can hardly be a more unpleasant sensation than the having any thing returned on our hands, which we have given with a reasonable hope of its contributing to the comfort of a friend. Why should she lose a pleasure which she has shewn herself so deserving of?"

"If it had been given to me in the first instance," said Fanny, "I

5. *niceness*: neatness, delicacy.

6. *neat*: elegantly formed, well-proportioned.

7. *drawback*: diminution, deduction.

8. *coincidence*: concurrence.

should not have thought of returning it; but being her brother's present, is not it fair to suppose that she would rather not part with it, when it is not wanted?"

"She must not suppose it not wanted, not acceptable at least; and its having been originally her brother's gift makes no difference, for as she was not prevented from offering, nor you from taking it on that account, it ought not to affect your keeping it. No doubt it is handsomer than mine, and fitter for a ball-room."

"No, it is not handsomer, not at all handsomer in its way, and for my purpose not half so fit. The chain will agree with William's cross beyond all comparison better than the necklace."

"For one night, Fanny, for only one night, if it *be* a sacrifice—I am sure you will, upon consideration, make that sacrifice rather than give pain to one who has been so studious of your comfort. Miss Crawford's attentions to you have been—not more than you were justly entitled to—I am the last person to think that *could be*— but they have been invariable; and to be returning them with what must have something the *air* of ingratitude, though I know it could never have the *meaning*, is not in your nature I am sure. Wear the necklace, as you are engaged to do to-morrow evening, and let the chain, which was not ordered with any reference to the ball, be kept for commoner occasions. This is my advice. I would not have the shadow of a coolness between the two whose intimacy I have been observing with the greatest pleasure, and in whose characters there is so much general resemblance in true generosity and natural delicacy as to make the few slight differences, resulting principally from situation,[9] no reasonable hindrance to a perfect friendship. I would not have the shadow of a coolness arise," he repeated, his voice sinking a little, "between the two dearest objects I have on earth."

He was gone as he spoke; and Fanny remained to tranquillize herself as she could. She was one of his two dearest—that must support her. But the other!—the first! She had never heard him speak so openly before, and though it told her no more than what she had long perceived, it was a stab;—for it told of his own convictions and views. They were decided. He would marry Miss Crawford. It was a stab, in spite of every long-standing expectation; and she was obliged to repeat again and again that she was one of his two dearest, before the words

9. The differences in situation he probably has most in mind are Mary's greater wealth and her being raised in a fashionable London environment instead of at Mansfield. Here and elsewhere, he underrates the more fundamental differences in character between Fanny and Mary, due to his love for Mary and his wish that she possess all the moral virtues he appreciates in Fanny.

A woman holding a letter.

[From *The Repository of arts, literature, fashions, manufactures, &c*, Vol. XI (1814), p. 36]

gave her any sensation. Could she believe Miss Crawford to deserve him, it would be—Oh! how different would it be—how far more tolerable! But he was deceived in her; he gave her merits which she had not; her faults were what they had ever been, but he saw them no longer. Till she had shed many tears over this deception, Fanny could not subdue her agitation; and the dejection which followed could only be relieved by the influence of fervent prayers for his happiness.

It was her intention, as she felt it to be her duty, to try to overcome all that was excessive, all that bordered on selfishness in her affection for Edmund. To call or to fancy it a loss, a disappointment, would be a presumption,[10] for which she had not words strong enough to satisfy her own humility. To think of him as Miss Crawford might be justified in thinking, would in her be insanity. To her, he could be nothing under any circumstances—nothing dearer than a friend. Why did such an idea occur to her even enough to be reprobated and forbidden? It ought not to have touched on the confines of her imagination. She would endeavour to be rational,[11] and to deserve the right of judging of Miss Crawford's character and the privilege of true solicitude for him by a sound intellect and an honest heart.[12]

She had all the heroism of principle, and was determined to do her duty; but having also many of the feelings of youth and nature, let her not be much wondered at if, after making all these good resolutions on the side of self-government,[13] she seized the scrap of paper on which Edmund had begun writing to her, as a treasure beyond all her hopes, and reading with the tenderest emotion these words, "My very dear Fanny, you must do me the favour to accept"[14]—locked it up with the chain, as the dearest part of the gift. It was the only thing approaching to a letter which she had ever received from him; she might never receive another; it was impossible that she ever should receive another so perfectly gratifying in the occasion and the style. Two lines more prized had never fallen from the pen of the most distinguished author—never more completely blessed the researches of the fondest biographer. The enthusiasm of a woman's love is even beyond the biographer's.[15] To her, the hand-writing itself, independent of any thing it may convey, is a blessedness. Never were such characters cut[16] by any other human being, as Edmund's commonest hand-writing gave![17] This specimen, written in haste as it was, had

10. Disappointment would be a presumption because it would result from affection for Edmund, and she believes she has no right to that affection, because of their different social position, or Edmund's professed love for another, or both.

11. This ideal of subduing destructive or sinful emotion through reason and moral principle was a fundamental one of the time, and is articulated at various points by Jane Austen. In *Sense and Sensibility*, where she deals most directly with the issue, the principal heroine exemplifies this ideal over the course of the novel. Fanny is another example of such a heroic heroine, though in her case, perhaps more realistically, the author shows the heroine struggling more, and sometimes failing temporarily, in her efforts to control her feelings.

12. In other words, only if she lacked any special feelings toward Edmund, beyond that of a friend and relation, would she deserve to judge Miss Crawford and offer solicitude to him, for only then could she be sure that her judgment was not biased by jealousy and that her solicitude came purely from a wish for Edmund's own welfare (rather than a hope of making him like her). Fanny indicates again her exacting moral standards.

13. Meaning the government of herself. To "govern" one's self or one's passions was a common concept and expression then.

14. He got this far in his note before being interrupted by Fanny's entrance.

15. Biography was a popular genre of the time, and it is later described as a particular love of Fanny's.

16. *cut*: engraved. The reference is to characters or letters inscribed in stone or other hard material, as on a statue or public plaque.

17. *gave*: presented, portrayed. In other words, the characters he scribbled exceeded in quality even those engraved in stone.

not a fault; and there was a felicity in the flow of the first four words, in the arrangement of "My very dear Fanny," which she could have looked at for ever.

Having regulated her thoughts and comforted her feelings by this happy mixture of reason and weakness, she was able, in due time, to go down and resume her usual employments near her aunt Bertram, and pay her the usual observances[18] without any apparent want of spirits.

Thursday, predestined to hope and enjoyment, came; and opened with more kindness to Fanny than such self-willed, unmanageable days often volunteer, for soon after breakfast a very friendly note was brought from Mr. Crawford to William stating, that as he found himself obliged to go to London on the morrow for a few days, he could not help trying to procure a companion; and therefore hoped that if William could make up his mind to leave Mansfield half a day earlier than had been proposed, he would accept a place in his carriage.[19] Mr. Crawford meant to be in town by his uncle's accustomary[20] late dinner-hour,[21] and William was invited to dine with him at the Admiral's. The proposal was a very pleasant one to William himself, who enjoyed the idea of travelling post with four horses [22] and such a

Carriages stopping at a posting inn (by a leading caricaturist of the time).

[From Joseph Grego, *Rowlandson the Caricaturist*, Vol. I (London, 1880), p. 213]

18. *observances*: courtesies, attentions.

19. As revealed below, William was already planning to go to Portsmouth via London, and going with Henry would, in addition to providing him with a companion, save the cost of travel on the leg to London.

20. *accustomary*: usual.

21. Wealthy people, especially in London, tended to keep later hours. They could afford to use more artificial light in order to stay up later at night and to prepare and eat the main meal of the day after dark, and it was also much easier to go places in the evening in a city, with its paved and fairly well-lit streets, than in the country.

22. Traveling post is the standard means of long-distance travel in Austen's novels. It involved using a private carriage, either one's own or a rented one, and horses that were hired at posting stations, generally local inns, that existed approximately every ten miles along main routes. The horses would proceed at full gallop for this distance and then, upon arrival at the next station, be changed for a set of fresh horses that would gallop quickly for another ten miles. The system was very well developed by this time; inns had ample supplies of horses and were able to change those on incoming carriages very quickly, so travelers could proceed with no need to stop except for food or rest. Public coaches, plying the same routes and changing horses in the same manner, also existed, but their lower status and lesser privacy made genteel people avoid them. William's financial position, however, has forced him to use the cheaper public coach (which he will still use on the latter stage of this journey), and thus he appreciates the opportunity to go post. He also likes the idea of going with four horses because post travel usually involved only two; public coaches used more because of their larger size. Using four with a barouche, which was smaller than a coach, and with far fewer passengers, would allow the carriage to attain significantly greater speeds.

good humoured agreeable friend; and in likening it to going up with dispatches, was saying at once every thing in favour of its happiness and dignity which his imagination could suggest;[23] and Fanny, from a different motive, was exceedingly pleased: for the original plan was that William should go up by the mail from Northampton the following night,[24] which would not have allowed him an hour's rest before he must have got[25] into a Portsmouth coach;[26] and though this offer of Mr. Crawford's would rob her of many hours of his company, she was too happy in having William spared from the fatigue of such a journey, to think of any thing else. Sir Thomas approved of it for another reason. His nephew's introduction to Admiral Crawford might be of service. The Admiral he believed had interest.[27] Upon the whole, it was a very joyous note. Fanny's spirits lived on it half the morning, deriving some accession of pleasure from its writer being himself to go away.

As for the ball so near at hand, she had too many agitations and fears to have half the enjoyment in anticipation which she ought to have had, or must have been supposed to have, by the many young ladies looking forward to the same event in situations more at ease, but under circumstances of less novelty, less interest, less peculiar gratification than would be attributed to her. Miss Price, known only by name to half the people invited, was now to make her first appearance, and must be regarded as the Queen of the evening. Who could be happier than Miss Price? But Miss Price had not been brought up to the trade of *coming out*;[28] and had she known in what light this ball was, in general, considered respecting her, it would very much have lessened her comfort by increasing the fears she already had, of doing wrong and being looked at. To dance without much observation or any extraordinary fatigue, to have strength and partners for about half the evening, to dance a little with Edmund, and not a great deal with Mr. Crawford, to see William enjoy himself, and be able to keep away from her aunt Norris, was the height of her ambition, and seemed to comprehend her greatest possibility of happiness. As these were the best of her hopes, they could not always prevail; and in the course of a long morning, spent principally with her two aunts, she was often under the influence of much less sanguine views. William,

23. Ships in port could send dispatches to the central naval administration in London. William could have seen others assigned to the task and wished that he could perform it someday, spurred by its importance, the speed of travel involved, and the possibility that, if announcing a victory, he could be rewarded.

24. This means by the mail coach, a service established in 1784 for speedy transport of mail between towns and cities; prior to this people often sent their mail via public coach because it was faster. The coaches in England went between London and major towns, including Northampton, and traveled overnight, allowing the mail collected during the day in one place to arrive at another the following morning for delivery. The coaches could also carry a few paying passengers: the cost was greater than on a public coach, but the journey was faster; for a contemporary picture, giving a sense of the mail coach's speed, see the next page. By going this way on the night after the ball William would be able to sleep late after the ball, which normally went for many hours after midnight, and have the rest of the day at Mansfield, though it would also mean then having to spend the night on the coach. Going via London, instead of directly to Portsmouth, would add a little to the length of the journey, but not much: the latter distance on current roads was 120 miles, while the former was 138 miles.

25. *must have got*: would have needed to get.

26. Mail coaches toward London were scheduled to arrive early in the morning, and he would need, if going this way, to take a morning coach to Portsmouth because the distance, seventy-two miles, would require traveling all day.

27. *interest*: influence. Such influence was often critical for allowing an officer to win promotion.

28. The daughters of wealthy families, like Maria and Julia, were groomed for coming out, since their first appearance at a fashionable social event such as a ball was critical for what was in effect their profession or trade in life, securing marriage to a wealthy and high-ranking man. They would be carefully prepared for this appearance, by mothers, other female relatives, or governesses and servants. Fanny's poorer status and more limited expectation means she has undergone little of this preparation.

determined to make this last day a day of thorough enjoyment, was out snipe shooting;[29] Edmund, she had too much reason to suppose, was at the Parsonage; and left alone to bear the worrying of Mrs. Norris, who was cross because the housekeeper would have her own way with the supper,[30] and whom *she* could not avoid though the housekeeper might, Fanny was worn down at last to think every thing an evil belonging to the ball, and when sent off with a parting worry to dress, moved as languidly towards her own room, and felt as incapable of happiness as if she had been allowed no share in it.

As she walked slowly up stairs she thought of yesterday; it had been about the same hour that she had returned from the Parsonage, and found Edmund in the east room. — "Suppose I were to find him there again to-day!" said she to herself in a fond indulgence of fancy.

"Fanny," said a voice at that moment near her. Starting and looking up, she saw across the lobby she had just reached Edmund himself, standing at the head of a different staircase. He came towards her. "You look tired and fagged, Fanny. You have been walking too far."

"No, I have not been out at all."

"Then you have had fatigues within doors, which are worse. You had better have gone out."

Fanny, not liking to complain, found it easiest to make no answer; and though he looked at her with his usual kindness, she believed he had soon ceased to think of her countenance. He did not appear in spirits; something unconnected with her was probably amiss. They proceeded up stairs together, their rooms being on the same floor above.

"I come from Dr. Grant's," said Edmund presently. "You may guess my errand there, Fanny." And he looked so conscious, that Fanny could think but of one errand, which turned her too sick for speech. — "I wished to engage Miss Crawford for the two first dances," was the explanation that followed, and brought Fanny to life again, enabling her, as she found she was expected to speak, to utter something like an inquiry as to the result.

"Yes," he answered, "she is engaged to me; but (with a smile that did not sit easy) she says it is to be the last time that she ever will dance with me. She is not serious. I think, I hope, I am sure she is not serious — but I would rather not hear it. She never has danced with

29. Snipe are birds that inhabit marshes or other wet ground. In England they are found especially in low-lying areas in the east, which Northamptonshire is on the edge of. According to a contemporary guide to shooting birds (W. B. Daniel, *Rural Sports*), they "are scarcely good until November, when they get very fat." Thus William is hunting them at an appropriate time. Snipe are also difficult birds to hit; the term "sniper" derives from the skill needed to hunt them. For pictures of snipe and snipe hunting, see pp. 489 and 491.

30. A substantial supper was a standard part of a ball, for they went very late in the evening and the participants would become hungry from hours on the dance floor. The housekeeper is in charge of that, and would resent the interference of Mrs. Norris, who is shown regularly interfering in servants' affairs. The housekeeper's high rank in the domestic hierarchy would also make it easier for her to stand up to Mrs. Norris, particularly since Lady Bertram's indolence probably means that the housekeeper is rarely challenged or questioned by her mistress and thus has full rein when it comes to many household matters.

A mail coach.

[From Andrew Tuer, *The Follies and Fashions of our Grandfathers* (London, 1887), p. 326]

a clergyman she says, and she never *will*. For my own sake, I could wish there had been no ball just at—I mean not this very week, this very day—tomorrow I leave home."

Fanny struggled for speech, and said, "I am very sorry that any thing has occurred to distress you. This ought to be a day of pleasure. My uncle meant it so."

"Oh! yes, yes, and it will be a day of pleasure. It will all end right. I am only vexed for a moment. In fact, it is not that I consider the ball as ill-timed;—what does it signify? But, Fanny,"—stopping her by taking her hand, and speaking low and seriously, "you know what all this means. You see how it is; and could tell me, perhaps better than I could tell you, how and why I am vexed. Let me talk to you a little. You are a kind, kind listener. I have been pained by her manner this morning, and cannot get the better of it. I know her disposition to be as sweet and faultless as your own, but the influence of her former companions makes her seem, gives to her conversation, to her professed opinions, sometimes a tinge of wrong. She does not *think* evil, but she speaks it—speaks it in playfulness—and though I know it to be playfulness, it grieves me to the soul."

"The effect of education," said Fanny gently.

Edmund could not but agree to it. "Yes, that uncle and aunt! They have injured the finest mind!—for sometimes, Fanny, I own[31] to you, it does appear more than manner; it appears as if the mind itself was tainted."[32]

Fanny imagined this to be an appeal to her judgment, and therefore, after a moment's consideration, said, "If you only want me as a listener, cousin, I will be as useful as I can; but I am not qualified for an adviser. Do not ask advice of *me*. I am not competent."

"You are right, Fanny, to protest against such an office, but you need not be afraid. It is a subject on which I should never ask advice. It is the sort of subject on which it had better never be asked; and few I imagine do ask it, but when they want to be influenced against their conscience. I only want to talk to you."

"One thing more. Excuse the liberty—but take care *how* you talk to me. Do not tell me any thing now, which hereafter you may be sorry for. The time may come—"

31. *own*: acknowledge.

32. "Mind" and "manner" were often paired and contrasted in this period, with the first referring to inner character and the second to outer character or behavior.

Snipe.

[From W. B. Daniel, *Rural Sports* (London, 1807), p. 173]

The colour rushed into her cheeks as she spoke.[33]

"Dearest Fanny!" cried Edmund, pressing her hand to his lips, with almost as much warmth as if it had been Miss Crawford's, "you are all considerate thought!—But it is unnecessary here. The time will never come. No such time as you allude to will ever come. I begin to think it most improbable; the chances grow less and less. And even if it should—there will be nothing to be remembered by either you or me, that we need be afraid of, for I can never be ashamed of my own scruples;[34] and if they are removed, it must be by changes that will only raise her character the more by the recollection of the faults she once had.[35] You are the only being upon earth to whom I should say what I have said; but you have always known my opinion of her; you can bear me witness, Fanny, that I have never been blinded. How many a time have we talked over her little errors! You need not fear me. I have almost given up every serious idea of her; but I must be a blockhead indeed if, whatever befell me, I could think of your kindness and sympathy without the sincerest gratitude."

He had said enough to shake the experience of eighteen. He had said enough to give Fanny some happier feelings than she had lately known, and with a brighter look, she answered, "Yes, cousin, I am convinced that *you* would be incapable of any thing else, though perhaps some might not. I cannot be afraid of hearing any thing you wish to say. Do not check yourself. Tell me whatever you like."

They were now on the second floor, and the appearance of a housemaid prevented any further conversation.[36] For Fanny's present comfort it was concluded perhaps at the happiest moment; had he been able to talk another five minutes, there is no saying that he might not have talked away all Miss Crawford's faults and his own despondence. But as it was, they parted with looks on his side of grateful affection, and with some very precious sensations on her's. She had felt nothing like it for hours. Since the first joy from Mr. Crawford's note to William had worn away, she had been in a state absolutely their reverse; there had been no comfort around, no hope within her. Now, every thing was smiling. William's good fortune returned again upon her mind, and seemed of greater value than at

33. She means that if he does marry Mary Crawford he will regret having spoken ill of her now. Fanny feels morally obligated to issue this warning, though she finds mentioning this future event so horrible and embarrassing that she blushes and breaks off before she can actually speak of it more explicitly.

34. Meaning that even if, despite his current expectations, they do marry, he and Fanny will not need to be sorry for having spoken critically of Mary, since Edmund's current scruples or hesitations regarding her are based on moral principles he can never regret holding.

35. His scruples will be removed by her ceasing to object to his clerical career. In that case, recollecting the faults that made her object earlier will only raise his opinion of her current, reformed character.

36. The housemaid is coming to help Fanny dress for the ball, since there is no lady's maid who normally attends to this task.

Snipe shooting.

[From *The Repository of arts, literature, fashions, manufactures, &c*, Vol. IV (1810), p. 23]

first. The ball too—such an evening of pleasure before her! It was now a real animation! and she began to dress for it with much of the happy flutter which belongs to a ball. All went well—she did not dislike her own looks; and when she came to the necklaces again, her good fortune seemed complete, for upon trial the one given her by Miss Crawford would by no means go through the ring of the cross. She had, to oblige Edmund, resolved to wear it—but it was too large for the purpose. His therefore must be worn; and having, with delightful feelings, joined the chain and the cross, those memorials of the two most beloved of her heart, those dearest tokens so formed for each other by every thing real and imaginary[37]—and put them round her neck, and seen and felt how full of William and Edmund they were, she was able, without an effort, to resolve on wearing Miss Crawford's necklace too. She acknowledged it to be right. Miss Crawford had a claim; and when it was no longer to encroach on, to interfere with the stronger claims, the truer kindness of another, she could do her justice even with pleasure to herself. The necklace really looked very well; and Fanny left her room at last, comfortably satisfied with herself and all about her.

Her aunt Bertram had recollected her on this occasion, with an unusual degree of wakefulness. It had really occurred to her, unprompted, that Fanny, preparing for a ball, might be glad of better help than the upper housemaid's, and when dressed herself, she actually sent her own maid to assist her; too late of course to be of any use. Mrs. Chapman had just reached the attic floor,[38] when Miss Price came out of her room completely dressed, and only civilities were necessary—but Fanny felt her aunt's attention[39] almost as much as Lady Bertram or Mrs. Chapman could do themselves.

37. "Real and imaginary" probably means the reality of the chain and cross fitting together well and Fanny's imaginary sense of their being a special or intrinsic harmony between them, due to their coming from the two people she cherishes most.

38. Mrs. Chapman is the name of Lady Bertram's lady's maid. Such a maid, as an upper servant, would usually be called by her last name—without "Mrs." Lady Bertram, immediately afterward and elsewhere, simply calls her "Chapman." The "Mrs." is a courtesy of the author; she does the same in *Pride and Prejudice* with the housekeeper of the principal family, "Mrs. Hill," even though her employers always call her "Hill." People outside the family would use "Mrs." in speaking to or of her, and the author is probably in effect ascribing the same position to herself.

39. *attention*: act of courtesy.

A woman getting dressed with the help of her lady's maid.

[From *Works of James Gillray* (London, 1849), Figure 572]

Chapter Ten

*H*er uncle and both her aunts were in the drawing-room when Fanny went down. To the former she was an interesting object, and he saw with pleasure the general elegance of her appearance and her being in remarkably good looks. The neatness and propriety of her dress was all that he would allow himself to commend in her presence, but upon her leaving the room again soon afterwards, he spoke of her beauty with very decided praise.

"Yes," said Lady Bertram, "she looks very well. I sent Chapman to her."

"Look well! Oh yes," cried Mrs. Norris, "she has good reason to look well with all her advantages: brought up in this family as she has been, with all the benefit of her cousins' manners before her. Only think, my dear Sir Thomas, what extraordinary advantages you and I have been the means of giving her. The very gown you have been taking notice of, is your own generous present to her when dear Mrs. Rushworth married. What would she have been if we had not taken her by the hand?"

Sir Thomas said no more; but when they sat down to table the eyes of the two young men assured him, that the subject might be gently touched again when the ladies withdrew, with more success. Fanny saw that she was approved; and the consciousness of looking well, made her look still better. From a variety of causes she was happy, and she was soon made still happier; for in following her aunts out of the room,[1] Edmund, who was holding open the door, said as she passed him, "You must dance with me, Fanny; you must keep two dances for me; any two that you like, except the first."[2] She had nothing more to wish for. She had hardly ever been in a state so nearly approaching high spirits in her life. Her cousins' former gaiety on the day of a ball was no longer surprizing to her; she felt it to be indeed very charming, and was actually practising her steps about the drawing-room as long as she could be safe from the notice of her

1. The ladies are leaving the dining room while the gentlemen remain.

2. He has already engaged the first pair of dances with Mary Crawford.

Dance positions.

[From Thomas Wilson, *Analysis of Country Dancing* (London, 1808), front.]

aunt Norris, who was entirely taken up at first in fresh arranging and injuring the noble fire which the butler had prepared.[3]

Half an hour followed, that would have been at least languid under any other circumstances, but Fanny's happiness still prevailed. It was but[4] to think of her conversation with Edmund; and what was the restlessness of Mrs. Norris? What were the yawns of Lady Bertram?

The gentlemen joined them; and soon after began the sweet expectation of a carriage, when a general spirit of ease and enjoyment seemed diffused, and they all stood about and talked and laughed, and every moment had its pleasure and its hope. Fanny felt that there must be a struggle in Edmund's cheerfulness, but it was delightful to see the effort so successfully made.

When the carriages were really heard, when the guests began really to assemble, her own gaiety of heart was much subdued; the sight of so many strangers threw her back into herself; and besides the gravity and formality of the first great circle, which the manners of neither Sir Thomas nor Lady Bertram were of a kind to do away, she found herself occasionally called on to endure something worse. She was introduced here and there by her uncle, and forced to be spoken to, and to curtsey, and speak again. This was a hard duty, and she was never summoned to it, without looking at William, as he walked about at his ease in the back ground of the scene, and longing to be with him.

The entrance of the Grants and Crawfords was a favourable epoch. The stiffness of the meeting soon gave way before their popular manners and more diffused intimacies:—little groups were formed and every body grew comfortable. Fanny felt the advantage; and, drawing back from the toils of civility, would have been again most happy, could she have kept her eyes from wandering between Edmund and Mary Crawford. *She* looked all loveliness—and what might not be the end of it? Her own musings were brought to an end on perceiving Mr. Crawford before her, and her thoughts were put into another channel by his engaging her almost instantly for the two first dances. Her happiness on this occasion was very much à-la-mortal,[5] finely[6] chequered.[7] To be secure of a partner at first, was a most essential good—for the moment of beginning was now growing seriously near, and she so little understood her own claims as to think, that if Mr.

3. Preparing a fire in the fireplace was normally the job of lower servants, but the butler may take a special pride in doing the task on an important occasion like a ball.

4. *but*: only necessary.

5. *à-la-mortal*: in the style of mortals, or characteristic of mortal existence.

6. *finely*: delicately, carefully.

7. *chequered*: checkered, i.e., variegated, mixed.

A woman in ball dress.

[From *The Repository of arts, literature, fashions, manufactures, &c*, Vol. IX (1813), p. 368]

Crawford had not asked her, she must have been the last to be sought after, and should have received a partner only through a series of inquiry, and bustle, and interference which would have been terrible; but at the same time there was a pointedness in his manner of asking her, which she did not like, and she saw his eye glancing for a moment at her necklace—with a smile—she thought there was a smile—which made her blush and feel wretched. And though there was no second glance to disturb her, though his object seemed then to be only quietly agreeable, she could not get the better of her embarrassment, heightened as it was by the idea of his perceiving it, and had no composure till he turned away to some one else. Then she could gradually rise up to the genuine satisfaction of having a partner, a voluntary partner secured against[8] the dancing began.

When the company were moving into the ball-room she found herself for the first time near Miss Crawford, whose eyes and smiles were immediately and more unequivocally directed as her brother's had been, and who was beginning to speak on the subject, when Fanny, anxious to get the story over, hastened to give the explanation of the second necklace—the real chain. Miss Crawford listened; and all her intended compliments and insinuations to Fanny were forgotten; she felt only one thing; and her eyes, bright as they had been before, shewing they could yet be brighter, she exclaimed with eager pleasure, "Did he? Did Edmund? That was like himself. No other man would have thought of it. I honour him beyond expression." And she looked around as if longing to tell him so. He was not near, he was attending a party of ladies out of the room; and Mrs. Grant coming up to the two girls and taking an arm of each, they followed with the rest.

Fanny's heart sunk, but there was no leisure for thinking long even of Miss Crawford's feelings. They were in the ball-room, the violins were playing,[9] and her mind was in a flutter that forbad its fixing on any thing serious. She must watch the general arrangements and see how every thing was done.

In a few minutes Sir Thomas came to her, and asked if she were engaged; and the "Yes, sir, to Mr. Crawford," was exactly what he had intended to hear. Mr. Crawford was not far off; Sir Thomas brought him to her, saying something which discovered[10] to Fanny,

8. *against*: before.

9. They have hired an orchestra of professional musicians to play at the ball, and violins are its principal instrument.

10. *discovered*: disclosed, revealed.

Dancing.

[From *The Repository of arts, literature, fashions, manufactures, &c*, Vol. V (1811), p. 232]

that *she* was to lead the way and open the ball;[11] an idea that had never occurred to her before. Whenever she had thought on the minutiæ of the evening, it had been as a matter of course that Edmund would begin with Miss Crawford, and the impression was so strong, that though *her uncle* spoke the contrary, she could not help an exclamation of surprize, a hint of her unfitness, an entreaty even to be excused. To be urging her opinion against Sir Thomas's, was a proof of the extremity of the case, but such was her horror at the first suggestion, that she could actually look him in the face and say she hoped it might be settled otherwise; in vain however;— Sir Thomas smiled, tried to encourage her, and then looked too serious and said too decidedly—"It must be so, my dear," for her to hazard another word; and she found herself the next moment conducted by Mr. Crawford to the top of the room, and standing there to be joined by the rest of the dancers, couple after couple as they were formed.[12]

She could hardly believe it. To be placed above so many elegant young women! The distinction was too great. It was treating her like her cousins! And her thoughts flew to those absent cousins with most unfeigned and truly tender regret, that they were not at home to take their own place in the room, and have their share of a pleasure which would have been so very delightful to them. So often as she had heard them wish for a ball at home as the greatest of all felicities! And to have them away when it was given—and for *her* to be opening the ball—and with Mr. Crawford too! She hoped they would not envy her that distinction *now*; but when she looked back to the state of things in the autumn, to what they had all been to each other when once dancing in that house before, the present arrangement was almost more than she could understand herself.

The ball began. It was rather honour than happiness to Fanny, for the first dance at least; her partner was in excellent spirits and tried to impart them to her, but she was a great deal too much frightened to have any enjoyment, till she could suppose herself no longer looked at. Young, pretty, and gentle, however, she had no awkwardnesses that were not as good as graces, and there were few persons present that were not disposed to praise her. She was attractive, she was modest, she was Sir Thomas's niece, and she was soon said to be admired by

11. This means that she, with her partner, will take the lead during the first dance. This was a great honor, so Fanny is shocked. It was given according to social prominence as well as sometimes to commemorate a special occasion. In *Emma* the heroine is disappointed that another lady, of lower status, receives the honor because she is a recent bride. Sir Thomas may have selected Fanny for the honor because of her relationship to him, the host and probably the highest-ranking man there, or because this is the ball, being her first attended by the whole neighborhood, in which she effectively "comes out" (the earlier dance she participated in was a more intimate and casual affair—p. 224).

12. They are dancing in the standard country dance manner, which involves two facing rows of couples. She and Henry Crawford are at the top of their respective rows.

A ballroom.

[From John Swarbrick, *Robert Adam and his Brothers* (New York, 1915), p. 251]

Mr. Crawford. It was enough to give her general favour. Sir Thomas himself was watching her progress down the dance with much complacency;[13] he was proud of his niece, and without attributing all her personal beauty, as Mrs. Norris seemed to do, to her transplantation to Mansfield, he was pleased with himself for having supplied every thing else;—education and manners she owed to him.

Miss Crawford saw much of Sir Thomas's thoughts as he stood, and having, in spite of all his wrongs towards her,[14] a general prevailing desire of recommending herself to him, took an opportunity of stepping aside to say something agreeable of Fanny. Her praise was warm, and he received it as she could wish, joining in it as far as discretion, and politeness, and slowness of speech would allow, and certainly appearing to greater advantage on the subject, than his lady did, soon afterwards, when Mary, perceiving her on a sofa very near, turned round before she began to dance, to compliment her on Miss Price's looks.

"Yes, she does look very well," was Lady Bertram's placid reply. "Chapman helped her dress. I sent Chapman to her." Not but that she was really pleased to have Fanny admired; but she was so much more struck with her own kindness in sending Chapman to her, that she could not get it out of her head.

Miss Crawford knew Mrs. Norris too well to think of gratifying *her* by commendation of Fanny; to her, it was as the occasion offered.— "Ah! ma'am, how much we want dear Mrs. Rushworth and Julia to-night!" and Mrs. Norris paid her with as many smiles and courteous words as she had time for, amid so much occupation as she found for herself, in making up card-tables, giving hints to Sir Thomas, and trying to move all the chaperons to a better part of the room.[15]

Miss Crawford blundered most towards Fanny herself, in her intentions to please.[16] She meant to be giving her little heart a happy flutter, and filling her with sensations of delightful self-consequence; and misinterpreting Fanny's blushes, still thought she must be doing so—when she went to her after the two first dances and said, with a significant look, "perhaps *you* can tell me why my brother goes to town to-morrow. He says, he has business there, but will not tell me what. The first time he ever denied me his confidence! But this is

13. She and Henry begin by dancing together and at some point, depending on the nature of the dance, they progress down the space between rows; when they finish they take their position at the bottom, and wait for succeeding couples to follow the same procedure. When all have done that, and Fanny and Henry are again first in line, the dance is over.

14. His principal recent wrong, in her eyes, was his insistence that Edmund inhabit the parsonage once he takes over the clerical position at Thornton Lacey, rather than continue to live at Mansfield Park. She probably also blames him for his encouragement of Edmund's choice of a clerical career, and for the overall atmosphere of strict propriety he has imposed since his return home. Furthermore, she may still resent his cancellation of the play, which would have given Mary opportunities for open flirtation with Edmund as well as more general enjoyment.

15. Entire families, except children, would attend balls, but only younger people would usually dance. Older women served as chaperons by standing and sitting around the edge of the room; Mrs. Norris may think, or have decided to think, that they would observe better from a different position. Older men would often leave the dancing area and play cards.

16. Mary Crawford's efforts to please and flatter a variety of people, even those she has reason to dislike, such as Sir Thomas and Mrs. Norris, indicate her character. Her one failure, in the case of Fanny, results partly from not imagining Fanny is in love with Edmund—something that no one imagines, since she has kept it so secret—and partly from not suspecting Fanny's dislike of Henry. The latter is less excusable, for Fanny has revealed, in the considerable time she has recently spent with Mary, her strict moral standards and disinterest in social status, but Mary, while grasping some elements of Fanny's character, cannot really fathom someone with principles so contrary to her own.

what we all come to. All are supplanted sooner or later.[17] Now, I must apply to you for information. Pray what is Henry going for?"

Fanny protested her ignorance as steadily as her embarrassment allowed.

"Well, then," replied Miss Crawford laughing, "I must suppose it to be purely for the pleasure of conveying your brother and talking of you by the way."

Fanny was confused, but it was the confusion of discontent; while Miss Crawford wondered she did not smile, and thought her over-anxious, or thought her odd, or thought her any thing rather than insensible of pleasure in Henry's attentions. Fanny had a good deal of enjoyment in the course of the evening—but Henry's attentions had very little to do with it. She would much rather *not* have been asked by him again so very soon, and she wished she had not been obliged to suspect that his previous inquiries of Mrs. Norris, about the supper-hour, were all for the sake of securing her at that part of the evening.[18] But it was not to be avoided; he made her feel that she was the object of all; though she could not say that it was unpleasantly done, that there was indelicacy or ostentation in his manner—and sometimes, when he talked of William, he was really not un-agreeable, and shewed even a warmth of heart which did him credit. But still his attentions made no part of her satisfaction. She was happy whenever she looked at William, and saw how perfectly he was enjoying himself, in every five minutes that she could walk about with him and hear his account of his partners; she was happy in knowing herself admired, and she was happy in having the two dances with Edmund still to look forward to, during the greatest part of the evening, her hand being so eagerly sought after,[19] that her indefinite engagement with *him* was in continual perspective. She was happy even when they did take place; but not from any flow of spirits on his side, or any such expressions of tender gallantry as had blessed the morning. His mind was fagged, and her happiness sprung from being the friend with whom it could find repose. "I am worn out with civility," said he. "I have been talking incessantly all night, and with nothing to say. But with *you*, Fanny, there may be peace. You will not want to be talked to. Let us have the luxury of silence." Fanny would hardly even speak her agreement. A weariness arising

17. Mary is teasing Fanny about having supplanted her in Henry's confidence, but is not thinking of her as a possible wife for Henry (p. 528).

18. He wishes to secure a seat next to Fanny at supper.

19. Her having opened the ball, and her being Sir Thomas's niece, have made her a desired partner among the men at the ball. The good looks she has been displaying are probably a further inducement.

A lady with a fan.

[From *The Repository of arts, literature, fashions, manufactures, &c*, Vol. X (1813), p. 369]

probably, in great measure, from the same feelings which he had acknowledged in the morning, was peculiarly to be respected, and they went down their two dances together with such sober tranquillity as might satisfy any looker-on, that Sir Thomas had been bringing up no wife for his younger son.

The evening had afforded Edmund little pleasure. Miss Crawford had been in gay spirits when they first danced together, but it was not her gaiety that could do him good; it rather sank than raised his comfort; and afterwards—for he found himself still impelled to seek her again, she had absolutely pained him by her manner of speaking of the profession to which he was now on the point of belonging. They had talked—and they had been silent—he had reasoned—she had ridiculed—and they had parted at last with mutual vexation. Fanny, not able to refrain entirely from observing them, had seen enough to be tolerably satisfied. It was barbarous to be happy when Edmund was suffering. Yet some happiness must and would arise, from the very conviction, that he did suffer.[20]

When her two dances with him were over, her inclination and strength for more were pretty well at an end; and Sir Thomas having seen her rather walk than dance down the shortening set,[21] breathless and with her hand at her side, gave his orders for her sitting down entirely. From that time, Mr. Crawford sat down likewise.

"Poor Fanny!" cried William, coming for a moment to visit her and working away his partner's fan as if for life:[22]—"how soon she is knocked up![23] Why, the sport is but just begun. I hope we shall keep it up these two hours. How can you be tired so soon?"

"So soon! my good friend," said Sir Thomas, producing his watch with all necessary caution—"it is three o'clock, and your sister is not used to these sort of hours."[24]

"Well then, Fanny, you shall not get up to-morrow before I go. Sleep as long as you can and never mind me."

"Oh! William."

"What! Did she think of being up before you set off?"

"Oh! yes, sir," cried Fanny, rising eagerly from her seat to be nearer her uncle, "I must get up and breakfast with him. It will be the last time you know, the last morning."

20. Her pleasure at Edmund's quarreling with Mary, and his consequent unhappiness, could be seen as pure jealousy, and therefore a bad reflection on her character, though it surely also results from her belief that Mary is unworthy of Edmund and thus that he will benefit if he does not marry her.

21. The set of facing rows of dancers is becoming shorter as people drop out from exhaustion. Those still participating are supposed to proceed down the rows by dancing, but Fanny can only walk droopingly.

22. Ladies regularly carried fans during this period, especially at formal occasions like a ball. Fans could enhance a woman's appearance, for they tended to be elaborately decorated, often with hand-painted scenes. They also could be used as aids to flirtation or as a means of signaling to people through the way they were positioned or moved. Finally, they could serve the purpose seen here, that of combating the heat: rooms at parties and balls could become hot because of the number of people, and those dancing would become further heated from their exertions.

23. *knocked up*: exhausted.

24. Dances could go very late. Jane Austen describes such a ball in a letter: "We began at 10, supped at 1, & were at Deane [where she was staying] before 5" (Nov. 20, 1800).

A fan of the time.

[From Alice Morse Earle, *Two Centuries of Costume in America* (New York, 1903), p. 496]

"You had better not.—He is to have breakfasted and be gone by half past nine.—Mr. Crawford, I think you call for him at half past nine?"[25]

Fanny was too urgent, however, and had too many tears in her eyes for denial; and it ended in a gracious, "Well, well," which was permission.

"Yes, half past nine," said Crawford to William, as the latter was leaving them, "and I shall be punctual, for there will be no kind sister to get up for *me*." And in a lower tone to Fanny, "I shall have only a desolate house to hurry from. Your brother will find my ideas of time and his own very different to-morrow."[26]

After a short consideration, Sir Thomas asked Crawford to join the early breakfast party in that house instead of eating alone; he should himself be of it; and the readiness with which his invitation was accepted, convinced him that the suspicions whence, he must confess to himself, this very ball had in great measure sprung, were well founded. Mr. Crawford was in love with Fanny. He had a pleasing anticipation of what would be. His niece, meanwhile, did not thank him for what he had just done. She had hoped to have William all to herself, the last morning. It would have been an unspeakable indulgence. But though her wishes were overthrown there was no spirit of murmuring[27] within her. On the contrary, she was so totally unused to have her pleasure consulted, or to have any thing take place at all in the way she could desire, that she was more disposed to wonder and rejoice in having carried her point so far, than to repine at the counteraction which followed.

Shortly afterwards, Sir Thomas was again interfering a little with her inclination, by advising her to go immediately to bed. "Advise" was his word, but it was the advice of absolute power, and she had only to rise and, with Mr. Crawford's very cordial adieus, pass quietly away; stopping at the entrance door, like the Lady of Branxholm Hall, "one moment and no more,"[28] to view the happy scene, and take a last look at the five or six determined couple, who were still hard at work—and then, creeping slowly up the principal staircase, pursued by the ceaseless country-dance,[29] feverish with hopes and fears, soup and negus,[30] sore-footed and fatigued, restless and

25. This is a little earlier than usual for breakfast among those of this social rank, but Henry has already indicated that he wishes to leave in time to reach London before his uncle's dinner hour.

26. Henry is impressed by Fanny's affection for her brother, as he was earlier when William first arrived (p. 428). In *Pride and Prejudice* the hero receives an early positive impression of the heroine, one he refers to after he proposes, because of her affection and kindness toward her sister.

27. *murmuring*: grumbling, discontent.

28. This line is from Walter Scott's popular narrative poem *The Lay of the Last Minstrel*; Fanny quoted lines from it during the visit to Sotherton (p. 166). In this passage the Lady of Branxholm Hall starts to enter a hall in order to summon a man for a mission, but as she does, she spies her son engaged in childish play. At this point,

> The Ladye forgot her purpose high,
>   One moment and no more;
> One moment gaz'd with a mother's eye,
>   As she paused at the arched door:

For a contemporary illustration of this character, see the following page.

29. Meaning the music for the country dance, the type of dance they are doing.

30. Soup was often served at balls; in *Pride and Prejudice* the host of an upcoming ball declares he will set a date for it as soon as his cook has made enough white soup, a popular soup for parties. Negus is a drink often served toward the end of evening gatherings, particularly in the winter, for it was a warm drink that was considered fortifying. It is served toward the end of a ball in Jane Austen's unfinished novel *The Watsons*. It consists of boiling water, wine, calves-foot jelly, lemon, and spices.

agitated, yet feeling, in spite of every thing, that a ball was indeed delightful.

In thus sending her away, Sir Thomas perhaps might not be thinking merely of her health. It might occur to him, that Mr. Crawford had been sitting by her long enough, or he might mean to recommend her as a wife by shewing her persuadableness.[31]

Ball dress.

[From *The Repository of arts, literature, fashions, manufactures, &c*, Vol. VII (1812), p. 120]

31. The ideal of a persuadable wife was common in this society. This would not necessarily mean a wife who was completely submissive or who never expressed an opinion, but one who tended to defer to her husband's judgment and who was never obstinate in asserting her own position. Sir Thomas assumes it is a quality that would appeal particularly to a potential husband.

"The Lady of Branxholm soliciting Deloraine to go for the Magic Book."

[From James Merigot, *The Amateur's Portfolio, or the New Drawing Magazine*, Vol. II (London, 1815–1816), No. 2, Plate 3]

Chapter Eleven

*T*he ball was over—and the breakfast was soon over too; the last kiss was given, and William was gone. Mr. Crawford had, as he foretold, been very punctual, and short and pleasant had been the meal.

After seeing William to the last moment, Fanny walked back into the breakfast-room with a very saddened heart to grieve over the melancholy change; and there her uncle kindly left her to cry in peace, conceiving perhaps that the deserted chair of each young man might exercise her tender enthusiasm, and that the remaining cold pork bones and mustard in William's plate, might but divide her feelings with the broken egg-shells in Mr. Crawford's.[1] She sat and cried *con amore*[2] as her uncle intended, but it was con amore fraternal and no other. William was gone, and she now felt as if she had wasted half his visit in idle cares and selfish solicitudes unconnected with him.

Fanny's disposition was such that she could never even think of her aunt Norris in the meagreness and cheerlessness of her own small house, without reproaching herself for some little want of attention to her when they had been last together; much less could her feelings acquit her of having done and said and thought every thing by William, that was due to him for a whole fortnight.

It was a heavy,[3] melancholy day.—Soon after the second breakfast,[4] Edmund bad them good bye for a week, and mounted his horse for Peterborough,[5] and then all were gone. Nothing remained of last night but remembrances, which she had nobody to share in. She talked to her aunt Bertram—she must talk to somebody of the ball,[6] but her aunt had seen so little of what passed, and had so little curiosity, that it was heavy work. Lady Bertram was not certain of any body's dress, or any body's place at supper, but her own. "She could not recollect what it was that she had heard about one of the Miss Maddoxes, or what it was that Lady Prescott had noticed in Fanny;[7]

1.   Henry's and William's breakfasts are more substantial than the usual morning fare of the time, which consisted of breads or cakes along with tea, coffee, or hot cocoa. They may feel that such a meal will reduce their need to stop for refreshment while traveling to London.

2.   con amore: with or from love.

3.   *heavy*: overcast with dark clouds, gloomy.

4.   The second breakfast was that taken by those besides the travelers and Fanny, who have no special reason to rise earlier than the usual breakfast time, especially after staying up so late the night before.

5.   Edmund is probably going on horseback only to Northampton, where he will then travel post using a carriage (his horse could be ridden back to Mansfield by a servant or someone working at the inn where he catches the carriage). The distance to Peterborough is more than forty miles, which on horseback would mean several extended stops to allow the horse to rest.

6.   Jane Austen identifies discussing a ball as a favorite feminine activity: in *Pride and Prejudice*, after an assembly dance, she writes, "That the Miss Lucases and the Miss Bennets should meet to talk over a ball was absolutely necessary; and the morning after the assembly brought the former to Long-bourn to hear and to communicate." Fanny will soon be able to satisfy this impulse with Mary Crawford and Mrs. Grant (p. 514).

7.   This is the only mention of another titled person in the area. "Lady" could mean she is the wife of a lord and thus outranks the Bertrams, though if that were the case, she and her family would likely have been mentioned and discussed before, due to the prestige of having people of that rank in the vicinity. She also could be a baronet's wife, like Lady Bertram, or the wife of a knight, a rank lower than the Bertrams'. Any of those possibilities would have justified having her open the ball instead of Fanny, but she is probably older and thus simply a spectator at the dance who was observing Fanny and relating her observations to Lady Bertram.

she was not sure whether Colonel Harrison had been talking of Mr. Crawford or of William,[8] when he said he was the finest young man in the room; somebody had whispered something to her, she had forgot to ask Sir Thomas what it could be." And these were her longest speeches and clearest communications; the rest was only a languid "Yes—yes—very well—did you? did he?—I did not see *that*—I should not know one from the other." This was very bad. It was only better than Mrs. Norris's sharp answers would have been; but she being gone home with all the supernumerary jellies to nurse a sick maid,[9] there was peace and good humour in their little party, though it could not boast much beside.

The evening was heavy like the day—"I cannot think what is the matter with me!" said Lady Bertram, when the tea-things were removed.[10] "I feel quite stupid. It must be sitting up so late last night. Fanny, you must do something to keep me awake. I cannot work. Fetch the cards,—I feel so very stupid."[11]

The cards were brought, and Fanny played at cribbage with her aunt till bed-time;[12] and as Sir Thomas was reading to himself, no sounds were heard in the room for the next two hours beyond the reckonings of the game—"And *that* makes thirty-one;—four in hand and eight in crib.—You are to deal, ma'am; shall I deal for you?"[13] Fanny thought and thought again of the difference which twenty-four hours had made in that room, and all that part of the house. Last night it had been hope and smiles, bustle and motion, noise and brilliancy[14] in the drawing-room, and out of the drawing-room, and every where. Now it was languor, and all but solitude.

A good night's rest improved her spirits. She could think of William the next day more cheerfully, and as the morning afforded her an opportunity of talking over Thursday night with Mrs. Grant and Miss Crawford, in a very handsome style, with all the heightenings of imagination and all the laughs of playfulness which are so essential to the shade of a departed ball, she could afterwards bring her mind without much effort into its everyday state, and easily conform to the tranquillity of the present quiet week.

They were indeed a smaller party than she had ever known there for a whole day together, and *he* was gone on whom the comfort and cheerfulness of every family-meeting and every meal chiefly

8.   Military officers were a common element in genteel society. They could be on temporary leave, or commanding a local regiment (though none is ever mentioned here); they also could be retired, perhaps most likely in this case. In all Austen's novels except this one and *Pride and Prejudice*, a retired army or naval officer is an important character.

9.   The jellies were part of the supper at the ball. Mrs. Norris naturally wishes to procure for herself any that are left over, and is happy to claim the needs of her maid as a justification, whether or not the maid is really ill.

10.   Tea things are items used for evening tea. They included a container of boiling water, tea (and possibly coffee), sugar, milk or cream, breads and cakes, and various utensils and dishes, including cups, saucers, a creamer, and plates. For contemporary examples of tea things, see the following page and p. 521.

11.   *stupid*: stupefied.

12.   Cribbage is a card game that had been played in England for several centuries before this. It is usually a game for two, but can be played by more.

13.   Fanny is commenting on the game. Cribbage consists of two parts: In the first the participants alternate playing single cards from their hands, with points scored if their card can form combinations with cards just played or can collectively add up to fifteen or thirty-one. In the second part the players add up the points from the combinations in their own hands and in the crib, formed by the cards earlier discarded by each player (the points in the crib go to the dealer, with players alternating in that role).

14.   *brilliancy*: brightness, luster. The principal reference here is to the bright lighting during the dance, for dances and fancy evening parties were the only times that large amounts of artificial light were used. An additional connotation of more general splendor may also be intended.

depended. But this must be learned to be endured. He would soon be always gone;[15] and she was thankful that she could now sit in the same room with her uncle, hear his voice, receive his questions, and even answer them without such wretched feelings as she had formerly known.

"We miss our two young men," was Sir Thomas's observation on both the first and second day, as they formed their very reduced circle after dinner; and in consideration of Fanny's swimming[16] eyes, nothing more was said on the first day than to drink their good health; but on the second it led to something farther. William was kindly commended and his promotion hoped for. "And there is no reason to suppose," added Sir Thomas, "but that his visits to us may now be tolerably frequent. As to Edmund, we must learn to do without him. This will be the last winter of his belonging to us, as he has done." "Yes," said Lady Bertram, "but I wish he was not going away. They are all going away I think. I wish they would stay at home."

This wish was levelled[17] principally at Julia, who had just applied for permission to go to town with Maria;[18] and as Sir Thomas thought it best for each daughter that the permission should be granted, Lady Bertram, though in her own good nature she would not have prevented it, was lamenting the change it made in the prospect of Julia's return, which would otherwise have taken place about this time. A great deal of good sense followed on Sir Thomas's side, tending to reconcile his wife to the arrangement. Every thing that a considerate parent *ought* to feel was advanced for her use;[19] and every thing that an affectionate mother *must* feel in promoting her children's enjoyment, was attributed to her nature. Lady Bertram agreed to it all with a calm "Yes"—and at the end of a quarter of an hour's silent consideration, spontaneously observed, "Sir Thomas, I have been thinking—and I am very glad we took Fanny as we did, for now the others are away, we feel the good of it."

Sir Thomas immediately improved this compliment by adding, "Very true. We shew Fanny what a good girl we think her by praising her to her face—she is now a very valuable companion. If we have been kind to *her*, she is now quite as necessary to *us*."

"Yes," said Lady Bertram presently—"and it is a comfort to think that we shall always have *her*."

15. They mean Edmund, who will shortly return from this current excursion but will not long afterward depart Mansfield for full-time residence elsewhere.

16. *swimming*: watery, full of tears.

17. *levelled*: directed.

18. Maria and Mr. Rushworth have finished their time in Brighton (they have been there more than a month) and, as originally planned (pp. 374–376), are now heading to their house in London. Julia wishes to continue living with Maria, most likely because of the far greater opportunities for social life and entertainment in the capital, while Maria doubtless welcomes the continued presence of a close companion besides her husband.

19. *use*: benefit.

A *cup and saucer.*

[From MacIver Percival, *Old English Furniture and its Surroundings* (New York, 1920), Plate XIV, no. 4]

Sir Thomas paused, half smiled, glanced at his niece, and then gravely replied, "She will never leave us, I hope, till invited to some other home that may reasonably promise her greater happiness than she knows here."

"And *that* is not very likely to be, Sir Thomas. Who should invite her? Maria might be very glad to see her at Sotherton now and then, but she would not think of asking her to live there—and I am sure she is better off here—and besides I cannot do without her."

The week which passed so quietly and peaceably at the great house in Mansfield,[20] had a very different character at the Parsonage. To the young lady at least in each family, it brought very different feelings. What was tranquillity and comfort to Fanny was tediousness and vexation to Mary. Something arose from difference of disposition and habit—one so easily satisfied, the other so unused to endure; but still more might be imputed to difference of circumstances. In some points of interest they were exactly opposed to each other. To Fanny's mind, Edmund's absence was really in its cause and its tendency a relief. To Mary it was every way painful. She felt the want of his society every day, almost every hour; and was too much in want of it to derive any thing but irritation from considering the object for which he went. He could not have devised any thing more likely to raise his consequence than this week's absence, occurring as it did at the very time of her brother's going away, of William Price's going too, and completing the sort of general break-up of a party which had been so animated. She felt it keenly. They were now a miserable trio,[21] confined within doors by a series of rain and snow, with nothing to do and no variety to hope for. Angry as she was with Edmund for adhering to his own notions and acting on them in defiance of her (and she had been so angry that they had hardly parted friends at the ball), she could not help thinking of him continually when absent, dwelling on his merit and affection, and longing again for the almost daily meetings they lately had. His absence was unnecessarily long. He should not have planned such an absence—he should not have left home for a week, when her own departure from Mansfield was so near. Then she began to blame herself. She wished she had not spoken so warmly in their last conversation. She was afraid she had used some strong—some contemptuous expressions in speaking of

20. This week includes Christmas (the ball was on the 22nd), but the holiday is not mentioned here—though Mary Crawford alludes to "Christmas gaieties" on p. 522. In fact, Christmas was not a major holiday at this time. It had been more extensively celebrated in England in earlier times, but the custom had declined in the seventeenth century, partly under the influence of Puritanism. It was now mainly an occasion for parties and feasting, which is what Mary has in mind. Most of the things we now associate with Christmas, including a tree, presents, and cards, emerged later in the nineteenth century, when the holiday again became a major occasion.

21. The trio are Mary and the two Grants.

A woman drinking tea.

[From *The Repository of arts, literature, fashions, manufactures, &c*, Vol. XIV (1815), p. 240]

the clergy, and *that* should not have been. It was ill-bred[22] — it was wrong. She wished such words unsaid with all her heart.

Her vexation did not end with the week. All this was bad, but she had still more to feel when Friday came round again and brought no Edmund[23] — when Saturday came and still no Edmund — and when, through the slight communication with the other family which Sunday produced,[24] she learnt that he had actually written home to defer his return, having promised to remain some days longer with his friend!

If she had felt impatience and regret before — if she had been sorry for what she said, and feared its too strong effect on him, she now felt and feared it all tenfold more. She had, moreover, to contend with one disagreeable emotion entirely new to her — jealousy. His friend Mr. Owen had sisters — He might find them attractive. But at any rate his staying away at a time, when, according to all preceding plans, she was to remove to London, meant something that she could not bear. Had Henry returned, as he talked of doing, at the end of three or four days, she should now have been leaving Mansfield. It became absolutely necessary for her to get to Fanny and try to learn something more. She could not live any longer in such solitary wretchedness; and she made her way to the Park, through difficulties of walking which she had deemed unconquerable a week before, for the chance of hearing a little in addition, for the sake of at least hearing his name.

The first half hour was lost, for Fanny and Lady Bertram were together, and unless she had Fanny to herself she could hope for nothing. But at last Lady Bertram left the room — and then almost immediately Miss Crawford thus began, with a voice as well regulated as she could[25] — "And how do *you* like your cousin Edmund's staying away so long? — Being the only young person at home, I consider *you* as the greatest sufferer. — You must miss him. Does his staying longer surprise you?"

"I do not know," said Fanny hesitatingly. — "Yes — I had not particularly expected it."

"Perhaps he will always stay longer than he talks of. It is the general way all young men do."[26]

22. *ill-bred*: rude. As often, Mary's principal regrets concern lack of manners. Her focus on bad manners may also be a way of venting her more fundamental dissatisfaction, regarding Edmund's absence, without acknowledging to herself how deeply she still cares for him.

23. He left the day after the ball, which was on a Thursday, and planned to be gone only a week. Mary has clearly been counting the days.

24. Both families would attend church on Sunday, and while there greet each other and probably engage in brief conversation.

25. She wishes to regulate or control her voice in order to avoid signaling to Fanny how anxious and distressed she is about Edmund.

26. Young men had a freedom to go where they liked compared with young women, especially when it came to visiting distant places, and many wealthy young men, who had no pressing work obligations, took full advantage of this freedom to exercise flexibility in the length of their visits. Mary is probably judging particularly by her brother, who has already shown a willingness to change his plans whenever it suits him.

A hot water jug, a creamer, and a teapot.

[From MacIver Percival, *Old English Furniture and its Surroundings* (New York, 1920), pp. 176 and 177]

"He did not, the only time he went to see Mr. Owen before."

"He finds the house more agreeable *now*.—He is a very—a very pleasing young man himself, and I cannot help being rather concerned at not seeing him again before I go to London, as will now undoubtedly be the case.—I am looking for Henry every day, and as soon as he comes there will be nothing to detain me at Mansfield. I should like to have seen him once more, I confess. But you must give my compliments to him. Yes—I think it must be compliments. Is not there a something wanted, Miss Price, in our language—a something between compliments and—and love—to suit the sort of friendly acquaintance we have had together?—So many months acquaintance!—But compliments may be sufficient here.—Was his letter a long one?—Does he give you much account of what he is doing?—Is it Christmas gaieties that he is staying for?"

"I only heard a part of the letter; it was to my uncle—but I believe it was very short; indeed I am sure it was but a few lines. All that I heard was that his friend had pressed him to stay longer, and that he had agreed to do so. A *few* days longer, or *some* days longer, I am not quite sure which."

"Oh! if he wrote to his father—But I thought it might have been to Lady Bertram or you. But if he wrote to his father, no wonder he was concise. Who could write chat[27] to Sir Thomas? If he had written to you, there would have been more particulars. You would have heard of balls and parties.—He would have sent you a description of every thing and every body. How many Miss Owens are there?"

"Three grown up."

"Are they musical?"

"I do not at all know. I never heard."

"That is the first question, you know," said Miss Crawford, trying to appear gay and unconcerned, "which every woman who plays herself is sure to ask about another. But it is very foolish to ask questions about any young ladies—about any three sisters just grown up; for one knows, without being told, exactly what they are—all very accomplished and pleasing,[28] and *one* very pretty. There is a beauty in every family.—It is a regular thing. Two play on the pianoforte, and one on the harp[29]—and all sing—or would sing if they were

27. *chat*: small talk.

28. Because being accomplished, and being pleasing, were two of the most valued qualities in young ladies, praising them for these qualities was a standard courtesy. In *Pride and Prejudice* a man declares that all young ladies are "so very accomplished," since "I am sure I never heard a young lady spoken of for the first time, without being informed that she was very accomplished." Mary's words suggest a similar experience, along with a more critical perspective on whether the praise is universally valid.

29. The pianoforte was the most popular instrument for young ladies, and the harp was next. A family of three daughters might have one play the harp in order to create more variety of sound when they all played; furnishing music for the home was one of the principal justifications for teaching young ladies music. Mary does not mention drawing, the other principal form of female accomplishment: she may be less inclined to think of it, since she plays music rather than draws, or she may focus on music because another important reason for teaching young women to play was that it helped them attract a potential mate, and Mary is concerned about that possibility with regard to Edmund.

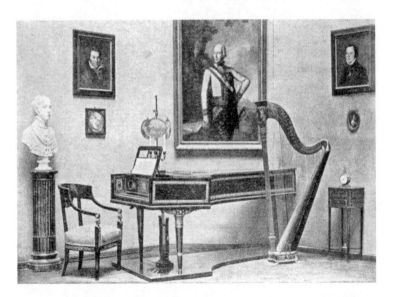

An interior of the time with a pianoforte and a harp.

[From Max von Boehn, *Modes & Manners of the Nineteenth Century*, Vol. I (London, 1909), p. 67]

taught—or sing all the better for not being taught—or something like it."[30]

"I know nothing of the Miss Owens," said Fanny calmly.

"You know nothing and you care less, as people say. Never did tone express indifference plainer. Indeed how can one care for those one has never seen?—Well, when your cousin comes back, he will find Mansfield very quiet;—all the noisy ones gone, your brother and mine and myself. I do not like the idea of leaving Mrs. Grant now the time draws near. She does not like my going."

Fanny felt obliged to speak. "You cannot doubt your being missed by many," said she. "You will be very much missed."

Miss Crawford turned her eye on her, as if wanting to hear or see more, and then laughingly said, "Oh! yes, missed as every noisy evil is missed when it is taken away; that is, there is a great difference felt. But I am not fishing; don't compliment me. If I *am* missed, it will appear. I may be discovered by those who want to see me. I shall not be in any doubtful,[31] or distant, or unapproachable region."[32]

Now Fanny could not bring herself to speak, and Miss Crawford was disappointed; for she had hoped to hear some pleasant assurance of her power, from one who she thought must know; and her spirits were clouded again.

"The Miss Owens," said she soon afterwards—"Suppose you were to have one of the Miss Owens settled at Thornton Lacey; how should you like it? Stranger things have happened. I dare say they are trying for it. And they are quite in the right, for it would be a very pretty[33] establishment for them. I do not at all wonder or blame them.—It is every body's duty to do as well for themselves as they can.[34] Sir Thomas Bertram's son is somebody; and now, he is in their own line. Their father is a clergyman and their brother is a clergyman, and they are all clergymen together. He is their lawful property, he fairly belongs to them.[35] You don't speak, Fanny—Miss Price—you don't speak.—But honestly now, do not you rather expect it than otherwise?"

"No," said Fanny stoutly, "I do not expect it at all."

"Not at all!"—cried Miss Crawford with alacrity. "I wonder at that. But I dare say you know exactly—I always imagine you are—perhaps you do not think him likely to marry at all—or not at present."

30. Mary's wording satirizes the general polite urge to find some way to praise young ladies, regardless of the circumstances. Many ladies were given singing lessons, for the same reasons as they were taught to play instruments.

31. *doubtful*: uncertain.

32. She will be in London.

33. *pretty*: nice, proper.

34. Mary has earlier articulated her sense of a "duty" to pursue their interest, especially by seeking an advantageous marriage. She also assumes that a marriage to Edmund would be materially advantageous for the Miss Owens, something she does not believe for herself. She has a good foundation for this assumption, since children of clergy were unlikely to receive ample inheritances, as Mary herself has, because income from a clerical position cannot be passed on to children.

35. Daughters of clergymen might be more likely to marry clergy themselves, but it was by no means a universal practice: the heroine of *Northanger Abbey* does that, though her husband's being a clergyman does not factor overtly into her decision. Jane Austen's mother was the daughter of a clergyman and married one; however, Jane and her sister both became engaged to men in other lines.

"No, I do not," said Fanny softly—hoping she did not err either in the belief or the acknowledgment of it.[36]

Her companion looked at her keenly; and gathering greater spirit from the blush soon produced from such a look, only said, "He is best off as he is," and turned[37] the subject.

36. She hopes she does not err in her belief that Edmund will not marry, since she does not wish him to wed Mary, the only present candidate. She also hopes she does not err by acknowledging her doubt, because she might be presuming more knowledge of Edmund than she has a right to claim or because it might give Mary a false impression of the situation, which Fanny in truth cannot really know.

37. *turned*: changed.

A view of a road through a village.

[From Humphry Repton, *Fragments on the Theory and Practice of Landscape Gardening* (London, 1816), p. 233]

Chapter Twelve

*M*iss Crawford's uneasiness was much lightened by this conversation, and she walked home again in spirits which might have defied almost another week of the same small party in the same bad weather, had they been put to the proof; but as that very evening brought her brother down from London again in quite, or more than quite, his usual cheerfulness, she had nothing further to try her own. His still refusing to tell her what he had gone for, was but the promotion of gaiety; a day before it might have irritated, but now it was a pleasant joke—suspected only of concealing something planned as a pleasant surprize to herself. And the next day *did* bring a surprize to her. Henry had said he should just go and ask the Bertrams how they did, and be back in ten minutes—but he was gone above an hour; and when his sister, who had been waiting for him to walk with her in the garden, met him at last most impatiently in the sweep,[1] and cried out, "My dear Henry, where can you possibly have been all this time?" he had only to say that he had been sitting with Lady Bertram and Fanny.

"Sitting with them an hour and half!" exclaimed Mary.

But this was only the beginning of her surprize.

"Yes, Mary," said he, drawing her arm within his, and walking along the sweep as if not knowing where he was—"I could not get away sooner—Fanny looked so lovely!—I am quite determined, Mary. My mind is entirely made up. Will it astonish you? No—You must be aware that I am quite determined to marry Fanny Price."

The surprize was now complete; for in spite of whatever his consciousness might suggest, a suspicion of his having any such views[2] had never entered his sister's imagination; and she looked so truly the astonishment she felt, that he was obliged to repeat what he had said, and more fully and more solemnly. The conviction of his determination once admitted, it was not unwelcome. There was even pleasure

1. A sweep was a curved drive for carriages that leads to a house.

2. *views*: intentions.

A grand house (Normanton Park, Rutlandshire) with a circular sweep in front.

[From John Preston Neale, *Views of the Seats of Noblemen and Gentlemen*, Vol. V (London, 1822)]

with the surprize. Mary was in a state of mind to rejoice in a connection with the Bertram family, and to be not displeased with her brother's marrying a little beneath him.

"Yes, Mary," was Henry's concluding assurance, "I am fairly caught. You know with what idle designs I began—but this is the end of them. I have (I flatter myself) made no inconsiderable progress in her affections; but my own are entirely fixed."

"Lucky, lucky girl!" cried Mary as soon as she could speak—"what a match for her![3] My dearest Henry, this must be my *first* feeling; but my *second*, which you shall have as sincerely, is that I approve your choice from my soul, and foresee your happiness as heartily as I wish and desire it. You will have a sweet little wife; all gratitude and devotion. Exactly what you deserve. What an amazing match for her! Mrs. Norris often talks of her luck; what will she say now? The delight of all the family indeed! And she has some *true* friends in it.[4] How *they* will rejoice! But tell me all about it. Talk to me for ever. When did you begin to think seriously about her?"

Nothing could be more impossible than to answer such a question, though nothing be more agreeable than to have it asked. "How the pleasing plague had stolen on him"[5] he could not say, and before he had expressed the same sentiment with a little variation of words three times over, his sister eagerly interrupted him with, "Ah! my dear Henry, and this is what took you to London! This was your business! You chose to consult the Admiral, before you made up your mind."

But this he stoutly denied. He knew his uncle too well to consult him on any matrimonial scheme. The Admiral hated marriage, and thought it never pardonable in a young man of independent fortune.[6]

"When Fanny is known to him," continued Henry, "he will doat on her. She is exactly the woman to do away every prejudice of such a man as the Admiral, for she is exactly such a woman as he thinks does not exist in the world. She is the very impossibility he would describe[7]—if indeed he has now delicacy of language enough to embody[8] his own ideas.[9] But till it is absolutely settled—settled beyond all interference, he shall know nothing of the matter. No,

3. She is mainly lucky in Mary's eyes because she has attracted a husband as rich and high-ranking as Henry despite her poverty and undistinguished family origin. She probably also considers Fanny lucky due to Henry's personal qualifications.

4. She knows Edmund is a true friend to Fanny, and she may believe Sir Thomas is also.

5. The quotation is from a song by the eighteenth-century poet William Whitehead entitled "The Je ne scai Quoi, A Song." It occurs at the end of the first stanza:

> Yes, I'm in love, I feel it now
>   And Caelia has undone me;
> And yet I'll swear I can't tell how
>   The pleasing plague stole on me.

6. In introducing Admiral Crawford, the narrator stated that he and his wife agreed in nothing other than affection for Henry and Mary, and even there they each had a different exclusive favorite. Hence he was likely unhappy in his own marriage and now dislikes the institution. He could still excuse a man's marrying if he needed the money it would bring, but that would not be the case with a wealthy young man.

7. His experience with his wife presumably soured him, or reinforced misogynistic tendencies he already had. Also, living now with a mistress, and perhaps having had others, he could have been further confirmed in his prejudices by dealing with women who were far from morally pure and who may have been thoroughly mercenary in their motives (his reported character does not suggest he is someone who would inspire real affection in a mistress).

8. *embody*: express, give form to.

9. Naval men were known for coarse and profane language, and Admiral Crawford's private life and amorous experiences would have naturally coarsened his ideas and language further.

Mary, you are quite mistaken. You have not discovered my business yet!"[10]

"Well, well, I am satisfied. I know now to whom it must relate, and am in no hurry for the rest. Fanny Price—Wonderful—quite wonderful!—That Mansfield should have done so much for—that *you* should have found your fate in Mansfield! But you are quite right, you could not have chosen better. There is not a better girl in the world, and you do not want for fortune; and as to her connections, they are more than good. The Bertrams are undoubtedly some of the first people in this country. She is niece to Sir Thomas Bertram; that will be enough for the world. But go on, go on. Tell me more. What are your plans? Does she know her own happiness?"

"No."

"What are you waiting for?"

"For—for very little more than opportunity. Mary, she is not like her cousins; but I think I shall not ask in vain."

"Oh! no, you cannot. Were you even less pleasing—supposing her not to love you already (of which however I can have little doubt), you would be safe. The gentleness and gratitude of her disposition would secure her all your own immediately. From my soul I do not think she would marry you *without* love; that is, if there is a girl in the world capable of being uninfluenced by ambition, I can suppose it her; but ask her to love you, and she will never have the heart to refuse."

As soon as her eagerness could rest in silence, he was as happy to tell as she could be to listen, and a conversation followed almost as deeply interesting to her as to himself, though he had in fact nothing to relate but his own sensations, nothing to dwell on but Fanny's charms.—Fanny's beauty of face and figure, Fanny's graces of manner and goodness of heart were the exhaustless theme. The gentleness, modesty, and sweetness of her character were warmly expatiated on, that sweetness which makes so essential a part of every woman's worth in the judgment of man, that though he sometimes loves where it is not, he can never believe it absent. Her temper he had good reason to depend on and to praise. He had often seen it tried. Was there one of the family, excepting Edmund, who had not

10. His business, which concerned William rather than Fanny, will be revealed in the next chapter.

Walking dress of the time.

[From Andrew Tuer, *The Follies and Fashions of our Grandfathers* (London, 1887), p. 326]

in some way or other continually exercised her patience and for-bearance? Her affections were evidently strong. To see her with her brother! What could more delightfully prove that the warmth of her heart was equal to its gentleness?—What could be more encourag-ing to a man who had her love in view? Then, her understanding[11] was beyond every suspicion, quick and clear; and her manners were the mirror of her own modest and elegant mind.[12] Nor was this all. Henry Crawford had too much sense not to feel the worth of good principles in a wife, though he was too little accustomed to serious reflection to know them by their proper name;[13] but when he talked of her having such a steadiness and regularity of conduct, such a high notion of honour, and such an observance of decorum as might war-rant any man in the fullest dependence on her faith and integrity,[14] he expressed what was inspired by the knowledge of her being well principled and religious.[15]

"I could so wholly and absolutely confide in her," said he; "and *that* is what I want."

Well might his sister, believing as she really did that his opinion of Fanny Price was scarcely beyond her merits, rejoice in her prospects.

"The more I think of it," she cried, "the more am I convinced that you are doing quite right, and though I should never have selected Fanny Price as the girl most likely to attach you, I am now persuaded she is the very one to make you happy. Your wicked project upon her peace turns out a clever thought indeed. You will both find your good in it."

"It was bad, very bad in me against such a creature! but I did not know her then.[16] And she shall have no reason to lament the hour that first put it into my head. I will make her very happy, Mary, hap-pier than she has ever yet been herself, or ever seen any body else. I will not take her from Northamptonshire. I shall let Everingham,[17] and rent a place in this neighbourhood—perhaps Stanwix Lodge.[18] I shall let a seven years' lease of Everingham.[19] I am sure of an excel-lent tenant at half a word. I could name three people now, who would give me my own terms and thank me."

"Ha!" cried Mary, "settle in Northamptonshire! That is pleasant! Then we shall be all together."

11. *understanding*: mind, intelligence.

12. Meaning her outer behavior perfectly expresses her fine inner character.

13. Extended philosophical discussion and analysis of moral principles were common in writings of the time; a work Fanny was earlier described as reading, Johnson's *The Idler*, was a prime example. Jane Austen's own work, both in her explicit authorial reflections and in the moral themes embodied in her stories, shows the influence of such writings. Such philosophical discussions were seen as valuable aids to help people understand true moral principles and thereby appreciate others' goodness as well as improve their own moral character.

14. He would be thinking particularly of his ability to rely on her sexual integrity—not simply that she would not cheat on him but also that she would never behave in a way that could give rise to suspicion or scandalous rumors. Coming from a background of fashionable London society, where sexual infidelity, and gossip about it, were more common than among the country gentry, he would naturally be inclined to worry about that.

15. The idea of the close connection of moral principles and religion, and the need for religion as a basis of morality, was a basic belief of the time, seen at various points in Jane Austen's writings.

16. Henry, even as he expresses regret for his bad behavior, reveals a laxness in his moral attitude by arguing that making a woman fall in love with you when you have no intention of returning the affection is not wicked if the victim is an ordinary woman without the special virtue of someone like Fanny.

17. Owners of grand estates sometimes let them (rented them to a tenant). The principal family in *Persuasion* does that, and in *Pride and Prejudice* the hero arrives in the neighborhood of the heroine because his best friend has rented a grand house there.

18. "Lodge" was often used as part of the name of a grand house. Jane Austen may mean the name to relate to Stanwyck, a village in northeast Northamptonshire that is around fifteen miles from the likely location of Mansfield. But it is not clear whether she, who had never traveled to this part of England, had ever heard of the village, which had fewer than five hundred people at the time, and Henry would probably wish to be closer than fifteen miles to Mansfield.

19. Not all leases were for this duration. Henry's declaration expresses his enthusiasm about the impending marriage and his adoption of a completely new course in life.

When she had spoken it, she recollected herself, and wished it unsaid; but there was no need of confusion,[20] for her brother saw her only as the supposed inmate of Mansfield Parsonage, and replied but to invite her in the kindest manner to his own house, and to claim the best right in her.

"You must give us more than half your time," said he; "I cannot admit Mrs. Grant to have an equal claim with Fanny and myself, for we shall both have a right in you. Fanny will be so truly your sister!"

Mary had only to be grateful and give general assurances; but she was now very fully purposed[21] to be the guest of neither brother nor sister many months longer.

"You will divide your year between London and Northampton-shire?"

"Yes."

"That's right; and in London, of course, a house of your own;[22] no longer with the Admiral. My dearest Henry, the advantage to you of getting away from the Admiral before your manners are hurt by the contagion of his, before you have contracted any of his foolish opin-ions, or learnt to sit over your dinner, as if it were the best blessing of life![23]—*You* are not sensible of the gain, for your regard for him has blinded you; but, in my estimation, your marrying early may be the saving of you. To have seen you grow like the Admiral in word or deed, look or gesture, would have broken my heart."

"Well, well, we do not think quite alike here. The Admiral has his faults, but he is a very good man, and has been more than a father to me. Few fathers would have let me have my own way half so much.[24] You must not prejudice Fanny against him. I must have them love one another."

Mary refrained from saying what she felt, that there could not be two persons in existence, whose characters and manners were less accordant; time would discover it to him; but she could not help *this* reflection on the Admiral. "Henry, I think so highly of Fanny Price, that if I could suppose the next Mrs. Crawford would have half the reason which my poor ill used aunt had to abhor the very name, I would prevent the marriage, if possible;[25] but I know you, I know that a wife you *loved* would be the happiest of women, and that even

20. *confusion*: embarrassment, perturbation.

21. *purposed*: determined, resolved.

22. Henry already spends part of his time in London, and undoubtedly appreciates its many opportunities for diversions; he also probably has companions he would wish to continue seeing. Having a house in London, and spending at least part of the year there, was standard for people wealthy enough to afford it (and only a small minority of the population could do that while also living part of the year elsewhere). An important attraction that could never be found in a rural area was the presence of so many people of their own high social level. Neither Henry nor Mary has apparently thought about whether Fanny would like or fit in with the fashionable London social whirl.

23. His foolish opinions are, at least in part, his disdain for marriage and women. His love of a good dinner above all other pleasures could be a natural attitude for a wealthy man, especially one without active employment, to develop as he aged, one reason for Mary to fear Henry's following in Admiral Crawford's path.

24. This is Henry's principal criterion for a good father. It is notable that he defends his uncle after having earlier admitted his irrational prejudice regarding women and his thorough indelicacy of language.

25. This gives a further sense of the misery of their aunt and uncle's marriage, this time from the perspective of the wife. A wife could suffer far more from a miserable marriage due to the extremely dependent legal position of married women at the time.

when you ceased to love, she would yet find in you the liberality and good-breeding of a gentleman."[26]

The impossibility of not doing every thing in the world to make Fanny Price happy, or of ceasing to love Fanny Price, was of course the ground-work of his eloquent answer.[27]

"Had you seen her this morning, Mary," he continued, "attending with such ineffable sweetness and patience, to all the demands of her aunt's stupidity, working with her, and for her, her colour beautifully heightened as she leant over the work,[28] then returning to her seat to finish a note which she was previously engaged in writing for that stupid woman's service, and all this with such unpretending gentleness, so much as if it were a matter of course that she was not to have a moment at her own command, her hair arranged as neatly as it always is, and one little curl falling forward as she wrote,[29] which she now and then shook back, and in the midst of all this, still speaking at intervals to *me*, or listening, and as if she liked to listen to what I said. Had you seen her so, Mary, you would not have implied the possibility of her power over my heart ever ceasing."

"My dearest Henry," cried Mary, stopping short,[30] and smiling in his face, "how glad I am to see you so much in love! It quite delights me. But what will Mrs. Rushworth and Julia say?"

"I care neither what they say, nor what they feel. They will now see what sort of woman it is that can attach me, that can attach a man of sense. I wish the discovery may do them any good. And they will now see their cousin treated as she ought to be, and I wish they may be heartily ashamed of their own abominable neglect and unkindness. They will be angry," he added, after a moment's silence, and in a cooler tone, "Mrs. Rushworth will be very angry. It will be a bitter pill to her; that is, like other bitter pills, it will have two moments ill-flavour, and then be swallowed and forgotten;[31] for I am not such a coxcomb[32] as to suppose her feelings more lasting than other women's, though *I* was the object of them.[33] Yes, Mary, my Fanny will feel a difference indeed, a daily, hourly difference, in the behaviour of every being who approaches her; and it will be the completion of my happiness to know that I am the doer of it, that I am the person to give the consequence so justly her due. Now she is dependent, helpless, friendless, neglected, forgotten."

26. Mary envisions the probability of Henry's love fading, though she also believes that his natural generosity and courtesy ensure that he would continue to treat his wife decently. Mary's statement thus combines a worldly skepticism about the possibility and need for continued love in a marriage with a genuine concern for Fanny's welfare.

27. This again shows Henry's almost extravagant enthusiasm. He also showed great enthusiasm about the play before moving on to new interests, though in that case he was stopped by external events.

28. *work*: needlework.

29. Her hair is pinned up, for grown women almost never let their hair down except in bed, but one strand is falling loose. Curls were popular in women's hairstyles then; for an example, see the following page. In fact, the principal surviving portrait of Jane Austen shows her in curls.

30. They have been walking during this conversation.

31. This turns out to be a complete error regarding Maria.

32. *coxcomb*: fop; conceited, foolish man.

33. His belief in the ephemeral nature of most women's romantic feelings is one reason for his willingness to engage in flirtations, though he probably also developed this belief at least in part as a way to justify his behavior. It is also the reason for his mistaken estimate of Maria's feelings.

"Nay, Henry, not by all, not forgotten by all, not friendless or forgotten. Her cousin Edmund never forgets her."

"Edmund—True, I believe he is (generally speaking) kind to her; and so is Sir Thomas in his way, but it is the way of a rich, superior, longworded, arbitrary uncle. What can Sir Thomas and Edmund together do, what *do* they do for her happiness, comfort, honour, and dignity in the world to[34] what I *shall* do?"

An admiral.

[From William Alexander, *Picturesque Representations of the Dress and Manners of the English* (London, 1813), Plate 34]

34. *to*: compared to.

A contemporary portrait of a young woman with curled hair.

[From *Lawrence* (Master in Art) (Boston, 1907), p. 11]

Chapter Thirteen

*H*enry Crawford was at Mansfield Park again the next morning, and at an earlier hour than common visiting warrants. The two ladies were together in the breakfast-room, and fortunately for him, Lady Bertram was on the very point of quitting it as he entered.[1] She was almost at the door, and not chusing by any means to take so much trouble in vain,[2] she still went on, after a civil reception, a short sentence about being waited for, and a "Let Sir Thomas know," to the servant.

Henry, overjoyed to have her go, bowed and watched her off,[3] and without losing another moment, turned instantly to Fanny, and taking out some letters said, with a most animated look, "I must acknowledge myself infinitely obliged to any creature who gives me such an opportunity of seeing you alone: I have been wishing it more than you can have any idea. Knowing as I do what your feelings as a sister are, I could hardly have borne that any one in the house should share with you in the first knowledge of the news I now bring. He is made. Your brother is a Lieutenant. I have the infinite satisfaction of congratulating you on your brother's promotion. Here are the letters which announce it, this moment come to hand.[4] You will, perhaps, like to see them."

Fanny could not speak, but he did not want her to speak. To see the expression of her eyes, the change of her complexion, the progress of her feelings, their doubt, confusion, and felicity, was enough. She took the letters as he gave them. The first was from the Admiral to inform his nephew, in a few words, of his having succeeded in the object he had undertaken, the promotion of young Price, and inclosing two more, one from the Secretary of the First Lord to a friend,[5] whom the Admiral had set to work in the business, the other from that friend to himself,[6] by which it appeared that his Lordship had the very great happiness of attending to the recommendation of

1. They probably eat breakfast at ten, which was a standard time for wealthy people. When William and Henry left together, their breakfast, which finished at nine-thirty, was followed by a second breakfast for the others (p. 512). Hence it is probably between ten-thirty and eleven now, which would be considered too early for normal visiting. The common routine was for people to stay indoors early in the day, and only venture out later to go on visits or engage in other activities.

2. The standard response would be for her to sit down again and greet the visitor, but doing that and then afterward getting up again and proceeding to the door is too much effort for her.

3. Bowing is a more formal gesture than normal for this situation; Henry probably bows because it allows him to make a polite gesture of greeting without delaying Lady Bertram's departure, as a verbal greeting would.

4. *to hand*: into my possession.

5. This is the secretary of the First Lord of the Admiralty, whom William earlier identified as the person he would most like to be connected to for the sake of obtaining a promotion. It is possible that the secretary handled the matter himself, even though the letter below speaks of the effort of "his Lordship."

6. This shows how Admiral Crawford procured William's promotion. He contacted a friend who possessed influence, because of personal or family connections or because of his own prominence and importance, and this friend asked a favor of either the First Lord or the secretary. Jane Austen was very familiar with these matters from the advancement of her naval brothers through Austen family connections. Her oldest brother James's father-in-law, General Mathew, had a niece married to Admiral Gambier, who was a member of the Admiralty Board, the governing body of the navy headed by the First Lord. This connection allowed Jane Austen's father to apply to Admiral Gambier, which led to a written reply quoted by Austen in a letter to her sister. Gambier wrote, regarding Charles Austen, "I have mentioned to the Board of Admiralty his wish to be in a Frigate, and when a proper opportunity offers & it is judged that he has taken his Turn in a small Ship, I hope he will be removed," and, regarding Francis Austen, "I am glad I can give you the assurance that his promotion is likely to take place very soon, as Lord Spencer [the First Lord] has been so good as to say he would include him in an arrangement in that quarter" (Dec. 24, 1798). A few days later she writes that General Mathew has sent a "very friendly" letter "transcribing one from Admiral Gambier to the General" that reveals that Frank has been promoted and Charles transferred to a frigate (Dec. 28, 1798).

Sir Charles,[7] that Sir Charles was much delighted in having such an opportunity of proving his regard for Admiral Crawford,[8] and that the circumstance of Mr. William Price's commission as second Lieutenant of H. M. sloop Thrush,[9] being made out,[10] was spreading general joy through a wide circle of great people.[11]

While her hand was trembling under these letters, her eye running from one to the other, and her heart swelling with emotion,[12] Crawford thus continued, with unfeigned eagerness, to express his interest in the event.

"I will not talk of my own happiness," said he, "great as it is, for I think only of yours. Compared with you, who has a right to be happy? I have almost grudged myself my own prior knowledge of what you ought to have known before all the world. I have not lost a moment, however. The post was late this morning, but there has not been since, a moment's delay. How impatient, how anxious, how wild I have been on the subject, I will not attempt to describe; how severely mortified, how cruelly disappointed, in not having it finished while I was in London! I was kept there from day to day in the hope of it, for nothing less dear to me than such an object would have detained me half the time from Mansfield. But though my uncle entered into my wishes with all the warmth I could desire, and exerted himself immediately, there were difficulties from the absence of one friend, and the engagements of another,[13] which at last I could no longer bear to stay the end of, and knowing in what good hands I left the cause, I came away on Monday,[14] trusting that many posts would not pass before I should be followed by such very letters as these. My uncle, who is the very best man in the world, has exerted himself, as I knew he would after seeing your brother. He was delighted with him. I would not allow myself yesterday to say *how* delighted, or to repeat half that the Admiral said in his praise.[15] I deferred it all, till his praise should be proved the praise of a friend, as this day *does* prove it. *Now* I may say that even *I* could not require William Price to excite a greater interest, or be followed by warmer wishes and higher commendation, than were most voluntarily bestowed by my uncle, after the evening they passed together."

"Has this been all *your* doing then?" cried Fanny. "Good Heaven! how very, very kind! Have you really—was it by *your* desire—I beg

7. The navy had many "Sirs," especially at the highest level. Some had received a knighthood or baronetcy for meritorious service; others were sons of baronets.

8. The wording of the two preceding clauses, with their "very great happiness of attending" and "opportunity of proving his regard for," repeats or paraphrases the kind of phrases used in such formal letters.

9. A sloop was the smallest of the three main types of navy vessels; the other two were a frigate (see the picture on p. 557) and, largest of all, a ship of the line, or man-of-war. A sloop's main functions were to patrol the coasts, to protect commercial vessels, and to attack enemy commercial ships. Because of its small size the *Thrush* has only two lieutenants, the commissioned officers who assist the captain; William is now the lower ranking of the two. "H. M.," in the ship's official name (which would be used in a formal announcement), stands for "His Majesty's."

10. *made out*: accomplished, achieved.

11. This is more official phraseology, for the promotion of an obscure person like William Price would hardly be "spreading general joy," especially among "a wide circle of great [i.e., important or high-ranking] people."

12. Jane Austen consistently expresses great joy in letters relating the success and promotion of her naval brothers. In the first letter mentioned above, quoting the admiral's promise of assistance, she immediately adds, "There!—I may now finish my letter, & go & hang myself, for I can neither write nor do anything which will not appear insipid to you after this." In the second, a short one sent solely to announce the news (contrary to her usual practice of writing only long letters), she starts by writing, "Frank is made," and, after giving the details, adds that as soon as her sister has "cried a little for Joy," she can learn the good news about Charles.

13. The friend who was not absent, but was engaged and thus could not act immediately, was presumably the Sir Charles mentioned earlier. Admiral Crawford's having two friends potentially able to offer assistance indicates his prominence and good connections.

14. This is ten days after he left Mansfield with William (on a Friday); see chronology, pp. 857–858.

15. He would have seen William only on the evening they arrived in London, for William had to leave for Portsmouth the next day.

your pardon, but I am bewildered. Did Admiral Crawford apply?—
how was it?—I am stupified."

Henry was most happy to make it more intelligible, by beginning
at an earlier stage, and explaining very particularly what he had done.
His last journey to London had been undertaken with no other view
than that of introducing her brother in Hill-street,[16] and prevailing on
the Admiral to exert whatever interest he might have for getting him
on. This had been his business. He had communicated it to no creature; he had not breathed a syllable of it even to Mary; while uncertain of the issue, he could not have borne any participation of his
feelings, but this had been his business; and he spoke with such a glow
of what his solicitude had been, and used such strong expressions, was
so abounding in the *deepest interest,* in *twofold motives,* in *views and
wishes more than could be told,* that Fanny could not have remained
insensible of his drift, had she been able to attend; but her heart was so
full and her senses still so astonished, that she could listen but imperfectly even to what he told her of William, and saying only when he
paused, "How kind! how very kind! Oh! Mr. Crawford, we are infinitely obliged to you. Dearest, dearest William!" she jumped up and
moved in haste towards the door, crying out, "I will go to my uncle.
My uncle ought to know it as soon as possible." But this could not be
suffered. The opportunity was too fair, and his feelings too impatient.
He was after her immediately. "She must not go, she must allow him
five minutes longer," and he took her hand and led her back to her
seat,[17] and was in the middle of his further explanation, before she
had suspected for what she was detained. When she did understand
it, however, and found herself expected to believe that *she* had created
sensations which his heart had never known before, and that every
thing he had done for William, was to be placed to the account of[18]
his excessive and unequalled attachment to her, she was exceedingly
distressed, and for some moments unable to speak. She considered
it all as nonsense, as mere trifling and gallantry,[19] which meant only
to deceive for the hour; she could not but feel that it was treating her
improperly and unworthily, and in such a way as she had not deserved;
but it was like himself, and entirely of a piece with what she had seen
before; and she would not allow herself to shew half the displeasure
she felt, because he had been conferring an obligation, which no want

16. Hill Street has already been mentioned as the fashionable London address of Admiral Crawford.

17. A man would normally not engage in such physical contact with a woman unless she was related or married to him. In this case he is inspired by his hope that they will shortly become engaged, which will permit further liberties. Moreover, taking her hand to guide her is not as intimate as holding hands.

18. *placed to the account of*: credited to.

19. *gallantry*: amorous intrigue, flirtation.

Grosvenor Square, which is very close to Hill Street.

[From *The Repository of arts, literature, fashions, manufactures, &c*, Vol. X (1813), p. 275]

of delicacy on his part could make a trifle to her. While her heart was still bounding with joy and gratitude on William's behalf, she could not be severely resentful of any thing that injured only herself; and after having twice drawn back her hand, and twice attempted in vain to turn away from him, she got up and said only, with much agitation, "Don't, Mr. Crawford, pray don't. I beg you would not. This is a sort of talking which is very unpleasant to me. I must go away. I cannot bear it." But he was still talking on, describing his affection, soliciting a return, and, finally, in words so plain as to bear but one meaning even to *her*, offering himself, hand, fortune, every thing to her acceptance. It was so; he had said it. Her astonishment and confusion increased; and though still not knowing how to suppose him serious, she could hardly stand.[20] He pressed for an answer.

"No, no, no," she cried, hiding her face. "This is all nonsense. Do not distress me. I can hear no more of this. Your kindness to William makes me more obliged to you than words can express; but I do not want, I cannot bear, I must not listen to such—No, no, don't think of me. But you are *not* thinking of me. I know it is all nothing."

She had burst away from him, and at that moment Sir Thomas was heard speaking to a servant in his way towards the room they were in. It was no time for further assurances or entreaty, though to part with her at a moment when her modesty alone seemed to his sanguine and pre-assured mind to stand in the way of the happiness he sought, was a cruel necessity.[21]—She rushed out at an opposite door from the one her uncle was approaching, and was walking up and down the east room in the utmost confusion of contrary feelings, before Sir Thomas's politeness or apologies were over, or he had reached the beginning of the joyful intelligence, which his visitor came to communicate.

She was feeling, thinking, trembling, about every thing;—agitated, happy, miserable, infinitely obliged, absolutely angry. It was all beyond belief! He was inexcusable, incomprehensible!—But such were his habits, that he could do nothing without a mixture of evil. He had previously made her the happiest of human beings, and now he had insulted[22]—she knew not what to say—how to class or how to regard it. She would not have him be serious, and yet what could excuse the use of such words and offers, if they meant but to trifle?

20. *stand*: remain.

21. He is completely confident she will accept him, a confidence that has some basis in his wealth and social position, which would make most women in Fanny's social and economic situation happy to say yes. Henry has also consistently experienced great success with women of higher rank than Fanny. In *Pride and Prejudice* the hero makes his first proposal to the heroine with misplaced confidence, based on his knowledge of his high status and wealth.

22. Her first impulse is to regard his proposal as an insult, since she cannot believe he was serious.

Naval officers dining on board ship.

[From Alfred Burton, *The adventures of Johnny Newcome in the Navy* (London, 1818; 1904 reprint), p. 34]

But William was a Lieutenant. —*That* was a fact beyond a doubt and without an alloy. She would think of it for ever and forget all the rest. Mr. Crawford would certainly never address her so again: he must have seen how unwelcome it was to her; and in that case, how gratefully she could esteem him for his friendship to William!

She would not stir farther from the east room than the head of the great staircase,[23] till she had satisfied herself of Mr. Crawford's having left the house; but when convinced of his being gone, she was eager to go down and be with her uncle, and have all the happiness of his joy as well as her own, and all the benefit of his information or his conjectures as to what would now be William's destination. Sir Thomas was as joyful as she could desire, and very kind and communicative; and she had so comfortable a talk with him about William as to make her feel as if nothing had occurred to vex her, till she found towards the close that Mr. Crawford was engaged to return and dine there that very day. This was a most unwelcome hearing, for though *he* might think nothing of what had passed, it would be quite distressing to her to see him again so soon.

She tried to get the better of it, tried very hard as the dinner hour approached, to feel and appear as usual; but it was quite impossible for her not to look most shy and uncomfortable when their visitor entered the room. She could not have supposed it in the power of any concurrence of circumstances to give her so many painful sensations on the first day of hearing of William's promotion.

Mr. Crawford was not only in the room; he was soon close to her. He had a note to deliver from his sister.[24] Fanny could not look at him, but there was no consciousness of past folly in his voice. She opened her note immediately, glad to have any thing to do, and happy, as she read it, to feel that the fidgettings of her aunt Norris, who was also to dine there, screened her a little from view.

"MY DEAR FANNY, *for so I may now always call you, to the infinite relief of a tongue that has been stumbling at Miss Price for at least the last six weeks*[25] —*I cannot let my brother go without sending you a few lines of general congratulation, and giving my most joyful consent and approval. —Go on, my dear Fanny, and without fear; there can be no difficulties worth naming. I chuse to suppose that the assurance of my consent will be something; so, you may smile upon him with your*

23. The "great staircase" is a large central staircase, a common feature of homes like this. The space at its head, or top, is on the same level as the east room, the room Fanny uses during the day.

24. Mary Crawford, unlike Henry, has not been invited for dinner. Sir Thomas presumably has invited Henry only so that, with fewer others present, he will be able to focus more on Fanny.

25. Women could call each other by their first names if they were related or close friends. Mary has already been leaning toward use of the first name, though not sure if her intimacy with Fanny is great enough to justify it. But once Fanny has become engaged to her brother, as Mary believes is in the process of happening, she no longer needs to hesitate. She is actually being presumptuous in already saying "Fanny," for as the later part of her note indicates, Henry has not reported any definite affirmative from Fanny.

A grand staircase of the eighteenth century.

[From J. Alfred Gotch, *The English Home from Charles I to George IV* (New York, 1918), p. 350]

sweetest smiles this afternoon,[26] *and send him back to me even happier than he goes.*

Yours affectionately,
M. C."

These were not expressions[27] to do Fanny any good; for though she read in too much haste and confusion to form the clearest judgment of Miss Crawford's meaning, it was evident that she meant to compliment her on her brother's attachment and even to *appear* to believe it serious. She did not know what to do, or what to think. There was wretchedness in the idea of its being serious; there was perplexity and agitation every way. She was distressed whenever Mr. Crawford spoke to her, and he spoke to her much too often; and she was afraid there was a something in his voice and manner in addressing her, very different from what they were when he talked to the others. Her comfort in that day's dinner was quite destroyed; she could hardly eat any thing; and when Sir Thomas good humouredly observed, that joy had taken away her appetite, she was ready to sink with shame, from the dread of Mr. Crawford's interpretation; for though nothing could have tempted her to turn her eyes to the right hand where he sat, she felt that *his* were immediately directed towards her.

She was more silent than ever. She would hardly join even when William was the subject, for his commission came all from the right hand too, and there was pain in the connection.

She thought Lady Bertram sat longer than ever, and began to be in despair of ever getting away;[28] but at last they were in the drawing-room and she was able to think as she would, while her aunts finished the subject of William's appointment in their own style.

Mrs. Norris seemed as much delighted with the saving it would be to Sir Thomas, as with any part of it. "*Now* William would be able to keep himself, which would make a vast difference to his uncle, for it was unknown how much he had cost his uncle; and indeed it would make some difference in *her* presents too. She was very glad that she had given William what she did at parting, very glad indeed that it had been in her power, without material inconvenience just at that time, to give him something rather considerable; that is, for *her*, with *her* limited means, for now it would all be useful in helping

26. Since the afternoon is the period just after dinner (see p. 225, note 21), Henry and Fanny will be together then.

27. *expressions*: declarations, statements.

28. Lady Bertram, as the mistress of the house, rises to signal to the other ladies that it is time to leave the gentlemen in the dining room.

A woman writing.

[From *The Repository of arts, literature, fashions, manufactures, &c*, Vol. X (1813), p. 116]

to fit up[29] his cabin. She knew he must be at some expense, that he would have many things to buy,[30] though to be sure his father and mother would be able to put him in the way of[31] getting every thing very cheap—but she was very glad that she had contributed her mite towards it."[32]

"I am glad you gave him something considerable," said Lady Bertram, with most unsuspicious calmness—"for *I* gave him only 10*l*."[33]

"Indeed!" cried Mrs. Norris, reddening. "Upon my word, he must have gone off with his pockets well lined! and at no expense for his journey to London either!"

"Sir Thomas told me 10*l*. would be enough."

Mrs. Norris, being not at all inclined to question its sufficiency, began to take the matter in another point.[34]

"It is amazing," said she, "how much young people cost their friends,[35] what with bringing them up and putting them out in the world! They little think how much it comes to, or what their parents, or their uncles and aunts pay for them in the course of the year. Now, here are my sister Price's children;—take them all together, I dare say nobody would believe what a sum they cost Sir Thomas every year, to say nothing of what *I* do for them."

"Very true, sister, as you say. But, poor things! they cannot help it; and you know it makes very little difference to Sir Thomas. Fanny, William must not forget my shawl, if he goes to the East Indies;[36] and I shall give him a commission for any thing else that is worth having. I wish he may go to the East Indies, that I may have my shawl. I think I will have two shawls, Fanny."

Fanny, meanwhile, speaking only when she could not help it, was very earnestly trying to understand what Mr. and Miss Crawford were at. There was every thing in the world *against* their being serious, but his words and manner. Every thing natural, probable, reasonable was against it; all their habits and ways of thinking, and all her own demerits.—How could *she* have excited serious attachment in a man, who had seen so many, and been admired by so many, and flirted with so many, infinitely her superiors[37]—who seemed so little open to serious impressions, even where pains had been taken to please him—who thought so slightly, so carelessly, so unfeelingly on all such points—who was every thing to every body, and seemed to

29. *fit up*: furnish.

30. Both midshipmen and officers were required to provide their own furnishings. But midshipmen shared a berth and slept in a hammock, while each officer had his own cabin in which he would install a regular bed and other furniture. This could represent a considerable expenditure for a new officer.

31. *in the way of*: in a likely position for.

32. "Her mite" alludes to a famous gospel story, told in Mark and Luke, about a poor widow who contributes "two mites" (in the King James translation, then in universal use in England) to the temple in Jerusalem, and is praised by Jesus for giving more than others, because "all these have of their abundance cast in unto the offerings of God: but she of her penury hath cast in all the living that she had." Mrs. Norris's citation of it represents a supreme irony, for, in complete contrast to the woman in the story, she is a widow with ample wealth who contributes almost nothing to others.

33. Ten pounds is a generous sum for William. As a lieutenant he will earn just under eight and a half pounds per month, and he earned less as a midshipman.

34. Mrs. Norris has clearly given less, even though she called her gift considerable while Lady Bertram speaks of "only" ten pounds. In his *A Memoir of Jane Austen*, her nephew James Edward Austen-Leigh states that his aunt, when asked for more information about her characters than is furnished in the novels, stated that Mrs. Norris gave William one pound.

35. *friends*: relations.

36. The East Indies meant India and Southeast Asia, and cashmere shawls from India were highly valued. British naval ships did sometimes go there, due to British holdings in India, and if his did, William would probably have an opportunity to go ashore and purchase items from local merchants.

37. She means her social superiors, and she also, given her own modesty, probably thinks of them as superior in their personal qualities and accomplishments as well.

find no one essential to him?—And further, how could it be supposed that his sister, with all her high[38] and worldly[39] notions of matrimony, would be forwarding any thing of a serious nature in such a quarter?[40] Nothing could be more unnatural in either. Fanny was ashamed of her own doubts. Every thing might be possible rather than serious attachment or serious approbation of it toward her. She had quite convinced herself of this before Sir Thomas and Mr. Crawford joined them. The difficulty was in maintaining the conviction quite so absolutely after Mr. Crawford was in the room; for once or twice a look seemed forced on her which she did not know how to class among the common meaning; in any other man at least, she would have said that it meant something very earnest, very pointed. But she still tried to believe it no more than what he might often have expressed towards her cousins and fifty other women.

She thought he was wishing to speak to her unheard by the rest. She fancied he was trying for it the whole evening at intervals, whenever Sir Thomas was out of the room, or at all engaged with Mrs. Norris, and she carefully refused him every opportunity.[41]

At last—it seemed an at last to Fanny's nervousness, though not remarkably late,—he began to talk of going away; but the comfort of the sound was impaired by his turning to her the next moment, and saying, "Have you nothing to send to Mary? No answer to her note? She will be disappointed if she receives nothing from you. Pray write to her, if it be only a line."

"Oh! yes, certainly," cried Fanny, rising in haste, the haste of embarrassment and of wanting to get away—"I will write directly."

She went accordingly to the table, where she was in the habit of writing for her aunt, and prepared her materials without knowing what in the world to say![42] She had read Miss Crawford's note only once; and how to reply to any thing so imperfectly understood was most distressing. Quite unpractised in such sort of note-writing, had there been time for scruples and fears as to style, she would have felt them in abundance; but something must be instantly written, and with only one decided feeling, that of wishing not to appear to think any thing really intended, she wrote thus, in great trembling both of spirits and hand:

38. *high*: focused on exalted rank or social station.

39. *worldly*: devoted to success and money.

40. Fanny has heard Mary speak of marriage in those terms, though here she undervalues Mary's genuine appreciation of Fanny's virtues.

41. Social rules prohibit Henry from simply calling her aside to speak with him alone. Courting couples often found it difficult to have purely private conversations, so a person who wished to avoid such a conversation could usually do so without much trouble.

42. These would be her materials for writing, including paper, a pen, an inkwell, and a sander (see p. 475, note 2).

Two frigates off Dover cliffs.

[From James Merigot, *The Amateur's Portfolio, or the New Drawing Magazine*, Vol. II (London, 1815–1816), No. 5, Plate 5]

"I AM very much obliged to you, my dear Miss Crawford,[43] for your kind congratulations, as far as they relate to my dearest William.[44] The rest of your note I know means nothing; but I am so unequal to any thing of the sort, that I hope you will excuse my begging you to take no further notice.[45] I have seen too much of Mr. Crawford not to understand his manners; if he understood me as well, he would, I dare say, behave differently. I do not know what I write, but it would be a great favour of you never to mention the subject again. With thanks for the honour of your note,

I remain, dear Miss Crawford,

&c. &c."[46]

The conclusion was scarcely intelligible from increasing fright, for she found that Mr. Crawford, under pretence of receiving the note, was coming towards her.

"You cannot think I mean to hurry you," said he, in an under voice, perceiving the amazing trepidation with which she made up the note; "you cannot think I have any such object. Do not hurry yourself, I entreat."

"Oh! I thank you, I have quite done, just done—it will be ready in a moment—I am very much obliged to you—if you will be so good as to give *that* to Miss Crawford."

The note was held out and must be taken; and as she instantly and with averted eyes walked towards the fireplace, where sat the others, he had nothing to do but to go in good earnest.

Fanny thought she had never known a day of greater agitation, both of pain and pleasure; but happily the pleasure was not of a sort to die with the day—for every day would restore the knowledge of William's advancement, whereas the pain she hoped would return no more. She had no doubt that her note must appear excessively ill-written, that the language would disgrace a child,[47] for her distress had allowed no arrangement;[48] but at least it would assure them both of her being neither imposed on, nor gratified by Mr. Crawford's attentions.

END OF VOL. II.

43. Fanny continues to call her "Miss Crawford."

44. Actually, in her note Mary offered only "general congratulation," and her subsequent words, "giving my joyful consent and approval," signal that her congratulations related to Fanny only, not William.

45. The wording, though vague and unclear due to Fanny's confused state of mind, seems to suggest she considers the rest of Mary's note to be a joke or deception.

46. "&c. &c." simply abbreviates the rest of the standard ending of such a note, which would include Fanny's name.

47. Fanny again shows her high standards, for while the content of her note was confused, the language had no serious fault.

48. *arrangement*: orderly arrangement or organization (of her thoughts).

VOLUME THREE

Chapter One

*F*anny had by no means forgotten Mr. Crawford, when she awoke the next morning; but she remembered the purport of her note, and was not less sanguine, as to its effect, than she had been the night before. If Mr. Crawford would but go away!—That was what she most earnestly desired;—go and take his sister with him, as he was to do, and as he returned to Mansfield on purpose to do. And why it was not done already, she could not devise,[1] for Miss Crawford certainly wanted no delay.—Fanny had hoped, in the course of his yesterday's visit, to hear the day named; but he had only spoken of their journey as what would take place ere long.

Having so satisfactorily settled the conviction her note would convey, she could not but be astonished to see Mr. Crawford, as she accidentally did, coming up to the house again, and at an hour as early as the day before.—His coming might have nothing to do with her, but she must avoid seeing him if possible; and being then in her way up stairs, she resolved there to remain, during the whole of his visit, unless actually sent for; and as Mrs. Norris was still in the house, there seemed little danger of her being wanted.

She sat some time in a good deal of agitation, listening, trembling, and fearing to be sent for every moment; but as no footsteps approached the east room, she grew gradually composed, could sit down, and be able to employ herself, and able to hope that Mr. Crawford had come, and would go without her being obliged to know any thing of the matter.

Nearly half an hour had passed, and she was growing very comfortable, when suddenly the sound of a step in regular approach was heard—a heavy step, an unusual step in that part of the house; it was her uncle's; she knew it as well as his voice; she had trembled at it as often, and began to tremble again, at the idea of his coming up

1. *devise*: conceive, imagine.

A woman with a shawl.

[From *The Repository of arts, literature, fashions, manufactures, &c*, Vol. XIV (1815), p. 51]

to speak to her, whatever might be the subject.—It was indeed Sir Thomas, who opened the door, and asked if she were there, and if he might come in. The terror of his former occasional visits to that room seemed all renewed, and she felt as if he were going to examine her again in French and English.[2]

She was all attention, however, in placing a chair for him, and trying to appear honoured; and in her agitation, had quite over-looked the deficiencies of her apartment,[3] till he, stopping short as he entered, said, with much surprise, "Why have you no fire to-day?"

There was snow on the ground, and she was sitting in a shawl. She hesitated.

"I am not cold, Sir—I never sit here long at this time of year."

"But,—you have a fire in general?"

"No, Sir."

"How comes this about; here must be some mistake. I understood that you had the use of this room by way of[4] making you perfectly comfortable.—In your bedchamber I know you *cannot* have a fire.[5] Here is some great misapprehension which must be rectified. It is highly unfit for you to sit—be it only half an hour a day, without a fire. You are not strong. You are chilly. Your aunt cannot be aware of this."

Fanny would rather have been silent, but being obliged to speak, she could not forbear, in justice to the aunt she loved best, from saying something in which the words "my aunt Norris" were distin-guishable.

"I understand," cried her uncle recollecting himself, and not wanting to hear more—"I understand. Your aunt Norris has always been an advocate, and very judiciously, for young people's being brought up without unnecessary indulgences; but there should be moderation in every thing.—She is also very hardy herself, which of course will influence her in her opinion of the wants of others. And on another account too, I can perfectly comprehend.—I know what her sentiments have always been. The principle was good in itself, but it may have been, and I believe *has been* carried too far in your case.[6]—I am aware that there has been sometimes, in some points, a misplaced distinction; but I think too well of you, Fanny, to suppose you will ever harbour resentment on that account.—You have an

2. French was earlier mentioned as part of her schooling. Fanny had a governess, but Sir Thomas obviously played some role in her education as well. He may have decided, knowing that his wife would do nothing in this regard, that Fanny, and presumably his own children, would benefit from a second person guiding their studies.

3. *apartment*: room.

4. *by way of*: for the purpose of.

5. Her bedchamber, or bedroom, is an attic room, and so does not have a fireplace in it.

6. The principle was one enunciated by Sir Thomas when they first decided to adopt Fanny, namely that since she is not a Miss Bertram and will be inferior to Sir Thomas's children in fortune and expectations, some degree of inequality and distinction must be maintained between her and the Bertram children. Mrs. Norris has followed this principle vigorously, while also forgetting, as Sir Thomas admits now, the other principle he also pronounced initially of not imposing too unequal a status on Fanny. In admitting this, and clearly intending to remedy the fault, Sir Thomas demonstrates his basic decency and fair-mindedness, but in doing so only now, after eight years, he shows what has long marred his good instincts—namely, his distance from the daily affairs of the family and his failure to observe much that is happening there.

understanding, which will prevent you from receiving things only in part, and judging partially by the event.—You will take in the whole of the past, you will consider times, persons, and probabilities, and you will feel that *they* were not least your friends who were educating and preparing you for that mediocrity of condition[7] which *seemed* to be your lot.[8]—Though their caution may prove eventually unnecessary, it was kindly meant; and of this you may be assured, that every advantage of affluence will be doubled by the little privations and restrictions that may have been imposed. I am sure you will not disappoint my opinion of you, by failing at any time to treat your aunt Norris with the respect and attention that are due to her.—But enough of this. Sit down, my dear. I must speak to you for a few minutes, but I will not detain you long."

Fanny obeyed, with eyes cast down and colour rising.—After a moment's pause, Sir Thomas, trying to suppress a smile, went on.

"You are not aware, perhaps, that I have had a visitor this morning.—I had not been long in my own room, after breakfast, when Mr. Crawford was shewn in.—His errand you may probably conjecture."

Fanny's colour grew deeper and deeper; and her uncle perceiving that she was embarrassed to a degree that made either speaking or looking up quite impossible, turned away his own eyes, and without any farther pause, proceeded in his account of Mr. Crawford's visit.

Mr. Crawford's business had been to declare himself the lover of Fanny, make decided proposals for her, and intreat the sanction of the uncle, who seemed to stand in the place of her parents;[9] and he had done it all so well, so openly, so liberally, so properly, that Sir Thomas, feeling, moreover, his own replies, and his own remarks to have been very much to the purpose—was exceedingly happy to give the particulars of their conversation—and, little aware of what was passing in his niece's mind, conceived that by such details he must be gratifying her far more than himself. He talked therefore for several minutes without Fanny's daring to interrupt him.—She had hardly even attained the wish to do it. Her mind was in too much confusion. She had changed her position, and with her eyes fixed intently on one of the windows, was listening to her uncle, in the utmost perturbation and dismay.—For a moment he ceased, but she had barely become conscious of it, when, rising from his chair, he

7. *condition*: social rank or position.

8. Meaning that since it appeared Fanny would also remain in a mediocre or modest position in life, those who prepared her for that lot, by not treating her like Maria and Julia, were actually behaving properly toward her, i.e., as her friends.

9. Social norms dictated that a marriage not occur without a father's approval (or mother's, if there were no father). Usually the couple would agree to an engagement and then ask parental permission. Henry started on that path, but, having failed to receive a positive answer from Fanny, has turned to asking Sir Thomas, probably with the expectation that her uncle's sanction will help overcome her hesitation and diffidence (which is all that Henry believes is impeding her assent).

said, "And now, Fanny, having performed one part of my commission, and shewn you every thing placed on a basis the most assured and satisfactory, I may execute the remainder by prevailing on you to accompany me down stairs, where—though I cannot but presume on having been no unacceptable companion myself, I must submit to your finding one still better worth listening to.—Mr. Crawford, as you have perhaps foreseen, is yet in the house. He is in my room, and hoping to see you there."

There was a look, a start, an exclamation, on hearing this, which astonished Sir Thomas; but what was his increase of astonishment on hearing her exclaim—"Oh! no, Sir, I cannot, indeed I cannot go down to him. Mr. Crawford ought to know—he must know that—I told him enough yesterday to convince him—he spoke to me on this subject yesterday—and I told him without disguise that it was very disagreeable to me, and quite out of my power to return his good opinion."

"I do not catch your meaning," said Sir Thomas, sitting down again.—"Out of your power to return his good opinion! what is all this? I know he spoke to you yesterday, and (as far as I understand), received as much encouragement to proceed as a well-judging young woman could permit herself to give.[10] I was very much pleased with what I collected[11] to have been your behaviour on the occasion; it shewed a discretion highly to be commended. But now, when he has made his overtures so properly, and honourably[12]—what are your scruples *now*?"

"You are mistaken, Sir,"—cried Fanny, forced by the anxiety of the moment even to tell her uncle that he was wrong—"You are quite mistaken. How could Mr. Crawford say such a thing? I gave him no encouragement yesterday—On the contrary, I told him—I cannot recollect my exact words—but I am sure I told him that I would not listen to him, that it was very unpleasant to me in every respect, and that I begged him never to talk to me in that manner again.—I am sure I said as much as that and more; and I should have said still more,—if I had been quite certain of his meaning any thing seriously, but I did not like to be—I could not bear to be—imputing more than might be intended.[13] I thought it might all pass for nothing with *him*."

10. Women were strongly urged to be modest and cautious in responding to a man's overtures, though not to the point of refusing a man they mean to accept. Sir Thomas's unusually stringent interpretation of the ideal of modesty reflects his own strict moral standards, as well as, most likely, his hope and expectation that Fanny will accept Henry Crawford and thus that her hesitation could not result from any intent to refuse him.

11. *collected*: gathered.

12. That is, by seeking a parent's (or stand-in parent's) permission first.

13. Fanny's halting speech indicates her distress and confusion. Usually, though often reluctant to open her mouth, she speaks smoothly and eloquently when she does.

She could say no more; her breath was almost gone.

"Am I to understand," said Sir Thomas, after a few moments silence, "that you mean to *refuse* Mr. Crawford?"

"Yes, Sir."

"Refuse him?"

"Yes, Sir."

"Refuse Mr. Crawford! Upon what plea? For what reason?"

"I—I cannot like him, Sir, well enough to marry him."

"This is very strange!" said Sir Thomas, in a voice of calm displeasure. "There is something in this which my comprehension does not reach. Here is a young man wishing to pay his addresses to[14] you, with every thing to recommend him; not merely situation in life, fortune, and character, but with more than common agreeableness, with address[15] and conversation pleasing to every body.[16] And he is not an acquaintance of to-day, you have now known him some time. His sister, moreover, is your intimate friend, and he has been doing *that* for your brother, which I should suppose would have been almost sufficient recommendation to you, had there been no other. It is very uncertain when my interest might have got William on. He has done it already."

"Yes," said Fanny, in a faint voice, and looking down with fresh shame; and she did feel almost ashamed of herself, after such a picture as her uncle had drawn, for not liking Mr. Crawford.

"You must have been aware," continued Sir Thomas, presently, "you must have been some time aware of a particularity in Mr. Crawford's manners to you. This cannot have taken you by surprise. You must have observed his attentions; and though you always received them very properly (I have no accusation to make on that head), I never perceived them to be unpleasant to you. I am half inclined to think, Fanny, that you do not quite know your own feelings."

"Oh! yes, Sir, indeed I do. His attentions were always—what I did not like."

Sir Thomas looked at her with deeper surprise. "This is beyond me," said he. "This requires explanation. Young as you are, and having seen scarcely any one, it is hardly possible that your affections—"[17]

He paused and eyed her fixedly. He saw her lips formed into a *no*,

14. *pay his addresses to*: court, propose marriage.

15. *address*: outward demeanor or manner.

16. Sir Thomas's reasons give a sense of his priorities, and thus the reason why Fanny's behavior is so beyond his comprehension. In mentioning Henry Crawford's virtues he mostly refers to his wealth and social position, as well as his surface manners and agreeableness. He does mention character, and Henry has done nothing before Sir Thomas to indicate a bad character. But Sir Thomas has also had little opportunity to observe him: less than a month passed between the time Henry returned to Mansfield and decided to stay and flirt with Fanny and the time he left after the ball with William. Moreover, during that time Sir Thomas has mostly seen him in company, and there has never been a mention of a sustained conversation between the two men. Somebody deeply concerned with the true inner character of a potential suitor for a niece, or daughter, would not draw such thoroughly positive conclusions on such a limited basis.

17. He is asking, very tentatively, if she has developed affections for anyone else.

though the sound was inarticulate, but her face was like scarlet. That, however, in so modest a girl might be very compatible with innocence;[18] and chusing at least to appear satisfied, he quickly added, "No, no, I know *that* is quite out of the question—quite impossible.[19] Well, there is nothing more to be said."

And for a few minutes he did say nothing. He was deep in thought.[20] His niece was deep in thought likewise, trying to harden and prepare herself against farther questioning. She would rather die than own the truth,[21] and she hoped by a little reflection to fortify herself beyond betraying it.

"Independently of the interest which Mr. Crawford's *choice* seemed to justify," said Sir Thomas, beginning again, and very composedly, "his wishing to marry at all so early is recommendatory[22] to me. I am an advocate for early marriages, where there are means in proportion, and would have every young man, with a sufficient income, settle[23] as soon after four and twenty as he can. This is so much my opinion, that I am sorry to think how little likely my own eldest son, your cousin, Mr. Bertram, is to marry early; but at present, as far as I can judge, matrimony makes no part of his plans or thoughts. I wish he were more likely to fix."[24] Here was a glance at Fanny.[25] "Edmund I consider from his disposition and habits as much more likely to marry early than his brother. *He*, indeed, I have lately thought has seen the woman he could love, which, I am convinced, my eldest son has not. Am I right? Do you agree with me, my dear?"[26]

"Yes, Sir."

It was gently, but it was calmly said, and Sir Thomas was easy on the score of the cousins. But the removal of his alarm did his niece no service; as her unaccountableness was confirmed, his displeasure increased; and getting up and walking about the room, with a frown, which Fanny could picture to herself, though she dared not lift up her eyes, he shortly afterwards, and in a voice of authority, said, "Have you any reason, child, to think ill of Mr. Crawford's temper?"

"No, Sir."

She longed to add, "but of his principles I have"; but her heart sunk under the appalling[27] prospect of discussion, explanation, and probably non-conviction. Her ill opinion of him was founded chiefly

18. In other words, extreme blushing might indicate she is in love, but he tells himself that a very modest girl also could blush from embarrassment just from being asked about such a subject.

19. His *"that"* probably refers to her falling in love with either Tom or Edmund. Sir Thomas knows that they, along with Henry, are the only unmarried young men she has really gotten to know and thus the possible alternative objects of her affection. This possibility disturbs him, though he would like to dismiss it, which is why he so peremptorily declares it "out of the question," why he adduces modesty to explain her blush, and why he chooses "at least to appear satisfied."

20. His next speech, raising the topic of Tom and Edmund in regard to Fanny, suggests that is why he is now deep in thought. He is too intelligent to dismiss completely the idea of affection there, now that the possibility has been raised by her behavior and her current reaction, and it is a matter that touches him very deeply, even more than the issue of marriage between Fanny and Henry.

21. Meaning the truth of her affection for Edmund.

22. *recommendatory*: praiseworthy, serving as a recommendation.

23. *settle*: marry.

24. *fix*: settle down.

25. His glance is intended to ascertain Fanny's reaction. While continuing to discuss Henry Crawford, he has also managed to introduce Tom and his marital state into the conversation, observing Fanny as he does so.

26. Having apparently elicited no reaction from Fanny regarding Tom, he turns to Edmund's romantic situation and asks Fanny to comment on it. As indicated immediately afterward, her answer finally satisfies him and he can return to the matter of Fanny and Henry.

27. *appalling*: dismaying, terrifying.

on observations, which, for her cousins' sake, she could scarcely dare
mention to their father. Maria and Julia—and especially Maria, were
so closely implicated in Mr. Crawford's misconduct, that she could
not give his character,[28] such as she believed it, without betraying
them. She had hoped that to a man like her uncle, so discerning, so
honourable, so good, the simple acknowledgment of settled *dislike*
on her side, would have been sufficient. To her infinite grief she
found it was not.

Sir Thomas came towards the table where she sat in trembling
wretchedness, and with a good deal of cold sternness, said, "It is of
no use, I perceive, to talk to you. We had better put an end to this
most mortifying conference. Mr. Crawford must not be kept longer
waiting. I will, therefore, only add, as thinking it my duty to mark my
opinion of your conduct—that you have disappointed every expectation I had formed, and proved yourself of a character the very reverse
of what I had supposed. For I *had*, Fanny, as I think my behaviour
must have shewn, formed a very favourable opinion of you from the
period of my return to England. I had thought you peculiarly free
from wilfulness of temper, self-conceit, and every tendency to that
independence of spirit, which prevails so much in modern days,[29]
even in young women, and which in young women is offensive
and disgusting[30] beyond all common offence.[31] But you have now
shewn me that you can be wilful and perverse, that you can and
will decide for yourself, without any consideration or deference for
those who have surely some right to guide you—without even asking
their advice. You have shewn yourself very, very different from any
thing that I had imagined.[32] The advantage or disadvantage of your
family—of your parents—your brothers and sisters—never seems to
have had a moment's share in your thoughts on this occasion. How
they might be benefited, how *they* must rejoice in such an establishment[33] for you—is nothing to *you*.[34] You think only of yourself;
and because you do not feel for Mr. Crawford exactly what a young,
heated fancy imagines to be necessary for happiness,[35] you resolve to
refuse him at once, without wishing even for a little time to consider
of it—a little more time for cool consideration, and for really examining your own inclinations—and are, in a wild fit of folly, throwing
away from you such an opportunity of being settled in life, eligibly,

28. *give his character*: describe or reveal his character.

29. Preceding decades ("modern days" to Sir Thomas) had witnessed cultural and political currents that encouraged personal autonomy and independence, as well as rebelliousness in many cases. The most significant examples were the democratic revolutions of the time, most notably the French one. These had frequently failed, the problems and violence of the French Revolution had spurred a reaction against many of its ideals, and a truly revolutionary spirit remained confined to a minority of the population, but even in the rest, more muted traces of this spirit had begun to penetrate and lead to limited changes in behavior and attitude. Many writers of the time commented on this, and frequently, like Sir Thomas, expressed their disapproval.

30. *disgusting*: distasteful.

31. In keeping with the conservative outlook described above, independence of spirit was often regarded in negative terms, since it placed personal desires over social, familial, and religious obligations. This was considered especially bad among women and young people, for they were expected to submit to familial authority; hence independence of spirit would be worst of all in young women.

32. His surprise results in part from his previous observation of Fanny's deference and timidity. She does reveal in response to Henry's proposal a firmness that surprises everyone, but the reason is that previously her submissiveness reflected her belief in her moral obligation to behave so, whereas now her moral principles tell her to stand firm and resist, since she is being asked to marry a man she considers morally defective.

33. *establishment*: marriage, or position created by marriage.

34. This is a pertinent point, for Fanny's marriage to a man as wealthy as Henry would place her in a position to offer considerable help to her parents and siblings.

35. He assumes she has been influenced by ideals of extreme romantic love, which the many highly sentimental novels of the period often depicted and celebrated. Jane Austen often ridicules such novels, as well as extravagantly romantic conceptions of love. But she also upholds more rational and moderate notions of romantic love, and she consistently supports the idea that, as she says in a letter to her niece on the subject of marriage, "Anything is to be preferred or endured rather than marrying without Affection" (Nov. 18, 1814).

honourably, nobly[36] settled, as will, probably, never occur to you again.[37] Here is a young man of sense, of character, of temper,[38] of manners, and of fortune, exceedingly attached to you, and seeking your hand in the most handsome and disinterested way; and let me tell you, Fanny, that you may live eighteen years longer in the world, without being addressed by a man of half Mr. Crawford's estate, or a tenth part of his merits. Gladly would I have bestowed either of my own daughters on him. Maria is nobly married—but had Mr. Crawford sought Julia's hand, I should have given it to him with superior and more heartfelt satisfaction than I gave Maria's to Mr. Rushworth." After half a moment's pause—"And I should have been very much surprised had either of my daughters, on receiving a proposal of marriage at any time, which might carry with it only *half* the eligibility of *this*, immediately and peremptorily, and without paying my opinion or my regard the compliment of any consultation, put a decided negative on it. I should have been much surprised, and much hurt, by such a proceeding. I should have thought it a gross violation of duty and respect. *You* are not to be judged by the same rule. You do not owe me the duty of a child. But, Fanny, if your heart can acquit you of *ingratitude*—"

He ceased. Fanny was by this time crying so bitterly, that angry as he was, he would not press that article[39] farther. Her heart was almost broke by such a picture of what she appeared to him; by such accusations, so heavy, so multiplied, so rising in dreadful gradation! Self-willed, obstinate, selfish, and ungrateful. He thought her all this. She had deceived his expectations; she had lost his good opinion. What was to become of her?

"I am very sorry," said she inarticulately through her tears, "I am very sorry indeed."

"Sorry! yes, I hope you are sorry; and you will probably have reason to be long sorry for this day's transactions."

"If it were possible for me to do otherwise," said she with another strong effort, "but I am so perfectly convinced that I could never make him happy, and that I should be miserable myself."

Another burst of tears; but in spite of that burst, and in spite of that great black word *miserable*, which served to introduce it, Sir Thomas began to think a little relenting, a little change of inclination, might

36. *nobly*: superbly (especially in a social sense).

37. Fanny's lack of money, except what Sir Thomas chooses to give her, and her relatively low family origins mean that Henry Crawford does represent a marital opportunity that, in social and economic terms, she is unlikely ever to come close to matching in the future.

38. *temper*: mental composure and equanimity.

39. *article*: subject.

have something to do with it; and to augur favourably from the personal intreaty of the young man himself. He knew her to be very timid, and exceedingly nervous; and thought it not improbable that her mind might be in such a state, as a little time, a little pressing, a little patience, and a little impatience, a judicious mixture of all on the lover's side, might work their usual effect on. If the gentleman would but persevere, if he had but love enough to persevere—Sir Thomas began to have hopes; and these reflections having passed across his mind and cheered it, "Well," said he, in a tone of becoming gravity, but of less anger, "well, child, dry up your tears. There is no use in these tears; they can do no good. You must now come down stairs with me. Mr. Crawford has been kept waiting too long already. You must give him your own answer; we cannot expect him to be satisfied with less; and you only can explain to him the grounds of that misconception of your sentiments, which, unfortunately for himself, he certainly has imbibed. I am totally unequal to it."

But Fanny shewed such reluctance, such misery, at the idea of going down to him, that Sir Thomas, after a little consideration, judged it better to indulge her. His hopes from both gentleman and lady suffered a small depression in consequence; but when he looked at his niece, and saw the state of feature and complexion which her crying had brought her into, he thought there might be as much lost as gained by an immediate interview. With a few words, therefore, of no particular meaning, he walked off by himself, leaving his poor niece to sit and cry over what had passed, with very wretched feelings.

Her mind was all disorder. The past, present, future, every thing was terrible. But her uncle's anger gave her the severest pain of all. Selfish and ungrateful! to have appeared so to him! She was miserable for ever. She had no one to take her part, to counsel, or speak for her. Her only friend was absent. He might have softened his father; but all, perhaps all, would think her selfish and ungrateful. She might have to endure the reproach again and again; she might hear it, or see it, or know it to exist for ever in every connection[40] about her.[41] She could not but feel some resentment against Mr. Crawford; yet, if he really loved her, and were unhappy too!—it was all wretchedness together.

40. *connection*: relative, family member.

41. This represents another terrible possibility for Fanny if she persists in rejecting Henry Crawford. Her otherwise poor marital prospects mean she may end up spending the rest of her life as a dependent relation among the Bertrams, and they, knowing she refused an advantageous offer of marriage that could have relieved them permanently of the need to support her, could resent her, thereby making her life of spinsterhood and dependence even more miserable.

In about a quarter of an hour her uncle returned; she was almost ready to faint at the sight of him. He spoke calmly, however, without austerity, without reproach, and she revived a little. There was comfort too in his words, as well as his manner, for he began with, "Mr. Crawford is gone; he has just left me. I need not repeat what has passed. I do not want to add to any thing you may now be feeling, by an account of what he has felt. Suffice it, that he has behaved in the most gentleman-like and generous[42] manner; and has confirmed me in a most favourable opinion of his understanding, heart, and temper. Upon my representation of what you were suffering, he immediately, and with the greatest delicacy, ceased to urge to see you for the present."

Here Fanny, who had looked up, looked down again. "Of course," continued her uncle, "it cannot be supposed but that he should request to speak with you alone, be it only for five minutes; a request too natural, a claim too just to be denied. But there is no time fixed, perhaps to-morrow, or whenever your spirits are composed enough. For the present you have only to tranquillize yourself. Check these tears; they do but exhaust you. If, as I am willing to suppose, you wish to shew me any observance,[43] you will not give way to these emotions, but endeavour to reason yourself into a stronger frame of mind. I advise you to go out, the air will do you good; go out for an hour on the gravel, you will have the shrubbery to yourself and will be the better for air and exercise.[44] And, Fanny, (turning back again for a moment) I shall make no mention below of what has passed; I shall not even tell your aunt Bertram. There is no occasion for spreading the disappointment; say nothing about it yourself."

This was an order to be most joyfully obeyed; this was an act of kindness which Fanny felt at her heart. To be spared from her aunt Norris's interminable reproaches!—he left her in a glow of gratitude. Any thing might be bearable rather than such reproaches. Even to see Mr. Crawford would be less overpowering.

She walked out directly as her uncle recommended, and followed his advice throughout, as far as she could; did check her tears, did earnestly try to compose her spirits, and strengthen her mind. She wished to prove to him that she did desire his comfort, and sought to regain his favour; and he had given her another strong motive

42. *generous*: noble, magnanimous.

43. *observance*: respect, deference.

44. Gravel was prized in gardens because it remained drier than grass or dirt, a particularly strong consideration during the winter, when conditions were often damp.

A woman in morning dress.

[From *The Repository of arts, literature, fashions, manufactures, &c*, Vol. VII (1812), p. 246]

for exertion, in keeping the whole affair from the knowledge of her aunts. Not to excite suspicion by her look or manner was now an object worth attaining; and she felt equal to almost any thing that might save her from her aunt Norris.

She was struck, quite struck, when on returning from her walk, and going into the east room again, the first thing which caught her eye was a fire lighted and burning. A fire! it seemed too much; just at that time to be giving her such an indulgence, was exciting even painful gratitude. She wondered that Sir Thomas could have leisure to think of such a trifle again; but she soon found, from the voluntary information of the housemaid, who came in to attend it, that so it was to be every day. Sir Thomas had given orders for it.

"I must be a brute indeed, if I can be really ungrateful!" said she in soliloquy; "Heaven defend me from being ungrateful!"

She saw nothing more of her uncle, nor of her aunt Norris, till they met at dinner. Her uncle's behaviour to her was then as nearly as possible what it had been before; she was sure he did not mean there should be any change, and that it was only her own conscience that could fancy any; but her aunt was soon quarrelling with her: and when she found how much and how unpleasantly her having only walked out without her aunt's knowledge could be dwelt on, she felt all the reason she had to bless the kindness which saved her from the same spirit of reproach, exerted on a more momentous subject.

"If I had known you were going out, I should have got you just to go as far as my house with some orders for Nanny," said she, "which I have since, to my very great inconvenience, been obliged to go and carry myself. I could very ill spare the time, and you might have saved me the trouble, if you would only have been so good as to let us know you were going out. It would have made no difference to you, I suppose, whether you had walked in the shrubbery, or gone to my house."

"I recommended the shrubbery to Fanny as the dryest place," said Sir Thomas.

"Oh," said Mrs. Norris with a moment's check, "that was very kind of you, Sir Thomas; but you do not know how dry the path is to my house. Fanny would have had quite as good a walk there, I assure you; with the advantage of being of some use, and obliging her aunt:

A woman in evening dress.

[From *The Repository of arts, literature, fashions, manufactures, &c*, Vol. VI (1811), p. 226]

it is all her fault. If she would but have let us know she was going out—but there is a something about Fanny, I have often observed it before,—she likes to go her own way to work; she does not like to be dictated to; she takes her own independent walk whenever she can; she certainly has a little spirit of secrecy, and independence, and nonsense,[45] about her, which I would advise her to get the better of."

As a general reflection on Fanny, Sir Thomas thought nothing could be more unjust, though he had been so lately expressing the same sentiments himself, and he tried to turn the conversation; tried repeatedly before he could succeed; for Mrs. Norris had not discernment enough to perceive, either now, or at any other time, to what degree he thought well of his niece, or how very far he was from wishing to have his own children's merits set off by the depreciation of hers. She was talking *at* Fanny, and resenting this private walk half through the dinner.

It was over, however, at last; and the evening set in with more composure to Fanny, and more cheerfulness of spirits than she could have hoped for after so stormy a morning; but she trusted, in the first place, that she had done right, that her judgment had not misled her; for the purity of her intentions she could answer; and she was willing to hope, secondly, that her uncle's displeasure was abating, and would abate farther as he considered the matter with more impartiality, and felt, as a good man must feel, how wretched, and how unpardonable, how hopeless and how wicked it was, to marry without affection.

When the meeting with which she was threatened for the morrow was past, she could not but flatter herself that the subject would be finally concluded, and Mr. Crawford once gone from Mansfield, that every thing would soon be as if no such subject had existed. She would not, could not believe, that Mr. Crawford's affection for her could distress him long; his mind was not of that sort. London would soon bring its cure. In London he would soon learn to wonder at his infatuation, and be thankful for the right reason in her, which had saved him from its evil consequences.

While Fanny's mind was engaged in these sort of hopes, her uncle was soon after tea called out of the room; an occurrence too common to strike her, and she thought nothing of it till the butler re-

45. *nonsense*: ridiculous or senseless behavior—as in a phrase such as "let's have no nonsense."

A woman in walking dress.

[From *The Repository of arts, literature, fashions, manufactures, &c*, Vol. VI (1811), p. 302]

appeared ten minutes afterwards, and advancing decidedly towards herself, said, "Sir Thomas wishes to speak with you, Ma'am, in his own room." Then it occurred to her what might be going on; a suspicion rushed over her mind which drove the colour from her cheeks; but instantly rising, she was preparing to obey, when Mrs. Norris called out, "Stay, stay, Fanny! what are you about?—where are you going?—don't be in such a hurry. Depend upon it, it is not you that are wanted; depend upon it it is me; (looking at the butler) but you are so very eager to put yourself forward. What should Sir Thomas want you for? It is me, Baddeley, you mean; I am coming this moment. You mean me, Baddeley, I am sure; Sir Thomas wants me, not Miss Price."[46]

But Baddeley was stout. "No, Ma'am, it is Miss Price, I am certain of its being Miss Price." And there was a half smile with the words which meant, "I do not think *you* would answer the purpose at all."[47]

Mrs. Norris, much discontented, was obliged to compose herself to work again; and Fanny, walking off in agitating consciousness, found herself, as she anticipated, in another minute alone with Mr. Crawford.

46. She says "Miss Price" because that is what the butler calls her.

47. Mrs. Norris, who frequently tries to dictate to or interfere with the servants, is undoubtedly very unpopular among them. Normally, however, their position means they cannot argue or answer back, so Baddeley probably relishes the opportunity to confound Mrs. Norris while strictly performing his duties. He smiles also at the ridiculousness of Mrs. Norris being the one Mr. Crawford wishes a private conference with.

Chapter Two

*T*he conference was neither so short, nor so conclusive, as the lady had designed. The gentleman was not so easily satisfied. He had all the disposition to persevere that Sir Thomas could wish him. He had vanity, which strongly inclined him, in the first place, to think she did love him, though she might not know it herself; and which, secondly, when constrained at last to admit that she did know her own present feelings, convinced him that he should be able in time to make those feelings what he wished.

He was in love, very much in love; and it was a love which, operating on an active, sanguine spirit, of more warmth than delicacy,[1] made her affection appear of greater consequence, because it was withheld, and determined him to have the glory, as well as the felicity, of forcing her to love him.

He would not despair: he would not desist. He had every well-grounded reason for solid attachment; he knew her to have all the worth that could justify the warmest hopes of lasting happiness with her; her conduct at this very time, by speaking[2] the disinterestedness and delicacy of her character (qualities which he believed most rare indeed),[3] was of a sort to heighten all his wishes, and confirm all his resolutions. He knew not that he had a pre-engaged heart to attack. Of *that*, he had no suspicion. He considered her rather as one who had never thought on the subject enough to be in danger; who had been guarded[4] by youth, a youth of mind as lovely as of person;[5] whose modesty had prevented her from understanding his attentions, and who was still overpowered by the suddenness of addresses so wholly unexpected, and the novelty of a situation which her fancy had never taken into account.

Must it not follow of course, that when he was understood, he should succeed? — he believed it fully. Love such as his, in a man like himself, must with perseverance secure a return, and at no great distance; and he had so much delight in the idea of obliging her to love

1. *delicacy*: sensitivity to others' feelings.

2. *speaking*: indicating, testifying to.

3. Most women he has met in fashionable London society, including those he has flirted with, were probably very interested in wealth and social position, as his sister is. Thus he is surprised and impressed by Fanny's indifference to these matters, as well as by the general moral delicacy and refinement she displays.

4. *guarded*: preserved.

5. *person*: physical appearance.

him in a very short time, that her not loving him now was scarcely regretted. A little difficulty to be overcome, was no evil to Henry Crawford. He rather derived spirits[6] from it. He had been apt to gain hearts too easily. His situation was new and animating.

To Fanny, however, who had known too much opposition all her life, to find any charm in it, all this was unintelligible. She found that he did mean to persevere; but how he could, after such language from her as she felt herself obliged to use, was not to be understood. She told him, that she did not love him, could not love him, was sure she never should love him: that such a change was quite impossible, that the subject was most painful to her, that she must intreat him never to mention it again, to allow her to leave him at once, and let it be considered as concluded for ever. And when farther pressed, had added, that in her opinion their dispositions were so totally dissimilar, as to make mutual affection incompatible; and that they were unfitted for each other by nature, education, and habit. All this she had said, and with the earnestness of sincerity; yet this was not enough, for he immediately denied there being anything uncongenial in their characters, or anything unfriendly[7] in their situations;[8] and positively declared, that he would still love, and still hope!

Fanny knew her own meaning, but was no judge of her own manner. Her manner was incurably gentle, and she was not aware how much it concealed the sternness of her purpose.[9] Her diffidence, gratitude, and softness, made every expression of indifference seem almost an effort of self-denial; seem at least, to be giving nearly as much pain to herself as to him. Mr. Crawford was no longer the Mr. Crawford who, as the clandestine, insidious, treacherous admirer of Maria Bertram, had been her abhorrence, whom she had hated to see or to speak to, in whom she could believe no good quality to exist, and whose power, even of being agreeable, she had barely acknowledged. He was now the Mr. Crawford who was addressing herself with ardent, disinterested, love; whose feelings were apparently become all that was honourable and upright, whose views of happiness were all fixed on a marriage of attachment;[10] who was pouring out his sense of her merits, describing and describing again his affection, proving, as far as words could prove it, and in the language, tone, and spirit of a man of talent too, that he sought her for

6. *spirits*: vigor, ardor.

7. *unfriendly*: unfavorable.

8. *situations*: social conditions or status.

9. Fanny's incomprehension of her own effect on others is the converse of their incomprehension of her. It results from the gulf between her inner strength and her outer softness, which also makes others fail to appreciate the determination lying beneath her gentle demeanor.

10. *attachment*: affection. Henry's proposal has raised her opinion of him, for it shows that he is willing to overlook considerations of social or financial advantage on such an all-important matter.

her gentleness, and her goodness; and to complete the whole, he was now the Mr. Crawford who had procured William's promotion!

Here was a change! and here were claims which could not but operate. She might have disdained him in all the dignity of angry virtue, in the grounds of Sotherton, or the theatre at Mansfield Park; but he approached her now with rights that demanded different treatment. She must be courteous, and she must be compassionate. She must have a sensation of being honoured, and whether thinking of herself or her brother, she must have a strong feeling of gratitude. The effect of the whole was a manner so pitying and agitated, and words intermingled with her refusal so expressive of obligation[11] and concern, that to a temper of vanity and hope like Crawford's, the truth, or at least the strength of her indifference, might well be questionable; and he was not so irrational as Fanny considered him, in the professions of persevering, assiduous, and not desponding attachment which closed the interview.

It was with reluctance that he suffered her to go, but there was no look of despair in parting to bely his words, or give her hopes of his being less unreasonable than he professed himself.

Now she was angry. Some resentment did arise at a perseverance so selfish and ungenerous. Here was again a want[12] of delicacy and regard for others which had formerly so struck and disgusted her. Here was again a something of the same Mr. Crawford whom she had so reprobated before. How evidently was there a gross want of feeling and humanity where his own pleasure was concerned—And, alas! how always known no principle to supply as a duty what the heart was deficient in.[13] Had her own affections been as free—as perhaps they ought to have been—he never could have engaged[14] them.

So thought Fanny in good truth and sober sadness, as she sat musing over that too great indulgence and luxury of a fire upstairs— wondering at the past and present, wondering at what was yet to come, and in a nervous agitation which made nothing clear to her but the persuasion of her being never under any circumstances able to love Mr. Crawford, and the felicity of having a fire to sit over and think of it.

Sir Thomas was obliged or obliged himself to wait till the morrow for a knowledge of what had passed between the young people. He

11. *obligation*: obligingness, civility.

12. *want*: lack.

13. In other words, not only does he lack feeling or sympathy in many cases, but he also lacks sufficient principles to make him behave correctly even when his heart does not lead him right.

14. *engaged*: gained.

An aristocratic man of the time (Lord Castlereigh).

[From Lord Ronald Sutherland Gower, *Sir Thomas Lawrence* (London, 1900), p. 12]

then saw Mr. Crawford, and received his account.—The first feeling was disappointment: he had hoped better things; he had thought that an hour's intreaty from a young man like Crawford could not have worked so little change on a gentle tempered girl like Fanny; but there was speedy comfort in the determined views and sanguine perseverance of the lover; and when seeing such confidence of success in the principal, Sir Thomas was soon able to depend on it himself.

Nothing was omitted, on his side, of civility, compliment, or kindness, that might assist the plan. Mr. Crawford's steadiness was honoured, and Fanny was praised, and the connection was still the most desirable in the world. At Mansfield Park Mr. Crawford would always be welcome; he had only to consult his own judgment and feelings as to the frequency of his visits, at present or in future. In all his niece's family and friends there could be but one opinion, one wish on the subject; the influence of all who loved her must incline one way.

Every thing was said that could encourage, every encouragement received with grateful joy, and the gentlemen parted the best of friends.

Satisfied that the cause was now on a footing the most proper and hopeful, Sir Thomas resolved to abstain from all farther importunity with his niece, and to shew no open interference. Upon her disposition he believed kindness might be the best way of working. Intreaty should be from one quarter only. The forbearance of her family on a point, respecting which she could be in no doubt of their wishes, might be their surest means of forwarding it. Accordingly, on this principle Sir Thomas took the first opportunity of saying to her, with a mild gravity, intended to be overcoming, "Well, Fanny, I have seen Mr. Crawford again, and learn from him exactly how matters stand between you. He is a most extraordinary young man, and whatever be the event,[15] you must feel that you have created an attachment of no common character; though, young as you are, and little acquainted with the transient, varying, unsteady nature of love, as it generally exists, you cannot be struck as I am with all that is wonderful in a perseverance of this sort, against discouragement. With him, it is entirely a matter of feeling; he claims no merit in it, perhaps is entitled to none. Yet, having chosen so well, his constancy

15. *event*: outcome.

A contemporary portrait of a young woman (Mrs. Bannister).

[From Lord Ronald Sutherland Gower, *Sir Thomas Lawrence* (London, 1900), p. 164]

has a respectable stamp. Had his choice been less unexceptionable, I should have condemned his persevering."

"Indeed, Sir," said Fanny, "I am very sorry that Mr. Crawford should continue to—I know that it is paying me a very great compliment, and I feel most undeservedly honoured, but I am so perfectly convinced, and I have told him so, that it never will be in my power—"

"My dear," interrupted Sir Thomas, "there is no occasion for this. Your feelings are as well known to me, as my wishes and regrets must be to you. There is nothing more to be said or done. From this hour, the subject is never to be revived between us. You will have nothing to fear, or to be agitated about. You cannot suppose me capable of trying to persuade you to marry against your inclinations. Your happiness and advantage are all that I have in view, and nothing is required of you but to bear with Mr. Crawford's endeavours to convince you, that they may not be incompatible with his. He proceeds at his own risk. You are on safe ground. I have engaged for your seeing him whenever he calls, as you might have done, had nothing of this sort occurred. You will see him with the rest of us, in the same manner, and as much as you can, dismissing the recollection of every thing unpleasant. He leaves Northamptonshire so soon, that even this slight sacrifice cannot be often demanded. The future must be very uncertain. And now, my dear Fanny, this subject is closed between us."

The promised departure was all that Fanny could think of with much satisfaction. Her uncle's kind expressions, however, and forbearing manner, were sensibly felt; and when she considered how much of the truth was unknown to him, she believed she had no right to wonder at the line of conduct he pursued. He who had married a daughter to Mr. Rushworth. Romantic delicacy was certainly not to be expected from him.[16] She must do her duty, and trust that time might make her duty easier than it now was.

She could not, though only eighteen, suppose Mr. Crawford's attachment would hold out for ever; she could not but imagine that steady, unceasing discouragement from herself would put an end to it in time. How much time she might, in her own fancy, allot for its dominion, is another concern. It would not be fair to enquire into a young lady's exact estimate of her own perfections.

16. "Romantic delicacy" is a keen sensitivity to the rights of love and feeling, a quality that would have kept its possessor from ever approving a marriage so lacking in affection, at least on the bride's side, as that of Maria and Mr. Rushworth. Interestingly, the one other case where Jane Austen uses this phrase is in describing Mrs. Dashwood, the mother of the heroines in *Sense and Sensibility*, and there romantic delicacy is criticized for keeping Mrs. Dashwood from exercising common sense and prudence in the matter of her daughter's romance with a man who has acted strangely and mysteriously. Clearly Jane Austen, as in so many matters, seeks a mean between extremes.

In spite of his intended silence, Sir Thomas found himself once more obliged to mention the subject to his niece, to prepare her briefly for its being imparted to her aunts; a measure which he would still have avoided, if possible, but which became necessary from the totally opposite feelings of Mr. Crawford, as to any secrecy of proceeding. He had no idea of concealment. It was all known at the parsonage, where he loved to talk over the future with both his sisters; and it would be rather gratifying to him to have enlightened witnesses of the progress of his success. When Sir Thomas understood this, he felt the necessity of making his own wife and sister-in-law acquainted with the business without delay; though on Fanny's account, he almost dreaded the effect of the communication to Mrs. Norris as much as Fanny herself. He deprecated her mistaken, but well-meaning zeal. Sir Thomas, indeed, was, by this time, not very far from classing Mrs. Norris as one of those well-meaning people, who are always doing mistaken and very disagreeable things.

Mrs. Norris, however, relieved him. He pressed for the strictest forbearance and silence towards their niece; she not only promised, but did observe it. She only looked her increased ill-will. Angry she was, bitterly angry; but she was more angry with Fanny for having received such an offer, than for refusing it. It was an injury and affront to Julia, who ought to have been Mr. Crawford's choice; and, independently of that, she disliked Fanny, because she had neglected her; and she would have grudged such an elevation to one whom she had been always trying to depress.

Sir Thomas gave her more credit for discretion on the occasion than she deserved; and Fanny could have blessed her for allowing her only to see her displeasure, and not to hear it.

Lady Bertram took it differently. She had been a beauty, and a prosperous beauty, all her life; and beauty and wealth were all that excited her respect. To know Fanny to be sought in marriage by a man of fortune, raised her, therefore, very much in her opinion. By convincing her that Fanny *was* very pretty, which she had been doubting[17] about before, and that she would be advantageously married, it made her feel a sort of credit in calling her niece.

"Well, Fanny," said she, as soon as they were alone together afterwards,—and she really had known something like impatience,

17. *doubting*: wondering.

A woman with a book.

[From *The Repository of arts, literature, fashions, manufactures, &c*, Vol. XIV (1815), p. 304]

to be alone with her, and her countenance, as she spoke, had extraordinary animation—"Well, Fanny, I have had a very agreeable surprise this morning. I must just speak of it *once*, I told Sir Thomas I must *once*, and then I shall have done.[18] I give you joy, my dear niece."—And looking at her complacently, she added, "Humph—We certainly are a handsome family."

Fanny coloured, and doubted at first what to say; when hoping to assail her on her vulnerable side, she presently answered—

"My dear aunt, *you* cannot wish me to do differently from what I have done, I am sure. *You* cannot wish me to marry; for you would miss me, should not you?—Yes, I am sure you would miss me too much for that."

"No, my dear, I should not think of missing you, when such an offer as this comes in your way. I could do very well without you, if you were married to a man of such good estate as Mr. Crawford. And you must be aware, Fanny, that it is every young woman's duty to accept such a very unexceptionable offer as this."[19]

This was almost the only rule of conduct, the only piece of advice, which Fanny had ever received from her aunt in the course of eight years and a half.—It silenced her. She felt how unprofitable contention would be. If her aunt's feelings were against her, nothing could be hoped from attacking her understanding. Lady Bertram was quite talkative.

"I will tell you what, Fanny," said she.—"I am sure he fell in love with you at the ball, I am sure the mischief was done that evening. You did look remarkably well. Every body said so. Sir Thomas said so. And you know you had Chapman to help you dress. I am very glad I sent Chapman to you. I shall tell Sir Thomas that I am sure it was done that evening."—And still pursuing the same cheerful thoughts, she soon afterwards added,—"And I will tell you what, Fanny—which is more than I did for Maria—the next time Pug has a litter you shall have a puppy."[20]

18. *have done*: cease, desist.

19. This echoes her daughter Maria's earlier thinking, in which she, being "now in her twenty-first year, . . . was beginning to think matrimony a duty" (p. 76). Marriage was in effect the profession of women, especially women of high rank, and thus achieving a good one could be seen as a duty, a fulfillment of the path in life they had been created and bred to follow.

20. Earlier Pug was called by a masculine pronoun, first by Lady Bertram and then by the author (pp. 144 and 154). Yet now it seems Pug has had a litter. This has led to some speculation among those commenting on the novel. One possibility is simply that Jane Austen erred, though she rarely does, and this is such an elementary mistake that she presumably would have caught it, especially since this novel underwent two editions overseen by her. Another is that the first, male dog died, and was replaced by a female, and Lady Bertram calls both Pug out of her usual indolence; however, only six months passed between the earlier mention of Pug and this one, and that is not much time to acquire a new dog who then has a litter. Finally, as one scholar (John Sutherland) speculates, it is possible Lady Bertram, from typical negligence, says "has a litter" when she really means "sires a litter": pugs, as valuable purebred dogs, would normally reproduce through arranged matings, and the owners of the male could arrange to receive a portion of the resulting litter; these may be the puppies Lady Bertram has in mind.

Chapter Three

*E*dmund had great things to hear on his return. Many surprises were awaiting him. The first that occurred was not least in interest,—the appearance of Henry Crawford and his sister walking together through the village, as he rode into it.—He had concluded,—he had meant them to be far distant. His absence had been extended beyond a fortnight purposely to avoid Miss Crawford.[1] He was returning to Mansfield with spirits ready to feed on melancholy remembrances, and tender associations, when her own fair self was before him, leaning on her brother's arm; and he found himself receiving a welcome, unquestionably friendly from the woman whom, two moments before, he had been thinking of as seventy miles off, and as farther, much farther from him in inclination than any distance could express.

Her reception of him was of a sort which he could not have hoped for, had he expected to see her. Coming as he did from such a purport fulfilled as had taken him away, he would have expected any thing rather than a look of satisfaction, and words of simple, pleasant meaning. It was enough to set his heart in a glow, and to bring him home in the properest state for feeling the full value of the other joyful surprises at hand.

William's promotion, with all its particulars, he was soon master of; and with such a secret provision of comfort within his own breast to help the joy, he found in it a source of most gratifying sensation, and unvarying cheerfulness all dinner-time.

After dinner, when he and his father were alone, he had Fanny's history; and then all the great events of the last fortnight, and the present situation of matters at Mansfield were known to him.

Fanny suspected what was going on. They sat so much longer than usual in the dining parlour, that she was sure they must be talking of her; and when tea at last brought them away,[2] and she was to be

1. Edmund expected Mary to have left by this point, for she had spoken of leaving when January came, and it is now the 9th or 10th of the month (see chronology, p. 858). Henry's proposal to Fanny has interfered with their original plan for him to come to Mansfield and take Mary back to London.

2. Tea is served, usually an hour or a little more after dinner, in the drawing room, where the ladies have been waiting for them.

A grand dining room of the period.

[From Chandler R. Clifford, *Period Furnishings* (New York, 1922), p. 192]

seen by Edmund again, she felt dreadfully guilty. He came to her, sat down by her, took her hand, and pressed it kindly; and at that moment she thought that, but for the occupation and the scene which the tea-things afforded,[3] she must have[4] betrayed her emotion in some unpardonable excess.

He was not intending, however, by such action, to be conveying to her that unqualified approbation and encouragement which her hopes drew from it. It was designed only to express his participation in all that interested her, and to tell her that he had been hearing what quickened every feeling of affection. He was, in fact, entirely on his father's side of the question. His surprise was not so great as his father's, at her refusing Crawford, because, so far from supposing her to consider him with anything like a preference, he had always believed it to be rather the reverse, and could imagine her to be taken perfectly unprepared, but Sir Thomas could not regard the connection as more desirable than he did. It had every recommendation to him, and while honouring her for what she had done under the influence of her present indifference, honouring her in rather stronger terms than Sir Thomas could quite echo, he was most earnest in hoping, and sanguine in believing, that it would be a match at last, and that, united by mutual affection, it would appear that their dispositions were as exactly fitted to make them blessed in each other, as he was now beginning seriously to consider them. Crawford had been too precipitate. He had not given her time to attach herself. He had begun at the wrong end. With such powers as his, however, and such a disposition as hers, Edmund trusted that every thing would work out a happy conclusion. Meanwhile, he saw enough of Fanny's embarrassment to make him scrupulously guard against exciting it a second time, by any word, or look, or movement.

Crawford called the next day, and on the score of Edmund's return, Sir Thomas felt himself more than licensed to ask him to stay[5] dinner; it was really a necessary compliment. He staid of course, and Edmund had then ample opportunity for observing how he sped[6] with Fanny, and what degree of immediate encouragement for him might be extracted from her manners; and it was so little, so very very little, (every chance, every possibility of it, resting upon her embar-

3. One or more ladies of the house usually performed the tasks of making tea—the servants would bring a container of hot water—and of then serving it along with the coffee, if that was wanted, and breads or cakes. Lady Bertram's indolence probably means that Fanny regularly performs this service, except possibly when Maria or Julia is there.

4. *must have*: would certainly have.

5. *stay*: stay for.

6. *sped*: succeeded, prospered. This was the original meaning of "speed."

Reading aloud.

[From William Combe, *The Tour of Doctor Syntax in Search of the Picturesque* (London, 1817; 1903 reprint), p. 175]

rassment only, if there was not hope in her confusion, there was hope in nothing else), that he was almost ready to wonder at his friend's perseverance.—Fanny was worth it all; he held her to be worth every effort of patience, every exertion of mind—but he did not think he could have gone on himself with any woman breathing, without something more to warm his courage than his eyes could discern in hers.[7] He was very willing to hope that Crawford saw clearer; and this was the most comfortable conclusion for his friend that he could come to from all that he observed to pass before, and at, and after dinner.

In the evening a few circumstances occurred which he thought more promising. When he and Crawford walked into the drawing-room, his mother and Fanny were sitting as intently and silently at work as if there were nothing else to care for. Edmund could not help noticing their apparently deep tranquillity.

"We have not been so silent all the time," replied his mother. "Fanny has been reading to me, and only put the book down upon hearing you coming."—And sure enough there was a book on the table which had the air of being very recently closed, a volume of Shakespeare.[8]—"She often reads to me out of those books; and she was in the middle of a very fine speech of that man's—What's his name, Fanny?[9]—when we heard your footsteps."

Crawford took the volume. "Let me have the pleasure of finishing that speech to your ladyship," said he. "I shall find it immediately." And by carefully giving way to the inclination of the leaves, he did find it, or within a page or two,[10] quite near enough to satisfy Lady Bertram, who assured him, as soon as he mentioned the name of Cardinal Wolsey, that he had got the very speech.[11]—Not a look, or an offer of help had Fanny given; not a syllable for or against. All her attention was for her work. She seemed determined to be interested by nothing else. But taste was too strong in her. She could not abstract her mind five minutes; she was forced to listen; his reading was capital, and her pleasure in good reading extreme. To *good* reading, however, she had been long used; her uncle read well—her cousins all—Edmund very well; but in Mr. Crawford's reading there was a variety of excellence beyond[12] what she had ever met with. The King, the Queen, Buckingham, Wolsey, Cromwell,[13] all were given

7. Edmund has already shown a more cautious spirit than Henry in his romantic affairs, as well as in other matters.

8. This could be one of a vast array of editions of Shakespeare then available. Starting in the eighteenth century many editions were published, with an average of one a year by the later part of the century (though some of these were reprints of earlier editions). Some were scholarly, and others were designed to make Shakespeare more accessible to the general public.

9. Their edition of Shakespeare was published in multiple books, or volumes. That was generally the case with his works, and many other books as well, including Austen's novels. One reason was the thickness of paper, which limited how many pages could be bound in a single volume.

10. Because the pages in books were thick and stiff, they usually retained the impression of where they had been most recently opened and handled.

11. The play they are reading is *Henry VIII* (1613), one of Shakespeare's last plays and one believed now to have been a collaboration with John Fletcher (at that time it was believed to be only by Shakespeare). Cardinal Wolsey, Henry VIII's leading minister for much of his reign, is one of the principal characters. He has many lines, including a number of long speeches, so it is highly possible that, as the narrative implies, Henry has not found the exact speech that Fanny had been reading.

12. *beyond*: superior to.

13. These are most of the main characters. In addition to the king and Wolsey, they are: Catherine of Aragon (called Katherine by Shakespeare), Henry's first queen; the Duke of Buckingham, an enemy of Wolsey whose execution for treason dominates the early part of the play; and Thomas Cromwell, who became the king's leading minister after Wolsey fell from power.

in turn; for with the happiest knack, the happiest power of jumping and guessing, he could always light, at will, on the best scene, or the best speeches of each; and whether it were dignity or pride, or tenderness or remorse, or whatever were to be expressed, he could do it with equal beauty.—It was truly dramatic.[14]—His acting had first taught Fanny what pleasure a play might give, and his reading brought all his acting before her again; nay, perhaps with greater enjoyment, for it came unexpectedly, and with no such drawback as she had been used to suffer in seeing him on the stage with Miss Bertram.

Edmund watched the progress of her attention, and was amused and gratified by seeing how she gradually slackened in the needlework, which, at the beginning, seemed to occupy her totally; how it fell from her hand while she sat motionless over it—and at last, how the eyes which had appeared so studiously to avoid him throughout the day, were turned and fixed on Crawford, fixed on him for minutes, fixed on him in short till the attraction drew Crawford's upon her, and the book was closed, and the charm was broken. Then, she was shrinking again into herself, and blushing and working as hard as ever; but it had been enough to give Edmund encouragement for his friend, and as he cordially thanked him, he hoped to be expressing Fanny's secret feelings too.

"That play must be a favourite with you," said he; "You read as if you knew it well."

"It will be a favourite I believe from this hour," replied Crawford;— "but I do not think I have had a volume of Shakespeare in my hand before, since I was fifteen.[15]—I once saw Henry the 8th acted.—Or I have heard of it from somebody who did[16]—I am not certain which. But Shakespeare one gets acquainted with without knowing how. It is a part of an Englishman's constitution. His thoughts and beauties are so spread abroad[17] that one touches them every where, one is intimate with him by instinct.—No man of any brain can open at a good part of one of his plays, without falling into the flow of his meaning immediately."[18]

"No doubt, one is familiar with Shakespeare in a degree," said Edmund, "from one's earliest years. His celebrated passages are quoted by every body; they are in half the books we open, and we all talk Shakespeare, use his similes, and describe with his descrip-

14. Henry has shown this chameleon-like ability previously, and here he gives a particularly vivid display of it by embodying such a variety of emotions and characters, many of whom differ fundamentally from himself. This ability is one of the keys to his character, and it shapes his actions and decisions throughout the novel. For example, his love of flirtation is motivated, at least in part, by his enjoyment of playing the role of the lover, both for its intrinsic pleasures and because he knows how good he is at it—it was frustration at his initial failure in appealing to Fanny that first spurred him to devote himself to pursuing her.

15. He would have had it in his hands as a schoolboy. Tom Bertram earlier related how he and Edmund recited Shakespearean speeches as boys as part of their education, and in *Northanger Abbey* the heroine's education includes learning famous passages from Shakespeare.

16. *Henry VIII* is one of the least performed Shakespeare plays at present, in part because of the complex court and aristocratic intrigues that dominate it and in part because it lacks a strong overarching plot. At this time it was more popular: stage records indicate it was the fifteenth most performed play (out of thirty-seven) in the second half of the eighteenth century. One reason was the number of dramatic long speeches in the play, a feature more popular in drama of the time (and one that now gives Henry Crawford a chance to shine). Court and aristocratic intrigues also had greater relevance in a society in which the monarch and aristocracy still exercised great political power; moreover, the central event of Henry's reign, the replacement of Roman Catholicism by the Church of England as the official religion, was still highly relevant to a nation in which most people were strong religious believers, Protestantism was a crucial element in national identity, and legal rights for Catholics were a hotly contested political issue.

At the same time, Jane Austen's choice of this play is likely a joke at the expense of Henry Crawford, the man who now performs it so well and is the namesake of the title character. Just as Henry has been wooing one woman after another, so Henry VIII is most notorious for going through one wife after another: he divorced his first and fourth wives, Catherine of Aragon and Anne of Cleves, and beheaded his second and fifth, Anne Boleyn and Catherine Howard (his third, Jane Seymour, died after childbirth, and his last, Catherine Parr, outlived him).

17. *abroad*: among people in general, in the world.

18. Shakespeare had been regarded with great respect from the time when his plays first appeared, though he had suffered a partial eclipse from the mid-seventeenth century to the mid-eighteenth, due to the prevailing taste for French classical drama, which operated according to sharply different principles. But in the mid-1700s he experienced a revival, one that included

tions;[19] but this is totally distinct from giving his sense as you gave it. To know him in bits and scraps, is common enough; to know him pretty thoroughly, is, perhaps, not uncommon; but to read him well aloud, is no every-day talent."

"Sir, you do me honour;" was Crawford's answer, with a bow of mock gravity.

Both gentlemen had a glance at Fanny, to see if a word of accordant praise could be extorted from her; yet both feeling that it could not be. Her praise had been given in her attention; *that* must content them.

Lady Bertram's admiration was expressed, and strongly too. "It was really like being at a play,"[20] said she. — "I wish Sir Thomas had been here."

Crawford was excessively pleased. — If Lady Bertram, with all her incompetency and languor, could feel this, the inference of what her niece, alive and enlightened as she was, must feel, was elevating.[21]

"You have a great turn for acting, I am sure, Mr. Crawford," said her Ladyship soon afterwards — "and I will tell you what, I think you will have a theatre, some time or other, at your house in Norfolk. I mean when you are settled there. I do, indeed. I think you will fit up a theatre at your house in Norfolk."

"Do you, Ma'am?" cried he with quickness. "No, no, that will never be. Your Ladyship is quite mistaken. No theatre at Everingham! Oh! no." — And he looked at Fanny with an expressive smile, which evidently meant, "that lady will never allow a theatre at Everingham."

Edmund saw it all, and saw Fanny so determined *not* to see it, as to make it clear that the voice was enough to convey the full meaning of the protestation; and such a quick consciousness of compliment, such a ready comprehension of a hint, he thought, was rather favourable than not.

The subject of reading aloud was farther discussed. The two young men were the only talkers, but they, standing by the fire, talked over the too common neglect of the qualification,[22] the total inattention to it, in the ordinary school-system for boys,[23] the consequently natural — yet in some instances almost unnatural degree of ignorance and uncouthness of men, of sensible and well-informed men,

increased writing about him as well as special celebrations in his honor, and that led him to be seen as a national icon.

19. Jane Austen's works contain a number of allusions to or quotations from Shakespeare, and they are found throughout writings of the period, whether novels, poetry, essays, or other forms.

20. Caroline Austen, in her *My Aunt Jane Austen: A Memoir* (1867), says, "She [Jane Austen] was considered to read aloud remarkably well. I did not often hear her but *once* I knew her to take up a volume of Evelina [a novel by Frances or Fanny Burney] and read a few pages of Mr. Smith and the Brangtons and I thought it was like a play."

21. *elevating*: exhilarating.

22. *qualification*: accomplishment, skill.

23. Education, at the elite public schools for boys that both Edmund and Henry attended, centered around mastery of Latin and Greek, especially the former, and often focused on memorization of passages in those languages. Reading aloud in English, and especially reading in an effective rhetorical manner, would not figure much in it.

A church service.

[From William Combe, *The Dance of Life* (London, 1817; 1903 reprint), p. 243]

when suddenly called to the necessity of reading aloud, which had fallen within their notice,[24] giving instances of blunders, and failures with their secondary causes, the want of management of the voice, of proper modulation and emphasis, of foresight and judgment, all proceeding from the first cause, want of early attention and habit;[25] and Fanny was listening again with great entertainment.

"Even in my profession"—said Edmund with a smile—"how little the art of reading has been studied! how little a clear manner, and good delivery, have been attended to! I speak rather of the past, however, than the present.—There is now a spirit of improvement abroad;[26] but among those who were ordained twenty, thirty, forty years ago, the larger number, to judge by their performance, must have thought reading was reading, and preaching was preaching. It is different now. The subject is more justly considered. It is felt that distinctness and energy may have weight in recommending the most solid truths; and, besides, there is more general observation[27] and taste, a more critical knowledge diffused, than formerly; in every congregation, there is a larger proportion who know a little of the matter, and who can judge and criticize."[28]

Edmund had already gone through the service once since his ordination;[29] and upon this being understood, he had a variety of questions from Crawford as to his feelings and success; questions which being made—though with the vivacity of friendly interest and quick taste—without any touch of that spirit of banter or air of levity which Edmund knew to be most offensive to Fanny, he had true pleasure in satisfying; and when Crawford proceeded to ask his opinion and give his own as to the properest manner in which particular passages in the service should be delivered, shewing it to be a subject on which he had thought before, and thought with judgment,[30] Edmund was still more and more pleased. This would be the way to Fanny's heart. She was not to be won by all that gallantry and wit, and good nature together, could do; or at least, she would not be won by them nearly so soon, without the assistance of sentiment and feeling, and seriousness on serious[31] subjects.

"Our liturgy," observed Crawford, "has beauties, which not even a careless, slovenly style of reading can destroy; but it has also redundancies and repetitions, which require good reading not to be felt.

24. The principal professions for men of their rank, aside from the army and navy, were politics, the church, and the law (specifically those lawyers who could appear in court). In all three, public speaking would play a critical role.

25. The two men's careful distinction between a first or principal cause and a secondary cause, and their use of this terminology, reflects the influence of the principles of logic that were an important part of the education they received.

26. Edmund probably refers partly to a general spirit of improvement that was manifested in various spheres, including proposals for political reform and the technical and mechanical innovations of the Industrial Revolution that had recently begun in Britain; a domestic example of this last appeared in *Northanger Abbey*, where "the improving hand" of the hero's father introduced new mechanical contrivances to increase the efficiency of household tasks. The earlier speculations in this novel of improving the grounds at Sotherton represent another example. At the same time, Edmund is probably also thinking of changes within the church itself, whose practices had become lax in many respects in the eighteenth century and which was now, under the influence of the evangelical movement, experiencing growing efforts to revive piety and devotion, improve religious practice, spread religious principles more widely, and raise moral standards in society.

27. *observation*: perception.

28. The overall educational and cultural level of the clergy had gradually risen over the previous century. One reason was higher clerical salaries, the result of agricultural improvements that meant more money for tithes (see p. 617 for a contemporary illustration of paying tithes), and the consequent greater ability of the church to attract quality candidates. Another was a general spread of schooling and education in society. A third was the greater ability of clergy to learn about the outside world, due to better communication and transportation, and to read widely, due to lower costs of books.

29. This was part of his preparation for being the clergyman for a parish.

30. The improvement of sermon delivery was a subject of debate and discussion at the time, and various writers offered theories and suggestions regarding the best way of preaching. Henry's extensive discussion of the subject probably results, at least in part, from his hope to impress Fanny.

31. *serious*: religious (though it could have a more general meaning, as it probably also does here).

*

For myself, at least, I must confess being not always so attentive as I ought to be—(here was a glance at Fanny) that nineteen times out of twenty I am thinking how such a prayer ought to be read, and longing to have it to read myself [32]—Did you speak?" stepping eagerly to Fanny, and addressing her in a softened voice; and upon her saying, "No," he added, "Are you sure you did not speak? I saw your lips move. I fancied you might be going to tell me I *ought* to be more attentive, and not *allow* my thoughts to wander. Are not you going to tell me so?"

"No, indeed, you know your duty too well for me to—even supposing—"

She stopt, felt herself getting into a puzzle, and could not be prevailed on to add another word, not by dint of several minutes of supplication and waiting. He then returned to his former station, and went on as if there had been no such tender interruption.

"A sermon, well delivered, is more uncommon even than prayers well read. A sermon, good in itself, is no rare thing. It is more difficult to speak well than to compose well; that is, the rules and trick [33] of composition are oftener an object of study. [34] A thoroughly good sermon, thoroughly well delivered, is a capital gratification. I can never hear such a one without the greatest admiration and respect, and more than half a mind to take orders and preach myself. [35] There is something in the eloquence of the pulpit, when it is really eloquence, which is entitled to the highest praise and honour. The preacher who can touch and affect such an heterogeneous mass of hearers, on subjects limited, and long worn thread-bare in all common hands; who can say any thing new or striking, any thing that rouses the attention, without offending the taste, or wearing out the feelings of his hearers, [36] is a man whom one could not (in his public capacity) honour enough. I should like to be such a man."

Edmund laughed.

"I should indeed. I never listened to a distinguished preacher in my life, without a sort of envy. But then, I must have a London audience. I could not preach, but to the educated; to those who were capable of estimating my composition. [37] And I do not know that I should be fond of preaching often; now and then, perhaps, once or twice in the spring, after being anxiously expected for half a dozen

32. Anglican worship was characterized by a lengthy and elaborate liturgy, which included repetition of certain formulas and the expounding of central points in more than one place. Because most of it would be the same each Sunday, with some variations for different occasions or periods of the church calendar, a worshipper would hear the same ceremony repeatedly. This was generally regarded as a virtue; it could help reinforce the points in the congregations' minds and also emphasize the venerability of the traditional doctrines of the church, which was regarded as an argument in their favor. But someone like Henry, who does not have deep religious beliefs and who loves novelty, could naturally find it tiring and look for ways both to improve it and to divert his mind while he is forced to listen. His statement also reveals the strong aesthetic sense he displays on various occasions.

33. *trick*: art, knack.

34. Rules of composition were a common subject of books at the time, many of them designed to help people teach composition to children.

35. One sees Henry again imagining himself in a role, though as in many cases, his longing is more a reaction to the circumstances of the moment than something that leads to a lasting resolution.

36. Jane Austen would probably agree with part of what Henry says: in a letter from the year she finished this novel she speaks of a clergyman she heard preach for the first time and declares, "he gave us an excellent Sermon—a little too eager sometimes in his delivery, but that is to *me* a better extreme than the want of animation, especially when it comes from the heart as in him" (Sept. 25, 1813).

37. London churches in wealthy parts of town would have a congregation consisting mostly of the well-educated and culturally sophisticated; for a contemporary picture of a London church, showing the beautiful architecture that added to the attraction of many of those in the capital, see p. 619. A rural congregation would consist primarily of uneducated laborers and their families, with a smaller number of middle-class families, and even fewer genteel families.

Sundays together;[38] but not for a constancy; it would not do for a constancy."[39]

Here Fanny, who could not but listen, involuntarily shook her head, and Crawford was instantly by her side again, intreating to know her meaning; and as Edmund perceived, by his drawing in a chair, and sitting down close by her, that it was to be a very thorough attack, that looks and undertones were to be well tried, he sank as quietly as possible into a corner, turned his back, and took up a newspaper, very sincerely wishing that dear little Fanny might be persuaded into explaining away that shake of the head to the satisfaction of her ardent lover; and as earnestly trying to bury every sound of the business from himself in murmurs of his own, over the various advertisements of "a most desirable estate in South Wales"—"To Parents and Guardians"—and a "Capital season'd Hunter."[40]

Fanny, meanwhile, vexed with herself for not having been as motionless as she was speechless, and grieved to the heart to see Edmund's arrangements, was trying, by every thing in the power of her modest gentle nature, to repulse Mr. Crawford, and avoid both his looks and enquiries; and he unrepulsable was persisting in both.

"What did that shake of the head mean?" said he. "What was it meant to express? Disapprobation, I fear. But of what?—What had I been saying to displease you?—Did you think me speaking improperly?—lightly, irreverently on the subject?—Only tell me if I was. Only tell me if I was wrong. I want to be set right. Nay, nay, I entreat you; for one moment put down your work. What did that shake of the head mean?"

In vain was her "Pray, Sir, don't—pray, Mr. Crawford," repeated twice over; and in vain did she try to move away—In the same low eager voice, and the same close neighbourhood,[41] he went on, re-urging the same questions as before. She grew more agitated and displeased.

"How can you, Sir? You quite astonish me—I wonder how you can"—

"Do I astonish you?"—said he. "Do you wonder? Is there any thing in my present intreaty that you do not understand? I will explain to you instantly all that makes me urge you in this manner, all that

38. A regular minister would preach twice every Sunday, so Henry is proposing something very different.

39. *for a constancy*: as a permanent arrangement.

40. Advertising was common in newspapers; some papers even had "Advertiser" in their title and ads frequently appeared on the front page. The ads Henry reads are common types: the first is from someone selling or leasing an estate; the second could be from someone seeking an apprentice (and thus a child) or seeking employment as a governess or nurse in a family; the third is about selling a horse.

41. *neighbourhood*: vicinity.

Selling a horse.

[From William Combe, *The Tour of Doctor Syntax in Search of the Picturesque* (London, 1817; 1903 reprint), p. 134]

gives me an interest in what you look and do, and excites my present curiosity. I will not leave you to wonder long."

In spite of herself, she could not help half a smile, but she said nothing.

"You shook your head at my acknowledging that I should not like to engage in the duties of a clergyman always for a constancy. Yes, that was the word. Constancy, I am not afraid of the word. I would spell it, read it, write it with any body. I see nothing alarming in the word. Did you think I ought?"

"Perhaps, Sir," said Fanny, wearied at last into speaking — "perhaps, Sir, I thought it was a pity you did not always know yourself as well as you seemed to do at that moment."

Crawford, delighted to get her to speak at any rate, was determined to keep it up; and poor Fanny, who had hoped to silence him by such an extremity of reproof,[42] found herself sadly mistaken, and that it was only a change from one object of curiosity and one set of words to another. He had always something to intreat the explanation of. The opportunity was too fair. None such had occurred since his seeing her in her uncle's room, none such might occur again before his leaving Mansfield. Lady Bertram's being just on the other side of the table was a trifle, for she might always be considered as only half awake, and Edmund's advertisements were still of the first utility.

"Well," said Crawford, after a course of rapid questions and reluctant answers — "I am happier than I was, because I now understand more clearly your opinion of me. You think me unsteady — easily swayed by the whim of the moment — easily tempted — easily put aside. With such an opinion, no wonder that — But we shall see. — It is not by protestations that I shall endeavour to convince you I am wronged,[43] it is not by telling you that my affections are steady. My conduct shall speak for me — absence, distance, time shall speak for me. — *They* shall prove, that as far as you can be deserved by any body, I do deserve you. — You are infinitely my superior in merit; all *that* I know. — You have qualities which I had not before supposed to exist in such a degree in any human creature. You have some touches of the angel in you, beyond what — not merely beyond what one sees, because one never sees any thing like it — but beyond what one fancies might be. But still I am not frightened. It is not by equal-

42. Meaning the extreme nature of her reproof. In fact, it is extreme only in the eyes of someone like her, highly sensitive to others' harsh words and unwilling to use them herself.

43. *wronged*: maligned.

A clergyman receiving his tithes. Sometimes tithes would be paid in kind.

[From Malcolm Salaman, *Old English Colour Prints* (New York, 1909), Plate XXXI]

ity of merit that you can be won. That is out of the question. It is he
who sees and worships your merit the strongest, who loves you most
devotedly, that has the best right to a return. There I build my confidence. By that right I do and will deserve you; and when once convinced that my attachment is what I declare it, I know you too well
not to entertain the warmest hopes—Yes, dearest, sweetest Fanny—
Nay—(seeing her draw back displeased) forgive me.[44] Perhaps I have
as yet no right—but by what other name can I call you? Do you suppose you are ever present to my imagination under any other? No, it
is 'Fanny' that I think of all day, and dream of all night.—You have
given the name such reality of sweetness, that nothing else can now
be descriptive of you."

Fanny could hardly have kept her seat any longer, or have refrained
from at least trying to get away in spite of all the too public opposition she foresaw to it, had it not been for the sound of approaching
relief, the very sound which she had been long watching for, and
long thinking strangely delayed.

The solemn procession, headed by Baddeley, of tea-board, urn,
and cake-bearers, made its appearance,[45] and delivered her from a
grievous imprisonment of body and mind. Mr. Crawford was obliged
to move. She was at liberty, she was busy, she was protected.[46]

Edmund was not sorry to be admitted again among the number
of those who might speak and hear. But though the conference had
seemed full[47] long to him, and though on looking at Fanny he saw
rather a flush of vexation, he inclined to hope that so much could not
have been said and listened to, without some profit to the speaker.

44. She draws back because of the impropriety of his use of her first name.

45. This is a procession of the butler and some footmen with the tea things; in a grand house like this serving tea could be a highly formal ritual. A "tea-board" is a tea tray; on it are dishes and utensils as well as tea. The urn contains hot water for the tea.

46. She is now at liberty from being questioned, as she is busy making the tea, and she is protected from his continued presence by her side, since it would be rude for him to interfere with her task as well as the activities of serving and drinking and eating.

47. *full*: very.

St. Stephen, Walbrook, an elegant London church.

[From Fiona St. Aubyn, *Ackermann's Illustrated London,* illustrations by Augustus Pugin and Thomas Rowlandson (Ware, 1985), p. 29]

Chapter Four

*E*dmund had determined that it belonged entirely to Fanny to chuse whether her situation with regard to Crawford should be mentioned between them or not; and that if she did not lead the way, it should never be touched on by him; but after a day or two of mutual reserve,[1] he was induced by his father to change his mind, and try what his influence might do for his friend.

A day, and a very early day, was actually fixed for the Crawfords' departure; and Sir Thomas thought it might be as well to make one more effort for the young man before he left Mansfield, that all his professions and vows of unshaken attachment might have as much hope to sustain them as possible.

Sir Thomas was most cordially[2] anxious for the perfection of Mr. Crawford's character in that point. He wished him to be a model of constancy; and fancied the best means of effecting it would be by not trying him too long.

Edmund was not unwilling to be persuaded to engage in the business; he wanted to know Fanny's feelings. She had been used to consult him in every difficulty, and he loved her too well to bear to be denied her confidence now; he hoped to be of service to her, he thought he must be of service to her, whom else had she to open her heart to? If she did not need counsel, she must need the comfort of communication. Fanny estranged from him, silent and reserved, was an unnatural state of things; a state which he must break through, and which he could easily learn to think she was wanting him to break through.

"I will speak to her, Sir; I will take the first opportunity of speaking to her alone," was the result of such thoughts as these; and upon Sir Thomas's information of her being at that very time walking alone in the shrubbery, he instantly joined her.

"I am come to walk with you, Fanny," said he. "Shall I?" — (drawing her arm within his), "it is a long while since we have had a comfortable walk together."

1. *reserve*: reticence, nondisclosure.

2. *cordially*: heartily.

A woman drinking tea.

[From *The Repository of arts, literature, fashions, manufactures, &c*, Vol. XI (1814), p. 240]

She assented to it all rather by look than word. Her spirits were low.

"But, Fanny," he presently added, "in order to have a comfortable walk, something more is necessary than merely pacing this gravel together.[3] You must talk to me. I know you have something on your mind. I know what you are thinking of. You cannot suppose me uninformed. Am I to hear of it from every body but Fanny herself?"

Fanny, at once agitated and dejected, replied, "If you hear of it from every body, cousin, there can be nothing for me to tell."

"Not of facts, perhaps; but of feelings, Fanny. No one but you can tell me them. I do not mean to press you, however. If it is not what you wish yourself, I have done. I had thought it might be a relief."

"I am afraid we think too differently, for me to find any relief in talking of what I feel."

"Do you suppose that we think differently? I have no idea of it. I dare say, that on a comparison of our opinions, they would be found as much alike as they have been used to be: to the point—I consider Crawford's proposals as most advantageous and desirable, if you could return his affection. I consider it as most natural that all your family should wish you could return it; but that as you cannot, you have done exactly as you ought in refusing him. Can there be any disagreement between us here?"

"Oh no! But I thought you blamed me. I thought you were against me. This is such a comfort!"

"This comfort you might have had sooner, Fanny, had you sought it. But how could you possibly suppose me against you? How could you imagine me an advocate for marriage without love?[4] Were I even careless in general on such matters, how could you imagine me so where *your* happiness was at stake?"

"My uncle thought me wrong, and I knew he had been talking to you."

"As far as you have gone, Fanny, I think you perfectly right. I may be sorry, I may be surprised—though hardly *that*, for you had not had time to attach yourself; but I think you perfectly right. Can it admit of a question? It is disgraceful to us if it does. You did not love him—nothing could have justified your accepting him."

Fanny had not felt so comfortable for days and days.

3. The shrubbery was already described as having a gravel walk.

4. Jane Austen enunciated this principle in a letter, quoted on p. 573, note 35, and in a very similar passage in *Pride and Prejudice*: "do any thing rather than marry without affection." She followed this advice in her own life, for after accepting the offer of a man who was heir to a good property and could have offered her a much better home (at that point, before she had sold any novels, she was penniless and completely dependent on family charity), she decided the next day that her feelings for him did not justify marriage and she canceled the engagement, despite the resentment she knew this might arouse in the man's family, who were close with the Austens.

"So far your conduct has been faultless, and they were quite mistaken who wished you to do otherwise. But the matter does not end here. Crawford's is no common attachment; he perseveres, with the hope of creating that regard which had not been created before. This, we know, must be a work of time. But (with an affectionate smile), let him succeed at last, Fanny, let him succeed at last. You have proved yourself upright and disinterested, prove yourself grateful and tenderhearted; and then you will be the perfect model of a woman,[5] which I have always believed you born for."

"Oh! never, never, never; he never will succeed with me." And she spoke with a warmth which quite astonished Edmund, and which she blushed at the recollection of herself, when she saw his look, and heard him reply, "Never, Fanny, so very determined and positive! This is not like yourself, your rational self."

"I mean," she cried, sorrowfully, correcting herself, "that I *think*, I never shall, as far as the future can be answered for—I think I never shall return his regard."

"I must hope better things. I am aware, more aware than Crawford can be, that the man who means to make you love him (you having due notice of his intentions), must have very up-hill work, for there are all your early attachments, and habits, in battle array; and before he can get your heart for his own use, he has to unfasten it from all the holds upon things animate and inanimate, which so many years growth have confirmed, and which are considerably tightened for the moment by the very idea of separation. I know that the apprehension of being forced to quit Mansfield will for a time be arming you against him. I wish he had not been obliged to tell you what he was trying for. I wish he had known you as well as I do, Fanny. Between us, I think we should have won you. My theoretical and his practical knowledge together, could not have failed. He should have worked upon my plans. I must hope, however, that time proving him (as I firmly believe it will), to deserve you by his steady affection, will give him his reward. I cannot suppose that you have not the *wish* to love him—the natural wish of gratitude. You must have some feeling of that sort. You must be sorry for your own indifference."

"We are so totally unlike," said Fanny, avoiding a direct answer, "we are so very, very different in all our inclinations and ways, that I con-

5.   A tender heart was considered both a natural quality of a woman and a high virtue.

A man in daytime dress.

[From Elisabeth McClellan, *Historic Dress in America, 1800–1870* (Philadelphia, 1910), p. 421]

sider it as quite impossible we should ever be tolerably happy together, even if I *could* like him. There never were two people more dissimilar. We have not one taste in common. We should be miserable."

"You are mistaken, Fanny. The dissimilarity is not so strong. You are quite enough alike. You *have* tastes in common. You have moral and literary tastes in common. You have both warm hearts and benevolent feelings; and Fanny, who that heard him read, and saw you listen to Shakespeare the other night, will think you unfitted as companions? You forget yourself: there is a decided difference in your tempers,[6] I allow. He is lively,[7] you are serious; but so much the better;[8] his spirits will support yours. It is your disposition to be easily dejected, and to fancy difficulties greater than they are. His cheerfulness will counteract this. He sees difficulties no where; and his pleasantness and gaiety will be a constant support to you. Your being so far unlike, Fanny, does not in the smallest degree make against[9] the probability of your happiness together: do not imagine it. I am myself convinced that it is rather a favourable circumstance. I am perfectly persuaded that the tempers had better be unlike: I mean unlike in the flow of the spirits, in the manners, in the inclination for much or little company, in the propensity to talk or to be silent, to be grave or to be gay. Some opposition here is, I am thoroughly convinced, friendly to matrimonial happiness. I exclude extremes of course; and a very close resemblance in all those points would be the likeliest way to produce an extreme. A counteraction, gentle and continual, is the best safeguard of manners and conduct."

Full well could Fanny guess where his thoughts were now. Miss Crawford's power was all returning. He had been speaking of her cheerfully from the hour of his coming home. His avoiding her was quite at an end. He had dined at the parsonage only the preceding day.

After leaving him to his happier thoughts for some minutes, Fanny feeling it due to herself, returned to Mr. Crawford, and said, "It is not merely in *temper* that I consider him as totally unsuited to myself; though in *that* respect, I think the difference between us too great, infinitely too great; his spirits often oppress me—but there is something in him which I object to still more. I must say, cousin, that I cannot approve his character. I have not thought well of him from

6. *tempers*: dispositions, emotional qualities.

7. *lively*: merry, lighthearted.

8. He may also be thinking of himself and Mary here, for the same contrast exists between them.

9. *make against*: militate against, portend unfavorably toward.

the time of the play. I then saw him behaving, as it appeared to me, so very improperly and unfeelingly, I may speak of it now because it is all over—so improperly by poor Mr. Rushworth, not seeming to care how he exposed[10] or hurt him, and paying attentions to my cousin Maria, which—in short, at the time of the play, I received an impression which will never be got over."

"My dear Fanny," replied Edmund, scarcely hearing her to the end, "let us not, any of us, be judged by what we appeared at that period of general folly. The time of the play, is a time which I hate to recollect. Maria was wrong, Crawford was wrong, we were all wrong together; but none so wrong as myself. Compared with me, all the rest were blameless. I was playing the fool with my eyes open."[11]

"As a by-stander," said Fanny, "perhaps I saw more than you did; and I do think that Mr. Rushworth was sometimes very jealous."

"Very possibly. No wonder. Nothing could be more improper than the whole business. I am shocked whenever I think that Maria could be capable of it; but if she could undertake the part, we must not be surprised at the rest."

"Before the play, I am much mistaken, if *Julia* did not think he was paying her attentions."

"Julia!—I have heard before from some one of his being in love with Julia, but I could never see any thing of it. And Fanny, though I hope I do justice to my sisters' good qualities, I think it very possible that they might, one or both, be more desirous of being admired by Crawford, and might shew that desire rather more unguardedly than was perfectly prudent.[12] I can remember that they were evidently fond of his society; and with such encouragement, a man like Crawford, lively, and it may be a little unthinking, might be led on to—There could be nothing very striking, because it is clear that he had no pretensions; his heart was reserved for you. And I must say, that its being for you, has raised him inconceivably in my opinion. It does him the highest honour; it shews his proper estimation of the blessing of domestic happiness, and pure attachment. It proves him unspoilt by his uncle. It proves him, in short, every thing that I had been used to wish to believe him, and feared he was not."

"I am persuaded that he does not think as he ought, on serious subjects."

10. *exposed*: caused to look ridiculous.

11. This is another effect of Edmund's participation in the play: in addition to being too busy at the time to notice what Fanny did, he is currently too full of regrets about his own conduct to attend carefully to her discussion of others' more serious faults.

12. While Edmund's refusal to heed Fanny stems partly from his own regrets, and his focus on his romance with Mary, it also results from how subtle and skillful Henry was in his flirtation, so that only a careful and attentive observer would have noticed.

"Say rather, that he has not thought at all upon serious subjects, which I believe to be a good deal the case. How could it be otherwise, with such an education and adviser? Under the disadvantages, indeed, which both have had, is it not wonderful that they should be what they are? Crawford's *feelings*, I am ready to acknowledge, have hitherto been too much his guides. Happily, those feelings have generally been good.[13] You will supply the rest; and a most fortunate man he is to attach himself to such a creature—to a woman, who firm as a rock in her own principles, has a gentleness of character so well adapted to recommend them. He has chosen his partner, indeed, with rare felicity. He will make you happy, Fanny, I know he will make you happy; but you will make him every thing."

"I would not engage in such a charge," cried Fanny in a shrinking accent—"in such an office of high responsibility!"

"As usual, believing yourself unequal to anything!—fancying every thing too much for you! Well, though I may not be able to persuade you into different feelings, you will be persuaded into them I trust. I confess myself sincerely anxious that you may. I have no common interest in Crawford's well doing. Next to your happiness, Fanny, his has the first claim on me. You are aware of my having no common interest in Crawford."

Fanny was too well aware of it, to have anything to say; and they walked on together some fifty yards in mutual silence and abstraction. Edmund first began again:—

"I was very much pleased by her manner of speaking of it yesterday, particularly pleased, because I had not depended upon her seeing every thing in so just a light. I knew she was very fond of you, but yet I was afraid of her not estimating your worth to her brother, quite as it deserved, and of her regretting that he had not rather fixed on some woman of distinction,[14] or fortune. I was afraid of the bias of those worldly maxims, which she has been too much used to hear. But it was very different. She spoke of you, Fanny, just as she ought. She desires the connection[15] as warmly as your uncle or myself. We had a long talk about it. I should not have mentioned the subject, though very anxious to know her sentiments—but I had not been in the room five minutes, before she began, introducing it with all that openness of heart, and sweet peculiarity of manner, that spirit

13. Edmund's words touch on an important philosophical discussion in the eighteenth century. While traditional moral philosophies had focused on the need for reason or religion as the source of morality, and the guide to which people should turn, a new school of thought in the eighteenth century focused on the idea of the moral sense—inner feelings of goodness considered to be either innate or the natural product of human social life—as the source of morality. Edmund espouses the traditional emphasis on a source higher than feeling, as Jane Austen does at various points in her writings, but he also is willing to argue for a man's good feelings as offering at least a strong basis for hope of his acting well.

14. *distinction*: high rank.

15. *connection*: marriage, or link through marriage. All could be thinking of how a marriage between Fanny and Henry would link the two families closer together.

and ingenuousness, which are so much a part of herself. Mrs. Grant laughed at her for her rapidity."

"Was Mrs. Grant in the room, then?"[16]

"Yes, when I reached the house I found the two sisters together by themselves; and when once we had begun, we had not done with you, Fanny, till Crawford and Dr. Grant came in."

"It is above a week since I saw Miss Crawford."

"Yes, she laments it; yet owns it may have been best. You will see her, however, before she goes. She is very angry with you, Fanny; you must be prepared for that. She calls herself very angry, but you can imagine her anger. It is the regret and disappointment of a sister, who thinks her brother has a right to every thing he may wish for, at the first moment. She is hurt, as you would be for William; but she loves and esteems you with all her heart."

"I knew she would be very angry with me."

"My dearest Fanny," cried Edmund, pressing her arm closer to him, "do not let the idea of her anger distress you. It is anger to be talked of, rather than felt. Her heart is made for love and kindness, not for resentment. I wish you could have overheard her tribute of praise; I wish you could have seen her countenance, when she said that you *should* be Henry's wife. And I observed, that she always spoke of you as 'Fanny,' which she was never used to do; and it had a sound of most sisterly cordiality."

"And Mrs. Grant, did she say—did she speak—was she there all the time?"

"Yes, she was agreeing exactly with her sister. The surprise of your refusal, Fanny, seems to have been unbounded. That you could refuse such a man as Henry Crawford, seems more than they can understand. I said what I could for you; but in good truth, as they stated the case—you must prove yourself to be in your senses as soon as you can, by a different conduct; nothing else will satisfy them. But this is teazing you. I have done. Do not turn away from me."

"I *should* have thought," said Fanny, after a pause of recollection[17] and exertion, "that every woman must have felt the possibility of a man's not being approved, not being loved by some one of her sex, at least, let him be ever so generally agreeable. Let him have all the perfections in the world, I think it ought not to be set down as cer-

16. Since Henry has had no hesitation in telling others of his proposal, Mrs. Grant would know, and Fanny would be aware of that, but she still finds it distressing to have so many people discussing her and her affairs.

17. *recollection*: regaining her composure.

tain, that a man must be acceptable to every woman he may happen to like himself. But even supposing it is so, allowing Mr. Crawford to have all the claims which his sisters think he has, how was I to be prepared to meet him with any feeling answerable to his own? He took me wholly by surprise. I had not an idea that his behaviour to me before had any meaning; and surely I was not to be teaching myself to like him only because he was taking, what seemed, very idle notice of me. In my situation, it would have been the extreme of vanity to be forming expectations on Mr. Crawford. I am sure his sisters, rating him as they do, must have thought it so, supposing he had meant nothing. How then was I to be—to be in love with him the moment he said he was with me? How was I to have an attachment at his service, as soon as it was asked for? His sisters should consider me as well as him. The higher his deserts, the more improper for me ever to have thought of him. And, and—we think very differently of the nature of women, if they can imagine a woman so very soon capable of returning an affection as this seems to imply."

"My dear, dear Fanny, now I have the truth. I know this to be the truth; and most worthy of you are such feelings. I had attributed them to you before. I thought I could understand you. You have now given exactly the explanation which I ventured to make for you to your friend and Mrs. Grant, and they were both better satisfied, though your warm-hearted friend was still run away with a little, by the enthusiasm of her fondness for Henry. I told them, that you were of all human creatures the one, over whom habit had most power, and novelty least: and that the very circumstance of the novelty of Crawford's addresses[18] was against him. Their being so new and so recent was all in their disfavour; that you could tolerate nothing that you were not used to; and a great deal more to the same purpose, to give them a knowledge of your character. Miss Crawford made us laugh by her plans of encouragement for her brother. She meant to urge him to persevere in the hope of being loved in time, and of having his addresses most kindly received at the end of about ten years' happy marriage."

Fanny could with difficulty give the smile that was here asked for. Her feelings were all in revolt. She feared she had been doing wrong, saying too much, overacting the caution which she had been fancy-

18. *addresses*: courtship, application for marriage.

A woman taking a walk.

[From *The Repository of arts, literature, fashions, manufactures, &c,* Vol. VII (1812), p. 120]

ing necessary, in guarding against one evil, laying herself open to another, and to have Miss Crawford's liveliness[19] repeated to her at such a moment, and on such a subject, was a bitter aggravation.

Edmund saw weariness and distress in her face, and immediately resolved to forbear all farther discussion; and not even to mention the name of Crawford again, except as it might be connected with what *must* be agreeable to her. On this principle, he soon afterwards observed, "They go on Monday. You are sure therefore of seeing your friend either to-morrow or Sunday. They really go on Monday! and I was within a trifle of being persuaded to stay at Lessingby till that very day![20] I had almost promised it. What a difference it might have made! Those five or six days more at Lessingby might have been felt all my life!"[21]

"You were near staying there?"

"Very. I was most kindly pressed, and had nearly consented. Had I received any letter from Mansfield, to tell me how you were all going on, I believe I should certainly have stayed; but I knew nothing that had happened here for a fortnight, and felt that I had been away long enough."

"You spent your time pleasantly there."

"Yes; that is, it was the fault of my own mind if I did not. They were all very pleasant. I doubt their finding me so. I took uneasiness with me, and there was no getting rid of it till I was in Mansfield again."

"The Miss Owens—you liked them, did not you?"

"Yes, very well. Pleasant, good-humoured, unaffected girls. But I am spoilt, Fanny, for common female society. Good-humoured, unaffected girls, will not do for a man who has been used to sensible women. They are two distinct orders of being. You and Miss Crawford have made me too nice."[22]

Still, however, Fanny was oppressed and wearied; he saw it in her looks; it could not be talked away, and attempting it no more, he led her directly with the kind authority of a privileged guardian into the house.

19. *liveliness*: jocular or playful talk.

20. Lessingby is where he was staying while away; it could be the name of a village, or of the family's residence. It is not a real place.

21. Thus his return at this time has allowed him to rekindle the romance between him and Mary. It has not, however, led to a proposal, perhaps because she is leaving so soon. Had he returned in a week as he initially planned, instead of staying more than two weeks (see p. 512 and chronology, p. 858), there might have been sufficient time for their relationship to become close enough to inspire him to propose, and her to accept. But he stayed away longer because of her coldness and apparent rejection of him at the ball.

22. *nice*: demanding, particular.

Chapter Five

*E*dmund now believed himself perfectly acquainted with all that Fanny could tell, or could leave to be conjectured of her sentiments, and he was satisfied.—It had been, as he before presumed, too hasty a measure on Crawford's side, and time must be given to make the idea first familiar, and then agreeable to her. She must be used to the consideration of his being in love with her, and then a return of affection might not be very distant.

He gave this opinion as the result of the conversation, to his father; and recommended there being nothing more said to her, no farther attempts to influence or persuade; but that every thing should be left to Crawford's assiduities, and the natural workings of her own mind.

Sir Thomas promised that it should be so. Edmund's account of Fanny's disposition he could believe to be just, he supposed she had all those feelings, but he must consider it as very unfortunate that she *had*; for, less willing than his son to trust to the future, he could not help fearing that if such very long allowances of time and habit were necessary for her, she might not have persuaded herself into receiving his addresses properly, before the young man's inclination for paying them were over. There was nothing to be done, however, but to submit quietly, and hope the best.

The promised visit from her "friend," as Edmund called Miss Crawford, was a formidable threat to Fanny, and she lived in continual terror of it. As a sister, so partial and so angry, and so little scrupulous of what she said; and in another light,¹ so triumphant and secure,² she was in every way an object of painful alarm. Her displeasure, her penetration,³ and her happiness were all fearful to encounter; and the dependence⁴ of having others present when they met, was Fanny's only support in looking forward to it. She absented herself as little as possible from Lady Bertram, kept away from the east room, and took no solitary walk in the shrubbery, in her caution to avoid any sudden attack.

1. The "other light" is as a rival for Edmund's love.

2. *secure*: certain, confident (of Edmund's affection).

3. *penetration*: discernment, keenness of perception.

4. *dependence*: expectation.

She succeeded. She was safe in the breakfast-room, with her aunt, when Miss Crawford did come;[5] and the first misery over, and Miss Crawford looking and speaking with much less particularity of expression than she had anticipated, Fanny began to hope there would be nothing worse to be endured than an half-hour of moderate agitation. But here she hoped too much, Miss Crawford was not the slave of opportunity. She was determined to see Fanny alone, and therefore said to her tolerably soon, in a low voice, "I must speak to you for a few minutes somewhere"; words that Fanny felt all over her, in all her pulses, and all her nerves. Denial was impossible. Her habits of ready submission, on the contrary, made her almost instantly rise and lead the way out of the room. She did it with wretched feelings, but it was inevitable.

They were no sooner in the hall than all restraint of countenance was over on Miss Crawford's side. She immediately shook her head at Fanny with arch, yet affectionate reproach, and taking her hand, seemed hardly able to help beginning directly. She said nothing, however, but, "Sad, sad girl! I do not know when I shall have done scolding you," and had discretion enough to reserve the rest till they might be secure of having four walls to themselves. Fanny naturally turned up stairs, and took her guest to the apartment which was now always fit for comfortable use; opening the door, however, with a most aching heart, and feeling that she had a more distressing scene before her than ever that spot had yet witnessed.[6] But the evil ready to burst on her, was at least delayed by the sudden change in Miss Crawford's ideas;[7] by the strong effect on her mind which the finding herself in the east room again produced.

"Ha!" she cried, with instant animation, "am I here again? The east room. Once only was I in this room before!"—and after stopping to look about her, and seemingly to retrace all that had then passed, she added, "Once only before. Do you remember it? I came to rehearse. Your cousin came too; and we had a rehearsal. You were our audience and prompter. A delightful rehearsal. I shall never forget it. Here we were, just in this part of the room; here was your cousin, here was I, here were the chairs.—Oh! why will such things ever pass away?"

Happily for her companion, she wanted no answer. Her mind

5.   They are sitting in the breakfast room, not eating (breakfast itself would be too early for normal calls). Descriptions at other points indicate the breakfast room is a general sitting room for the morning. It probably faces east to capture the morning sun.

6.   In this room she earlier witnessed both Mary and Edmund's rehearsal of their affectionate scene from *Lovers' Vows*, and the bitter and painful scene when Sir Thomas called her ungrateful for refusing Henry. Those two scenes, especially the latter, were probably more distressing than anything she is likely to experience now, but Fanny's fearfulness makes her tend to exaggerate possible future distresses.

7.   *ideas*: thoughts.

A morning room of the period.

[From John Swarbrick, *Robert Adam and his Brothers* (New York, 1915), p. 243]

was entirely self-engrossed. She was in a reverie of sweet remembrances.

"The scene we were rehearsing was so very remarkable! The subject of it so very—very—what shall I say? He was to be describing and recommending matrimony to me. I think I see him now, trying to be as demure and composed as Anhalt ought, through the two long speeches. 'When two sympathetic hearts meet in the marriage state, matrimony may be called a happy life.'[8] I suppose no time can ever wear out the impression I have of his looks and voice, as he said those words. It was curious, very curious, that we should have such a scene to play! If I had the power of recalling any one week of my existence, it should be that week, that acting week. Say what you would, Fanny,[9] it should be *that*;[10] for I never knew such exquisite happiness in any other. His sturdy spirit to bend as it did! Oh! it was sweet beyond expression.[11] But alas! that very evening destroyed it all. That very evening brought your most unwelcome uncle. Poor Sir Thomas, who was glad to see you? Yet, Fanny, do not imagine I would now speak disrespectfully of Sir Thomas, though I certainly did hate him for many a week. No, I do him justice now. He is just what the head of such a family should be. Nay, in sober sadness,[12] I believe I now love you all." And having said so, with a degree of tenderness and consciousness which Fanny had never seen in her before, and now thought only too becoming, she turned away for a moment to recover herself. "I have had a little fit since I came into this room, as you may perceive," said she presently, with a playful smile, "but it is over now; so let us sit down and be comfortable; for as to scolding you, Fanny, which I came fully intending to do, I have not the heart for it when it comes to the point." And embracing her very affectionately,—"Good, gentle Fanny! when I think of this being the last time of seeing you; for I do not know how long—I feel it quite impossible to do any thing but love you."

Fanny was affected.[13] She had not foreseen anything of this, and her feelings could seldom withstand the melancholy influence of the word "last." She cried as if she had loved Miss Crawford more than she possibly could; and Miss Crawford, yet farther softened by the sight of such emotion, hung about her with fondness, and said, "I hate to leave you. I shall see no one half so amiable[14] where I am going. Who says we shall not be sisters? I know we shall. I feel that

8.   This is the beginning of a long speech during the extended scene where Amelia and Anhalt end up declaring their love for each other, in which Anhalt evokes the beauty and joy of a harmonious marriage. In saying "two speeches" she may be thinking of the companion speech, coming immediately after, in which Anhalt evokes the horrors of a marriage of disharmony. She would naturally prefer to remember the opening lines of the first speech. Anhalt is supposed to remain very composed, for he is trying to act as Amelia's tutor and moral guide. Mary's words suggest that Edmund, who by general accounts was not a very good actor, had trouble maintaining sufficient composure.

9.   Here and elsewhere Mary calls her "Fanny," while Fanny continues to say "Miss Crawford." Mary's usage is negligent by the rules of the day, especially since Fanny's indicates she does not agree that they are sufficiently intimate friends to justify such familiarity.

10.   She alludes to Fanny's disapproval of their acting.

11.   It is notable that what is most sweet to her is the feeling of power at having bent another's will to her own.

12.   *sober sadness*: dispassionate seriousness or earnestness.

13.   *affected*: moved.

14.   *amiable*: kind, good-natured, worthy of being loved.

we are born to be connected; and those tears convince me that you feel it too, dear Fanny."

Fanny roused herself, and replying only in part, said, "But you are only going from one set of friends to another. You are going to a very particular friend."

"Yes, very true. Mrs. Fraser has been my intimate friend for years. But I have not the least inclination to go near her. I can think only of the friends I am leaving; my excellent sister, yourself, and the Bertrams in general. You have all so much more *heart* among you, than one finds in the world at large. You all give me a feeling of being able to trust and confide in you; which, in common intercourse, one knows nothing of. I wish I had settled with Mrs. Fraser not to go to her till after Easter, a much better time for the visit—but now I cannot put her off. And when I have done with her, I must go to her sister, Lady Stornaway, because *she* was rather my most particular friend of the two; but I have not cared much for *her* these three years."

After this speech, the two girls sat many minutes silent, each thoughtful; Fanny meditating on the different sorts of friendship in the world,[15] Mary on something of less philosophic tendency. *She* first spoke again.

"How perfectly I remember my resolving to look for you up stairs; and setting off to find my way to the east room, without having an idea whereabouts it was! How well I remember what I was thinking of as I came along; and my looking in and seeing you here, sitting at this table at work; and then your cousin's astonishment when he opened the door at seeing me here! To be sure, your uncle's returning that very evening! There never was anything quite like it."

Another short fit of abstraction followed—when, shaking it off, she thus attacked her companion.

"Why, Fanny, you are absolutely in a reverie! Thinking, I hope, of one who is always thinking of you. Oh! that I could transport you for a short time into our circle in town, that you might understand how your power over Henry is thought of there! Oh! the envyings and heart-burnings of dozens and dozens! the wonder, the incredulity that will be felt at hearing what you have done! For as to secrecy, Henry is quite the hero of an old romance, and glories in his chains.[16] You should come to London, to know how to estimate

15. Fanny is reacting to Mary's calling Mrs. Fraser and Lady Stornaway her "intimate friend for years" and her "most particular friend" while also proclaiming her disinclination to see either of them. Mary says this in part to contrast her longtime and putatively close London friends with her more recent and more genuine Mansfield ones. But she also seems unaware of how contradictory her words are. The contradiction stems from being decent and sensitive enough to recognize the faults of her fashionable friends but still devoted enough to the world of smart London society to be unable to cease her attachment to it. Notably, she recognizes how different her Mansfield friends (most notably Fanny and Edmund) are in fundamental qualities of kindness and trustworthiness from her previous acquaintance. At the same time, she fails to perceive that they have those qualities in part because they are not products of Mary's London world and have interests and principles completely opposed to it.

16. A romance at this time meant a story that was usually set in distant times and places and involved larger-than-life characters and incidents. A novel, in contrast, generally meant a story set in the current world, with characters and situations like those in ordinary life. Jane Austen often ridiculed romances for their extravagances and lack of realism, and when asked to write one, responded that "I could not sit seriously down to write a serious Romance under any other motive than to save my Life, & if it were indispensable for me to keep it up & never relax into laughing at myself or other people, I am sure I should be hung before I had finished the first Chapter" (April 1, 1816). Romances had been the dominant type of narrative literature prior to the eighteenth century, when novels, as defined here, first emerged as a major genre. These romances, especially the older ones, often included lovers who were absolutely devoted to each other and ready to make any sacrifice, and often placed them in situations where they were forced to undergo great ordeals for the sake of their love. Many were influenced by medieval ideas of chivalry, which could involve a male lover binding himself by an oath to his beloved and never being able to renounce her no matter how much he suffers or what obstacles arise. In presenting himself as such a character Henry is again adopting a new role, and undoubtedly enjoying the attention and comment it attracts—though without necessarily being insincere in his devotion to Fanny.

your conquest. If you were to see how he is courted, and how I am courted for his sake! Now I am well aware, that I shall not be half so welcome to Mrs. Fraser in consequence of his situation with you. When she comes to know the truth, she will very likely wish me in Northamptonshire again;[17] for there is a daughter of Mr. Fraser by a first wife, whom she is wild to get married, and wants Henry to take.[18] Oh! she has been trying for him to such a degree! Innocent and quiet as you sit here, you cannot have an idea of the *sensation* that you will be occasioning, of the curiosity there will be to see you, of the endless questions I shall have to answer! Poor Margaret Fraser will be at me for ever about your eyes and your teeth, and how you do your hair, and who makes your shoes.[19] I wish Margaret were married, for my poor friend's sake, for I look upon the Frasers to be about as unhappy as most other married people. And yet it was a most desirable match for Janet at the time. We were all delighted. She could not do otherwise than accept him, for he was rich, and she had nothing;[20] but he turns out ill-tempered, and *exigeant*;[21] and wants a young woman, a beautiful young woman of five-and-twenty, to be as steady as himself.[22] And my friend does not manage him well; she does not seem to know how to make the best of it. There is a spirit of irritation, which, to say nothing worse, is certainly very ill-bred. In their house I shall call to mind the conjugal manners of Mansfield Parsonage with respect. Even Dr. Grant does shew a thorough confidence in my sister, and a certain consideration for her judgment, which makes one feel there *is* attachment; but of that, I shall see nothing with the Frasers. I shall be at Mansfield for ever, Fanny.[23] My own sister as a wife, Sir Thomas Bertram as a husband, are my standards of perfection. Poor Janet has been sadly taken in;[24] and yet there was nothing improper on her side; she did not run into the match inconsiderately,[25] there was no want of foresight. She took three days to consider of his proposals; and during those three days asked the advice of every body connected with her, whose opinion was worth having;[26] and especially applied to my late dear aunt, whose knowledge of the world made her judgment very generally and deservedly looked up to by all the young people of her acquaintance; and she was decidedly in favour of Mr. Fraser. This seems as if nothing were a security for matrimonial

17. Presumably she will resent Mary because of Henry's behavior.

18. Her motive is likely a wish to get rid of this stepdaughter, who probably creates complications in her household. This, like her resentment of Mary, signals the nature of her character.

19. At this time shoes could be bought ready-made, but they also could be custom ordered to fit the individual buyer. Mary's friends in London, being wealthy and very concerned with fashion and looks (as shown by their asking only about Fanny's appearance, rather than any other quality), would have their own shoes specially made, and assume that others would likewise.

20. This shows the mercenary attitude to marriage that makes Fanny such a wonder, and also echoes Lady Bertram's comment about a duty to accept an offer from a wealthy and high-ranking man.

21. exigeant: exacting, demanding. The word is in italics because it is a French word that had not become standard English.

22. This suggests he is much older. The marriage of a rich old man with a beautiful young woman, and the frequent infidelity of the latter, was a common subject of satire.

23. She means she will have Mansfield continually in her thoughts.

24. This case probably played a significant role in Mary's earlier statement that everyone is taken in, i.e., deceived, in marriage (p. 90).

25. inconsiderately: rashly, carelessly.

26. According to Mary, taking three days to consider a marriage proposal and inquire about the groom means there was no want, or lack, of foresight.

comfort![27] I have not so much to say for my friend Flora, who jilted a very nice young man in the Blues,[28] for the sake of that horrid Lord Stornaway, who has about as much sense, Fanny, as Mr. Rushworth, but much worse looking, and with a blackguard character. I *had* my doubts at the time about her being right, for he has not even the air of a gentleman, and now, I am sure, she was wrong. By the by, Flora Ross was dying for Henry the first winter she came out. But were I to attempt to tell you of all the women whom I have known to be in love with him, I should never have done. It is you only, you, insensible Fanny, who can think of him with any thing like indifference. But are you so insensible as you profess yourself? No, no, I see you are not."

There was indeed so deep a blush over Fanny's face at that moment, as might warrant strong suspicion in a predisposed mind.

"Excellent creature! I will not teaze you. Every thing shall take its course. But dear Fanny, you must allow that you were not so absolutely unprepared to have the question asked as your cousin fancies. It is not possible, but that you must have had some thoughts on the subject, some surmises as to what might be. You must have seen that he was trying to please you, by every attention in his power. Was not he devoted to you at the ball? And then before the ball, the necklace! Oh! you received it just as it was meant. You were as conscious as heart could desire. I remember it perfectly."

"Do you mean then that your brother knew of the necklace beforehand? Oh! Miss Crawford, *that* was not fair."

"Knew of it! it was his own doing entirely, his own thought. I am ashamed to say, that it had never entered my head; but I was delighted to act on his proposal, for both your sakes."

"I will not say," replied Fanny, "that I was not half afraid at the time of its being so;[29] for there was something in your look that frightened me—but not at first—I was as unsuspicious of it at first!—indeed, indeed I was. It is as true as that I sit here. And had I had an idea of it, nothing should have induced me to accept the necklace. As to your brother's behaviour, certainly I was sensible of a particularity, I had been sensible of it some little time, perhaps two or three weeks; but then I considered it as meaning nothing, I put it down as simply being his way, and was as far from supposing as from wishing him to

27. This is an example of Jane Austen's technique of allowing a character to reveal, and condemn, herself through her own words. She draws the sweeping conclusion that her friend's failure shows there is no way to know how a marriage will turn out, instead of drawing the more logical inference that there was a problem in her friend's method or in the reliability of the people she consulted.

28. "The Blues" is the Royal Horse Guard Blues, an elite cavalry regiment based in London that acted as royal bodyguards and that was very prestigious.

29. For Mary's maneuvering, Fanny's suspicions, and Henry's reaction to seeing the necklace on Fanny, which strengthened her suspicions, see pp. 466–472 and 498.

have any serious thoughts of me. I had not, Miss Crawford, been an inattentive observer of what was passing between him and some part of this family in the summer and autumn. I was quiet, but I was not blind. I could not but see that Mr. Crawford allowed himself in[30] gallantries which did mean nothing."

"Ah! I cannot deny it. He has now and then been a sad flirt, and cared very little for the havock he might be making in young ladies' affections. I have often scolded him for it, but it is his only fault; and there is this to be said, that very few young ladies have any affections worth caring for. And then, Fanny, the glory of fixing[31] one who has been shot at by so many; of having it in one's power to pay off the debts of one's sex! Oh, I am sure it is not in woman's nature to refuse such a triumph."[32]

Fanny shook her head. "I cannot think well of a man who sports[33] with any woman's feelings; and there may often be a great deal more suffered than a stander-by[34] can judge of."[35]

"I do not defend him. I leave him entirely to your mercy; and when he has got you at Everingham, I do not care how much you lecture him. But this I will say, that his fault, the liking to make girls a little in love with him, is not half so dangerous to a wife's happiness, as a tendency to fall in love himself, which he has never been addicted to. And I do seriously and truly believe that he is attached to you in a way that he never was to any woman before; that he loves you with all his heart, and will love you as nearly for ever as possible. If any man ever loved a woman for ever, I think Henry will do as much for you."

Fanny could not avoid a faint smile, but had nothing to say.

"I cannot imagine Henry ever to have been happier," continued Mary, presently, "than when he had succeeded in getting your brother's commission."

She had made a sure push at Fanny's feelings here.

"Oh! yes. How very, very kind of him!"

"I know he must have exerted himself very much, for I know the parties he had to move. The Admiral hates trouble, and scorns asking favours; and there are so many young men's claims to be attended to in the same way,[36] that a friendship and energy, not very determined, is easily put by.[37] What a happy creature William must be! I wish we could see him."

30. *allowed himself in*: permitted himself to indulge in.

31. *fixing*: securing the affection of.

32. Again Mary sees triumphing over another as the most glorious pleasure and achievement in love. She also reveals a contradictory attitude toward her own sex, calling for Fanny to get revenge for the wrongs suffered by women just after she has declared the worthlessness of most ladies' affections. Two pretentious characters, Miss Bingley in *Pride and Prejudice* and Mrs. Elton in *Emma*, express similarly contradictory sentiments on questions of female value or rights.

33. *sports*: amuses himself.

34. *stander-by*: bystander.

35. Fanny's statement is interesting, since she was a bystander who observed keenly the relationship of Julia and Maria with Henry, and Julia's misery when he chose Maria. She may be suggesting that less attentive bystanders like Mary failed to observe nearly as much, or she may be ackowledging the limitations of her observations, and suggesting that the wounded feelings may be even worse than what she perceived.

36. There were more young men like William seeking promotion than could be satisfied, and a man like Admiral Crawford probably would receive many pleas for assistance.

37. *put by*: set aside.

Poor Fanny's mind was thrown into the most distressing of all its varieties.[38] The recollection of what had been done for William was always the most powerful disturber of every decision against Mr. Crawford; and she sat thinking deeply of it till Mary, who had been first watching her complacently, and then musing on something else, suddenly called her attention, by saying, "I should like to sit talking with you here all day, but we must not forget the ladies below, and so good bye, my dear, my amiable, my excellent Fanny, for though we shall nominally part in the breakfast-parlour, I must take leave of you here. And I do take leave, longing for a happy re-union, and trusting, that when we meet again, it will be under circumstances which may open our hearts to each other without any remnant or shadow of reserve."

A very, very kind embrace, and some agitation of manner, accompanied these words.

"I shall see your cousin in town soon; he talks of being there tolerably soon; and Sir Thomas, I dare say, in the course of the spring;[39] and your eldest cousin and the Rushworths and Julia I am sure of meeting again and again, and all but you. I have two favours to ask, Fanny; one is your correspondence. You must write to me. And the other, that you will often call on Mrs. Grant and make her amends for my being gone."

The first, at least, of these favours Fanny would rather not have been asked; but it was impossible for her to refuse the correspondence; it was impossible for her even not to accede to it more readily than her own judgment authorized. There was no resisting so much apparent affection. Her disposition was peculiarly calculated[40] to value a fond treatment, and from having hitherto known so little of it, she was the more overcome by Miss Crawford's. Besides, there was gratitude towards her, for having made their tête à tête so much less painful than her fears had predicted.

It was over, and she had escaped without reproaches and without detection. Her secret was still her own; and while that was the case, she thought she could resign herself to almost every thing.

In the evening there was another parting. Henry Crawford came and sat some time with them; and her spirits not being previously in the strongest state, her heart was softened for a while towards him —

38. *varieties*: variations.

39. Spring was the standard time for the meeting of Parliament, of which Sir Thomas is a member.

40. *calculated*: suited, apt.

because he really seemed to feel.—Quite unlike his usual self, he scarcely said any thing. He was evidently oppressed,[41] and Fanny must grieve for him, though hoping she might never see him again till he were the husband of some other woman.

When it came to the moment of parting, he would take her hand, he would not be denied it; he said nothing, however, or nothing that she heard, and when he had left the room, she was better pleased that such a token of friendship had passed.[42]

On the morrow the Crawfords were gone.

41. *oppressed*: depressed.

42. *passed*: been conveyed. Her pleasure indicates some softening in her attitude toward him, though she still thinks of him only as a friend, and she can feel pleased only once he has left the room.

A contemporary portrait of an aristocratic woman (the Countess of Dysart).

[From Sir Walter Armstrong, *Lawrence* (London, 1913), p. 38]

Chapter Six

*M*r. Crawford gone, Sir Thomas's next object was, that he should be missed, and he entertained great hope that his niece would find a blank in the loss of those attentions which at the time she had felt, or fancied an evil. She had tasted of consequence in its most flattering form; and he did hope that the loss of it, the sinking again into nothing, would awaken very wholesome regrets in her mind.—He watched her with this idea—but he could hardly tell with what success. He hardly knew whether there were any difference in her spirits or not. She was always so gentle and retiring, that her emotions were beyond his discrimination.[1] He did not understand her; he felt that he did not; and therefore applied to Edmund to tell him how she stood affected on the present occasion, and whether she were more or less happy than she had been.

Edmund did not discern any symptoms of regret, and thought his father a little unreasonable in supposing the first three or four days could produce any.

What chiefly surprised Edmund was, that Crawford's sister, the friend and companion, who had been so much to her, should not be more visibly regretted. He wondered that Fanny spoke so seldom of *her*, and had so little voluntarily to say of her concern at this separation.

Alas! it was this sister, this friend and companion, who was now the chief bane of Fanny's comfort.—If she could have believed Mary's future fate as unconnected with Mansfield, as she was determined the brother's should be, if she could have hoped her return thither, to be as distant as she was much inclined to think his, she would have been light of heart indeed; but the more she recollected and observed, the more deeply was she convinced that every thing was now in a fairer train[2] for Miss Crawford's marrying Edmund than it had ever been before.—On his side, the inclination was stronger, on hers less equivocal. His objections, the scruples of his integrity, seemed all

1. *discrimination*: perception.

2. *in a fairer train*: on a better or more certain course.

done away—nobody could tell how; and the doubts and hesitations of her ambition were equally got over—and equally without apparent reason. It could only be imputed to increasing attachment. His good and her bad feelings yielded to love, and such love must unite them. He was to go to town, as soon as some business relative to Thornton Lacey were completed—perhaps, within a fortnight, he talked of going, he loved to talk of it; and when once with her again, Fanny could not doubt the rest.—Her acceptance must be as certain as his offer; and yet, there were bad feelings still remaining which made the prospect of it most sorrowful to her, independently—she believed independently of self.

In their very last conversation, Miss Crawford, in spite of some amiable sensations, and much personal kindness, had still been Miss Crawford, still shewn a mind led astray and bewildered, and without any suspicion of being so; darkened, yet fancying itself light. She might love, but she did not deserve Edmund by any other sentiment. Fanny believed there was scarcely a second feeling in common between them; and she may be forgiven by older sages, for looking on the chance of Miss Crawford's future improvement as nearly desperate, for thinking that if Edmund's influence in this season of love, had already done so little in clearing her judgment, and regulating her notions, his worth would be finally wasted on her even in years of matrimony.

Experience might have hoped more for any young people, so circumstanced, and impartiality would not have denied to Miss Crawford's nature, that participation of[3] the general nature of women, which would lead her to adopt the opinions of the man she loved and respected, as her own.—But as such were Fanny's persuasions, she suffered very much from them, and could never speak of Miss Crawford without pain.[4]

Sir Thomas, meanwhile, went on with his own hopes, and his own observations, still feeling a right, by all his knowledge of human nature, to expect to see the effect of the loss of power and consequence, on his niece's spirits, and the past attentions of the lover producing a craving for their return; and he was soon afterwards able to account for his not yet completely and indubitably seeing all this, by the prospect of another visitor, whose approach he could allow to

3. *participation of*: partaking of, sharing in.

4. Thus the author shows some of the limitations of Fanny's judgment, even while picturing her generally as wise and virtuous. Also, the vision presented here of a marriage between Edmund and Mary is ambivalent: it would not be ideal, given Mary's flaws and the conflict of their natures, but it would not necessarily be bad either.

Admiral Nelson, the most renowned admiral of the age, in full dress uniform.
[From J. R. Green, *A Short History of the English People*, Vol. IV (New York, 1903), p. 1762]

be quite enough to support the spirits he was watching.—William had obtained a ten days' leave of absence to be given to Northamptonshire, and was coming, the happiest of lieutenants, because the latest made, to shew his happiness and describe his uniform.

He came; and he would have been delighted to shew his uniform there too, had not cruel custom prohibited its appearance except on duty.[5] So the uniform remained at Portsmouth, and Edmund conjectured that before Fanny had any chance of seeing it, all its own freshness, and all the freshness of its wearer's feelings, must be worn away. It would be sunk into a badge of disgrace; for what can be more unbecoming, or more worthless, than the uniform of a lieutenant, who has been a lieutenant a year or two, and sees others made commanders before him?[6] So reasoned Edmund, till his father made him the confident[7] of a scheme which placed Fanny's chance of seeing the 2d lieutenant of H. M. S. Thrush, in all his glory in another light.

This scheme was that she should accompany her brother back to Portsmouth, and spend a little time with her own family.[8] It had occurred to Sir Thomas, in one of his dignified musings, as a right and desirable measure; but before he absolutely made up his mind, he consulted his son. Edmund considered it every way, and saw nothing but what was right. The thing was good in itself, and could not be done at a better time; and he had no doubt of it being highly agreeable to Fanny. This was enough to determine Sir Thomas; and a decisive "then so it shall be," closed that stage of the business; Sir Thomas retiring from it with some feelings of satisfaction, and views of good over and above what he had communicated to his son, for his prime motive in sending her away, had very little to do with the propriety of her seeing her parents again, and nothing at all with any idea of making her happy. He certainly wished her to go willingly, but he as certainly wished her to be heartily sick of home before her visit ended; and that a little abstinence from the elegancies and luxuries of Mansfield Park, would bring her mind into a sober state, and incline her to a juster estimate of the value of that home of greater permanence, and equal comfort, of which she had the offer.

It was a medicinal project upon his niece's understanding, which he must consider as at present diseased. A residence of eight or nine years in the abode of wealth and plenty had a little disordered her

5. Naval officers did not wear their uniforms while off duty. Each rank of officer had a distinctive uniform.

6. Commander was the next rank above lieutenant. It allowed an officer to captain a small vessel like a sloop.

7. *confident*: confidant.

8. Fanny would then be able to see William's uniform, because, once in Portsmouth and back on duty, he would wear it when he went ashore. This

A luxurious room of the time, such as Sir Thomas hopes Fanny will miss when at her parents.

[From K. Warren Clouston, *The Chippendale Period in English Furniture* (New York, 1897), p. 149]

powers of comparing and judging. Her father's house would, in all probability, teach her the value of a good income; and he trusted that she would be the wiser and happier woman, all her life, for the experiment he had devised.

Had Fanny been at all addicted to raptures, she must have had a strong attack of them, when she first understood what was intended, when her uncle first made her the offer of visiting the parents and brothers, and sisters, from whom she had been divided, almost half her life, of returning for a couple of months to the scenes of her infancy, with William for the protector and companion of her journey; and the certainty of continuing to see William to the last hour of his remaining on land. Had she ever given way to bursts of delight, it must have been then, for she was delighted, but her happiness was of a quiet, deep, heart-swelling sort; and though never a great talker, she was always more inclined to silence when feeling most strongly. At the moment she could only thank and accept. Afterwards, when familiarized with the visions of enjoyment so suddenly opened, she could speak more largely to William and Edmund of what she felt; but still there were emotions of tenderness that could not be clothed in words—The remembrance of all her earliest pleasures, and of what she had suffered in being torn from them, came over her with renewed strength, and it seemed as if to be at home again, would heal every pain that had since grown out of the separation. To be in the centre of such a circle, loved by so many, and more loved by all than she had ever been before, to feel affection without fear or restraint, to feel herself the equal of those who surrounded her,[9] to be at peace from all mention of the Crawfords, safe from every look which could be fancied a reproach on their account!—This was a prospect to be dwelt on with a fondness that could be but half acknowledged.

Edmund too—to be two months from *him* (and perhaps, she might be allowed to make her absence three) must do her good. At a distance unassailed[10] by his looks or his kindness, and safe from the perpetual irritation of knowing his heart, and striving to avoid his confidence, she should be able to reason herself into a properer state; she should be able to think of him as in London, and arranging every thing there, without wretchedness.—What might have been hard to bear at Mansfield, was to become a slight evil at Portsmouth.

is Fanny's first visit to her family in the eight and a half years since she came to Mansfield. As a woman, she needs a male escort, and thus an earlier visit would have required Tom or Edmund to make a special trip to Portsmouth and back to take her, and then again to bring her home. Now she can accompany William on the way there.

9. This indicates that while Fanny has become attached to Mansfield Park and those living there, and has never complained of her treatment, she has continually suffered, at least to some degree, from the perpetual reminders of her social inferiority.

10. *unassailed*: unaffected.

A luxurious room of the time.

[From K. Warren Clouston, *The Chippendale Period in English Furniture* (New York, 1897), p. 183]

The only drawback was the doubt of her Aunt Bertram's being comfortable without her. She was of use to no one else; but *there* she might be missed to a degree that she did not like to think of; and that part of the arrangement was, indeed, the hardest for Sir Thomas to accomplish, and what only *he* could have accomplished at all.

But he was master at Mansfield Park. When he had really resolved on any measure, he could always carry it through; and now by dint of long talking on the subject, explaining and dwelling on the duty of Fanny's sometimes seeing her family, he did induce his wife to let her go; obtaining it rather from submission, however, than conviction, for Lady Bertram was convinced of very little more than that Sir Thomas thought Fanny ought to go, and therefore that she must. In the calmness of her own dressing room,[11] in the impartial flow of her own meditations, unbiassed by his bewildering statements, she could not acknowledge any necessity for Fanny's ever going near a father and mother who had done without her so long, while she was so useful to herself.—And as to the not missing her, which under Mrs. Norris's discussion was the point attempted to be proved, she set herself very steadily against admitting any such thing.

Sir Thomas had appealed to her reason, conscience, and dignity.[12] He called it a sacrifice, and demanded it of her goodness and self-command as such. But Mrs. Norris wanted to persuade her that Fanny could be very well spared—(*She* being ready to give up all her own time to her as requested) and in short could not really be wanted or missed.

"That may be, sister,"—was all Lady Bertram's reply—"I dare say you are very right, but I am sure I shall miss her very much."

The next step was to communicate with Portsmouth. Fanny wrote to offer herself; and her mother's answer, though short, was so kind, a few simple lines expressed so natural and motherly a joy in the prospect of seeing her child again, as to confirm all the daughter's views of happiness in being with her—convincing her that she should now find a warm and affectionate friend in the "Mamma" who had certainly shewn no remarkable fondness for her formerly; but this she could easily suppose to have been her own fault, or her own fancy. She had probably alienated Love[13] by the helplessness and fretfulness of a fearful temper, or been unreasonable in wanting a

11. Her dressing room is attached to her bedroom, and thus is a private chamber where she can be alone with her thoughts.

12. To appeal to her dignity would be to remind her that it would be degrading or undignified to allow an inconvenience like this to upset or disorient her. The next sentence speaks of his calling upon her self-command; maintaining one's self-command and dignity in the face of the vicissitudes of life was considered an aristocratic virtue.

13. "Love" is capitalized in the original. This presumably signals Fanny's current exalted and idealized vision of her mother's love, similar to religious believers capitalizing "Lord" or other sacred concepts.

larger share than any one among so many could deserve. Now, when she knew better how to be useful and how to forbear, and when her mother could be no longer occupied by the incessant demands of a house full of little children, there would be leisure and inclination for every comfort, and they should soon be what mother and daughter ought to be to each other.

William was almost as happy in the plan as his sister. It would be the greatest pleasure to him to have her there to the last moment before he sailed, and perhaps find her there still when he came in, from his first cruise![14] And besides, he wanted her so very much to see the Thrush before she went out of harbour[15] (the Thrush was certainly the finest sloop in the service). And there were several improvements in the dock-yard, too, which he quite longed to shew her.[16]

He did not scruple[17] to add, that her being at home for a while would be a great advantage to every body.

"I do not know how it is," said he, "but we seem to want some of your nice ways and orderliness at my father's. The house is always in confusion. You will set things going in a better way, I am sure. You will tell my mother how it all ought to be, and you will be so useful to Susan, and you will teach Betsey, and make the boys love and mind you. How right and comfortable[18] it will all be!"

By the time Mrs. Price's answer arrived, there remained but a very few days more to be spent at Mansfield; and for part of one of those days the young travellers were in a good deal of alarm on the subject of their journey, for when the mode of it came to be talked of, and Mrs. Norris found that all her anxiety to save her brother-in-law's money was vain, and that in spite of her wishes and hints for a less expensive conveyance of Fanny, they were to travel post,[19] when she saw Sir Thomas actually give William notes for the purpose,[20] she was struck with the idea of there being room for a third in the carriage,[21] and suddenly seized with a strong inclination to go with them—to go and see her poor dear sister Price. She proclaimed her thoughts. She must say that she had more than half a mind to go with the young people; it would be such an indulgence[22] to her; she had not seen her poor dear sister Price for more than twenty years; and it would be a help to the young people in their journey to have

14. Sloops often patrolled the home coast and waters, and if this was the mission of the *Thrush* it might return to base in less than two months. Larger ships tended to go to distant seas and oceans, and their cruises could last for years at a time.

15. To go out of harbor is not the same as sailing, for it meant the ship would anchor in a nearby waterway to await orders to sail, and officers in the ship might still have an opportunity to come ashore. But only when still in harbor could a civilian like Fanny see her.

16. The dockyard was an enormous industrial complex for building and repairing ships, and was considered the leading sight in Portsmouth. For more, see p. 721, note 5, and p. 725, note 17.

17. *scruple*: hesitate.

18. *comfortable*: pleasant, enjoyable.

19. Her idea was for them to use the public coach. William seems to have traveled that way on his own, but Sir Thomas probably feels that Fanny deserves better. In addition, the difference in cost would not be as great for two passengers, for renting a carriage and horses cost the same for one or for two people, whereas riding coach meant buying a fare for each person.

20. These are bank notes. Coins were used for most everyday transactions, but notes were preferred for larger sums of money.

21. The standard carriage for traveling post, a chaise, accommodated three passengers.

22. *indulgence*: gratification.

her older head to manage for them;[23] and she could not help think-ing her poor dear sister Price would feel it very unkind of her not to come by such an opportunity.

William and Fanny were horror-struck at the idea.

All the comfort of their comfortable journey would be destroyed at once. With woeful countenances they looked at each other. Their suspense lasted an hour or two. No one interfered to encourage or dissuade. Mrs. Norris was left to settle the matter by herself; and it ended to the infinite joy of her nephew and niece, in the recollection that she could not possibly be spared from Mansfield Park at present; that she was a great deal too necessary to Sir Thomas and Lady Ber-tram for her to be able to answer it to herself to leave them even for a week, and therefore must certainly sacrifice every other pleasure to that of being useful to them.

It had, in fact, occurred to her, that, though taken to Portsmouth for nothing, it would be hardly possible for her to avoid paying her own expenses back again.[24] So, her poor dear sister Price was left to all the disappointment of her missing such an opportunity; and another twenty years' absence, perhaps, begun.

Edmund's plans were affected by this Portsmouth journey, this absence of Fanny's. He too had a sacrifice to make to Mansfield Park, as well as his aunt. He had intended, about this time, to be going to London,[25] but he could not leave his father and mother just when every body else of most importance to their comfort, was leav-ing them; and with an effort, felt but not boasted of, he delayed for a week or two longer a journey which he was looking forward to, with the hope of its fixing his happiness for ever.

He told Fanny of it. She knew so much already, that she must know every thing. It made the substance of one other confidential discourse about Miss Crawford; and Fanny was the more affected from feeling it to be the last time in which Miss Crawford's name would ever be mentioned between them with any remains of liberty. Once afterwards, she was alluded to by him. Lady Bertram had been telling her niece in the evening to write to her soon and often, and promising to be a good correspondent herself; and Edmund, at a convenient moment, then added, in a whisper, "And *I* shall write to you, Fanny, when I have any thing worth writing about; any thing to

23. Traveling post did not involve any great difficulty, but, as on any journey, mishaps could occur—once when Jane Austen was traveling she left a valuable item at an earlier stop and had to take steps to retrieve it—and Mrs. Norris seizes on any possible justification for her presence, particularly one that allows her to claim she is being useful.

24. Sir Thomas will almost certainly pay Fanny's passage back, but that will occur only after two months, and Mrs. Norris would not stay that long, especially since her choices would be to stay with the Prices, who are not affluent, or to rent her own accommodation.

25. Edmund wishes to go to London to see Mary, and seems to intend to propose to her there.

say, that I think you will like to hear, and that you will not hear so soon from any other quarter." Had she doubted his meaning while she listened, the glow in his face, when she looked up at him, would have been decisive.

For this letter she must try to arm herself. That a letter from Edmund should be a subject of terror! She began to feel that she had not yet gone through all the changes of opinion and sentiment, which the progress of time and variation of circumstances occasion in this world of changes. The vicissitudes of the human mind had not yet been exhausted by her.

Poor Fanny! though going, as she did, willingly and eagerly, the last evening at Mansfield Park must still be wretchedness. Her heart was completely sad at parting. She had tears for every room in the house, much more for every beloved inhabitant. She clung to her aunt, because she would miss her; she kissed the hand of her uncle with struggling sobs, because she had displeased him; and as for Edmund, she could neither speak, nor look, nor think, when the last moment came with *him*, and it was not till it was over that she knew he was giving her the affectionate farewell of a brother.

All this passed over night, for the journey was to begin very early in the morning; and when the small, diminished party met at breakfast, William and Fanny were talked of as already advanced one stage.[26]

26. The first stage is to Northampton. Since breakfast is probably at ten, it makes sense for the travelers to leave earlier, for the journey takes more than a day and they do not wish to arrive late on the second day.

Carriage dress, such as Fanny might wear for her journey.

[From *The Repository of arts, literature, fashions, manufactures, &c*, Vol. VI (1811), p. 302]

Chapter Seven

*T*he novelty of travelling, and the happiness of being with William, soon produced their natural effect on Fanny's spirits, when Mansfield Park was fairly left behind, and by the time their first stage was ended, and they were to quit Sir Thomas's carriage, she was able to take leave of the old coachman,[1] and send back proper messages, with cheerful looks.

Of pleasant talk between the brother and sister, there was no end. Every thing supplied an amusement to the high glee of William's mind, and he was full of frolic and joke, in the intervals of their higher-toned subjects, all of which ended, if they did not begin, in praise of the Thrush, conjectures how she would be employed, schemes for an action with some superior force,[2] which (supposing the first lieutenant out of the way—and William was not very merciful to the first lieutenant) was to give himself the next step as soon as possible,[3] or speculations upon prize money, which was to be generously distributed at home,[4] with only the reservation of enough to make the little cottage comfortable, in which he and Fanny were to pass all their middle and latter life together.[5]

Fanny's immediate concerns, as far as they involved Mr. Crawford, made no part of their conversation. William knew what had passed, and from his heart lamented that his sister's feelings should be so cold towards a man whom he must consider as the first of human characters; but he was of an age to be all for love,[6] and therefore unable to blame; and knowing her wish on the subject, he would not distress her by the slightest allusion.

She had reason to suppose herself not yet forgotten by Mr. Crawford.—She had heard repeatedly from his sister within the three weeks which had passed since their leaving Mansfield, and in each letter there had been a few lines from himself, warm and determined like his speeches.[7] It was a correspondence which Fanny found quite as unpleasant as she had feared. Miss Crawford's style

1.   They have used Sir Thomas's carriage, driven by the family coachman, on the initial stage to Northampton. There they will rent a post-chaise at an inn to use for the rest of their journey.

2.   An attack on a superior force would offer the opportunity for more glory and more prize money. Ships of the British navy often attacked larger enemy vessels, for the superior seamanship of the British compared with most other navies gave them an advantage.

3.   If the first lieutenant was out of the way, most likely through being killed or wounded in battle, William would step into his place and be better positioned to win acclaim for a victory that could in turn lead to another promotion.

4.   Meaning distributed among his family in Portsmouth. Naval officers could sometimes gain large amounts through prize money seized from defeated ships, though it would usually require more than one action, and sloops were less likely to gain prize money than frigates, the next largest type of ship.

5.   This is probably a long-standing plan, made when both William and Fanny were children. Their modest circumstances led them to envisage only a cottage rather than a grander dwelling.

6.   The phrase "all for love" alludes to a famous drama of that name written in 1677 by the leading poet John Dryden.

7.   Mary writes so assiduously to Fanny partly for the sake of her brother: social rules forbade unmarried men and women from corresponding, so Henry can communicate with Fanny only through his sister's letters.

All Souls College, Oxford (see the next page).

[From Rudolph Ackermann, A History of the University of Oxford, Vol. I (London, 1814), p. 210]

of writing, lively and affectionate, was itself an evil, independent of what she was thus forced into reading from the brother's pen, for Edmund would never rest till she had read the chief[8] of the letter to him,[9] and then she had to listen to his admiration of her language, and the warmth of her attachments.—There had, in fact, been so much of message, of allusion, of recollection, so much of Mansfield in every letter, that Fanny could not but suppose it meant for him to hear; and to find herself forced into a purpose of that kind, compelled into a correspondence which was bringing her the addresses of the man she did not love, and obliging her to administer to the adverse passion of the man she did, was cruelly mortifying. Here, too, her present removal promised advantage. When no longer under the same roof with Edmund, she trusted that Miss Crawford would have no motive for writing, strong enough to overcome the trouble, and that at Portsmouth their correspondence would dwindle into nothing.

With such thoughts as these among ten hundred others, Fanny proceeded in her journey, safely and cheerfully, and as expeditiously as could rationally be hoped in the dirty[10] month of February. They entered Oxford, but she could take only a hasty glimpse of Edmund's College as they passed along,[11] and made no stop any where, till they reached Newbury,[12] where a comfortable meal, uniting dinner and supper,[13] wound up the enjoyments and fatigues of the day.

The next morning saw them off again at an early hour; and with no events and no delays they regularly[14] advanced, and were in the environs of Portsmouth while there was yet daylight for Fanny to look around her, and wonder at the new buildings.—They passed the Drawbridge, and entered the town;[15] and the light was only beginning to fail,[16] as, guided by William's powerful voice, they were rattled into a narrow street,[17] leading from the high street,[18] and drawn up before the door of a small house now inhabited by Mr. Price.

Fanny was all agitation and flutter—all hope and apprehension. The moment they stopt, a trollopy[19]-looking maid-servant, seemingly in waiting for them at the door, stept forward, and more intent on telling the news, than giving them any help, immediately began with "the Thrush is gone out of harbour, please Sir, and one of the officers has been here to"—She was interrupted by a fine tall boy of eleven

8. *chief*: greater part.

9. Being able to communicate with Edmund through this means is probably another reason for her letters, since the same rules prevented her writing to him directly.

10. *dirty*: muddy.

11. Oxford is along the most direct route to Portsmouth. The university was divided into colleges, and all students were enrolled in one.

12. Newbury is sixty-eight miles from Northampton by current roads; this would take them around nine hours by current speeds, on top of less than an hour to get from Mansfield to Northampton. For the locations of Newbury, Oxford, and Portsmouth, see map, p. 882.

13. They did not arrive at their destination until after the normal dinnertime, and they need to rise early the next morning for another long day, so they wish to retire before the later supper hour. Hence a single large meal at the inn substitutes for both dinner and supper.

14. *regularly*: steadily.

15. The main town of Portsmouth was surrounded by fortifications, a legacy of its long being a major naval base. According to contemporary travelers, access to the town was no longer guarded, but it still required going through one of several gates; Landport Gate, at the northeastern edge of town, was the one normally used by those traveling to Portsmouth (see map, p. 884). A narrow channel of water lay just outside the fortifications, so those entering or leaving needed to cross a drawbridge. Because the compact town had long been completely built up, the population expanded into surrounding areas, so Fanny sees new buildings only outside the drawbridge. Since that time Portsmouth has expanded further and incorporated these surrounding areas, and the small central part is now called Old Portsmouth. Jane Austen was familiar with Portsmouth, since she lived for three years in the nearby town of Southampton.

16. It is now early February (see chronology, p. 859), so daytime ends early.

17. The streets of Portsmouth were paved, so carriage wheels would rattle. In *Persuasion* the author mentions the substantial noise made by carriages and carts going along the streets of Bath, also paved. Thus William must speak loudly to the driver.

18. The high street, as in many English towns, is the principal street. Since Portsmouth was old and crowded, a side street would be narrow.

19. *trollopy*: slovenly, untidy; or sluttish (as in current English).

years old, who rushing out of the house, pushed the maid aside, and while William was opening the chaise door himself,[20] called out, "you are just in time. We have been looking for you this half hour. The Thrush went out of harbour this morning. I saw her. It was a beautiful sight. And they think she will have her orders in a day or two.[21] And Mr. Campbell was here at four o'clock, to ask for you; he has got one of the Thrush's boats,[22] and is going off to her at six, and hoped you would be here in time to go with him."

A stare or two at Fanny, as William helped her out of the carriage, was all the voluntary notice which this brother bestowed;—but he made no objection to her kissing him, though still entirely engaged in detailing farther particulars of the Thrush's going out of harbour, in which he had a strong right of interest, being to commence his career of seamanship in her at this very time.[23]

Another moment, and Fanny was in the narrow entrance-passage of the house, and in her mother's arms, who met her there with looks of true kindness, and with features which Fanny loved the more, because they brought her aunt Bertram's before her; and there were her two sisters, Susan, a well-grown fine girl of fourteen, and Betsey, the youngest of the family, about five—both glad to see her in their way, though with no advantage of manner[24] in receiving her. But manner Fanny did not want. Would they but love her, she should be satisfied.

She was then taken into a parlour,[25] so small that her first conviction was of its being only a passage-room to something better,[26] and she stood for a moment expecting to be invited on; but when she saw there was no other door, and that there were signs of habitation before her, she called back her thoughts, reproved herself, and grieved lest they should have been suspected. Her mother, however, could not stay long enough to suspect any thing. She was gone again to the street door, to welcome William. "Oh! my dear William, how glad I am to see you. But have you heard about the Thrush? She is gone out of harbour already, three days before we had any thought of it; and I do not know what I am to do about Sam's things, they will never be ready in time; for she may have her orders to-morrow, perhaps.[27] It takes me quite unawares. And now you must be off for Spithead too.[28] Campbell has been here, quite in a worry about you;

20. The servant should open the door.

21. These are her orders to sail.

22. Ships had small rowboats for traveling to land or to other ships; for a contemporary picture, see p. 687.

23. William also first went to sea at eleven or twelve; current regulations stated that eleven was the youngest age for sons of officers to enter the service (others were supposed to wait until age thirteen). Regulations also dictated that a boy aspiring to become an officer serve three years as a "volunteer" before ascending to midshipman, the rank William held until recently. In practice, many with good naval connections could arrange for their sons to start as midshipmen. Whether that has happened in this case is uncertain, but it is probable that either his father or brother arranged for him to start on William's ship by talking to the captain, who had wide latitude to select personnel under him.

24. *manner*: deportment, social polish.

25. Parlor was the usual name, along with drawing room, for a sitting or living room. A parlor was smaller and less luxurious.

26. Older houses—and those in Portsmouth would tend to be old—often had rooms serving as passages to others, since they generally did not have corridors.

27. Sam is the brother going on the *Thrush* with William, which is why she worries that his things will not be ready when the ship sails.

28. Spithead is the part of the strait separating the English mainland from the Isle of Wight opposite Portsmouth (see maps, pp. 882 and 884). It is approximately five miles long and two miles wide. The name derives from an adjacent sandbank, called the Spit, stretching along the mainland shore. It is well protected from winds off the English Channel, and was where ships preparing to leave Portsmouth gathered while awaiting their orders.

and now, what shall we do? I thought to have had such a comfortable evening with you, and here everything comes upon me at once."[29]

Her son answered cheerfully, telling her that every thing was always for the best; and making light of his own inconvenience, in being obliged to hurry away so soon.

"To be sure, I had much rather she had stayed in harbour, that I might have sat a few hours with you in comfort; but as there is a boat ashore, I had better go off at once, and there is no help for it. Whereabouts does the Thrush lay at Spithead? Near the Canopus?[30] But no matter—here's Fanny in the parlour, and why should we stay in the passage?—Come, mother, you have hardly looked at your own dear Fanny yet."

In they both came, and Mrs. Price having kindly kissed her daughter again, and commented a little on her growth, began with very natural solicitude to feel for their fatigues and wants as travellers.

"Poor dears! how tired you must both be!—and now what will you have? I began to think you would never come. Betsey and I have been watching for you this half hour.[31] And when did you get anything to eat? And what would you like to have now? I could not tell whether you would be for some meat, or only a dish of tea after your journey,[32] or else I would have got something ready. And now I am afraid Campbell will be here, before there is time to dress[33] a steak, and we have no butcher at hand. It is very inconvenient to have no butcher in the street. We were better off in our last house. Perhaps you would like some tea, as soon as it can be got."

They both declared they should prefer it to anything. "Then, Betsey, my dear, run into the kitchen, and see if Rebecca has put the water on; and tell her to bring in the tea-things as soon as she can. I wish we could get the bell mended[34]—but Betsey is a very handy little messenger."

Betsey went with alacrity; proud to shew her abilities before her fine[35] new sister.

"Dear me!" continued the anxious mother, "what a sad fire we have got, and I dare say you are both starved[36] with cold. Draw your chair nearer, my dear. I cannot think what Rebecca has been about. I am sure I told her to bring some coals half an hour ago.[37] Susan, *you* should have taken care of the fire."

29. This is the first speech of Mrs. Price, and it reveals characteristics she will continue to display: incompetence and negligence in managing household affairs, a tendency toward complaining and self-pity, and an indifference toward Fanny.

30. The *Canopus* is the name of an actual ship captained in 1805 and 1806 by Jane Austen's brother Francis. On p. 682 she also uses the name of the ship he was captaining at the time of this novel, the *Elephant*. She had written to him, asking, "And by the bye—shall you object to my mentioning the *Elephant* in it, & two or three other of your old Ships?—I *have* done it, but it shall not stay, to make you angry.—They are only just mentioned" (July 6, 1813). In the end these were the only two ships of Francis's she mentions; she also uses the names of two of her brother Charles's (see p. 683, note 53). Both the *Canopus* and the *Elephant* were ships of the line; the former was part of the fleet commanded by Admiral Nelson that won the famous Battle of Trafalgar, though to Francis's great regret the ship was away on a separate mission at the time of the battle.

31. Their expecting William and Fanny to arrive at almost the exact time they do demonstrates the predictability of travel times, due to the uniformly good quality of the main roads and the well-developed system of traveling post. William probably conveyed his estimate of their arrival time in a letter.

32. Tea was originally served in bowl-like dishes until, in the late eighteenth century, cups with handles appeared. But the term "dish of tea" continued to be used for a while; it may have lingered especially long with those, like Mrs. Price, who were less affluent and thus slower to purchase items in the newer style.

33. *dress*: cook, prepare.

34. This is the bell to call servants; for more, see p. 267, note 13.

35. *fine*: refined, elegant.

36. *starved*: perished or afflicted from cold.

37. This is the only reference to coal in Austen's novels. In rural areas, where her novels are mostly set, wood was used for fires. But in large towns, wood was scarcer, for it needed to be transported from farther away. Coal was cheaper, especially for coastal towns like Portsmouth, since it was easier to ship it there from Newcastle, a large town on the northeast coast that was the center of England's coal mining industry.

"I was up stairs, mamma, moving my things"; said Susan, in a fearless, self-defending tone, which startled Fanny. "You know you had but just settled that my sister Fanny and I should have the other room; and I could not get Rebecca to give me any help."

Farther discussion was prevented by various bustles; first, the driver came to be paid[38]—then there was a squabble between Sam and Rebecca, about the manner of carrying up his sister's trunk, which he would manage all his own way; and lastly in walked Mr. Price himself, his own loud voice preceding him, as with something of the oath[39] kind he kicked away his son's portmanteau,[40] and his daughter's band-box in the passage,[41] and called out for a candle; no candle was brought, however, and he walked into the room.

Fanny, with doubting feelings, had risen to meet him, but sank down again on finding herself undistinguished in the dusk, and unthought of. With a friendly shake of his son's hand, and an eager voice, he instantly began—"Ha! welcome back, my boy. Glad to see you. Have you heard the news? The Thrush went out of harbour this morning. Sharp is the word, you see.[42] By G—,[43] you are just in time. The doctor has been here enquiring for you;[44] he has got one of the boats, and is to be off for Spithead by six, so you had better go with him. I have been to Turner's about your mess;[45] it is all in a way[46] to

A naval battle between a British frigate and a French frigate.
[From Constance Hill, *Jane Austen; her Home and her Friends* (London, 1904), p. 42]

38. It is notable that, after all that has happened since William and Fanny's arrival, the carriage driver has yet to be paid.

39. *oath*: curse, profane word or expression.

40. A portmanteau is a case or bag for traveling; it would contain William's clothes and other effects.

41. A bandbox is a lightweight, delicate box that was used particularly for women's hats; this is separate from Fanny's trunk, already mentioned. In *Pride and Prejudice*, the heroine and her sisters have bandboxes with them during one journey, and Jane Austen, in a letter describing her arrival in London for a visit to her brother Henry, mentions taking possession of her bedroom and unpacking her bandbox (March 2, 1814).

42. "Sharp" was "alert" in the first edition. Jane Austen probably changed it because "alert," in a naval context, meant specifically being on the watch or lookout, and that would not be appropriate in this context. From this point until the end of the paragraph she made a number of alterations between editions, the only substantial ones in the novel. One of her naval brothers almost certainly informed her of the more correct terminology that a man familiar with naval matters like Mr. Price would use.

43. G—: God. This would be considered improper to print in full, since it involved taking the Lord's name in vain. This is an example of Mr. Price's oaths; the author may have imagined him using others that she did not dare to print even in abbreviated form. Naval men were notorious for using profane language.

44. The doctor is the ship's surgeon. Surgeons were naturally important figures on naval ships, needed to deal with wounds from accidents and battle and with the continual threat of disease in crowded ships. They often had surgeon's mates assisting them.

45. Turner's was an actual store in Portsmouth. "Mess" was "things" in the first edition and probably means the same. One meaning of "mess" then was a quantity or collection of food, and the term may have been used in the navy to refer to other supplies as well. The most common use of "mess" then was for a group of men on a naval ship (or in an army unit) who dined together, with all who served on ship being part of a mess; it could also refer to the place where they dined. Hence another possibility is that Mr. Price means "things for your mess," in which case the ungrammatical abbreviation would be a further sign of his informality and lack of polish.

46. *in a way*: likely, or on track.

be done. I should not wonder if you had your orders to-morrow; but you cannot sail with this wind, if you are to cruize to the westward; and Captain Walsh thinks you will certainly have a cruize to the westward, with the Elephant. By G—, I wish you may.[47] But old Scholey was saying just now, that he thought you would be sent first to the Texel.[48] Well, well, we are ready, whatever happens. But by G—, you lost a fine sight by not being here in the morning to see the Thrush go out of harbour. I would not have been out of the way[49] for a thousand pounds. Old Scholey ran in at breakfast time, to say she had slipped her moorings and was coming out.[50] I jumped up, and made but two steps to the platform.[51] If ever there was a perfect beauty afloat, she is one; and there she lays at Spithead, and anybody in England would take her for an eight-and-twenty.[52] I was upon the platform two hours this afternoon, looking at her. She lays close to the Endymion, between her and the Cleopatra,[53] just to the eastward of the sheer hulk."[54]

"Ha!" cried William, "*that's* just where I should have put her myself. It's the best birth[55] at Spithead. But here is my sister, Sir, here is Fanny"; turning and leading her forward;—"it is so dark you do not see her."

With an acknowledgement that he had quite forgot her, Mr. Price now received his daughter; and, having given her a cordial hug, and observed that she was grown into a woman, and he supposed would be wanting a husband soon, seemed very much inclined to forget her again.

Fanny shrunk back to her seat, with feelings sadly pained by his language and his smell of spirits;[56] and he talked on only to his son, and only of the Thrush, though William, warmly interested, as he was, in that subject, more than once tried to make his father think of Fanny, and her long absence and long journey.

After sitting some time longer, a candle was obtained; but, as there was still no appearance of tea, nor, from Betsey's reports from the kitchen, much hope of any under a considerable period, William determined to go and change his dress, and make the necessary preparations for his removal on board directly,[57] that he might have his tea in comfort afterwards.

As he left the room, two rosy-faced boys, ragged and dirty, about

47. Heading to the west would be more likely to mean a long cruise to more distant seas, since ships sailed westward toward most other parts of the world, and this would offer greater possibilities of glory and distinction, and of prize money. The distinction of such a cruise would be further increased if the *Thrush* were to accompany an enormous ship of the line like the *Elephant*.

48. The Texel Channel, east of Portsmouth, was the principal access for ships sailing from Holland, which was then occupied by France. Britain maintained a regular blockade there.

49. *out of the way*: absent.

50. "Had slipped her moorings" is a substitute for the first edition's "was under weigh." The latter expression is used when a ship is anchored to the bottom and then raises (or weighs) its anchor in order to sail. Ships in Portsmouth Harbor, however, were attached to moorings rather than anchored, and thus "slipped her moorings" is more accurate. One perceives here the exacting standards of experienced naval officers like Jane Austen's brothers; the speaker, Mr. Price, would probably be just as particular in his choice of words.

51. The Platform is an ideal viewing spot; for more, see p. 737, note 7.

52. An "eight-and-twenty" is a ship with that number of cannons. Ships were rated by their quantity of guns. A twenty-eight-gun ship was the smallest type of frigate. Sloops had between eight and eighteen guns.

53. The *Endymion* and the *Cleopatra* were both frigates; Jane Austen's brother Charles served as lieutenant on the first and captained the second. This sentence involves the most extensive of her changes between editions. The first edition has "lays just astern of the Endymion, with the Cleopatra at the larboard." But a ship at anchorage does not position herself relative to ships at her side ("larboard" means port, or the left side of a ship when facing forward). Thus in the revised version the *Thrush* is simply "between" the other two ships, which could mean being behind one ship and in front of the other, the manner in which ships at anchorage are normally positioned.

54. A "sheer hulk" is a hulk, i.e., an old disused ship, that is now permanently moored and fitted with shears, an elaborate mechanical device used to hoist heavy equipment and to fit and remove masts on ships.

55. *birth*: berth.

56. Men connected with the navy were known for heavy drinking.

57. He needs to change into his uniform for going on board the ship, since he will now be on duty.

eight and nine years old, rushed into it just released from school,[58] and coming eagerly to see their sister, and tell that the Thrush was gone out of harbour; Tom and Charles: Charles had been born since Fanny's going away, but Tom she had often helped to nurse, and now felt a particular pleasure in seeing again. Both were kissed very tenderly, but Tom she wanted to keep by her, to try to trace the features of the baby she had loved, and talk to him[59] of his infant preference of herself. Tom, however, had no mind for such treatment: he came home, not to stand and be talked to, but to run about and make a noise; and both boys had soon burst away from her, and slammed the parlour door till her temples ached.

She had now seen all that were at home; there remained only two brothers between herself and Susan, one of whom was a clerk in a public office in London,[60] and the other midshipman on board an Indiaman.[61] But though she had *seen* all the members of the family, she had not yet *heard* all the noise they could make. Another quarter of an hour brought her a great deal more. William was soon calling out from the landing-place[62] of the second story,[63] for his mother and for Rebecca. He was in distress for something that he had left there, and did not find again. A key was mislaid,[64] Betsey accused of having got at his new hat,[65] and some slight, but essential alteration of his uniform waistcoat,[66] which he had been promised to have done for him, entirely neglected.

Mrs. Price, Rebecca, and Betsey, all went up to defend themselves, all talking together, but Rebecca loudest, and the job was to be done, as well as it could, in a great hurry; William trying in vain to send Betsey down again, or keep her from being troublesome where she was; the whole of which, as almost every door in the house was open, could be plainly distinguished in the parlour, except when drowned at intervals by the superior noise of Sam, Tom, and Charles chasing each other up and down stairs, and tumbling about and hallooing.[67]

Fanny was almost stunned. The smallness of the house, and thinness of the walls, brought every thing so close to her, that, added to the fatigue of her journey, and all her recent agitation, she hardly knew how to bear it. *Within* the room all was tranquil enough, for Susan having disappeared with the others, there were soon only her father and herself remaining; and he taking out a newspaper—the

58. They are going to a local day school. This would be a private school, for no government schools existed.

59. Both editions published in Jane Austen's lifetime have "talked to," followed by a comma, instead of "talk to him." That wording, which suggests her having talked to him when he was an infant rather than talking to him now, makes less sense, especially since the comma after "talked to" would make the remainder of the sentence ungrammatical. Moreover, the next sentence indicates that she is talking to the boy now. Therefore the original wording was likely a mistake in the first edition that was not noticed and corrected in the second.

60. A public office is a building or set of buildings for a governmental department.

61. An Indiaman was a merchant ship trading with the East Indies, especially a ship of the East India Company, a commercial company that governed the British possessions in India at this time. Serving on a merchant ship was less prestigious than serving in the navy. It is possible that the family had been unable to procure a naval berth for this brother, but that William's promotion to lieutenant has made him better able to help Sam.

62. *landing-place*: landing on stairs.

63. This is two stories above the ground floor; that is why he needs to call out from the landing, to make himself heard far below. Urban houses tended to be narrow, with many floors.

64. This would be a key to a drawer or a storage box.

65. The hat is part of his new uniform; naval officers wore large and impressive hats when on duty.

66. *waistcoat*: vest.

67. *hallooing*: shouting.

accustomary loan of a neighbour,[68] applied himself to studying it, without seeming to recollect her existence. The solitary candle was held between himself and the paper, without any reference to her possible convenience; but she had nothing to do, and was glad to have the light screened from her aching head, as she sat in bewildered, broken, sorrowful contemplation.

She was at home. But alas! it was not such a home, she had not such a welcome, as—she checked herself; she was unreasonable. What right had she to be of importance to her family? She could have none, so long lost sight of! William's concerns must be dearest—they always had been—and he had every right. Yet to have so little said or asked about herself—to have scarcely an enquiry made after Mansfield! It did pain her to have Mansfield forgotten; the friends who had done so much—the dear, dear friends! But here, one subject swallowed up all the rest. Perhaps it must be so. The destination of the Thrush must be now preeminently interesting. A day or two might shew the difference. *She* only was to blame. Yet she thought it would not have been so at Mansfield. No, in her uncle's house there would have been a consideration of times and seasons, a regulation of subject, a propriety,[69] an attention towards every body which there was not here.

The only interruption which thoughts like these received for nearly half an hour, was from a sudden burst of her father's, not at all calculated to compose them. At a more than ordinary pitch of thumping and hallooing in the passage, he exclaimed, "Devil take those young dogs! How they are singing out! Ay, Sam's voice louder than all the rest! That boy is fit for a boatswain.[70] Holla—you there—Sam—stop your confounded pipe,[71] or I shall be after you."

This threat was so palpably disregarded, that though within five minutes afterwards the three boys all burst into the room together and sat down, Fanny could not consider it as a proof of any thing more than their being for the time thoroughly fagged,[72] which their hot faces and panting breaths seemed to prove—especially as they were still kicking each other's shins, and hallooing out at sudden starts immediately under their father's eye.

The next opening of the door brought something more welcome; it was for the tea-things, which she had begun almost to despair of see-

68. Newspapers were costly, so he saves money by reading a neighbor's, after the latter is finished. This is why he is reading it so late in the day.

69. *propriety*: appropriateness, adherence to what is right and proper.

70. A boatswain was responsible for the sails and rigging of the ship; he also supervised other activities on deck, and summoned the crew onto the deck and ensured they worked vigilantly. He was constantly barking out orders and instructions, as well as chastisements, and doing so under frequently very noisy conditions, so a loud voice was an essential qualification.

71. *pipe*: voice.

72. *fagged*: worn out.

A naval ship with small boats rowing toward it.

[From J. R. Green, *A Short History of the English People*, Vol. IV (New York, 1903), p. 1827]

ing that evening. Susan and an attendant girl, whose inferior appearance informed Fanny, to her great surprise, that she had previously seen the upper servant,[73] brought in every thing necessary for the meal; Susan looking as she put the kettle on the fire and glanced at her sister, as if divided between the agreeable triumph of shewing her activity[74] and usefulness, and the dread of being thought to demean herself by such an office.[75] "She had been into the kitchen," she said, "to hurry Sally and help make the toast,[76] and spread the bread and butter — or she did not know when they should have got tea — and she was sure her sister must want something after her journey."

Fanny was very thankful. She could not but own that she should be very glad of a little tea, and Susan immediately set about making it, as if pleased to have the employment all to herself; and with only a little unnecessary bustle, and some few injudicious attempts at keeping her brothers in better order than she could, acquitted herself very well. Fanny's spirit was as much refreshed as her body; her head and heart were soon the better for such well-timed kindness. Susan had an open, sensible countenance; she was like William — and Fanny hoped to find her like him in disposition and good will towards herself.

In this more placid state of things William re-entered, followed not far behind by his mother and Betsey. He, complete in his Lieutenant's uniform, looking and moving all the taller, firmer, and more graceful for it,[77] and with the happiest smile over his face, walked up directly to Fanny — who, rising from her seat, looked at him for a moment in speechless admiration, and then threw her arms round his neck to sob out her various emotions of pain and pleasure.

Anxious not to appear unhappy, she soon recovered herself: and wiping away her tears, was able to notice and admire all the striking parts of his dress[78] — listening with reviving spirits to his cheerful hopes of being on shore some part of every day before they sailed, and even of getting her to Spithead to see the sloop.

The next bustle brought in Mr. Campbell, the Surgeon of the Thrush, a very well behaved young man, who came to call for his friend, and for whom there was with some contrivance found a chair, and with some hasty washing of the young tea-maker's, a cup and saucer; and after another quarter of an hour of earnest talk between

73. The Prices have two servants. Though Rebecca is of higher status, and hence called the upper servant here, both are low-ranking in a general sense and so are called by their first names. Only in larger houses, with more servants and greater specialization of tasks, would some have enough status to be true upper servants entitled to be called by their last names.

74. *activity*: energy, vigor.

75. A mark of gentility for a woman was not needing to engage in basic household chores like boiling a kettle. Putting the kettle on the fire, in the room where tea is served, also marks a sharp difference with Mansfield Park. There the water was boiled in the kitchen by servants, out of sight of the family, and then brought into the drawing room in an urn.

76. Sally is the lesser servant just mentioned. Susan's having to go into the kitchen and perform such chores marks a further distinction from life at Mansfield Park. Toast was made over an open fire.

77. At this time William is not wearing his full dress uniform, which included an epaulette on one shoulder, white lapels, and a little gold lace (higher ranks than lieutenants had even fancier trimmings), for that was worn only on formal occasions. But even the undress uniform worn most of the time featured an impressive blue coat with a narrow white trim, and white breeches.

78. *dress*: attire.

the gentlemen, noise rising upon noise, and bustle upon bustle, men and boys at last all in motion together, the moment came for setting off; every thing was ready, William took leave, and all of them were gone—for the three boys, in spite of their mother's intreaty, determined to see their brother and Mr. Campbell to the sally-port;[79] and Mr. Price walked off at the same time to carry back his neighbour's newspaper.

Something like tranquillity might now be hoped for, and accordingly, when Rebecca had been prevailed on to carry away the tea-things, and Mrs. Price had walked about the room some time looking for a shirt sleeve,[80] which Betsey at last hunted out from a drawer in the kitchen, the small party of females were pretty well composed, and the mother having lamented again over the impossibility of getting Sam ready in time, was at leisure to think of her eldest daughter and the friends she had come from.

A few enquiries began; but one of the earliest—"How did her sister Bertram manage about her servants? Was she as much plagued as herself to get tolerable servants?"—soon led her mind away from Northamptonshire, and fixed it on her own domestic grievances; and the shocking character of all the Portsmouth servants, of whom she believed her own two were the very worst, engrossed her completely.[81] The Bertrams were all forgotten in detailing the faults of Rebecca, against whom Susan had also much to depose,[82] and little Betsey a great deal more, and who did seem so thoroughly without a single recommendation, that Fanny could not help modestly presuming that her mother meant to part with her when her year was up.[83]

"Her year!" cried Mrs. Price; "I am sure I hope I shall be rid of her before she has staid a year, for that will not be up till November. Servants are come to such a pass, my dear, in Portsmouth, that it is quite a miracle if one keeps them more than half-a-year.[84] I have no hope of ever being settled; and if I was to part with Rebecca, I should only get something worse. And yet I do not think I am a very difficult mistress to please—and I am sure the place is easy enough, for there is always a girl under her, and I often do half the work myself."

Fanny was silent; but not from being convinced that there might not be a remedy found for some of these evils. As she now sat looking at Betsey, she could not but think particularly of another sister, a very

79. A sally port is an opening in fortifications. In Portsmouth that was where boats would embark for ships anchored at Spithead.

80. At this time shirtsleeves were often made separately from the body of a shirt; the two parts were sewn together by the purchaser. Buying them in separate pieces was cheaper. Mrs. Price is presumably looking for a shirtsleeve to do such sewing, most likely for a shirt for William. Jane Austen refers more than once in her letters to making shirts for her brothers, by which she meant sewing the pieces together.

81. One inspiration for Mrs. Price's trouble with servants could be Jane Austen's own experience in Southampton, when she, her mother, and her sister were living in fairly pinched material circumstances. In one of Austen's letters from there she mentions one servant's being inexplicably away during an important time, a second's limited competence, and a third's having to be dismissed for being "so very drunken and negligent" (Jan. 20, 1809).

82. *depose*: declare, testify.

83. She has been hired for a year.

84. Servants, like other paid workers, often left their existing employment to seek better jobs, especially in a family like the Prices who could not pay high

Southampton High Street.
[From *The Repository of arts, literature, fashions, manufactures, &c*, Vol. VII (1812), p. 281]

pretty little girl, whom she had left there not much younger when she went into Northamptonshire, who had died a few years afterwards. There had been something remarkably amiable about her. Fanny, in those early days, had preferred her to Susan; and when the news of her death had at last reached Mansfield, had for a short time been quite afflicted.—The sight of Betsey brought the image of little Mary back again, but she would not have pained her mother by alluding to her, for the world.—While considering her with these ideas, Betsey, at a small distance, was holding out something to catch her eyes, meaning to screen it at the same time from Susan's.

"What have you got there, my love?" said Fanny, "come and shew it to me."

It was a silver knife. Up jumped Susan, claiming it as her own, and trying to get it away; but the child ran to her mother's protection, and Susan could only reproach, which she did very warmly, and evidently hoping to interest Fanny on her side. "It was very hard that she was not to have her *own* knife; it was her own knife; little sister Mary had left it to her upon her death-bed, and she ought to have had it to keep herself long ago.[85] But mamma kept it from her, and was always letting Betsey get hold of it; and the end of it would be that Betsey would spoil it, and get it for her own, though mamma had *promised* her that Betsey should not have it in her own hands."

Fanny was quite shocked. Every feeling of duty, honour, and tenderness was wounded by her sister's speech and her mother's reply.[86]

"Now, Susan," cried Mrs. Price in a complaining voice, "now, how can you be so cross? You are always quarrelling about that knife. I wish you would not be so quarrelsome. Poor little Betsey; how cross Susan is to you! But you should not have taken it out, my dear, when I sent you to the drawer. You know I told you not to touch it, because Susan is so cross about it.[87] I must hide it another time, Betsey. Poor Mary little thought it would be such a bone of contention when she gave it me to keep, only two hours before she died. Poor little soul! she could but just speak to be heard, and she said so prettily, 'Let sister Susan have my knife, mamma, when I am dead and buried.'— Poor little dear! she was so fond of it, Fanny, that she would have it lay by her in bed, all through her illness. It was the gift of her good godmother, old Mrs. Admiral Maxwell,[88] only six weeks before she

wages and in an urban area where there were many other job opportunities. Servants also left if they decided to get married, and most servants tended to be young people who hoped to save up money through their work to enable them to marry.

85. A knife is a basic accessory for household tasks, which girls and women in a family like this, one that could not rely on servants for most of those tasks, would use frequently and strongly value. "Knife" did not have any aggressive connotation at this time: a blade used as a weapon was called a dagger.

86. A girl's duty would be to honor her mother in her speech and behavior, whatever her mother's faults. Susan's speech also reveals a distinct lack of tenderness in her quickness to blame her mother and accuse her of unfairness.

87. Mrs. Price blatantly takes one daughter's side against another, which represents a transgression both of duty and of maternal tenderness.

88. The Prices probably had a connection with the wife, or widow, of Admiral Maxwell that induced her to become godmother to the girl.

A mother with children.

[From Randall Davies, *English Society of the Eighteenth Century in Contemporary Art* (London, 1907), p. 52]

was taken for death. Poor little sweet creature! Well, she was taken away from evil to come. My own Betsey, (fondling her), *you* have not the luck of such a good godmother. Aunt Norris lives too far off, to think of such little people as you."[89]

Fanny had indeed nothing to convey from aunt Norris, but a message to say she hoped her goddaughter was a good girl, and learnt her book. There had been at one moment a slight murmur in the drawing-room at Mansfield Park, about sending her a Prayer-book;[90] but no second sound had been heard of such a purpose. Mrs. Norris, however, had gone home and taken down two old Prayer-books of her husband, with that idea, but upon examination, the ardour of generosity went off.[91] One was found to have too small a print for a child's eyes, and the other to be too cumbersome for her to carry about.

Fanny fatigued and fatigued again, was thankful to accept the first invitation of going to bed; and before Betsey had finished her cry at being allowed to sit up only one hour extraordinary in honour of sister, she was off, leaving all below in confusion and noise again, the boys begging for toasted cheese, her father calling out for his rum and water,[92] and Rebecca never where she ought to be.

There was nothing to raise her spirits in the confined and scantily-furnished chamber that she was to share with Susan. The smallness of the rooms above and below indeed, and the narrowness of the passage and staircase, struck her beyond her imagination. She soon learnt to think with respect of her own little attic at Mansfield Park, in *that* house reckoned too small for anybody's comfort.

89. This child, five years old, was born after the reconciliation of the Prices with Mrs. Norris and the Bertrams, allowing Mrs. Norris to be her godmother. It is possible she was named after Mrs. Norris, whose name is Elizabeth, one of the most common female names of the time.

90. A prayer book was a common possession that could be considered especially appropriate for a child. It could also be a suitable gift for a godmother.

91. *went off*: passed away, ceased.

92. Rum was a popular drink with sailors. Mr. Price could have acquired a taste for it while at sea, and it would be widely available in Portsmouth.

A sailor.

[From William Alexander, *Picturesque Representations of the Dress and Manners of the English* (London, 1813), Plate 18]

Chapter Eight

*C*ould Sir Thomas have seen all his niece's feelings, when she wrote her first letter to her aunt, he would not have despaired; for though a good night's rest, a pleasant morning, the hope of soon seeing William again, and the comparatively quiet state of the house, from Tom and Charles being gone to school, Sam on some project of his own, and her father on his usual lounges,[1] enabled her to express herself cheerfully on the subject of home, there were still to her own perfect consciousness, many drawbacks suppressed. Could he have seen only half that she felt before the end of a week, he would have thought Mr. Crawford sure of her, and been delighted with his own sagacity.

Before the week ended, it was all disappointment. In the first place, William was gone. The Thrush had had her orders, the wind had changed, and he was sailed[2] within four days from their reaching Portsmouth; and during those days, she had seen him only twice, in a short and hurried way, when he had come ashore on duty. There had been no free conversation, no walk on the ramparts,[3] no visit to the dock-yard,[4] no acquaintance with the Thrush—nothing of all that they had planned and depended on. Every thing in that quarter failed her, except William's affection. His last thought on leaving home was for her. He stepped back again to the door to say, "Take care of Fanny, mother. She is tender, and not used to rough it like the rest of us. I charge you, take care of Fanny."

William was gone;—and the home he had left her in was—Fanny could not conceal it from herself—in almost every respect, the very reverse of what she could have wished. It was the abode of noise, disorder, and impropriety. Nobody was in their right place, nothing was done as it ought to be. She could not respect her parents, as she had hoped. On her father, her confidence had not been sanguine, but he was more negligent of his family, his habits were worse, and his manners coarser, than she had been prepared for. He did not want

1. *lounges*: strolls.

2. *was sailed*: had sailed. "To be" was sometimes used instead of "to have" to form the past tense, a legacy of an earlier time when "to be" was even more commonly used for this purpose.

3. The ramparts were the fortifications that surrounded Portsmouth, extending more than a mile. They had walks at the top, and the views they offered made them popular. Stairs at various points along the ramparts allowed access from below, and trees were planted along them to make them more attractive.

4. For the dockyards, the leading sight in Portsmouth, see p. 721, note 5.

Posting a letter.
[From Andrew Tuer, *Old London Street Cries* (London, 1885), p. 57]

abilities;[5] but he had no curiosity, and no information[6] beyond his profession; he read only the newspaper and the navy-list;[7] he talked only of the dock-yard, the harbour, Spithead, and the Motherbank;[8] he swore and he drank, he was dirty and gross.[9] She had never been able to recal anything approaching to tenderness in his former treatment of herself. There had remained only a general impression of roughness and loudness; and now he scarcely ever noticed her, but to make her the object of a coarse joke.

Her disappointment in her mother was greater; *there* she had hoped much, and found almost nothing. Every flattering scheme of being of consequence to her soon fell to the ground.[10] Mrs. Price was not unkind—but, instead of gaining on her affection and confidence, and becoming more and more dear, her daughter never met with greater kindness from her, than on the first day of her arrival. The instinct of nature was soon satisfied, and Mrs. Price's attachment had no other source.[11] Her heart and her time were already quite full; she had neither leisure nor affection to bestow on Fanny. Her daughters never had been much to her. She was fond of her sons, especially of William, but Betsey was the first of her girls whom she had ever much regarded. To her she was most injudiciously indulgent. William was her pride; Betsey, her darling; and John, Richard, Sam, Tom, and Charles,[12] occupied all the rest of her maternal solicitude, alternately her worries and her comforts. These shared her heart; her time was given chiefly to her house and her servants. Her days were spent in a kind of slow bustle; always busy without getting on, always behindhand[13] and lamenting it, without altering her ways; wishing to be an economist,[14] without contrivance[15] or regularity;[16] dissatisfied with her servants, without skill to make them better, and whether helping, or reprimanding, or indulging them, without any power of engaging[17] their respect.[18]

Of her two sisters, Mrs. Price very much more resembled Lady Bertram than Mrs. Norris. She was a manager by necessity, without any of Mrs. Norris's inclination for it, or any of her activity. Her disposition was naturally easy and indolent, like Lady Bertram's; and a situation of similar affluence and do-nothingness would have been much more suited to her capacity, than the exertions and self-denials

5. *want abilities*: lack mental endowments or intelligence.

6. *information*: knowledge.

7. The navy list, or *Steele's Original and Correct List of the Royal Navy*, was a publication that included a list of all the active ships in the navy, with their number of guns, current station, and (in most cases) commanding officer. It also contained a list of all naval officers, grouped according to rank and revealing the date they attained that rank. The publication, which had been coming out in regular updated versions for several decades, was sufficiently popular that in 1814, the year this novel was published, the navy began publishing its own list.

8. The Motherbank was an area of shallow water to the immediate south and southwest of Spithead. Ships would often anchor there.

9. *gross*: unrefined, uncultured.

10. *fell to the ground*: came to nothing, was given up.

11. The "instinct of nature" is her innate maternal tenderness, which in this case has not been reinforced by continuous contact over the years.

12. John and Richard were already described as being a clerk in London and serving on a merchant ship. This gives the Prices six boys and three girls, including Fanny; there was a fourth girl, Mary, who died.

13. *behindhand*: tardy (in the completion of her tasks).

14. That is, to be frugal and a good household manager.

15. *contrivance*: faculty of contriving; ingenuity.

16. *regularity*: orderliness.

17. *engaging*: gaining.

18. Managing servants was one of the most important tasks of the mistress of a household that could afford them. It would also require particular skill in a modest household like this where there were few servants and the mistress needed to be actively engaged in getting work done. In contrast, the Bertrams are able to afford a large staff of servants, each one able to specialize in particular tasks, and a highly professional housekeeper to manage the household well, despite the inability of Lady Bertram in this regard.

of the one, which her imprudent marriage had placed her in. She might have made just as good a woman of consequence as Lady Bertram, but Mrs. Norris would have been a more respectable mother of nine children, on a small income.[19]

Much of all this, Fanny could not but be sensible of. She might scruple to make use of the words, but she must and did feel that her mother was a partial, ill-judging parent, a dawdle,[20] a slattern, who neither taught nor restrained her children, whose house was the scene of mismanagement and discomfort from beginning to end, and who had no talent, no conversation,[21] no affection towards herself; no curiosity to know her better, no desire of her friendship, and no inclination for her company that could lessen her sense of such feelings.[22]

Fanny was very anxious to be useful, and not to appear above her home, or in any way disqualified or disinclined, by her foreign[23] education, from contributing her help to its comforts, and therefore set about working for Sam immediately, and by working early and late, with perseverance and great dispatch, did so much, that the boy was shipped off at last, with more than half his linen ready.[24] She had great pleasure in feeling her usefulness, but could not conceive how they would have managed without her.

Sam, loud and overbearing as he was, she rather regretted when he went, for he was clever and intelligent, and glad to be employed in any errand in the town; and though spurning the remonstrances of Susan, given as they were—though very reasonable in themselves, with ill-timed and powerless warmth, was beginning to be influenced by Fanny's services, and gentle persuasions; and she found that the best of the three younger ones was gone in him; Tom and Charles being at least as many years as they were his juniors distant from that age of feeling and reason, which might suggest the expediency of making friends, and of endeavouring to be less disagreeable. Their sister soon despaired of making the smallest impression on *them*; they were quite untameable by any means of address which she had spirits or time to attempt.[25] Every afternoon brought a return of their riotous games all over the house; and she very early learnt to sigh at the approach of Saturday's constant half holiday.[26]

19. This praise of Mrs. Norris, as limited as it is, demonstrates Jane Austen's realism and fairness regarding her characters. Mrs. Norris is perhaps the most odious of all characters in her novels, one whose nasty characteristics are constantly on display. But the author is still willing to admit that Mrs. Norris's particular qualities could, within a certain context, prove useful and beneficial.

20. *dawdle*: dawdler, lazy person.

21. Meaning no ability or willingness to engage in worthwhile conversation.

22. Fanny's harsh verdict on her parents, especially her mother, as well as her similar verdict on her family home, has been criticized by many readers and commentators as being snobbish and insensitive. But she is actually typical of Austen's heroines in this regard. All, except the heroine of *Northanger Abbey*, have one or more parents who are fundamentally flawed, and all recognize these flaws. Their ability to do this and to make decisions on their own without parental guidance is presented as a mark of maturity and wisdom. If Fanny differs, it is only in having parents who are particularly faulty and a home that, partly due to the Prices' relative poverty, inflicts greater misery on her. Moreover, all of Austen's heroines combine knowledge of parental flaws with continuing love and concern for their parents, respect for their authority, avoidance of behavior that would challenge or dishonor them in public, and serious efforts to remedy any defects or dangers they cause. Fanny shows this here, too, though her longtime separation from her parents and her natural timidity render her less able to effect any improvement. Jane Austen lived with a similar situation. Her letters to her sister include critical comments about their mother, usually presented in a casual way that suggests that she and her sister had often exchanged similar opinions in person. But the letters also evince a strong love and concern for her mother, and by all accounts Jane Austen was always a dutiful and caring daughter.

23. *foreign*: alien, different.

24. His linen are his clothes, especially his shirts and undergarments. Her assistance probably includes sewing some of them, a skill she has often been shown exercising at Mansfield Park, though she probably makes mostly decorative items there.

25. Meaning ways of speaking to them or dealing with them that she had the vigor and assertiveness, as well as time, to try.

26. A half holiday, i.e., one for half the day, was common for schools on Saturday.

Betsey too, a spoilt child, trained up to think the alphabet her greatest enemy,[27] left to be with the servants at her pleasure, and then encouraged to report any evil of them,[28] she was almost as ready to despair of being able to love or assist; and of Susan's temper, she had many doubts. Her continual disagreements with her mother, her rash squabbles with Tom and Charles, and petulance with Betsey, were at least so distressing to Fanny, that though admitting they were by no means without provocation, she feared the disposition that could push them to such length must be far from amiable, and from affording any repose to herself.[29]

Such was the home which was to put Mansfield out of her head, and teach her to think of her cousin Edmund with moderated feelings. On the contrary, she could think of nothing but Mansfield, its beloved inmates,[30] its happy ways. Every thing where she now was was in full contrast to it. The elegance, propriety, regularity, harmony—and perhaps, above all, the peace and tranquillity of Mansfield, were brought to her remembrance every hour of the day, by the prevalence of every thing opposite to them *here*.[31]

The living in incessant noise was to a frame and temper, delicate and nervous like Fanny's, an evil which no super-added elegance or harmony could have entirely atoned for. It was the greatest misery of all. At Mansfield, no sounds of contention, no raised voice, no abrupt bursts, no tread of violence was ever heard; all proceeded in a regular course of cheerful orderliness; every body had their due importance; every body's feelings were consulted. If tenderness could be ever supposed wanting, good sense and good breeding supplied its place;[32] and as to the little irritations, sometimes introduced by aunt Norris, they were short, they were trifling, they were as a drop of water to the ocean, compared with the ceaseless tumult of her present abode. Here, every body was noisy, every voice was loud (excepting, perhaps, her mother's, which resembled the soft monotony of Lady Bertram's, only worn into fretfulness).—Whatever was wanted, was halloo'd for, and the servants halloo'd out their excuses from the kitchen. The doors were in constant banging, the stairs were never at rest, nothing was done without a clatter, nobody sat still, and nobody could command attention when they spoke.

27. Her mother is in charge of teaching the child to read, which was standard practice, except in very wealthy homes that hired governesses from a young age for their children. The description suggests Mrs. Price has so far either refrained from doing so, due to the girl's resistance, or done so badly.

28. Children often spent time with servants, but some writers warned of the bad effects of too much time so spent. Of course, any such harm would only be exacerbated by a child's being encouraged to spy on the servants.

29. *from affording any repose to herself*: far from likely to furnish any repose to Fanny. Thus here Fanny, as at Mansfield Park, suffers neglect and isolation that further compounds the general difficulties of her situation, with the main difference being that here she has no Edmund to relieve her isolation.

30. *inmates*: inhabitants.

31. In this respect Sir Thomas's design regarding Fanny is working; his expectation of her reaction to her home has proven more prescient than her idealistic hopes, mentioned again in the first sentence of the paragraph. Sir Thomas was wrong, however, to expect that she would be primarily affected by missing Mansfield Park's affluence. Instead, more intangible moral qualities are what she mostly regrets, so her change does not foretell any necessary alteration in her attitude to Henry Crawford.

32. One effect of Fanny's treatment is to teach her to appreciate the benefits of good breeding or manners. The Bertrams, along with the Crawfords, present a variety of cases in which politeness and outward refinement are accompanied by serious moral defects, most notably lack of concern for others. The Prices, however, with similar moral defects, demonstrate that lack of politeness significantly exacerbates them. In contrast, a woman like Lady Bertram, who almost never thinks of other people, much less does anything for them, still avoids inflicting misery on others, and provides at least benign companionship, because of her self-restraint and fine manners.

In a review of the two houses, as they appeared to her before the end of a week, Fanny was tempted to apply to them Dr. Johnson's celebrated judgment as to matrimony and celibacy,[33] and say, that though Mansfield Park might have some pains, Portsmouth could have no pleasures.[34]

A fashionable London interior of the time.

[From E. Beresford Chancellor, *The XVIIIth Century in London* (New York, 1921), p. 227]

33. *celibacy*: a single or unmarried state.

34. The famous line is "Marriage has many pains, but celibacy has no plea-sures." It is spoken by Princess Nekayah in *Rasselas* (1759), a philosophical novel by Samuel Johnson on the inevitable disappointments and miseries of life that is set in an imaginary African kingdom.

Burlington House, a leading London house.

[From E. Beresford Chancellor, *The XVIIIth Century in London* (New York, 1921), p. 163]

Chapter Nine

*F*anny was right enough in not expecting to hear from Miss Crawford now, at the rapid rate in which their correspondence had begun; Mary's next letter was after a decidedly longer interval than the last, but she was not right in supposing that such an interval would be felt a great relief to herself.—Here was another strange revolution of mind!—She was really glad to receive the letter when it did come. In her present exile from good society, and distance from every thing that had been wont to interest her, a letter from one belonging to the set where her heart lived, written with affection, and some degree of elegance, was thoroughly acceptable.—The usual plea of increasing engagements was made in excuse for not having written to her earlier, "and now that I have begun,"[1] she continued, "my letter will not be worth your reading, for there will be no little offering of love at the end, no three or four lines passionées[2] from the most devoted H. C. in the world,[3] for Henry is in Norfolk; business called him to Everingham ten days ago,[4] or perhaps he only pretended the call, for the sake of being travelling[5] at the same time that you were. But there he is, and, by the by, his absence may sufficiently account for any remissness of his sister's in writing, for there has been no 'well, Mary, when do you write to Fanny?—is not it time for you to write to Fanny?' to spur me on. At last, after various attempts at meeting, I have seen your cousins, 'dear Julia and dearest Mrs. Rushworth'; they found me at home yesterday, and we were glad to see each other again.[6] We *seemed very* glad to see each other,[7] and I do really think we were a little.—We had a vast deal to say.—Shall I tell you how Mrs. Rushworth looked when your name was mentioned? I did not use to think her wanting in self-possession, but she had not quite enough for the demands of yesterday.[8] Upon the whole Julia was in the best looks of the two, at least after you were spoken of. There was no recovering the complexion from the moment that I spoke of 'Fanny,' and spoke of her

1.   This marks the beginning of a phase in which many of the plot developments are related by letter, because Fanny is now isolated from all the other
important characters. Jane Austen also uses the letters to reveal character,
something she does regularly in her other novels. An inspiration for this was
the epistolary novel, one entirely told via letters, the mode in which a large
proportion of eighteenth-century novels were written. In some of her stories
Austen used the epistolary technique; the first version of either *Sense and Sensibility* or *Pride and Prejudice* may have been written in this way.

2.   *passionées*: impassioned. Using this French word, Mary also follows the
rule in French of placing the adjective after the noun it modifies.

3.   In Mary's earlier letters to Fanny she included brief greetings to Fanny
from Henry, i.e., H.C.

4.   His business would relate to the management of his estate there.

5.   *being travelling*: traveling.

6.   They presumably called on each other previously when the other party
was either not there or not receiving visitors. A common custom, when people
did not wish for visitors, was to have the servant tell callers that the person
being sought was not at home; hence, by saying she was finally "at home"
Mary may mean that on earlier occasions she was simply not receiving visitors. Etiquette dictated that when one called on another party who was not at
home, one left a visiting card with one's name on it; this ritual was especially
prevalent in cities and towns. This is how Mary knows the other two women
called on her earlier.

7.   Meaning they displayed enthusiasm, which would be proper etiquette,
though their real feelings were obviously more mixed. Mary's placing quotation marks around the words "dear" and "dearest" may also signal her sense of
the artificiality of their friendliness.

8.   Maria was feeling jealousy of Fanny. It is probably especially galling to
Maria that, though she is the eldest girl in a wealthy family and an acknowledged beauty, the man she fell in love with instead proposed to her socially
insignificant cousin, whom Maria always condescended to and who was
never considered a great beauty or likely to marry well. The extent of her jealousy is shown by her lack of self-possession, for not only does that violate the
upper-class ideal of a calm and self-controlled demeanor, but it might also
reveal her state of mind and lead to humiliating gossip.

as a sister should.[9]—But Mrs. Rushworth's day of good looks will come; we have cards for her first party on the 28th.[10]—Then she will be in beauty, for she will open one of the best houses in Wimpole Street.[11] I was in it two years ago, when it was Lady Lascelles's, and prefer it to almost any I know in London, and certainly she will then feel—to use a vulgar phrase—that she has got her pennyworth for her penny.[12] Henry could not have afforded her such a house. I hope she will recollect it, and be satisfied, as well she may, with moving the queen of a palace, though the king may appear best in the back ground; and as I have no desire to tease[13] her, I shall never *force* your name upon her again. She will grow sober by degrees.—From all that I hear and guess, Baron Wildenhaim's attentions to Julia continue,[14] but I do not know that he has any serious encouragement. She ought to do better. A poor honourable is no catch,[15] and I cannot imagine any liking in the case, for, take away his rants,[16] and the poor Baron has nothing. What a difference a vowel makes!—if his rents were but equal to his rants![17]—Your cousin Edmund moves slowly; detained, perchance, by parish duties. There may be some old woman at Thornton Lacey to be converted.[18] I am unwilling to fancy myself neglected for a *young* one. Adieu, my dear sweet Fanny, this is a long letter from London; write me a pretty one in reply to gladden Henry's eyes, when he comes back—and send me an account of all the dashing young captains whom you disdain for his sake."[19]

There was great food for meditation in this letter, and chiefly for unpleasant meditation; and yet, with all the uneasiness it supplied, it connected her with the absent, it told her of people and things about whom she had never felt so much curiosity as now, and she would have been glad to have been sure of such a letter every week. Her correspondence with her aunt Bertram was her only concern of higher interest.

As for any society in Portsmouth, that could at all make amends for deficiencies at home, there were none within the circle of her father's and mother's acquaintance to afford her the smallest satisfaction; she saw nobody in whose favour she could wish to overcome her own shyness and reserve. The men appeared to her all coarse,

9. Meaning as one who expects to become Fanny's sister. This would include calling her "Fanny" instead of "Miss Price" (though Mary's mention of that will only anger Fanny when she reads it).

10. These are her cards of invitation. This marks her debut as a hostess in London society.

11. Wimpole Street is in the fashionable Marylebone district of West London (see the picture on the next page). Marylebone is adjacent to Mayfair, and after the latter was developed in the first half of the eighteenth century, builders turned to Marylebone and created similar housing for the wealthy there. Most of the wealthy characters in Austen's novels inhabit Mayfair or Marylebone when they visit or reside in London. By opening the house Mary means that Maria will now establish it as a place for fashionable entertaining.

12. Meaning she has gotten her money's worth for what she paid (a penny is a single pence—see p. 105, note 19). The price she paid was being married to a foolish man, but once she is able to use his vast wealth to establish herself as a leading London hostess, she can feel it was worth it.

13. *tease*: annoy, irritate.

14. Baron Wildenhaim is Yates, for that is the character he played in *Lovers' Vows*. The appropriateness of the name is enhanced by Yates's being the son of a baron.

15. By an "honourable" she means a man with that courtesy title, which is applied to a son of an earl, viscount, or baron.

16. She refers to Yates's ranting while acting in the play.

17. Rents are income from an estate. Owners of estates leased the land to farmers, whose rents constituted the bulk of the owners' income. When the income of male characters in Austen's novels who possess estates is described, as in the case of Henry Crawford, that means principally the amount they receive annually in rents. Yates does have an estate, but because he is a younger son it is a small one, see p. 830 and p. 831, note 4.

18. Mary exhibits the same snobbery that Henry showed in his talk of wanting to be a preacher only in a fine parish in London, for the old woman she envisions is likely poor. Mary's remarks indicate either her continued obtuseness regarding Fanny, for she should know that Fanny would hate a joke like that, or her devotion to making witty remarks whatever the consequences. Fanny would hate even more the allusion to Mary's relationship with Edmund, but Mary could not know that.

19. She is thinking of naval captains, whom she may regard as dashing because of the heroic nature, and high social status, of their profession.

the women all pert, every body under-bred;[20] and she gave as little contentment as she received from introductions either to old or new acquaintance. The young ladies who approached her at first with some respect, in consideration of her coming from a Baronet's family, were soon offended by what they termed "airs"—for as she neither played on the pianoforte nor wore fine pelisses,[21] they could, on farther observation, admit no right of superiority.[22]

The first solid consolation which Fanny received for the evils of home, the first which her judgment could entirely approve, and which gave any promise of durability, was in a better knowledge of Susan, and a hope of being of service to her. Susan had always behaved pleasantly to herself, but the determined character of her general manners had astonished and alarmed her, and it was at least a fortnight before she began to understand a disposition so totally different from her own. Susan saw that much was wrong at home, and wanted to set it right. That a girl of fourteen, acting only on her own unassisted reason, should err in the method of reform was not wonderful;[23] and Fanny soon became more disposed to admire the natural light of the mind which could so early distinguish justly, than to censure severely the faults of conduct to which it led. Susan was only acting on the same truths, and pursuing the same system,[24] which her own judgment acknowledged, but which her more supine and yielding temper would have shrunk from asserting. Susan tried to be useful, where *she* could only have gone away and cried; and that Susan was useful she could perceive; that things, bad as they were, would have been worse but for such interposition, and that both her mother and Betsey were restrained from some excesses of very offensive indulgence and vulgarity.

In every argument with her mother, Susan had in point of reason the advantage, and never was there any maternal tenderness to buy her off. The blind fondness which was for ever producing evil around her, *she* had never known. There was no gratitude for affection past or present, to make her better bear with its excesses to the others.

All this became gradually evident, and gradually placed Susan before her sister as an object of mingled compassion and respect. That her manner was wrong, however, at times very wrong—her measures often ill-chosen and ill-timed, and her looks and language

20. *under-bred*: lacking in manners and refinement.

21. Playing the pianoforte was probably the accomplishment most widely taught to genteel girls, and hence would be recognized as a mark of female status. A pelisse is a full-length female overcoat popular in this period; see the picture on the following page. Since it is February Fanny would wear one when venturing outside; she may not own one, or hers may be unimpressive.

22. Their lack of respect for Fanny indicates their lack of appreciation for less obvious qualities of gentility or refinement, such as politeness and a cultivated mind and good taste. Others, including Henry Crawford, do appreciate these qualities of hers.

23. *wonderful*: astonishing.

24. *system*: set of principles.

Cavendish Square, very close to the Rushworths' house on Wimpole Street.

[From *The Repository of arts, literature, fashions, manufactures, &c*, Vol. IX (1813), p. 178]

very often indefensible, Fanny could not cease to feel; but she began
to hope they might be rectified. Susan, she found, looked up to her
and wished for her good opinion; and new as any thing like an office
of authority was to Fanny, new as it was to imagine herself capable
of guiding or informing any one, she did resolve to give occasional
hints to Susan, and endeavour to exercise for her advantage the
juster notions of what was due to every body, and what would be
wisest for herself, which her own more favoured education had fixed
in her.

Her influence, or at least the consciousness and use of it, originated in an act of kindness by[25] Susan, which after many hesitations
of delicacy, she at last worked herself up to. It had very early occurred
to her, that a small sum of money might, perhaps, restore peace for
ever on the sore subject of the silver knife, canvassed[26] as it now was
continually, and the riches which she was in possession of herself,
her uncle having given her 10*l.* at parting, made her as able as she
was willing to be generous. But she was so wholly unused to confer
favours, except on the very poor, so unpractised in removing evils, or
bestowing kindnesses among her equals, and so fearful of appearing
to elevate herself as a great lady at home, that it took some time to
determine that it would not be unbecoming in her to make such a
present. It was made, however, at last; a silver knife was bought for
Betsey, and accepted with great delight, its newness giving it every
advantage over the other that could be desired; Susan was established in the full possession of her own. Betsey handsomely declaring
that now she had got one so much prettier herself, she should never
want *that* again—and no reproach seemed conveyed to the equally
satisfied mother, which Fanny had almost feared to be impossible.
The deed thoroughly answered,[27] a source of domestic altercation
was entirely done away, and it was the means of opening Susan's
heart to her, and giving her something more to love and be interested in. Susan shewed that she had delicacy;[28] pleased as she was
to be mistress of property which she had been struggling for at least
two years, she yet feared that her sister's judgment had been against
her, and that a reproof was designed her for having so struggled as to
make the purchase necessary for the tranquillity of the house.

25. *kindness by*: kindness to or toward. This use of "by" is found elsewhere in Austen's novels.

26. *canvassed*: discussed.

27. *answered*: satisfied or fulfilled its purpose.

28. *delicacy*: sense of what is proper and appropriate.

A woman in a fine pelisse.

[From *The Repository of arts, literature, fashions, manufactures, &c*, Vol. V (1811), p. 48]

Her temper was open.[29] She acknowledged her fears, blamed herself for having contended so warmly, and from that hour Fanny understanding the worth of her disposition, and perceiving how fully she was inclined to seek her good opinion and refer to her judgment, began to feel again the blessing of affection, and to entertain the hope of being useful to a mind so much in need of help, and so much deserving it. She gave advice; advice too sound to be resisted by a good understanding, and given so mildly and considerately as not to irritate an imperfect temper; and she had the happiness of observing its good effects not unfrequently; more was not expected by one, who, while seeing all the obligation and expediency of submission and forbearance, saw also with sympathetic acuteness of feeling, all that must be hourly grating to a girl like Susan. Her greatest wonder on the subject soon became—not that Susan should have been provoked into disrespect and impatience against her better knowledge—but that so much better knowledge, so many good notions, should have been hers at all; and that, brought up in the midst of negligence and error, she should have formed such proper opinions of what ought to be—she, who had had no cousin Edmund to direct her thoughts or fix her principles.[30]

The intimacy thus begun between them was a material advantage to each. By sitting together up stairs, they avoided a great deal of the disturbance of the house; Fanny had peace, and Susan learnt to think it no misfortune to be quietly employed. They sat without a fire; but *that* was a privation familiar even to Fanny, and she suffered the less because reminded by it of the east room. It was the only point of resemblance. In space, light, furniture,[31] and prospect,[32] there was nothing alike in the two apartments; and she often heaved a sigh at the remembrance of all her books and boxes, and various comforts there. By degrees the girls came to spend the chief of the morning up stairs, at first only in working[33] and talking; but after a few days, the remembrance of the said books grew so potent and stimulative, that Fanny found it impossible not to try for books again. There were none in her father's house; but wealth is luxurious[34] and daring—and some of hers found its way to a circulating library. She became a subscriber[35]—amazed at being any thing in *propria persona*,[36] amazed at her own doings in every way; to be a renter, a

29. *open*: sincere, unreserved.

30. This gives a sense of Jane Austen's mixed opinion on the subject of nature versus nurture. She acknowledges inborn dispositions, for Susan's ability to value and assert good principles despite her background indicates an inherent inclination. But her lack of a good upbringing and guidance has kept her from putting the principles into practice well. At other points in the novel, in discussing wealthy characters who were spoiled in various ways, the author gives much weight to education and nurture.

31. *furniture*: furnishings.

32. *prospect*: view of the outside.

33. *working*: needlework.

34. *luxurious*: given to luxury and self-indulgence.

35. A circulating library was a private enterprise that allowed people to subscribe for a fee and borrow books (there were no public lending libraries then). Usually they were part of bookshops. They had spread throughout England during the eighteenth century and become fixtures in towns of any size. They lent a great variety of books, though they were most associated with novels, the most popular genre.

36. *in* propria persona: in one's own person. Jane Austen made a mistake with the Latin here by not italicizing the "in," for it is part of the Latin phrase (though it is possible the omission was a printer's error). She did not know Latin, for it was almost never taught to girls, but because of the importance of it in male education, Latin phrases abounded in contemporary literature, so she would be familiar with the phrase and its meaning.

chuser of books! And to be having any one's improvement in view in her choice! But so it was. Susan had read nothing, and Fanny longed to give her a share in her own first pleasures, and inspire a taste for the biography and poetry which she delighted in herself.[37]

In this occupation she hoped, moreover, to bury some of the recollections of Mansfield which were too apt to seize her mind if her fingers only were busy; and especially at this time, hoped it might be useful in diverting her thoughts from pursuing Edmund to London, whither, on the authority of her aunt's last letter, she knew he was gone. She had no doubt of what would ensue. The promised notification was hanging over her head. The postman's knock within the neighbourhood[38] was beginning to bring its daily terrors[39]—and if reading could banish the idea for even half an hour, it was something gained.

A London bookstore.

[From *The Repository of arts, literature, fashions, manufactures, &c,* Vol. I (1809), p. 251]

37. When Edmund visited Fanny in her room earlier (p. 292), he identified the three books she was currently reading as poetry, biography, and a collection of essays.

38. The postman delivered the mail; in an urban area he would stop by each house.

39. Her terror is that it will bring a letter from either Mary or Edmund announcing their engagement.

Postal delivery.

[From William Alexander, *Picturesque Representations of the Dress and Manners of the English* (London, 1813), Plate 24]

Chapter Ten

A week was gone since Edmund might be supposed in town, and Fanny had heard nothing of him. There were three different conclusions to be drawn from his silence, between which her mind was in fluctuation; each of them at times being held the most probable. Either his going had been again delayed, or he had yet procured no opportunity of seeing Miss Crawford alone—or, he was too happy for letter writing!

One morning about this time, Fanny having now been nearly four weeks from Mansfield—a point which she never failed to think over and calculate every day—as she and Susan were preparing to remove as usual up stairs, they were stopt by the knock of a visitor, whom they felt they could not avoid, from Rebecca's alertness[1] in going to the door, a duty which always interested her beyond any other.

It was a gentleman's voice; it was a voice that Fanny was just turning pale about, when Mr. Crawford walked into the room.

Good sense, like hers, will always act when really called upon; and she found that she had been able to name him to her mother, and recal her remembrance of the name, as that of "William's friend," though she could not previously have believed herself capable of uttering a syllable at such a moment. The consciousness of his being known there only as William's friend, was some support. Having introduced him, however, and being all re-seated, the terrors that occurred of what this visit might lead to were overpowering, and she fancied herself on the point of fainting away.

While trying to keep herself alive, their visitor, who had at first approached her with as animated a countenance as ever, was wisely and kindly keeping his eyes away, and giving her time to recover, while he devoted himself entirely to her mother, addressing her, and attending to her with the utmost politeness and propriety, at the same time with a degree of friendliness—of interest at least—which was making his manner perfect.

1. *alertness*: briskness, rapidity.

A contemporary picture of Portsmouth Point, showing its raucous and licentious character—see p. 723, note 13.

[From Joseph Grego, *Rowlandson the Caricaturist*, Vol. II (London, 1880), p. 285]

Mrs. Price's manners were also at their best. Warmed by the sight of such a friend to her son, and regulated by the wish of appearing to advantage before him, she was overflowing with gratitude, artless, maternal gratitude, which could not be unpleasing. Mr. Price was out, which she regretted very much. Fanny was just recovered enough to feel that *she* could not regret it; for to her many other sources of uneasiness was added the severe one of shame for the home in which he found her. She might scold herself for the weakness, but there was no scolding it away. She was ashamed, and she would have been yet more ashamed of her father, than of all the rest.

They talked of William, a subject on which Mrs. Price could never tire; and Mr. Crawford was as warm in his commendation, as even her heart could wish. She felt that she had never seen so agreeable a man in her life; and was only astonished to find, that so great[2] and so agreeable as he was, he should be come down to Portsmouth neither on a visit to the port-admiral, nor the commissioner,[3] nor yet with the intention of going over to the island,[4] nor of seeing the Dock-yard.[5] Nothing of all that she had been used to think of as the proof of importance, or the employment of wealth, had brought him to Portsmouth. He had reached it late the night before, was come for a day or two, was staying at the Crown,[6] had accidentally[7] met with a navy officer or two of his acquaintance, since his arrival, but had no object of that kind in coming.

By the time he had given all this information, it was not unreasonable to suppose, that Fanny might be looked at and spoken to; and she was tolerably able to bear his eye, and hear that he had spent half an hour with his sister, the evening before his leaving London; that she had sent her best and kindest love, but had had no time for writing; that he thought himself lucky in seeing Mary for even half an hour, having spent scarcely twenty-four hours in London after his return from Norfolk,[8] before he set off again; that her cousin Edmund was in town, had been in town, he understood, a few days; that he had not seen him, himself, but that he was well, had left them all well at Mansfield, and was to dine, as yesterday, with the Frasers.[9]

Fanny listened collectedly even to the last-mentioned circumstance; nay, it seemed a relief to her worn mind to be at any certainty;

2. *great*: socially important, high-ranking.

3. The port admiral and the commissioner were the two principal naval authorities in Portsmouth. The first was in charge of active ships and crew there; the second was in charge of the dockyard.

4. "The island" is the nearby Isle of Wight; Fanny also referred to it that way when she came to Mansfield Park. The Isle of Wight was a popular destination for tourists, one praised for its natural beauties by guidebooks of the time.

5. Contemporary travelers universally identified the dockyard as the main object of their visit to Portsmouth. The British navy maintained a complex of dockyards at its principal bases for the purpose of repairing and refitting its ships, as well as building new ships. The one at Portsmouth was the largest, and in fact one of the largest industrial enterprises in the world, employing several thousand skilled workers (whereas at the time almost all other forms of production occurred in small enterprises). Its approximate dimensions were half a mile in one direction, and a quarter to a third of a mile in the other. In the complex were almost thirty-five buildings, along with other features, including eight docks and a large pond for storing masts. A continual stream of ships passed through the dockyard, some for minor repairs and some for complete refittings, a process that usually took several months, since it required the replacement of substantial sections of the ships (whose wood and metal parts would inevitably decay after several years at sea).

6. The Crown was one of the leading inns in Portsmouth. A contemporary history, in addition to naming it as the inn where the London mail coach originates, states that in 1814, when the crowned heads of Europe arrived in England after the victory over Napoleon, the Prince Regent, the reigning British sovereign, held a ball for royalty at the Crown (Lake Allen, *The History of Portsmouth*, 1817). Many towns had inns with that name; one in *Emma* plays an important role in the plot.

7. *accidentally*: by chance, fortuitously.

8. Henry was in Norfolk for three weeks; see chronology, p. 859.

9. Mary is staying with the Frasers, so this means dining with her as well.

and the words, "then by this time it is all settled," passed internally, without more evidence of emotion[10] than a faint blush.

After talking a little more about Mansfield, a subject in which her interest was most apparent, Crawford began to hint at the expediency of an early walk; — "It was a lovely morning, and at that season of the year a fine morning so often turned off,[11] that it was wisest for everybody not to delay their exercise"; and such hints producing nothing, he soon proceeded to a positive recommendation to Mrs. Price and her daughters, to take their walk without loss of time. Now they came to an understanding. Mrs. Price, it appeared, scarcely ever stirred out of doors, except of a Sunday; she owned she could seldom, with her large family, find time for a walk.[12] — "Would she not then persuade her daughters to take advantage of such weather, and allow him the pleasure of attending them?" — Mrs. Price was greatly obliged, and very complying. "Her daughters were very much confined — Portsmouth was a sad place — they did not often get out[13] — and she knew they had some errands in the town, which they would be very glad to do." — And the consequence was, that Fanny, strange as it was — strange, awkward, and distressing — found herself and Susan, within ten minutes, walking towards the High Street, with Mr. Crawford.

It was soon pain upon pain, confusion upon confusion; for they were hardly in the High Street, before they met her father, whose appearance was not the better from its being Saturday.[14] He stopt; and, ungentlemanlike as he looked, Fanny was obliged to introduce him to Mr. Crawford. She could not have a doubt of the manner in which Mr. Crawford must be struck. He must be ashamed and disgusted altogether. He must soon give her up, and cease to have the smallest inclination for the match; and yet, though she had been so much wanting his affection to be cured, this was a sort of cure that would be almost as bad as the complaint; and I believe, there is scarcely a young lady in the united kingdoms,[15] who would not rather put up with the misfortune of being sought by a clever, agreeable man, than have him driven away by the vulgarity of her nearest relations.[16]

Mr. Crawford probably could not regard his future father-in-law with any idea of taking him for a model in dress; but (as Fanny

10. *emotion*: agitation.

11. *turned off*: changed for the worse.

12. He could not ask only Fanny to walk with him, for he does not wish to embarrass her by showing his interest in her, and it would be improper for an unmarried man and woman to take a walk alone together.

13. She could be thinking either of the physical atmosphere, meaning a crowded town with narrow streets, or of the moral atmosphere. The latter was influenced by the many ordinary sailors on leave at any given time. They would take advantage of a break from months confined on ship to enjoy themselves to the full, which often meant heavy drinking and rowdiness in the street. It also often meant going to prostitutes, and Portsmouth was notorious for the number of such women. One visitor described his arrival at Portsmouth Point, the place where sailors embarked, "where there is scarcely anything but public houses" (i.e., taverns serving alcohol), including one whose sign declared, "if you do not pay for what you call [order], you may expect a broken head." He adds, "I never was more disgusted with human nature, than in passing from this place to the dock-yard; drunken sailors and their infamous associates met us at every step" (*A Tour through England, described in a series of letters from a young gentleman to his sister*; 1806). Not all of Portsmouth was this bad, but it still was a less-than-ideal place for Fanny and Susan to stroll around. For a contemporary picture of Portsmouth Point, in all its rowdiness and licentiousness, see p. 719.

14. He, and perhaps his friends, probably drink more heavily on Saturday, knowing they will not be able to purchase alcohol in a tavern on the next day. During the late eighteenth century a drive to improve public morals, connected with the burgeoning evangelical movement, led to severe prohibitions on the public sale of alcohol on Sunday in most of England.

15. These are the kingdoms of Britain and Ireland. They had long been separate kingdoms with separate parliaments, though both under the same monarch. But in 1801 they were joined, forming the United Kingdom of Great Britain and Ireland. The author's usage is a legacy of this earlier state.

16. Fanny faces a situation that almost all Austen's heroines face, that of being embarrassed or chagrined by the conduct of some members of her own family. This always places the heroine in a difficult position of maintaining outward respectfulness while feeling shame at family members' behavior, and it becomes in many cases an important test of character.

instantly, and to her great relief discerned), her father was a very different man, a very different Mr. Price in his behaviour to this most highly-respected stranger, from what he was in his own family at home. His manners now, though not polished, were more than passable; they were grateful, animated, manly; his expressions were those of an attached father, and a sensible man;—his loud tones did very well in the open air, and there was not a single oath to be heard. Such was his instinctive compliment to the good manners of Mr. Crawford; and be the consequence what it might, Fanny's immediate feelings were infinitely soothed.

The conclusion of the two gentlemen's civilities was an offer of Mr. Price's to take Mr. Crawford into the dock-yard, which Mr. Crawford, desirous of accepting as a favour, what was intended as such, though he had seen the dock-yard again and again;[17] and hoping to be so much the longer with Fanny, was very gratefully disposed to avail himself of, if the Miss Prices were not afraid of the fatigue; and as it was somehow or other ascertained, or inferred, or at least acted upon, that they were not at all afraid, to the dock-yard they were all to go; and, but for Mr. Crawford, Mr. Price would have turned thither directly, without the smallest consideration for his daughters' errands in the High Street. He took care, however, that they should be allowed to go to the shops they came out expressly to visit; and it did not delay them long, for Fanny could so little bear to excite impatience, or be waited for, that before the gentlemen, as they stood at the door, could do more than begin upon the last naval regulations,[18] or settle the number of three deckers now in commission,[19] their companions were ready to proceed.

They were then to set forward for the dock-yard at once, and the walk would have been conducted (according to Mr. Crawford's opinion) in a singular manner, had Mr. Price been allowed the entire regulation of it, as the two girls, he found, would have been left to follow, and keep up with them, or not, as they could, while they walked on together at their own hasty pace. He was able to introduce some improvement occasionally, though by no means to the extent he wished; he absolutely would not walk away from them; and, at any crossing, or any crowd, when Mr. Price was only

17. Places like dockyards were major tourist attractions. Guidebooks of the time included industrial sights as well as places of natural beauty and grand houses. In *Pride and Prejudice* the heroine and her aunt and uncle include in their tour of parts of England a stop at Birmingham, a major manufacturing center noted for its factories. Such places were a novelty and also a source of national pride, for Britain, which was going through the early phase of the Industrial Revolution, was far ahead of any other country in the development of such facilities. Naval dockyards would appeal to this pride, due to the worldwide preeminence of the British navy and its vital role in national defense against Napoleon. The dockyards were also notable for making extensive use of the steam engine, the most important of all inventions in this stage of the Industrial Revolution.

18. The navy frequently issued new regulations regarding a variety of matters; for example, the rules governing uniforms were altered in 1813, the year Jane Austen finished writing this novel. The ongoing intensive war with France presented a continual series of new challenges and problems that often required changes in naval policy and procedure.

19. Three-deckers were the largest of all naval ships. The term referred to the number of gun decks; ships also had a top deck above their guns and storage decks beneath them. Most three-deckers had more than a hundred guns: the HMS *Victory*, Admiral Nelson's flagship at the Battle of Trafalgar, which is still on display at the naval museum in Portsmouth, had 104 guns. Three-

British ships of the line, or men-of-war. The one on the left is a two-decker; the one on the right, a three-decker.

[From A. T. Mahon, *The Life of Nelson* (Boston, 1897), p. 180]

calling out, "Come, girls—come, Fan—come, Sue[20]—take care of yourselves—keep a sharp look out," he would give them his particular attendance.

Once fairly in the dock-yard, he began to reckon upon some happy intercourse with Fanny, as they were very soon joined by a brother lounger[21] of Mr. Price's, who was come to take his daily survey of how things went on, and who must prove a far more worthy companion than himself; and after a time the two officers seemed very well satisfied in going about together and discussing matters of equal and never-failing interest, while the young people sat down upon some timbers in the yard, or found a seat on board a vessel in the stocks which they all went to look at.[22] Fanny was most conveniently in want[23] of rest. Crawford could not have wished her more fatigued or more ready to sit down; but he could have wished her sister away. A quick looking girl of Susan's age was the very worst third in the world—totally different from Lady Bertram—all eyes and ears; and there was no introducing the main point before her. He must content himself with being only generally agreeable, and letting Susan have her share of entertainment, with the indulgence, now and then, of a look or hint for the better informed and conscious Fanny. Norfolk was what he had mostly to talk of; there he had been some time, and every thing there was rising in importance from his present schemes. Such a man could come from no place, no society, without importing something to amuse; his journeys and his acquaintance were all of use, and Susan was entertained in a way quite new to her. For Fanny, somewhat more was related than the accidental agreeableness of the parties he had been in. For her approbation, the particular reason of his going into Norfolk at all, at this unusual time of year, was given.[24] It had been real business, relative to the renewal of a lease in which the welfare of a large and (he believed) industrious family was at stake.[25] He had suspected his agent of some underhand dealing—of meaning to bias him against the deserving[26]—and he had determined to go himself, and thoroughly investigate the merits of the case. He had gone, had done even more good than he had foreseen, had been useful to more than his first plan had comprehended, and was now able to congratulate himself upon it, and to feel, that in performing

deckers were very expensive and were sometimes unwieldy to sail, but their firepower made them valuable and, most important of all for men like Mr. Price, their enormous size made them impressive sights and objects of fascination. The small number in existence made it possible to estimate how many were in commission: twenty-five in 1813. The navy had just over a thousand ships in total in 1813, its peak year (the number started to decline in the following year, when Napoleon surrendered).

20. His use of abbreviated versions of his daughters' names reflects greater informality than prevailed at Mansfield Park.

21. *lounger*: idler.

22. As the description suggests, they are walking freely in the dockyard. People were allowed to enter and walk about if they applied at the entrance, and two officers, whether marine or navy, would be able to enter easily, along with their companions. Because ships were primarily made of wood, much of the dockyard complex was occupied by storage areas for timber. A vessel in the stocks is one under repair or construction (stocks are frames or supports for vessels out of water); they were also a prominent feature of the dockyard.

23. *want*: need.

24. It is unusual because this is the height of the social season in London (the reason Mary chose to go to London at this point), and because there are no outdoor activities at his estate to tempt him now that the shooting and hunting seasons are over and summer, which offers other outdoor opportunities, is still far away. He may have gone there, and attended to the business he describes, for the purpose of impressing Fanny.

25. Leases for tenants on estates usually ran for a number of years and would need to be renewed periodically. The custom was to allow the existing family to continue, especially since such families had often held the lease for generations. But the terms were subject to renegotiation, and owners might attempt to raise the rate beyond what a family could pay or decide to install a new tenant who seemed more promising.

26. His agent, most likely his steward, supervises the management of the estate and deals with the tenants. Previous descriptions of Henry suggest that he has spent little time dealing with the estate himself, which means his agent has probably had a very free hand and ample opportunity to engage in underhanded activity if so inclined.

a duty, he had secured agreeable recollections for his own mind.[27] He had introduced himself to some tenants, whom he had never seen before;[28] he had begun making acquaintance[29] with cottages whose very existence, though on his own estate, had been hitherto unknown to him.[30] This was aimed, and well aimed, at Fanny. It was pleasing to hear him speak so properly; here, he had been acting as he ought to do. To be the friend of the poor and oppressed! Nothing could be more grateful to her, and she was on the point of giving him an approving look when it was all frightened off, by his adding a something too pointed of his hoping soon to have an assistant, a friend, a guide in every plan of utility or charity for Everingham,[31] a somebody that would make Everingham and all about it, a dearer object than it had ever been yet.

She turned away, and wished he would not say such things. She was willing to allow he might have more good qualities than she had been wont to suppose. She began to feel the possibility of his turning out well at last; but he was and must ever be completely unsuited to her, and ought not to think of her.

He perceived that enough had been said of Everingham, and that it would be as well to talk of something else, and turned to Mansfield. He could not have chosen better; that was a topic to bring back her attention and her looks almost instantly. It was a real indulgence to her to hear or to speak of Mansfield. Now so long divided from every body who knew the place, she felt it quite the voice of a friend when he mentioned it, and led the way to her fond exclamations in praise of its beauties and comforts, and by his honourable tribute to its inhabitants allowed her to gratify her own heart in the warmest eulogium, in speaking of her uncle as all that was clever and good, and her aunt as having the sweetest of all sweet tempers.

He had a great attachment to Mansfield himself; he said so; he looked forward with the hope of spending much, very much of his time there—always there, or in the neighbourhood. He particularly built upon a very happy summer and autumn there this year;[32] he felt that it would be so; he depended upon it; a summer and autumn infinitely superior to the last. As animated, as diversified, as social— but with circumstances of superiority undescribable.[33]

27. The idea of the pleasure produced by virtuous action had been prominent in the philosophical writings and literature of the preceding century. It was often seen as a critical basis for virtue. At the same time, Henry's citing of this reward for his good deed shows him once again focusing on himself rather than others.

28. This indicates Henry's previous neglect. Most estate owners would at least know their tenants, especially since the prevailing practice was to rent large blocks of land to a small number of tenants.

29. *making acquaintance*: becoming acquainted.

30. The cottages are likely for ordinary agricultural laborers, hired by the farmers renting the land. Such cottages were frequently in poor shape, with the inhabitants living in some degree of squalor (see the pictures below and on p. 739). There was a significant movement that continued through the nineteenth century to improve the conditions of these cottages and their inhabitants. The heroine of George Eliot's *Middlemarch*, which is set a little after the time of Jane Austen, engages in substantial efforts in this direction.

31. The wife of a landowner could assist or collaborate with her husband in such projects, and even take the lead when it came to charity for the poor.

32. These are the times when wealthy people were most likely to be in the countryside.

33. Meaning with Fanny as his wife.

A cottage.

[From George Williamson, *George Morland: His Life and Works* (London, 1907), p. 14]

"Mansfield, Sotherton, Thornton Lacey,"[34] he continued, "what a society will be comprised in those houses![35] And at Michaelmas,[36] perhaps, a fourth may be added, some small hunting-box[37] in the vicinity of every thing so dear—for as to any partnership in Thornton Lacey, as Edmund Bertram once good-humouredly proposed,[38] I hope I foresee two objections, two fair, excellent, irresistible objections to that plan."[39]

Fanny was doubly silenced here; though when the moment was passed, could regret that she had not forced herself into the acknowledged comprehension of one half of his meaning, and encouraged him to say something more of his sister and Edmund. It was a subject which she must learn to speak of, and the weakness that shrunk from it would soon be quite unpardonable.

When Mr. Price and his friend had seen all that they wished, or had time for, the others were ready to return; and in the course of their walk back, Mr. Crawford contrived a minute's privacy for telling Fanny that his only business in Portsmouth was to see her, that he was come down for a couple of days on her account and hers only, and because he could not endure a longer total separation. She was sorry, really sorry; and yet, in spite of this and the two or three other things which she wished he had not said, she thought him altogether improved since she had seen him; he was much more gentle, obliging, and attentive to other people's feelings than he had ever been at Mansfield; she had never seen him so agreeable—so *near* being agreeable; his behaviour to her father could not offend, and there was something particularly kind and proper in the notice he took of Susan. He was decidedly improved. She wished the next day over, she wished he had come only for one day—but it was not so very bad as she would have expected; the pleasure of talking of Mansfield was so very great!

Before they parted, she had to thank him for another pleasure, and one of no trivial kind. Her father asked him to do them the honour of taking his mutton with them, and Fanny had time for only one thrill of horror, before he declared himself prevented by a prior engagement. He was engaged to dinner already both for that day and the next; he had met with some acquaintance at the Crown who would not be denied; he should have the honour, however, of waiting on[40]

34. Thus he is also thinking of Edmund, and of Maria and Mr. Rushworth, who will presumably be back at Sotherton during the same period. There is no indication, regarding Maria, that he sees her as anything other than a friend and a relation of Fanny; Mary's letters from London make no mention of a meeting between Henry and Maria.

35. Henry displays his usual enthusiasm and bent for plans and projects for the future.

36. *Michaelmas*: September 29.

37. *hunting-box*: a small house used during the hunting season. The term "box" also applied to houses occupied for the sake of other sports.

38. At the Grants' dinner party, Henry, after being rebuffed in his proposal of renting the parsonage at Thornton Lacey from Edmund, was invited by Edmund to "come to me as a friend. Consider the house as half your own every winter" (p. 450).

39. The two objections to Henry and Edmund sharing a house are Fanny, as his wife, and Mary, as Edmund's. His use of "fair" and "irresistible" are certain signs he is referring, in typical chivalrous fashion, to women.

40. *waiting on*: calling upon.

them again on the morrow, &c. and so they parted—Fanny in a state
of actual felicity from escaping so horrible an evil!

To have had him join their family dinner-party and see all their
deficiencies would have been dreadful! Rebecca's cookery and
Rebecca's waiting, and Betsey's eating at table without restraint, and
pulling every thing about as she chose, were what Fanny herself was
not yet enough inured to, for her often to make a tolerable meal. *She*
was nice[41] only from natural delicacy, but *he* had been brought up in
a school of luxury and epicurism.[42]

A contemporary illustration of a gentleman giving money to the poor.

[From Joseph Grego, *Rowlandson the Caricaturist*, Vol. I (London, 1880), p. 316]

41. *nice*: fastidious, refined in one's taste.

42. *epicurism*: fine dining, cultivated taste in food.

A wealthy lady giving money to the poor. (The clothing is from a slightly earlier period.)

[From Malcolm Salaman, *Old English Colour Prints* (New York, 1909), Plate XI]

Chapter Eleven

*T*he Prices were just setting off for church the next day when Mr. Crawford appeared again. He came—not to stop—but to join them; he was asked to go with them to the Garrison chapel,[1] which was exactly what he had intended, and they all walked thither together.

The family were now seen to advantage. Nature had given them no inconsiderable share of beauty, and every Sunday dressed them in their cleanest skins and best attire. Sunday always brought this comfort to Fanny, and on this Sunday she felt it more than ever. Her poor mother now did not look so very unworthy of being Lady Bertram's sister as she was but too apt to look. It often grieved her to the heart—to think of the contrast between them—to think that where nature had made so little difference, circumstances should have made so much, and that her mother, as handsome as Lady Bertram, and some years her junior, should have an appearance so much more worn and faded, so comfortless, so slatternly, so shabby. But Sunday made her a very creditable and tolerably cheerful looking Mrs. Price, coming abroad[2] with a fine family of children, feeling a little respite of her weekly cares, and only discomposed if she saw her boys run into danger, or Rebecca pass by with a flower in her hat.[3]

In chapel they were obliged to divide,[4] but Mr. Crawford took care not to be divided from the female branch; and after chapel he still continued with them, and made one in the family party on the ramparts.

Mrs. Price took her weekly walk on the ramparts every fine Sunday throughout the year, always going directly after morning service and staying till dinner-time. It was her public place; there she met her acquaintance, heard a little news, talked over the badness of the Portsmouth servants, and wound up her spirits for the six days ensuing.[5]

1. The Garrison chapel is a church in Portsmouth. Built in the 1200s, it still stands, though it suffered heavy damage during World War II.

2. *abroad*: out of doors, outside one's home.

3. Rebecca is her servant, and a flower in her hat would be a sign of dressing above her station. Many people at the time, specifically those wealthy enough to afford servants, complained of their overly fine dressing, especially that of female servants. Differences in rank were considered essential for the proper ordering of society and were expressed in part by differences in clothing. Mrs. Price's inability to spend a lot on her own dress or her family's probably makes her especially sensitive to a servant's elevating herself in this way. Another concern was that desire for fine clothes could tempt a servant to steal money (a regular worry among employers). Mrs. Norris earlier spoke with approval of the housekeeper at Sotherton dismissing two housemaids for wearing white gowns (p. 204), which were considered elegant, and in *Persuasion* a woman complains to the heroine of the excessive finery of her daughter-in-law's maid and worries it may corrupt her own servants. The problem, from employers' perspective, had become more acute in recent times because increasing prosperity and decreasing prices for clothes (a product of industrial advances) permitted more servants to buy them. Pictures from the period often show servants and other laborers dressed in good clothing of the latest fashion.

4. They are too large a family for everyone to occupy the same pew.

5. An analogy with a clock or watch is probably intended by "wound up": just as a mechanical timepiece (the only type then) needs regular winding, this refreshment of her spirits will set her wheels in motion for the upcoming week.

Thither they now went; Mr. Crawford most happy to consider the Miss Prices as his peculiar charge; and before they had been there long—somehow or other—there was no saying how—Fanny could not have believed it—but he was walking between them with an arm of each under his, and she did not know how to prevent or put an end to it. It made her uncomfortable for a time—but yet there were enjoyments in the day and in the view which would be felt.

The day was uncommonly lovely. It was really March;[6] but it was April in its mild air, brisk soft wind, and bright sun, occasionally clouded for a minute; and every thing looked so beautiful under the influence of such a sky, the effects of the shadows pursuing each other, on the ships at Spithead and the island beyond, with the ever-varying hues of the sea now at high water, dancing in its glee and dashing against the ramparts with so fine a sound,[7] produced alto-gether such a combination of charms for Fanny, as made her gradu-ally almost careless of the circumstances under which she felt them. Nay, had she been without his arm, she would soon have known that she needed it, for she wanted strength for a two hours' saunter of this kind, coming as it generally did upon a week's previous inactivity. Fanny was beginning to feel the effect of being debarred from her usual, regular exercise; she had lost ground as to health since her being in Portsmouth, and but for Mr. Crawford and the beauty of the weather, would soon have been knocked up[8] now.

The loveliness of the day, and of the view, he felt like herself. They often stopt with the same sentiment and taste, leaning against the wall, some minutes, to look and admire; and considering he was not Edmund, Fanny could not but allow that he was sufficiently open to the charms of nature, and very well able to express his admira-tion. She had a few tender reveries now and then, which he could sometimes take advantage of, to look in her face without detection; and the result of these looks was, that though as bewitching as ever, her face was less blooming than it ought to be.—She *said* she was very well, and did not like to be supposed otherwise; but take it all in all, he was convinced that her present residence could not be comfortable, and, therefore, could not be salutary for her, and he was growing anxious for her being again at Mansfield, where her own happiness, and his in seeing her, must be so much greater.

6. It is now early March; see chronology, p. 859.

7. The seaward section of the ramparts offers excellent views, particularly one stretch of it called the Platform (or sometimes Saluting Platform); see map, p. 884. A popular contemporary guide to England states in its description of Portsmouth, "From the Platform . . . is an extremely fine sea-view, including the anchorage at Spithead, and the Isle of Wight in the distance: the more contiguous scenes are scarcely less beautiful" (John Britton, *The Beauties of England and Wales*, Vol. VI, 1805). The Platform lies at the foot of High Street, off which the Prices' home stood, so they would have been able to reach it easily; Mr. Price described earlier having "made but two steps to the platform" in order to see William's ship leave the harbor (p. 682).

8. *knocked up*: worn out, exhausted.

"You have been here a month, I think?" said he.

"No. Not quite a month.—It is only four weeks tomorrow since I left Mansfield."

"You are a most accurate[9] and honest reckoner. I should call that a month."

"I did not arrive here till Tuesday evening."

"And it is to be a two months' visit, is not it?"

"Yes.—My uncle talked of two months. I suppose it will not be less."

"And how are you to be conveyed back again? Who comes for you?"

"I do not know. I have heard nothing about it yet from my aunt. Perhaps I may be to[10] stay longer. It may not be convenient for me to be fetched exactly at the two months' end."

After a moment's reflection, Mr. Crawford replied, "I know Mansfield, I know its way, I know its faults towards *you*. I know the danger of your being so far forgotten, as to have your comforts give way to the imaginary convenience of any single being in the family. I am aware that you may be left here week after week, if Sir Thomas cannot settle every thing for coming himself, or sending your aunt's maid for you, without involving the slightest alteration of the arrangements which he may have laid down for the next quarter of a year. This will not do. Two months is an ample allowance, I should think six weeks quite enough.—I am considering your sister's health," said he, addressing himself to Susan, "which I think the confinement of Portsmouth unfavourable to. She requires constant air and exercise. When you know her as well as I do, I am sure you will agree that she does, and that she ought never to be long banished from the free air, and liberty of the country.—If, therefore, (turning again to Fanny) you find yourself growing unwell, and any difficulties arise about your returning to Mansfield—without waiting for the two months to be ended—*that* must not be regarded as of any consequence, if you feel yourself at all less strong, or comfortable than usual, and will only let my sister know it, give her only the slightest hint, she and I will immediately come down, and take you back to Mansfield.[11] You know the ease, and the pleasure with which this would be done. You know all that would be felt on the occasion."

9. *accurate*: precise.

10. *be to*: be forced to, required to.

11. Social rules require them both to come, he in order to provide a male escort, and she because it would be improper for two unmarried and unrelated young people of the opposite sex to travel alone together.

A poor man in a cottage.

[From Sir Walter Gilbey and E. D. Cuming, *George Morland: His Life and Works* (London, 1907), p. 288]

Fanny thanked him, but tried to laugh it off.

"I am perfectly serious,"—he replied,—"as you perfectly know.—And I hope you will not be cruelly concealing any tendency to indisposition.—Indeed, you shall *not*, it shall not be in your power, for so long only as you positively say, in every letter to Mary, 'I am well.'—and I know you cannot speak or write a falsehood,—so long only shall you be considered as well."

Fanny thanked him again, but was affected and distressed to a degree that made it impossible for her to say much, or even to be certain of what she ought to say.—This was towards the close of their walk. He attended them to the last, and left them only at the door of their own house, when he knew them to be going to dinner, and therefore pretended to be waited for elsewhere.

"I wish you were not so tired,"—said he, still detaining Fanny after all the others were in the house; "I wish I left you in stronger health.—Is there any thing I can do for you in town? I have half an idea of going into Norfolk again soon. I am not satisfied about Maddison.[12]—I am sure he still means to impose on[13] me if possible, and get a cousin of his own into a certain mill,[14] which I design for somebody else.—I must come to an understanding with him. I must make him know that I will not be tricked on the south side of Everingham, any more than on the north, that I will be master of my own property. I was not explicit enough with him before.—The mischief[15] such a man does on an estate, both as to the credit[16] of his employer, and the welfare of the poor, is inconceivable. I have a great mind to go back into Norfolk directly, and put every thing at once on such a footing as cannot be afterwards swerved from.—Maddison is a clever fellow; I do not wish to displace him—provided he does not try to displace *me*;[17]—but it would be simple[18] to be duped by a man who has no right of creditor to dupe me—and worse than simple to let him give me a hard-hearted, griping[19] fellow for a tenant, instead of an honest man, to whom I have given half a promise already.—Would not it be worse than simple? Shall I go?—Do you advise it?"

"I advise!—you know very well what is right."

"Yes. When you give me your opinion, I always know what is right. Your judgment is my rule of right."

12. Maddison is his agent, mentioned earlier. He is of sufficient status to be called by his last name. Some agents, particularly the many who were also attorneys, were of high enough status to be called "Mr." as well.

13. *impose on*: deceive.

14. Many estates had mills; one is mentioned on the property of the leading landowner in *Emma*. One of the most famous works by the leading landscape painter John Constable is *Flatford Mill* (1816), which depicts a water mill. Mills had long been used to grind grain into flour, as Flatford Mill did. Others had been recently developed to power factories, an activity landowners were sometimes happy to promote on their property, though they would let somebody else manage the actual enterprise.

15. *mischief*: harm, injury.

16. *credit*: public standing, good name.

17. After having been able to manage the estate with almost no interference, Maddison would probably dislike having his practices suddenly examined and criticized, and might try to resist his employer's interference even if he was not doing anything underhanded.

18. *simple*: foolish, unwise.

19. *griping*: grasping, avaricious.

"Oh, no!—do not say so. We have all a better guide in ourselves, if we would attend to it, than any other person can be.[20] Good bye; I wish you a pleasant journey to-morrow."

"Is there nothing I can do for you in town?"

"Nothing, I am much obliged to you."

"Have you no message for anybody?"

"My love to your sister, if you please; and when you see my cousin—my cousin Edmund, I wish you would be so good as to say that—I suppose I shall soon hear from him."

"Certainly; and if he is lazy or negligent, I will write his excuses myself—"

He could say no more, for Fanny would be no longer detained. He pressed her hand, looked at her, and was gone. *He* went to while away the next three hours as he could, with his other acquaintance, till the best dinner that a capital inn afforded,[21] was ready for their enjoyment, and *she* turned in to her more simple one immediately.

Their general fare bore a very different character; and could he have suspected how many privations, besides that of exercise, she endured in her father's house, he would have wondered that her looks were not much more affected than he found them. She was so little equal to Rebecca's puddings, and Rebecca's hashes,[22] brought to table as they all were, with such accompaniments of half-cleaned plates, and not half-cleaned knives and forks, that she was very often constrained to defer her heartiest meal, till she could send her brothers in the evening for biscuits and buns.[23] After being nursed up at Mansfield, it was too late in the day to be hardened at Portsmouth; and though Sir Thomas, had he known all, might have thought his niece in the most promising way of being[24] starved, both mind and body, into a much juster value for Mr. Crawford's good company and good fortune, he would probably have feared to push his experiment farther, lest she might die under the cure.

Fanny was out of spirits all the rest of the day. Though tolerably secure of not seeing Mr. Crawford again, she could not help being low. It was parting with somebody of the nature of a friend; and though in one light glad to have him gone, it seemed as if she was now deserted by every body; it was a sort of renewed separation from Mansfield; and she could not think of his returning to town, and

20. Fanny enunciates here a basic principle of many Anglican thinkers of the time who argued that God has created a rational and harmonious universe that includes timeless principles of morality and has implanted in human beings the capacity, through their conscience, of grasping those principles and judging moral questions.

21. That Henry dines three hours later is a sign of the social gulf between him and the Prices, for while people lower in the social scale dined fairly early, those in fashionable London society could dine very late. In a letter Jane Austen mentions, with some embarrassment, dining at three-thirty in the afternoon (Dec. 18, 1798), while in *Pride and Prejudice* the hero and some wealthy friends, who are often in London, dine at six-thirty.

22. Puddings had for centuries been a basic feature of the English diet; they could be savory as well as sweet. Hashes arrived during the sixteenth and seventeenth centuries from France. That these appear to be the basics of the Prices' diet signals their limited means. Meat dishes—usually simply meat plus perhaps a sauce—were the staple of the diets of wealthy people, and puddings and hashes were only side dishes if served at all. During the period when Jane Austen lived in Southampton, under fairly straitened circumstances, she speaks in her letters of the poor quality of the food they sometimes consumed.

23. A biscuit was a small, flat, crisp piece of bread, generally dry and hard. Buns were usually a sweet cake or bread that could be held in the hand.

24. *in the most promising way of being*: in the most promising position to be, in the most promising likelihood of being.

being frequently with Mary and Edmund, without feelings so near akin to envy, as made her hate herself for having them.

Her dejection had no abatement from anything passing around her; a friend or two of her father's, as always happened if he was not with them, spent the long, long evening there; and from six o'clock to half past nine, there was little intermission of noise or grog.[25] She was very low. The wonderful improvement which she still fancied in Mr. Crawford, was the nearest to administering comfort of anything within the current of her thoughts. Not considering in how different a circle she had been just seeing him, nor how much might be owing to contrast, she was quite persuaded of his being astonishingly more gentle, and regardful of others, than formerly. And if in little things, must it not be so in great? So anxious for her health and comfort, so very feeling[26] as he now expressed himself, and really seemed, might not it be fairly supposed, that he would not much longer persevere in a suit so distressing to her?

25. Grog was a mixture of rum and water popular in the navy. Mr. Price and his friends would have acquired a taste for it there. It is a "long, long evening" and they are drinking at home because of laws against public serving of alcohol on Sunday.

26. *feeling*: tender, compassionate.

An inn in a town.

[From Geoffrey Holme, ed., *Early English Water-colour Drawings* (London, 1919), Plate XXV]

Chapter Twelve

*I*t was presumed that Mr. Crawford was travelling back to London, on the morrow, for nothing more was seen of him at Mr. Price's; and two days afterwards, it was a fact ascertained to Fanny by the following letter from his sister, opened and read by her, on another account, with the most anxious curiosity:[1]—

"I have to inform you, my dearest Fanny, that Henry has been down to Portsmouth to see you; that he had a delightful walk with you to the Dock-yard last Saturday, and one still more to be dwelt on the next day, on the ramparts; when the balmy air, the sparkling sea, and your sweet looks and conversation were altogether in the most delicious harmony, and afforded[2] sensations which are to raise[3] ecstacy even in retrospect. This, as well as I understand, is to be the substance of my information. He makes me write, but I do not know what else is to be communicated, except this said visit to Portsmouth, and these two said walks, and his introduction to your family, especially to a fair sister of your's, a fine girl of fifteen,[4] who was of the party on the ramparts, taking her first lesson, I presume, in love. I have not time for writing much, but it would be out of place if I had, for this is to be a mere letter of business, penned for the purpose of conveying necessary information, which could not be delayed without risk of evil. My dear, dear Fanny, if I had you here, how I would talk to you!—You should listen to me till you were tired, and advise me till you were still tired more; but it is impossible to put an hundredth part of my great[5] mind on paper, so I will abstain altogether, and leave you to guess what you like. I have no news for you. You have politics of course; and it would be too bad to plague you with the names of people and parties, that fill up my time.[6] I ought to have sent you an account of your cousin's first party, but I was lazy, and now it is too long ago; suffice it, that every thing was just as it ought to be, in a style that any of her connections must have been gratified to witness, and that her own dress and manners did her the

1. Henry left on Monday and arrived in London that evening, Mary wrote on Tuesday, and Fanny received her letter on Wednesday. Her curiosity is on the subject of Mary and Edmund, as indicated by what she first reflects upon after finishing the letter.

2. *afforded*: provided.

3. *raise*: arouse.

4. Susan was earlier stated to be fourteen, and this is confirmed in a later chapter. It is possible Henry was not told her age and simply guessed it.

5. *great*: full of emotions or thoughts.

6. By "parties" she could mean either social gatherings, large or small, that are connected with politics, or actual political parties or factions. At the time there were two main political parties in Britain, the Whigs and the Tories, though the term also could refer to smaller or more temporary factions. Politics was a central concern of fashionable London society, many of whose members were in Parliament.

St. George's, Hanover Square (see the next page).

[From E. Beresford Chancellor, *The XVIIIth Century in London* (New York, 1921), p. 199]

greatest credit. My friend Mrs. Fraser is mad for such a house, and it would not make *me* miserable. I go to Lady Stornaway after Easter. She seems in high spirits, and very happy. I fancy Lord S. is very good-humoured and pleasant in his own family, and I do not think him so very ill-looking as I did, at least one sees many worse. He will not do by the side of your cousin Edmund. Of the last-mentioned hero, what shall I say? If I avoided his name entirely, it would look suspicious. I will say, then, that we have seen him two or three times, and that my friends here are very much struck with his gentleman-like appearance. Mrs. Fraser (no bad judge), declares she knows but three men in town who have so good a person, height, and air;[7] and I must confess, when he dined here the other day, there were none to compare with him, and we were a party of sixteen. Luckily there is no distinction of dress now-a-days to tell tales,[8] but—but—but.

> *Your's, affectionately."*

"I had almost forgot (it was Edmund's fault, he gets into my head more than does me good), one very material[9] thing I had to say from Henry and myself, I mean about our taking you back into Northamptonshire. My dear little creature, do not stay at Portsmouth to lose your pretty looks. Those vile sea-breezes are the ruin of beauty and health. My poor aunt always felt affected, if within ten miles of the sea,[10] which the Admiral of course never believed, but I know it was so. I am at your service and Henry's, at an hour's notice. I should like the scheme, and we would make a little circuit, and shew you Everingham in our way, and perhaps you would not mind passing through London,[11] and seeing the inside of St. George's, Hanover-Square.[12] Only keep your cousin Edmund from me at such a time, I should not like to be tempted.[13] What a long letter!—one word more. Henry I find has some idea of going into Norfolk again upon some business that *you* approve, but this cannot possibly be permitted before the middle of next week, that is, he cannot any how be spared till after the 14th, for *we* have a party that evening. The value of a man like Henry on such an occasion, is what you can have no conception of; so you must take it upon my word, to be inestimable.[14] He will see the Rushworths, which I own I am not sorry for—

7. *air*: outward character, demeanor.

8. Meaning that at present, unlike in earlier times, clergymen dress like other men, so nothing alerts others to Edmund's being one. Mary does not wish her fashionable friends to see that the man she admires is a clergyman.

9. *material*: essential.

10. Her aunt may have been using that as an excuse to avoid being near her husband, who as an admiral would be serving at sea or in a port. Most medical opinion of the time praised the seaside as good for health.

11. Norfolk, where Everingham lies, is not at all on the route from Portsmouth to Northampton, but since it is not far to the east, they could follow a circular route going through it. This would also mean going through London, which lies along the most direct route from Portsmouth to Norfolk. See map, p. 882.

12. St. George's is a church in Hanover Square, in the middle of the highly fashionable Mayfair district. Mary may think of it because it is where she is attending church now (the address of the Frasers is never specified, but it is almost certainly in Mayfair or nearby). Her mention of it is likely meant to tease Fanny about getting married there to Henry. It is possible Jane Austen was familiar with the church: in her letters she mentions going to various London churches in her visits there. For a picture of the church, see the previous page.

13. If Edmund came while Fanny and Henry were getting married, Mary might be tempted to marry him. Her "but—but—but" at the end of the letter indicates she is wavering with regard to Edmund.

14. That Mary would insist on his staying for a party indicates her priorities.

having a little curiosity—and so I think has he, though he will not acknowledge it."[15]

This was a letter to be run through eagerly, to be read deliberately, to supply matter for much reflection, and to leave every thing in greater suspense than ever. The only certainty to be drawn from it was, that nothing decisive had yet taken place. Edmund had not yet spoken. How Miss Crawford really felt—how she meant to act, or might act without or against her meaning—whether his importance to her were quite what it had been before the last separation— whether if lessened it were likely to lessen more, or to recover itself, were subjects for endless conjecture, and to be thought of on that day and many days to come, without producing any conclusion. The idea that returned the oftenest, was that Miss Crawford, after proving herself cooled and staggered[16] by a return to London habits, would yet prove herself in the end too much attached to him, to give him up. She would try to be more ambitious than her heart would allow. She would hesitate, she would teaze, she would condition,[17] she would require a great deal, but she would finally accept. This was Fanny's most frequent expectation. A house in town!—*that* she thought must be impossible. Yet there was no saying what Miss Crawford might not ask. The prospect for her cousin grew worse and worse. The woman who could speak of him, and speak only of his appearance!—What an unworthy attachment!—To be deriving support from the commendations of Mrs. Fraser! *She* who had known him intimately half a year! Fanny was ashamed of her. Those parts of the letter which related only to Mr. Crawford and herself, touched her in comparison, slightly. Whether Mr. Crawford went into Norfolk before or after the 14th, was certainly no concern of her's, though, every thing considered, she thought he *would* go without delay. That Miss Crawford should endeavour to secure a meeting between him and Mrs. Rushworth, was all in her worst line of conduct, and grossly unkind and ill-judged; but she hoped *he* would not be actuated by any such degrading curiosity. He acknowledged no such inducement, and his sister ought to have given him credit for better feelings than her own.[18]

She was yet more impatient for another letter from town after receiving this, than she had been before; and for a few days, was so

15. Her wording implies that Henry is willing to stay for the party, though he will not admit to being curious to see how Maria and Julia will react to him.

16. *staggered*: made more hesitant or doubting or wavering.

17. *condition*: lay down terms, bargain.

18. It is notable that Fanny, who used to condemn Henry and Mary equally, is now more favorable to him.

A lady at the seaside.

[From *The Repository of arts, literature, fashions, manufactures, &c,* Vol. VI (1811), p. 226]

unsettled by it altogether, by what had come, and what might come, that her usual readings and conversation with Susan were much suspended. She could not command her attention as she wished. If Mr. Crawford remembered her message to her cousin, she thought it very likely, *most* likely, that he would write to her at all events; it would be most consistent with his usual kindness, and till she got rid of this idea, till it gradually wore off, by no letters appearing in the course of three or four days more, she was in a most restless, anxious state.

At length, a something like composure succeeded. Suspense[19] must be submitted to, and must not be allowed to wear her out, and make her useless. Time did something, her own exertions something more, and she resumed her attentions to Susan, and again awakened the same interest in them.

Susan was growing very fond of her, and though without any of the early delight in books, which had been so strong in Fanny, with a disposition much less inclined to sedentary pursuits, or to information for information's sake, she had so strong a desire of not *appearing* ignorant, as with a good clear understanding, made her a most attentive, profitable, thankful pupil. Fanny was her oracle. Fanny's explanations and remarks were a most important addition to every essay, or every chapter of history.[20] What Fanny told her of former times, dwelt more on her mind than the pages of Goldsmith;[21] and she paid her sister the compliment of preferring her style to that of any printed author. The early habit of reading was wanting.

Their conversations, however, were not always on subjects so high[22] as history or morals.[23] Others had their hour; and of lesser matters, none returned so often, or remained so long between them, as Mansfield Park, a description of the people, the manners, the amusements, the ways of Mansfield Park. Susan, who had an innate taste for the genteel and well-appointed,[24] was eager to hear, and Fanny could not but indulge herself in dwelling on so beloved a theme. She hoped it was not wrong; though after a time, Susan's very great admiration of every thing said or done in her uncle's house, and earnest longing to go into Northamptonshire, seemed almost to blame her for exciting feelings which could not be gratified.

Poor Susan was very little better fitted for home than her elder sister; and as Fanny grew thoroughly to understand this, she began

19. *Suspense*: delay, uncertainty.

20. Fanny may have chosen these subjects because she believed they were the most necessary for Susan's education. Earlier we were told that she most desired to inspire in her sister her own love of poetry and biography.

21. Oliver Goldsmith's four-volume *History of England* (1771) was a bestseller (Goldsmith also wrote poetry, essays, plays, and a novel, all of which were popular). It was often used to teach history to children. When she was young Jane Austen wrote a parody of Goldsmith, her only known work of nonfiction. She herself does not seem to have been a lover of history, though she recognized its value. In a letter to a friend she discusses a history she is reading and the possibility of relating its contents to her friend: the wording suggests that at least some of the book is more a matter of duty than of pleasure.

22. *high*: weighty, elevated.

23. Morals would refer to the essays. Essays of the time tended to be heavily focused on moral reflections; that is certainly true of those Fanny was earlier shown to be reading, in Samuel Johnson's *The Idler*.

24. *well-appointed*: nicely furnished.

to feel that when her own release from Portsmouth came, her happiness would have a material drawback in leaving Susan behind. That a girl so capable of being made, every thing good, should be left in such hands, distressed her more and more. Were *she* likely to have a home to invite her to, what a blessing it would be!—And had it been possible for her to return Mr. Crawford's regard, the probability of his being very far from objecting to such a measure, would have been the greatest increase of all her own comforts. She thought he was really good-tempered, and could fancy his entering into a plan of that sort, most pleasantly.

A woman leaving a bookshop. (The clothing is from a slightly earlier period.)

[From Randall Davies, *English Society of the Eighteenth Century in Contemporary Art* (London, 1907), p. 54]

Chapter Thirteen

Seven weeks of the two months were very nearly gone, when the one letter, the letter from Edmund so long expected, was put into Fanny's hands. As she opened and saw its length she prepared herself for a minute detail[1] of happiness and a profusion of love and praise towards the fortunate creature, who was now mistress of his fate. These were the contents.

"Mansfield Park.

"My dear Fanny,

"Excuse me that I have not written before. Crawford told me that you were wishing to hear from me, but I found it impossible to write from London, and persuaded myself that you would understand my silence. — Could I have sent a few happy lines, they should not have been wanting, but nothing of that nature was ever in my power. — I am returned to Mansfield in a less assured state than when I left it. My hopes are much weaker. — You are probably aware of this already. — So very fond of you as Miss Crawford is, it is most natural that she should tell you enough of her own feelings, to furnish a tolerable guess at mine. — I will not be prevented, however, from making my own communication. Our confidences in you need not clash. — I ask no questions. — There is something soothing in the idea, that we have the same friend, and that whatever unhappy differences of opinion may exist between us, we are united in our love of you. — It will be a comfort to me to tell you how things now are, and what are my present plans, if plans I can be said to have. — I have been returned since Saturday. I was three weeks in London, and saw her (for London) very often.[2] I had every attention from the Frasers that could be reasonably expected. I dare say I was not reasonable in carrying with me hopes of an intercourse at all like that of Mansfield. It was her manner, however, rather than any unfrequency of meeting. Had she been different when I did see her, I should have made no complaint, but from the very first she

1. *detail*: account.

2. He means that the busy social life and other diversions of London make it naturally harder for Mary to devote her time to him. He may be trying to excuse, to himself at least as much as to Fanny, the decreased attention he received from Mary there, to avoid concluding that it marks a decline in her interest in him.

A woman holding a letter.

[From *The Repository of arts, literature, fashions, manufactures, &c,* Vol. VII (1812), p. 179]

*was altered; my first reception was so unlike what I had hoped, that I had almost resolved on leaving London again directly.*³—*I need not particularize. You know the weak side of her character, and may imagine the sentiments and expressions which were torturing me. She was in high spirits, and surrounded by those who were giving all the support of their own bad sense to her too lively mind.*⁴ *I do not like Mrs. Fraser. She is a cold-hearted, vain woman, who has married entirely from convenience,*⁵ *and though evidently unhappy in her marriage, places*⁶ *her disappointment, not to faults of judgment or temper, or disproportion of age, but to her being after all, less affluent than many of her acquaintance, especially than her sister, Lady Stornaway, and is the determined supporter of every thing mercenary and ambitious, provided it be only mercenary and ambitious enough. I look upon her intimacy with those two sisters, as the greatest misfortune of her life and mine. They have been leading her astray for years. Could she be detached from them!—and sometimes I do not despair of it, for the affection appears to me principally on their side. They are very fond of her; but I am sure she does not love them as she loves you. When I think of her great attachment to you, indeed, and the whole of her judicious, upright conduct as a sister, she appears a very different creature, capable of every thing noble, and I am ready to blame myself for a too harsh construction*⁷ *of a playful manner. I cannot give her up, Fanny. She is the only woman in the world whom I could ever think of as a wife. If I did not believe that she had some regard for me, of course I should not say this, but I do believe it. I am convinced, that she is not without a decided preference. I have no jealousy of any individual. It is the influence of the fashionable world*⁸ *altogether that I am jealous of. It is the habits of wealth that I fear. Her ideas are not higher than her own fortune may warrant, but they are beyond what our incomes united could authorize.*⁹ *There is comfort, however, even here. I could better bear to lose her, because not rich enough, than because of my profession. That would only prove her affection not equal to sacrifices, which, in fact, I am scarcely justified in asking; and if I am refused, that, I think, will be the honest motive. Her prejudices, I trust, are not so strong as they were. You have my thoughts exactly as they arise, my dear Fanny; perhaps they are some times contradictory, but it will not be a less faithful picture of my mind. Having once begun, it is a plea-*

3. *directly*: immediately.

4. Mary was in London for five to six weeks before Edmund arrived (see chronology, pp. 858–859), so she had rehabituated herself to its ways and mores by the time, something also suggested in her letters to Fanny.

5. This is consistent with Mary's earlier description of the mercenary calculations behind her friend's marriage.

6. *places*: attributes.

7. *construction*: interpretation.

8. *the fashionable world*: high society.

9. Meaning that with twenty thousand pounds, a very large fortune for a woman, Mary could reasonably expect to marry a very wealthy man, with many thousands a year in income. But her fortune will provide an annual income of only a thousand a year (by the standard 5 percent return on investments in government bonds, in which people without land generally placed their money), and Edmund's income will probably be, at best, only a little larger than that, so they would have to live far more modestly than she hopes and expects to do.

sure to me to tell you all I feel. I cannot give her up. Connected, as we already are, and, I hope, are to be, to give up Mary Crawford, would be to give up the society of some of those most dear to me, to banish myself from the very houses and friends whom, under any other distress, I should turn to for consolation. The loss of Mary I must consider as comprehending the loss of Crawford and of Fanny. Were it a decided thing, an actual refusal, I hope I should know how to bear it, and how to endeavour to weaken her hold on my heart—and in the course of a few years—but I am writing nonsense—were I refused, I must bear it; and till I am, I can never cease to try for her. This is the truth. The only question is how? What may be the likeliest means? I have sometimes thought of going to London again after Easter, and sometimes resolved on doing nothing till she returns to Mansfield. Even now, she speaks with pleasure of being in Mansfield in June; but June is at a great distance, and I believe I shall write to her. I have nearly determined on explaining myself by letter. To be at an early certainty is a material object. My present state is miserably irksome. Considering every thing, I think a letter will be decidedly the best method of explanation.[10] I shall be able to write much that I could not say, and shall be giving her time for reflection before she resolves on her answer, and I am less afraid of the result of reflection than of an immediate hasty impulse; I think I am. My greatest danger would lie in her consulting Mrs. Fraser, and I at a distance, unable to help my own cause. A letter exposes to all the evil of consultation, and where the mind is any thing short of perfect decision, an adviser may, in an unlucky moment, lead it to do what it may afterwards regret. I must think this matter over a little.[11] This long letter, full of my own concerns alone, will be enough to tire even the friendship of a Fanny. The last time I saw Crawford was at Mrs. Fraser's party.[12] I am more and more satisfied with all that I see and hear of him. There is not a shadow of wavering. He thoroughly knows his own mind, and acts up to his resolutions—an inestimable quality. I could not see him, and my eldest sister in the same room, without recollecting what you once told me, and I acknowledge that they did not meet as friends. There was marked coolness on her side. They scarcely spoke. I saw him draw back surprised,[13] and I was sorry that Mrs. Rushworth should resent any former supposed slight to Miss Bertram. You will wish to hear my opinion of Maria's degree of com-

10. He means proposing to her as well as explaining himself to her. Proposing in person was the usual way at this time, but people could and did propose by letter. A character in *Emma* does so.

11. Edmund's reversing his just-reached decision in a letter reflects his confused and disordered state of mind. He jumps from topic to topic, often haphazardly, while always returning to the subject of Mary.

12. So Henry did attend the party, as Mary wished (p. 748), rather than heading immediately to his estate in Norfolk.

13. Henry's reaction shows that he no longer has any affection for Maria, but his surprise demonstrates that he still has no conception of how deeply she fell in love, and how deeply his abandonment wounded her.

The Pump Room, Bath, where people drank the hot mineral waters found in the town (see the following pages).

[From Emma Austen-Leigh, *Jane Austen and Bath* (London, 1939), p. 8]

fort as a wife. There is no appearance of unhappiness. I hope they get on pretty well together. I dined twice in Wimpole Street,[14] and might have been there oftener, but it is mortifying to be with Rushworth as a brother. Julia seems to enjoy London exceedingly. I had little enjoyment there — but have less here. We are not a lively party. You are very much wanted. I miss you more than I can express. My mother desires her best love, and hopes to hear from you soon. She talks of you almost every hour, and I am sorry to find how many weeks more she is likely to be without you. My father means to fetch you himself, but it will not be till after Easter, when he has business in town.[15] You are happy at Portsmouth, I hope, but this must not be a yearly visit. I want you at home, that I may have your opinion about Thornton Lacey. I have little heart for extensive improvements till I know that it will ever have a mistress.[16] I think I shall certainly write. It is quite settled that the Grants go to Bath; they leave Mansfield on Monday. I am glad of it. I am not comfortable enough to be fit for any body; but your aunt seems to feel out of luck that such an article of Mansfield news should fall to my pen instead of her's. Your's ever, my dearest Fanny."

"I never will — no, I certainly never will wish for a letter again," was Fanny's secret declaration, as she finished this. "What do they bring but disappointment and sorrow? — Not till after Easter! — How shall I bear it? — And my poor aunt talking of me every hour!"

Fanny checked the tendency of these thoughts as well as she could, but she was within half a minute of starting the idea, that Sir Thomas was quite unkind, both to her aunt and to herself. — As for the main subject of the letter — there was nothing in that to soothe irritation. She was almost vexed into displeasure, and anger, against Edmund. "There is no good in this delay," said she. "Why is not it settled? — He is blinded, and nothing will open his eyes, nothing can, after having had truths before him so long in vain. — He will marry her, and be poor and miserable. God grant that her influence do not make him cease to be respectable!" — She looked over the letter again. " 'So very fond of me!' 'tis nonsense all. She loves nobody but herself and her brother. Her friends leading her astray for years! She is quite as likely to have led *them* astray. They have all, perhaps, been corrupting one another; but if they are so much fonder of her than she is of them, she is the less likely to have been hurt, except by their

14. That is the location of the Rushworths' residence.

15. This is probably business relating to Parliament, which is now in session. Once in London, he will be almost halfway to Portsmouth, so coming to pick up Fanny will be less out of the way.

16. Henry had earlier advised significant improvements to the parsonage at Thornton Lacey, and though Edmund rejected such ambitious plans, he did acknowledge the need for some improvements (pp. 440–444).

The central complex in Bath, where the Grants are going; it contains the Pump Room and the principal baths.

[From Emma Austen-Leigh, *Jane Austen and Bath* (London, 1939), p. 46]

flattery. 'The only woman in the world, whom he could ever think of as a wife.' I firmly believe it. It is an attachment to govern his whole life. Accepted or refused, his heart is wedded to her for ever. 'The loss of Mary, I must consider as comprehending the loss of Crawford and Fanny.' Edmund, you do not know *me*. The families would never be connected, if you did not connect them! Oh! write, write. Finish it at once. Let there be an end of this suspense. Fix,[17] commit, condemn yourself."

Such sensations, however, were too near a kin to resentment to be long guiding Fanny's soliloquies. She was soon more softened and sorrowful.—His warm regard, his kind expressions, his confidential treatment touched her strongly. He was only too good to every body.—It was a letter, in short, which she would not but have had for the world, and which could never be valued enough. This was the end of it.

Every body at all addicted to letter writing, without having much to say, which will include a large proportion of the female world at least, must feel with Lady Bertram, that she was out of luck in having such a capital piece of Mansfield news, as the certainty of the Grants going to Bath, occur at a time when she could make no advantage of it, and will admit that it must have been very mortifying to her to see it fall to the share of her thankless son, and treated as concisely as possible at the end of a long letter, instead of having it to spread over the largest part of a page of her own.—For though Lady Bertram rather shone in the epistolary line, having early in her marriage, from the want of other employment, and the circumstance of Sir Thomas's being in Parliament, got into the way of making and keeping correspondents,[18] and formed for herself a very creditable, commonplace, amplifying style, so that a very little matter was enough for her; she could not do entirely without any; she must have something to write about, even to her niece, and being so soon to lose all the benefit of Dr. Grant's gouty symptoms and Mrs. Grant's morning calls,[19] it was very hard upon her to be deprived of one of the last epistolary uses she could put them to.

There was a rich amends, however, preparing for her. Lady Bertram's hour of good luck came. Within a few days from the receipt of Edmund's letter, Fanny had one from her aunt, beginning thus:—

17. *Fix*: decide definitely.

18. His being in Parliament may have encouraged her because it meant he had the power to frank all her letters, and thereby save her correspondents from having to pay the normal postage, which was expensive at the time (see p. 35, note 38). In addition, until the approximate time when Fanny came to live with them, which means most of their married life so far, she joined Sir Thomas in London every spring (p. 42). She would have been away for a few months from her sister and friends in Mansfield, and she could have made friends in London, whom she would be away from during the rest of the year. Both of these circumstances would give her reason to write letters.

19. Mrs. Grant probably pays regular morning calls to Lady Bertram, and tells her about her husband's troubles with gout, which furnishes Lady Bertram with letter material. Dr. Grant's gout has not previously been mentioned, but as an older, affluent man deeply devoted to the pleasures of the table, he is a very likely candidate for the ailment (for more on gout, see p. 21, note 81). They are probably going to Bath now because of his gout, since he is a "stay-at-home man" (p. 92) who would not wish normally to travel, and his wife usually caters to his desires. Many people went to Bath for the supposed healing powers of bathing in or drinking the abundant warm waters, and gout figured prominently among their ailments; in fact, it was commonly associated with the town. In both *Persuasion* and *Northanger Abbey* older male characters with gout go to Bath in search of a cure.

A man with gout.

[From Joseph Grego, *Rowlandson the Caricaturist*, Vol. I (London, 1880), p. 157]

"My dear Fanny,

"I take up my pen to communicate some very alarming intelligence, which I make no doubt will give you much concern."

This was a great deal better than to have to take up the pen to acquaint her with all the particulars of the Grants' intended journey, for the present intelligence was of a nature to promise occupation for the pen for many days to come, being no less than the dangerous illness of her eldest son, of which they had received notice by express,[20] a few hours before.

Tom had gone from London with a party of young men to Newmarket,[21] where a neglected fall, and a good deal of drinking, had brought on a fever; and when the party broke up, being unable to move, had been left by himself at the house of one of these young men, to the comforts of sickness and solitude, and the attendance only of servants. Instead of being soon well enough to follow his friends, as he had then hoped, his disorder increased considerably, and it was not long before he thought so ill of himself, as to be as ready as his physician to have a letter dispatched to Mansfield.[22]

"This distressing intelligence, as you may suppose," observed her Ladyship, after giving the substance of it, "has agitated us exceedingly, and we cannot prevent ourselves from being greatly alarmed, and apprehensive for the poor invalid, whose state Sir Thomas fears may be very critical; and Edmund kindly proposes attending his brother immediately, but I am happy to add, that Sir Thomas will not leave me on this distressing occasion, as it would be too trying for me. We shall greatly miss Edmund in our small circle, but I trust and hope he will find the poor invalid in a less alarming state than might be apprehended, and that he will be able to bring him to Mansfield shortly, which Sir Thomas proposes should be done, and thinks best on every account, and I flatter myself, the poor sufferer will soon be able to bear the removal without material inconvenience or injury. As I have little doubt of your feeling for us, my dear Fanny, under these distressing circumstances, I will write again very soon."

Fanny's feelings on the occasion were indeed considerably more warm and genuine than her aunt's style of writing. She felt truly for them all. Tom dangerously ill, Edmund gone to attend him, and the sadly small party remaining at Mansfield, were cares to shut out

20. *express*: express message or messenger. Such messengers could be hired to deliver a message that could not wait for the post.

21. Newmarket was the leading center in England for horse racing, a sport Tom was earlier shown pursuing with dedication. It is even possible his own horse was running in a race there. Newmarket's racing season was much longer than most; in 1809 it had thirty-nine days of racing. It was also a place for extensive socializing, which attracted many upper-class people because only those of their social rank were normally allowed to attend the races.

22. A physician was the most advanced type of medical man at the time; the other two types were surgeon and apothecary. Physicians were the only ones who had received a formal education and were considered gentlemen. They were few in number, so they tended to be concentrated in cities and large towns; people who lived elsewhere, even if wealthy, had to rely on surgeons or apothecaries for regular treatment. Newmarket would be a natural venue for physicians, because of the presence of visitors wealthy enough to afford their high fees. At the end of her life Jane Austen's family sent her to Winchester, the nearest large town, so she could consult a physician about the serious illness afflicting her. Unfortunately, the physician was unable to cure her, and she died in Winchester.

Weighing a horse, an important part of horse racing at places like Newmarket.

[From Ralph Nevill, *Old Sporting Prints* (London, 1908)]

every other care, or almost every other. She could just find selfish-ness enough to wonder whether Edmund *had* written to Miss Craw-ford before this summons came, but no sentiment dwelt long with her, that was not purely affectionate and disinterestedly anxious. Her aunt did not neglect her; she wrote again and again; they were receiving frequent accounts from Edmund, and these accounts were as regularly transmitted to Fanny, in the same diffuse style, and the same medley of trusts, hopes, and fears, all following and producing each other at hap-hazard. It was a sort of playing at being frightened. The sufferings which Lady Bertram did not see, had little power over her fancy; and she wrote very comfortably about agitation and anxi-ety, and poor invalids, till Tom was actually conveyed to Mansfield, and her own eyes had beheld his altered appearance. Then, a letter which she had been previously preparing for Fanny, was finished in a different style, in the language of real feeling and alarm; then, she wrote as she might have spoken. "He is just come, my dear Fanny, and is taken up stairs; and I am so shocked to see him, that I do not know what to do. I am sure he has been very ill. Poor Tom, I am quite grieved for him, and very much frightened, and so is Sir Thomas; and how glad I should be, if you were here to comfort me. But Sir Thomas hopes he will be better to-morrow, and says we must con-sider his journey."

The real solicitude now awakened in the maternal bosom was not soon over. Tom's extreme impatience to be removed to Mansfield, and experience those comforts of home and family which had been little thought of in uninterrupted health, had probably induced his being conveyed thither too early, as a return of fever came on,[23] and for a week he was in a more alarming state than ever. They were all very seriously frightened. Lady Bertram wrote her daily terrors to her niece, who might now be said to live upon letters, and pass all her time between suffering from that of to-day, and looking forward to to-morrow's. Without any particular affection for her eldest cousin, her tenderness of heart made her feel that she could not spare him; and the purity of her principles added yet a keener solicitude, when she considered how little useful, how little self-denying his life had (apparently) been.[24]

23. Travel was a rigorous experience, due to the rough roads and lack of good shock absorbers on carriages (see the illustration on the following page). Jane Austen's mother became very ill on one occasion after a long journey. Travel from Newbury to Northampton would take a full day by current speeds; see map, p. 882.

24. Her keener solicitude is her worry about what will happen to him in the afterlife. Having lived a selfish life, his soul is in danger of damnation.

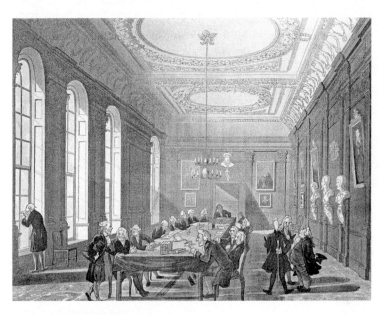

The College of Physicians.

[From Fiona St. Aubyn, *Ackermann's Illustrated London*, illustrations by Augustus Pugin and Thomas Rowlandson (Ware, 1985), p. 91]

Susan was her only companion and listener on this, as on more common occasions. Susan was always ready to hear and to sympathize. Nobody else could be interested in so remote an evil as illness, in a family above an hundred miles off—not even Mrs. Price, beyond a brief question or two if she saw her daughter with a letter in her hand, and now and then the quiet observation of "My poor sister Bertram must be in a great deal of trouble."

So long divided, and so differently situated, the ties of blood were little more than nothing. An attachment, originally as tranquil as their tempers, was now become a mere name. Mrs. Price did quite as much for Lady Bertram, as Lady Bertram would have done for Mrs. Price. Three or four Prices might have been swept away, any or all, except Fanny and William, and Lady Bertram would have thought little about it; or perhaps might have caught from Mrs. Norris's lips the cant of its being a very happy thing, and a great blessing to their poor dear sister Price to have them so well provided for.[25]

25. Those who died would now be well provided for, being united with God instead of suffering poverty on earth. The contrast between this attitude and Fanny's regarding the afterlife is that Fanny is not heartlessly supposing that someone's death could be a blessing for his or her loved ones.

A contemporary image of the discomforts of carriage travel.

[From Ralph Straus, *Carriages and Coaches* (London, 1912), p. 216]

Chapter Fourteen

*A*t about the week's end from his return to Mansfield, Tom's immediate danger was over, and he was so far pronounced safe, as to make his mother perfectly easy; for being now used to the sight of him in his suffering, helpless state, and hearing only the best, and never thinking beyond what she heard, with no disposition for alarm, and no aptitude at a hint,[1] Lady Bertram was the happiest subject in the world for a little medical imposition. The fever was subdued; the fever had been his complaint, of course he would soon be well again; Lady Bertram could think nothing less, and Fanny shared her aunt's security,[2] till she received a few lines from Edmund, written purposely to give her a clearer idea of his brother's situation, and acquaint her with the apprehensions which he and his father had imbibed from the physician, with respect to some strong hectic[3] symptoms, which seemed to seize the frame on the departure of the fever. They judged it best that Lady Bertram should not be harassed by alarms which, it was to be hoped, would prove unfounded; but there was no reason why Fanny should not know the truth. They were apprehensive for his lungs.[4]

A very few lines from Edmund shewed her the patient and the sick room in a juster and stronger light than all Lady Bertram's sheets of paper could do. There was hardly any one in the house who might have not described, from personal observation, better than herself; not one who was not more useful at times to her son. She could do nothing but glide in quietly and look at him; but, when able to talk or be talked to, or read to, Edmund was the companion he preferred. His aunt worried him by her cares, and Sir Thomas knew not how to bring down his conversation or his voice to the level of irritation and feebleness. Edmund was all in all. Fanny would certainly believe him so at least, and must find that her estimation of him was higher than ever when he appeared as the attendant, supporter, cheerer of a suffering brother. There was not only the debility of recent illness to

1.   Meaning no aptitude at discerning a hint.

2.   *security*: confidence, assurance.

3.   *hectic*: pertaining to a consumptive fever; see next note.

4.   This means they fear he has consumption, the current term for tuberculosis. The disease is a bacterial infection of the lungs; a regular fever or infection can make one more susceptible to catching it. It was a leading killer during this time, with no known cure; a few years after this novel, in 1821, the poet John Keats would die of tuberculosis at twenty-five, the same age as Tom Bertram is now.

assist; there was also, as she now learnt, nerves much affected,[5] spirits much depressed to calm and raise; and her own imagination added that there must be a mind to be properly guided.

The family were not consumptive, and she was more inclined to hope than fear for her cousin—except when she thought of Miss Crawford—but Miss Crawford gave her the idea of being the child of good luck, and to her selfishness and vanity it would be good luck to have Edmund the only son.[6]

Even in the sick chamber, the fortunate Mary was not forgotten. Edmund's letter had this postscript. "On the subject of my last, I had actually begun a letter when called away by Tom's illness, but I have now changed my mind, and fear to trust the influence of friends. When Tom is better, I shall go."

Such was the state of Mansfield, and so it continued, with scarcely any change till Easter. A line occasionally added by Edmund to his mother's letter was enough for Fanny's information. Tom's amendment was alarmingly slow.

Easter came—particularly late this year, as Fanny had most sorrowfully considered, on first learning that she had no chance of leaving Portsmouth till after it. It came, and she had yet heard nothing of her return—nothing even of the going to London, which was to precede her return. Her aunt often expressed a wish for her, but there was no notice, no message from the uncle on whom all depended. She supposed he could not yet leave his son, but it was a cruel, a terrible delay to her. The end of April was coming on; it would soon be almost three months instead of two that she had been absent from them all,[7] and that her days had been passing in a state of penance, which she loved them too well to hope they would thoroughly understand,[8]—and who could yet say when there might be leisure to think of, or fetch her?

Her eagerness, her impatience, her longings to be with them, were such as to bring a line or two of Cowper's Tirocinium for ever before her.—"With what intense desire she wants her home,"[9] was continually on her tongue, as the truest description of a yearning which she could not suppose any school-boy's bosom to feel more keenly.

When she had been coming to Portsmouth, she had loved to call it her home, had been fond of saying that she was going home; the

5. The term "nerves" was often used to refer to people's general bodily state, for medical opinion of the time attributed numerous ailments to bad nerves or nervous disorders.

6. If Tom dies, Edmund will be heir to Mansfield Park and the family estate, as well as the title of baronet. He would also give up being a clergyman, for such a position would be both unnecessary to support him and incompatible with the demands of managing a large estate.

7. She left Mansfield in early February.

8. Meaning her love for them makes her wish that they not understand how much she has been suffering, for that could cause them further pain.

9. William Cowper is the same poet Fanny quoted earlier in relation to the suggested improvements at Sotherton (p. 106; see also the accompanying note for general information about Cowper). "Tirocinium: Or, A Review of Schools" was published in 1785 with *The Task*, the more famous long poem that was the source of the earlier quotation. The line Fanny quotes here occurs in a passage about the homesickness of a boy away at boarding school (though it reads "he wants" rather than "she wants").

word had been very dear to her; and so it still was, but it must be applied to Mansfield. *That* was now the home. Portsmouth was Portsmouth; Mansfield was home. They had been long so arranged in the indulgence of her secret meditations; and nothing was more consolatory to her than to find her aunt using the same language.—"I cannot but say, I much regret your being from home at this distressing time, so very trying to my spirits.—I trust and hope, and sincerely wish you may never be absent from home so long again"—were most delightful sentences to her. Still, however, it was her private regale.[10]—Delicacy to her parents made her careful not to betray such a preference of her uncle's house: it was always, "when I go back into Northamptonshire, or when I return to Mansfield, I shall do so and so."—For a great while it was so; but at last the longing grew stronger, it overthrew caution, and she found herself talking of what she should do when she went home, before she was aware.— She reproached herself, coloured[11] and looked fearfully towards her father and mother. She need not have been uneasy. There was no sign of displeasure, or even of hearing her. They were perfectly free from any jealousy of Mansfield. She was as welcome to wish herself there, as to be there.

It was sad to Fanny to lose all the pleasures of spring. She had not known before what pleasures she *had* to lose in passing March and April in a town. She had not known before, how much the beginnings and progress of vegetation had delighted her.—What animation both of body and mind, she had derived from watching the advance of that season which cannot, in spite of its capriciousness, be unlovely, and seeing its increasing beauties, from the earliest flowers, in the warmest divisions of her aunt's garden,[12] to the opening of leaves of her uncle's plantations, and the glory of his woods.[13]—To be losing such pleasures was no trifle; to be losing them, because she was in the midst of closeness and noise, to have confinement, bad air,[14] bad smells, substituted for liberty, freshness, fragrance, and verdure, was infinitely worse;—but even these incitements[15] to regret, were feeble, compared with what arose from the conviction of being missed, by her best friends, and the longing to be useful to those who were wanting her!

Could she have been at home, she might have been of service to

10. *regale*: delight.

11. *coloured*: blushed.

12. Certain parts of the garden could be warmer because of their position in relation to the sun or wind, and gardens were often kept warmer by building walls around them, and in some cases even heating the walls with a fire.

13. The plantations differ from the woods in being planted trees. Thus they could contain young trees that do not exhibit the full glory of the mature trees of the woods.

14. Stale or foul air, in addition to being unpleasant, was also regarded as an acute danger to health. People were as yet unaware of microorganisms due to the lack of sufficiently powerful microscopes to see them, so medical opinion frequently attributed the spread of infectious diseases to poisonous atmospheres.

15. *incitements*: incentives.

every creature in the house. She felt that she must have been of use to all. To all, she must have saved some trouble of head or hand; and were it only in supporting the spirits of her aunt Bertram, keeping her from the evil of solitude, or the still greater evil of a restless, officious companion, too apt to be heightening danger in order to enhance her own importance,[16] her being there would have been a general good. She loved to fancy how she could have read to her aunt, how she could have talked to her, and tried at once to make her feel the blessing of what was, and prepare her mind for what might be; and how many walks up and down stairs she might have saved her, and how many messages she might have carried.

It astonished her that Tom's sisters could be satisfied with remaining in London at such a time—through an illness, which had now, under different degrees of danger, lasted several weeks.[17] *They* might return to Mansfield when they chose; travelling could be no difficulty to *them*, and she could not comprehend how both could still keep away.[18] If Mrs. Rushworth could imagine any interfering obligations, Julia was certainly able to quit London whenever she chose.—It appeared from one of her aunt's letters, that Julia had offered to return if wanted—but this was all.—It was evident that she would rather remain where she was.

Fanny was disposed to think the influence of London very much at war with all respectable attachments. She saw the proof of it in Miss Crawford, as well as in her cousins; *her* attachment to Edmund had been respectable, the most respectable part of her character, her friendship for herself, had at least been blameless.[19] Where was either sentiment now? It was so long since Fanny had had any letter from her, that she had some reason to think lightly of the friendship which had been so dwelt on.—It was weeks since she had heard any thing of Miss Crawford or of her other connections in town, except through Mansfield, and she was beginning to suppose that she might never know whether Mr. Crawford had gone into Norfolk again or not, till they met, and might never hear from his sister any more this spring, when the following letter was received to revive old, and create some new sensations.

"Forgive me, my dear Fanny, as soon as you can, for my long silence, and behave as if you could forgive me directly.[20] This is my

16. She means Mrs. Norris.

17. Nursing was one of the basic female tasks in the household. Most nursing was done at home by family members or servants; there were few professional nurses, and those who existed had not received any special training. Moreover, the severe limitations of current medicine meant that illnesses could last for a long time and the main treatment was continual nursing care. A young man's sisters would be expected to be willing to return home to help nurse him in a case where his life was threatened, especially since they know their mother is inadequate to the task and they have no other pressing obligations, such as children to care for.

18. They could easily return because London was only a day away, rather than two days, and because they could easily procure a man to escort them for such a journey: Edmund or Sir Thomas could come to London to pick them up, or a man they know in London could take them to Mansfield, Mr. Rushworth being an obvious possibility.

19. Blameless because she had nothing to gain in a material or social sense from the friendship.

20. Mary regularly asks forgiveness for faults and negligence. This indicates a perceptive consciousness of her wrongs, but also an inclination to rely on such appeals in lieu of making a serious effort to ameliorate her behavior.

Queen Square, in Bloomsbury, near Bedford Square (see p. 782).

[From *The Repository of arts, literature, fashions, manufactures, &c*, Vol. VIII (1812), p. 150]

modest request and expectation, for you are so good, that I depend upon being treated better than I deserve—and I write now to beg an immediate answer. I want to know the state of things at Mansfield Park, and you, no doubt, are perfectly able to give it. One should be a brute not to feel for the distress they are in—and from what I hear, poor Mr. Bertram has a bad chance of ultimate recovery. I thought little of his illness at first. I looked upon him as the sort of person to be made a fuss with,[21] and to make a fuss himself in any trifling disorder, and was chiefly concerned for those who had to nurse him; but now it is confidently asserted that he is really in a decline, that the symptoms are most alarming, and that part of the family, at least, are aware of it. If it be so, I am sure you must be included in that part, that discerning part, and therefore intreat you to let me know how far I have been rightly informed. I need not say how rejoiced I shall be to hear there has been any mistake, but the report is so prevalent, that I confess I cannot help trembling. To have such a fine young man cut off in the flower of his days, is most melancholy.[22] Poor Sir Thomas will feel it dreadfully. I really am quite agitated on the subject. Fanny, Fanny, I see you smile, and look cunning, but upon my honour, I never bribed a physician in my life.[23] Poor young man!—If he is to die, there will be *two* poor young men less in the world;[24] and with a fearless face and bold voice would I say to any one, that wealth and consequence could fall into no hands more deserving of them.[25] It was a foolish precipitation last Christmas,[26] but the evil of a few days may be blotted out in part. Varnish and gilding hide many stains.[27] It will be but the loss of the Esquire after his name.[28] With real affection, Fanny, like mine, more might be overlooked. Write to me by return of post,[29] judge of my anxiety, and do not trifle with it. Tell me the real truth, as you have it from the fountain head. And now, do not trouble yourself to be ashamed of either my feelings or your own.[30] Believe me, they are not only natural, they are philanthropic and virtuous. I put it to your conscience, whether 'Sir Edmund' would not do more good with all the Bertram property, than any other possible 'Sir.'[31] Had the Grants been at home, I would not have troubled you, but you are now the only one I can apply to for the truth, his sisters not being within my reach. Mrs. R. has been

21. *with*: about.

22. Being cut off in the flower of one's youth was a common expression at the time. "The flower of his days" was not nearly so common, but expresses the same idea.

23. The joke is that she might wish to bribe Tom's physician in order to ensure his death, and thereby make Edmund the heir.

24. Tom is currently poor in his physical state, and Edmund poor financially (by Mary's standards). Both their conditions will change if Tom dies.

25. "Consequence" is social consequence. She thinks he deserves it for being a better person, and probably believes that she would then have a fully deserving husband, one who had wealth joined to his moral and personal virtues.

26. The "precipitation," or precipitous action, was his becoming ordained.

27. That is, the stain of becoming a clergyman, an undesirable profession in the eyes of the fashionable world, will remain but be mostly covered up by the splendor of being heir to a wealthy estate and a baronetcy.

28. "Esquire" is a designation added, usually in formal contexts, to the name of a man of genteel status who lacks a title. It derives from "squire," the medieval term for a man just below a knight in status, and a current term for gentry landowners. Jane Austen affixed the abbreviated "Esq." to her male relatives' names in some letters to them, and in one to a nephew who had reached an age to be considered an adult gentleman, she says, "One reason for my writing to you now, is that I may have the pleasure of directing to you *Esq*^re" (Dec. 16, 1816). Edmund is now an esquire, but if he inherits someday instead of Tom he will drop the "Esquire" in favor of the more prestigious "Sir."

29. *return of post*: by the next mail. The term originally meant replying by sending back a message with the courier who delivered it, but that practice had gradually faded, leaving the term as a residue.

30. She assumes that Fanny would also be pleased by Edmund's elevation, due to her close friendship with him. This assumption, along with her open celebration of the possibility of Tom's death, shows how much she fails to understand Fanny. Her talk of not being ashamed demonstrates that she is aware that many would condemn her statements and attitude, but she still supposes that Fanny's personal biases would overcome such general moral principles.

31. A "Sir Edmund" would be in a position to exercise greater charity to the local poor, to supervise neighborhood affairs well, to be a responsible and decent landlord, and to assist family members and friends.

spending the Easter with the Aylmers at Twickenham[32] (as to be sure you know), and is not yet returned; and Julia is with the cousins, who live near Bedford Square; but I forgot their name and street.[33] Could I immediately apply to either, however, I should still prefer you, because it strikes me, that they have all along been so unwilling to have their own amusements cut up,[34] as to shut their eyes to the truth. I suppose, Mrs. R.'s Easter holidays will not last much longer; no doubt they are thorough holidays to her.[35] The Aylmers are pleasant people; and her husband away, she can have nothing but enjoyment. I give her credit for promoting his going dutifully down to Bath, to fetch his mother; but how will she and the dowager agree in one house?[36] Henry is not at hand, so I have nothing to say from him. Do not you think Edmund would have been in town again long ago, but for this illness?—Yours ever, Mary."

"I had actually began folding my letter, when Henry walked in; but he brings no intelligence to prevent my sending it. Mrs. R. knows a decline is apprehended; he saw her this morning, she returns to Wimpole Street today, the old lady is come. Now do not make yourself uneasy with any queer fancies, because he has been spending a few days at Richmond.[37] He does it every spring. Be assured, he cares for nobody but you. At this very moment, he is wild to see you, and occupied only in contriving the means for doing so, and for making his pleasure conduce to yours. In proof, he repeats, and more eagerly, what he said at Portsmouth, about our conveying you home, and I join him in it with all my soul. Dear Fanny, write directly, and tell us to come. It will do us all good.[38] He and I can go to the Parsonage, you know, and be no trouble to our friends at Mansfield Park. It would really be gratifying to see them all again, and a little addition of society might be of infinite use to them; and, as to yourself, you must feel yourself to be so wanted there, that you cannot in conscience (conscientious as you are), keep away, when you have the means of returning. I have not time or patience to give half Henry's messages; be satisfied, that the spirit of each and every one is unalterable affection."[39]

Fanny's disgust at the greater part of this letter, with her extreme reluctance to bring the writer of it and her cousin Edmund together, would have made her (as she felt), incapable of judging impartially

32. Twickenham, where Mary earlier said that Admiral Crawford had a summer place, was a town near London where many wealthy people had homes.

33. Bedford Square is in Bloomsbury, a middle-class area of London that was not as fashionable or wealthy as Mayfair or Marylebone. Mary may have deliberately not bothered to learn the name and street of this family from an unwillingness to associate herself with a less desirable neighborhood.

34. *cut up*: broken off, disrupted.

35. Thorough holidays because she is away from her husband.

36. Mary turns out to be prescient in imagining problems between Mr. Rushworth's mother and Maria. This is why she gives credit to Maria for promoting Mr. Rushworth's mission to Bath: Maria would know it is right for his mother to visit them, even though it could create complications for her, since she will now be living with the person who used to run her husband's household. Maria's main motive in encouraging him to go may have been to get him out of London for a brief time; she also may hope that with his mother to occupy much of his time once they are in London, he will wish to be less with his wife.

37. Richmond is next to Twickenham, and was also full of homes of the wealthy. Its location allows Henry to see Maria easily while she is in Twickenham, and Mary's report that he "saw her this morning" suggests he may be seeing her on a regular basis, rather than at special social events. This also means he has still not left London to perform the tasks on his estate he spoke of when he was with Fanny.

38. Mary's words exhibit a stronger longing to go to Mansfield than she expressed previously. She may wish to see Edmund, now that she thinks he is about to become a far more eligible mate, and she may wish to see Tom to gain a clearer sense of the chances of that. It is also possible that she fears Henry's time with Maria could prove dangerous to him. Henry himself, if he really was, as she states, even more eager than before about fetching Fanny, may be hoping that such a mission will tear him away from a situation he knows is becoming treacherous. Of course, if that were the case Henry could always leave of his own accord. But he has shown himself capable of knowing what is sensible and right without having the willpower to act on that knowledge if it is painful or inconvenient. His plea to Fanny about needing her help to carry out his improvements on his estate may even have stemmed, at least in part, from awareness of that feature of his character.

39. In other words, Henry may no longer be sending specific messages to Fanny, aside from a general wish of seeing her.

whether the concluding offer might be accepted or not. To herself, individually, it was most tempting. To be finding herself, perhaps, within three days, transported to Mansfield,[40] was an image of the greatest felicity—but it would have been a material drawback, to be owing such felicity to persons in whose feelings and conduct, at the present moment, she saw so much to condemn; the sister's feelings— the brother's conduct—*her* cold-hearted ambition—*his* thoughtless vanity. To have him still the acquaintance, the flirt, perhaps, of Mrs. Rushworth!—She was mortified.[41] She had thought better of him. Happily, however, she was not left to weigh and decide between opposite inclinations and doubtful notions of right; there was no occasion to determine, whether she ought to keep Edmund and Mary asunder or not. She had a rule to apply to, which settled every thing. Her awe of her uncle, and her dread of taking a liberty with him, made it instantly plain to her, what she had to do. She must absolutely decline the proposal. If he wanted, he would send for her; and even to offer an early return, was a presumption which hardly any thing would have seemed to justify. She thanked Miss Crawford, but gave a decided negative.[42]—"Her uncle, she understood, meant to fetch her; and as her cousin's illness had continued so many weeks without her being thought at all necessary, she must suppose her return would be unwelcome at present, and that she should be felt an incumbrance."

Her representation of her cousin's state at this time, was exactly according to her own belief of it, and such as she supposed would convey to the sanguine mind of her correspondent, the hope of every thing she was wishing for. Edmund would be forgiven for being a clergyman, it seemed, under certain conditions of wealth; and this she suspected, was all the conquest of prejudice, which he was so ready to congratulate himself upon. She had only learnt to think nothing of consequence but money.

40. It would take one day for Mary and Henry to reach Portsmouth from London, and then two days to travel to Mansfield.

41. Her mortification shows she had begun to take a real interest in Henry's welfare and his moral improvement, though her reaction to the news also shows that jealousy does not enter at all into her thoughts.

42. This decision will have apparently momentous consequences, though it is not certain if subsequent events would have been different if she had decided to accept Mary's offer.

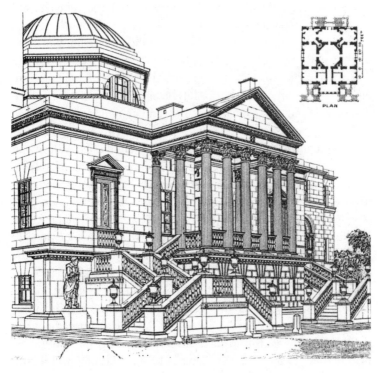

Chiswick House, a grand villa near Richmond and London.

[From J. Alfred Gotch, *The English Home from Charles I to George IV* (New York, 1918), p. 217]

Chapter Fifteen

*A*s Fanny could not doubt that her answer was conveying a real disappointment, she was rather in expectation, from her knowledge of Miss Crawford's temper, of being urged again; and though no second letter arrived for the space of a week, she had still the same feeling when it did come.

On receiving it, she could instantly decide on its containing little writing, and was persuaded of its having the air of a letter of haste and business.[1] Its object was unquestionable; and two moments were enough to start[2] the probability of its being merely to give her notice that they should be in Portsmouth that very day, and to throw her into all the agitation of doubting what she ought to do in such a case. If two moments, however, can surround with difficulties, a third can disperse them; and before she had opened the letter, the possibility of Mr. and Miss Crawford's having applied to her uncle and obtained his permission, was giving her ease.[3] This was the letter.

"A most scandalous, ill-natured rumour has just reached me, and I write, dear Fanny, to warn you against giving the least credit to it, should it spread into the country.[4] Depend upon it there is some mistake, and that a day or two will clear it up—at any rate, that Henry is blameless, and in spite of a moment's *etourderie*[5] thinks of nobody but you. Say not a word of it—hear nothing, surmise nothing, whisper nothing, till I write again. I am sure it will be all hushed up, and nothing proved but Rushworth's folly. If they are gone, I would lay my life they are only gone to Mansfield Park, and Julia with them.[6] But why would not you let us come for you? I wish you may not repent it.[7]

"*Yours, &c.*"

Fanny stood aghast. As no scandalous, ill-natured rumour had reached her, it was impossible for her to understand much of this strange letter. She could only perceive that it must relate to Wimpole

1. The expense of postage meant that people usually did not send short letters, which cost as much as a longer letter filling the page, unless they had urgent business to communicate. Many of Jane Austen's letters were written over the course of more than one day: if she finished the news for one day, and still had space on the page, she would wait to send it until she could add more news.

2. *start*: introduce.

3. This would obviate the main barrier to her return, the lack of permission from Sir Thomas.

4. *into the country*: outside London.

5. etourderie: thoughtless blunder (in French, which is why it is italicized).

6. What Henry has done, who may be with him, and what she means by "Rushworth's folly" will soon become clear.

7. The repentance she imagines is for losing Henry.

Street and Mr. Crawford, and only conjecture that something very imprudent had just occurred in that quarter to draw the notice of the world, and to excite her jealousy, in Miss Crawford's apprehension, if she heard it. Miss Crawford need not be alarmed for her. She was only sorry for the parties concerned and for Mansfield, if the report should spread so far; but she hoped it might not. If the Rushworths were gone themselves to Mansfield, as was to be inferred from what Miss Crawford said, it was not likely that any thing unpleasant should have preceded them, or at least should make any impression.

As to Mr. Crawford, she hoped it might give him a knowledge of his own disposition, convince him that he was not capable of being steadily attached to any one woman in the world, and shame him from persisting any longer in addressing herself.

It was very strange! She had begun to think he really loved her, and to fancy his affection for her something more than common — and his sister still said that he cared for nobody else. Yet there must have been some marked display of attentions to her cousin, there must have been some strong indiscretion, since her correspondent was not of a sort to regard a slight one.

Very uncomfortable she was and must continue till she heard from Miss Crawford again. It was impossible to banish the letter from her thoughts, and she could not relieve herself by speaking of it to any human being. Miss Crawford need not have urged secrecy with so much warmth, she might have trusted to her sense of what was due to her cousin.

The next day came and brought no second letter. Fanny was disappointed. She could still think of little else all the morning; but when her father came back in the afternoon with the daily newspaper as usual, she was so far from expecting any elucidation through such a channel, that the subject was for a moment out of her head.

She was deep in other musing. The remembrance of her first evening in that room, of her father and his newspaper came across her. No candle was *now* wanted. The sun was yet an hour and half above the horizon. She felt that she had, indeed, been three months there; and the sun's rays falling strongly into the parlour, instead of cheering, made her still more melancholy; for sun-shine appeared to her a totally different thing in a town and in the country.[8] Here, its power

8.   Jane Austen, after living the first twenty-five years of her life in the country, spent the next eight in the towns of Bath and Southampton. There are a
number of indications in her letters that overall she liked town life less and was
relieved when she finally returned to the country, going to the village where
she lived during the remainder of her life.

A woman with a letter.

[From *The Repository of arts, literature, fashions, manufactures, &c*, Vol. IX (1813), p. 303]

was only a glare, a stifling, sickly glare, serving but to bring forward stains and dirt that might otherwise have slept. There was neither health nor gaiety in sun-shine in a town. She sat in a blaze of oppressive heat, in a cloud of moving dust; and her eyes could only wander from the walls marked by her father's head, to the table cut and knotched by her brothers, where stood the tea-board never thoroughly cleaned, the cups and saucers wiped in streaks, the milk a mixture of motes floating in thin blue,[9] and the bread and butter growing every minute more greasy than even Rebecca's hands had first produced it. Her father read his newspaper, and her mother lamented over the ragged carpet as usual, while the tea was in preparation—and wished Rebecca would mend it;[10] and Fanny was first roused by his calling out to her, after humphing and considering over a particular paragraph—"What's the name of your great cousins in town, Fan?"

A moment's recollection enabled her to say, "Rushworth, Sir."

"And don't they live in Wimpole Street?"

"Yes, Sir."

"Then, there's the devil to pay among them, that's all. There, (holding out the paper to her)—much good may such fine[11] relations do you. I don't know what Sir Thomas may think of such matters; he may be too much of the courtier and fine gentleman to like his daughter the less.[12] But by G—— if she belonged to me, I'd give her the rope's end as long as I could stand over her.[13] A little flogging for man and woman too, would be the best way of preventing such things."[14]

Fanny read to herself that "it was with infinite concern the newspaper had to announce to the world, a matrimonial *fracas*[15] in the family of Mr. R. of Wimpole Street; the beautiful Mrs. R. whose name had not long been enrolled in the lists of hymen,[16] and who had promised to become so brilliant[17] a leader in the fashionable world, having quitted her husband's roof in company with the well known and captivating Mr. C. the intimate friend and associate of Mr. R. and it was not known,[18] even to the editor of the newspaper, whither they were gone."

"It is a mistake, Sir," said Fanny instantly; "it must be a mistake—it cannot be true—it must mean some other people."

9. Milk was not homogenized, so it would contain floating pieces of cream. It is possible worse substances are also present, as standards of hygiene, including for food and drink, were not high in towns at the time.

10. This vivid depiction of a shabby home has no equivalent elsewhere in Austen's novels, which mostly refrain from detailed physical description of places and, when they do, concentrate on houses and gardens of the wealthy. The passage reveals that Jane Austen was fully aware of this seamier side of life, so her decision to exclude it elsewhere results from a conscious artistic choice. In this case the description represents a fitting climax of Fanny's stay at her parents', intensifying her feeling that she really belongs to Mansfield.

11. *fine*: fancy, elegant. The term could be used in a pejorative sense.

12. He refers to a common belief in looser sexual morals among the upper classes; see note 19 below.

13. In the navy beating someone with a rope's end was a common informal method of punishment by officers; it coexisted with a variety of other harsh physical punishments, both formal and informal. Beating a daughter severely for sexual misbehavior was a long-standing custom outside the elite classes, though one that was perhaps talked about and threatened more than actually enforced.

14. Flogging was the main official punishment in the navy, one frequently inflicted on ordinary sailors. The cat-of-nine-tails, a short whip with nine separate thin knotted ropes, was most commonly used; a sailor would be bound standing and lashed repeatedly on his bare back with the cat. The entire crew was made to witness it, so a man like Mr. Price serving on a ship would have seen numerous instances of flogging.

15. fracas: uproar, disturbance.

16. This is a fancy way of saying she has not long been married; Hymen is the ancient Greek god of marriage.

17. *brilliant*: splendid, distinguished.

18. Accounts of elopements, and other misdeeds, among the fashionable elite were popular in newspapers. Use of initials was also standard: this prevented the parties from becoming infamous generally, while still giving enough information, including addresses, to allow those who knew them to guess their identity. In a letter Jane Austen, commenting on a case of adultery among

She spoke from the instinctive wish of delaying shame, she spoke with a resolution which sprung from despair, for she spoke what she did not, could not believe herself. It had been the shock of conviction as she read. The truth rushed on her; and how she could have spoken at all, how she could even have breathed—was afterwards matter of wonder to herself.

Mr. Price cared too little about the report, to make her much answer. "It might be all a lie," he acknowledged; "but so many fine ladies were going to the devil now-a-days that way, that there was no answering for anybody."[19]

"Indeed, I hope it is not true," said Mrs. Price plaintively, "it would be so very shocking!—If I have spoken once to Rebecca about that carpet, I am sure I have spoke at least a dozen times; have not I, Betsey?—And it would not be ten minutes work."

The horror of a mind like Fanny's, as it received the conviction of such guilt, and began to take in some part of the misery that must ensue, can hardly be described. At first, it was a sort of stupifaction; but every moment was quickening her perception of the horrible evil.[20] She could not doubt; she dared not indulge a hope of the paragraph being false. Miss Crawford's letter, which she had read so often as to make every line her own, was in frightful conformity with it. Her eager defence of her brother, her hope of its being *hushed up*, her evident agitation, were all of a piece with something very bad; and if there was a woman of character in existence,[21] who could treat as a trifle this sin of the first magnitude, who could try to gloss it over, and desire to have it unpunished, she could believe Miss Crawford to be the woman! Now she could see her own mistake as to *who* were gone—or *said* to be gone. It was not Mr. and Mrs. Rushworth, it was Mrs. Rushworth and Mr. Crawford.

Fanny seemed to herself never to have been shocked before. There was no possibility of rest. The evening passed, without a pause of misery, the night was totally sleepless. She passed only from feelings of sickness to shudderings of horror; and from hot fits of fever to cold. The event was so shocking, that there were moments even when her heart revolted from it as impossible—when she thought it could not be. A woman married only six months ago, a man professing himself devoted, even *engaged*, to another—that other her near

acquaintances, says, "A hint of it, with Initials, was in yesterday's Courier" (June 22, 1808).

19. The social elite was perceived to be rife with infidelity and other forms of sexual misbehavior. One reason was looser standards among the elite, something the Crawfords are an example of; another was that elite misbehavior was often widely publicized, unlike that of ordinary people, which made it seem more widespread. Both elite mores and public perception of them were influenced by the reigning sovereign of Britain, the Prince Regent, a notorious philanderer who was bitterly estranged from his wife; Jane Austen expresses her distaste for him in a letter. He helped set the tone for fashionable society and his misdeeds were widely covered. In her letters Austen mentions several cases of adultery in prominent aristocratic families that she had some acquaintance with, though she did not necessarily know the guilty parties personally. Her reaction shows a mixture of fascination and disgust that was probably typical of those following these scandals. In one case, that of the daughter of Lady Saye and Sele, Austen writes of spotting her at a ball in Bath: "I am proud to say that I have a very good eye at an Adulteress, for tho' repeatedly assured that another in the same party was the *She*, I fixed upon the right one from the first" (May 12, 1801). In another, that of Lady Caroline Paget, whose family was known for previous scandals, she declares, "What can be expected from a Paget, born & brought up in the centre of conjugal Infidelity & Divorces?—I will *not* be interested about Lady Caroline. I abhor all the race of Pagets" (March 13, 1817).

20. This shocked reaction was typical for the period. In *Pride and Prejudice* the heroine is prostrate with distress upon learning that her unmarried sister has run away with a man, a misdeed that would not be condemned as severely as adultery by a married person. Jane Austen's letters exhibit a strong reaction on her part toward such cases, even though they never involved anyone close to herself. At the same time, Fanny's extreme reaction, described over the next page, goes beyond what even many upright people would feel, and reflects both Fanny's very strict standards and her emotional sensitivity.

21. Mary is a woman of character because she would not commit such a transgression herself, in Fanny's estimation. It is notable that Fanny's shock and horror have not caused her to cease showing some justice to Mary.

relation—the whole family, both families connected as they were by tie upon tie, all friends, all intimate together!—it was too horrible a confusion of guilt, too gross a complication of evil, for human nature, not in a state of utter barbarism,[22] to be capable of!—yet her judgment told her it was so. *His* unsettled affections, wavering with his vanity, *Maria's* decided attachment, and no sufficient principle on either's side, gave it possibility—Miss Crawford's letter stampt it a fact.

What would be the consequence? Whom would it not injure? Whose views[23] might it not affect? Whose peace would it not cut up for ever? Miss Crawford herself—Edmund; but it was dangerous, perhaps, to tread such ground. She confined herself, or tried to confine herself to the simple, indubitable family-misery which must envelope all, if it were indeed a matter of certified guilt and public exposure. The mother's sufferings, the father's—there, she paused. Julia's, Tom's, Edmund's—there, a yet longer pause. They were the two on whom it would fall most horribly. Sir Thomas's parental solicitude, and high sense of honour and decorum, Edmund's upright principles, unsuspicious temper, and genuine strength of feeling,[24] made her think it scarcely possible for them to support life and reason under such disgrace; and it appeared to her, that as far as this world alone was concerned, the greatest blessing to every one of kindred with Mrs. Rushworth would be instant annihilation.[25]

Nothing happened the next day, or the next, to weaken her terrors. Two posts[26] came in, and brought no refutation, public or private. There was no second letter to explain away the first, from Miss Crawford; there was no intelligence from Mansfield, though it was now full[27] time for her to hear again from her aunt. This was an evil omen. She had, indeed, scarcely the shadow of a hope to soothe her mind, and was reduced to so low and wan and trembling a condition as no mother—not unkind, except Mrs. Price, could have overlooked, when the third day did bring the sickening knock, and a letter was again put into her hands. It bore the London postmark, and came from Edmund.[28]

"Dear Fanny,

You know our present wretchedness. May God support you under *your* share. We have been here two days, but there is nothing to be

22. The notion of civilization as progressively moving further away from conditions of barbarism was widespread in this society, and adherents of this ideal identified progress in morality and standards of behavior as at least as important as more material forms of progress.

23. *views*: expectations, plans, aspirations.

24. She makes a distinction between Sir Thomas and Edmund. The first, she believes, would be more concerned with outward honor, especially of the family, and with the breach of decorum and social rules. The second would be more concerned with the underlying moral wrongness of adultery. This does not mean that each man would disregard the other's reasons, only that they are not his first priority.

25. Meaning for the worldly welfare of those connected with Maria it would be best that she die, but from an otherworldly perspective it would be best for her to remain alive so she can repent of her sin and possibly gain eventual divine forgiveness. Maria's death would probably serve the practical interests of others in her family, due to the dishonor and social taint of being connected with an adulteress; in *Pride and Prejudice* the heroine worries that her sister's transgression will mar the marital chances of all the other sisters in the family. Of course, that does not mean that the Bertrams actually desire such an outcome: there is never any indication of that. As for Maria herself, social opinion often held that death was a preferred outcome in cases of adultery, especially for the woman, whose sin was regarded as particularly heinous (for more on this, see p. 841, note 40). This idea was given famous expression in a poem in Oliver Goldsmith's popular novel *The Vicar of Wakefield* (1766), a poem that Jane Austen humorously alludes to in *Emma*:

> When lovely woman stoops to folly,
>   And finds too late that men betray,
> What charm can soothe her melancholy,
>   What art can wash her guilt away?
> The only art her guilt to cover,
>   To hide her shame from every eye,
> To give repentance to her lover,
>   And wring his bosom—is to die.

26. *posts*: mail deliveries.

27. *full*: fully.

28. Letters had postmarks showing their origin. As explained below, and later, Edmund accompanied Sir Thomas to London to try to salvage the situation.

done. They cannot be traced. You may not have heard of the last blow—Julia's elopement; she is gone to Scotland with Yates.[29] She left London a few hours before we entered it. At any other time, this would have been felt dreadfully. Now it seems nothing, yet it is an heavy aggravation. My father is not overpowered. More cannot be hoped. He is still able to think and act; and I write, by his desire, to propose your returning home. He is anxious to get you there for my mother's sake. I shall be at Portsmouth the morning after you receive this, and hope to find you ready to set off for Mansfield. My father wishes you to invite Susan to go with you, for a few months.[30] Settle it as you like; say what is proper; I am sure you will feel such an instance of his kindness at such a moment! Do justice to his meaning, however I may confuse it.[31] You may imagine something of my present state. There is no end of the evil let loose upon us. You will see me early, by the mail.[32] Your's, &c."

Never had Fanny more wanted a cordial.[33] Never had she felt such a one as this letter contained. To-morrow! to leave Portsmouth to-morrow! She was, she felt she was, in the greatest danger of being exquisitely happy, while so many were miserable. The evil which brought such good to her! She dreaded lest she should learn to be insensible of it. To be going so soon, sent for so kindly, sent for as a comfort, and with leave to take Susan, was altogether such a combination of blessings as set her heart in a glow, and for a time, seemed to distance every pain, and make her incapable of suitably sharing the distress even of those whose distress she thought of most. Julia's elopement could affect her comparatively but little; she was amazed and shocked; but it could not occupy her, could not dwell on her mind. She was obliged to call herself[34] to think of it, and acknowl-edge it to be terrible and grievous, or it was escaping her, in the midst of all the agitating, pressing, joyful cares attending this summons to herself.

There is nothing like employment, active, indispensable employ-ment, for relieving sorrow. Employment, even melancholy, may dispel melancholy, and her occupations were hopeful. She had so much to do, that not even the horrible story of Mrs. Rushworth (now fixed[35] to the last point of certainty), could affect her as it had done

29. The laws of England forbade a couple from marrying without parental permission if either was under twenty-one. But the laws of Scotland allowed such marriages, and if the marriage occurred there it was recognized in English law. Hence young couples wishing to marry often went to Scotland; the town of Gretna Green, the first Scottish town on the main road from England, had a flourishing business in quick marriages. In this case, Julia is only twenty, and Sir Thomas has shown no inclination to consent to Yates as her husband.

30. Fanny has presumably mentioned Susan in her letters and perhaps even indicated Susan's interest in Mansfield Park or Fanny's own hope of remaining with and guiding her sister.

31. He means justice to his intention of helping Susan. Edmund fears that his agitation is making his letter incoherent.

32. He is taking the mail coach from London to Portsmouth (see p. 485, note 24), because it travels overnight, so he will arrive the next morning and be able to set out immediately to Mansfield. If he traveled by normal means, he would not arrive until the following evening, and thus have to depart a day later.

33. *cordial*: a substance to revive people or to assist their recovery from illness, or from shock in this case. There were a great variety of cordials, for no regulations existed regarding what could go in them or what claims could be made on their behalf. Many contained alcohol, which was often viewed as medicinal and could make the user feel better regardless of whether it had any other beneficial effect.

34. *call herself*: enjoin or command herself.

35. *fixed*: settled, confirmed.

before. She had not time to be miserable. Within twenty-four hours she was hoping to be gone; her father and mother must be spoken to, Susan prepared, every thing got ready. Business followed business;[36] the day was hardly long enough. The happiness she was imparting too, happiness very little alloyed by the black communication which must briefly precede it—the joyful consent of her father and mother to Susan's going with her—the general satisfaction with which the going of both seemed regarded—and the ecstacy of Susan herself, was all serving to support her spirits.

The affliction of the Bertrams was little felt in the family. Mrs. Price talked of her poor sister for a few minutes—but how to find any thing to hold Susan's clothes, because Rebecca took away all the boxes and spoilt them,[37] was much more in her thoughts, and as for Susan, now unexpectedly gratified in the first wish of her heart, and knowing nothing personally of those who had sinned, or of those who were sorrowing—if she could help rejoicing from beginning to end, it was as much as ought to be expected from human virtue at fourteen.

As nothing was really left for the decision of Mrs. Price, or the good offices of Rebecca, every thing was rationally and duly accomplished, and the girls were ready for the morrow. The advantage of much sleep to prepare them for their journey, was impossible. The cousin who was travelling towards them, could hardly have less than visited their agitated spirits, one all happiness, the other all varying and indescribable perturbation.[38]

By eight in the morning, Edmund was in the house. The girls heard his entrance from above, and Fanny went down. The idea of immediately seeing him, with the knowledge of what he must be suffering, brought back all her own first feelings. He so near her, and in misery. She was ready to sink,[39] as she entered the parlour. He was alone, and met her instantly; and she found herself pressed to his heart with only these words, just articulate, "My Fanny—my only sister—my only comfort now." She could say nothing; nor for some minutes could he say more.

He turned away to recover himself, and when he spoke again, though his voice still faltered, his manner showed the wish of self-

36. *business*: things to be done, or to be busy about.

37. Susan does not have a trunk, since she has never traveled before. Boxes were sometimes used for travel: in *Pride and Prejudice* three travelers returning home have boxes and parcels with them.

38. All three are similarly sleepless, for Edmund will probably achieve little sleep in the overnight coach.

39. *sink*: faint.

A mail coach.

[From William Pyne, *The Costume of Great Britain* (London, 1804; 1989 reprint), Plate LIV]

command, and the resolution of avoiding any farther allusion. "Have you breakfasted?—When shall you be ready?—Does Susan go?"—were questions following each other rapidly. His great object was to be off as soon as possible. When Mansfield was considered, time was precious; and the state of his own mind made him find relief only in motion. It was settled that he should order the carriage to the door in half an hour;[40] Fanny answered for their having breakfasted, and being quite ready in half an hour. He had already ate, and declined staying for their meal. He would walk round the ramparts, and join them with the carriage. He was gone again, glad to get away even from Fanny.

He looked very ill; evidently suffering under violent emotions, which he was determined to suppress. She knew it must be so, but it was terrible to her.

The carriage came; and he entered the house again at the same moment, just in time to spend a few minutes with the family, and be a witness—but that he saw nothing—of the tranquil manner in which the daughters were parted with, and just in time to prevent their sitting down to the breakfast table, which by dint of much unusual activity, was quite and completely ready as the carriage drove from the door. Fanny's last meal in her father's house was in character with her first; she was dismissed from it as hospitably as she had been welcomed.

How her heart swelled with joy and gratitude, as she passed the barriers of Portsmouth,[41] and how Susan's face wore its broadest smiles, may be easily conceived. Sitting forwards, however, and screened by her bonnet,[42] those smiles were unseen.

The journey was likely to be a silent one. Edmund's deep sighs often reached Fanny. Had he been alone with her, his heart must have opened in spite of every resolution; but Susan's presence drove him quite into himself, and his attempts to talk on indifferent subjects could never be long supported.

Fanny watched him with never-failing solicitude, and sometimes catching his eye, revived[43] an affectionate smile, which comforted her; but the first day's journey passed without her hearing a word from him on the subjects that were weighing him down. The next

40. This is a private chaise, which he probably hired at the inn where the mail coach arrived; he could have left it there awaiting his instructions.

41. The barriers are the fortifications and gate and drawbridge guarding the entrance to the town from the outside.

42. Bonnets had recently become popular for women. Because they fit close to the head, and the brim stuck out in front, the wearer's face was blocked from view for those looking from the side.

43. This was "received" in the 1814 edition, but changed to "revived" in the 1816 one. The first could have been a printer's error, or Jane Austen may have decided to change the word. "Received" has Edmund smiling on his own, "revived" has him being influenced by Fanny. Austen may have wished to emphasize Fanny's role in assisting his recovery from his anguish and despair, a role she will continue to play.

A bonnet (on left) and a hat.

[From *The Repository of arts, literature, fashions, manufactures, &c*, Vol. I (1809), p. 494]

morning produced a little more. Just before their setting out from Oxford, while Susan was stationed at a window, in eager observation of the departure of a large family from the inn, the other two were standing by the fire; and Edmund, particularly struck by the alteration in Fanny's looks, and from his ignorance of the daily evils of her father's house, attributing an undue share of the change, attributing *all* to the recent event, took her hand, and said in a low, but very expressive tone, "No wonder—you must feel it—you must suffer. How a man who had once loved, could desert you! But *your's*—your regard was new compared with—Fanny, think of *me!*"[44]

The first division of their journey occupied a long day, and brought them almost knocked up, to Oxford; but the second was over at a much earlier hour.[45] They were in the environs of Mansfield long before the usual dinner-time, and as they approached the beloved place, the hearts of both sisters sank a little. Fanny began to dread the meeting with her aunts and Tom, under so dreadful a humiliation; and Susan to feel with some anxiety, that all her best manners, all her lately acquired knowledge of what was practised here, was on the point of being called into action. Visions of good and ill breeding, of old vulgarisms and new gentilities were before her;[46] and she was meditating much upon silver forks, napkins, and finger glasses.[47] Fanny had been every where awake to the difference of the country since February; but, when they entered the Park, her perceptions and her pleasures were of the keenest sort. It was three months, full three months, since her quitting it; and the change was from winter to summer. Her eye fell every where on lawns and plantations of the freshest green; and the trees, though not fully clothed, were in that delightful state, when farther beauty is known to be at hand, and when, while much is actually given to the sight, more yet remains for the imagination. Her enjoyment, however, was for herself alone. Edmund could not share it. She looked at him, but he was leaning back, sunk in a deeper gloom than ever, and with eyes closed as if the view of cheerfulness oppressed him, and the lovely scenes of home must be shut out.

44. He is thinking of his loss of Mary, for he could never marry her now because of the family rift caused by Henry's behavior.

45. They stayed at the inn at Oxford, where Fanny and Edmund were talking before the fire. Portsmouth to Oxford was seventy-nine miles, which would take a little more than ten hours; that is why they are exhausted when they arrive. From there to Northampton is only forty-one miles, plus four miles to Mansfield.

46. Meaning forms of vulgar and of genteel behavior, the former being what she has experienced at home, and the latter what she will encounter at Mansfield Park and must adapt to.

47. These are all items she would not have used before. Most forks were made of steel; silver forks were used only by the wealthy, who also used separate forks for separate tasks, which means that Susan will have to remember when she should use which one. Napkins of some kind had been in use in earlier times, when people ate partly with their hands. The introduction of the fork into England in the late seventeenth century, which eliminated the need for using hands, led to the disuse of napkins for a while, but during the eighteenth century they were reintroduced in wealthy households. Finger glasses are placed next to each diner's plate to allow them to wash their fingers; they were used

Oxford High Street.

[From Rudolph Ackermann, *A History of the University of Oxford*, Vol. I (London, 1814), p. 27]

It made her melancholy again; and the knowledge of what must be enduring[48] there, invested even the house, modern, airy, and well situated as it was,[49] with a melancholy aspect.[50]

By one of the suffering party within, they were expected with such impatience as she had never known before. Fanny had scarcely passed the solemn-looking servants,[51] when Lady Bertram came from the drawing-room to meet her; came with no indolent step; and, falling on her neck, said, "Dear Fanny! now I shall be comfortable."

A modern house (Organ Hall, Hertfordshire) with large windows.

[From James Merigot, *The Amateur's Portfolio, or the New Drawing Magazine*, Vol. II (London, 1815–1816), No. 4, Plate 4]

by the wealthy during the dessert course, which often involved sticky items eaten by hand.

48. *enduring*: being endured.

49. Modern houses had larger windows than older ones, due to improvements in glass making. This would allow them to let in more air during a time of year such as this, May, when the temperature was pleasant. For the superior situation or position of modern houses, see p. 93, note 27.

50. *aspect*: appearance.

51. The servants line up in front of the house to greet those coming from far away, whether guests or members of the household.

A house with a large park (Normanton Park, Rutlandshire).

[From John Preston Neale, *Views of the Seats of Noblemen and Gentlemen*, Vol. V (London, 1822)]

Chapter Sixteen

*I*t had been a miserable party, each of the three believing them-selves most miserable. Mrs. Norris, however, as most attached to Maria, was really the greatest sufferer. Maria was her first favourite, the dearest of all; the match had been her own contriving, as she had been wont with such pride of heart to feel and say, and this conclu-sion of it almost overpowered her.

She was an altered creature, quieted, stupified, indifferent to every thing that passed. The being left with her sister and nephew, and all the house under her care, had been an advantage entirely thrown away; she had been unable to direct or dictate, or even fancy herself useful. When really touched by affliction, her active powers had been all benumbed; and neither Lady Bertram nor Tom had received from her the smallest support or attempt at support. She had done no more for them, than they had done for each other. They had been all solitary, helpless, and forlorn alike; and now the arrival of the others only established[1] her superiority in wretchedness. Her companions were relieved, but there was no good for *her*. Edmund was almost as welcome to his brother, as Fanny to her aunt; but Mrs. Norris, instead of having comfort from either, was but the more irri-tated by the sight of the person whom, in the blindness of her anger, she could have charged as the dæmon[2] of the piece.[3] Had Fanny accepted Mr. Crawford, this could not have happened.

Susan, too, was a grievance. She had not spirits to notice her in more than a few repulsive looks, but she felt her as a spy, and an intruder, and an indigent niece, and every thing most odious. By her other aunt, Susan was received with quiet kindness. Lady Bertram could not give her much time, or many words, but she felt her, as Fanny's sister, to have a claim at Mansfield, and was ready to kiss and like her; and Susan was more than satisfied, for she came perfectly aware, that nothing but ill humour was to be expected from Aunt Norris; and was so provided with happiness, so strong in that best

1. *established*: confirmed.

2. *dæmon*: demon, evil spirit.

3. *piece*: drama, play.

Landscaped grounds on an estate.

[From Humphry Repton, *The Art of Landscape Gardening* (Boston, 1907; reprint edition), p. 26]

of blessings, an escape from many certain evils, that she could have stood against a great deal more indifference than she met with from the others.

She was now left a good deal to herself, to get acquainted with the house and grounds as she could, and spent her days very happily in so doing, while those who might otherwise have attended to her, were shut up, or wholly occupied each with the person quite dependent on them, at this time, for every thing like comfort; Edmund trying to bury his own feelings in exertions for the relief of his brother's, and Fanny devoted to her aunt Bertram, returning to every former office,[4] with more than former zeal, and thinking she could never do enough for one who seemed so much to want her.

To talk over the dreadful business with Fanny, talk and lament, was all Lady Bertram's consolation. To be listened to and borne with, and hear the voice of kindness and sympathy in return, was every thing that could be done for her. To be otherwise comforted was out of the question. The case admitted of no comfort. Lady Bertram did not think deeply, but, guided by Sir Thomas, she thought justly on all important points; and she saw, therefore, in all its enormity, what had happened, and neither endeavoured herself, nor required Fanny to advise her, to think little of guilt and infamy.

Her affections were not acute, nor was her mind tenacious. After a time, Fanny found it not impossible to direct her thoughts to other subjects, and revive some interest in the usual occupations; but whenever Lady Bertram *was* fixed on the event, she could see it only in one light, as comprehending the loss of a daughter, and a disgrace never to be wiped off.[5]

Fanny learnt from her, all the particulars which had yet transpired. Her aunt was no very methodical narrator; but with the help of some letters to and from Sir Thomas, and what she already knew herself, and could reasonably combine, she was soon able to understand quite as much as she wished of the circumstances attending the story.

Mrs. Rushworth had gone, for the Easter holidays, to Twicken-ham, with a family whom she had just grown intimate with—a family of lively, agreeable manners, and probably of morals and discretion to suit—for to *their* house Mr. Crawford had constant access at all times. His having been in the same neighbourhood, Fanny already

4. *office*: task, function.

5. Meaning that though her daughter will continue to exist, she will no longer be able to see or communicate with her mother, or be truly considered one of the family.

knew. Mr. Rushworth had been gone, at this time, to Bath, to pass a few days with his mother, and bring her back to town, and Maria was with these friends without any restraint, without even Julia; for Julia had removed from Wimpole Street two or three weeks before, on a visit to some relations of Sir Thomas; a removal which her father and mother were now disposed to attribute to some view of convenience on Mr. Yates's account. Very soon after the Rushworths return to Wimpole Street, Sir Thomas had received a letter from an old and most particular friend in London, who hearing and witnessing a good deal to alarm him in that quarter, wrote to recommend Sir Thomas's coming to London himself, and using his influence with his daughter, to put an end to an intimacy which was already exposing her to unpleasant remarks, and evidently making Mr. Rushworth uneasy.

Sir Thomas was preparing to act upon this letter, without communicating its contents to any creature at Mansfield, when it was followed by another, sent express[6] from the same friend, to break to him the almost desperate situation in which affairs then stood with the young people. Mrs. Rushworth had left her husband's house; Mr. Rushworth had been in great anger and distress to *him* (Mr. Harding), for his advice;[7] Mr. Harding feared there had been *at least*, very flagrant indiscretion.[8] The maid-servant of Mrs. Rushworth, senior, threatened alarmingly.[9] He was doing all in his power to quiet every thing, with the hope of Mrs. Rushworth's return, but was so much counteracted in Wimpole Street by the influence of Mr. Rushworth's mother, that the worst consequences might be apprehended.

This dreadful communication could not be kept from the rest of the family. Sir Thomas set off; Edmund would go with him; and the others had been left in a state of wretchedness, inferior only to what followed the receipt of the next letters from London. Every thing was by that time public beyond a hope. The servant of Mrs. Rushworth, the mother, had exposure in her power, and, supported by her mistress, was not to be silenced. The two ladies, even in the short time they had been together, had disagreed; and the bitterness of the elder against her daughter-in-law might, perhaps, arise[10] almost as much from the personal disrespect with which she had herself been treated, as from sensibility[11] for her son.

6. *express*: by express message.

7. Mary, in her letter to Fanny, spoke of "Rushworth's folly" as being the main problem, one that would keep the affair from being hushed up (p. 786). She meant his telling others at this point of the departure of Henry and Mary.

8. Indiscretion would mean they had only gone away together, thereby provoking nasty rumors and making them look guilty, but had not committed actual adultery.

9. This is probably the elder Mrs. Rushworth's lady's maid. Servants would know what was happening, for such a dramatic event could not be kept from them. This maid, based on subsequent description, seems to be spreading the news under the instructions of her mistress, or with her encouragement.

10. *might . . . arise*: may have arisen.

11. *sensibility*: sensitivity, feeling.

However that might be, she was unmanageable. But had she been less obstinate, or of less weight with her son, who was always guided by the last speaker, by the person who could get hold of and shut him up, the case would still have been hopeless, for Mrs. Rushworth did not appear again, and there was every reason to conclude her to be concealed somewhere with Mr. Crawford, who had quitted his uncle's house, as for a journey, on the very day of her absenting herself.

Sir Thomas, however, remained yet a little longer in town, in the hope of discovering, and snatching her from farther vice, though all was lost on the side of character.[12]

His present state, Fanny could hardly bear to think of. There was but one of his children who was not at this time a source of misery to him. Tom's complaints had been greatly heightened by the shock of his sister's conduct, and his recovery so much thrown back by it, that even Lady Bertram had been struck by the difference, and all her alarms were regularly sent off to her husband; and Julia's elopement, the additional blow which had met him on his arrival in London, though its force had been deadened at the moment, must, she knew, be sorely felt. She saw that it was. His letters expressed how much he deplored it. Under any circumstances it would have been an unwelcome alliance,[13] but to have it so clandestinely formed, and such a period chosen for its completion, placed Julia's feelings in a most unfavourable light, and severely aggravated the folly of her choice. He called it a bad thing, done in the worst manner, and at the worst time; and though Julia was yet as more pardonable than Maria as folly than vice, he could not but regard the step she had taken, as opening the worst probabilities of a conclusion hereafter, like her sister's. Such was his opinion of the set into which she had thrown herself.

Fanny felt for him most acutely. He could have no comfort but in Edmund. Every other child must be racking his heart. His displeasure against herself she trusted, reasoning differently from Mrs. Norris, would now be done away. *She* should be justified. Mr. Crawford would have fully acquitted her conduct in refusing him, but this, though most material to herself, would be poor consolation to Sir Thomas. Her uncle's displeasure was terrible to her; but what could

12. *character*: reputation. If he separated her from Henry now, after they had been together only a few days, he would have limited her time spent in sin, but she would never be able to restore her public reputation as an honorable woman.

13. *alliance*: marriage.

A portrait of a woman (Elizabeth Jennings).

[From Sir Walter Armstrong, *Lawrence* (London, 1913), p. 64]

her justification, or her gratitude and attachment do for him? His stay[14] must be on Edmund alone.

She was mistaken, however, in supposing that Edmund gave his father no present pain. It was of a much less poignant nature than what the others excited; but Sir Thomas was considering his happiness as very deeply involved in the offence of his sister and friend, cut off by it as he must be from the woman, whom he had been pursuing with undoubted attachment, and strong probability of success; and who in every thing but this despicable brother, would have been so eligible[15] a connection. He was aware of what Edmund must be suffering on his own behalf in addition to all the rest, when they were in town; he had seen or conjectured his feelings, and having reason to think that *one* interview with Miss Crawford had taken place, from which Edmund derived only increased distress, had been as anxious on that account as on others, to get him out of town, and had engaged him in taking Fanny home to her aunt, with a view to his relief and benefit, no less than theirs. Fanny was not in the secret of her uncle's feelings, Sir Thomas not in the secret of Miss Crawford's character. Had he been privy to her conversation with his son, he would not have wished her to belong to him, though her twenty thousand pounds had been forty.

That Edmund must be for ever divided from Miss Crawford, did not admit of a doubt with Fanny; and yet, till she knew that he felt the same, her own conviction was insufficient. She thought he did, but she wanted to be assured of it. If he would now speak to her with the unreserve[16] which had sometimes been too much for her before, it would be most consoling; but *that* she found was not to be. She seldom saw him—never alone—he probably avoided being alone with her. What was to be inferred? That his judgment submitted to all his own peculiar[17] and bitter share of this family affliction, but that it was too keenly felt to be a subject of the slightest communication. This must be his state. He yielded, but it was with agonies, which did not admit of speech. Long, long would it be ere Miss Crawford's name passed his lips again, or she could hope for a renewal of such confidential intercourse as had been.

It *was* long. They reached Mansfield on Thursday, and it was not till Sunday evening that Edmund began to talk to her on the subject.

14. *stay*: reliance (for support).

15. *eligible*: desirable, proper.

16. *unreserve*: frankness, full disclosure.

17. *peculiar*: particular.

A lady in church.

[From *The Repository of arts, literature, fashions, manufactures, &c*, Vol. IV (1810), p. 242]

Sitting with her on Sunday evening—a wet Sunday evening—the very time of all others when if a friend is at hand the heart must be opened, and every thing told[18]—no one else in the room, except his mother, who, after hearing an affecting sermon, had cried herself to sleep[19]—it was impossible not to speak; and so, with the usual beginnings, hardly to be traced as to what came first, and the usual declaration that if she would listen to him for a few minutes, he should be very brief, and certainly never tax her kindness in the same way again—she need not fear a repetition—it would be a subject prohibited entirely—he entered upon the luxury of relating circumstances and sensations of the first interest to himself, to one of whose affectionate sympathy he was quite convinced.

How Fanny listened, with what curiosity and concern, what pain and what delight, how the agitation of his voice was watched, and how carefully her own eyes were fixed on any object but himself, may be imagined. The opening was alarming. He had seen Miss Crawford.[20] He had been invited to see her.[21] He had received a note from Lady Stornaway to beg him to call;[22] and regarding it as what was meant to be the last, last interview of friendship, and investing her with all the feelings of shame and wretchedness which Crawford's sister ought to have known, he had gone to her in such a state of mind, so softened, so devoted, as made it for a few moments impossible to Fanny's fears, that it should be the last. But as he proceeded in his story, these fears were over. She had met him, he said, with a serious—certainly a serious—even an agitated air; but before he had been able to speak one intelligible sentence, she had introduced the subject in a manner which he owned[23] had shocked him. "I heard you were in town," said she—"I wanted to see you. Let us talk over this sad business. What can equal the folly of our two relations?"—"I could not answer, but I believe my looks spoke. She felt reproved. Sometimes how quick to feel! With a graver look and voice she then added—'I do not mean to defend Henry at your sister's expense.' So she began—but how she went on, Fanny, is not fit—is hardly fit to be repeated to you. I cannot recal all her words. I would not dwell upon them if I could. Their substance was great anger at the *folly* of each. She reprobated her brother's folly in being drawn on by a woman whom he had never cared for, to do what must lose him the woman

18. Prevailing mores restricted many activities on Sunday, not only work but also certain forms of pleasure. So Sunday evening could be a time when people, having little other diversion, were ready to talk at length. Moreover, the church services they had attended earlier might put them in the mood for discussing their deepest and most serious concerns.

19. She heard the sermon at a service in the early evening. She may be especially susceptible to sermons now because of her distress over Maria.

20. This is the "one interview" believed on p. 814 by Sir Thomas to have occurred.

21. He saw her while in London with his father, shortly before he came to Portsmouth for Fanny.

22. Social etiquette forbids Mary, an unmarried woman, from sending Edmund a note, or visiting him, but Lady Stornaway, a married woman, can issue an invitation to him on Mary's behalf.

23. *owned*: admitted.

he adored; but still more the folly of—poor Maria, in sacrificing such a situation,[24] plunging into such difficulties, under the idea of being really loved by a man who had long ago made his indifference clear. Guess what I must have felt. To hear the woman whom—no harsher name than folly given!—So voluntarily, so freely, so coolly to canvass it!—No reluctance, no horror, no feminine—shall I say? no modest loathings![25]—This is what the world[26] does. For where, Fanny, shall we find a woman whom nature had so richly endowed?—Spoilt, spoilt!—"

After a little reflection, he went on with a sort of desperate calmness—"I will tell you every thing, and then have done[27] for ever. She saw it only as folly, and that folly stamped only by exposure. The want of common discretion, of caution—his going down to Richmond for the whole time of her being at Twickenham—her putting herself in the power of a servant;—it was the detection in short—Oh! Fanny, it was the detection, not the offence which she reprobated. It was the imprudence which had brought things to extremity, and obliged her brother to give up every dearer plan, in order to fly with her."

He stopt.—"And what," said Fanny, (believing herself required to speak), "what could you say?"

"Nothing, nothing to be understood. I was like a man stunned. She went on, began to talk of you;—yes, then she began to talk of you, regretting, as well she might, the loss of such a——. There she spoke very rationally. But she has always done justice to you. 'He has thrown away,' said she, 'such a woman as he will never see again. She would have fixed[28] him, she would have made him happy for ever.'—My dearest Fanny, I am giving you I hope more pleasure than pain by this retrospect of what might have been—but what never can be now. You do not wish me to be silent?—if you do, give me but a look, a word, and I have done."[29]

No look or word was given.

"Thank God!" said he. "We were all disposed to wonder—but it seems to have been the merciful appointment of Providence that the heart which knew no guile,[30] should not suffer. She spoke of you with high praise and warm affection; yet, even here, there was alloy, a dash of evil—for in the midst of it she could exclaim 'Why, would not she have him? It is all her fault. Simple girl!—I shall never

24. Meaning her high social and economic position as Mrs. Rushworth.

25. His idea is that women's natural modesty should give them an instinctive loathing of sexual misconduct. Mary trivializes the sin by calling it mere "folly."

26. *world*: fashionable world, high society.

27. *have done*: cease.

28. *fixed*: settled, given stability to.

29. He worries that talk of her missed opportunity to marry Henry will distress her or fill her with regret.

30. This expression has biblical echoes, probably intended by the author (this is one of only two times she uses the word "guile" in all her writings, including her letters). The two especially pertinent passages are the second verse of Psalm 32, "Blessed is the man unto whom the Lord imputeth not iniquity, and in whose spirit there is no guile," and the forty-seventh verse of the first chapter of John, "Jesus saw Nathaniel coming to him, and saith of him, 'Behold an Israelite indeed, in whom is no guile!'" As a clergyman Edmund would naturally tend to use biblical phrases.

A mansion in Twickenham.

[From John Malcolm, *Anecdotes of the Manners and Customs of London* (London, 1808)]

forgive her. Had she accepted him as she ought, they might now have been on the point of marriage, and Henry would have been too happy and too busy to want any other object. He would have taken no pains to be on terms with Mrs. Rushworth again. It would have all ended in a regular standing flirtation, in yearly meetings at Sotherton and Everingham.'[31] Could you have believed it possible?—But the charm is broken. My eyes are opened."

"Cruel!" said Fanny—"quite cruel! At such a moment to give way to gaiety and to speak with lightness,[32] and to you!—Absolute cruelty."[33]

"Cruelty, do you call it?—We differ there. No, her's is not a cruel nature. I do not consider her as meaning to wound my feelings. The evil lies yet deeper; in her total ignorance, unsuspiciousness of there being such feelings, in a perversion of mind which made it natural to her to treat the subject as she did. She was speaking only, as she had been used to hear others speak, as she imagined every body else would speak. Her's are not faults of temper. She would not voluntarily give unnecessary pain to any one, and though I may deceive myself, I cannot but think that for me, for my feelings, she would— Her's are faults of principle, Fanny, of blunted delicacy and a corrupted, vitiated mind. Perhaps it is best for me—since it leaves me so little to regret.—Not so, however. Gladly would I submit to all the increased pain of losing her, rather than have to think of her as I do. I told her so."

"Did you?"

"Yes, when I left her I told her so."

"How long were you together?"

"Five and twenty minutes. Well, she went on to say, that what remained now to be done, was to bring about a marriage between them. She spoke of it, Fanny, with a steadier voice than I can." He was obliged to pause more than once as he continued. "'We must persuade Henry to marry her,'[34] said she, 'and what with honour, and the certainty of having shut himself out for ever from Fanny, I do not despair of it. Fanny he must give up. I do not think that even *he* could now hope to succeed with one of her stamp, and therefore I hope we may find no insuperable difficulty. My influence, which is not small, shall all go that way; and, when once married, and prop-

31. Henry's connection to the Bertrams if he married Fanny would have given him and Fanny good reason to visit the Rushworths at Sotherton once a year, and for the latter to pay an annual visit to Everingham. Mary is envisioning a scenario in which Henry and Maria regularly flirt in front of their own spouses, which would horrify Fanny in particular and make her miserable in her marriage. At the same time, it corresponds to the mores of the fashionable society in which Mary has lived, for such flirtations between married people were often tolerated as long as they led to nothing serious, and spouses were supposed to turn a blind eye.

32. *lightness*: frivolity.

33. Cruel because of the distress Edmund is feeling due to Maria's action.

34. A marriage could happen after a divorce of the Rushworths; for the laws governing divorce, see p. 835, note 12.

erly supported by her own family, people of respectability as they are, she may recover her footing in society to a certain degree. In some circles, we know, she would never be admitted, but with good dinners, and large parties, there will always be those who will be glad of her acquaintance;[35] and there is, undoubtedly, more liberality[36] and candour[37] on those points than formerly.[38] What I advise is, that your father be quiet. Do not let him injure his own cause by interference. Persuade him to let things take their course. If by any officious exertions of his, she is induced to leave Henry's protection,[39] there will be much less chance of his marrying her, than if she remain with him. I know how he is likely to be influenced. Let Sir Thomas trust to his honour and compassion, and it may all end well; but if he get his daughter away, it will be destroying the chief hold.'"[40]

After repeating this, Edmund was so much affected, that Fanny, watching him with silent, but most tender concern, was almost sorry that the subject had been entered on at all. It was long before he could speak again. At last, "Now, Fanny," said he, "I shall soon have done. I have told you the substance of all that she said. As soon as I could speak, I replied that I had not supposed it possible, coming in such a state of mind into that house, as I had done, that any thing could occur to make me suffer more, but that she had been inflicting deeper wounds in almost every sentence. That, though I had, in the course of our acquaintance, been often sensible of some difference in our opinions, on points too, of some moment, it had not entered my imagination to conceive the difference could be such as she had now proved it. That the manner in which she treated the dreadful crime committed by her brother and my sister—(with whom lay the greater seduction I pretended not to say)—but the manner in which she spoke of the crime itself, giving it every reproach but the right, considering its ill consequences only as they were to be braved or overborne by a defiance of decency and impudence[41] in wrong; and, last of all, and above all, recommending to us a compliance, a compromise, an acquiescence, in the continuance of the sin, on the chance of a marriage which, thinking as I now thought of her brother, should rather be prevented than sought—all this together most grievously convinced me that I had never understood her before, and that, as far as related to mind,[42] it had been the creature

35. Opinions varied regarding how strict and unforgiving to be toward people who had committed adultery or been divorced (the latter was also considered scandalous then). They would certainly not have been accepted in most parts of England, but in London they probably could find some people, including those in a similar situation, who would associate with them.

36. *liberality*: open-mindedness, freedom from prejudice.

37. *candour*: generosity, willingness to think favorably of others.

38. Mary perceives this change, but it is uncertain if she is correct. The general movement in society at large was toward greater strictness regarding sexual and other behavior. This was partly because of the influence of the evangelical movement, which had spread to some portion of the aristocracy as well, even as other members of high society were influenced in the opposite direction by the licentious example of the Prince Regent. Mary may be judging by her own immediate circle and friends, as well as by her wish for such a change.

39. His protection most of all means living with him. Social mores forbade a young woman from living on her own; without him or the protection of her family Maria would have a difficult time even finding an inn to stay in or a residence to rent.

40. His honor could make him feel bound to marry someone who had abandoned her marriage for his sake, and with his collaboration. His compassion would make him not wish to leave her and render her completely helpless and defenseless. But if she left him to go with her father, Henry could conclude that she had, by her own volition, ceased to be his responsibility.

41. *impudence*: shamelessness.

42. Meaning, as far as his estimate of her character (i.e., mind), particularly her moral character, was concerned.

of my own imagination, not Miss Crawford, that I had been too apt to dwell on for many months past. That, perhaps it was best for me; I had less to regret in sacrificing a friendship—feelings—hopes which must, at any rate, have been torn from me now. And yet, that I must and would confess, that, could I have restored her to what she had appeared to me before, I would infinitely prefer any increase of the pain of parting, for the sake of carrying with me the right of tenderness and esteem.[43] This is what I said—the purport of it—but, as you may imagine, not spoken so collectedly or methodically as I have repeated it to you. She was astonished, exceedingly astonished—more than astonished. I saw her change countenance. She turned extremely red. I imagined I saw a mixture of many feelings—a great, though short struggle—half a wish of yielding to truths, half a sense of shame—but habit, habit carried it. She would have laughed if she could. It was a sort of laugh, as she answered, 'A pretty good lecture upon my word. Was it part of your last sermon? At this rate, you will soon reform every body at Mansfield and Thornton Lacey; and when I hear of you next, it may be as a celebrated preacher in some great society of Methodists, or as a missionary into foreign parts.'[44] She tried to speak carelessly; but she was not so careless as she wanted to appear. I only said in reply, that from my heart I wished her well, and earnestly hoped that she might soon learn to think more justly, and not owe the most valuable knowledge we could any of us acquire—the knowledge of ourselves and of our duty—to the lessons of affliction,[45] and immediately left the room. I had gone a few steps, Fanny, when I heard the door open behind me. 'Mr. Bertram,' said she. I looked back. 'Mr. Bertram,' said she, with a smile—but it was a smile ill-suited to the conversation that had passed, a saucy playful smile, seeming to invite, in order to subdue me; at least, it appeared so to me. I resisted; it was the impulse of the moment to resist, and still walked on. I have since—sometimes—for a moment—regretted that I did not go back; but I know I was right; and such has been the end of our acquaintance! And what an acquaintance has it been! How have I been deceived! Equally in brother and sister deceived! I thank you for your patience, Fanny. This has been the greatest relief, and now we will have done."

And such was Fanny's dependence on his words, that for five

43. That is, he wishes he could still feel tenderly toward her and think well of her, even if it made their separation more painful.

44. Methodism was a movement that developed in the eighteenth century to promote a more fervent devotion and practice of religion. It won many adherents, especially among the poorer classes. Methodists were noted for their zeal and for their emphasis on highly emotional preaching. Many devout English people went abroad as missionaries to spread Christianity, a process assisted by the increasing reach of British trade and military power, including colonization, around the world. Mary's idea is that once Edmund has reformed, in a religious and moral sense, everyone at Thornton Lacey and Mansfield, he will then seek a new, even more ambitious venue for his proselytizing zeal.

45. Affliction was often seen as a punishment by God, and a means of teaching important moral and religious truths to people, but Edmund's fondness for Mary makes him wish she will be able to learn without suffering.

A clergyman.

[From Elisabeth McClellan, *Historic Dress in America, 1800–1870* (Philadelphia, 1910), p. 421]

minutes she thought they *had* done. Then, however, it all came on again, or something very like it, and nothing less than Lady Bertram's rousing thoroughly up, could really close such a conversation. Till that happened, they continued to talk of Miss Crawford alone, and how she had attached him, and how delightful nature had made her, and how excellent she would have been, had she fallen into good hands earlier. Fanny, now at liberty to speak openly, felt more than justified in adding to his knowledge of her real character, by some hint of what share his brother's state of health might be supposed to have in her wish for a complete reconciliation.[46] This was not an agreeable intimation. Nature resisted it for a while. It would have been a vast deal pleasanter to have had her more disinterested in her attachment; but his vanity was not of a strength to fight long against reason. He submitted to believe, that Tom's illness had influenced her; only reserving for himself this consoling thought, that considering the many counteractions of opposing habits, she had certainly been *more* attached to him than could have been expected, and for his sake been more near doing right. Fanny thought exactly the same; and they were also quite agreed in their opinion of the lasting effect, the indelible impression, which such a disappointment must make on his mind. Time would undoubtedly abate somewhat[47] of his sufferings, but still it was a sort of thing which he never could get entirely the better of; and as to his ever meeting with any other woman who could—it was too impossible to be named but with indignation. Fanny's friendship was all that he had to cling to.

46. Fanny's intervention is well timed, whether consciously or unconsciously. Edmund has just begun, once again, to relent in his condemnation of Mary, and Fanny, not wishing him to do that for both his sake and her own, delivers the coup de grâce by telling him of Mary's letter expressing hope for Tom's death and Edmund's eventual inheritance of Mansfield Park.

47. *somewhat*: something.

Evening dress.

[From Andrew Tuer, *The Follies and Fashions of our Grandfathers* (London, 1887), p. 54]

Chapter Seventeen

*L*et other pens dwell on guilt and misery. I quit such odious subjects as soon as I can, impatient to restore every body, not greatly in fault themselves, to tolerable comfort, and to have done with all the rest.[1]

My Fanny indeed at this very time, I have the satisfaction of knowing, must have been happy in spite of every thing.[2] She must have been a happy creature in spite of all that she felt or thought she felt, for the distress of those around her. She had sources of delight that must force their way. She was returned to Mansfield Park, she was useful, she was beloved; she was safe from Mr. Crawford, and when Sir Thomas came back she had every proof that could be given in his then melancholy state of spirits, of his perfect approbation and increased regard; and happy as all this must make her, she would still have been happy without any of it, for Edmund was no longer the dupe of Miss Crawford.

It is true, that Edmund was very far from happy himself. He was suffering from disappointment and regret, grieving over what was, and wishing for what could never be. She knew it was so, and was sorry; but it was with a sorrow so founded on satisfaction, so tending to ease, and so much in harmony with every dearest sensation, that there are few who might not have been glad to exchange their greatest gaiety for it.

Sir Thomas, poor Sir Thomas, a parent, and conscious of errors in his own conduct as a parent, was the longest to suffer. He felt that he ought not to have allowed the marriage, that his daughter's sentiments had been sufficiently known to him to render him culpable in authorizing it, that in so doing he had sacrificed the right to the expedient, and been governed by motives of selfishness and worldly[3] wisdom. These were reflections that required some time to soften; but time will do almost every thing, and though little comfort arose

1. The opening of this chapter represents an unusual case of overt authorial interpolation by Jane Austen, speaking in her own person and treating her story as a piece of fiction that she can manipulate as she wishes. She does this occasionally in all her novels, but usually in a briefer and more subtle manner. The exception is her earliest work, *Northanger Abbey*, where the authorial voice continually intrudes. That, however, is a comical work that is in part a sustained satire and commentary on novels themselves. *Mansfield Park*, however, is a highly serious and realistic novel, and the narrator's intrusion here, as well as in other parts of this concluding chapter, has been criticized as incongruous with the rest of the story.

This incongruity serves a purpose. As one fine study of the author puts it, the fundamental difficulty of the novel is that "the violent act which precipitates the catastrophe (though carefully kept below the level of tragedy) is not essentially comic; nor can it be made to appear so, without breach of the author's moral purpose" (Mary Lascelles, *Jane Austen and Her Art*, p. 76). Austen's vision here, as elsewhere, is fundamentally comic, involving a happy resolution of the story, especially for the heroine. The grim developments of the several penultimate chapters, however, threaten a different resolution and set a somber tone. Hence the unexpected opening of this chapter serves to wrench the reader back toward a lighter perspective and expectations, and thereby prepare the way for the mostly harmonious resolution of the plot.

2. "My Fanny" is a unique formulation in Austen's novels. While always evincing sympathy for her heroines, the author never otherwise refers to one in so intimate a manner. This may reflect an almost maternal tenderness for Fanny Price, due to her timidity and sensitivity and to the extensive tribulations she suffers over the course of the story.

3. *worldly*: devoted to success and money.

on Mrs. Rushworth's side for the misery she had occasioned, comfort was to be found greater than he had supposed, in his other children. Julia's match became a less desperate business than he had considered it at first. She was humble and wishing to be forgiven, and Mr. Yates, desirous of being really received into the family, was disposed to look up to him and be guided. He was not very solid; but there was a hope of his becoming less trifling—of his being at least tolerably domestic and quiet; and, at any rate, there was comfort in finding his estate rather more, and his debts much less,[4] than he had feared, and in being consulted and treated as the friend best worth attending to. There was comfort also in Tom, who gradually regained his health, without regaining the thoughtlessness and selfishness of his previous habits. He was the better for ever for his illness. He had suffered, and he had learnt to think, two advantages that he had never known before; and the self-reproach arising from the deplorable event in Wimpole Street, to which he felt himself accessary by all the dangerous intimacy of his unjustifiable theatre, made an impression on his mind which, at the age of six-and-twenty, with no want of sense, or good companions, was durable in its happy effects. He became what he ought to be, useful to his father, steady and quiet, and not living merely for himself.

Here was comfort indeed! and quite as soon as Sir Thomas could place dependence[5] on such sources of good, Edmund was contributing to his father's ease by improvement in the only point in which *he* had given him pain before—improvement in his spirits. After wandering about and sitting under trees with Fanny all the summer evenings, he had so well talked his mind into submission, as to be very tolerably cheerful again.

These were the circumstances and the hopes which gradually brought their alleviation to Sir Thomas, deadening his sense of what was lost, and in part reconciling him to himself; though the anguish arising from the conviction of his own errors in the education of his daughters, was never to be entirely done away.

Too late he became aware how unfavourable to the character of any young people, must be the totally opposite treatment which Maria and Julia had been always experiencing at home, where the

4. Many wealthy young men like Mr. Yates, pursuing a life of pleasure among their friends, went heavily into debt. As the younger son, Yates will not inherit the main family estate, but he has been given another estate to help sustain him. Landed families sometimes owned smaller properties separate from the main estate, which they might bequeath to a younger son instead of cash. Another possible explanation here is the custom mentioned earlier in an exchange between Edmund and Mary, that of a childless uncle bequeathing an estate to the younger son.

5. *dependence*: confidence.

excessive indulgence and flattery of their aunt had been continually contrasted with his own severity. He saw how ill he had judged, in expecting to counteract what was wrong in Mrs. Norris, by its reverse in himself, clearly saw that he had but increased the evil, by teaching them to repress their spirits in his presence, as to make their real disposition unknown to him, and sending them for all their indulgences to a person who had been able to attach them only by the blindness of her affection, and the excess of her praise.

Here had been grievous mismanagement; but, bad as it was, he gradually grew to feel that it had not been the most direful mistake in his plan of education. Something must have been wanting *within*, or time would have worn away much of its ill effect. He feared that principle, active principle, had been wanting, that they had never been properly taught to govern their inclinations and tempers, by that sense of duty which can alone suffice.[6] They had been instructed theoretically in their religion, but never required to bring it into daily practice.[7] To be distinguished for elegance and accomplishments— the authorized object of their youth—could have had no useful influence that way, no moral effect on the mind. He had meant them to be good, but his cares had been directed to the understanding and manners,[8] not the disposition;[9] and of the necessity of self-denial and humility, he feared they had never heard from any lips that could profit them.[10]

Bitterly did he deplore a deficiency which now he could scarcely comprehend to have been possible. Wretchedly did he feel, that with all the cost and care of an anxious and expensive education, he had brought up his daughters, without their understanding their first duties, or his being acquainted with their character and temper.

The high spirit and strong passions of Mrs. Rushworth especially, were made known to him only in their sad result. She was not to be prevailed on to leave Mr. Crawford. She hoped to marry him, and they continued together till she was obliged to be convinced that such hope was vain, and till the disappointment and wretchedness arising from the conviction, rendered her temper so bad, and her feelings for him so like hatred,[11] as to make them for a while each other's punishment, and then induce a voluntary separation.

6. The author described this defect of their education early in the novel (p. 40); she now has shown its full consequence.

7. Religion was considered the fundamental foundation of morality, and much of the religious doctrines and teaching of the Anglican Church centered around moral conduct. Hence those who had not been taught or led to practice religious precepts might neglect basic moral duties.

8. *understanding and manners*: mind and conduct.

9. *disposition*: general mental character, especially in relation to moral qualities.

10. That is, could convince them of this truth, and thereby be profitable or beneficial to them. The only sources of this lesson, with Sir Thomas having neglected to impart it and both Lady Bertram and Mrs. Norris, for different reasons, having not even tried, would have been perhaps their governess or the local clergyman, neither of whom had much influence with them.

11. She comes to hate him because he, by his willingness to run off with her but unwillingness to marry her, has effectively left her ruined. She knows that despite his conduct he can always resume his previous life, though with some inconveniences from the public scandal, but because women were judged more harshly she has thrown away all possibility of a decent and respectable existence.

She had lived with him to be reproached as the ruin of all his happiness in Fanny, and carried away no better consolation in leaving him, than that she *had* divided them. What can exceed the misery of such a mind in such a situation?

Mr. Rushworth had no difficulty in procuring a divorce;[12] and so ended a marriage contracted under such circumstances as to make any better end, the effect of good luck, not to be reckoned on. She had despised him, and loved another—and he had been very much aware that it was so. The indignities of stupidity, and the disappointments of selfish passion, can excite little pity. His punishment followed his conduct, as did a deeper punishment, the deeper guilt of his wife. *He* was released from the engagement to be mortified and unhappy, till some other pretty girl could attract him into matrimony again, and he might set forward on a second, and it is to be hoped, more prosperous[13] trial of the state—if duped, to be duped at least with good humour and good luck; while *she* must withdraw with infinitely stronger feelings to a retirement and reproach, which could allow no second spring of hope or character.[14]

Where she could be placed, became a subject of most melancholy and momentous consultation. Mrs. Norris, whose attachment seemed to augment with the demerits of her niece, would have had her received at home, and countenanced by them all. Sir Thomas would not hear of it, and Mrs. Norris's anger against Fanny was so much the greater, from considering *her* residence there as the motive. She persisted in placing his scruples to *her* account, though Sir Thomas very solemnly assured her, that had there been no young woman in question, had there been no young person of either sex belonging to him, to be endangered by the society, or hurt by the character of Mrs. Rushworth, he would never have offered so great an insult to the neighbourhood, as to expect it to notice[15] her.[16] As a daughter—he hoped a penitent one—she should be protected by him, and secured in every comfort, and supported by every encouragement to do right, which their relative situations admitted; but farther than *that*, he would not go. Maria had destroyed her own character, and he would not by a vain attempt to restore what never could be restored, be affording his sanction to vice, or in seeking to lessen its disgrace, be anywise accessary to

12. Divorce was in principle legally prohibited, and was in practice extremely difficult to obtain. The only official way to get one was for Parliament to pass a private bill, meaning a bill applying only to select individuals, that granted a divorce. This was available only to aggrieved husbands, and Parliament also required that such a husband first pursue a case in ecclesiastical court to obtain a separation from his wife and a civil suit in a common law court to obtain damages from the wife's lover (this latter was called a criminal conversation suit). The costs of these legal actions, especially the criminal conversation suit, were so high that only men of great wealth could pursue them. Mr. Rushworth, however, is such a man, and since the evidence of Maria's and Henry's guilt is very strong, he would be certain to gain his bill of divorce. He also might gain a large amount in damages from Henry Crawford in his civil suit, for the court sometimes granted judgments in the thousands of pounds.

13. *prosperous*: fortunate, successful.

14. She could never hope to regain her public reputation.

15. *notice*: acknowledge, treat courteously.

16. A fundamental principle of the time was the importance of the community, and the need for all its members to uphold its essential standards. By

The Court of King's Bench, where a man applying for divorce would go to sue his wife's lover for damages.

[From Fiona St. Aubyn, *Ackermann's Illustrated London*, illustrations by Augustus Pugin and Thomas Rowlandson (Ware, 1985), p. 69]

introducing such misery in another man's family, as he had known himself.[17]

It ended in Mrs. Norris's resolving to quit Mansfield, and devote herself to her unfortunate Maria,[18] and in an establishment[19] being formed for them in another country[20]—remote and private, where, shut up together with little society,[21] on one side no affection, on the other, no judgment, it may be reasonably supposed that their tempers became their mutual punishment.[22]

Mrs. Norris's removal from Mansfield was the great supplementary comfort of Sir Thomas's life. His opinion of her had been sinking from the day of his return from Antigua; in every transaction together from that period, in their daily intercourse, in business, or in chat, she had been regularly losing ground in his esteem, and convincing him that either time had done her much disservice, or that he had considerably overrated her sense, and wonderfully borne with her manners before. He had felt her as an hourly evil, which was so much the worse, as there seemed no chance of its ceasing but with life; she seemed a part of himself, that must be borne for ever. To be relieved from her, therefore, was so great a felicity, that had she not left bitter remembrances behind her, there might have been danger of his learning almost to approve the evil which produced such a good.

She was regretted by no one at Mansfield. She had never been able to attach even those she loved best, and since Mrs. Rushworth's elopement, her temper had been in a state of such irritation, as to make her every where tormenting. Not even Fanny had tears for aunt Norris—not even when she was gone for ever.

That Julia escaped better than Maria was owing, in some measure, to a favourable difference of disposition and circumstance, but in a greater to her having been less the darling of that very aunt, less flattered, and less spoilt. Her beauty and acquirements[23] had held but a second place. She had been always used to think herself a little inferior to Maria. Her temper was naturally the easiest of the two; her feelings, though quick, were more controulable; and education had not given her so very hurtful a degree of self-consequence.

She had submitted the best to the disappointment in Henry Crawford. After the first bitterness of the conviction of being slighted was

bringing an adulteress into this community as a member of its leading family, he would be violating that principle and pressuring his neighbors, through his own social prestige, to recognize and associate with someone whom they would not approve.

17. The example of a prominent titled family forgiving a daughter guilty of adultery could potentially encourage other women tempted by adultery to think the consequences might not be so dire.

18. The plausibility of Mrs. Norris's action can be questioned, for while she has shown a strong affection for Maria, she has also shown a consistently stronger concern for herself, and in going to live with Maria she is abandoning her comfortable home in Mansfield village and her place among the Bertrams for a very restricted existence. She may have sensed, with Sir Thomas's growing coldness toward her as well as Fanny's rising status and Susan's presence, that her position at Mansfield was deteriorating. Being able to take sole charge of Maria and become the unimpeded manager of a household might therefore look more attractive. Moreover, since Sir Thomas will doubtless underwrite the expenses of his daughter's household, and Mrs. Norris has ample funds of her own, their household should be comfortable financially. Even so, it could be argued that here the author has sacrificed a degree of plausibility and realism of character to her wish, stated at the opening of the chapter, to mete out just deserts to everyone.

19. *establishment*: household, residence.

20. *country*: county.

21. The neighbors in their vicinity, at least the genteel neighbors, would disdain social contact with them.

22. A question that often arises is why Maria suffers such a worse fate than the character in *Pride and Prejudice*, Lydia Bennet, who runs off and lives with a man, when both are unmarried. One reason is that Lydia's action was considered less heinous because she did not break marriage vows or betray a husband; moreover, allowances would be made for her because of her youth, as she was only sixteen. Another is that she does eventually marry the man she eloped with. This results from bribery of her seducer rather than from any worth or action of her own, but it still means that she ends up in a respectable situation, and while the taint of her immoral action remains, that action occurred discreetly and privately, unlike Maria's highly publicized affair.

23. *acquirements*: accomplishments.

over, she had been tolerably soon in a fair way of[24] not thinking of him again; and when the acquaintance was renewed in town, and Mr. Rushworth's house became Crawford's object, she had had the merit of withdrawing herself from it, and of chusing that time to pay a visit to her other friends, in order to secure herself from being again too much attracted.[25] This had been her motive in going to her cousins. Mr. Yates's convenience had had nothing to do with it. She had been allowing his attentions some time, but with very little idea of ever accepting him; and, had not her sister's conduct burst forth as it did, and her increased dread of her father and of home, on that event—imagining its certain consequence to herself would be greater severity and restraint[26]—made her hastily resolve on avoiding such immediate horrors at all risks, it is probable that Mr. Yates would never have succeeded. She had not eloped with any worse feelings than those of selfish alarm. It had appeared to her the only thing to be done. Maria's guilt had induced Julia's folly.

Henry Crawford, ruined by early independence[27] and bad domestic example, indulged in the freaks[28] of a cold-blooded vanity a little too long. Once it had, by an opening undesigned and unmerited, led him into the way of happiness. Could he have been satisfied with the conquest of one amiable woman's affections, could he have found sufficient exultation in overcoming the reluctance, in working himself into the esteem and tenderness of Fanny Price, there would have been every probability of success and felicity for him. His affection had already done something. Her influence over him had already given him some influence over her. Would he have deserved more, there can be no doubt that more would have been obtained; especially when that marriage had taken place, which would have given him the assistance of her conscience in subduing her first inclination,[29] and brought them very often together. Would he have persevered, and uprightly, Fanny must have been his reward—and a reward very voluntarily bestowed—within a reasonable period from Edmund's marrying Mary.[30]

Had he done as he intended, and as he knew he ought, by going down to Everingham after his return from Portsmouth, he might have been deciding his own happy destiny. But he was pressed to stay for Mrs. Fraser's party; his staying was made of flattering con-

24. *in a fair way of*: in a good state of mind for, advancing in the direction of.

25. She shows more wisdom and self-knowledge here than Maria, who begins by being cool to Henry, but soon succumbs again to his charm.

26. She fears she will be kept at home and forbidden to travel or to see other people except under parental supervision.

27. *independence*: financial independence.

28. *freaks*: caprices, whims.

29. Her first inclination was her love for Edmund, but once he was married to Mary she would have felt obligated to suppress and overcome that love, since it now would have been adulterous in spirit.

30. Thus Jane Austen envisions a possible alternative ending to her story, one in which all the main characters experience a dramatically different fate. Notably, she does not suggest that this different ending would have been disastrous, though she does not specify exactly how happy or successful these alternative marriages would have been.

sequence, and he was to meet Mrs. Rushworth there. Curiosity and vanity were both engaged,[31] and the temptation of immediate pleasure was too strong for a mind unused to make any sacrifice to right; he resolved to defer his Norfolk journey, resolved that writing should answer the purpose of it,[32] or that its purpose was unimportant—and staid. He saw Mrs. Rushworth, was received by her with a coldness which ought to have been repulsive,[33] and have established apparent indifference between them for ever; but he was mortified, he could not bear to be thrown off by the woman whose smiles had been so wholly at his command; he must exert himself to subdue so proud a display of resentment; it was anger on Fanny's account; he must get the better of it, and make Mrs. Rushworth Maria Bertram again in her treatment of himself.[34]

In this spirit he began the attack; and by animated perseverance had soon re-established the sort of familiar intercourse—of gallantry[35]—of flirtation which bounded his views,[36] but in triumphing over the discretion, which, though beginning in anger, might have saved them both,[37] he had put himself in the power of feelings on her side, more strong than he had supposed.—She loved him; there was no withdrawing attentions, avowedly dear to her. He was entangled by his own vanity, with as little excuse of love as possible,[38] and without the smallest inconstancy of mind towards her cousin.—To keep Fanny and the Bertrams from a knowledge of what was passing became his first object. Secrecy could not have been more desirable for Mrs. Rushworth's credit than he felt it for his own.—When he returned from Richmond, he would have been glad to see Mrs. Rushworth no more.—All that followed was the result of her imprudence; and he went off with her at last, because he could not help it, regretting Fanny, even at the moment, but regretting her infinitely more, when all the bustle of the intrigue was over, and a very few months had taught him, by the force of contrast, to place a yet higher value on the sweetness of her temper, the purity of her mind, and the excellence of her principles.

That punishment, the public punishment of disgrace, should in a just measure attend *his* share of the offence, is, we know, not one of the barriers, which society gives to virtue.[39] In this world, the penalty is less equal than could be wished;[40] but without presuming to look

31. Mary stated in her letter to Fanny that she required Henry to stay because of the value of his presence for the party (p. 748), but this shows that he acted on different, purely selfish motives.

32. Meaning he would write to his agent giving instructions on what he wanted to be done. His earlier objections to trusting the agent are now easily swept aside.

33. *repulsive*: repellent.

34. Henry's actions could be seen as implausible, given the ardent love of Fanny he has shown and that the author still attributes to him. But there is a plausible basis for his adopting a course that goes so completely against his interests and inclinations. One explanation is that it happens in stages, through a series of smaller steps that he never would have taken had he anticipated their ultimate result. Another is that he has already displayed traits that make him susceptible to this kind of temptation: a competitive spirit, the belief that things will always work out for him (even when he has done wrong), hastiness and impulsiveness, and a fickleness that drives him to continually seek novelty. Perhaps most of all, a cold and angry Maria probably represented the same kind of irresistible challenge to his seductive skills as a virtuous and shy Fanny had. And since his first extended flirtation with Maria had had no lasting consequences, he may have felt confident this one would not either, particularly as this time she had so much more to lose.

35. *gallantry*: amorous intimacy.

36. *bounded his views*: limited his aspirations. Meaning he only aspired to reestablishing their earlier condition of pleasant flirtation and friendly conversation (which is how he, though not Maria, had seen it).

37. Maria's "discretion" was her initial reluctance to converse and be friendly with him. This reluctance, though it stemmed from resentment rather than genuine discretion, could have prevented further involvement had Henry not striven to overcome it.

38. Having bestowed such gallant attentions on her, it would have been callous and dishonorable to disavow them once she embraced them and returned them so strongly. Similar reasons end up compelling him to run away with her when she takes the initiative in that direction.

39. *virtue*: sexual chastity.

40. Jane Austen refers to a long-standing double standard in judging male and female sexual misbehavior. Its basic justification specifically in relation to

forward to a juster appointment hereafter,[41] we may fairly consider a man of sense like Henry Crawford, to be providing for himself no small portion of vexation and regret—vexation that must rise sometimes to self-reproach, and regret to wretchedness—in having so requited hospitality, so injured family peace, so forfeited his best, most estimable and endeared acquaintance, and so lost the woman whom he had rationally, as well as passionately loved.

After what had passed to wound and alienate the two families, the continuance of the Bertrams and Grants in such close neighbourhood[42] would have been most distressing; but the absence of the latter, for some months purposely lengthened,[43] ended very fortunately in the necessity, or at least the practicability of a permanent removal. Dr. Grant, through an interest[44] on which he had almost ceased to form hopes, succeeded to[45] a stall in Westminster, which, as affording an occasion for leaving Mansfield, an excuse for residence in London, and an increase of income to answer[46] the expenses of the change,[47] was highly acceptable to those who went, and those who staid.

Mrs. Grant, with a temper to love and be loved, must have gone with some regret, from the scenes and people she had been used to; but the same happiness of disposition must in any place and any

Westminster Abbey.

[From *The Repository of arts, literature, fashions, manufactures, &c*, Vol. II (1809), p. 51]

marital infidelity, was that maternity was always known while paternity was not. Hence an adulterous wife could saddle her husband with a child who was not his own, with no way for him to know or prove the child's illegitimacy. This possibility threatened many of the foundations of society: a husband's commitment to marriage, children's ability to be certain of their fathers, and a property owner's ability to pass on his property and position to his true heirs. This made wifely infidelity far more heinous in its effect, and was seen to justify harsher punishments as well as sharper restrictions on women's freedom to prevent their pursuing illicit relationships. Samuel Johnson expressed it this way: "Confusion of progeny constitutes the essence of the crime; and therefore a woman who breaks her marriage vow is much more criminal than a man who does it. A man, to be sure, is criminal in the sight of God; but he does not do his wife a very material injury, if he does not insult her; if, for instance, from mere wantonness of appetite, he steals privately to her chambermaid."

Jane Austen's criticism of the double standard represents one of the only overt pieces of social criticism in her novels. It is still notable that she calls only for lessening the difference in treatment between men and women, rather than eliminating it. Moreover, her call is for increasing punishment for men rather than relaxing it for women. In fact, virtually no one at the time called for relaxing a strict standard of female chastity. Even Mary Wollstonecraft, whose *Vindication of the Rights of Women* (1792) constitutes one of the first major statements of feminist principles, still asserts the need for women to be sexually pure; one of her arguments for improved education for women, her principal focus, is that making women more rational will enable them to better safeguard their virtue.

41. That is, a superior allotment of justice in the next world. The author does not presume to look forward to this because that would be to anticipate the inevitably mysterious workings of divine justice.

42. *neighbourhood*: proximity.

43. This refers to their stay in Bath, already under way. They have stayed away longer than planned, to avoid the Bertrams.

44. *interest*: connection.

45. *succeeded to*: was appointed to (in the wake of someone else).

46. *answer*: compensate for.

47. A stall is a position as a canon at a cathedral or collegiate church; canons are responsible for administering the institution. Westminster Abbey is one of the two such entities in London (the other being St. Paul's Cathedral). Mrs. Grant earlier expressed a wish for her husband to be someday appointed dean of one of these (p. 392), a dean being the head clergyman. Being a canon is

society, secure her a great deal to enjoy, and she had again a home to offer Mary; and Mary had had enough of her own friends, enough of vanity, ambition, love, and disappointment in the course of the last half year, to be in need of the true kindness of her sister's heart, and the rational tranquillity of her ways. — They lived together; and when Dr. Grant had brought on apoplexy and death,[48] by three great institutionary dinners in one week,[49] they still lived together; for Mary, though perfectly resolved against ever attaching herself to a younger brother again, was long in finding among the dashing representatives,[50] or idle heir apparents,[51] who were at the command of her beauty, and her 20,000*l.* any one who could satisfy the better taste she had acquired at Mansfield, whose character and manners could authorize a hope of the domestic happiness she had there learnt to estimate,[52] or put Edmund Bertram sufficiently out of her head.

Edmund had greatly the advantage of her in this respect. He had not to wait and wish with vacant affections for an object worthy to succeed her in them. Scarcely had he done regretting Mary Crawford, and observing to Fanny how impossible it was that he should ever meet with such another woman, before it began to strike him whether a very different kind of woman might not do just as well — or a great deal better; whether Fanny herself were not growing as dear, as important to him in all her smiles, and all her ways, as Mary Crawford had ever been; and whether it might not be a possible, an hopeful undertaking to persuade her that her warm and sisterly regard for him would be foundation enough for wedded love.

I purposely abstain from dates on this occasion, that every one may be at liberty to fix their own, aware that the cure of unconquerable passions, and the transfer of unchanging attachments, must vary much as to time in different people.[53] — I only intreat every body to believe that exactly at the time when it was quite natural that it should be so, and not a week earlier, Edmund did cease to care about Miss Crawford, and became as anxious to marry Fanny, as Fanny herself could desire.

With such a regard for her, indeed, as his had long been, a regard founded on the most endearing claims of innocence and helplessness, and completed by every recommendation of growing worth,

not as good, but it is still a desirable position, and one that allows them to live in London. That its increase in income balances the increased cost of living in London, which was considerable, indicates the importance of the position.

48. Dr. Grant was earlier described by Tom as tending toward apoplexy, the term for a stroke or other sudden seizures.

49. Meaning dinners relating to the church, his institution. These were probably official banquets involving church dignities, and thus extensive heavy eating and drinking, which was thought to contribute to apoplexy.

50. *representatives*: heirs.

51. *heir apparents*: those who will inherit after the current holder dies. They are contrasted here with eldest sons who have already inherited and who can be dashing because they have acquired the full means to display their prominence ("dashing" then often meant fashionably showy). In contrast, heirs apparent can merely wait idly for their fortune to come; such young men would be given an allowance by the existing estate holder (usually their father) that enabled them to live comfortably, but on far less than the income they expect to eventually enjoy.

52. *estimate*: value, appreciate.

53. The author is having fun with one of her most frequent satirical targets, the idea of "unconquerable passions" or "unchanging sentiments." She is also mocking Edmund's certainty that he will never get over his romantic suffering or ever meet again a suitable replacement for Mary (p. 826)—though it is a gentle mockery, derived from knowing how normal such sentiments are to those disappointed in love. In fact, by appealing to "every one . . . to fix their own" estimate of how long romantic recovery takes, she is relying on her readers' likely acquaintance with the phenomenon of dejection and despair followed by eventual recuperation. All this gives a reason for Austen's uncharacteristic vagueness about dates. There is also no need for her to be precise here, since the outcome will not vary according to how long it takes, and, unlike in the body of the novel, there are no concurrent events that need to be chronologically coordinated and reconciled with this one.

what could be more natural than the change? Loving, guiding, protecting her, as he had been doing ever since her being ten years old, her mind in so great a degree formed by his care, and her comfort depending on his kindness, an object to him of such close and peculiar interest, dearer by all his own importance with her than any one else at Mansfield, what was there now to add, but that he should learn to prefer soft light eyes to sparkling dark ones.—And being always with her, and always talking confidentially, and his feelings exactly in that favourable state which a recent disappointment gives, those soft light eyes could not be very long in obtaining the pre-eminence.

Having once set out, and felt that he had done so, on this road to happiness, there was nothing on the side of prudence to stop him or make his progress slow; no doubts of her deserving, no fears from opposition of taste, no need of drawing new hopes of happiness from dissimilarity of temper. Her mind, disposition, opinions, and habits wanted no half concealment, no self deception on the present, no reliance on future improvement. Even in the midst of his late infatuation, he had acknowledged Fanny's mental superiority. What must be his sense of it now, therefore? She was of course only too good for him; but as nobody minds having what is too good for them, he was very steadily earnest in the pursuit of the blessing, and it was not possible that encouragement from her should be long wanting. Timid, anxious, doubting as she was, it was still impossible that such tenderness as hers should not, at times, hold out the strongest hope of success, though it remained for a later period to tell him the whole delightful and astonishing truth. His happiness in knowing himself to have been so long the beloved of such a heart, must have been great enough to warrant any strength of language in which he could clothe it to her or to himself; it must have been a delightful happiness! But there was happiness elsewhere which no description can reach. Let no one presume to give the feelings of a young woman on receiving the assurance of that affection of which she has scarcely allowed herself to entertain a hope.

Their own inclinations ascertained, there were no difficulties behind,[54] no drawback of poverty or parent. It was a match which Sir Thomas's wishes had even forestalled.[55] Sick of ambitious and mercenary connections, prizing more and more the sterling good

54. *behind*: remaining, still to come.

55. *forestalled*: anticipated.

Westminster Abbey.

[From Fiona St. Aubyn, *Ackermann's Illustrated London*, illustrations by Augustus Pugin and Thomas Rowlandson (Ware, 1985), p. 85]

of principle and temper, and chiefly anxious to bind by the strongest securities all that remained to him of domestic felicity, he had pondered with genuine satisfaction on the more than possibility of the two young friends finding their mutual consolation in each other for all that had occurred of disappointment to either; and the joyful consent which met Edmund's application, the high sense of having realised a great acquisition in the promise of Fanny for a daughter, formed just such a contrast with his early opinion on the subject when the poor little girl's coming had been first agitated,[56] as time is for ever producing between the plans and decisions of mortals, for their own instruction, and their neighbour's entertainment.[57]

Fanny was indeed the daughter that he wanted. His charitable kindness had been rearing a prime comfort for himself. His liberality[58] had a rich repayment, and the general goodness of his intentions by her, deserved it. He might have made her childhood happier; but it had been an error of judgment only which had given him the appearance of harshness, and deprived him of her early love; and now, on really knowing each other, their mutual attachment became very strong. After settling her at Thornton Lacey with every kind attention to her comfort, the object of almost every day was to see her there, or to get her away from it.

Selfishly dear as she had long been to Lady Bertram, she could not be parted with willingly by *her*. No happiness of son or niece could make her wish the marriage. But it was possible to part with her, because Susan remained to supply her place. — Susan became the stationary niece — delighted to be so! — and equally well adapted for it by a readiness of mind, and an inclination for usefulness, as Fanny had been by sweetness of temper, and strong feelings of gratitude. Susan could never be spared. First as a comfort to Fanny, then as an auxiliary, and last as her substitute, she was established at Mansfield, with every appearance of equal permanency. Her more fearless disposition and happier nerves made every thing easy to her there. — With quickness in understanding the tempers of those she had to deal with, and no natural timidity to restrain any consequent wishes, she was soon welcome, and useful to all; and after Fanny's removal, succeeded so naturally to her influence over the hourly comfort of her aunt, as gradually to become, perhaps, the most beloved of the

56. *agitated*: discussed, raised for consideration.

57. The foiling of plans and decisions by subsequent events provides valuable lessons for those involved, and amusement for neighbors who can look on with detached curiosity and bemusement. Jane Austen exhibits this latter attitude on many occasions in her letters, as she comments on the foibles and failures and misadventures of those around her; she also does not exempt herself from this scrutiny.

58. *liberality*: generosity.

A *marriage ceremony*.

[From William Combe, *The Dance of Life* (London, 1817; 1903 reprint), p. 234]

two.—In *her* usefulness, in Fanny's excellence, in William's continued good conduct, and rising fame, and in the general well-doing
and success of the other members of the family, all assisting to
advance each other,[59] and doing credit to his countenance[60] and aid,
Sir Thomas saw repeated, and for ever repeated reason to rejoice in
what he had done for them all, and acknowledge the advantages of
early hardship and discipline, and the consciousness of being born to
struggle and endure.[61]

With so much true merit and true love, and no want of fortune or
friends, the happiness of the married cousins must appear as secure
as earthly happiness can be.—Equally formed for domestic life, and
attached to country pleasures, their home was the home of affection
and comfort; and to complete the picture of good, the acquisition
of Mansfield living by the death of Dr. Grant,[62] occurred just after
they had been married long enough to begin to want an increase of
income,[63] and feel their distance from the paternal abode an inconvenience.

On that event they removed to Mansfield,[64] and the parsonage
there, which under each of its two former owners, Fanny had never
been able to approach but with some painful sensation of restraint or
alarm, soon grew as dear to her heart, and as thoroughly perfect in
her eyes, as every thing else, within the view and patronage of Mansfield Park, had long been.

FINIS

59. This means the children of the Price family. This is a more positive assessment of the Price siblings than was apparent during Fanny's stay at Portsmouth, but it is possible that as the children reached maturity they adopted a responsible and helpful attitude toward one another.

60. *countenance*: support, favor.

61. He may be thinking of the contrast between the Price children's cooperative spirit and most of his own children, who were almost exclusively concerned with themselves. Fanny, though growing up at Mansfield, represents another lesson in the benefits of hardship and not always getting one's way.

62. Once appointed to the Mansfield living, Dr. Grant had the right to remain in it until he died; even after he received his appointment in London he retained this living and the income attached to it, and hired a curate to perform the duties (as he did while he was visiting Bath). But once Dr. Grant died, Sir Thomas was able to appoint Edmund as the next holder.

63. Meaning long enough for Fanny to be pregnant, and thus for them to know they soon will have another mouth to feed.

64. Edmund would retain the lesser living of Thornton Lacey, but hire a curate to do its duties.

A contemporary picture of a visit to a new mother.

[From Joseph Grego, *Rowlandson the Caricaturist*, Vol. II (London, 1880), p. 313]

Chronology

Jane Austen provides one exact date in *Mansfield Park* (Thursday, December 22), along with a number of specifics concerning times of year, intervals between events, and days of the week, and from these it is possible to develop a good outline of the chronology of the novel.

Year Seven	Frances Ward marries Mr. Price *It is later because Mrs. Norris is already married, but it could not be much afterward, since the eldest Price is only six years younger than Tom Bertram.*	6
Year Eight	William Price born *He is ten when Mrs. Price writes to Sir Thomas.*	10
Year Nine	Fanny Price born *She is two years younger than Julia (p. 28).*	12
Years Ten to Twelve	John and Richard Price born *They are mentioned here as the next oldest, and their ages, never given, can be inferred.*	698
Year Thirteen	Susan Price born *She is fourteen when Fanny visits (at eighteen).*	676
Years Fourteen to Fifteen	Mary Price born *She is described as having been a little under five when Fanny left (having just turned ten).*	690–692
Year Sixteen	Sam Price born *He is eleven when Fanny visits.*	674–676
Year Eighteen	Tom Price born *He is nine when Fanny visits.*	682–684
Year Eighteen	Mrs. Price writes to Sir Thomas for help *It is eleven years since her marriage.*	10
Year Nineteen	Charles Price born *He is eight when Fanny visits.*	682–684
Year Nineteen	Sir Thomas offers to adopt Fanny *This is "within a twelvemonth" of Mrs. Price's letter.*	12–18
Year Nineteen	Fanny comes to Mansfield Park	26
Years Nineteen to Twenty	William goes to sea *This happens "soon after Fanny's removal."*	44
Year Twenty-Two	Betsey Price born *She is "about five" when Fanny visits.*	676
Year Twenty-Two—?	Mary Price dies *This is "a few years after" Fanny's departure.*	692

Year Twenty-Four	Mr. Norris dies *Fanny is "about fifteen."*	46
Year Twenty-Four: Late Autumn	The Grants arrive in Mansfield *This occurs soon after Mr. Norris's death. It was "hardly . . . a year" until the next event (p. 64).*	62
Year Twenty-Five: Probably October	Sir Thomas and Tom leave for Antigua *They expect to be gone "nearly a twelvemonth," and to return in September (p. 72). Fanny is sixteen (p. 66).*	64
Year Twenty-Six: Winter	Maria and Julia mix in society	68–70
Year Twenty-Six: March	Fanny's pony dies *It is in the spring, and she has no horse to ride during April and May.*	70
Year Twenty-Six: Summer	Edmund returns, gives Fanny a horse *It is after May, but before the next event.*	72–74
Year Twenty-Six: Autumn	Tom returns from Antigua	74
Year Twenty-Seven: Winter	Maria becomes engaged to Mr. Rushworth	76–78
Year Twenty-Seven: Early July	Beginning of main action of the novel; Mary and Henry Crawford arrive in Mansfield *Fanny is just eighteen. Early July can be derived from Henry's departure "seven weeks" later, at the end of August (p. 222).*	80
Early to Mid-July	Julia and Maria become interested in Henry *This was within a week of his arrival.*	86
Mid-July	Tom leaves Mansfield Park *Six weeks pass until he returns at the end of August (p. 220).*	100
Mid- to Late July	Discussion of Sotherton Court over dinner *Soon after Tom's departure.*	100
Next Day	Fanny and Edmund discuss Mary	124
Late July	Edmund falling in love with Mary	126–128

Early August	Mr. Rushworth issues invitations to Sotherton *This is two weeks after the dinner.*	146
Early to Mid-August	Visit to Sotherton *This is less than a week from the invitation, for Mr. Rushworth asks whether "Wednesday would suit" (p. 146).*	154
Mid-August	Letters arrive announcing Sir Thomas's return *This occurs "soon afterwards" (referring to the previous event); "the middle of November was three months off."*	206
End of August	Tom returns to Mansfield Park	220
End of August/ Beginning of September	Henry Crawford leaves *He needs to be at his own estate during "the beginning of September."*	220
Mid-September	Henry Crawford returns *He comes "at the time appointed," which was "a fortnight" (p. 220).*	222
Late September	Mr. Yates's arrival; Fanny's first ball *Time is unspecified, but it does not seem long after Henry's return.*	224
Late September	Mr. Yates inspires the idea of doing a play *Soon after above, for Mr. Yates talks of little else, and the others are quickly inspired.*	232–234
Early October	Rehearsals for the play *Mary later describes it as a week (p. 642).*	308

VOLUME II

Early to Mid-October	Return of Sir Thomas *Tom speaks of "incessant rains" for many days since the 3rd (p. 334). See also timing of next event.*	322–324
Mid-October (Two Days Later)	Departure of Henry Crawford *He returns at end of November (see below), after being gone "six weeks" (p. 418).*	354–356
Mid-October	Departure of Mr. Yates *This was "Another day or two" after Henry Crawford's departure.*	358

Late October	Sir Thomas asks Maria if she wishes to cancel the engagement *There had been "three or four days after Henry Crawford's leaving," plus "another three or four days" (p. 372).*	368–370
Very Early November	Mrs. Rushworth retires to Bath	374
Early to Mid-November	Maria marries Mr. Rushworth *It was "before the middle of the . . . month."*	374
Late November	Fanny becomes intimate with Mary Crawford	378–382
Very Late November	Fanny and Mary talk in the garden *It is still November (p. 390); Mary says it is "nearly five months" since her arrival, which was early July (p. 386).*	384
Next Day	Fanny dines at the Grants'; Henry Crawford arrives	396, 408
A Day Later	Henry announces plan to flirt with Fanny	418
Early December	Letter from William Price announcing his return *This was "a few days" after the previous event.*	422
December 9 (probable)	William arrives at Mansfield Park *He leaves on the 23rd, after having been there "a whole fortnight" (p. 512). It is also "scarcely ten days" since dinner at the Grants'.*	424
Early to Mid-December	Large dinner party at the Grants' *Time is unspecified.*	434
Next Day	Sir Thomas decides to hold a ball	458
Wednesday, December 21	Fanny consults Mary about jewelry for the ball *Date can be known from its being the day before the ball.*	466
Thursday, December 22	Large ball at Mansfield Park *Described earlier as "the 22d" (p. 460) and as Thursday (p. 466).*	494
Friday, December 23	Departure of William, Henry, and Edmund	512

Sunday, January 1	Mary learns Edmund is staying away longer	**520**
Monday, January 2	Mary talks to Fanny about Edmund Henry returns in the evening	**520** **528**
Tuesday, January 3	Henry tells Mary he intends to marry Fanny	**528**
Wednesday, January 4	Henry proposes	**542–546**

VOLUME III

Thursday, January 5	Sir Thomas speaks to Fanny about proposal	**560–562**
Friday, January 6	Henry tells Sir Thomas and Fanny he will persist despite her refusal	**582–586**
Saturday, January 7	Sir Thomas speaks to Henry again	**590–592**
Monday, **January 9,** **or Tuesday,** **January 10**	Edmund returns *He later says, regarding Mary's departure (see below), he would have missed her if he had stayed away "five or six days more" (p. 636).*	**600**
Next Day	Henry visits, reads from Shakespeare	**602–604**
Thursday, January 12	Edmund dines at the Grants *It was "the preceding day" before the next event.*	**626**
Friday, January 13	Edmund speaks to Fanny of Henry's proposal *He says that tomorrow is Saturday (p. 636).*	**620**
Sunday, January 15	Mary speaks to Fanny Henry says good-bye to Fanny *They leave the next day.*	**640** **652–654**
Monday, January 16	Mary and Henry leave Mansfield *It was stated earlier to be Monday (p. 636).*	**654**
End of January	William arrives at Mansfield Park *He has ten days' leave; it is not certain whether days of departure and return are counted.*	**660**

Monday, **February 6**	Fanny and William leave for Portsmouth *It is three weeks since the Crawfords'* *departure; she later says they left on Monday* *(p. 738).*	672
	Henry travels to his estate in Norfolk *He traveled the same time as Fanny (could be* *next day instead, since his is a one-day trip).*	706
Tuesday, **February 7**	Fanny and William arrive in Portsmouth	674
Saturday, **February 11**	William's ship sails *It was "within four days" of his arrival.*	696
Thursday, **February 16** **(probable)**	Mary writes to Fanny *She says Henry left for Norfolk ten days ago.*	706
Saturday, **February 25**	Edmund travels to London *Henry (see below) says Edmund came a few* *days before Henry himself. Later Edmund* *says he was there three weeks, and he left on* *a Saturday (p. 756).*	720
Tuesday, **February 28**	Maria's first London party *Mentioned in Mary's letter to Fanny.*	708
Wednesday, **March 1** **(assuming no** **leap year)**	Henry returns to London *He says he spent "scarcely twenty-four hours"* *in London until he traveled to Portsmouth,* *and both journeys would take all day.*	720
Friday, March 3	Henry travels from London to Portsmouth	720
Saturday, **March 4**	Henry visits Fanny *Stated to be a Saturday (p. 722).*	718
Sunday, March 5	Henry sees Fanny again	734
Monday, **March 6**	Henry returns to London	746
Wednesday, **March 8**	Fanny receives letter from Mary	746
Tuesday, **March 14**	Henry sees Maria at Mrs. Fraser's party *Mary mentions it being this date in her letter* *to Fanny (p. 748).*	838–840
Saturday, **March 18**	Edmund returns to Mansfield from London *See next event for dating.*	756

Friday, March 24 (rough estimate)	Fanny receives letter from Edmund *He wrote it after he returned to Mansfield, perhaps several days later. "Seven weeks" are "very nearly gone" in Fanny's absence from Mansfield, which started on Monday, February 6.*	756
Monday, March 27	The Grants leave for Bath	762
Same Day, or a Day or Two Later	Fanny learns of Tom's illness *This was "Within a few days from the receipt of Edmund's letter."*	764–766
Beginning of April	Edmund brings Tom home *Lady Bertram, in her letter to Fanny, says this will happen "shortly" (p. 766).*	768
Early to Mid-April	Tom begins to improve *"At about the week's end from his return."*	772
Mid- to Late April	Mr. Rushworth in Bath; Henry seeing Maria *It is around Easter, which was late (p. 774).*	780–782
Late April	Fanny still in Portsmouth, wanting to leave	774
End of April	Fanny receives a letter from Mary about Tom *This occurs a week before Mary's next letter (p. 786)—see below.*	778–780
End of April/ Early May	Increasing intimacy between Maria and Henry	808–810
Early May	Sir Thomas's friend Mr. Harding writes to him about danger; Sir Thomas prepares to act	810
Thursday, May 5 (probable date)	Maria and Henry run away together Mr. Rushworth agitated, talks to Mr. Harding; latter sends express message to Sir Thomas *This likely happened on the same day; Mary speaks of "Rushworth's folly" in her letter to Fanny—see next two entries.*	810–812 810

	Mary writes to Fanny about scandalous rumor	786
	The day of the week can be established from subsequent events; the date is a logical guess, based upon Fanny's arriving in Portsmouth on February 7, and two days after this, her having "been three months there" (p. 788).	
Friday, May 6	Fanny receives letter from Mary	786
	Julia elopes with Mr. Yates	796
	They left "a few hours before" Sir Thomas and Edmund arrived.	
	Sir Thomas and Edmund travel to London	794
	Edmund, writing to Fanny on Monday, says they have been two days in London; he presumably counts only the two full days there.	
Saturday, May 7	Fanny sees newspaper story about scandal involving Maria and Henry	790
	This was the next day (p. 788).	
Between Saturday and Tuesday	Edmund sees Mary	816
	While he is in London; day not specified.	
Monday, May 8	Edmund writes to Fanny	794
Tuesday, May 9	Fanny receives letter from Edmund	794
	This was three days after hearing of the affair.	
	Edmund leaves for Portsmouth in evening on overnight mail coach	796
Wednesday, May 10	Edmund arrives, leaves with Fanny and Susan	798–800
Thursday, May 11	They arrive at Mansfield	802
	It is the next day; later said to be Thursday (p. 814).	
Sunday, May 12	Fanny and Edmund talk about Mary	814–816
Summer	Edmund recovers some of his cheerfulness	830
	Henry and Maria separate	832
	"A very few months had taught him" to regret Fanny, by contrast with Maria (p. 840).	

Autumn	Dr. Grant gets a position in London *Previously the absence of the Grants from* *Mansfield was "for some months purposely* *lengthened."*	842
	Maria and Mrs. Norris go to live in a remote location	834–836
	Mr. Rushworth procures a divorce *Autumn is a guess.*	834
Late in the Year, or Early Next Year	Edmund and Fanny marry *The interval of time is deliberately left vague.* *This estimate seems logical.*	844–846
A Year Later (estimate)	Fanny is pregnant; Dr. Grant dies; Edmund and Fanny move back to Mansfield *This would be year twenty-nine or thirty,* *depending on the exact lengths of time before* *the marriage, and between that and the* *pregnancy and return to Mansfield.*	850

It is improbable that Jane Austen followed an exact calendar in composing *Mansfield Park*. If she had, she would have used the calendars for 1808 and 1809, for 1808 was the most recent year prior to the composition (in 1812–1813) that contained a Thursday, December 22, the one specific day and date in the novel. But the novel also states that the following Easter was "particularly late," whereas Easter of 1809 was early, on April 2. Moreover, there is every indication that Jane Austen, as in all her novels, intended the story to occur contemporaneously with its composition. Hence it is likely she selected the one specific date arbitrarily, and otherwise imagined the action according to general knowledge of the sequence of the year and intervals of time.

Reference

The Oxford Illustrated Jane Austen, vol. 3, edited by R. W. Chapman (Oxford, 1933).

Bibliography

EDITIONS OF *MANSFIELD PARK*

Chapman, R. W., ed., *The Novels of Jane Austen, Vol. III: Mansfield Park* (Oxford, 1934)

Johnson, Claudia, ed., *Mansfield Park: A Norton Critical Edition* (New York, 1998)

Wiltshire, John, ed., *The Cambridge Edition of the Works of Jane Austen: Mansfield Park* (Cambridge, 2005)

WORKS BY JANE AUSTEN

The Cambridge Edition of the Works of Jane Austen (Cambridge, 2005–2009)

Jane Austen's Letters, ed. by Deirdre Le Faye (Oxford, 2011)

The Oxford Illustrated Jane Austen, 6 vols., ed. by R. W. Chapman (Oxford, 1988)

WORKS RELATING TO JANE AUSTEN

Biographical

Austen, Caroline, *Reminiscences of Caroline Austen* (Guildford, Surrey, 1986)

Austen-Leigh, J. E., *A Memoir of Jane Austen and Other Family Recollections* (Oxford, 2002; originally published 1871)

Austen-Leigh, William, and Richard Arthur Austen-Leigh, *Jane Austen: A Family Record*, revised and enlarged by Deirdre Le Faye (Boston, 1989)

Byrne, Paula, *The Real Jane Austen: A Life in Small Things* (New York, 2013)

Harman, Claire, *Jane's Fame: How Jane Austen Conquered the World* (Edinburgh, 2009)

Le Faye, Deirdre, *Jane Austen: The World of Her Novels* (New York, 2002)

Llewelyn, Margaret, *Jane Austen: A Character Study* (London, 1977)

Ross, Josephine, *Jane Austen: A Companion* (New Brunswick, NJ, 2003)

Tomalin, Claire, *Jane Austen: A Life* (New York, 1997)

Tucker, George Holbert, *Jane Austen's Family* (Stroud, Gloucestershire, 1998)
——, *Jane Austen the Woman* (New York, 1994)
Wilson, Kim, *At Home with Jane Austen* (New York, 2014)

Critical

Auerbach, Emily, *Searching for Jane Austen* (Madison, WI, 2004)
Bush, Douglas, *Jane Austen* (New York, 1975)
Butler, Marilyn, *Jane Austen and the War of Ideas* (Oxford, 1975)
Cecil, Lord David, *A Portrait of Jane Austen* (New York, 1979)
Cockshut, A. O. J., *Man and Woman: A Study of Love and the Novel, 1740–1940* (New York, 1978)
Colby, R. A., *Fiction with a Purpose: Major and Minor Nineteenth-Century Novels* (Bloomington, IN, 1967)
Craik, W. A., *Jane Austen: The Six Novels* (London, 1965)
Devlin, D. D., *Jane Austen and Education* (London, 1975)
Donoghue, Denis, *England, Their England: Commentaries on English Language and Literature* (Berkeley, 1988)
Duckworth, Alistair M., *The Improvement of the Estate: A Study of Jane Austen's Novels* (Baltimore, 1971)
Emsley, Sarah, *Jane Austen's Philosophy of the Virtues* (New York, 2005)
Fleishman, Avrom, *A Reading of Mansfield Park* (Baltimore, 1977)
Gooneratne, Yasmine, *Jane Austen* (Cambridge, 1970)
Grey, J. David, ed., *The Jane Austen Companion* (New York, 1986)
Hardy, Barbara, *A Reading of Jane Austen* (New York, 1979)
Horwitz, Barbara, *Jane Austen and the Question of Women's Education* (New York, 1991)
Jenkyns, Richard, *A Fine Brush on Ivory: An Appreciation of Jane Austen* (New York, 2004)
Lascelles, Mary, *Jane Austen and Her Art* (Oxford, 1939)
Littlewood, Ian, ed., *Jane Austen: Critical Assessmemts*, 4 vols. (Mountfield, East Sussex, 1998)
Lodge, David, *Language of Fiction: Essays in Criticism and Verbal Analysis of the English Novel* (New York, 1966)
Mandal, Anthony, *Jane Austen and the Popular Novel: The Determined Author* (Basingstoke, Hampshire, 2007)
Moler, Kenneth L., *Jane Austen's Art of Illusion* (Lincoln, NE, 1968)
Mooneyham, Laura, *Romance, Language and Education in Jane Austen's Novels* (New York, 1988)
Morini, Massimiliano, *Jane Austen's Narrative Techniques: A Stylistic and Pragmatic Analysis* (Farnham, Surrey, 2009)
Morris, Ivor, *Jane Austen and the Interplay of Character* (London, 1999)
Mullan, John, *What Matters in Jane Austen: Twenty Puzzles Solved* (New York, 2012)
Nabokov, Vladimir, *Lectures on Literature* (New York, 1980)

Nardin, Jane, *Those Elegant Decorums: The Concept of Propriety in Jane Austen's Novels* (Albany, NY, 1973)

Odmark, John, *An Understanding of Jane Austen's Novels* (Oxford, 1981)

Pollock, Walter, *Jane Austen: Her Contemporaries and Herself* (London, 1899)

Roberts, Warren, *Jane Austen and the French Revolution* (New York, 1979)

Ruderman, Anne C., *The Pleasures of Virtue: Political Thought in the Novels of Jane Austen* (Lanham, MD, 1995)

Scheuermann, Mona, *Reading Jane Austen* (New York, 2009)

Scott, P. J. M., *Jane Austen* (London, 1982)

Southam, B. C., ed., *Jane Austen: The Critical Heritage*, 2 vols. (London, 1968–87)

Sutherland, John, *Can Jane Eyre Be Happy? More Puzzles in Classic Fiction* (New York, 1997)

Tave, Stuart, *Some Words of Jane Austen* (Chicago, 1973)

Villard, Léonie, *Jane Austen: A French Appreciation* (London, 1924)

Watt, Ian, ed., *Jane Austen: A Collection of Critical Essays* (Englewood Cliffs, NJ, 1963)

Weisenfarth, Joseph, *The Errand of Form: An Assay of Jane Austen's Art* (New York, 1967)

WORKS OF HISTORICAL BACKGROUND

General Histories and Reference

Adkins, Roy and Lesley, *Jane Austen's England* (New York, 2013)

Burton, Elizabeth, *The Pageant of Georgian England* (New York, 1967)

Craik, W. A., *Jane Austen in Her Time* (London, 1969)

Daunton, M. J., *Progress and Poverty: An Economic and Social History of Britain, 1700–1850* (Oxford, 1995)

Fullerton, Susannah, *Jane Austen and Crime* (Madison, WI, 2006)

Halevy, Elie, *A History of the English People in the Nineteenth Century, Vol. I: England in 1815*, translated by E. I. Watkin and D. A. Barker, 2nd ed. (London, 1949)

Harvey, A. D., *Britain in the Early Nineteenth Century* (New York, 1978)

Hole, Christina, *English Home-Life, 1500–1800* (London, 1947)

Jaeger, Muriel, *Before Victoria: Changing Standards & Behaviour* (London, 1956)

McKendrick, Neil, John Brewer, and J. H. Plumb, *The Birth of a Consumer Society: The Commercialization of Eighteenth-Century England* (Bloomington, IN, 1982)

Olsen, Kirstin, *All Things Austen: An Encyclopedia of Austen's World*, 2 vols. (Westport, CT, 2005)

Porter, Roy, *English Society in the Eighteenth Century*, rev. ed. (London, 1990)

Quinlan, Maurice J., *Victorian Prelude: A History of English Manners* (Hamden, CT, 1965)

Rule, John, *Albion's People: English Society, 1714–1815* (London, 1992)

Todd, Janet, ed., *Jane Austen in Context* (New York, 2005)

Uglow, Jenny, *In These Times: Living in Britain Through Napoleon's War, 1793–1815* (New York, 2014)

White, R. J., *Life in Regency England* (London, 1963)

Language of the Period

The Compact Edition of the Oxford English Dictionary (Oxford, 1971)

Johnson, Samuel, *Dictionary of the English Language*, ed. by Alexander Chalmers (London, 1994; reprint of 1843 ed.)

Lane, Maggie, *Jane Austen and Names* (Bristol, 2002)

Page, Norman, *The Language of Jane Austen* (Oxford, 1972)

Phillipps, K. C., *Jane Austen's English* (London, 1970)

Pinion, F. B., *A Jane Austen Companion* (London, 1973)

Schapera, I., *Kinship Terminology in Jane Austen's Novels* (London, 1977)

Stokes, Myra, *The Language of Jane Austen: A Study of Some Aspects of Her Vocabulary* (New York, 1991)

Tucker, Susie, *Protean Shape: A Study in Eighteenth-Century Vocabulary and Usage* (London, 1967)

Cultural and Literary Background

Bradbrook, Frank W., *Jane Austen and Her Predecessors* (Cambridge, 1966)

Bredvold, Louis I., *The Natural History of Sensibility* (Detroit, 1962)

Brewer, John, *The Pleasures of the Imagination: English Culture in the Eighteenth Century* (New York, 1997)

Feingold, Richard, *Nature and Society: Later Eighteenth-Century Uses of the Pastoral and Georgic* (New Brunswick, NJ, 1978)

Foster, James, *The History of the Pre-Romantic Novel in England* (New York, 1949)

Gaull, Marilyn, *English Romanticism: The Human Context* (New York, 1988)

Holmes, Richard, *The Age of Wonder: How the Romantic Generation Discovered the Beauty and Terror of Science* (New York, 2008)

Jones, Ann H., *Ideas and Innovations: Best Sellers of Jane Austen's Age* (New York, 1986)

Kelly, Gary, *English Fiction of the Romantic Period, 1789–1830* (London, 1989)

McCalman, Iain, ed., *An Oxford Companion to the Romantic Age: British Culture, 1776–1832* (Oxford, 1999)

Spadafora, David, *The Idea of Progress in Eighteenth-Century Britain* (New Haven, 1990)

Sweet, Rosemary, *Antiquaries: The Discovery of the Past in Eighteenth-Century Britain* (London, 2004)

Tompkins, Joyce, *The Popular Novel in England, 1770–1800* (Lincoln, NE, 1961)

Irish Stereotypes

Edgeworth, Richard Lovell and Maria, *Essay on Irish Bulls* (London, 1802)
Truninger, Annelise, *Paddy and the Paycock: A Study of the Stage Irishman from Shakespeare to O'Casey* (Bern, 1976)

Shakespeare

Franklin, Colin, *Shakespeare Domesticated: The Eighteenth-Century Editions* (Aldershot, Hampshire, 1991)
Marder, Louis, *His Exits and Entrances: The Story of Shakespeare's Reputation* (Philadelphia, 1963)
Smith, David Nichol, *Shakespeare in the Eighteenth Century* (Oxford, 1928; 1967 reprint)
Taylor, Gary, *Reinventing Shakespeare: A Cultural History from the Restoration to the Present* (New York, 1989)
Wells, Stanley, *Shakespeare: For All Time* (Oxford, 2003)

Marriage and the Family

Bailey, Joanne, *Unquiet Lives: Marriage and Marriage Breakdown in England, 1660–1800* (Cambridge, 2003)
Fletcher, Anthony, *Growing Up in England: The Experience of Childhood, 1600–1914* (New Haven, 2008)
Harvey, A. D., *Sex in Georgian England: Attitudes and Prejudices from the 1720s to the 1820s* (New York, 1994)
Jones, Hazel, *Jane Austen and Marriage* (London, 2009)
Lane, Maggie, *Growing Older with Jane Austen* (London, 2014)
Probert, Rebecca, *Marriage Law and Practice in the Long Eighteenth Century: A Reassessment* (Cambridge, 2009)
Selwyn, David, *Jane Austen and Children* (London, 2010)
Stone, Lawrence, *The Family, Sex and Marriage in England, 1500–1800* (London, 1977)
——, *The Road to Divorce: England 1530–1987* (Oxford, 1990)
Tadmor, Naomi, *Family and Friends in Eighteenth-Century England: Household, Kinship, and Patronage* (Cambridge, 2001)
Trumbach, Randolph, *The Rise of the Egalitarian Family: Aristocratic Kinship and Domestic Relations in Eighteenth-Century England* (New York, 1978)
Wolfram, Sybil, *In-Laws and Outlaws: Kinship and Marriage in England* (Beckenham, Kent, 1987)

The Position of Women

Barker, Hannah, and Elaine Chalus, eds., *Women's History: Britain, 1700–1850: An Introduction* (London, 2005)

Martin, Joanna, *Wives and Daughters: Women and Children in the Georgian Country House* (London, 2004)

Shoemaker, Robert B., *Gender in English Society, 1650–1850: The Emergence of Separate Spheres?* (London, 1998)

Tague, Ingrid H., *Women of Quality: Accepting and Contesting Ideals of Femininity in England, 1690–1760* (Woodbridge, Suffolk, 2002)

Vickery, Amanda, *The Gentleman's Daughter: Women's Lives in Georgian England* (London, 1998)

Housekeeping and Servants

Adams, Samuel and Sarah, *The Complete Servant* (Lewes, East Sussex, 1989; originally published 1825)

Davidson, Caroline, *A Woman's Work Is Never Done: A History of Housework in the British Isles, 1650–1950* (London, 1982)

Dillon, Maureen, *Artificial Sunshine: A Social History of Domestic Lighting* (London, 2002)

Hardyment, Christina, *Home Comfort: A History of Domestic Arrangements* (Chicago, 1992)

Hecht, J. Jean, *The Domestic Servant Class in Eighteenth-Century England* (London, 1956)

Hill, Bridget, *Servants: English Domestics in the Eighteenth Century* (Oxford, 1996)

Horn, Pamela, *Flunkeys and Scullions: Life Below Stairs in Georgian England* (Stroud, Gloucestershire, 2004)

——, *The Rise and Fall of the Victorian Servant* (Stroud, Gloucestershire, 2004)

Sambrook, Pamela, *The Country House Servant* (Stroud, Gloucestershire, 1999)

Turner, E. S., *What the Butler Saw: 250 Years of the Servant Problem* (New York, 1962)

Entails and Settlements

English, Barbara, and John Saville, *Strict Settlement: A Guide for Historians* (Hull, Yorkshire, 1983)

Erickson, Amy Louise, *Women and Property in Early Modern England* (London, 1993)

Habakkuk, John, *Marriage, Debt and the Estates System: English Landownership, 1650–1950* (Oxford, 1994)

Money and Finance

Burnett, John, *A History of the Cost of Living* (Harmondsworth, Middlesex, 1969)

Daunton, M. J., *Progress and Poverty: An Economic and Social History of Britain, 1700–1850* (Oxford, 1995)

Josset, C. R., *Money in Great Britain and Ireland* (Dawlish, Devon, 1971)

Landed Society

Beckett, J. V., *The Aristocracy in England, 1660–1914* (Oxford, 1986)
Book of the Ranks and Dignities of British Society, attributed to Charles Lamb (London, 1805; reprinted 1924)
Bourne, J. M., *Patronage and Society in Nineteenth-Century England* (London, 1986)
Bush, M. L., *The English Aristocracy: A Comparative Synthesis* (Manchester, 1984)
Cannon, John, *Aristocratic Century: The Peerage of Eighteenth-Century England* (Cambridge, 1984)
Greene, D. J., "Jane Austen and the Peerage," *PMLA* 68 (1953): 1017–31.
Harte, Negley, and Roland Quinault, eds., *Land and Society in Britain, 1700–1914* (Manchester, 1996)
Langford, Paul, *Public Life and the Propertied Englishman, 1689–1798* (Oxford, 1991)
Mingay, G. E., *English Landed Society in the Eighteenth Century* (London, 1963)
——, *The Gentry: The Rise and Fall of a Ruling Class* (New York, 1976)
Thompson, F. M. L., *English Landed Society in the Nineteenth Century* (London, 1963)

The Rural World

Bettey, J. H., *Estates and the English Countryside* (London, 1993)
Bovill, E. W., *English Country Life, 1780–1830* (London, 1962)
Bushaway, Bob, *By Rite: Custom, Ceremony and Community in England 1700–1800* (London, 1982)
Darby, H. C., ed., *A New Historical Geography of England* (Cambridge, 1973)
Eastwood, David, *Governing Rural England: Tradition and Transformation in Local Government, 1780–1840* (Oxford, 1994)
——, *Government and Community in the English Provinces, 1700–1870* (New York, 1997)
Keith-Lucas, Brian, *The Unreformed Local Government System* (London, 1980)
Le Faye, Deirdre, *Jane Austen's Country Life* (London, 2014)
Mingay, G. E., *Land and Society in England, 1750–1850* (London, 1994)
Rackham, Oliver, *The History of the Countryside* (London, 1986)
Rowley, Trevor, *Villages in the Landscape* (London, 1978)
Thirsk, Joan, ed., *The English Rural Landscape* (Oxford, 2000)
Wade Martins, Susanna, *Farmers, Landlords, and Landscapes: Rural Britain, 1720 to 1870* (Macclesfield, Cheshire, 2004)
Williamson, Tom, *The Transformation of Rural England: Farmers and the Landscape, 1700–1870* (Exeter, Devon, 2002)
Williamson, Tom, and Liz Bellamy, *Property and Landscape: A Social History of Land Ownership and the English Countryside* (London, 1987)

Urban Life

Berg, Maxine, *Luxury and Pleasure in Eighteenth-Century Britain* (New York, 2005)

Corfield, P. J., *The Impact of English Towns, 1700–1800* (Oxford, 1982)

Cruickshank, Daniel, and Neil Burton, *Life in the Georgian City* (London, 1990)

Girouard, Mark, *The English Town: A History of Urban Life* (New Haven, 1990)

Raven, James, *Judging New Wealth: Popular Publishing and Responses to Commerce in England, 1750–1800* (Oxford, 1992)

Sweet, Rosemary, *English Town, 1680–1840: Government, Society and Culture* (New York, 1999)

London

Porter, Roy, *London: A Social History* (Cambridge, MA, 1994)

Sheppard, Francis, *London: A History* (New York, 1998)

Weinreb, Ben, and Christopher Hibbert, *The London Encyclopedia* (Bethesda, MD, 1986)

The Professions and the Army

Corfield, Penelope J., *Power and the Professions in Britain, 1700–1850* (New York, 1995)

Holmes, Richard, *Redcoat: The British Soldier in the Age of Horse and Musket* (London, 2001)

Reader, W. J., *Professional Men: The Rise of the Professional Classes in Nineteenth-Century England* (London, 1966)

The Church and the Clergy

Collins, Irene, *Jane Austen and the Clergy* (London, 1994)

Gibson, William, *A Social History of the Domestic Chaplain, 1530–1810* (London, 1997)

Jacob, W. M., *The Clerical Profession in the Long Eighteenth Century, 1680–1840* (Oxford, 2007)

Jarvis, William, *Jane Austen and Religion* (Witney, Oxfordshire, 1996)

Legg, J. Wickham, *English Church Life from the Restoration to the Tractarian Movement* (London, 1914)

Sykes, Norman, *Church and State in England in the XVIIIth Century* (Hamden, CT, 1962)

Virgin, Peter, *The Church in an Age of Negligence: Ecclesiastical Structure and Problems of Church Reform 1700–1840* (Cambridge, 1989)

Webb, Sidney and Beatrice, *The History of Liquor Licensing in England, Principally from 1700 to 1830* (London, 1903)

Whitaker, Wilfred Barnett, *The Eighteenth-Century English Sunday* (London, 1940)

White, Laura Mooneyham, *Jane Austen's Anglicanism* (Farnham, Surrey, 2011)

Yates, Nigel, *Eighteenth-Century Britain: Religion and Politics, 1714–1815* (Edinburgh, 2008)

The Navy

Coad, Jonathan G., *The Royal Dockyards, 1690–1850: Architectural and Engineering Works of the Sailing Navy* (Aldershot, Hampshire, 1989)

Hill, J. R., ed., *The Oxford Illustrated History of the Royal Navy* (Oxford, 1995)

Hubback, John H., *Jane Austen's Sailor Brothers* (London, 1906)

Lavery, Brian, *Nelson's Navy: The Ships, Men and Organisation, 1793–1815* (London, 1989)

Lewis, Michael, *A Social History of the Navy, 1793–1815* (London, 1960)

———, *Spithead: An Informal History* (London, 1972)

Lincoln, Margarette, *Representing the Royal Navy: British Sea Power, 1750–1815* (Aldershot, Hampshire, 2002)

Lipscomb, F. W., *Heritage of Sea Power: The Story of Portsmouth* (London, 1967)

Marcus, G. J., *Heart of Oak: A Survey of British Sea Power in the Georgian Era* (London, 1975)

McDougall, Philip, *Royal Dockyards* (North Pomfret, VT, 1982)

Morriss, Roger, *The Royal Dockyards During the Revolutionary and Napoleonic Wars* (Leicester, 1983)

Rodger, N. A. M., *The Command of the Ocean: A Naval History of Britain, 1649–1815* (New York, 2006)

———, *The Wooden World: An Anatomy of the Georgian Navy* (New York, 1986)

Southam, Brian, *Jane Austen and the Navy* (London, 2005)

Medicine

Buchan, William, *Domestic Medicine* (New York, 1815; based on London ed.)

Floud, Roderick, et al., *Height, Health, and History: Nutritional Status in the United Kingdom, 1750–1980* (Cambridge, 1990)

Loudon, Irvine, *Medical Care and the General Practitioner, 1750–1850* (Oxford, 1986)

Porter, Roy, and Dorothy Porter, *In Sickness and in Health: The British Experience, 1650–1850* (New York, 1989)

———, *Patient's Progress: Doctors and Doctoring in Eighteenth-Century England* (Stanford, CA, 1989)

Porter, Roy, and G. S. Rousseau, *Gout: The Patrician Malady* (New Haven, 1998)

Shah, Sonia, *The Fever: How Malaria Has Ruled Humankind for 500,000 Years* (New York, 2010)

Law and Lawyers

Lemmings, David, *Professors of the Law: Barristers and English Legal Culture in the Eighteenth Century* (Oxford, 2000)

Robson, Robert, *The Attorney in Eighteenth-Century England* (Cambridge, 1959)

Education

Borer, Mary Cathcart, *Willingly to School: A History of Women's Education* (Guildford, Surrey, 1975)

Brock, M. G., and M. C. Curthoys, eds., *The History of the University of Oxford, Vol. VI: Nineteenth-Century Oxford, Part 1* (Oxford, 1997)

Chandos, John, *Boys Together: English Public Schools, 1800–1864* (New Haven, 1984)

Gardiner, Dorothy, *English Girlhood at School: A Study of Women's Education Through Twelve Centuries* (London, 1929)

Hans, Nicholas, *New Trends in Education in the Eighteenth Century* (London, 1951)

Kamm, Josephine, *Hope Deferred: Girls' Education in English History* (London, 1965)

Lyte, H. C. Maxwell, *A History of Eton College, 1440–1884* (London, 1889)

Midgley, Graham, *University Life in Eighteenth-Century Oxford* (New Haven, 1996)

The Oxford University Calendar for the Year 1814 (Oxford, 1814)

Sutherland, L. S., and L. G. Mitchell, eds., *The History of the University of Oxford, Vol. V: The Eighteenth Century* (Oxford, 1986)

Books and Libraries

Fergus, Jan, *Provincial Readers in Eighteenth-Century England* (Oxford, 2006)

Hamlyn, H. M., "Eighteenth-Century Circulating Libraries in England," *Library*, Fifth Series I (1947): 197–218.

Kaufman, Paul, *The Community Library: A Chapter in English Social History* (Philadelphia, 1967)

St. Clair, William, *The Reading Nation in the Romantic Period* (Cambridge, 2004)

The Press

Barker, Hannah, *Newspapers, Politics and English Society, 1695–1855* (Harlow, Essex, 2000)

Black, Jeremy, *The English Press, 1621–1861* (Stroud, Gloucestershire, 2001)

Christie, Ian, "British Newspapers in the Later Georgian Age," in *Myth and Reality in Late-Eighteenth-Century British Politics and Other Papers* (Berkeley, 1970)

Clarke, Bob, *From Grub Street to Fleet Street: An Illustrated History of English Newspapers to 1899* (Aldershot, Hampshire, 2004)

Writing and the Postal Service

Finlay, Michael, *Western Writing Implements in the Age of the Quill Pen* (Carlisle, Cumbria, 1990)

Hemmeon, J. C., *The History of the British Post Office* (Cambridge, MA, 1912)

Joyce, Herbert, *The History of the Post Office* (London, 1893)

Kay, F. George, *Royal Mail: The Story of the Posts in England from the Time of Edward IVth to the Present Day* (London, 1951)

Marshall, C. F. Dendy, *The British Post Office: From Its Beginnings to the End of 1925* (London, 1926)

Robinson, Howard, *The British Post Office: A History* (Princeton, 1948)

Transportation

Anderson, R. C. and J. M., *Quicksilver: A Hundred Years of Coaching, 1750–1850* (Newton Abbot, Devon, 1973)

Copeland, John, *Roads and Their Traffic* (Newton Abbot, Devon, 1968)

Felton, William, *A Treatise on Carriages* (London, 1796)

Jackman, W. T., *The Development of Transportation in Modern England* (London, 1962)

Jones, Hazel, *Jane Austen's Journeys* (London, 2014)

MacKinnon, Honourable Mr. Justice (F. D.), "Topography and Travel in Jane Austen's Novels," *The Cornhill Magazine*, series 3, vol. 59 (1925): 184–99.

McCausland, Hugh, *The English Carriage* (London, 1948)

Pawson, Eric, *Transport and Economy: The Turnpike Roads of Eighteenth-Century Britain* (New York, 1977)

Tarr, Laszlo, *A History of the Carriage* (New York, 1969)

Leisure and Amusement

Crawford, T. S., *History of the Umbrella* (New York, 1970)

Hoyle's Games Improved, Consisting of Practical Treatises on Whist, Quadrille, Piquet, etc., revised and corrected by Charles Jones, Esq. (London, 1800)

Parlett, David, *A History of Card Games* (New York, 1991)

Pimlott, J. A. R., *The Englishman's Christmas: A Social History* (Atlantic Highlands, NJ, 1998)

Selwyn, David, *Jane Austen and Leisure* (London, 1999)

Strutt, Joseph, *Sports and Pastimes of the People of England* (London, 1810)

Theater

Byrne, Paula, *Jane Austen and the Theatre* (London, 2002)

Donohue, Joseph W., *Theatre in the Age of Keen* (Oxford, 1975)

Hogan, Charles Beecher, *The London Stage, 1776–1800: A Critical Introduction* (Carbondale, IL, 1968)

———, *Shakespeare in the Theatre, 1701–1800: A Record of Performances in London, 1751–1800* (Oxford, 1957)

Hume, Robert D., ed., *The London Theatre World, 1660–1800* (Carbondale, IL, 1980)

Leacroft, Richard, *The Development of the English Playhouse* (Ithaca, NY, 1973)

MacKintosh, Iain, *The Georgian Playhouse: Actors, Artists, Audiences and Architecture, 1730–1830* (London, 1975)

Nicoll, Allardyce, *A History of Late Eighteenth Century Drama, 1750–1800* (Cambridge, 1927)

Rosenfeld, Sybil, *Temples of Thespis: Some Private Theatres and Theatricals in England and Wales, 1700–1820* (London, 1978)

Southern, Richard, *The Georgian Playhouse* (London, 1948)

Styan, J. L., *The English Stage: A History of Drama and Performance* (Cambridge, 1996)

Taylor, George, *History of the Amateur Theatre* (Melksham, Wiltshire, 1976)

Music

Busby, Thomas, *A Dictionary of Music, Theoretical and Practical*, 4th ed. (London, 1813)

Hart, Miriam, *Hardly an Innocent Diversion: Music in the Life and Writings of Jane Austen* (Athens, OH, 1999)

Johnstone, H. D., and Roger Fiske, *The Blackwell History of Music in Britain: The Eighteenth Century* (Oxford, 1990)

Loesser, Arthur, *Men, Women and Pianos: A Social History* (New York, 1954)

Piggott, Patrick, *The Innocent Diversion: A Study of Music in the Life and Writings of Jane Austen* (London, 1979)

Rensch, Roslyn, *Harps and Harpists* (Bloomington, 1989)

Rubin, Emanuel, *The English Glee in the Reign of George III: Participatory Art Music for an Urban Society* (Warren, MI, 2003)

Temperley, Nicholas, ed., *The Romantic Age, 1800–1914* (London, 1981)

Dance

Fullerton, Susannah, *A Dance with Jane Austen: How a Novelist and Her Characters Went to the Ball* (London, 2012)

Richardson, Philip J. S., *The Social Dances of the Nineteenth Century in England* (London, 1960)

Wilson, Thomas, *Analysis of Country Dancing* (London, 1808)

———, *The Complete System of English Country Dancing* (London, 1820)

Sports

Billett, Michael, *A History of English Country Sports* (London, 1994)

Brailsford, Dennis, *A Taste for Diversions: Sport in Georgian England* (Cambridge, 1999)

Carr, Raymond, *English Fox Hunting: A History* (London, 1986)

Daniel, W. B., *Rural Sports, Vol. III: Birds* (London, 1807)

Griffin, Emma, *Blood Sport: Hunting in Britain Since 1066* (New Haven, 2007)

Huggins, Mike, *Flat Racing and British Society, 1790–1914: A Social and Economic History* (Portland, OR, 2000)

Longrigg, Roger, *The English Squire and His Sport* (New York, 1977)

———, *The History of Horse Racing* (New York, 1972)

Munsche, P. B., *Gentlemen and Poachers: The English Game Laws, 1671–1831* (Cambridge, 1981)

Russell, Nicholas, *Like Engend'ring Like: Heredity and Animal Breeding in Early Modern England* (Cambridge, 1986)

Vamplew, Wray, *The Turf: A Social and Economic History of Horse Racing* (London, 1976)

Pug Dogs

Ash, Edward, *Dogs: Their History and Development, Vol. II* (London, 1927)

Lee, Rawdon, *A History and Description of the Modern Dogs of Great Britain and Ireland: Non-Sporting Division* (London, 1894)

Rogers, Katharine M., *First Friend: A History of Dogs and Humans* (New York, 2005)

The Seaside and Spas

Feltham, John, *A Guide to All the Watering and Sea-Bathing Places* (London, 1804)

Hembry, Phyllis, *The English Spa* (London, 1990)

McIntyre, Sylvia, "Bath: The Rise of a Resort Town, 1660–1800," in Peter Clark, ed., *Country Towns in Pre-Industrial England* (Leicester, 1981)

Walton, John K., *The English Seaside Resort: A Social History, 1750–1914* (New York, 1983)

Walvin, James, *Beside the Seaside: A Social History of the Popular Seaside Holiday* (London, 1978)

Gardens and Landscaping

Batey, Mavis, *Jane Austen and the English Landscape* (Chicago, 1996)

Daniels, Stephen, *Humphry Repton: Landscape Gardening and the Geography of Georgian England* (New Haven, 1999)

Gilpin, William, *Remarks on Forest Scenery and Other Woodland Views* (London, 1808)

Hadfield, Miles, *Landscape with Trees* (London, 1967)

Hooker, William, *Pomona Londinensis: Containing Colored Engravings of the Most Esteemed Fruits Cultivated in the British Gardens, with a Descriptive Account of Each Variety*, Vol. I (London, 1818)

Hyams, Edward, *Capability Brown and Humphry Repton* (New York, 1971)

Jackson-Stops, Gervase, *The Country House Garden: A Grand Tour* (Boston, 1987)

Jacques, David, *Georgian Gardens: The Reign of Nature* (Portland, OR, 1984)

Laird, Mark, *The Flowering of the Landscape Garden: English Pleasure Grounds, 1720–1800* (Philadelphia, 1999)

Marshall, Charles, *A Plain and Easy Introduction to the Knowledge and Practice of Gardening* (London, 1805)

Quest-Ritson, Charles, *The English Garden: A Social History* (London, 2001)

Repton, Humphry, *The Art of Landscape Gardening* (Boston, 1907)

Stroud, Dorothy, *Humphry Repton* (London, 1962)

Stuart, David, *Georgian Gardens* (London, 1979)

——, *The Kitchen Garden: A Historical Guide to Traditional Crops* (London, 1984)

Thacker, Christopher, *The History of Gardens* (Berkeley, 1979)

Williamson, Tom, *Polite Landscapes: Gardens and Society in Eighteenth-Century England* (Baltimore, 1995)

Wilson, C. Anne, *The Country House Kitchen Garden, 1600–1950* (Thrupp, Oxfordshire, and Stroud, Gloucestershire, 1998)

Wilson, Kim, *In the Garden with Jane Austen* (London, 2008)

Flowers

Fogg, H. G. Witham, *History of Popular Garden Plants from A to Z* (London, 1977)

Hollingsworth, Buckner, *Flower Chronicles* (New Brunswick, NJ, 1958)

Potter, Jennifer, *The Rose: A True History* (London, 2010)

Houses

Chambers, James, *The English House* (New York, 1985)

Christie, Christopher, *The British Country House in the Eighteenth Century* (New York, 2000)

Girouard, Mark, *Life in the English Country House: A Social and Architectural History* (New Haven, 1978)

——, *Town and Country* (New Haven, 1992)

Jackson-Stops, Gervase, et al., eds., *The Fashioning and Functioning of the British Country House* (Washington, DC, 1989)

Jackson-Stops, Gervase, and James Pipkin, *The English Country House: A Grand Tour* (Boston, 1985)

Pevsner, Nikolaus, "The Architectural Setting of Jane Austen's Novels," *Journal of the Warburg and Courtauld Institutes* 31 (1968): 404–22.

Reid, Richard, *The Georgian House and Its Details* (Bath, 1989)

Tristram, Philippa, *Living Space in Fact and Fiction* (London, 1989)

Wilson, Richard, and Alan Mackley, *Creating Paradise: The Building of the English Country House, 1660–1880* (London, 2000)

Interior Decoration

Blakemore, Robbie G., *History of Interior Design Furniture: From Ancient Egypt to Nineteenth-Century Europe* (New York, 1997)

Bly, John, *Discovering English Furniture* (Aylesbury, Buckinghamshire, 1976)

Boyce, Charles, *Dictionary of Furniture* (New York, 2001)

Calloway, Stephen, ed., *The Elements of Style: A Practical Encyclopedia of Interior Architectural Details from 1485 to the Present* (New York, 1991)

Crowley, John E., *The Invention of Comfort: Sensibilities and Design in Early Modern America and Early Modern Britain* (Baltimore, 2001)

Edwards, Ralph, and L. G. G. Ramsey, *The Connoisseur's Period Guides to the Houses, Decoration, Furnishing and Chattels of the Classic Periods, Vol. 4: The Late Georgian Period, 1760–1810,* and *Vol. 5: The Regency Period, 1810–1830* (London, 1958)

Fastnedge, Ralph, *English Furniture Styles: From 1500 to 1830* (London, 1955)

Gloag, John, *Georgian Grace: A Social History of Design from 1660 to 1830* (London, 1956)

Jourdain, Margaret, *English Interior Decoration, 1500–1830: A Study in the Development of Design* (London, 1950)

——, *Regency Furniture, 1795–1830* (London, 1965)

Jourdain, Margaret, and F. Rose, *English Furniture: The Georgian Period (1750–1830)* (London, 1953)

Morley, John, *The History of Furniture: Twenty-Five Centuries of Style and Design in the Western Tradition* (Boston, 1999)

——, *Regency Design, 1790–1840* (London, 1993)

Parissien, Steven, *Adam Style* (Washington, DC, 1992)

——, *The Georgian House in America and Britain* (New York, 1995)

——, *Regency Style* (Washington, DC, 1992)

Rogers, John, *English Furniture* (Feltham, 1967)

Smith, Charles Saumarez, *Eighteenth-Century Decoration: Design and the Domestic Interior in England* (New York, 1993)

Snodin, Michael, and John Styles, *Design and the Decorative Arts: Georgian Britain, 1714–1837* (London, 2004)

Thornton, Peter, *Authentic Decor: The Domestic Interior, 1620–1920* (New York, 1984)

——, *Form & Decoration: Innovation in the Decorative Arts, 1470–1870* (London, 1998)

Vickery, Amanda, *Behind Closed Doors: At Home in Georgian England* (New Haven, 2009)

Watkins, Susan, *Jane Austen in Style* (New York, 1996)

Female Decorative Activities

Beck, Thomasina, *The Embroiderer's Story: Needlework from the Renaissance to the Present Day* (Devon, 1995)

Bermingham, Ann, *Learning to Draw: Studies in the Cultural History of a Polite and Useful Art* (New Haven, 2000)

Forest, Jennifer, *Jane Austen's Sewing Box* (Millers Point, New South Wales, 2009)

Hughes, Therle, *English Domestic Needlework, 1660–1860* (London, 1961)

Rogers, Gay Ann, *Illustrated History of Needlework Tools* (London, 1983)

Taunton, Nerylla, *Antique Needlework Tools and Embroideries* (Woodbridge, Suffolk, 1997)

The Young Lady's Book: A Manual of Elegant Recreations, Exercises, and Pursuits (London, 1829)

Transparencies

Imison, John, *Elements of Science and Art* (London, 1803)

Roberts, James, *Introductory Lessons, with Familiar Examples in Landscape* (London, 1800)

Smith, James, *The Panorama of Science and Art* (Liverpool, 1815)

Jewelry

Evans, Joan, *History of Jewellery, 1100–1870* (London, 1953)

Scarisbrick, Diana, *Jewellery in Britain: A Dcoumentary, Social, Literary, and Artistic Survey* (Wilby, Suffolk, 1984)

Beauty and Fashion

Ashelford, Jane, *The Art of Dress: Clothes and Society, 1500–1914* (New York, 1996)

Byrde, Penelope, *A Frivolous Distinction: Fashion and Needlework in the Works of Jane Austen* (Bristol, 1979)

Corson, Richard, *Fashions in Hair: The First Five Thousand Years* (New York, 1965)

Cunnington, C. Willett, *English Women's Clothing in the Nineteenth Century* (Mineola, NY, 1990; originally published 1937)

Downing, Sarah Jane, *Fashion in the Time of Jane Austen* (Oxford, 2010)

Ewing, Elizabeth, *Everyday Dress, 1650–1900* (London, 1984)

Foster, Vanda, *Visual History of Costume: The Nineteenth Century* (London, 1984)

Harris, Jennifer, ed., *Textiles, 5,000 Years: An International History and Illustrated Survey* (New York, 1993)

Lady of Distinction, *The Mirror of the Graces; or, The English Lady's Costume* (London, 1811)

Mackrell, Alice, *Shawls, Stoles and Scarves* (London, 1986)

Pratt, Lucy, and Linda Woolley, *Shoes* (London, 1999)

Sherrow, Victoria, *Encyclopedia of Hair: A Cultural History* (Westport, CT, 2006)

Styles, John, *Dress of the People: Everyday Fashion in Eighteenth-Century England* (New Haven, 2007)

Swann, June, *Shoes* (London, 1982)

Food and Dining

Black, Maggie, and Deirdre Le Faye, *The Jane Austen Cookbook* (Chicago, 1995)

Drummond, J. C., and Anne Wilbraham, *The Englishman's Food: Five Centuries of English Diet* (London, 1991)

Glanville, Philippa, and Hilary Young, eds., *Elegant Eating: Four Hundred Years of Dining with Style* (London, 2002)

Hartley, Dorothy, *Food in England* (London, 1954)

Hickman, Peggy, *A Jane Austen Household Book, with Martha Lloyd's Recipes* (North Pomfret, VT, 1977)

Johnson, Hugh, *Vintage: The Story of Wine* (New York, 1989)

Lane, Maggie, *Jane Austen and Food* (London, 1995)

Lehmann, Gilly, *The British Housewife: Cookery Books, Cooking and Society in Eighteenth-Century Britain* (Totnes, Devon, 2003)

Palmer, Arnold, *Movable Feasts* (New York, 1952)

Paston-Williams, Sara, *The Art of Dining: A History of Cooking and Eating* (London, 1993)

Wilson, C. Anne, *Food and Drink in Britain: From the Stone Age to Recent Times* (London, 1973)

Etiquette

Cunnington, Phyllis, and Catherine Lucas, *Costume for Births, Marriages, & Deaths* (New York, 1972)

Fritzer, Penelope Joan, *Jane Austen and Eighteenth-Century Courtesy Books* (Westport, CT, 1997)

Morgan, Marjorie, *Manners, Morals and Class in England, 1774–1858* (New York, 1994)

Ross, Josephine, *Jane Austen's Guide to Good Manners* (New York, 2006)

Wildeblood, Joan, *The Polite World: A Guide to the Deportment of the English in Former Times* (London, 1973)

Female Conduct Books

Advice of a Mother to Her Daughter, by the Marchioness of Lambert; *A Father's Legacy to His Daughters,* by Dr. Gregory; and *The Lady's New Year's Gift, or, Advice to a Daughter,* by Lord Halifax, in *Angelica's Ladies Library* (London, 1794)

Burton, John, *Lectures on Female Education and Manners* (London, 1793; reprint ed., New York, 1970)

Chapone, Hester, *Letters on the Improvement of the Mind* (Walpole, NH, 1802; first published London, 1773)

Gisborne, Thomas, *An Enquiry into the Duties of the Female Sex* (London, 1796)

Trusler, John, *Principles of Politeness, and of Knowing the World, in Two Parts* (London, 1800)

Fashionable Society

Erickson, Carolly, *Our Tempestuous Day: A History of Regency England* (New York, 1986)

Greig, Hannah, *The Beau Monde: Fashionable Society in Georgian London* (Oxford, 2013)

SLAVERY AND THE WEST INDIES

Clarkson, Thomas, *The History of the Rise, Progress, and Accomplishment of the Abolition of the African Slave-Trade by the British Parliament* (London, 1808; 1968 reprint)

Dyde, Brian, *A History of Antigua: The Unsuspected Isle* (London, 2000)

Edwards, Bryan, *The History, Civil and Commercial, of the British West Indies* (London, 1819)

Goveia, Elsa, *Slave Society in British Leeward Islands at the End of the Eighteenth Century* (New Haven, 1965)

Knox-Shaw, Peter, *Jane Austen and the Enlightenment* (Cambridge, 2004)

Oldfield, J. R., *Popular Politics and British Anti-Slavery: The Mobilisation of Public Opinion Against the Slave Trade* (London, 1998)

Ragatz, Lowell Joseph, *The Fall of the Planter Class in the British Caribbean: A Study in Social and Economic History* (New York, 1963)

Walvin, James, *England, Slaves and Freedom, 1776–1838* (Jackson, MS, 1986)

——, ed., *Slavery and British Society, 1776–1846* (Baton Rouge, 1982)

Ward, J. R., *British West Indian Slavery: The Process of Amelioration* (Oxford, 1988)

White, Gabrielle D. V., *Jane Austen in the Context of Abolition: "A fling at the slave trade"* (Basingstoke, Hampshire, 2006)

Maps

ENGLAND

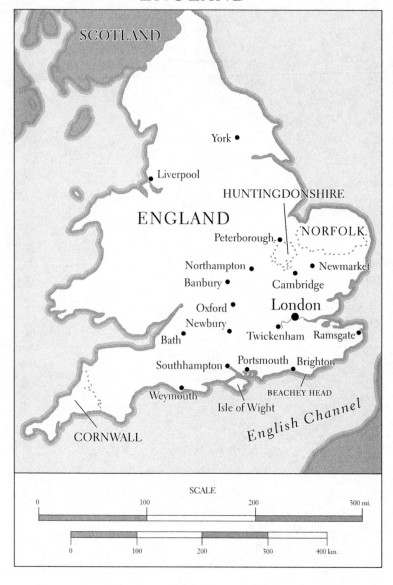

SCOTLAND

York •

Liverpool •

HUNTINGDONSHIRE

ENGLAND

NORFOLK

Peterborough •

Northampton •

• Newmarket

Banbury •

Cambridge

Oxford •

London

Newbury •

Bath •

Twickenham

Ramsgate •

Southhampton •

Portsmouth •

Brighton •

Weymouth •

Isle of Wight

BEACHEY HEAD

CORNWALL

English Channel

SCALE

0   100   200   300 mi.

0   100   200   300   400 km.

Banbury: Where Henry hopes to spend the night on his way to Bath from Mansfield.

Bath: Leading resort town where Henry goes and where Mrs. Rushworth retires.

Beachey Head: Promontory that William uses as a point of reference for Brighton.

Brighton: Seaside resort where Maria and Mr. Rushworth spend their honeymoon.

Cambridge: Where Henry attended university.

Cornwall: County where Mr. Yates first engaged in private theatricals.

Huntingdonshire: County where Lady Bertram, Mrs. Norris, and Mrs. Price are from.

Isle of Wight: Island forming the channel that made Portsmouth an excellent naval base; called "the Island" by Portsmouth residents.

Liverpool: Large port city where Sir Thomas arrives when returning from Antigua.

Newbury: Where Fanny and William spend the night when going to Portsmouth from Mansfield.

Newmarket: Leading center of horse racing; where Tom Bertram becomes ill.

Norfolk: County where Henry owns an estate.

Northampton: Principal town of the County of Northampton, where most of the story occurs; Mansfield Park lies approximately four miles north of Northampton.

Oxford: Where Edmund attended university, and where he and Fanny spend the night when returning to Mansfield from Portsmouth.

Peterborough: Cathedral town where Edmund goes to be ordained.

Portsmouth: Port town containing the principal naval base of Britain; where Fanny is from and where she visits her family.

Ramsgate: Seaside resort visited earlier by Tom.

Scotland: Where Julia and Mr. Yates elope.

Southampton: Port town where Jane Austen lived for three years and acquired the knowledge of Portsmouth she used in the novel.

Twickenham: Popular town for the wealthy where Admiral Crawford bought a cottage and where Henry and Maria advance their illicit flirtation.

Weymouth: Seaside resort where Tom met Mr. Yates.

York: One of the places Henry Crawford claims he would return from at an hour's notice if summoned to Mansfield Park.

PORTSMOUTH

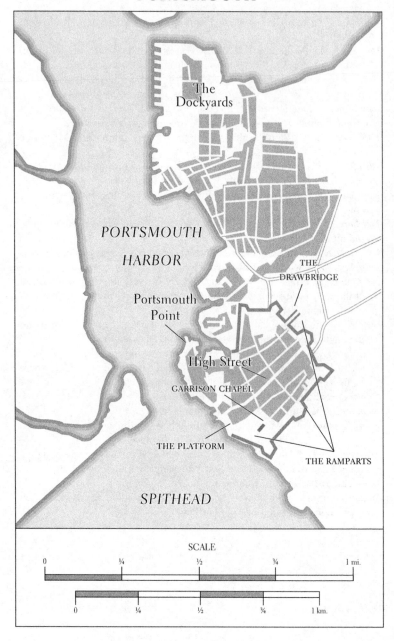

The Dockyards

PORTSMOUTH

HARBOR

Portsmouth Point

THE DRAWBRIDGE

High Street

GARRISON CHAPEL

THE PLATFORM

THE RAMPARTS

SPITHEAD

SCALE

0   ¼   ½   ¾   1 mi.

0   ¼   ½   ¾   1 km.

The Dockyards: Large complex for building and repairing ships; where Fanny, her sister, her father, and Henry Crawford go after Henry arrives.

The Drawbridge (at Landport Gate): Where Fanny and William enter into the town of Portsmouth proper.

Garrison Chapel: Church where the Prices worship.

High Street: Main street in Portsmouth; the Prices live on a small street off High Street.

The Platform: Popular viewing area where Mr. Price sees William's ship leave the harbor for Spithead.

Portsmouth Point: Where sailors embark and an area notorious for licentious behavior.

The Ramparts: Fortifications surrounding Portsmouth, and also a popular place for walking and enjoying the view.

Spithead: Channel separating Portsmouth from the Isle of Wight and the principal anchorage for naval ships using the Portsmouth base.

THE ANNOTATED PERSUASION

From the editor of the popular *Annotated Pride and Prejudice* comes an annotated edition of Jane Austen's *Persuasion* that makes the beloved novel an even more satisfying and fulfilling read. Here is the complete text of *Persuasion* with hundreds of annotations on facing pages, including explanations of historical context; citations from Austen's life, letters, and other writings; definitions and clarifications; literary comments and analysis; and plentiful maps and illustrations. Packed with all kinds of illuminating information—from what Bath and Lyme looked like at the time to how "bathing machines" at seaside resorts were used to how Wentworth could have made a fortune from the Napoleonic Wars—David M. Shapard's delightfully entertaining edition brings Austen's novel of second chances vividly to life.

Fiction

ALSO AVAILABLE

The Annotated Northanger Abbey

ANCHOR BOOKS
Available wherever books are sold.
www.anchorbooks.com